The Missing and the Dead

Stuart MacBride

W F HOWES LTD

This large print edition published in 2015 by
W F Howes Ltd
Unit 4, Rearsby Business Park, Gaddesby Lane,
Rearsby, Leicester LE7 4YH

1 3 5 7 9 10 8 6 4 2

First published in the United Kingdom in 2015
by HarperCollins*Publishers*

A CIP catalogue record for this book is available
from the British Library

ISBN 978 1 51001 455 8

Typeset by Palimpsest Book Production Limited,
Falkirk, Stirlingshire

Printed and bound in Great Britain
by TJ International Ltd, Padstow, Cornwall

For the brave loons and quines
who made Grampian Police
the great force it was

WITHOUT WHOM

As always I've received a lot of help from a lot of people while I was writing this book and I'd like to thank: Ishbel Gall, Prof. Lorna Dawson, Prof. Dave Barclay, Dr James Grieve, and Prof. Sue Black, for all their forensic cleverness; Deputy Divisional Commander Mark Cooper, Sergeant Bruce Crawford, the excellent officers and support staff of B Division, everyone at the Mintlaw Road Policing Unit, Alison Cowie, Lisa Shand, and all the OST instructors; Fiona, Magnus, and Alan; Sarah Hodgson, Jane Johnson, Julia Wisdom, Louise Swannell, Oliver Malcolm, Sarah Collett, Roger Cazalet, Kate Elton, Sarah Benton, Damon Greeney, Kate Stephenson, Lucy Dauman, Anne O'Brien, Marie Goldie, the DC Bishopbriggs Wild Brigade, and all the lovely people at HarperCollins (you're all great); and Phil Patterson and the team at Marjacq Scripts, for keeping my cat in shoes all these years.

More thanks to the naughty Alex, Nadine, Dave, Maureen, Al, Donna, Zoë, Mark, Peter, Russel, Chris, Christopher, Scott, and Catherine. And Russell (who inspired Bikini Golf).

A number of people have helped raise a lot of money for charity by bidding to have a character named after them in this book: Dean Scott, Syd Fraser, and Denise Wishart (Tony's mum).

And, as per tradition, saving the best for last: Fiona and Grendel.

I've taken the occasional liberty with the street names and geography of the northeast, for what, I hope, are obvious reasons. But I've been entirely accurate about how beautiful the place is. Don't take my word for it – get up there and see for yourself. It's great.

RUN.

CHAPTER 1

Faster. Sharp leaves whip past her ears, skeletal bushes and shrubs snatch at her ankles as she lurches into the next garden, breath trailing in her wake. Bare feet burning through the crisp, frozen grass.

He's getting louder, shouting and crashing and swearing through hedges in the gloom behind her. Getting closer.

Oh God . . .

She scrambles over a tall wooden fence, dislodging a flurry of frost. There's a sharp ripping sound and the hem of her summer dress leaves a chunk of itself behind. The sandpit rushes up to meet her, knocking the breath from her lungs.

Please . . .

Not like this . . .

Not flat on her back in a stranger's garden.

Above her, the sky fades from dirty grey to dark, filthy, orange. Tiny winks of light forge across it – a plane on its way south. The sound of a radio wafts out from an open kitchen window somewhere. The smoky smear of a roaring log fire. A small child screaming that it's not tired yet.

3

Up!

She scrambles to her feet and out onto the slippery crunch of frozen lawn, her shoes lost many gardens back. Tights laddered and torn, painted toenails on grubby feet. Breath searing her lungs, making a wall of fog around her head.

Run.

Straight across to the opposite side as the back door opens and a man comes out, cup of tea in one hand. Mouth hanging open. 'Hoy! What do you think you're—'

She doesn't stop. Bends almost in half and charges into the thick leylandii hedge. The jagged green scrapes at her cheeks. A sharp pain slashes across her calf.

RUN!

If He catches her, that's it. He'll drag her back to the dark. Lock her away from the sun and the world and the people who love her. Make her *suffer.*

She bursts out the other side.

A woman squats in the middle of the lawn next to a border terrier. She's wearing a blue plastic bag on her hand like a glove, hovering it over a mound of steaming brown. Her eyes snap wide, eyebrows up. Staring. 'Oh my God, are you . . .?'

His voice bellows out across the twilight. 'COME BACK HERE!'

Don't stop. Never stop. Don't let him catch up. Not now.

Not after all she's been through.

It's not fair.

She takes a deep breath and runs.

'God's sake . . .' Logan shoved his way out of a thick wad of hedge into another big garden and staggered to a halt. Spat out bitter shreds of green that tasted like pine disinfectant.

A woman caught in the act of poop-scooping stared up at him.

He dragged out his Airwave handset and pointed it at her. 'Which way?'

The hand wrapped in the carrier bag came up and trembled towards the neighbour's fence.

Brilliant . . .

'Thanks.' Logan pressed the button and ran for it. 'Tell Biohazard Bob to get the car round to Hillview Drive, it's . . .' He scrambled onto the roof of a wee plastic bike-shed thing, shoes skidding on the frosty plastic. From there to the top of a narrow brick wall. Squinted out over a patchwork of darkened gardens and ones bathed in the glow of house lights. 'It's the junction with Hillview Terrace.'

Detective Chief Inspector Steel's smoky voice rasped out of the handset's speaker. *'How have you no' caught the wee sod yet?'*

'Don't start. It's . . . Woah.' A wobble. Both hands out, windmilling. Then frozen, bent forward over an eight-foot drop into a patch of Brussels sprouts.

'What have I told you about screwing this up?'

Blah, blah, blah.

The gardens stretched away in front, behind, and to the right – backing onto the next road over. No sign of her. 'Where the hell are you?'

There – forcing her way through a copse of rowan and ash, making for the hedge on the other side. Two more gardens and she'd be out on the road.

Right.

Logan hit the send button again. 'I need you to—' His left shoe parted company with the wall. 'AAAAAAAARGH!' Cracking through dark green spears, sending little green bombs flying, and thumping into the frozen earth below. THUMP. 'Officer down!'

'*Laz? Jesus, what the hell's . . .*' Steel's voice faded for a second. '*You! I want an armed response unit and an ambulance round to—*'

'Gah . . .' He scrabbled upright, bits of squashed Brussels sprouts sticking to his dirt-smeared suit. 'Officer back up again!'

'*Are you taking the—*'

The handset went in his pocket again and he sprinted for the fence. Clambered over it as Steel's foul-mouthed complaints crackled away to themselves.

Across the next garden in a dozen strides, onto a box hedge then up over another slab of brick.

She was struggling with a wall of rosebushes, their thorned snaking branches digging into her blue summer dress, slicing ribbons of blood from

6

her arms and legs. Blonde hair caught in the spines.

'YOU! STOP RIGHT THERE!'

'Please no, please no, please no . . .'

Logan dropped into the garden.

She wrenched herself free and disappeared towards the last house on the road, leaving her scalp behind . . . No, not a scalp – a *wig*.

He sprinted. Jumped. Almost cleared the bush. Crashed through the privet on the other side, head first. Tumbled.

On his feet.

There!

He rugby-tackled her by the gate, his shoulder slamming into the small of her back, sending them both crunching onto the gravel. Sharp stones dug into his knees and side. The smell of dust and cat scratched into the air.

And she SCREAMED. No words, just a high-pitched bellow, face scarlet, spittle flying, eyes like chunks of granite. Stubble visible through the pancake makeup that covered her thorn-torn cheeks. Breath a sour cloud of grey in the cold air. Hands curled into fists, battering against Logan's chest and arms.

A fist flashed at Logan's face and he grabbed it. 'Cut it out! I'm detaining you under—'

'KILL YOU!' The other hand wrapped itself around his throat and squeezed. Nails digging into his skin, sharp and stinging.

Sod that. Logan snapped his head back, then

whipped it forward. *Crack* – right into the bridge of her nose.

A grunt and she let go, beads of blood spattering against his cheek. Warm and wet.

He snatched at her wrist, pulled till the hand was folded forward at ninety degrees, and leaned on the joint.

The struggling stopped, replaced by a sucking hiss of pain. Adam's apple bobbing. Scarlet dripping across her lips. 'Let me go, you *bastard*!' Not a woman's voice at all, getting deeper with every word. 'I didn't do anything!'

Logan hauled out his cuffs and snapped them on the twisted wrist, using the whole thing as a lever against the strained joint.

'Where's Stephen Bisset?'

'HELP! RAPE!'

More pressure. 'I'm not asking you again – where is he?'

'Aaaaagh . . . You're breaking my wrist! . . . Please, I don't—'

One more push.

'OK! OK! God . . .' A deep breath through gritted, blood-stained, teeth. Then a grin. 'He's dying. All on his own, in the dark. He's *dying*. And there's nothing you can do about it.'

CHAPTER 2

The windscreen wipers squealed and groaned their way across the glass, clearing the dusting of tiny white flakes. The council hadn't taken the Christmas decorations down yet: snowmen, and holly sprigs, and bells, and reindeer, and Santas shone bright against the darkness.

Ten days ago and the whole place would have been heaving – Hogmanay, like a hundred Friday nights all squished into one – but now it was deserted. Everyone would be huddled up at home, nursing Christmas overdrafts and longing for payday.

The pool car's wheels hissed through the slush. No traffic – the only other vehicles were parked at the side of the road, being slowly bleached by the falling snow.

Logan turned in his seat and scowled into the back of the car as they made the turn onto the North Deeside Road. 'Last chance, Graham.'

Graham Stirling sat hunched forwards, hands cuffed in front of him now, dabbing at his blood-crusted nostrils with grubby fingers. Voice thick and flat. 'You broke my nose . . .'

Sitting next to him, Biohazard Bob sniffed. 'Aye, and you didn't even say thank you, did you?' The single thick eyebrow that lurked above his eyes made a hairy V-shape. He leaned in, so close one of his big sticky-out ears brushed Stirling's forehead. 'Now answer the question: where's Stephen Bisset?'

'I need to go to hospital.'

'You need a stiff kicking is what you need.' Biohazard curled a hand into a hairy fist. 'Now tell us where Bisset is, or so help me God, I'm going to—'

'Detective Sergeant Marshall! *Enough.*' Logan bared his teeth. 'We don't assault prisoners in police cars.'

Biohazard sat back in his seat. Lowered his fist. 'Aye, it makes a mess of the upholstery. Rennie: find somewhere quiet to park. Somewhere dark.'

DS Rennie pulled the car to a halt at the pedestrian crossing, tip-tapping his fingers on the steering wheel as a pair of well-dressed men staggered across the road. Arms wrapped around each other's shoulders. Singing an old Rod Stewart tune. Oblivious as the snow got heavier.

Their suits looked a lot more expensive than Rennie's. Their haircuts too – his stuck up in a blond mop above his pink-cheeked face, neck disappearing into a shirt collar two sizes too big for it. Like a wee boy playing dress-up in his dad's clothes. He glanced over his shoulder. 'You want the court to know you cooperated, don't you, Graham? That you helped? Might save you a couple of years inside?'

Silence.

Stirling picked a clot of blood from the skin beneath his nose and wiped it on the tattered fabric of his dress.

'The DI's serious, Graham, he's not going to ask you again. Why not do yourself a favour and tell him what he needs to know?'

A pause. Then Stirling looked up. Smiled. 'OK.'

Biohazard pulled out an Airwave handset. ''Bout time. Come on then – address?'

His pink tongue emerged, slid its way around pale lips. 'No. You and the boy have to get out. I talk to him,' pointing at Logan, 'or we go back to the station and you get me a lawyer.'

'Don't be stupid, Stirling, we're not—'

'No comment.'

Logan sighed. 'This is idiotic, it's—'

'You heard me: no comment. They get out, or you get me a lawyer.'

Rennie's face pinched. 'Guv?'

'No comment.'

Logan rubbed his eyes. 'Out. Both of you.'

'Guv, I don't think that's—'

'I know. Now: out.'

Rennie stared at Biohazard.

Pause.

Biohazard shrugged. Then climbed out onto the empty pavement.

A beat later, Rennie killed the engine and followed him. 'Still think this is a bad idea.'

Clunk, the door shut, leaving Logan and Graham Stirling alone in the car.

'Talk.'

'The forest on the Slug Road. There's a track off into the trees, you need a key for the gate. An . . . an old forestry worker's shack hidden away in there, *miles* from anywhere.' The smile grew hazy, the eyes too, as if he was reliving something. 'If you're lucky, Steve might still be alive.'

Logan took out his handset. 'Right. We'll—'

'You'll never find it without me. It's not on any maps. Can't even see it on Google Earth.' Stirling leaned forward. 'Search all you like: by the time you find him, Steve Bisset will be long dead.'

The pool car's headlights cast long jagged shadows between the trees, its warning strobes glittering blue-and-white against the needles. Catching the thick flakes of snow and making them shine, caught in their slow-motion dance to the forest floor.

Logan shifted his footing on the frozen, rutted track. Ran his torch along the treeline.

Middle of nowhere.

He wiped a drip from the end of his nose. 'Well, what was I supposed to do? Let him no-comment till Stephen Bisset dies?'

The track snaked off further into the darkness, bordered on both sides by tussocks of grass, slowly disappearing under the falling snow, glowing in the torchlight.

On the other end of the phone, Steel groaned. *'Could you no' have let the nasty wee sod fall down the stairs a few times? We're no' allowed to—'*

'You want to tell Stephen's family we let him freeze to death, all alone, in a shack in the forest, because we were more concerned with following procedure than saving his life?'

'Laz, it's no' that simple, we—'

'Because if that's what you want, tell me now and we'll head back to HQ. You can help Dr Simms pick out a body-bag. Probably still got some nice Christmas paper knocking about, you could use that. Wrap his corpse up with a bow on top.'

'Will you shut up and—'

'Maybe something with kittens and teddy bears on it, so Bisset's kids won't mind so much?'

Silence.

'Hello?'

'All right, all right. But he better be alive. And another thing—'

He hung up and marched over to the pool car.

Biohazard leaned against the bonnet, arms folded, shoulders hunched, one cowboy boot up on the bumper. Nose going bright red, the tips of his taxi-door ears too. He spat. Nodded at the ill-fitting suit behind the steering wheel. 'The wee loon's right, this is daft.'

'Yeah, well, I've cleared it with the boss, so we're doing it.'

A sniff. 'What if Danny the Drag Queen tries it on when you're out there?'

Logan peered around Biohazard's shoulder.

Stirling was slumped in the rear seat, blood dried to a black mask that hid the lower half of his face. Bruises already darkening the skin beneath both eyes. The blue sundress all mud-stained and tatty after the chase through the gardens. Shivering.

'Think I'll risk it.' Logan pulled out the canister of CS gas from his jacket pocket, ran his thumb-nail across the join between the safety cap and the body. 'But just in case, get his hands cuffed behind him. And I want the pair of you ready to charge in.'

Logan popped open the back door and leaned into the car. It smelled of sweat and fear and rusting meat. 'Out.'

Twigs snapped beneath his feet as they picked their way between the grey-brown branches, following the circle of light cast by Logan's torch. A tiny dot, adrift on an ocean of darkness.

Something *moved* out there. Little scampering feet and claws that skittered away into the night.

Logan flicked the torch in its direction. 'How much further?'

He jerked his chin to the left. 'That way.' The words plumed out from his mouth in a glowing cloud, caught in the torchlight. Curling away into the night. Dragon's breath.

Down a slope, into a depression lined with brambles and the curled remains of long-dead ferns, already sagging under the weight of snow. More falling from the sickly dark sky.

Stirling's feet clumped about in Rennie's shoes, the scuffed black brogues and white socks looking huge beneath the torn sundress and laddered tights.

Up the other side, through the ferns – brittle foliage wrapping around Logan's trousers, leaving cold wet fingerprints. 'Why him? Why Stephen Bisset?'

'Why?' A shrug. The torchlight glinted off the handcuffs' metal bars, secured behind his back, fingers laced together as if they were taking a casual stroll along the beach. 'Why not?' A small sigh. 'Because he was *there*.'

Logan checked his watch. Fifteen minutes. Another five, and that was it: call this charade off. Call in a dog team. Get the helicopter up from Strathclyde with a thermal-imaging camera. Assuming Steel could pull enough rank to get them to fly this far north on a Friday night in January.

They stumbled on between the silent trees. Fallen pine needles made ochre drifts between the snaking roots, the branches too thick to let the snow through.

He stopped, pulled up his sleeve – exposing his watch again. 'Time's up. I'm not sodding about here any longer.' He grabbed the plastic bar in the middle of the handcuffs and dragged Stirling to a halt. 'This is a waste of time, isn't it? You're never going to show me where Stephen Bisset is. You want him dead so he can't testify against you.'

Stirling turned. Stared at Logan. Face lit from beneath by the torch, like someone telling a camp-fire horror story. Tilted his head to the left. 'You see?'

Logan stepped away. Swung the torch's beam in an arc across the trees, raking the needle-strewn forest floor with darting shadows . . .

A sagging wooden structure lurked between the trunks, in a space that barely counted as a clearing, partially hidden by a wall of skeletal brambles.

Stirling's voice dropped to a serrated-edged whisper. 'He's in there.'

Another step. Then stop.

Logan turned. Shone the torch right in Stirling's face, making him flinch and shy back, eyes clamped shut. Then took out his handcuff key. 'On your knees.'

A thick stainless-steel padlock secured the shack's door. It had four numerical tumblers built into the base, its hasp connecting a pair of heavy metal plates – one fixed to the door, the other to the surround. Both set up so the screw heads were inaccessible.

Logan flicked the torch beam towards Stirling. 'Combination?'

He was still on his knees, both arms wrapped around the tree trunk, as if he was giving it a hug. Hands cuffed together on the other side. Cheek pressed hard against the bark. 'One, seven, zero, seven.'

The dials were stiff, awkward, but they turned after a bit of fiddling. Squeaking against Logan's blue-nitrile-gloved fingertips. Clicking as they lined up into the right order. The hasp popped open and he slipped the padlock free of the metal plates. Slipped it into an evidence bag.

Pushed the door.

Almost as stiff as the padlock wheels, it creaked open and the stench of dirty bodies and blood and piss and shite collapsed over Logan. Making him step back.

Deep breath.

He stepped over the threshold. 'Stephen? Stephen Bisset? It's OK, you're safe now; it's the police.'

Bloody hell – it was actually colder *inside* the shack.

The torch picked out a stack of poles and saws and chains. Then a heap of logs and an old tarpaulin. Then a cast-iron stove missing its door. Then a pile of filthy blankets.

'Stephen? Hello?'

Logan reached out and picked one of the poles from the stack. Smooth and shiny from countless hands over countless years. A bill hook rattled on the end, the screws all loose and rusted. 'Stephen? I've come to take you home.'

He slipped the hook under the nearest blanket and lifted.

Oh Christ . . .

Outside. The cold air clawed at the sweat peppering his face. Deep breath.

Logan rested his forehead against a tree, bark rough against his skin. The smell of pine nowhere near strong enough to wash away the shack's corrupt stench.

Don't be sick.

Be professional.

Oh God . . .

Deep breath.

'I . . .' His throat closed, strangling the words. Pressed his forehead into the bark so hard it stung. Tried again. 'I should kick the living shit out of you.'

Stirling's voice oozed out from the darkness. 'He's beautiful, isn't he?'

The phone trembled in Logan's hands as he dug it out and called Steel. 'I've found Stephen Bisset.'

There was a whoop from the other end. Then, *'Laz, I could French you. Is he . . .?'*

'No.' Though if he ever woke up, he'd probably wish he was. 'I need an ambulance, and an SEB goon-squad, and a Crime Scene Manager, and someone to stop me stringing Graham Bloody Stirling up from the nearest tree.'

CHAPTER 3

Big Tony Campbell slung his jacket over the back of his chair and slumped down. Aberdeen City's Divisional Commander, the Big Boss, Arse-Kicker In Chief: a large man, with broad shoulders and hands to match. His bald head gleamed in the last rays of a dying sun, seeping across the rooftops of the city and into the office. The only hairs loyal enough to cling on above the neckline were his eyebrows – heavy, black, and bushy.

He pointed to the seat on the other side of the polished wooden desk. 'Sit.' Then swivelled around and hunched down, giving Logan a perfect view of his shirt coming untucked from the waistband of his trousers. Exposing a swathe of thick dark fur.

Logan settled into the nominated seat and stifled a yawn, covering it with his hand as Big Tony Campbell re-emerged with a bottle of Highland Park in one hand and two crystal tumblers in the other. They went on the desk.

A healthy portion of whisky glugged into both glasses, then the Divisional Commander handed one over. 'They tell me Stephen Bisset's going to live.'

Logan licked his teeth – rough and unbrushed. 'Yes, sir.'

'Might've been better if you'd arrived too late.' His fingers hovered over the folder that sat in front of the computer. He didn't touch the manila surface, as if it might be infectious. 'Castrated, teeth ripped out, chest slashed open and "implants" forced inside, repeatedly raped . . . Never mind all the broken bones.' The corners of his mouth curdled. 'A non-elective sex change courtesy of Jack the Ripper. Still . . .'

He raised his glass and Logan did the same. Clinking the two together, before taking a sip.

Warmth slid all the way down into Logan's belly, leaving smoky footprints behind.

The Divisional Commander spun his seat around till it faced the window. Gazed out over his domain as darkness claimed it. Took another drink. 'Your boss tells me you're not really cut out to be an Acting Detective Inspector.'

'Does she now?' Backstabbing cow . . .

Well, unless this was promotion time? Time to stop *acting* up and make the step for real. With the pay rise that went with it. OK, so he wouldn't get overtime any more, but swings and round-abouts. Logan sat up straighter in his chair. 'Actually, sir, I think she's—'

'Don't get me wrong,' the Divisional Commander held up a hand, 'it's not that you *can't* do the job

20

– the Bisset investigation more than proves that – but she seems to think you don't *like* doing it. The man management, the spreadsheets, the meetings, the budget balancing.' Another sip. 'Is she right?'

Don't fidget.

'Well, sir, it's . . . Detective Chief Inspector Steel, sometimes—'

'You see, Logan,' he turned back, a smile stretching his face, 'it's important to me that my officers achieve their full potential. And it's my privilege and *duty* to help them do that.' A little salute with the tumbler. 'Especially when I can give them the tools they need to shine.'

Oh no.

Don't say it.

Not the two words *no* police officer *ever* wanted to hear.

The whisky curdled in Logan's stomach. His smile was lemon-rind and ashes, but he pulled it on anyway. 'Sir?'

Please don't . . .

'I think I've got a development opportunity that would be *perfect* for you.'

Too late.

— MONDAY BACKSHIFT —

CROMARTY: SEVEN TO EIGHT, RISING. OCCASIONALLY SEVERE.

CHAPTER 4

'. . . and while we're on the subject: guess who gets out today?' Logan let the pause grow as the two officers stared at him. 'Alex Williams.'

A groan.

The Constables' Office wasn't a big room. Magnolia, with a big pinboard covered in mugshots on one wall next to a whiteboard; posters, reports, notices, calendars, and more whiteboards on the others. Scuffed blue carpet tiles covered in layers of tea and coffee stains. A workbench on two sides doubling as desks; four office chairs – plastic scratched, foam-rubber poking out of frayed-edged fabric; the same number of steam-powered computers; Logan and two other officers, all kitted up and ready for the off. A throat-tickling smell of stale feet, pickled onion crisps, and shoe polish.

Logan rubbed a hand across the stubble covering his head. 'So I'm putting a grade one flag on the house. Anything happens, I want someone there in under five minutes.'

Deano fiddled with the CS gas canister clipped to the front of his fluorescent yellow high-vis waist-coat, twisting the gunmetal canister round and round in its leather case with big spanner fingers. Winding the spiral bungee cord attached to the base in knots. His broad shoulders stretched the black police-issue T-shirt tight. Even slouched in the swivel chair he was clearly the tallest person in the room. 'Tenner says they make it till Wednesday.'

Constable Nicholson pulled the sides of her mouth down and dug her hands into the gap between her stabproof vest and her black uniform top. Hunched her shoulders, setting the no-nonsense black bob wobbling. Scowled. 'Hospital or mortuary?'

Deano stuck his head on one side. The overhead light glinted against the thinning patch of hair at the top of his forehead. Grey hair swept back at the sides. 'I'm going to say . . . hospital.'

She pulled out a hand – it had a small tartan wallet in it. 'I'll take: mortuary by Saturday.' Then blinked at Logan. 'Sarge?'

'Are you and Constable Scott *seriously* taking bets on when someone's going to assault or murder their partner?'

Shrug.

'OK.' He dug a hand into his pocket. 'I'll have a fiver on: nobody dies.'

Deano accepted the cash and hid it away. 'Fool to yourself, Sarge. But far be it from me to dampen your faith in—'

'Sorry.' The door banged open and Constable Quirrel backed into the room, carrying a tray loaded with four mugs and a plate of rowies. Thin-faced, with a number-two haircut of pale ginger and a set of watery blue eyes. A least a head shorter than everyone else in the room. 'What? What did I miss?'

'Alex Williams got released.'

'Is it six months already?' Quirrel handed out the mugs – starting with Logan – then worked his way around the room with the plate. He took the last rowie and slotted his narrow bum into the only vacant chair. 'Bags I don't have to—'

'Tufty,' Logan pointed at him, 'I hereby deputize you to go tell Alex's partner, "It's that time again."'

'But, Sa-arge . . .' His eyebrows bunched for a moment, scrunching up his eyes. Then a smile. 'Wouldn't it be *better* if someone from Domestic Abuse did it? You know, laid out all the options? They're the experts, and we wouldn't want to—'

'Do what you're told.' Logan took a bite of rowie, chomping through the waxy crust and into the butter, lard, and salty goodness inside. 'And try not to be a dick while you're there. Last thing you need is more complaints.' A nod. 'Next.'

Deano clicked the mouse and the image on the computer screen changed to a photo of a small-ish fishing boat – rust-streaked along one side of the blue hull, the name '*COPPER-TUN WANDERER*' picked out in fading white paint. The picture sat beside one of a middle-aged man in a bright orange jacket, hair hanging damp around his leathery face, bottle of beer in one hand, what looked like a dirty big haddock in the other.

It was all written across the bottom of the PowerPoint slide, but Logan read it out anyway. 'Charles "Craggie" Anderson, fifty-two, missing for a week and a bit now. Tufty?'

'Yeah . . .' Constable Quirrel pulled out his notebook and flicked through to near the end. 'Spoke to his friends and neighbours again: he's not been in touch. Got on to the Coastguard and there's no sign of the *Copper-Tun* washing up anywhere. Waiting to hear back from ports in Orkney, Shetland, and Norway in case he's done a runner.'

'Right. When you've been round Alex Williams's, you and Deano hit Whitehills, Macduff, Portsoy, and Gardenstown. Do a door-to-door of all the boats. Did anyone see Charles Anderson the night he went missing? Anyone hear where he was going? Did he have any money problems? You know the drill.'

Deano nodded. 'Sarge.'

'And keep Tufty on a tighter leash this time, OK? Never known a probationer to get in so much trouble.'

Quirrel blushed. 'How was I supposed to know she wasn't wearing any pants?'

'I repeat: tighter leash. That's five missing persons we've got on the books now. Be nice if we could *actually* find this one.' Pause. 'Last, and by all means least, we have a new edict from on high. We are Moray and Aberdeenshire Division. From this point on anyone caught calling it the "Mire" gets a spanking. Any questions?'

Deano gave the canister of CS one last fiddle. 'Aye, is that the good kind of spanking, or the bad kind?'

'You're disturbed, you know that, don't you?' Logan finished his rowie and sooked the grease from his finger. Stood. 'Deano and Tufty, you're in the Postman Pat van. Janet and me are away to spin some druggies.'

'Sarge?' Nicholson took the patrol car round the hairpin bend, changing down for the hill. Off to the left, the North Sea shone like a polished stone. Yachts and tiny fishing boats bobbed lazily in the harbour.

Made a nice change after the horrible weekend.

On the other side of the bay, Macduff shone in the afternoon sunshine.

Then the view was swallowed by the pale harling walls of the Railway Inn. Old-fashioned Scottish houses lined the road, all towered over by the intimidating grey Victorian bulk of the Health Centre. Nicholson shifted her hands along the steering wheel, voice light and carefree. 'Sarge, has anyone spoken to you about the pool? You know, how it's going?'

Logan unzipped one of the pockets on his stab-proof and pulled out a packet of Polos. Liberated one from its foil prison. Popped the mint in his mouth and crunched. 'Take it from me: CID's a

29

mug's game.' The stabproof vest was like a fist, squeezing his chest with every breath. Handcuffs clicking against the seatbelt clasp. Extendable baton poking into his thigh. Limb restraints digging into the small of his back. Bet Batman's utility belt never gave him this much gyp. 'Still don't see why you want to join.' Crunch, crunch, crunch. 'Polo?' Wiggling the pack at her.

Past the junction and the road widened out into Castle Street with its much grander houses. Nicholson waved at an old woman having a sneaky fag outside the Castle Bar. 'Come on, Sarge, you were CID for years. You *know* why.'

Logan popped another Polo. 'Yeah, in the old days, maybe. Now they hive off all the interesting bits of the job and give them to specialist groups. If you're not on the Major Investigation Team you're not going to catch a murder.' He counted each one off on his fingers. 'Then there's Rape Teams, Violence-Reduction Teams, Domestic Abuse Teams, Drugs Teams, Housebreaking Teams, blah, blah, blah teams.' A shrug. 'All that's left for CID is the boring crap no one else wants to do.'

Right, onto Seafield Street. Climbing again, Banff Bay glinting in the rear-view mirror. The sky above, saltire blue. Unblemished by clouds or airplane-trail scars.

'Didn't stop you catching Graham Stirling, did it?'

True.

Logan smiled. 'Forget CID, Janet. *Divisional* policing – that's where all the cool kids are.'

Her shoulders slumped a bit.

The houses on the right were huge. He turned his head to watch them drift by. 'How much do you think one of those cost?' All fancy granite with cornices and bay windows and those raised blocks around the doors, windows, and gable ends. Grey slate roofs and manicured gardens. The occasional gnome.

Nicholson sighed. 'More than we'll ever make.'

'Don't get me wrong, the Sergeant's Hoose will be nice when it's finished, but I'm tired of living out of boxes.'

A call crackled out of the car's radio. *'Control to Bravo India, hello?'*

'Aye, aye.' Logan turned the volume up. 'Must be something big if they're bothering the boss.'

'Come on, Sarge, I don't want to be one of those cops who spends their whole career in one place. Got a glass ceiling to shatter.'

A woman's voice came through the speakers, deep and smooth: *'Bravo India to Control, safe to talk.'*

'Aye, ma'am, we've got another Cashline machine gone walkabout. Owner says they got aboot twenty-seven grand of stock as well. Broch Braw Buys, on Gallowhill Road, Fraserburgh.'

Not another one.

'Twenty-seven thousand pounds? Who's he trying to kid?'

'So he says, like.'

'Sarge?'

Past the bowling green, and the houses got a lot more councily. Semidetached with streaked harling walls and rusting satellite dishes.

'Probably swinging for a hefty insurance claim. Get the scene secured and I'll be there soon as I can . . .'

Logan turned the radio down again. Have to pop past Broch Braw Buys later and see what was going on. But with any luck it'd be someone else's problem by then.

'Sarge, are you—'

'How about this: I'm off to court tomorrow for the trial. You want to be in charge while I'm gone? I mean, you couldn't be Duty Sergeant, but you could run the team.'

Nicholson chewed on the inside of her cheek.

'It'll look good on your CV. You can start doing some of the briefings too. It all helps.'

'Deal.' She leaned forward, squinting against the sunshine at the cars droning towards them. 'That boy on his mobile phone?'

Logan shielded his eyes. 'The ugly one in the blue Fiesta?'

The Fiesta rumbled past, followed by three other vehicles. Then a tiny gap . . . Then a Passat.

Nicholson's finger jabbed one of the buttons mounted in the middle of the dashboard and the unit's blues flickered into life. Another button and a short siren woop blared out.

The Passat's driver slammed the brakes on, slithering to a halt about six feet away. An auld mannie goggled out at them, hands curled into fists around the steering wheel, tartan bunnet all squint on his head.

She gave him a nod, then pulled a U-turn. Put her foot down. The acceleration pushed Logan into his seat. Added its weight to the stabproof vest's crushing fist.

Cars parted before them, clearing the way through to the blue Fiesta with the ugly driver. The thing was shiny and polished, like new. Nicholson wheeched up right behind it and tapped the horn. The siren changed tone. Insistent. Demanding.

Mr Ugly glanced back at them, his face a curdled mess through the rear window. A pause . . . then he pulled in to the kerb.

Nicholson parked behind him. She fiddled with the Airwave clipped to the front of her vest. 'Control, I need a PNC check on a blue Fiesta.'

Logan reached into the back of the patrol car for his hat and climbed out into the sunshine. Shook one leg like a dog getting its belly scratched. Bloody police-issue trousers were made of burning ants and sandpaper. He did a slow walk around the Fiesta to the driver's window. Rapped his knuckles on the glass.

It buzzed down and Mr Ugly glared up at him. 'What?' The word came out like a gob of phlegm from a crooked mouth full of crooked teeth. Definitely a Birmingham accent. Thick eyebrows, broad face, dimpled chin, a spattering of angry red spots along the line of his jaw.

OK. Going to be one of those.

Logan unhooked the elastic band holding his body-worn video shut and slipped the front down, setting it recording. 'You do know it's an offence to use your mobile phone while driving, don't you, sir?'

A scowl. 'I wasn't using no mobile.'

'We saw you, sir.'

He faced the front again. Worked his jaw, making the fault line of spots ripple. A couple of volcanoes in the chain ready to blow. 'Prove it.'

'Name?'

Silence. More tectonic activity. Then, 'Martyn Baker, with a "Y". Sixteenth December, Nineteen Ninety-Three. Thirty-eight Dresden Road, Sparkbrook. Birmingham.'

Name, date of birth, and address. The crook's version of name, rank, and serial number. Just like that. No stranger to giving his details to the police, then. Logan printed it all down in his notebook. 'Stay in the vehicle, sir.' Then around to the boot of the car and onto Control for a background check.

Nicholson pulled on her peaked cap and sauntered over, thumbs tucked into the armholes of her stabproof, like Rumpole of the Bailey. She jerked her chin up. 'Sarge? Car's registered to a Martyn Baker—'

'Nineteen Ninety-Three, thirty-eight Dresden Road, Birmingham?'

'That's him. AKA Paul Butcher, AKA Dave

34

Brooks. Got a sheet two miles long: housebreaking, aggravated assault, possession of a Class A, possession with intent, beat the crap out of his girlfriend *and* his mum . . . Bit of a charmer, by all accounts.'

'Certainly failed the attitude test.' Logan looked back at the car. Baker's narrowed eyes were right there in the rear-view mirror. Staring at them. 'Any outstanding warrants?'

'Not so much as an overdue library book.' She shifted from foot to foot. 'You want to do him for the phone?'

'Denies it.'

A snort. 'Really? Law-abiding citizen like him?'

The Airwave clipped to Logan's chest bleeped four times: a point-to-point call. A quick glance and there was PC Scott's shoulder number on the screen. His voice boomed out of the speaker. *'Shire Uniform Seven, it's Dean, you safe to talk?'*

He hunched one shoulder forward, tilting his head so his mouth was up against the microphone. Pressed the button. 'Go ahead, Deano.'

'Got ourselves an assault in Whitehills. The Drookit Haddie on Harbour Place. Bunch of scrotes gave an old boy a battering. Me and Tufty are waiting for the ambulance.'

'Suspects?'

'Nah: everyone in the pub's come down with amnesia. And Maggie's been on – there's a coo loose on the B9031 round about Gamrie.'

'OK. We'll see to it. Make sure you get the CCTV from the pub.'

35

Nicholson's face soured. 'A *cow* wandering about on the road. Not exactly *Silence of the Lambs*, is it?'

'Careful what you wish for.' Logan let go of the handset and turned back to Mr Ugly's Fiesta. 'Not all it's cracked up to be.'

'So . . . what are we going to do with Plukey Pete?'

But Logan was already walking up to the driver's window. 'Tell me, Martyn-with-a-"Y", what brings you all the way from thirty-eight Dresden Road, Birmingham, to the streets of sunny Banff?'

Another dose of the evil eye. 'Personal, isn't it. Now you done? 'Cos you're infringing my right to free movement and that.'

'I see . . .' He drummed his fingers on the roof of the car. 'You know what, Mr Baker, I was going to let you off with a warning, but I have reason to believe you wouldn't pay any attention to it. As such, I'm confiscating your mobile phone as evidence—'

'Aw, bugger *off*!' The line of spots simmered. 'You're not taking my bloody phone.'

'Under Common Law I have the power to seize any items suspected to be used in the execution of a crime. Or would you like me to do you for resisting instead?' Logan popped his wrist forward and checked his watch. 'I've got a couple of hours to spare. Step out of the car, Mr Baker.'

Baker folded over until his forehead brushed the steering wheel. '*Fine.*' Then dug in his pocket and came out with a big Samsung job, the case all battered and scratched. The screen cobwebbed with cracks radiating out from the bottom left corner. He handed it over. 'Happy?'

'Delirious, sir. I'll make out a receipt for the phone.' But he took his time over it. 'Drive carefully, Mr Baker.' A smile. 'We'll be keeping an eye out to make sure you're OK.'

Nicholson stared after the Fiesta as it drove away. 'Think he's dealing? Making a delivery? Maybe on the run from someone?'

'Or D, all of the above . . .' Logan slipped the phone into a brown paper evidence bag. Labelled it. 'But who knows, maybe he's off for a romantic assignation with a nice sheep?' Dumped the bag in the boot of the patrol car. 'Speaking of animal husbandry, that cow's not going to round itself up.'

CHAPTER 5

'. . . *says you're not to forget about your appraisal today.*'

Logan hit the talk button on his Airwave handset. 'Depends on how things pan out. Janet and me are busy keeping the good people of Aberdeenshire North safe from scoundrels and scallywags.'

Fields rolled past the car's windows, shiny and green, dark walls of gorse aflame with burning yellow flowers. Ahead, in a break between the hills, cliffs disappeared down into the North Sea.

Maggie's voice dropped to a hard whisper. '*Sergeant McRae, you* are *going to tell her I'm needing a wee pay rise, aren't you? Only with Bill's back being what it is, we—*'

'Can't promise anything, but I'll try. Assuming we get finished here in good time.' Logan shifted in his seat. Pointed out through the windscreen as they crowned the brow of yet another hill. 'There we go.'

A big brown bullock waddled down the middle of the road. Broad shouldered and thick bottomed. Tail flicking from side to side. Horns weaving back and forth as it lumbered along.

'*The Inspector says you're not to put it off again. Appraisals have to be in by Wednesday.*'

Nicholson leaned on the horn. *Breeeeeeeeeep.*

The cow didn't even flinch.

'*She really was quite insistent.*'

'OK, OK. Tell her we'll be back at the station about . . .' Logan checked his watch. 'Better make it half four. Twenty to five. *Ish.*'

'*Will do.*' And Maggie was gone.

Nicholson tried the horn again. *Breeeeeeeeeep.* Nothing. 'I went to police college for this? *Months* at Tulliallan. Two years as a probationer . . .' *Breeeeeeeeeep.* She buzzed down her window. 'Come on, you hairy bugger, get off the road!'

Logan swivelled in his seat. Empty fields, all around. Not a single head of livestock to be seen, other than the one clomping its way down the middle of the road. 'No idea where he came from.' Off to the left, a swathe of green was peppered with big round bales wrapped in black plastic. 'We'll stick him in there.' Logan undid his seatbelt. 'Come on.'

Nicholson scowled. 'This is what happens when they don't let us carry tasers.'

'Gah . . .' Nicholson shoved the gate shut and hauled the pin back, making the spring squeal. Let go and it clacked into place. She spat twice. Then a third time. Wiped a hand through the mud that caked her face from one ear to the other. More covered the front of her high-vis waistcoat.

39

Lumps of it wodged in the armholes of her stab-proof. Another gob of muddy spittle. Then a glower in his direction. 'Where all the cool kids are, my arse.'

Logan shrugged. 'You imagine what would happen if someone came round the corner doing sixty and hit that?' Pointing at the big brown beast, who was at least three shades cleaner than Nicholson. 'They'd have to scoop you into your body-bag like eleven stone of mince.'

She wiped her hands down the front of her vest, smearing the filth. 'You saying I'm fat?'

'Come back here, you wee sod!' Logan vaulted the low garden wall and sprinted across the lawn, knees pumping. One hand clamping the peaked cap to his head, the other clutching his extendable baton in its holder. Stopping it from jiggling about with every other step.

The wee sod in question kept on running. Sneakers flashing their white bellies, his arms and legs going like pistons, hoodie flapping behind him like an obscene pink tongue.

Over into the next garden.

Crashing straight through a bed of nasturtiums and pansies. The owners sat on a bench against the house, sharing a bottle of wine. On their feet and shaking fists as the Wee Sod battered past.

A hedge separated this property from the next one. He leapt it, almost lost his footing on the other side. His shoulder bag slipped, thumped into the lawn. Tins of spray paint clattered across the grass like WWII bombs.

'I said, come back here!'

The Wee Sod risked a grin over his shoulder. Freckled face, no more than twelve. Maybe thirteen. Curly red hair and dimpled cheeks.

Then THUMP – Nicholson slammed into him from the side with the kind of rugby tackle that would've done the nation proud at Murrayfield.

They went careening across the lawn in a tumble of limbs, coming to rest in a clatter of pots and gnomes.

Logan slowed to a jog, then a halt as Nicholson scrambled to her feet, then hauled the Wee Sod upright by his hoodie.

She spat out a blade of grass. 'When someone yells, "Stop, police!" you sodding well *stop*.'

He wriggled a couple of times, didn't get anywhere, then hung limp.

'Well?' She gave him a little shake. 'What've you got to say for yourself?'

He bit his top lip. Then shrugged. 'It's a comment on our political elite and the disenfranchisement and disengagement of the common man.' His voice tried out three octaves along the way.

'Spray-painting willies on a Conservative Party billboard doesn't count as political commentary.'

'Does too.'

She pushed him at Logan, then dragged out her notebook. 'Name?'

He tensed, as if he was about to bolt again.

Logan grabbed him by the shoulders. 'You want a go in the handcuffs? Because I can arrange that.'

He looked up, over his shoulder. A blush filled in the pale skin between his freckles. 'You're not going to tell my mum, are you?'

Nicholson poked him with her pen. '*Name?*'

'I mean, they lord it over us from Edinburgh, don't they? Our political masters. No one really cares what we think any more. We're like drones to them, only instead of honey they grow fat on our taxes.'

Logan pulled his chin in. '*Our* taxes? You're, what, thirteen? When did you last pay any tax?'

'Workers control the means of production.'

Nicholson poked him again. 'You've got one more chance, then I'm doing you for refusing to give your details. Now: *name?*'

He took a deep breath. Stared down at his trainers. 'Geoffrey Lovejoy.' Then a sniff, and his head came up again, eyes glinting. 'I'm a political prisoner. I demand you call the United Nations. Power to the people!'

Logan looked up from his notebook. 'And you're sure you'd recognize her again if you saw her?'

The shopkeeper nodded, setting a crowd of chins on a Mexican wave. 'Absolutely. She had half a dozen bottles of Chanel Number Five, a handful of Touche Éclat concealer, Elizabeth Arden, and every single bit of Paco Rabanne we had on display!' He swept a hand towards the other side of the chemist's, where the front door was being held open by a little old lady wearing a plastic headscarf. 'Scooped them up and ran off without so much as a blush. Our Stacey chased her, but . . .' A shrug.

Nicholson's stabproof was beginning to look as if she'd smeared it with camouflage paint – green grass stains mingling with the mud from their run-in with the escaped cow. It wasn't a good look. She pointed at the security camera bolted to the wall behind the till. 'You get it on CCTV?'

A blush swept across the puffy cheeks. 'It's plastic. I bought it off eBay for a fiver.'

Nicholson pointed. 'Is that not Liam Barden?'

On the other side of the road, a chubby man in an Aberdeen Football Club shirt walked into the Co-op.

Logan frowned as the automatic door closed, hiding the man and his bright-red shiny shirt. 'You sure?'

'Certain.' She parked outside the shop. 'Well . . . eighty percent. You got the ID sheet?'

He dug into the glove compartment and came out with four creased sheets of A4, stapled together. Two photos on each sheet, along with names and details of when and where they went missing. Liam Barden was on the third page: grinning away at a Caley Thistle match, both thumbs up, and what looked like a gravy stain splodging the Orion

43

Group logo on his blue-and-red football top. A wee gold thistle glinted on a golden chain around Liam's neck. Very classy. A proper Ratners special.

Liam shared the printout with a picture of everyone's favourite drug-dealing scumbag, Jack Simpson – jagged tribal tattoos on his neck, sunken cheeks, pierced nose and ears.

He'd also grown a Hitler moustache, a pair of glasses, Frankenstein's Monster bolts, and a blacked-out tooth. There was even a speech balloon with 'I HAS A SEXY!!!' written in it.

'For God's sake.' Logan held the sheet out. 'How many times do I have to tell people *not* to draw things on missing persons photos?'

'Don't look at me: don't even own a blue biro.'

'How would *you* feel if one of your relatives went missing and someone scrawled all over *their* picture? Jack Simpson's a nasty wee git, but he deserves the same treatment as everyone else.'

'It wasn't me!'

'Like working with a bunch of three-year-olds . . .'

Still: had to admit that the photo of Liam Barden did look a bit like the guy who'd gone into the store. Heavyset, balding from the back, toothy smile. 'Only problem is, what's happened to his moustache?'

'Maybe he shaved it off?' Nicholson unbuckled and climbed out into the sunshine. Pulled her hat on. 'You coming?'

'And why's he dumped Inverness Caley Thistle

for AFC?' Logan joined her on the pavement. Held out the sheet again. 'See?'

She frowned at the picture. 'Not illegal to support more than one club. Besides, think how stoked his wife and kids will be if we find him.'

Which was more than could be said for Jack Simpson. Missing for ten days already and not even his mum wanted him back. If he hadn't owed his granny money, he probably wouldn't even have been reported missing.

Logan turned the page. 'And why does no one update these things?' He rummaged through the zip-pockets on his stabproof vest. Frowned. Took out his notebook. Put it away again. 'Sodding Hector.' He held out a hand. 'Lend me a pen?'

She handed one over and Logan drew a thick X over the face of a little boy on the bottom of page four. 'We found Ian Dickinson four days ago.'

'You take my word for it – next one you can score off is Liam Barden.' Nicholson straightened her cap and marched into the Co-op.

Logan took a lick of his ice lolly, working his way through the raspberry coating to the cheap vanilla inside. Sun warm on the back of his neck. 'Well, it was worth a go.'

'Could have sworn it was him.' Nicholson worked her left arm around in a circle – Cornetto making chocolaty dribbles in her other hand as they wandered down the hill.

'How's the shoulder?'

45

A shrug. 'Still say we should've arrested the vandalizing wee sod.'

'Then we'd have to take him all the way to Fraserburgh for processing, and that's you and me off the streets for at least two hours. With Deano and Tufty still up the hospital, who's going to look after the good people of Banff and Macduff?'

'That's not the point, he's—'

'All the kid did was draw a big willy on a billboard. Some people might think our prospective Conservative MSP looks much better with a big willy sprayed all over him. At least Citizen Geoffrey's taking an interest in the political process.'

Four bleeps sounded from his Airwave handset. *'Sergeant McRae?'*

Another lick of lolly. 'Go ahead, Maggie, safe to talk.'

'Are you forgetting someone?'

They crossed over to the other side of the road. 'Am I?'

The reply came back as a hiss. *'Inspector McGregor! I told you, she needs to do your appraisal.'*

Damn. 'How pissed-off is she?'

A wee dog barked and barked and barked as they passed, pogoing up and down behind a little wrought-iron gate.

'You said you'd be back here by twenty-to. And it's nearly five.'

'We're . . .' Another lick of lolly, catching an

ice-cream tear. 'We're in the middle of something here, Maggie. Can't we reschedule for tomorrow?'

Silence.

Around the corner and onto Low Street with its bars and shops and cafés.

'Maggie?'

'You want me to dignify that with an answer? And you're supposed to put in a word for me – how are you going to do that if she's in a foul mood?'

'OK, OK. Tell her . . . half past five.'

Past the Cats Protection League and the whisky shop.

'All right. I'll try. But make sure you're not late.' Maggie signed off.

The gift shop next door had obviously started selling papers, because a little folding placard thing sat on the pavement outside it: 'LIVERPOOL SHOOTING ~ PICTURES EXCLUSIVE'.

He'd barely got the Airwave back in its twisty holder when the handset bleeped again. *'Sarge? Aye, it's Dean. Safe to talk?'*

'Deano. You and Tufty finished at the hospital yet, or are you planning on skiving the whole shift?'

'Still there, Sarge. Got a missing person for you.'

Another road led off to the right. Long, thin, dark, and claustrophobic. Rows of terraced buildings on either side, tall enough to block out the sunshine and leave the patchy tarmac blanketed in shadow. Raw grey walls and dark slate roofs. The occasional one painted with aging whitewash

– standing out like a filled tooth in a broken mouth. 'Do you mean you've found someone who's missing? Or that someone else has disappeared?'

'Aye. One Neil Wood, owns a B-and-B on the Shortgate Lane, Peterhead. His dad says Wood's been gone for three, maybe four days.'

'So take his details.' A bite of lolly, before it collapsed off the stick, then Logan froze. Pointed with his other hand.

Up ahead, loitering in the doorway of a boarded-up shop was a stick-thin woman in a baggy T-shirt and pink tracksuit bottoms. Filthy Ugg boots on her feet. Roll-up cigarette cupped in her hand as if it was going to give away her position to snipers in the enemy trenches.

Nicholson squinted. 'You jammy sod.'

'Not jammy, Constable, skill.'

'Sarge? You still there?'

'Look, Deano, you've been doing this longer than I have. You know the drill – you take his details and fill out a misper form. And maybe we find him, and maybe we don't. It's not—'

'The old boy who got a kicking in Whitehills is Neil Wood's dad. Seems the guys did it because of who his son is. Turns out Neil Wood's a stot. Did eight years for abusing kids in Tayside. Got out of Peterhead, couldn't go home, settled here. Bought a B-and-B and moved his dad up from down south to live with him, 'cos the old guy's got heart problems.'

'And now he's disappeared.'

'Which is why I'm not just filling in a form.'

'That's all we need.'

The woman turned her back, one hand scratching away at the crook of her arm, making the cigarette smoke curl and coil around her fingers. Couldn't be long until she spotted them.

'Deano, get onto the Offender Management Unit. Find out who's meant to be monitoring Wood, and tell them to get their finger out. We do *not* want someone like that running around our patch with no idea where he is. Tell them to get a lookout request on the go.'

'Will do.'

'Right, now bugger off, we've got a druggie to spin.'

A nod to Nicholson and they ditched the ice creams in a bin and marched down the road.

'Anything?' Logan shifted his grip on the skeletal arm as Nicholson rummaged her way through the leopard-skin-print handbag. Big enough to take a breezeblock or a small child.

A delivery van grumbled by, the Tesco Logo emblazoned down one side, trailing a cloud of dust behind it.

Warm golden light washed the gap between two buildings.

It was big enough to fit another house, but if there had been one on the site, it was long gone. Now it doubled as a dirt-floored car park and access through to the garages and lock-ups that ran along the rear of the gardens.

Weeds jungled at the base of the five-foot wall that formed either side of the gateless entry to the secret land beyond. Shutting the three of them off from the street.

Nicholson held up a golden pen thing in one blue-nitrile-gloved-hand. 'This is a bit fancy, isn't it, Kirstin? Touche Éclat? I've seen it in Boots – stuff costs a fortune.'

Kirstin Rattray shrugged one bony shoulder. The motion caused the neck of her baggy T-shirt to slip far enough to expose a bright-green bra strap stretched taut over semi-skimmed skin. 'Found it, didn't I?' A small flock of purple lovebites perched in the crook of her neck. Eighties hair and dark circles under her eyes. Cheekbones you could peel tatties with.

'Right. Course you did. What about these?' Nicholson pulled out two lots of Chanel No. 5, still in their boxes, then one of Paco Rabanne. 'You find them, too?'

Kirstin's bottom lip disappeared between her teeth. Eyes down to the left. 'You planted that. Never seen them before.'

'Don't be a spaz, Kirstin. Did you rob them yourself? Or did someone do it for you?'

'I should get a lawyer and that. Sue you for false thingummy.'

'Ooh and a brand new iPhone too.' Nicholson wiggled it at Logan. 'When I was on the dole it was a red-letter day if I could afford to buy chips and pants the same week. Now it's all smartphones and perfume.' Back to their new friend. 'Let me guess: you found it?'

Kirstin's head fell back so she was staring up at the warm blue sky. A breath hissed out. Her knees sagged an inch or two. 'What do you want?'

'World peace for me. Sarge?'

Logan frowned. 'I'm partial to Maltesers, myself.'

'Look, I've got a little girl. Amy. She's three, I swear on her *life* I never nicked nothing.'

'Really? Then how come you match the description of the woman who pilfered a heap of perfume and makeup from Fisher's the Chemists? And how come your handbag's full of the stuff that got robbed?'

'Told you, I found it.' She stuck her hand out. 'Now can I get me bag back?'

'Sarge?'

Logan let go of the thin pale arm. 'Police Scotland thanks you for your cooperation, and for handing in the items you "found". Very public spirited. We'll try to return them to their rightful owners.' He scribbled out another receipt. 'Now, we've got to make a quick stop at the station – prior engagement – but after that, why don't we all pop over to yours and see if we can't turn up anything else you've "found" recently? Voluntarily.'

Kirstin's head drooped back again. 'Sodding hell . . .'

51

CHAPTER 6

Kirstin scowled up at him from the bench in Interview Room Two. Both hands in front of her, fingers knotting and twisting, while Nicholson leaned back against the wall behind her.

The vertical blinds were closed, but the light was still painfully bright in the small room. The panic strip all shiny and unused. A creased chunk of flip-chart paper was pinned to one wall. Far more chairs than would ever be needed in an interview cluttered the grey carpet.

Logan gave Kirstin a smile, then slipped out and closed the door behind him.

Into the front hall, with its elaborate beige, brown, blue, and white tiles. They didn't really go with the walls – white to the waist-high rail, then pastel blue above. The Response Level sign was just visible through the open door to the stairwell. Apparently, today's terrorism threat level was 'FABULOUS!' in big block capitals.

Bloody day shift . . .

Logan replaced it with the official 'MODERATE'

then punched his access code into the keypad to get through to the main office.

It was all scuffed blue carpet tiles, magnolia walls, boxy plastic ducting, and slightly grubby ceiling tiles. Two desks, back-to-back, corralled in by blue fuzzy cubicle walls. Another barricade of the same blue fuzz separating the front desk – little more than a wide shelf with a roller shutter above it – from the reception area.

Maggie had one of the small square locker doors open, so she could fiddle an Airwave handset into its charger. A tall woman in black trousers, shiny shoes and a pink silk blouse. Grey hair pulled back in a ponytail. Sharp, bird-like features. She twitched her head towards the front desk's barricade, with its covering of posters and notices. 'Where have you been?'

'Saving society from a one-woman shoplifting crime-spree.' He clunked open the filing cabinet in the corner and rifled through it. 'Any messages?'

'That horrible Detective Chief Inspector Steel called. Then Nelson Street: they say you can't have the Big Car back till tomorrow—'

'You're *kidding*. Sick of not having a car with a proper radio in it.'

'Well, you'll have to sing along with yourself then, won't you. They need to put in a whole new CCTV system.'

'Again?'

'Take it up with Sergeant Muir. I'm not the one who left Stinky Sammy Wilson unsupervised in the back. Oh, and Louise from Sunny Glen was on the phone an hour ago.'

Logan froze, one hand on the thick manila folder marked 'B DIVISION ~ STAFF APPRAISALS'. He cleared his throat. 'Something wrong?'

'Oh, no, nothing bad. She wants to talk to you about changing your girlfriend's medication, that's all.' Maggie picked a couple of yellow Post-its from her desk and held them out. 'Here you go.'

So it wasn't an emergency. Nothing bad had happened. The breath huffed out of him, leaving a metallic taste behind. As if he'd been sucking on copper wire. 'Thanks, Maggie.' He took the proffered Post-its. 'Any chance you could order up some more Biros? Hector's nicked all mine again.'

'Hmmph.' A small selection of today's papers were draped over the partition of her cubicle. The *Press and Journal* had 'STORMS BATTER NORTHEAST COAST' in big letters across the front page and a photo of waves crashing over the harbour wall in Peterhead. *Aberdeen Examiner* – 'WOODLAND RIPPER TRIAL OPENS' stretched above a photo of Graham Stirling grinning away at a party somewhere. And the *Daily Mail* had gone for, 'DRIVE-BY SHOOTING KILLERS ON THE RUN' with a picture of a bus stop and blurry figures sealed off behind a line of blue-and-white 'POLICE' tape. 'LIVERPOOL POLICE

Launch Nationwide Manhunt For Gangland Murderers.'

Maggie grabbed the *Aberdeen Examiner* and slipped it under her arm. 'Right. I'd better get on. Bill's stovies won't make themselves.' She pulled on a multi-coloured hiking jacket and picked up her bag. 'Don't forget to put in a good word for my extra five percent.' She disappeared out the door to the tradesman's entrance, humming what sounded like 'Onward, Christian Soldiers'.

Took all sorts.

And *five* percent? What planet did she beam down from? Lucky if she got three quid and a box of staples.

He grabbed the appraisals folder, clanged the filing-cabinet drawer shut, then flicked through the Post-its. Groaned when he got to the one about Steel.

'Call DCI Steel about Graham Stirling ~ Urgent.'

Brilliant.

He pulled out his phone and selected her name from the contacts list. Listened to it ring.

Steel's gravelly voice rasped in his ear. *'About time. You all prepped for your testimony tomorrow? Cause if you're no', I'll—'*

'Yes, I'm all prepped. It's fine.' He settled his bum against the photocopier.

'Better be. Last thing we need is Graham Stirling back on the streets. You see what the press are calling him now? The—'

'The Woodland Ripper. I know. It's *fine*. Open-and-shut case. Graham Stirling isn't going anywhere but jail for the next sixteen to life.'

'*Good.*' There was a sooking noise, then she was back. '*Susan says are you remembering Jasmine has a dance competition Saturday? 'Cos you're going whether you like it or not.*'

'Saturday?'

'*There an echo in here? Aye, Saturday. She's been lolloping about the house for weeks, driving me and her mum mad. Don't see why we should be the only ones to suffer.*'

'What time?'

'*Half twelve. I've got you down for a pair of tickets. That's twelve quid you owe me. And* before *you ask: you're no' taking your mother.*'

As if.

Logan's shoulders dipped. 'I can't make half twelve. Saturday's dayshift – won't get off till three.' He pushed through the door and into the stairwell, his footsteps echoing on the tiled floor. 'Tell Jasmine I'm sorry.'

'*Oh no you don't. I'm no' doing your dirty work for you. You* can call *your* daughter and tell her why Daddy can't be arsed turning up for anything any more.*'

He closed his eyes and thunked the side of his head against the wall. 'We've been over this.'

'*Far be it from me to—*'

'You got me transferred up here! This is your fault.' He scuffed his way up to the first floor. 'What am I supposed to do, go AWOL in the middle of a shift? This isn't CID, OK? Divisional policing doesn't work like that.' Took a left at the top of the stairs and stopped outside the blue door: 'BANFF & BUCHAN ~ INSPECTOR'. A brass nameplate had been slid into the holder above the notice: 'WENDY McGREGOR'.

'*Wah, wah, wah. Pity poor Logan.*' Steel had another sook. '*You're lucky I'm no'*—'

He hung up on her. Switched his phone off. Rammed it into his pocket. Stood there, grinding his teeth for a bit.

As if he didn't have enough to worry about.

Deep breath.

Count to ten.

Shoulders back.

Then Logan reached out and knocked on the Duty Inspector's door.

'Come.'

He stepped into the room. About the same size as the one he had to share downstairs, only with a new blue carpet and chairs that didn't look as if they would self-destruct if you even thought about sitting on them. A round coffee table and a shiny desk. Two pinboards on opposite walls – almost completely covered in maps. And a stunning view from the corner windows, out over Banff harbour and the bay.

The Inspector sat behind her desk, black T-shirt complete with two shiny pips on each of the attached epaulettes. Hair swept back from her heart-shaped face, greying at the temples. She took her glasses off and pointed at one of the visitors' chairs. 'You actually turned up? Are you sure you're feeling all right? Couldn't come up with an excuse to wriggle out of it?'

Warmth spread between his shoulder blades, tickled the tips of his ears. 'Operational priorities . . .'

'Sit. Sit.' She pulled out a notepad and a silver pen. 'So, four months back in uniform.'

He sank into the chair and plonked his folder on the desk. 'How did you get on at Broch Braw Buys?'

'Definitely our friends the Cashline Ram-Raiders. In and out in less than two minutes. If you're in Fraserburgh tonight, do me a favour and pop past. It's about time we caught these idiots.'

'I can go now, if you like?'

'No you don't. Appraisals.'

Worth a try. He poked the folder. 'All up to date. A couple of the probationers could do with a bit more supervision, and Greeny in Peterhead needs a boot up the backside, but other than that everyone's getting on well.'

'What about you?'

'I want to get Constable Scott on the diploma course. It's about time he got promoted to sergeant.'

She smiled at him. 'No: what about *your* performance?'

Ah. He sat forward, hands clasped in his lap. 'I'm doing OK.'

Inspector McGregor pulled a sheet of paper from her in-tray, stuck her glasses on again, and peered at it. '"As Duty Sergeant, Logan McRae continues to integrate well with the various sections of B Division. He manages two teams of constables, in addition to his own team of four, and provides appropriate support to the resident sergeants at both Fraserburgh and Peterhead stations. Sergeant McRae assists with managing service delivery to the Local Policing Area and regularly engages with service partners to deal with local challenges. He has excellent interpersonal skills and responds well to direction."'

Logan didn't move. 'Direction?'

A shrug. 'Well, I had to put something.' She gave the paper a shoogle and went back to reading. 'Since he arrived in Banff, clear-up rates have improved in B Division with particular success being seen in tackling the problems associated with drug usage, such as housebreaking, antisocial behaviour, and dealing.' She put the form down again. 'Anything else I should add?'

'Maggie wants a pay rise. Five percent.'

'Five percent?' Inspector McGregor curled her top lip. 'Has she been helping herself to that cannabis we seized last week?'

'Can you imagine what would happen if she left? Who else is going to fill in all Maggie's forms, update STORM, manage the productions and the office. Order pens when Hector nicks them all. *And* she's the only one who can work the station CCTV.'

The Inspector took off her glasses and huffed a breath onto the lenses. Polished them on the hem of her black T-shirt. 'Logan, the rest of the support staff will be lucky if they get one percent, never mind five.'

He held up his hands. 'I promised I'd ask. She—'

The Inspector's Airwave bleeped. *'Bravo India, safe to talk?'*

She sighed. Sagged a little. Then pressed the button. 'Go ahead.'

'Aye, the SEB have turned up at last from Aberdeen. They're all talking overtime to deal with the ram-raid at Broch Braw Buys. Say it's going to take at least six hours. You OK to approve?'

Inspector McGregor stared at the ceiling for a moment. 'Fine. But tell them they've got four hours, not six. They're not dragging this out, twiddling their thumbs on my budget.'

'Will do.'

She dumped the handset into a drawer and thumped it shut. 'A bit of career advice, Logan: never, *ever*, volunteer to be Duty Inspector.' There was a brief pause as she clattered something out on her computer keyboard. Then sat back again. 'Right: what about your development actions for the next four months?'

'War on drugs. I want Frankie Ferris in the cells before summer's out.'

Something painful crawled across the Inspector's face. 'Frankie Ferris. Again.'

Shrug. 'He's got two strikes for Class A drug-trafficking. One more and he wins a giant stuffed

60

panda and a mandatory seven-stretch. What's not to like?'

'You're obsessed.' She shook her head and scribbled it down in her notepad. 'Any chance you can have something a bit more cuddly too? An increase in community engagement? How about . . .' her tongue poked out of the corner of her mouth then she read out what she was writing: '"I aim to build stronger ties with the residents of Banff, Macduff, and Portsoy. I feel that leveraging community-liaison opportunities will add value to Police Scotland's offerings through the exploitation of soft intelligence."'

Logan stared at her. 'Leveraging added value?'

'You're never going to get past sergeant if you don't learn management speak. Soon as you hit inspector it's like waking up in a foreign country where everyone's got catch-phrase Tourette's. Last divisional meeting I was at, someone came out with, "How do we incentivize our stakeholders to embrace three-sixty-degree thinking a hundred and ten percent of the time." Honest to God, not even the hint of a smile.'

Logan pinched the bridge of his nose. Someone had set a rat loose behind his eyes. Clawing and biting.

Nicholson patted him on the arm. 'Never mind, Sarge, only seven hours to go.'

Kirstin Rattray's flat sat on the top floor of a lumpen block of grey on Saint Catherine Street. It was to one end of a row of soulless buildings that loomed over the smaller, traditional, Scottish houses on the other side of the road. Threatening to beat them up and steal their lunch money.

It wasn't so much furnished as . . . manky. Peeling wallpaper in the kitchen. Cracked tiles in a bathroom that looked as if it hadn't seen a bottle of bleach in years. A smell of damp and sweat and dirty washing in the bedroom. The view from the lounge was terrific, down the hill, over the surrounding rooftops and out to sea. The view inside the lounge was a different matter.

Kirstin slumped down on a tatty brown corduroy couch. A fake oil painting – the kind you could order from a photo at Tesco or Argos – was mounted in a gaudy gilt frame above the fireplace. A mousy-haired little girl of two or three grinned from the canvas with a gap-toothed mouth. Button nose. Shiny eyes. A teddy bear and a couple of dinosaurs were arranged along the mantelpiece beneath her picture. Like a shrine.

It was the only clean bit of the flat.

Nicholson pulled a laptop out from behind the bookcase. 'Anything else?'

A bony shrug.

The pile on the coffee table had grown to a decent size. Phones, MP3 players, a bit of jewellery, two hundred quid in cash, and assorted perfumes and makeup.

Logan picked up a new-ish smartphone, the case squeaking in his blue-gloved fingers as he turned it over. 'Lot of this doesn't look shoplifty, Kirstin.

It looks breakey-and-entery. When did you turn to burglary?'

She kept her eyes on the dark brown stain on the cushion next to her. 'Told you: didn't nick anything. Found it.'

'I'll bet we can match most of this stuff to crime reports.'

'It's not mine!'

Nicholson put the laptop down then pulled the stained seat cushion from the sofa. A biscuit tin nestled amongst the rusting springs and torn support fabric. The picture on the lid had Jammie Dodgers and those weird pink ring things. 'Well, well, well . . .'

On the couch, Kirstin glanced at the biscuit tin and away again. Squirmed. 'That's nothing to do with me . . .'

Nicholson picked up the tin and opened it. Stared for a moment. 'Sarge?' She held it out. A handful of tinfoil wrappers sat inside, along with a tiny Ziploc bag of white powder; a thumbnail-sized nub of brown, wrapped in clingfilm; and a pack of Rizla rolling papers.

Kirstin folded forwards till her chest rested against her knees, arms wrapped around her head. 'It's not *mine* . . .'

Logan dumped the phone back on the pile of 'found' electronics, then had a wee poke about in the biscuit tin. Definitely enough for possession. Maybe even possession with intent. 'So, Kirstin. Looks like you're a bit screwed.'

'It's not mine.' Voice muffled by her knees.

'Right. You *found* it.' He handed the tin back to Nicholson.

She put the top on again. 'What do you think Kirstin's looking at, Sarge? Four years? Maybe five?'

Logan bared his teeth and sooked a breath in. Grimaced. 'Depends who the Sheriff is. Harding's got a bee in his bunnet about drugs right now; might go as high as seven, if he thinks she's dealing.'

'I see . . .' Nicholson frowned off into the middle distance. Stroked her chin. Then snapped her fingers. 'I know! What if Kirstin here tried to cut a deal? You know, if she decided to scratch our backs?'

He folded his arms. 'Well, I suppose that would depend. I'm pretty itchy.'

Kirstin groaned. Sat up. Slumped backwards. Covered her face with her hands. 'You didn't hear it from me, OK?'

Silence.

'Didn't hear what, Kirstin?'

'Klingon and Gerbil got a shipment in from down south today.'

Nicholson slipped the biscuit tin into a large evidence bag. 'Coke? Heroin? Hash? Crack? Smack? Jellies? Strepsils? What?'

A shrug.

Logan frowned. Outside, the sound of a car droned past. 'This delivery: was it an ugly bloke in a shiny blue Fiesta? Birmingham accent?' Then ran a finger along his own jaw. 'Big line of plukes here? Calls himself Martyn-with-a-"Y", or Paul, or Dave?'

'Don't know. Never met him. But Gerbil's all excited cause he thinks he's in with the big boys now. Shooting his mouth off round here last night.' She dropped her hands away from her face. Stared up at the fake painting of the wee girl. 'You can't tell him I told you. He'll kill me.'

'Kevin "the Gerbil" McEwan? Got more chance of being gored by a sheep.' Logan jerked a thumb at the ceiling. 'On your feet.'

'You've got to *promise*! So my Amy doesn't grow up an orphan.'

Nicholson had her notebook out. 'Where are they keeping the stuff?'

Kirstin stared up at Logan. 'I only get to see my Amy on the weekends, with supervised visits from the social. I'm trying to change, I really *am*.' One hand scratching away at the crook of her arm. Picking the scabs off the needle marks. 'Please . . .'

'Not till you tell us where it is.'

'Klingon's place. His mum's away to Australia for a month.'

'Right.' Logan unhooked his Airwave and made for the door. Pointed back towards the pile of stuff on the coffee table. 'Nicholson – you get that lot bagged and tagged. I'll be outside.' He punched in Inspector McGregor's shoulder number on the way down the stairs. 'Bravo India from Shire Uniform Seven, safe to talk?'

'*Logan, are you heading up to Fraserburgh any time soon? Because this missing cashline machine is a total mess. How come we've not got anyone Crime-Scene-Manager-trained on shift?*'

'I want to raid an address in Banff.'

'*What: now?*'

'Soon as.' He pushed through the main door and out into the sunny evening. 'I've got intel that Kevin McEwan and Colin Spinney have taken possession of a big shipment from down south. Storing it at Spinney's house. If we move quick, we might catch them before it's broken up and disappeared.'

'*Klingon and Gerbil moving up in the world, are they?*'

'Trying to.'

Silence.

A seagull wheeled overhead, wings radiant-white against the flawless blue.

'Guv?'

'*We'd need corroboration.*'

'Got a file yay thick with people complaining about them dealing from Gerbil's flat.'

'*Hold on . . .*' Some muffled conversation. Then silence again.

Logan leaned back against the wall, one foot up on the dirty grey harling.

A second seagull joined the first, making slow loops, drifting away out to sea.

'*You still there? Email me an address and I'll get the warrant sorted. Too short notice to get the Operational Support Unit involved, but you can have one van, and two extra officers from Inverurie.*'

'I need them to be search-trained. And a dog team.'

'*You want jam on it, don't you?*'

'Best chance we've got of finding Klingon and Gerbil's stash.'

Sigh. '*I'll see what I can do. It's going to take a couple of hours to get everything sorted, though. Stick in the ground: we go at nine tonight.*'

'Thanks, Guv.'

'*Just make sure you find something.*'

The desk phone rang and rang and rang. Logan grabbed the Post-it note, stuck a finger in one ear, mobile phone clamped to the other, and marched out of the main office into the corridor. 'Sorry, what was that?'

Louise's voice crackled down the line. '*I'm not saying it's* definitely *going to be a problem, but we need to keep on top of it. Samantha's health has to be our top priority.*'

Past the canteen and the gents' toilet. Through into the Constables' Office.

More phones ringing – Nicholson scrabbling for a pad and scribbling things down. 'Uhuh, yes, sir. I will, sir.' She'd stripped off her protective gear, exposing muddy circles under the arms of her black T-shirt. Like filthy sweat stains.

He plonked the Post-it in the middle of the desk, in front of her.

She nodded.

'*This chest infection's been dragging on for a couple of weeks and I'd really like to see if we can shift it.*'

'And there's no risk?'

'There's always a risk when you change someone's medication. But a chest infection's a serious thing for someone who was in a coma for as long as Samantha.'

Nicholson must have finished her call, because she picked up the Post-it. Squinted at it. Then waved it at Logan. 'What?'

'OK, so let's fix her medication then.' He put a hand over the mouthpiece. 'It says, "We've got a dog unit coming from Aberdeen."'

'It does?' More squinting. 'You ever think about becoming a doctor?'

'Are you going to be up tomorrow?'

'Can't, I'm in court all day. Wednesday though: about ten?'

Nicholson grabbed a dry marker and stomped over to the whiteboard above the radiator. Printed 'DOG UNIT' in the column marked 'ASSETS'.

'Perfect. And we need to take another look at getting you formally appointed as Samantha's legal guardian.'

'I hate—'

'I know you do. But if you're going to make decisions about medical interventions we need something a bit more legally secure than simply being her boyfriend. It's important, Logan.'

A weight pressed down on his shoulders, making them sag. 'OK. We'll talk about it Wednesday.'

'Trust me: it's for the best. You'll see.' And she was gone.

Logan slid his phone back into a pocket then

turned to face the whiteboard. Inverurie had reneged on the two extra officers – something about a big barney going on outside Specsavers. But the Duty Inspector had managed to scare up one search-trained constable from Mintlaw and another from Fraserburgh. Add in Nicholson, Deano, Tufty, and Logan: that made six officers, one dog handler, a dirty big Alsatian, and a Labrador with a thing for sniffing out drugs.

Could have been worse. At least they only had the one address to hit. None of that double-dunt nonsense.

The office phone rang. Nicholson grabbed it. 'Banff station, how can I help?'

With any luck, that would be their warrant ready for collection. Colin 'Klingon' Spinney's mum was in for a bit of a shock when she got back from Australia.

Logan's Airwave bleeped.

'Sarge?' Deano.

'Safe to talk. Where are you? Grab Tufty and get back here, we've got an op to plan. Big drugs—'

'Aye, no.' Deep breath. *'Sarge, I need you down at Tarlair Swimming Pool. Right now.'*

'Don't be daft, it's—'

'Sarge, we've got a body. It's a wee girl.'

Bloody hell . . . A missing paedophile and a dead little girl, all in the same day. He grabbed his hat. 'We're on our way.'

CHAPTER 7

'. . .*What do you mean, "The drugs raid's on hold"?*'

Logan took hold of the grab handle above the passenger door as Nicholson floored it along Low Shore, past the boxy terraced houses of Newton Drive, siren wailing and lights flashing.

Inspector McGregor sounded as if she was chewing a wasp. *'Do you have any idea how many strings I had to pull to get you extra officers, a van, and a dog? Never mind the warrant, it's—'*

'We've got reports of a young girl's body at Tarlair Swimming Pool.'

The houses with their red pantile roofs faded in the rear-view mirror. Now there was nothing keeping the car company but the chain-link fence between it and the cliffs that hugged the left-hand side of the road.

A hissed breath. *'Should you not have led with that?'*

'Sorry, Guv. Constables Scott and Quirrel are securing the scene. We've got an ETA . . .?' He looked at Nicholson. Raised both eyebrows.

She changed down and threw them around the corner. 'Going as fast as I can . . .'

The needle hit ninety.

'Call it two minutes.'

The wastewater-treatment plant flashed by on the left, and Nicholson slammed on the brakes, swinging the car round into a steep hairpin bend. A squeal of tyres.

Tarlair Outdoor Swimming Pool appeared in the distance. A collection of boxy art deco buildings – not much bigger than a handful of Portacabins – were surrounded on three sides by cliffs, the fourth open to the sea. Their whitewashed walls going grey with neglect, caught by the evening sun. The two outdoor pools empty and decaying in front of them.

'Have we got an ID?'

Logan switched off the siren. 'Not yet. We've no support staff in Banff after five. Can you spare someone?'

The road dipped steeply down to another hairpin – gorse bushes like a sheet of rolling flame on the right, the bay on the left. Dark rocks making broken submarines and stranded ships in the glittering water. White foam marked the outward edges as the waves tried to shoulder them up onto the grey stony beach.

'Any idea if it's accidental, or . . .?'

'I hope so. We've got a missing paedophile on the books: Neil Wood. Disappeared three days ago. His father only reported it today.'

'That's all we need . . .' The sound became muffled, as if she'd stuck her hand over the

microphone, partially blocking her firing orders at someone in the background – telling someone to get the Scenes Examination Branch to hotfoot it over from the cashline job in Fraserburgh.

Smooth tarmac gave way to scabby potholes. Knee-high grass bordered the sides of the road, punctuated by the searching pink antennae of rosebay willowherb. The patrol car bumped across the pockmarked tarmac, then wallowed as Nicholson slowed. The sound of a mudflap grinding against the uneven surface.

The road gave up in a dead end, just before the entrance to the pool. One way in, one way out. Well, unless you wanted to work your way down the cliff path from the golf course.

Inspector McGregor's voice went from muffled to full volume again. *'Logan, I need to know if this was a suspicious death ASAP. Am I calling in an MIT or not? Then secure the scene. I'll be right there, soon as I get someone to run admin tasks for you.'*

Logan stuck his Airwave handset on its clip.

Deano and Tufty's little police van was parked in the middle of the road, between two jagged lumps of rock, blocking off the entrance to the site. The thing needed a wash, its white paintwork nearly grey with grime, but the stripe of blue-and-yellow blocks along the side glowed in the pool car's flashing lights.

No sign of either of them.

Nicholson hit the button, killing the blue-and-whites.

Silence.

Logan grabbed his hat. 'Get the tape out and secure the road. I want it blocked.' He turned in his seat, then pointed at the top of the hill, where the first hairpin was. 'Better make it other side of the water-treatment plant. Don't want some scumbag with a telephoto lens selling snaps to the tabloids.'

'Sarge.'

As soon as he clunked the passenger door shut again, she was reversing through the potholes. Did a sharp three-pointer, then accelerated off.

He turned. Picked his way around the police van. Punched Deano's badge number into the Airwave.

But before he could press send, Tufty appeared, scrambling across the pebbled beach, both arms held out as if he was walking the high wire. He paused. Slithered back a couple of steps. Waved. 'Sarge? Over here.'

Logan followed him across the pebble beach, avoiding the road. Broken kelp roots clung to the high-tide mark, pale and weathered, like a thousand human tibias. Everything smelled of ozone and salt, underpinned by a thin smear of rotting fish. He looked over his shoulder. 'Guy was down here taking photos for some urban-decay-project-thing. Young lad doing an HND in photography at Aberdeen College. Peed himself. Then battered it over to Macduff on his bike. Saw us at the harbour, and that was that.'

A nod. Pebbles crunched and shifted under Logan's feet. 'You confiscate the camera?'

'Deano got the SD card.' Tufty pointed off to the right, towards a crumbling concrete embankment. 'This way.'

'Why didn't your student call nine-nine-nine? Thought everyone had a mobile phone now.'

Tufty flashed a wee smile and a shrug. 'Panicked. Says he couldn't remember the number. Bit of a climb, sorry . . .' He clambered up the embankment, then up onto the grass. Then over an outcrop of lichen-covered rock.

'You sure you know where you're going?'

'Deano said there's no way anyone would come this way carrying a body. So, you know, common approach path.' More clambering and scrambling, and they were up on a ridge above the swimming pools. Tufty nodded. 'Down there.'

The site was split into two halves. In front of the main buildings were a set of wide amphitheatre steps in dark-grey stained concrete, the edges picked out in decaying whitewash. They enclosed a D-shaped shallow pool – dry as an abandoned riverbed – the wall between it and the main swimming area crumbling and partially collapsed. On the other side of the wall, water came halfway up. A stony beach at one side that couldn't have been an original feature, speckled with broken pipes and other bits of rusting flotsam. Then the sea wall, and then the blue expanse of the North Sea.

A dark shape was hunched at the far side of the

pool, a line of black-and-yellow tape trailing from one hand: 'CRIME SCENE – DO NOT ENTER'. Deano. He stuck both arms up and waved them. 'Sarge!'

It took a moment to pick out the body. Grey against grey.

Not a mistake then.

A couple of inches below the ridge they stood on lay the decaying flat roof of some sort of ancient pump house. No way in hell Logan was risking standing on that. 'Where's this common approach path go, then?'

Tufty pointed. 'Far as we can tell, he'd take her in a straight line from the entrance over there, along the side, take the walkway between the two bits, and dump her in the pool.' His shoulders drooped. 'I wanted to do some searching, but Deano won't let me go down. Says I've got to stay up here.'

Proper procedure. Wonders would never cease.

Logan eased himself down the rock face and onto the amphitheatre steps. No way to get to where Deano was without crossing the killer's route. Well, except for picking his way along the sea wall, but it looked narrow and slippery with green slime. And according to the sign at the entrance, it was a two-metre drop from there to the rocks, so sod that.

Assuming there *was* a killer.

He pointed at Tufty. 'As of now, you're acting Crime Scene Manager. You record the time and the date and everyone who's been near the body. Guard the entrance and make sure no one gets past you till I say so. No one. Don't care if it's the Chief Constable himself, he cools his heels in the car park till I say otherwise. Understand?'

'Sarge.'

Good.

He went right, dropped into the D-shaped inshore pool and made his way through the rubble and rubbish to the other side.

Deano jabbed a metal spike into a crack in the crumbling concrete at his feet, then looped the tape through the pig's tail at the top. Moved on to the next spike, unspooling a trail of crime-scene yellow behind him. He sighed. 'Poor wee sod.'

Logan stopped, level with the tape, and peered over the crumbling walkway. 'Suspicious?'

A grimace. 'When's a dead kid not?'

'True.' He scrambled up and ducked under the yellow-and-black cordon.

The wee girl couldn't be much more than five or six. The same age as Jasmine. Same hair colour . . .

Something knotted in the middle of his chest, compressed by the stabproof vest's squeezing fist until it was hard and sharp.

But it wasn't her.

Breath hissed out of him.

Deano put the roll of tape down. 'You OK, Sarge?'

Blink. Logan coughed the lump out of his throat. 'Yeah. It's . . . She looks like Jasmine.'

The girl lay on her front, three feet from the dirty concrete wall and the ramp down into the pool. She was half-in, half-out of the water. Head, arms and torso floating amongst the detritus, lower half stranded on the rocks.

One leg lay straight out behind her, the small red shoe pointing back towards the main building. Looked as if the strap across her ankle had got caught on a rusting length of broken pipe. Holding her in place. The other leg stuck out at nearly ninety degrees. White socks and a grey dress. All covered with a thin dusting of white crystals.

Her grey jumper was sodden – torn between the shoulders, and at the elbows, showing the white shirt underneath. A school uniform.

Skin was pale as snow, covered in small scratches and tiny triangular holes. Her hands swollen and white. Neck bent at an unnatural angle.

Her cheek rested against a submerged rock. Eyes open, staring out through the murky water. Mouth open. Pale blonde hair floating around her face. A big dent in her forehead.

Deano tied the length of tape off on the last metal post. 'You sure you're OK?'

A shrug. 'Yeah. Bit of a surprise, that's all.'

'See if I thought it was *my* daughter, I'd skin the scumbag alive . . .' He sniffed. 'Well you know: if I actually had any kids.'

Logan picked his way down the ramp, boots slithering on the weed-covered concrete, and squatted down at the edge of the water. Licked the tip of his index finger, then tapped it against the snagged red shoe. Pressed the finger against his tongue. Salt.

'Deano, when's high tide?'

'No idea. Can find out, though.'

'Definitely not an accident?' Inspector McGregor was cranked up to full volume, trying to compete with the siren of the car she was in. *'You're sure?'*

'As I can be, without screwing up the scene.' Logan marched back to the road, pulling off his blue nitrile gloves and stuffing them into an empty carrier bag. Fingers trembling, struggling with the plastic. 'Looks as if someone battered her head in, but there's no sign of blood on the walkway, or the wall, or the steps. So she didn't do it falling into the pool. Best guess: she was dead by the time she hit the water. Probably had been for a couple of hours. Must've been completely submerged at one point – her skirt, legs and shoes are covered in salt crystals.' He stopped, blew out a breath. 'Poor wee soul was only five or six.'

The second-hand roar of the siren wailed from his Airwave's speaker.

'Guv?'

'I'll be there in five minutes. You've secured the scene? And got a lookout request on the go for Neil Wood?'

'Deano handed it off to the OMU soon as we knew the guy was missing. Don't know if they've done it or not.'

'For God's sake, Logan, it's—'

'You said, get back to you ASAP.' The carrier bag went in his pocket. 'Thought that made it top priority.'

A sigh, barely audible over the background noise. *'Suppose you're right.'*

Deano scrambled up the shingle beach, back onto the road. Stopped and shook one leg, as if he'd stood in a puddle. Waves hushed against the pebbled shore.

'Guv, you still there?'

'Yes. Fine. I'm getting the MIT up from Aberdeen. Make sure no one touches anything till I get there.'

'Already got Constable Quirrel as acting CSM.'

'Tufty's our Crime Scene Manager? . . . Wonderful . . . We're all doomed.' This time she was gone for good.

Deano marched over – one shoe leaving damp footprints on the age-dulled tarmac – while Logan punched in the badge number of the admin assistant Inspector McGregor had dug up for them.

The woman on the other end picked up. *'Sergeant McRae?'*

'I need you to run a check on all missing persons aged eleven and under.' The wee girl looked a lot younger than that, but there was no point taking any risks. 'Female. Blonde hair. Wearing a school uniform – grey with white socks and shirt. Red shoes and tie. No school badge on the jumper.'

'Where am I looking?'

Deano stopped in front of him, pointed at himself. Mouthed, 'Anything needing doing?'

'Better start with the Northeast and expand it from there. Go UK wide if you have to.' He took his finger off the transmit button. 'Deano, whoever you spoke to at the Offender Management Unit – give them a poke and make sure they've got a lookout request on for Neil Wood. I want him picked up.'

'Sarge.'

'. . . *OK, I've got three mispers that match the age range in the Northeast . . .*' The clatter of fingers on keyboard. '*Two are female . . . One red-haired, one brown. Sure yours hasn't dyed her hair?*'

He pulled out his mobile and scrolled through the photos he'd taken. That pale little face, staring down at the stones. Deep breath. 'Far as I can tell. Eyebrows match the hair colour, anyway.'

'*Then we're going to have to search further out. Might take me a while. How far back do you want me to go: one month, two, three?*'

'Better give it two years. Just because she only turned up today, doesn't mean she's not been missing for a long, long time.'

A sigh. Then, '*Josef Bloody Fritzl has a lot to answer for.*'

'Email me if you get anything.' Logan clipped the handset back in place.

Deano was on the other side of the police van, marching back and forth with one squelchy shoe. '. . . oh no you don't. I *told* you he was missing. I *told* you to get a lookout request and . . . No, no, no, no, no: this is *your* cock-up, sunshine, not mine.'

Brilliant.

As if today could get any worse.

The cliffs were washed with blood, shadows long and dark as the sun sank into the North Sea. Painting the grass in shades of amber and gold. Glinting on the chain-link fence.

Nicholson tucked her hands into the armholes of her stabproof, covered now with a clean high-vis waistcoat. Shrugged her shoulders up round her ears and kept them there, peaked cap wedged on top of her head. 'Getting a bit nippy.'

Logan rocked on the balls of his feet. Shoulders back. Hands clasped behind him. Chin up. 'No slouching.'

A double line of blue-and-white 'POLICE' tape stretched between the end of the chain-link fence and the telegraph pole on the other side of the road. A handful of rusty cars were parked in front of the cordon, their drivers and passengers sitting on the bonnets, cameras and microphones hanging idle. Waiting. The Sky TV outside broadcast van partially blocked the entrance to the wastewater plant, a journalist in a fleece and serious expression doing a piece to camera. The BBC doing the same a couple of hundred yards behind them.

'Feel like a right turnip.' But Nicholson stood upright anyway. 'Stuck here like a pair of willies while everyone else is off doing proper police work.'

'Pair of *Wallies*. Not willies.'

81

'I know what I said.' She turned back to the patrol car. 'Don't suppose we've got any of those nice padded jackets in the boot, do we?'

A sigh. 'Go on then.'

An unmarked car came to a halt on the other side of the barrier tape and the nightshift Duty Inspector climbed out. Held up his hands as a swarm of lenses turned in his direction. When he spoke, the words came out as a thick roll of bunged-up vowels. 'We're not making any comment at this time. Thank you.' He turned his back on them, ducked under the tape and marched up to Logan. Kept his voice low. 'Bunch of vultures.' A waft of Vicks VapoRub and menthol sweets.

'Guv.'

Inspector Fettes tucked his peaked cap under his arm. His hands were huge – completely out of proportion with the rest of him – and covered with freckles. His cheeks and nose were a freckle playground too, reaching all the way up his forehead to a magnificent mop of red hair. He nodded at the road, where it snaked off down the hill. 'Inspector McGregor still down there?'

'You taking over?'

'Got enough on my plate running the division as it is. Wendy can hold the fort here till her shift ends. Wanted to make sure I'm up to speed before she heads home.'

Logan's phone vibrated in his pocket. 'Sorry.' He pulled it out – an email from the support officer in Elgin, listing all the young girls reported missing

82

in the UK for the last two years, filtered for hair colour. None of the photographs worked on his phone. 'Bloody typical.'

'Problem?'

'Someone's emailed through photos of all the missing girls on file, but they won't display.' He gave the side of the phone a slap. It didn't help.

Of course, the photos only mattered if she'd actually been reported missing . . .

Inspector Fettes sniffed. Dabbed at his nose with a hanky. 'Still, I suppose it's not *really* our problem any more, is it?'

'Like they'd trust us with a murder.' Logan put his useless phone away again. 'No: the Major Investigation Team turns up an hour ago, in a blaze of flashing lights and sirens, and takes it off our hands. Thanks for your help, now sod off and go guard the scene for the rest of the night.'

'Tossers.'

'Exactly what I was thinking, Guv.'

Another sniff. 'Speak of the devil . . .'

A battered Vauxhall grumbled up the hill from the swimming pool, and rattled to a halt next to the patrol car. Sat there with its engine running.

Probably expected him to abandon his post and rush over to see what they wanted.

Well, tough.

Inspector Fettes popped his hat on his head. 'Suppose I'd better go make myself useful.' He headed over to the Vauxhall. Leaned on the roof and spoke to someone through the open window.

Pointed at Logan. Then stood back up and marched off down the road towards Tarlair Outdoor Swimming Pool.

Nicholson reappeared, hauling on a big fluorescent jacket with reflective strips. Nodded at the idling Vauxhall. 'Something happen?'

Logan faced front again. 'Doubt it.'

She checked her watch. 'Soon be time for tenses. Nice cuppa and a chocolate éclair.'

'No tenses for us tonight.'

'Oh . . .' Her face drooped. 'Elevenses?'

'We should be so lucky.'

The Vauxhall's passenger door opened and a dishevelled head poked out. Hair like an angry weasel had rampaged through a haystack. The creases deepened around her mouth. Voice like sandpaper on a rusty pipe. 'Laz! Stop dicking about.'

Nicholson raised an eyebrow. 'Laz?'

'Don't ask.'

Detective Chief Inspector Steel clambered out of the car. Slightly hunched in her wrinkled grey trouser suit. Black overcoat. Blue silk shirt. She waved at him. 'Get your arse over here.'

Pause.

'Sarge?'

Sigh. 'OK. You stay here. No one—'

'Yeah, "None shall pass", I get it.'

He turned and walked over to the Vauxhall.

'About sodding time.' Steel hooked a thumb over her shoulder. 'Come on, you and me's going for a walk.'

CHAPTER 8

They stopped at the top of the hill, over-looking the bay and the abandoned outdoor swimming pool. Steel waded into the knee-deep grass, then settled onto the park bench someone had erected years ago to make a viewing point. Back when councils still had money for things like that. She produced an electronic cigarette and took a deep puff, setting the tip glowing blue. Trickled out a stream of vapour from her nose. 'Well this is a bloody mess.'

Logan sat next to her, engulfed in the throat-catching smell of perfume and mints. He pointed down to the pools, where a phalanx of bodies in white SOC suits picked their way around the far side. Two marquees sat beside the old building, both glowing with their internal lights. Three patrol cars. Two police vans. A big Range Rover. And a scruffy Transit van. 'Any idea who she is yet?'

Steel jammed the e-cigarette into the corner of her mouth and took an envelope out of her pocket. 'Came today. Haven't dared look yet. Susan's terrified.'

'Going from the look of her, she can't have been

dead long. Maybe a day? Possibly two? We're lucky the seagulls didn't find her first.'

'Right.' Steel ran a finger along the envelope's seal, ripping it open. Then ferreted out the sheet inside. Stuck the whole lot on her lap. 'I can't look.'

'Put on your glasses then.'

She stared at him. 'I don't *need* glasses. It's important, OK?' She poked the sheet of paper. 'This is a big deal.'

'And a dead wee girl isn't?'

Another long drag on the fake cigarette. 'Got a point.'

'Look . . .' He cleared his throat. Took off his peaked cap and held it in his lap. 'I know it means a lot to Susan. But maybe she needs to . . .'

Steel just stared, mouth hanging open.

'What?'

'What the hell did you do to your *head*?' She reached out and scrubbed her hand across the back of it. 'It's like a velour egg.'

'Get off.' He scooted away to the edge of the bench.

'Who cut your hair? You tell me and we'll go round right now and beat the crap out of them. You look like an angry scrotum!'

'*I* cut it.' He slapped her hand away as she went in for seconds. 'Got a set of clippers off the internet.'

'One born every minute.' She took another puff on her e-cigarette. Glanced down at the paperwork in her lap. 'Pathologist's examining the wee girl now. Quick once-over then off to Aberdeen. Post mortem tomorrow.'

'You got any idea how much a haircut costs these days? Don't get anything like the same overtime I did in CID. And with the pension contribution going up . . .'

'Right now it looks like a blow to the head. Something solid and cylindrical. Best guess: he bashed her head in with a metal pipe. Find out more tomorrow when they cut her open.'

Logan screwed his hands together, knotting the fingers tight. 'When I saw her lying there, all twisted in her school uniform . . . For a heartbeat, I thought it was Jasmine.'

Steel draped an arm along the back of the bench. Gave Logan a little squeeze. 'Don't be such a big girl's blouse. She's home with her mum.'

'Who's SIO?'

'Officially, our beloved Detective Superintendent Young is the all-powerful Senior Investigating Officer. But it'll be Finnie's face on the TV. Dead wee girl. Paedo on the run. Got to bring out the big guns for something like that.' A sniff. Then she poked herself in the chest a couple of times with her thumb. 'No prizes for guessing who'll be doing all the work though.'

'I'd put my money on whatever poor sod you've got running around after you.'

'Damn straight.' She blew out a breath. Pulled her shoulders back. 'Right.' Picked up the sheet of paper from her lap. Paused. Then thrust it at Logan. 'I can't. You read it.'

He smoothed out the crumpled sheet. '"Dear Mrs Wallace-Steel, I write to inform you of the combined test results from your first-trimester nuchal translucency scan and bloodwork, taken on the"—'

'Get to the point!'

'Fine.' Logan skimmed the page with his finger. 'Blah, blah, blah . . . HCG is normal, but the PAPP-dash-A is elevated. Given Susan's age, they're going for a one in five hundred chance of the foetus having Down's syndrome.'

'Oh thank God.' Steel let her head fall back and covered her face with her hands. Then sat up again, frowning. 'One in five hundred. That's good, isn't it?'

No idea.

He manufactured a smile. 'Course it is.'

'Ha!' She slapped him on the back. 'You're going to be a daddy again!' The smile froze and Steel checked over her shoulder, as if someone might be lurking in the long grass. Her voice dropped to a raspy whisper. 'But if your mum asks, it wasn't you, OK? Someone else did the squirt-in-a-cup thing. Don't want her going all stalkery over this one like she did with Jasmine. I've had verrucas easier to shake off than that woman.'

'Tell me about it.' Logan stood. 'Look, any monkey in uniform could guard the cordon. And you've got heaps of bodies here.'

'Want me to release you from your servitude?'

'The whole team. Got a division to look after.'

The tip of Steel's artificial cigarette glowed. 'One in five hundred.' She grinned. 'Ah, go on then. I'm feeling generous.'

He marched back up the road. Tapped Nicholson on the shoulder. Lowered his voice to a whisper. 'Looks like tenses are on again.'

Logan swivelled his chair left and right, phone in one hand, mouse in the other. Scrolling through his team's actions on STORM. Waiting for the Sergeant at Fraserburgh station to pick up.

The sound of telephones and stomping feet came from overhead. Like elephants in cheap machine-washable suits. A pair of them thundered past the open door to the Sergeants' Office, trumpeting about getting a HOLMES suite set up and which of the bunnets was going to have to make the tea.

Logan stretched the phone cord to its full length and reached out with his leg. Caught the edge of the door with his foot and shoved. It banged shut.

A not-quite big enough room: two cupboards locked away behind white panelled doors; a pair of desks, back to back so the occupants could face each other over creaky black computers; some metal cabinets and overflowing in-trays. A line of body-worn video units winking their green lights at him as the mouse moved onto the next set of action.

Click.

Deano was all up to date. As was Nicholson. But Tufty . . .

God's sake. It was like having a five-year-old. Three assaults, two burglaries, and a purse-snatching, all needing following up.

He clicked on the first assault, wedged the phone between his ear and shoulder, and battered a remark into the system, fingers sparking across the keyboard.

Follow this up ASAP – this action has been open too long. I want it updated!

Finally, someone picked up in Fraserburgh and a rough male voice echoed out of the phone: *'Billy Broch's House of Horrors, how may I direct your call?'*

'Sergeant Smith, is that any way to answer the station telephone?'

'Knew it was you by the number. What's this I hear about you and your numpties turning up a body?'

'Dead child.'

'Aw, no . . . Sorry. No one said.'

'What are you and your hired thugs up to the night?'

'They inflict you with an MIT yet?'

More footsteps, stomping overhead. 'They've commandeered most of upstairs. *And* the night shift. Can you get a couple of bodies down Fraserburgh harbour? I need a door-to-door on the boats – looking for any intel you can get on Charles "Craggie" Anderson. Went missing a week ago. No sign of him or the *Copper-Tun Wanderer.*'

'You coming to see our cashline-machine-shaped hole later?'

'Planning on it. Anything else?'

The sound of air being sucked between teeth. *'Let's see. New today: two potential bail violations, three domestics, couple of complaints about that traveller camp outside Rosehearty, handful of break-ins, and we're looking for a druggie who's been snatching handbags. Otherwise it's same old, same old. What about your drugs raid? You still needing Constable King-Kong McMahon?'*

'On hold. Going to try again Wednesday, if they let me.'

A knock on the door. A muffled voice: 'Sarge?'

'Come in, Tufty. Got to go, Bill. Try and behave till I get there, OK?'

'No promises.'

Logan hung up as Constable Quirrel sidled into the room. 'Well?'

He glanced back over his shoulder like a really bad sneak thief. Dropped his voice to a whisper. 'Tenses in the cellblock.'

'Old one or the new one?'

'Ah . . .' A grimace. 'Forgot to ask.'

'. . . and don't get me started on that *prick* Dawson!' Nicholson paced the scuffed grey floor, her hands jabbing out at random angles as she went. She marched straight through one of the two open, thick, blue metal doors and into the darkened cell beyond. Turned and stamped back

91

into the room again. 'Do you know what he said to me? Do you?'

The new cellblock was a low-ceilinged room that smelled of lemon-scented cleaner and flaky pastry. The cells empty and immaculate, barely used since they were installed a decade ago, but still kitted out with their thin plastic mattresses and stainless-steel toilets. Waiting for the day when they had enough staff to open it up again. As if that was ever going to happen.

Logan leaned against the door through to the garage, Deano the one through to the older part of the building while Tufty handed out the pastries. 'No, but I'm sure you're going to tell us.'

'He said—'

'On second thoughts, don't.' Logan pointed at the office chair behind the custody desk. 'Sit. Deep breaths. And calm down.'

'But, Sarge, he—'

'Down. Arse in chair. Now.'

Whatever she said under her breath, it probably wasn't polite, but she thumped down in the chair and folded her arms.

'Thank you.' Logan helped himself to a bite of maple pecan twist. Talking with his mouth full. 'For better, or worse, we're lumbered with these guys. Some of them will be tossers, some of them won't. But I don't want *any* of you lowering your-selves to that level, am I understood?'

Pink bloomed across Nicholson's cheeks. She stared at her boots.

Deano sighed. 'She's only letting off steam.'

'I don't care. And that goes for *all* of you. We are a professional modern police force. I will *not* have you letting B Division down by acting like sulky children.'

The response was a barely audible, 'Yes, Sarge,' from Nicholson. 'Sorry, Sarge.'

Logan nodded. Had a sip of tea. Hot and milky. 'Now that we're all calm and grown-up again, what did he say?'

'Sexist scumbag thought I was going to make the tea for them!' Nicholson ripped a bite out of her apple turnover, getting flakes of pastry all down the front of her black T-shirt.

Tufty handed her a mug. 'What did you do?'

'Smiled sweetly and said, "Yes, Guv."' Her shoulders dipped. 'What was I supposed to do? Kick off in the canteen?'

Logan nodded back towards the older part of the building, where the main office was. 'You want me to have a word?'

She grimaced. 'Think that's going to help me get into CID? Constable Janet Nicholson, chippy feminist?'

'Maybe not.' But that didn't mean they were going to get away with it. Logan took another bite of pastry. 'I'm off to Fraserburgh after. Might do Peterhead too, depends if anything comes up.' He pointed at Deano. 'You and Tufty keep hitting the harbours. Janet, take the other car and drift by Alex Williams's place every half-hour. Can't stop the two of them getting back together, but we *can* let Alex know we're watching.'

A nod. 'Sarge.'

'When you're not there, do a general sweep of the area. Everyone needs to remember that *we're* the ones keeping the peace here, not some MIT bunch of bum-weasels.'

The patrol car slid into New Pitsligo, the grey buildings and grey streets washed with amber streetlight. Going the long way round to Fraserburgh. Taking a detour through the wee town's side streets. Peering into front and back gardens. Doing exactly the same thing he'd told Nicholson to do. Being seen. Flying the flag for community policing. Letting people know he was out there.

Singing along to whatever tune popped into his head as the car radio crackled and bleeped with snippets from the investigation going on at Tarlair Outdoor Swimming Pool. Fingertip search of a cliff, by torchlight. Someone was off their rocker.

And still no sign of anything turning up.

Back onto the A950. Then a left onto the Strichen road. Blackened fields. Clumps of trees looming from the shadows. Stars like tiny LEDs sprinkled across treacle. The moon a ball of darkness with a faint sliver of white on one edge. A flock of sheep, their eyes shining like vampires' in the headlights.

His Airwave bleeped, cutting off a spirited rendition of the Birds Eye Steakhouse Grills advert: 'Hope it's chips, it's chips . . .' He took one hand off the wheel and clicked the button. 'Go ahead, safe to talk.'

'*Sarge, it's Janet. Been past Alex Williams's – they're both sitting in the lounge, watching the TV. You'd think butter wouldn't melt. I mean, after what Williams did . . .*'

'I know. Keep an eye out. I'm winning that bet – no one dies.'

'*See if someone tried to do that to me? I'd have their kneecaps off.*'

'No one gets crippled either.'

A pause.

'*Sarge?*'

'What?'

'*Why haven't I got a nickname? I mean Stewart's Tufty, Dean's Deano. Even you've got one. I'm just Janet. Or Nicholson. Is it because I'm a woman?*'

'You're kidding, right?' Frown. 'Well . . . what do you want to be called?'

'*Oh no you don't – only tosspots pick their own nickname.*'

'We could call you Constable Pain-in-the-Hoop?'

'*Funny.*' Voice flat. '*Good job I'm wearing my stabproof vest, razor-sharp wit like that. Ha. Ha. Etc.*'

'Listen, do me a favour: have a bit of a drive round on Rundle Avenue. I want Frankie Ferris to know we're watching him. Keep him on edge.'

'God: a cow on the road, a bit of standing about behind a cordon, and the chance to kerb-crawl past a druggie scumbag's house for the rest of the shift? All in one day? You're right, why would anyone want to abandon that for a life in CID?'

Strichen was as small as it was quiet. But Logan gave it the same treatment – up and down the side streets. Look at me, I'm a police officer. Your taxes at work. The only thing even vaguely noteworthy was the naked man duct-taped to the 'Stop' sign outside the town hall on the corner of Bridge Street and the High Street.

Well . . . he was *probably* naked. It was difficult to tell under all the treacle and feathers. And they hadn't exactly skimped on the duct tape either.

Logan buzzed down the pool car's passenger window. Leaned across the seats. 'You OK?'

Mr Tar-And-Feathers blinked back at him, then released a lazy grin. 'I'm . . . I'm getting mar . . . married!' The words all slurred and wobbly.

'Congratulations.' He buzzed the window back up again and headed off northwest towards Fraserburgh.

'Control to Shire Uniform Seven.'

Logan looked left and right. No one else in the aisle. All alone with the rows and rows of soup tins. He pressed the button on his handset. 'Safe to talk.'

'*You're in Fraserburgh tonight? Anywhere near Arran Court?*'

'No idea. I'm in that Tesco on South Harbour Road.' The tattie and leek was cheap. But not as cheap as the lentil.

'*Neighbours are worried about a Mrs Bairden at number twenty-six. Not been seen since yesterday morning. History of heart problems. Not answering the door or the phone.*'

Lentil it is. Three tins went in the basket, joining the multipack of generic salt-and-vinegar and a bog-standard loaf of white.

'Give me five minutes.'

'*Will do.*'

Quick march, round the corner and a few aisles down, where the medicines and toothpaste lurked. Condoms, pile cream, antacids, eyedrops . . . Ah. There they were. Laxatives.

It'd break the weekly budget, but what the hell. Sometimes you had to live a little.

He picked two different brands at random and flipped them over to read the instructions.

A tap on his shoulder.

Logan turned to see a young woman in the standard blue-short-sleeved-shirt-and-black-trouser uniform. An 'ASK ME ABOUT CAR INSURANCE' badge pinned above the one with her name on it: 'AMANDA'. She smiled up at him. 'Are you looking for something specific?'

'Do you have anything really strong and quick-acting?'

She picked a green-and-yellow packet from the shelf. 'My nan uses these – gentle, predictable relief.'

'Nah. I'm looking for something a bit more aggressive. Wire-brush and Dettol time. Got anything that fits the bill?'

CHAPTER 9

Arran Court. A single row of terraced houses: white harling walls, slate roofs; the occasional block of dark wood connecting upper and lower windows. The street was hidden away in Fraserburgh's winding knot of cul-de-sacs. Surrounded by the back gardens of other buildings. A small patch of green sat opposite, lit by the yellow glow of a concrete lamp post. A handful of cars parked in front.

Logan counted the doors off, and stuck the patrol car in front of number twenty-six.

Three middle-aged women formed a clot by the garden gate. Two of them sitting on the low wall between it and number twenty-five. The third pacing back and forth, leaving cigarette trails in the street-lit air. All of them in pyjamas and dressing gowns.

Peaked cap on, out into the night. Logan clunked the car door shut and marched over. 'Does anyone have keys?'

The woman with the cigarette stopped pacing and stared at him. Face souring. 'You think we'd be standing here like lumps if we did?'

'How about relatives? Or maybe a carer?'

One of the wall-sitters shook her head. 'Her daughter, Sandra, lives three streets over, but she's in Edinburgh for a thing.'

He stepped through the gate. 'And you're sure she's not gone out somewhere? Night out in Aberdeen? Visiting friends in Peterhead?'

Number three sniffed. 'She's got a heart condition. What if she's dead?'

Logan tried the door handle. Locked.

No lights on inside.

'OK, let's try round the back.' He pointed at Mrs Cigarette. 'Do you have the daughter's mobile number?'

She dug a mobile from her dressing-gown pocket, poked at the screen, then held the thing out. 'Ringing.'

He took it. Stuck it against his ear as he marched to the end of the street and slipped around the side of the last house. A little lane ran between the back of Arran Court and the rear of the next street over. Logan counted his way along the patchwork of wooden fences to number twenty-six as the mobile phone rang. And rang. And rang.

And finally, *'Hello?'* A woman's voice, thin and nervous.

'Is this Sandra Bairden?'

There wasn't a gate into the back garden. Instead, a seven-foot-tall woven wood screen stretched the length of the garden. It wobbled when he grabbed hold of it.

'*Who is this?*'

'I'm a police officer. I don't want to worry you, Sandra, but your mum's neighbours are concerned about her.'

He put one foot on the low brick wall and pulled himself up. A single light was on in the house, shining faintly through a small pane of rippled glass. Probably the bathroom. The garden wreathed in gloom.

'*Oh God . . . Is it her heart?*'

'Could be nothing at all. We just want to make sure she's OK.' He gave the fence another shoogle. Better do it quick before the whole thing came crashing down. Up and over. Thumping down with both feet in a vegetable patch.

'*I . . . I knew I shouldn't have left her alone . . . But it was a work thing and—*'

'Let's not jump to any conclusions.' Crunching out through the woody stalks of leeks on parade, the air filled with the sharp scent of fresh onion. Back door. 'Do you know if your mother keeps a spare key anywhere on the property? Under a plant pot? Something like that?' He unclipped his torch from the stabproof and clicked it on. Swept the LED beam around the garden.

'*No, definitely not. She's very security conscious . . .*' A sob rattled from the phone's speaker. '*Please let her be all right . . .*'

One of those ridiculous half-terrier garden ornaments sat by the back door – as if the dog was digging its way through the paving slab down to the house foundations. He nudged it over with his toe. A single key was taped to the underside.

Yeah, because that was the *last* place a burglar would look.

He pinned the phone between ear and shoulder, picked the key up and slipped it into the back-door lock. 'It's OK, I'm letting myself in now.'

The kitchen was in darkness. 'Mrs Bairden? Hello?'

Silence.

'Oh my God, she's dead, isn't she?'

'Mrs Bairden? It's the police, are you OK?' He clicked on the light. Yellow and blue tiles on the walls, grey faux-marble worktop, white units.

Through into the hall. *Click.* Photos on the walls, leading up the stairs: an overweight little girl playing with a big hairy dog, the same girl in school uniform with missing front teeth, then getting older, married, looking more tired and more worn down as she aged.

'Why did I have to come to Edinburgh . . .?'

'Mrs Bairden? Hello?'

Up to the landing.

Light seeped out under the bathroom door, the drone of an extractor fan, muffled by the door.

Logan knocked. 'Mrs Bairden? Are you in there?'

He tried the handle. Locked.

'I'm so stupid . . .'

Another knock. 'Mrs Bairden?' He stuck his ear against the door. Was that a voice? Barely audible under the extractor fan's incessant buzz. 'Mrs Bairden, I'm coming in.'

Logan pulled a handful of change from his trouser pocket. Took a two-pence piece and slotted the edge of it into the little twiddly thing beneath the handle. Twisted it left till the lock went clack.

The door swung open, revealing a small bathroom clarted in pink floral tiles. A salmon-coloured suite. And a very pale old lady – naked in the bathtub, surrounded by filthy water. Thin grey hair. Sunken cheeks. One shoulder hunched. The left side of her mouth drooping.

Logan stuck the mobile phone on mute. Popped it on the pink cistern, next to the Spanish flamenco-dancer toilet-roll cosy. And knelt beside the bath. Put two fingers against Mrs Bairden's neck.

Then grabbed his Airwave and called for an ambulance.

'. . . *join us after the break when Josie and Marshal have to decide who's*—'

Logan poked the remote and the voice-over idiot on the TV was replaced by canned laughter on some mediocre sitcom.

The Fraserburgh station canteen was empty, except for him and the furniture. The blinds on the round window pulled tight, jaundiced light seeping through from the street outside.

His cheapo lentil soup wasn't too bad with a good slug of chilli sauce – pilfered from the back

103

of the cupboard. The bottle had 'ERIN'S ~ HANDS OFF YOU THIEVING SODS!' printed across it in angry black Sharpie letters. As if that was going to do any good.

Leave food lying about in a police station and you deserved everything you got.

A bleep from his Airwave. *'Anyone in the vicinity of Cruden Bay, we've got reports of an IC-One male threatening to commit suicide . . .'*

He ripped a chunk off the slice of toast and dipped it in the soup. Butter made round shiny slicks on the surface.

A dog-eared copy of the *Aberdeen Examiner* lay open on the table in front of him. Big two-page spread about the first day of Graham Stirling's trial. 'FAMILY'S AGONY OVER "SICK CLAIMS"' and a big photo of Stephen Bisset, taken before Stirling got his hands on him. A smiling, unremarkable man, in a blue jumper and white shirt. Side parting and a cheesy grin. Holding a baby in his arms. His teenaged kids stood at his shoulders, with matching eyes, smiles, and long black hair: 'HAPPY FAMILIES: LEFT TO RIGHT ➜ DAVID (17), STEPHEN (41), BABY DAVINA (3 MONTHS), AND CATHERINE (14)'.

Logan flipped the page to an opinion piece about a woman who'd scalded her husband with chip fat. Had another dunk of toast in his soup. Scanned an article about the drive-by execution of three gang members down in Liverpool. Another about a member of the Scottish Parliament caught thrashing out a 'private member's bill' in the women's toilets after hours.

His Airwave bleeped, then DCI Steel's gravelly tones ground out of the speaker. *'Laz? Where the hell are you?'*

Great – couldn't even eat his cheapo soup in peace.

He thumbed the button. 'Busy. What do you want?'

'How come I can't find anything in this warren you call a police station? Where are the marker pens?'

A spoonful of lumpy lentil. 'Hector nicks them all.'

'Who the hell is Hector? I'll kick his bum for him.'

'Too late for that: he died years ago.'

'Hilarious. Where's the damn pens?'

'And now he haunts the corridors of Banff station, terrifying probationers and anyone foolish enough to venture upstairs after dark . . . Wooo-oooo-ooohhhh-ooo!'

Silence.

He crunched on a mouthful of toast.

'You finished?'

'What? Not my fault. He's the station ghost, and every time a pen goes missing, it's Hector's fault. Try the old VIPER room on the top floor, next to the shower room. There's usually a box up there.'

'When you getting back? I need to go round all the registered stots, fiddlers, nonces, and paedos in the area.'

'So? You've got every spare body in the northeast: go visiting. Knock yourself out.'

'*Need me some local knowledge.*'

'Your team—'

'*Are a bunch of numpties. Wouldn't trust them to interview their bums for love bites. So . . .?*'

More soup. 'Depends if I get free later. I'll let you know.' Ha, no chance. 'Got to go.'

Another dollop of stolen hot sauce. Definitely improved the taste.

The door opened behind him. 'Sarge.'

He looked back over his shoulder and gave a one-spoon salute. 'Syd. How's the menagerie?'

A shrug. 'Enzo's OK, but Lusso bit Dino. Right on the bum.' Constable Fraser's black, police-issue fleece was frayed around the collar and sleeves, the thick leather dog lead draped across his shoulders and clipped together behind his back. Like BDSM braces. Black-and-white checked 'POLICE' baseball hat on his head, the brim worn and hairy on one side. The less than subtle waft of *Eau de Labrador*. 'Don't know what he'd been doing, but he probably deserved it.'

Logan stared at him. 'Your dog *bit* Deano? He bit Constable Scott? When did this happen?'

'What?' Syd curled his top lip, pulled his chin back into his neck. Then the frown slipped from his face. 'Ah, OK, no, not Deano, *Dino*. D.I.N.O. My Alsatian. He likes to wind the other two up.'

Thank God for that. Logan hissed out the breath he'd been holding. The paperwork would've been horrendous.

Syd clumped over to the kitchen that took up

one corner of the large room. Stuck a Tupperware box in the microwave and set it humming.

'*I need a car over to Market Street, Macduff. Reports of an elderly woman in distress wandering the street.*'

Nicholson's voice barked out of the Airwave handset. '*Roger that, Control – on my way.*'

Logan went back to his soup. 'You not out searching Tarlair?'

'Nope. You cancelled that drugs op, so me and Enzo ended up checking suspicious packages down the post office. Got three lots of coke, two of resin, and a teeny-tiny bit of heroin. Probably has a street value of eight pounds fifty, but every little helps.'

Ding.

Syd went rummaging in the cutlery drawer and carried the Tupperware back to the table. Pulled out the chair two down from Logan and settled in. Creaked the top off the container. The smell of rich Indian spices wafted out, covering the one of wet dog. 'Know if they've ID'd the girl yet?'

'MIT's handling it. Think they'd tell me?'

'Probably not.' A fork dug into the curry, pulled out a mound of chickpeas and onion. 'What's happening with your warrant? Me and the hairy loons were looking forward to that.' He took off his baseball cap, exposing a swathe of shiny scalp, fringed with close-cropped grey. 'Got nothing special on tomorrow, if you're up for it?'

'Can't – got the Stirling trial. Maybe Wednesday? Assuming they'll give me the bodies with this

Tarlair thing going on.' A spoonful of lentils helps the bitterness go down. 'Surprised they've not got you out there sniffing round the swimming pool too.'

'No one ever calls in the dogs as a first resort.' Another forkful of chickpeas. 'More fool them.'

'I'll see what I can do.'

Another handset bleep. *'Control to Bravo India One, safe to talk?'*

Syd pointed at the TV. 'You watching this pish?'

'Just on for the company, to be honest.'

The Duty Inspector's voice yawned out of the speaker: *'Go ahead.'*

'Cool.' He grabbed the remote and went spinning through the channels. 'You hear about Barney Massie? Up running that fatal RTA in Kirkwall, when he gets a challenge on his team's expenses.'

'Co-op in Aberchirder's had its front window panned in and the Cashline machine taken.'

A groan came from the Airwave. *'Not another one . . .'* A sigh. A pause. Then the Duty Inspector was back. *'OK. I'll be right over.'*

'Some wee numptie in Tulliallan calls him up to give him a roasting: "What's all these claims for flights? Did no one even *think* of taking the train?"'

Logan stared at him. 'To *Orkney?*'

'Exactly.' More chickpeas. 'The job is well and truly buggered.' Another jab at the remote produced a repeat of *Chewin' the Fat* – a pair of sailors chuntering out filth while their boat heaved through a storm. 'Still, only eight paydays to go.'

'Thanks. Rub it in. I'm stuck here till I'm sixty-five.'

On the TV, the seamen were replaced by Ford Kiernan buying a pie and a Paris bun.

'Got a big farewell bash planned: thirty years of keeping Grampian Police on the straight and narrow.'

Logan sucked in a breath. 'Better watch that kind of rebellious talk. There is no Grampian Police, there is only Police Scotland. All bow to our conquering overlords.'

'Ah, screw them. What they going to do, fire me?'

There wasn't much to see at Broch Braw Buys at five to midnight on a Monday night.

It was wedged between the Coral betting shop and a chip shop. Both closed for the evening. The Kenya Bar and Lounge on the corner had its door shut, the metal gate locked over the top. The sound of hoovering rattled out from somewhere inside.

Logan closed the pool car's door and crunched his way through little cubes of broken glass.

They'd obviously used the same tactics to get into the place and steal its cash machine, because the shop's front window was now boarded up with chipboard. Someone had stapled a poster right in the middle of the raw wood: '£1,000.00 REWARD FOR ANY INFORMATION LEADING TO THE BASTARD'S WHO DID THIS GETTING THEIR LEGS BROKEN!!!'

Logan reached out and tore it down. While a

nice sentiment, it wasn't exactly legal. And besides, that misplaced apostrophe grated.

He stood on the pavement and did a slow three-sixty.

Fraserburgh was quiet: no sound but the far-off burr of the occasional vehicle cruising some distant street. Not cold, but not exactly warm either. The roads washed in anaemic sodium light.

When did the call to the Duty Inspector come through? Couldn't have been much more than half three. So whoever it was going round nicking cash machines, they were either getting bolder, or stupider. Or maybe they simply had a schedule to keep?

Four cash machines in three days. If there wasn't a Major Investigation Team set loose on the case already, there would be by tomorrow morning. Earnest-faced plainclothes officers stomping about the countryside with their hobnail boots and fighting suits. Getting on everyone's nerves and lording it over the poor sods in uniform who'd have to clear up the mess they left behind.

Divisional policing, that's where all the cool kids were . . .

CHAPTER 10

The countryside swept past, dark and blurred, the road ahead picked out by the patrol car's headlights. Glinting back from the cats' eyes. A pulsing off-and-on glow as Logan tore down the dotted white line.

A sea of stars stretched from horizon to horizon. The water an expanse of slate grey to the left, bordered by cliffs. The distant glimmer of house lights.

Logan battered to the end of 'Started Out With Nothin'', drove in silence for a minute, then launched into 'Living Is a Problem Because Everything Dies'. Making up half of the words as he went along.

Sooner the Big Car was back with its working radio, the better. Honestly, it—

His Airwave gave the point-to-point quadruple bleep. *'Shire Uniform Seven, safe to talk?'*

'Go ahead, Deano.'

'Got a couple of guys in Gardenstown who think they saw Charles Anderson, Sunday last. Said he was off his face with the drink and spewing his hoop over the side of his boat.'

'Anything else?'

'Been talking in the pub earlier about going up to Papa Bank or Foula Waters, hunting haddies.'

Better than nothing.

Logan tapped his fingertips against the stubbly hair above his ear. 'So, maybe he's not missing at all. Maybe he's gone fishing?'

'Still should be answering his radio, unless the power's gone. Could be adrift, middle of the North Sea?'

'Pretty certain the radio has to have batteries. Health and Safety.'

'True.'

Round the next bend, and the bright lights of Macduff twinkled in the distance. 'Tell Tufty to get the kettle on. I'll be home in five.'

More dark fields. More cloudy silhouettes of trees. Then 'WELCOME TO MACDUFF'. Someone had hung a white sheet, with 'HAPPY 40TH BIRTHDAY CAZ!!!!!' splodged across it in black paint, under the limits sign. A couple of gaily coloured balloons were tied to the posts, sagging like a miserable clown's testes.

Logan took a quick detour down Moray Street, with its blocky grey buildings. Then stopped at the bottom – the junction with High Shore. Two choices. Right: back to the station, or left: towards the Tarlair Outdoor Swimming Pool?

The dashboard clock glowed '00:30' at him.

Wasn't as if he could contribute anything. Much more likely he'd get roped into doing something that could probably be accomplished by half a dozen traffic cones.

Right it was. Past the quaint wee houses, following the curving road, their dormer windows staring out across the sea as it hissed against the pebble beach.

Bleep. *'Anyone in the vicinity of Rosehearty? We've got a report of an assault ongoing outside the traveller camp . . .'*

Pause. Two. Three . . .

Then someone caved. *'Sergeant Smith to Control, on my way. Tell McMahon and Barrow to get their fingers out and join me there.'*

Past the aquarium – closed for refurbishment. A caravan sat in front of the temporary mesh fence encircling the oversized barnacle-shaped building, surrounded by orange traffic cones. A scruffy scarecrow in a filthy tracksuit sat on the caravan's top step, smoking. Hand cupped around the cigar-ette, trying to hide its light from snipers.

As if anyone would waste a bullet on Sammy Wilson.

Logan pulled into the entrance, drifting slowly past the big red buoy that decorated the middle of the car park.

His Airwave gave its point-to-point bleeps again, and DCI Steel's voice growled out into the car. *'How come you've no' called me back yet?'*

'I'm busy.' Logan slowed. Poked the button marked 'LEFT ALLEY' and a spotlight lanced out and caught Sammy Wilson full in the face.

All bones and angles and taut sallow skin. Flecked with stubble, dirt and bruises.

Sammy shrank back against the caravan, one arm up, covering his eyes.

Logan wound down the window. 'Evening, Sammy.'

A wince. Then a sniff. And Sammy Wilson peered out from behind his grim sleeve. 'Not doing nothing.'

'Sure you're not.'

'Hoy! You still there?'

'No. This is a recording. Leave a message after the beep.' He let go of the talk button and pointed at the temporary fencing with its warning notices. 'You're not planning on doing something I'd disapprove of, are you, Sammy? Bit of breaking and entering, maybe? Wheeching bits of kit off the building site?'

'Nah, I'd never. Nope. Not me. Not a thief and that.'

Logan stared at him.

He shrugged one shoulder. Stared down at his feet. 'Suppose I could sod off.'

'Probably for the best. Don't want someone getting the wrong idea.'

He hauled himself to his feet and scuffed away up Market Street, leaving a coil of cigarette smoke behind.

'You can be a right dick, you know that, don't you?' Steel cleared her throat. *'Anyway, it's no' like I'm asking for much: a wee hand to talk to your local sex offenders, that's all.'*

'I'm not the one being a dick.' He put the car in gear again, heading down Laing Street and along the front. 'You've got the biggest team in the division. Use it.'

'You want the murdering pervert who did this to get away? That what you want?'

To the left, a hodgepodge of old-fashioned Scottish buildings faced out over the railing to the harbour walls and the still, grey mass of the North Sea. Some of them wore grey harling, some dressed granite, some painted white.

'Shift finishes in half an hour.'

'You're no' telling me that sodding off home for a Pot Noodle and a spot of onanism is more important than catching a wee girl's murderer, are you?'

'And I'm in court tomorrow.'

Past the Macduff Arms, all shuttered and quiet.

'Oh, don't be such a big Jessie. It's just a couple of sex offenders. No' like we'll be that long at it.'

The Bayview Hotel had some sort of wedding reception going on – a knot of wobbly blokes in kilts smoking cigarettes and laughing on the pavement in front.

'You're authorizing the overtime, are you?'

'Ah . . .'

No one outside Bert's. A couple of women getting money from the Bank of Scotland cash machine. Nothing doing at the Highland Haven Hotel.

Nice and peaceful. Quiet. Like his Airwave's speaker.

Then the harbour gave way to industrial units and the bus depot.

He thumbed the button again. 'Well, *are* you?'

'It's no' as easy as—'

'This isn't CID. We get sod all for the first half-hour of unplanned overtime, after that it's on the clock. I'm not running a charity here.'

The buildings faded in the pool car's rear-view mirror. Banff twinkled on the other side of the bay.

More silence from Steel. Then, finally, *'OK, OK, overtime. You're a greedy—'*

'I'm not greedy, I'm skint. You got any idea how much of a pay-cut came with the "development opportunity" you lumbered me with? I'm living on bargain-basement soup and pappy sliced white.'

'That's no' my fault! How was I supposed to know Big Tony Campbell would stick you in a bunnet in the arse-end of nowhere?' Her voice dropped to what was probably meant to be a sultry purr. *'Come on: you and me, questioning sex offenders like the good old days.'*

'Yeah, well . . . Too late to do anything about it tonight anyway.' Up and over the bridge into Banff.

'Laz, Laz, Laz. Did you learn nothing *from our time together? It's never too late to rattle a nonce.'*

Nicholson leaned forward from the back seat. 'I want to say thank you, again, for the opportunity to work on the Tarlair Major Investigation Team.'

Sitting in the passenger seat, Steel took a long draw on her e-cigarette, setting the tip glowing blue. 'Calm down, eh? No one likes a brown-noser.' Then poked Logan in the shoulder. 'Are we there yet?'

'For the last time: we'll get there when we get there.'

A shrug. 'No' my fault you drive like an old lady, Laz.'

Nicholson tapped Steel on the arm. 'Erm . . . Why do you call him "Laz"?'

'Short for Lazarus. You remember the Mastrick Monster? Laz here caught him. Got into a knife fight on top of a tower block.'

'It *wasn't* a knife fight.'

'Who's telling this story, you or me?' Another puff. 'Knife fight.'

Nicholson frowned. 'But why Lazarus?'

''Cause our wee boy here got himself killed stone dead.'

Her eyes went wide in the rear-view mirror. 'What happened?'

Logan shifted his grip on the steering wheel. Took the turning onto Duff Street. 'I got better.'

Steel sniffed. 'Are we there yet?'

'Shut up.'

The short man blinked back at them from behind thick-framed spectacles. 'I'm sorry?' He clutched his dressing gown tight shut across his chest, hiding the patchwork of scars and shiny cigarette burns. Ran his other hand across the shiny top of his shiny head.

Steel scooted forward, until she was sitting right on the edge of the armchair. 'No' a difficult question, is it, Markyboy? Where were you?'

He puffed out his cheeks. Shrugged. 'Here, probably. I don't really like to go out much. After . . .' Mark Brussels cleared his throat. 'Well, it's probably for the best. Probably. I mean, you hear stories, don't you? People on the register getting beaten up.' He flapped a hand at the outside world. Then pressed his knees together. 'People on the register going missing.'

She pulled out her e-cigarette and gave it a sook. 'Missing like Neil Wood?'

'Been a lot of that kind of thing going on. Kickings. Disappearings. Concerned citizens taking it out on poor sods like us.'

'Poor sods?' She hauled out her list. 'Says here you abused girls as young as seven over a twelve-year period.'

Logan rocked back and forwards on the balls of his feet. 'When'd you last get a supervisory visit, Mr Brussels?'

The clock on the mantelpiece ticked into the silence. A small smelly terrier snored on its back in a tartan beanbag in the corner. A radio in another room, played saccharine boy-band pop. The floorboard creaked overhead as Nicholson crept about, pretending she was off to the toilet. Have to have a word with her about not sounding like an elephant in tap shoes.

Steel puffed out her cheeks. 'Come on, Markyboy,

118

it's like pulling teeth here. When'd you last get a visit from the Perv Patrol?'

'Well . . .' His eyes slid towards the zombie-grey gaze of the off television. 'They said I wasn't really a risk any more, so I could go to once every six weeks. To be honest, I miss the company.' He stood. 'Can I get anyone a cup of tea?'

'Sounds like a load of old bollocks to me, Billyboy.' Steel stuck her feet up on the low coffee table. Had a squint about. 'Someone like you, passing up a sweet young thing in a school uniform? Nah, that's no' your style.'

The man in the beige cardigan stared at her with striking blue eyes that lurked beneath heavy white eyebrows. 'It's *William*, not "Billyboy", and I'll thank you to get your feet *off* my furniture.' Spine ironing-board stiff, grey hair swept back from a high forehead. 'It's bad enough you turn up at this ungodly hour, the least you can do is have the civility not to treat my home like whatever kind of pigsty you live in.'

Logan stepped forward. 'Perhaps—'

'No, no, no.' Steel held up a hand. 'Billyboy's got every right to moan if he wants to.' She grinned at him with unnaturally white teeth. '"Pigsty", because we're police officers. Very droll. Your file didn't say you were such a wit.' She took her feet off the table. 'What it *does* say is you've got a thing for wee girls. Four to nine years old, wasn't it?'

His face hardened – a granite slab with a hooked nose. 'That was nothing more than scurrilous rumour. The whole trial was a farce from start to finish. A sick vendetta by a handful of ignorant troglodytes!'

The sound of a toilet flushing rattled the pipes behind the wall.

Steel pursed her lips – the wrinkles lined up to turn her mouth into a rouged cat's bumhole. 'Good enough for the jury to give you eight years, though, wasn't it?'

'Vile *lies*.'

'What was it the tabloids called you? No, don't tell me . . . Ah, got it: Dr Kidfiddler!'

Yes, because that was helping.

Logan took out his notebook. 'Mr Gilcomston—'

'*Doctor*. It's Dr Gilcomston.'

'Dr Gilcomston, has anyone threatened you? Implied they were going to attack you?'

'Ignorance runs rampant throughout our society, Sergeant.'

Steel rested her chin on her hands. 'And no one's tried to make contact?' She fluttered her eyelashes at him. 'Maybe, oh, I don't know, someone like Neil Wood?'

A pause. 'If you're implying I've got anything to do with that *pervert*, I resent it.'

The lounge door opened and Nicholson stepped into the room. 'Sorry about that. Must have been something I ate.'

Gilcomston shuddered. 'Well, I hope you cleaned

120

the bowl after you. I have no desire to clean up your *filth*.'

That halogen smile broke across Steel's face again. '"Filth!" Another excellent police pun. You're like Oscar Bleeding Wilde today, aren't you, Billyboy?'

Logan dropped his voice to a whisper. 'All I'm saying is we might get on better if you weren't so rude to everyone.'

Steel settled into the leather settee, stretched her arms along the back. 'No' bad here, is it? Wonder how much this place cost?'

It was a Victorian pile on Church Street with big bay windows and a garden to match. Hunting prints on the wall, pine cones and potpourri in the grate, beneath an ornate marble fireplace. Upright piano. Glass-fronted bookcase full of leather volumes. Standard lamps holding the night at bay.

'Dr Gilcomston—'

'Is a dirty scumbag. And he's no' a doctor either – got struck off after the conviction.'

Nicholson folded her hands behind her back. 'Am I on piddling duty again?'

Steel drummed her fingers on the tobacco-coloured leather. 'Got to play to your strengths.'

She sighed. Wrapped her arms around herself. 'People will think I've got cystitis.'

The lounge door swung open and a large woman in a twinset sailed into the room like a lavender barge. Half-moon glasses on the end of her round

121

nose. Only the pair of fluffy slippers, scuffing on the old woollen carpet, gave away the fact that she'd been roused from bed a little after one in the morning. She lowered a tray laden with scones and cups and a teapot onto the glass-topped coffee table. 'Who's got cystitis?'

Steel hooked a thumb at Nicholson. 'Been going all night like a leaky bathtub.'

There was a small pause, then Nicholson rubbed both knees together. 'Actually, sorry to bother you, but could I . . .?'

'There's one by the back door, or the top of the stairs on the left.'

'Thanks.' And she was gone.

Mrs Twinset settled into a wing-backed leather chair. 'Now, is this about these stupid threats?'

Logan took out his notebook. 'Threats, Mrs Bartholomew?'

'Yes, threats. Thrust through my letter box, like some sort of takeaway menu. "You will burn in hell for everything that you have done. God will not save you. We are coming." That kind of thing.' A snort. '"We are coming." Honestly, some people have no sense of propriety. Still, that's the age we live in, I suppose.' She picked up the teapot. 'Now, shall I be mother?'

Steel smiled. 'That no' how you got into trouble in the first place?'

A chubby rumpled face peered out at them through the gap between the door and the frame.

Streetlights thickened the dark circles beneath his eyes as he looked them up and down. 'You got any idea what time it is?'

Steel popped her wrist forward, so her watch poked from the end of her sleeve. 'Yup. Now you going to invite us in for a chat, or are we going to drag you down the nick?'

Nicholson climbed into the car. 'How many's that now?'

Logan started the engine. 'Eleven.'

'Pfff . . .' She sagged in the rear-view mirror. 'Your old boss is . . . different.'

DCI Steel paced up and down the pavement in front of the terraced houses, mobile phone clamped to her ear, puffing away on her e-cigarette. One hand flailed away, emphasizing whatever point she was making, even though there was no way whoever was on the other end of the phone could see it.

'Oh, she's that all right.' Logan stretched the knots out of his neck. 'On the plus side, we might have a new nickname for you.'

Nicholson covered her eyes with one hand. 'Sarge, I swear to God, if "Piddler" is the next word out of your mouth, I'm going to strangle you with your own limb restraints.'

A grin. 'Wouldn't dream of it.'

She turned to stare out at the houses. A light was on in the flat they'd just visited, the curtains held open – a figure silhouetted in the gap. Tall, thin, long hair. Then the curtains fell shut again.

Nicholson went on staring. 'Looked far too young to fiddle with little girls, didn't he? Barely out of nappies himself.'

'Still think it's all glamour and glory on a Major Investigation Team?'

'Kind of thought it'd be more . . .' A shrug. 'You know.'

Steel hung up and stuffed the phone in her pocket. Stomped back towards the car.

Logan nodded. 'If it's any consolation, you're following a long line of officers in a noble tradition.'

'Designated piddler?'

'I used to have to do it all the time. "Oh, I'm bursting for a pee, can I use your toilet?" Then go rummaging through drawers and cupboards while whichever boss it was asked stupid questions.'

'Yeah . . .' Nicholson's mouth stretched out and down, the tendons sticking out in her neck. 'You wouldn't *believe* some of the things I've found tonight. I mean, not kiddie porn or anything, but dildos, and lube, and rubbery things like Ping-Pong balls on a string.' She curled her top lip. 'That doctor guy had a butt plug, a ball gag, and furry handcuffs. I mean, can you *imagine* him all oiled up and—'

The passenger door clunked open and Steel tumbled into the seat. Produced her list of sex offenders and a pen, then drew a thick red line through the address of the young man who interfered with little girls. 'Right. Next up – Windy Brae.'

Logan stifled a yawn. Then tapped the dashboard clock. 'That's twenty past two. I've got court tomorrow, remember?'

'Worried you'll no' get enough beauty sleep? Trust me, that boat sailed when you got the shaved-scrotum haircut.'

He opened his mouth . . . Closed it again. Turned to stare at her. 'Why are you here?'

'Told you: trying to catch a wee girl's—'

'Oh no you don't. This . . .' He pointed up at the flat. 'Trolling through the registered sex offenders? That's no job for a detective chief inspector. That's a sergeant, maybe DI at most.'

She closed her door. 'Nothing wrong in taking pride in your work, is there?'

'You pissed someone off, didn't you? That's why you're here: it's a punishment. You said something you shouldn't to Finnie or Young.'

Steel yanked the seatbelt down and rammed it into place. 'Oh . . . sod off.'

CHAPTER 11

Logan checked his watch. 'Right, fifteen more minutes and we're done.'

Steel shuffled her feet as Nicholson thumbed the bell again. The cottage sat on the brow of a hill, overlooking the cliffs and the sea – still and silent, washed like pewter by the thin smear of light from the crescent moon. Nothing but fields and gorse for miles.

A plume of e-cigarette steam snaked up into the starry night. 'You used to be a lot more fun.'

'Just because *you're* on nightshift, it doesn't mean we are too. Some of us have got court tomorrow. Supposed to get eleven hours between the end of any shift and having to give evidence; that's gone for a Burton.'

'Don't say I'm never good to you: Swanson's heading into Aberdeen first thing with a bunch of productions from the search – she'll give you a lift. You can snore all the way.'

Nicholson backed away from the door. Stared up at the windows. 'Maybe he's not in?'

Another puff. 'Try round the back.'

She clicked on her LED torch and picked her

way past the rose bushes and round the side of the cottage.

Steel stuffed her hands in her pockets, fake fag clamped between her teeth. 'Don't know what you're moaning about. Case is watertight – Graham Stirling's spending the rest of his natural playing hide the soap with rapists and murderers.'

Logan leaned back against the wall. Yawned. Stretched his arms and legs. 'So, come on then: Nicholson's not here any more, what did you do?'

'Sod all.' She took a deep drag. Hissed out a thin stream of vapour. 'Ever occur to you I might miss this?'

'Knocking up sex offenders in the middle of the night?'

'No' sex offenders . . .' She pulled out a hand and thumped him on the chest. '*This*. You and me: Cagney and Lacey; Holmes and Watson; Dalziel and Pascoe.'

Laurel and Hardy, more like.

'Thought you had Rennie now.'

'Rennie's no' the same. He cries when I make fun of him. And McKenzie's one poke away from an aneurism.'

An owl hooted in the fields behind the cottage. Followed by what sounded like someone knocking over a stack of flowerpots and some muffled swearing.

Logan frowned out into the night. 'You think there's anything to this sex offenders getting attacked and going missing thing? That's twice we've heard about it.'

'Twice out of what, twenty paedos? No' exactly statistically significant, is it?'

'Three, if you count Mrs Bartholomew's "Burn in Hell" threat. *And* Neil Wood's dad got beaten up today. Well, technically yesterday, but you know what I mean.'

Steel took another long drag. 'Not like they don't deserve it, is it?'

All the parking slots outside the station were taken – a mix of patrol and unmarked pool cars, all bathed in the thin sodium light. The car park out front was full too. Among the more everyday vehicles loomed a couple of police pods and a Transit in full riot gear, its front grille raised like a surprised monobrow.

Logan found them a parking spot further down the street.

Steel creaked her way out of the passenger seat and paused on the pavement for a big stretch. Her blue silk shirt rode up, exposing a slash of dead-fish skin and a bellybutton. 'Pffff . . .' She had a scratch. 'Any chance of something to eat? Starving.'

Logan nodded back towards the station. 'Vending machine in the canteen. Crisps, caffeinated drinks, and chocolate.'

Her eyebrows tented in the middle, bringing out the puppy eyes. 'No chips?'

Nicholson bounced out from the back of the

car, following them along the pavement. 'The baker's opens at five. They do a great chicken-curry pie.'

Steel checked her watch, then sagged. 'An hour and twenty minutes . . . Be a skeleton by then.'

'Good, you can keep Hector company.' Logan thumbed the code into the keypad by the trades-men's entrance. Then covered his mouth for a long shuddering yawn.

The sound of telephones filtered through the building. Raised voices. Someone laughing.

Nicholson pointed down the corridor towards the Constables' Office. 'Paperwork first, Sarge?'

'Do your actions, then sod off home. Put down for three hours' overtime.' He turned to Steel. 'That's fair, isn't it?'

'Bloody bunnets, eating my budget . . .' Steel turned and lumbered into the main office.

Two PCs sat at Maggie's desk, one typing things into a spreadsheet while the other hunched over a pile of evidence bags. Reading out the label numbers as his mate logged them in.

Someone in a charcoal-grey suit was at the other desk, tongue poking out the side of her mouth as she picked at her keyboard with two fingers. Wrinkles furrowed the gap between her eyebrows, a mass of frizzy brown hair tied back in a wobbly half-bun-half-ponytail-thing.

Not one of them looked up until Steel clicked her fingers three times. 'Hoy, Becky: any messages?'

The woman in the suit flinched. Grabbed the

stack of Post-it notes beside her. 'Body's arrived at Aberdeen, Boss. PM's set for half nine. DS Rennie wants to call off the search till dawn. Says it's too dark to—'

More finger snaps. 'I *can* read, DS McKenzie: give.'

Becky handed over the Post-its. Her jaw tightened, the muscles flexing. 'Yes, Boss.'

Steel flicked through the yellow squares, holding them at arm's length and squinting. 'Pfff . . . Is there no bugger in the whole force who can make a decision on their own?' She stuffed them into a pocket. 'If anyone needs me, I'll be upstairs. In the ladies. Making smells.' She paused on the threshold to the hall. 'And see if you can rustle up a cup of tea, eh? And something to eat.' Then slouched off into the hall and away up the stairs.

Beat. Two. Three. Four. And the smile died on Becky's face. Eyes narrowed on the closing door. Voice a serrated-blade whisper. 'What did your last slave die of, you old *bag*?'

She turned and stomped off towards the canteen.

Looked as if Steel was right: one prod away from an aneurism.

Nothing like running a happy team.

Logan crossed to the Sergeants' Office and opened the door. Then froze.

A thin bloke in a blue suit was sitting in *his* seat. Feet up on *his* desk. Scratching himself on the back of the head with a biro, mobile phone clamped to his ear. '. . . yeah, that's what I

130

thought . . .' A frown. Then he glanced in Logan's direction: long nose, trendy hair quiffed up at the front, designer stubble. 'Get lost, I'm on the phone. . . . No, not you, Guv. Some fanny in uniform. . . . Yeah . . .' Then laughter.

Logan nodded. Stepped into the room, and slammed the door behind him, hard enough to make the dick in the suit flinch.

'And you are?'

The guy licked his lips. Took his feet off the desk. Squared his shoulders. 'On the phone.'

Probably too young to be a boss, but with these fast-track programmes you never knew. 'And tell me, *Inspector*, how long do you plan on using my office?'

'Sorry, Guv, give me a minute.' He held the phone against his chest, covering the mouthpiece. 'It's Detective Sergeant. Detective Sergeant Dawson. MIT.'

'Ah, I *see*.'

Dawson – the sexist scumbag who thought it was Nicholson's job to act as charlady.

Logan unclipped his belt and thunked it down on top of the little grey filing cabinet all the notebooks had to go in at the end of the shift. 'Well, if I'd known that, I would *never* have bothered you.' He dug his fingertips into the join on the side of his stabproof vest, hauled the Velcro flaps apart, then did the same with the shoulder strip above it. Slipped the whole thing off. 'Big important man like you, clearly has more important things to worry about than the running of B Division.'

A smile cracked across Dawson the Dick's face. 'You and me got a problem?'

'No, no, no. Wouldn't dream of it.' He hung his vest on the hook behind the door. 'How about I get one of my team to make you a nice cup of tea?'

Dawson's mouth hung open for a moment, accompanied by a frown, and then the smile was back. Broad and magnanimous on that trendy little face. 'That's . . . very cool of you, Sergeant. Thanks. Milk, two sugars.'

'Not a problem at all.' Logan held up both hands, palms out. 'I'll get out of your hair.'

Back through into the main office.

Becky stormed past, mug in one hand, packet of crisps in the other. Swearing under her breath as she pushed through into the hall, making for the upper floors.

Through into the Constables' Office.

Nicholson was poking away at her computer keyboard, filling in her actions for the day.

He leaned back against the work-surface desk. 'You'll never guess who I just met.'

She looked up. 'Santa?'

'Your favourite sexist scumbag, DS Dawson.'

'Urgh . . .' She went back to her keyboard, thumping away harder than before. 'Hope he gets syphilis. From an angry Rottweiler.'

'Wouldn't put it past—'

The Constables' Office door banged open and there was the PC who'd been banging evidence-label numbers into a spreadsheet: broad-faced with little black flecks along the underside of his double chin, as if he'd shaved in a hurry. 'Yeah, hi. Sorry.' A sniff. 'Listen, DS Dawson says if you guys are making tea anyway: we need three with milk and one sugar; four with milk; two white coffees; and one black, two sugars. Don't suppose you've got any Earl Grey, do you? The boss is partial.'

Nicholson was on her feet. 'Now you listen to me, you f—'

'It'll be our pleasure.' Logan stood. Patted Nicholson on the shoulder. 'Isn't that right, Constable?'

A pause.

The guy with the scabby chin shrugged. 'Only doing what I'm told.'

She hissed out a breath. 'Yes, Sarge.'

Nicholson thumped the mugs into a line on the counter beside the sink. All ten of them. Stuck the kettle on to boil, then plonked teabags and spoons of instant coffee in the requisite ones.

Logan leaned back against the vending machine, crumpling the notice saying that prices were going up again. 'Don't forget the milk.'

A scowl. 'Still don't see why we have to run around after—'

'Because we are *good* little parochial police officer

teuchters who know their place.' Sticking out his left arm, Logan grabbed the canteen door and shoved. It swung shut with a clunk.

The room was a washed-out shade of industrial magnolia. Recycling bins, a vending machine, and a TV-on-a-shelf took up one side; a blue worktop-table sat in the middle; kitchen units, cooker and sink against the opposite wall. A concrete garden gnome stood on the windowsill – someone had painted his eyes in with Tipp-Ex and black marker, given him a thick pair of sinister eyebrows, and added a cut-out paper knife to one hand. Presumably so he could guard the piggy bank.

Logan picked up the pottery pig and gave it a shoogle. It barely rattled.

Nicholson pointed. 'See? They're not even putting in for teas and coffees! Freeloading—'

'All right.' Logan dug into his fleece pockets. 'How we doing with the kettle?'

She checked. 'Nearly.' Then pouted. 'I mean, come on, Sarge, this isn't *fair*.'

'We're helping our fellow officers to a tasty hot beverage. Nothing wrong with that.'

Nicholson dumped the big carton of semi-skimmed down next to the cooker. 'Why are you taking this so bloody calmly?'

'Because *I* am a grown-up.' He held up the drugs he'd purchased from the Fraserburgh Tesco. 'Four boxes of violent, unpredictable relief.' He tossed one to Nicholson. 'What's the recommended dose?'

Frowning, she scanned the instructions. 'One tablet before bedtime. Why are—'

'What do you think: three or four per mug?'

She shifted from foot to foot. 'Won't they . . . you know, taste it?'

'Not the way you make tea. Grind them up first, then let's see if we can't scare up some biscuits for our *honoured* guests.'

CHAPTER 12

Sunlight streamed in through the thin curtains. The smell of damp, still alive under the combined assault of two plug-in air fresheners – bruised, but fighting back. The bleeping warble of an upbeat song on the alarm-clock radio.

Logan rolled over and thumped the snooze button. Lay back and stared at the collection of brown stains on the ceiling. That one looked like a buffalo. That one like a dismembered foot. That one like . . . Norway?

The walls weren't much better – covered in peeling paper, painted a revolting shade of blackcurrant mousse. Curling away from the plaster.

Home, sweet home.

A massive yawn grabbed him, stretching his arms and legs beneath the duvet. Leaving him limp and blinking.

Seven a.m. A whole two and a half hours' sleep.

Come on: up. Graham Stirling wasn't going to convict himself.

Logan rolled out of bed and padded to the window, bare feet scuffing on the bare floorboards. Pulled one side of the curtain back an inch.

Crystal-meth sky with high wispy clouds. The tide out, exposing a swathe of pale-blonde sand from here to the River Deveron. Lines of white rippling the sea. A yacht sailing off into the blue.

'Unngh . . .' Scratch. Yawn.

Cthulhu popped up on the windowsill beside him, landing in ghostly silence. Made a prooping noise, then butted her head against his arm. Small and fluffy, with stripes and a tail nearly as big as the rest of her put together. He rubbed one of her hairy ears, making her grimace and lean into it, purring.

The clock radio lurched into life again. The end of the warbling song replaced by a cheery woman's voice. *'I don't know about you, but I like it!'*

The purring stopped. Cthulhu shook her head then thumped back to the floorboards – landing like a sack of bricks – and padded off, tail straight up. Business to attend to.

'News and weather coming up at half past nine. And we'll have more on the hunt for missing forty-three-year-old, Neil Wood. But first, here's the latest hit single from Monster Mouse Machine . . .'

Sod that. Time for a quick shower, then off to Aberdeen.

'All right, all right, I'm coming . . .' Logan wrapped the towel around his middle, slipped his wet feet into his slippers and scuffed down the bare stairs as the bell kept up its brrrrrrrringing wail. Along the hall to the front door. Wrenched it open. 'What?'

Oh . . . *great.*

DCI Steel raised an eyebrow, took a long slow draw on the e-cigarette sticking out the corner of her mouth. 'I'm flattered, but I don't think my wife would approve.' Steel's hair was all squashed on one side, the other looked as if it had filed for independence from her head. Thick, dark circles crowded the bags beneath her eyes. More dark circles beneath the arms of the same blue silk shirt she'd had on the night before. Jacket slung over one shoulder, heavy carrier bag in her other hand. She nodded at his midriff. 'Nice scars though.'

He folded his arms over the shiny puckered lines.

She frowned. 'You've lost weight. What happened to the cuddly chunky-monkey McRae we all know and love? Just skin and bones now.'

'You try humphing a stone-and-a-bit of equipment around for ten hours every day.'

A minibus full of old ladies rumbled past, pale creased faces pressed to the window. Assorted whoops and obscene hand gestures.

Steel waved back at them. 'Well, you going to stand there dripping, with your willy hanging out, or are you going to invite me in?'

He grunted, turned and shuffled back inside. 'Can't be long – catching a hurl into Aberdeen with Swanson, remember?'

Steel clunked the door shut behind her, then whistled. 'Wow. Rennie was right, you *do* live in a craphole.'

The wallpaper was stripped off in the stairwell

138

and the hall, the lathe and plaster crumbling and stained. Grey flex drooped from the ceiling, dangling a single bare bulb like an unsniffed runny nose. Dust and fluff made little drifts on every step of the stairs, dark varnish chipped and faded on either side of the paler strip where the carpet had been. No carpet on the floor either. Small cracked patches of linoleum made scabs on the wooden boards.

She opened a door off the hall. The room on the other side was nothing but stacks and stacks of file-boxes. Not quite floor to ceiling, but close to it. 'This your porn collection? Nearly as big as mine.'

He clumped up the stairs in his slippers. 'Station's been using this place as an overflow file storage for decades. Kettle's in the kitchen. Make yourself useful.'

By the time he'd come back down, all dried and dressed in Police-Scotland black, she was in the lounge, an open bottle of beer clutched to her chest. Frowning at the stacks of books on the mantelpiece.

A small TV balanced on a packing box. A bargain-basement couch from the charity shop. A folding chair. Two stepladders draped with dust sheets and a stack of paint tins and brushes. Bags of plaster.

He dumped his black fleece on the couch. Tucked his T-shirt into his itchy trousers. Picked up Cthulhu's water and food bowls from their placemat in the corner. 'It's seven in the morning. Where did you get beer?'

'Confiscated it.' A swig. 'Laz, seriously, this place is a dump. And no' a nice one either, this is the kind of dump where you've got to go see your doctor afterwards to get the bad news. Half the windows are boarded up!'

Logan carried the bowls through to the kitchen. The units might have been cheap, but they were new and they were clean. A fresh coat of cheerful yellow on the walls. A row of potted herbs on the windowsill, drinking in the morning sun.

Through the glass, Banff police station lurked on the opposite corner of the small square. Three storeys of dirty sandstone, with a fake balcony over the main entrance and curly carved bits holding up various lintels. Stone urn-shaped things decorated the front edge of the roof. If it wasn't for the blue-and-white 'POLICE' sign and the sprawl of patrol cars and vans parked outside, it could have passed for an ancient hotel.

A handful of reporters wandered about out front, drinking from Styrofoam cups and sunning themselves in the early morning glow. Waiting . . .

Logan emptied out the kettle, filled it, and put it on to boil. 'You want a tea?'

Steel appeared in the doorway. 'How long's it going to take you to do this place up: five years? Ten?'

'It's a work in progress.'

'Pfff . . .' Then she dug into her plastic bag and

pulled out a copy of the *Daily Mail*. Slapped it down on the working surface. 'Looks like your PC Nicholson's no' the only thing that's leaky up here.'

Most of the front page was taken up with a photo of Neil Wood, beneath the headline, 'SICKO SEARCH ~ Police Hunt For Missing Paedophile'. There was even a small inset photo of the outdoor pool at Tarlair.

'Well, don't look at *my* team, this is your bunch of numpties.' He dug Cthulhu's bowl into the bag of dried cat food. 'So what happened with the dead girl?'

'Post mortem's at half nine. Messrs Young and Finnie in attendance, while yours truly gets to grab a whole five hours to herself . . .' A jaw-cracking yawn, followed by a burp. Then a shudder. And another mouthful of beer. 'Been on since seven yesterday morning. Two kebabs, three gallons of coffee, two proper cigarettes, a poke of chips, five tins of Red Bull, someone else's sandwich, a bag of cheese-and-onion, and a beer.' She raised it in salute. 'Doing wonders for my diet.'

Logan washed out the water bowl and filled it with fresh. 'So join divisional, that'll shift a few pounds.'

'Cheeky sod.' Another swig. 'And the leak *can't* have come from my numpties. Most of them spent the night carpet-bombing the porcelain. Was like the battle of Dresden in that station last night.' A nod. 'Luckily I'm made of sterner stuff.'

Lucky she got DS McKenzie to make a cuppa

before Logan and Nicholson got their poisoned round in, more like.

He dried his hands on a tea towel. Did his best to look innocent. 'Do me a favour?'

'If it involves me getting naked too: no.'

'Pair of local scrotes got a big shipment of drugs from down south. I've got a warrant for a raid. Couldn't go in yesterday because of the wee girl . . .' Through to the lounge to put Cthulhu's bowls back where they'd come from. 'If we leave it much longer, they'll cut the shipment up and disappear it out onto the streets. And *you've* got all the spare bodies in the division.' Then into the kitchen again.

'Would you stop charging about? Making me seasick.' She knocked back the rest of her beer. Clunked the bottle down on the worktop. Sagged. 'When, and how many?'

'Tomorrow evening. Say . . . four OSU, and a drugs dog? Syd Fraser's good, if we can get him.'

A massive yawn left her shuddering and stretching – shoulders up around her ears, arms locked, elbows out. 'How long?'

'Two hours. Ish.' A quick rummage in the cupboard for a bowl and the box of waxy own-brand cornflakes. 'About your dead girl – you're searching the outdoor swimming pool, and the car park, and the buildings, right?' Flakes in the bowl. 'What if she wasn't dumped there?'

Steel produced a bottle opener and clicked the top off another beer. 'She didn't fly there on her own. Body had to get there somehow.'

'There's green weed and slime all around the main pool, *especially* on the seaward side. That's only going to grow if the wall's regularly underwater. And given we had a couple days of rough weather over the weekend . . .?'

She stared at him. Then covered her face with her hands. 'Sodding hell. She washed in from the sea.'

'Sure you don't want a cup of tea?'

'Want a pee.'

'Top of the stairs.'

Her footsteps clumped up the bare steps. Then the clunk of a door closing.

Logan sploshed milk on the flakes and checked his phone – a voicemail from Deano and a text from his mother. *That* got deleted unread.

'Sarge, Deano. Listen, we're having a barbecue at ours, Thursday evening. A mate's come into some steaks, if you fancy it? Give us a shout back.'

Why not? Be nice to have something that actually looked like real meat for a change. And by then Graham Stirling would be heading off to Barlinnie for the rest of his unnatural. Plus: they'd have raided Klingon and Gerbil's place. Big haul of drugs, mentions in dispatches, medals, and a parade. Time to celebrate.

It was too early to call Deano back. So Logan wolfed down the cornflakes, slipped his phone in his pocket, and a slice of bargain-basement white into the toaster. Stuck his head out into the hall. 'Hurry up: I've got to go in a minute.'

143

No reply.

'OK, I'll leave a spare key on the table for you. You can let yourself out.'

Silence.

'Listen,' he walked to the bottom of the stairs, 'thought I'd pop past and see Susan while I'm in town. See how she's getting on. She at home today?'

Nothing.

Maybe she hadn't been so lucky with the poisoned tea after all?

'Hello?' The steps creaked beneath his feet, all the way up. 'You've not fallen in, have you?' When he knocked on the bathroom door, it swung open.

Thankfully Steel wasn't sitting on the toilet with her trousers around her ankles. The room was empty – freshly tiled with a new bathroom suite. Cheap, but serviceable. Even if it had taken weeks to put in.

'Hello?'

A jagged rasp, like a wood-saw hacking away at a sheet of corrugated metal, came from the bedroom. Then a pause. Then another one.

He put a hand on the door and swung it open. There she was: lying flat on her back, on his bed, with both feet still on the floor. One arm flung out to the left, the other hand draped over her right boob. Mouth wide open. Snoring.

Wonderful.

He swung her legs up onto the duvet, pulled off her boots, then pulled a blanket over her.

A 'Proooop?' came from the hallway. Cthulhu sauntered in and hopped up on the bed beside Steel. Treddled the blanket for a minute, then turned round twice and settled onto the pillow beside her head.

'Disloyal little sod.'

Logan closed the door and left them to it.

Logan shifted his fleece to the other hand and let himself into the station. The unnatural-pine scent of disinfectant and air freshener clawed its way into his nose, itched at the back of his throat. As if someone was trying to cover up a terrible smell.

Keep a straight face.

He poked his head into the Constables' Office: no one there. A couple of cardboard boxes sat in the middle of the room – piled high with brown-paper evidence bags – but other than that, it was the same slightly scruffy collection of posters, notices and in-trays laden with paperwork.

No one in the canteen. No one in the main office either.

Two abandoned papers hung folded over the edge of the partition by Maggie's desk – an *Aberdeen Examiner* and an *Evening Express*. One had gone with an aerial photo of Tarlair Outdoor Swimming Pool, with a silhouette inset of what was meant to be a little girl: 'Body Found In Neglected Northeast Beauty Spot'. The other featured a head-and-shoulders of Neil Wood: 'DID MISSING PAEDOPHILE KILL TRAGIC

SCHOOLGIRL?' A tiny article in the sidebar was titled, 'STIRLING TRIAL CONTINUES'. Would have thought it deserved more page space than that, considering what Graham Stirling had done to Stephen Bisset.

Logan did a three-sixty. 'Hello? Anyone home?'

Maybe the MIT had caught whoever killed the little girl and sodded off back where they'd come from? That'd be nice . . .

He got out his keys and opened the little blue locker with his name on it. Unhooked his Airwave handset from its charger. Switched it on and slipped it into his fleece pocket. Then pushed through into the Sergeants' Office.

Stopped.

DS Dawson was sitting in *his* seat again. Only not looking quite so cocky this time.

His face was a pale shade of grey, the bags under his eyes a smudgy, bruised colour. His quiff had lost its arrogant strut and dangled limply across his shiny forehead. He looked up as Logan closed the door. Grimaced. Stuck one hand to his stomach as a coffee-percolator-gurgle rumbled somewhere inside it. 'What you doing in? Thought you were backshift.'

Logan did his best not to smile. 'You look a bit rough.'

'Urgh . . . Think we hit a dodgy kebab shop last night. Half the station's been welded to the bogs since back of four.'

'That *is* a pity.' He unlocked the little grey filing

146

cabinet and pulled out the drawer with his notebook in it. Popped it into a pocket. 'Supposed to be getting a hurl into Aberdeen with Swanson. You seen her?'

'I ended up stuck in the cells for two hours – only bog that was free.' Dawson puffed out his cheeks and rubbed at his growling stomach. 'Never touching another doner as long as I live.'

'Sounds dreadful.' Don't grin. *Don't* grin. 'So, Swanson?'

'No idea. All I know is everyone ran off to break up some fight outside the— Urgh . . .' Another roll of gurgling thunder. 'Oh God . . .' He grabbed the desk. Paused. Took a deep breath. Let it out in a long slow hiss. 'No, I'm OK . . .'

Logan pulled on the most sympathetic face he could. 'Well, as I've got a couple of minutes, how about I make you a nice cup of tea?'

Constable Swanson shifted her grip on the steering wheel, hunched forward in her seat as they roared around the bend, heading south on the A947. Big hands; broad face; scruffy brown hair streaked with blonde like a humbug, tied up in a bun. Glasses. 'I'm really, really sorry. Only these two auld mannies were really laying into each other. Fists and false-teeth flying everywhere.' She grimaced. 'Sorry.'

'Told you: it's OK. As long as I'm at the High Court for nine, we're fine.' Logan took out his phone as they thundered over the Castleton Bridge. No new messages.

A constant burble of calls murmured from his Airwave handset – B Division going about its daily business.

'*Suspected overdose on Crooked Lane, Peterhead.*'

'*Anyone in the vicinity of Asda's in Fraserburgh? Shoplifter's been apprehended by store security.*'

'*All units, lookout request for one Tony Wishart, IC-one male, eighteen years old, dark hair. Outstanding apprehension warrant for burglary.*'

'*Getting complaints of a domestic disturbance in Whitehills, any unit free to attend? Priority one.*'

Logan turned the volume down and wriggled in his seat. Settling further into the fabric.

Nice not to be wearing a stabproof vest and equipment belt for a change.

Outside the window, vivid green fields and trees swooshed past. The hissing soundtrack of tyre noise joining the Airwave's chatter and the throaty growl of the patrol car's engine. The rattle of the blue plastic crate on the back seat. Their car swept around another bend, and the rustle of the crate's evidence bags joined the music.

Swanson grimaced at him. 'Just have to hope we don't catch the rush hour heading into Dyce. Don't know if going via Inverurie's worse or—'

'We'll be fine. Labs won't do anything with your stuff till this afternoon anyway.' He reclined his seat a couple of notches, tipped his peaked cap forwards so it covered his eyes and nose. 'And if it's getting tight, we'll blues-and-twos it. Don't think the Powers That Be will complain if it helps put Graham Stirling away.' He stretched out. Stifled a yawn. Sighed.

'Sarge?'

'What?'

'You don't snore, do you?'

'About to find out.'

The round of applause started as soon as Logan walked into the CID office. Beige walls, grubby ceiling tiles, grubbier carpet tiles, whiteboards covered in notes and lines. It was smaller than the old one, but then so was the team – whittled down by all the other specialist units that had sprung up with the change from Grampian Police to Police Scotland. But the half-dozen officers who were there gave him a standing ovation, a mug of milky tea, and a bacon buttie.

Biohazard slapped him on the back and popped the cap on a bottle of tomato sauce. Squirted it into the buttie. 'Got to keep your strength up for today.'

'Ta. When are you giving evidence?'

'Tomorrow morning.' He stuck the tomato sauce back on his desk. 'Course, by then it'll all be over.'

The others drifted back to their desks and their phones while Biohazard led him over to a file-box by the printer, with 'NOTEBOOKS' in heavy black marker letters. 'Took the liberty.'

Logan had a bite of buttie. It was lukewarm, but it tasted of smoky victory as he rummaged through the box for the notebooks he'd had when they'd been after Graham Stirling. Popped them onto the printer. 'What about Rennie?'

'Tomorrow afternoon. Assuming he can find his way back down here from your Teuchter backwater.'

'Watch it, you.' Logan had another mouthful, washing it down with a slurp of tea. 'Any idea how it's going so far?'

'You know how it is. Yesterday was all opening arguments and weaselling. Nothing for the jury to get its teeth into. Speaking of which . . .' Biohazard picked up a green folder and handed it over. 'They're going for mock-ups.'

He stuffed the last third of the buttie in his mouth and flicked through the folder's contents. Instead of the actual crime-scene photographs, someone had mocked up a body in the computer and modelled Stephen Bisset's wounds onto it. Nice and sanitized and safe for the fifteen boys and girls who'd be sending Graham Stirling to jail in a couple of days.

Logan slipped the pictures back where they'd come from. Checked his watch. 'Better get going. You know what the Fiscal's like before a big one.' He downed the last of his tea in one. 'Drinks after?'

'You better believe it.' A grin split across Biohazard Bob's face, all teeth and chubby cheeks. 'Steel's even put fifty quid in the kitty.'

'About time.' Logan stuck his old notebooks in his fleece pockets. 'Right, better get going.'

A wink. 'It's a shoo-in.' Then he screwed up one side of his face and leaned to the left. A high-pitched squeak. Then a grin. 'For luck, like.'

The smell was like being battered about the head with a mouldy badger. Logan backed off, eyes stinging. Waving a hand in front of his face. 'God . . . What have you been *eating*?'

The grin got bigger. 'Oh yeah, Stirling's going *down*.'

CHAPTER 13

The sound of murmured voices oozed out from the Witness Room. Logan tucked his peaked cap under one arm and pulled out his mobile. Headed through the doors to the stairwell, selecting Deano's number from the contacts as he climbed up to the next landing. Leaned against the windowsill as the phone rang. Outside, Marischal Street's granite terrace reached away down the hill, took a break for the bridge over the dual carriageway, then finished up at the harbour. Three storeys of grey stone, flecks of mica glittering in the sunshine. Rooftop dormers mirroring back the glare. A supply vessel loomed at the bottom of the road, its yellow-and-black hull streaked with lines of rust.

Probably start off in Blackfriars after the trial. Couple of pints, then across the road to Archies for pie-and-chips and more beer. Then on to the Illicit Still. The Prince of Wales. Ma Cameron's . . . All the old haunts. Maybe even—

'Hello?'

'Deano? Logan. Yeah, thanks, barbecue sounds good.'

'Cool. Janet and Tufty are coming too. Got a box of ribeyes big as your head.'

'We're on for the warrant tomorrow. Got the extra bodies.'

'Even better. Be good to finally get Gerbil and that idiot Klingon banged up.'

'Can you get the team to keep an eye on the place tonight? Probably peeing in the wind, but I don't want them cutting their shipment up and wheeching it out till we've had a chance to dunt their door in. Keep it low-key though.'

'Will do.'

'You need me to bring something on Thursday?'

'Potato salad? Coleslaw? Something like that. Aye, and not from a tub: homemade. Oops, got to go – don't want to burn my cornbread.'

Logan almost had his phone back in his pocket when it blared out its generic ringtone. 'Sod . . .' He pulled it out. Unknown number. Hit the button. 'Logan McRae.'

Silence.

'Hello?'

A thin, nervous voice filled his ear. *'Is this . . . is this Sergeant McRae? You saved my mum's life last night.'*

Frown. He did? 'Oh, Mrs *Bairden*.' The old woman in the bath.

A heavy-set man in a black robe, white bow tie and wing collar, appeared through the door on the next landing down. Scanned the stairs down to the floor below, then looked up at Logan. Small ears and small nose, eyes hidden in folds of drooping grey. The Macer checked the clipboard in his hand. 'Sergeant McRae?'

Logan nodded, held a hand up. Back to the phone: 'Is she OK?'

'The doctors say she had a stroke. If you hadn't got to her . . .' Pause. *'Thank you.'*

Warmth spread through his chest, like a sip of malt whisky. 'Glad I could help.'

'Sergeant McRae, they're ready for you.' A frown. 'And you shouldn't be using your mobile phone in here.'

'Really, really thank you . . .'

'It was my pleasure. Wish her well for me.'

'Sergeant McRae, I must insist—'

'Sorry, I've got to go. I'm in court today.'

'Yes, yes, of course. Thank you . . .'

When she'd hung up, he smiled. Switched off his phone and slipped it back into his pocket. Put his peaked cap on his head and marched downstairs to where the Macer was waiting. Patted him on the shoulder. 'You know, some days, I remember why I joined the police.'

The courtroom didn't look anything like the ones on the TV. It was bright and modern, with pale varnished wood and cream-coloured walls. Long and narrow, divided in half by a waist-high partition. A cross-section of Aberdonians had squeezed themselves into the rows of public seating, faces shining in the warm room. The table for the press

154

was packed with hunched men in sweat-ringed shirts, tapping away into laptops or scribbling into notepads.

In the middle of the partition, an eight-foot-high screen of bullet-proof glass wrapped around three sides of the defendant's box. Graham Stirling sat flanked by two *huge* G4S guards. He'd dropped the blue sundress for a sombre suit – his hair longer than it had been, curling around his ears. Looking more like an accountant than a manipulative, vicious, sexual predator. He turned his head, avoiding Logan's eyes.

Should think so too.

A large oval wooden table took up most of the space on this side of the partition. Prosecution team on one side: an Advocate Depute and his junior in their black robes, suits, and ties; and sitting next to them, the Procurator Fiscal in grey pinstripe with matching hair and military moustache. The defence team sat on the other side: the QC and his devil in robes, short wigs, and white bow ties; the instructing solicitor looked as if he should be selling houses in Elgin.

The court clerk was stationed between them, like a referee in No Man's Land. The jury lurked behind the defence, facing the witness stand, flanked by flat-screen TVs. Another two huge screens on opposite walls to display evidence on.

No mahogany. No Victorian pseudo-gothic twiddly bits. No smell of antique cigarettes seeping out of threadbare carpet tiles. The only nod to antiquity was the carved coat of arms hanging over the Judge's seat and the mace mounted on the wall beside it.

Well, that and the Judge's outfit.

She straightened her white robe – stained a mild shade of pink, presumably because of the two big red crosses on the front of it and a washing machine on too hot a cycle. Her short white wig sat on top of her long grey hair. A pair of severe glasses perched on the bridge of her long thin nose. One hand stroking the tip of her pointy chin, watching as Logan took the stand.

The Macer waited until Logan was in place, before turning to the Judge. 'M'Lady, we have witness number six, Sergeant Logan McRae.'

'I see.' She stood, held up her right hand. 'Sergeant McRae, repeat after me: I swear by Almighty God, that the evidence I shall give shall be the truth, the whole truth, and nothing but the truth.'

'So, Sergeant McRae,' Sandy Moir-Farquharson took off his glasses and polished them on the hem of his black robe, 'are you seriously expecting the jury to believe it was a *coincidence* that you happened to be in Cults that evening?' He slipped his glasses back on and smiled. It emphasized the twist in his nose. Grey hair swept back from the temples, the bald spot at the top covered by the short white wig. A suit that probably cost more than Logan made in six months peeking out between the front of his robes.

Logan pulled his shoulders back. 'That's not what I'm saying at all. Graham Stirling was there, attempting to acquire a second victim, so—'

'Objection.' He turned a smile on the Judge. 'Milady, the witness is indulging in supposition.'

A nod. 'Sustained.' The Judge peered down at the witness stand. 'Sergeant McRae, please restrict yourself to the *facts*.'

'I am, Milady. Graham Stirling was placing anonymous personal ads in the *Aberdeen Examiner*, looking for men interested in having a sexual liaison with a pre-operative transsexual. On the advice of our forensic psychologist, we responded to one of them and arranged to meet—'

'We'll get to that, Sergeant.' Moir-Farquharson checked his notes. Probably just for show. The slimy little sod would have all this memorized. 'Now, you claimed in your statement that you'd given chase through the back gardens of Hillview Drive, because there was, and I quote, "Something suspicious about the figure in the blue sundress." Is that right? In what way suspicious?'

'. . . and did anyone else hear this alleged confession, Sergeant?'

The clock mounted on the wall ticked away to itself.

Motes of dust hung in the light streaming in through the windows.

'Sergeant?'

Logan flicked over a couple of pages in his old

notebook. 'Graham Stirling said, "Stephen Bisset is dying in the dark and there is nothing you can do about it."'

Moir-Farquharson shook his head. 'No, Sergeant, I didn't ask you what you *claim* to have heard, I asked if anyone could corroborate it.'

Tick. Tick. Tick . . .

'We were alone in the garden at that point, but—'

'I thought not.' The smile was wide and white. Good dental work. Couldn't even see where most of his teeth had been kicked out. 'So, you assaulted Graham Stirling: headbutting him and breaking his nose. Tried to break his wrist, and then miraculously got this confession that no one else heard.'

The prosecution's Advocate Depute was on his feet. One arm jabbed out at his learned colleague. 'Objection!' Long grey curls swept back from a high forehead and pinched face. Voice a booming Morningside: 'Sergeant McRae applied reasonable force in restraining a suspect who was *vigorously* resisting arrest. To paint this as some sort of confession obtained by torture is disingenuous, to say the least.'

Moir-Farquharson held up a hand. 'My apologies, Milady. No such implication was intended.'

'Uncorroborated confessions seem to be something of a trademark of your evidence, don't they, Sergeant? I refer, of course, to the one allegedly obtained by yourself in the back of the unmarked police car.'

Tick. Tick. Tick . . .

Logan straightened his police-issue T-shirt. 'Graham Stirling insisted my colleagues leave the car before he would talk.'

'So no corroboration.'

'We believed, correctly, that there was a clear and imminent danger to Stephen Bisset's life. It was important to—'

'Your statement claims you were told,' he held up a sheath of paper and peered at it over the top of his glasses, '"You will never find the shack without me, it is not on any maps. By the time you find him, Stephen Bisset will be dead." Is that correct?'

'It is.'

'How very convenient . . .'

'Tell me, Sergeant McRae, is it normal Police Scotland practice to deny a suspect access to a solicitor on their arrest?'

God's sake . . .

'These were unusual circumstances, Stephen Bisset was seriously injured and dying—'

'You have heard of Cadder versus HM Advocate, haven't you, Sergeant? Do you make a habit of contravening your suspects' human rights?'

Tick. Tick. Tick . . .

'Sergeant?'

'We didn't . . . I took the decision that, given the time constraints, it was more important to save Stephen Bisset's life!'

'I see.' Moir-Farquharson turned to the jury. 'So, yet *again*, ladies and gentlemen, Sergeant McRae decided to ignore procedure, bend the rules, and cut *another* corner.'

'To recap: once more, we have only your word for it, Sergeant?'

Deep breaths. Calm.

Logan stared straight ahead. 'Graham Stirling refused to show me where the shack was, unless DS Rennie and DS Marshall remained behind at the car. My choices were to go with him, or let Stephen Bisset die.'

A sigh. A shake of the head. Then a turn to the jury. 'Bending the rules, yet again.'

'I had no choice! And he knew the combination to the padlock, he—'

'You make a disturbing habit of ignoring procedure, Sergeant McRae. How do we know that your sense of right and wrong isn't similarly compromised? How far *will* you go to obtain a conviction?'

'Objection!'

'I put it to you, Sergeant McRae, that you nominated Graham Stirling as being responsible for Stephen Bisset's disappearance and manufactured the circumstances and evidence to fit.'

'That's *not* true. We found evidence that Stephen Bisset had responded to Stirling's personal ad, seeking sex with what he believed to be a pre-operative transsexual and—'

'LIAR!' A young man was on his feet in the public seating area. Shoulder-length black hair, black tie, a shirt that still had the creases from where it had been folded in the packet. Thin face flushed and swollen around the eyes. Spit glowing in the sunlight. 'YOU'RE A LIAR! MY DAD WOULDN'T DO THAT!'

The Sheriff cracked her gavel against her desk, three sharp raps. 'Mr Bisset, I won't tell you again. While the court is sympathetic to your distress, it—'

'YOU'RE A LIAR!'

The young woman sitting next to him grabbed his arm, trying to pull him back down into his seat. She had the same dark hair, the same thin face. 'David, don't . . .'

'DAD WASN'T A PERVERT!'

Another three raps. 'That's *enough*, Mr Bisset. This court isn't—'

'MAKE HIM TELL THE TRUTH!'

'Clerk, I want this man removed.'

And all the way through it, Graham Stirling didn't move. He sat there, still, silent. Blinking slowly. A million miles away as his victim's children were escorted from the room.

'Are you denying that you threatened to *kill* Graham Stirling, Sergeant McRae?'

Logan's fingernails dug into the pale wood of the witness stand. 'I did *not* threaten to kill him.'

'Really?' A look of surprise. 'So you deny saying, "I should kick the living shit out of you."?'

Tick. Tick. Tick . . .

'Sergeant?'

'I don't remember. I'd just discovered Stephen Bisset. He'd been—'

'How about this one. Did you, or did you not tell your superior officer, "I need an ambulance and someone to stop me stringing Graham Bloody Stirling up from the nearest tree"?'

Logan hunched over the sink. Drips fell from his face, making ripples in the water that spread out in overlapping rings. He dug his hands into the basin again and sploshed more on his face. Cold against his skin. Leaching away the burning heat.

Bastard.

The court toilets were clean enough, filled with the scent of air-freshener and disinfectant.

Another faceful of water. Letting it drip back into the bowl. All those overlapping circles, knotting together then fading away, leaving nothing behind to show that they'd ever existed.

His phone buzzed on the surface between the sinks. Then the 'Imperial March' sounded.

DCI Steel.

Ignore it. Let it go to voicemail.

The toilet door thumped open and the Procurator Fiscal marched in: short grey hair combed forward above scowling eyebrows. His military moustache bristled, the mouth behind it chewing through the words in a booming Glaswegian accent that was

162

far too big for someone who barely scraped five foot four. 'What the sodding *hell* was that?'

'What was I supposed to do, lie under oath?'

'Of course not. But . . . It . . .' In four steps he was at the nearest cubicle door. It got a kick with a highly polished brogue. A pause. Then the Fiscal ran a finger along his moustache, as if making sure everything was in order. 'They've effectively killed Stirling's confession. After that little farce, it's going to be ruled inadmissible.'

Logan grabbed a handful of green paper towels, stacked by the broken hand-drier. 'I didn't have any choice, OK?' Scrubbed his face with the gritty green sheets. Dropped them in the bin. 'If I'd stuck to procedure, Stephen Bisset would be dead now. He'd probably still be missing, lying out there, rotting in a shack in the middle of the BLOODY FOREST!' Logan closed his eyes, pinched the bridge of his nose and squeezed, screwed his face up. Breathed out. 'Sorry.'

The Fiscal made a hissing noise, as if he was deflating. 'You could've recorded his confession on your mobile phone. Could've used your Airwave to broadcast it. *Something*.'

Logan's head fell back, thumped against the wall. Did it again. And once more for luck. 'I know.'

'Yes, well, I suppose Descartes was right: hindsight is a treacherous mirror. We just have to hope the DNA evidence convinces them.'

Sitting next to the sink, Logan's phone started

in on the 'Imperial March' again. He let his hands fall at his sides. 'You going to need me again?'

The phone rang out onto voicemail.

The PF cleared his throat. 'I think you've probably done enough.'

Logan's phone burst into song as he was thumping down the stairs. Not the 'Imperial March' this time, but the theme tune to the Muppets. He checked the screen: 'NICHOLSON'.

His thumb jabbed the button. 'Is it important? Because now's *really* not a good time.'

'Sarge? It's Janet. Thought you'd like to know – we got the Big Car back.'

He made it to the ground floor. 'Janet, I genuinely couldn't give less of a toss if—'

'Smells fusty though. Like something's died in there.' Her voice went all whispery. *'Look, about the teas and coffees last night . . . I kind of . . . feel a bit, you know, guilty.'*

'Sod them. I will not have a bunch of MIT scumbags treating anyone on my team like a glorified Mrs Doyle.'

'Yeah, but . . . they're working a murder enquiry, and from what I heard most of them spent half the night impersonating a Soyuz rocket.'

He slipped out of the side entrance, onto Marischal Street, avoiding the media scrum at the High Court's front doors. 'And?'

A pause. *'It's a wee girl, Sarge.'*

Someone beeped their horn. There was a taxi

parked in the middle of the road, blocking traffic while it picked up a fare.

A wee *dead* girl . . . Nicholson had a point.

Perfect: more guilt.

'If it makes you feel any better, they weren't going to achieve anything last night anyway.' He crossed over to the other side. No point heading up the hill, that'd put him in the camera's firing lines again. 'One: everyone and their maiden aunt is already out looking for Neil Wood. Two: until they identify her, they can't build a viable list of suspects. Three: with no ID and no witnesses, there's very little they can do until the post-mortem results are in.' He reached the opposite pavement. New plan: cross the bridge, down the steps onto Shore Lane, and he could go around the back of the Castlegate. Sneak into Divisional Headquarters via East North Street. 'Giving a bunch of arrogant sexist tossers a dose of the squits doesn't change any of that.'

A long slow breath. Then, *'Thanks, Sarge.'*

'Besides, I double-dosed DS Dawson this morning.'

'Urgh . . . I know I said I wanted to kill him, but I didn't mean we should actually—'

Whatever she said next, it was drowned out. 'YOU!'

Logan stopped. Turned.

The young man from the court – the one with the long black hair – was climbing out of the taxi. Glaring at him. 'YOU LYING BASTARD!' Stephen Bisset's son.

Great, because today wasn't *special* enough.

'Sorry, Janet, got to go.' Logan hung up. Put the phone back in his fleece pocket. Held his hands out. 'I need you to calm down.'

He'd loosened his tie and it dangled around his neck like a waiting noose. 'YOU LIED. WHY DID YOU *LIE*?'

His sister clambered out of the taxi behind him. Close up, she was obviously younger than him. Barely a teenager. 'David, come on, we spoke about this. If you calm—'

'I WILL NOT CALM DOWN!' His face was heading an unhealthy shade of reddish-purple, tears streaking his cheeks. 'DAD IS NOT A PERVERT!' He stormed down the hill towards Logan, hands curled into fists. 'YOU LIED!'

For God's sake . . .

'I didn't lie. We followed the trail of messages, that's how we found your dad. He—'

'SHUT UP! YOU SHUT YOUR LYING MOUTH!'

His sister caught up with him, grabbed his arm like she'd done in court. 'You have to *stop* this.'

'No! He lied, Catherine, he lied under oath!'

'It's OK, it's OK. Shhh . . .' She tried to pull him back towards the taxi, but he wouldn't budge. 'Come on, David, let's go home. Please?'

Logan backed off a step. 'Look, I'm sorry if it upsets you, but I didn't lie. I did everything I could to get your dad back safe and sound.' Yeah, because *that* worked.

David Bisset bared his teeth, forced the words out between them as if they were made of acid. 'You call that safe and sound?' He jabbed a finger in the rough direction of Aberdeen Royal Infirmary. 'Do you? HE'D BE BETTER OFF DEAD!'

'I know it's difficult, but—'

'LIAR!' David Bisset shook his sister off and lunged, fists swinging. Wide and amateur. No idea what he was doing.

Logan sidestepped, grabbed one of the flailing arms and twisted it round behind David's back. Slapped his other hand down on David's elbow, locked the wrist into place and closed the gap. Reached out and took hold of the other shoulder and pulled him upright.

Classic hammer lock and bar.

'LET GO! LET GO YOU—'

Logan put the pressure on.

'AAAAARGH!'

'Calm down.'

The girl, Catherine, snatched at the sleeve of Logan's fleece. 'Please, he didn't mean anything, he's upset, *please* don't hurt him.'

'GET OFF ME!'

'Are you going to calm down?'

'Please, it's not his fault. He's upset . . . We all are.'

David went quiet. Breath hissing in and out through his gritted teeth.

'Are we all calm? David? Are we good?'

She chewed on her fingernails. 'David, *please* don't . . .'

His breathing slowed. He stopped struggling. His head dipped. 'I'm sorry.'

'OK.' Logan released his grip. Stepped away. 'No harm done.'

David leaned against the granite wall of the nearest building, one hand rubbing his abused shoulder. He stared down at his feet. 'Dad's not a pervert.'

'If it's any help, I know what it's like—'

'No.' His jaw tightened, the words barely making it out between gritted teeth. 'You don't. You don't have any bloody clue.'

Deep breath. 'My girlfriend fell.' Logan turned and pointed down Marischal Street, at the top-floor flat that belonged to someone else now. 'Right there. Five storeys, straight down. Four years in a coma. I know what it's like to have someone you love hurt and stuck in a hospital bed, unable to move or talk.' He cleared his throat. 'It's horrible. And it's not fair. And it stinks. But he's still your dad.'

David glared back, mouth a hard trembling line.

Then his sister took his arm and led him back towards the taxi. 'Come on, David. Let's go home. It's OK.'

'He's not a pervert . . .'

'I know.'

They climbed back into the taxi, him hunched over, one hand wiping the tears from his eyes, her rubbing his back between the shoulder blades.

Logan stood where he was as the taxi drove past him.

David was in full flood now, face screwed up, back heaving. But his sister stared out of the window, her eyes locked on Logan's. Face dead and expressionless.

And then they were gone. Down to the bottom of Marischal Street and left, disappearing onto Regent Quay.

Graham Stirling ruined more than Stephen Bisset's life, he screwed up Bisset's kids too. Screwed them up so much they might never get past the sight of their father lying on his back in the High Dependency Unit with tubes and wires hooking him up to machines and drips and bags.

Four months and he'd barely moved. Hadn't said a word. Just lay there.

A small shiver danced across the back of Logan's neck.

Four months as a stump of a man, waiting for death. And Logan couldn't even put the bastard who'd done it behind bars.

David Bisset had been right to have a go at him. He deserved it.

Logan's seat rattled as the big diesel engine changed down to climb the hill. Outside the windows, granite tenements shone in the afternoon light.

Trees glowed green and gold. Roses made frozen scarlet fireworks in gardens.

He dug into his carrier bag and pulled out the first tin of beer. Still cold from the chiller cabinet. Little beads of condensation prickling on the metal surface. He clicked the tab, took a deep swig. Ground his teeth together and swallowed. Bitter. Which fitted perfectly.

The number 35 was nearly empty. A couple of oldies sat up front near the driver. Neither of them talking – him buried in his newspaper, her staring out of the window. Leaving Logan with most of the bus to himself.

Another swig.

Bloody Sandy Moir-Bloody-Farquharson.

What the hell was he supposed to do: let Stephen Bisset die?

He took his peaked cap off the seat next to him and stuffed it in the carrier bag. Followed it up with the epaulettes off his T-shirt. OK, so the sleeves still had 'POLICE' embroidered on them, but rolling them up a couple of turns hid that. Now he was just another skinhead, dressed in black, drinking cheap beer at the back of a bus. Glowering out at the city as the driver took them through Berryden, past Aberdeen Royal Infirmary, through Bucksburn, Dyce, then out into the countryside.

Tin number two died in his hands. He crushed the empty and dumped it in the bag.

Fields and sheep and cattle slid by outside the

windows. Green land, blue sky, and happy little fluffy sodding clouds.

Should've been raining. Should've been hammering it down from a slate-grey sky, wind battering the bus and whipping the trees.

Logan's phone went again. Not the 'Imperial March' for a change: unrecognized number.

His thumb hovered over the button. Pressed it. 'Hello?'

Steel's voice bellowed into his ear. *'How could you possibly screw this up? Simple, open-and-shut case. What the hell's wrong with you?'*

'It wasn't my—'

'Do you have any idea what the Big Brass are doing right now? They're getting a dirty big stake sharpened, so they can ram it up my backside and roast me on an open fire!'

'I didn't—'

'All the man-hours we put into that investigation and it's ruined!*'*

'There's still the DNA evidence. It'll—'

'YOU TOOK STIRLING TO THE BLOODY CRIME SCENE!' Silence. She was probably counting to ten. Then she was back, sounding as if she'd dropped something heavy on her foot. *'Hissing Sid's screaming cross-contamination. Never mind sending the bastard down, we'll be lucky if we get out of this without Graham Stirling suing our arses off! It's—'*

Logan hung up.

Three seconds later, his phone started ringing again. Then the Airwave handset joined in.

He turned them both off. Rammed them deep into his fleece pockets.

Opened another tin of beer.

So much for celebrating.

CHAPTER 14

The sound of happy-clappy piano and guitars dragged Logan up from the depths, hurling him into Wednesday morning.

'And we've got more smashing hits of the Eighties after the news and weather with Bernie.'

He slumped back on the bed, one hand over his eyes while the other fumbled for the alarm-clock radio.

'Thanks, Clyde. Merseyside Police confirmed this morning that one of the women killed in the drive-by shooting in Liverpool on Sunday was Mary Ann Nasrallah, an undercover police officer. We'll have more on that later this morning. Next, the hunt for missing sex offender Neil Wood enters its second day as—'

Logan slapped the radio into silent submission.

Should've switched the damn thing off before crashing last night.

Something dark and spiky throbbed behind his eyeballs. It coated the back of his throat with grit and bitterness. Made everything taste of cheap supermarket whisky. Then it sank its teeth into his bladder.

Unnngh . . .

The world was a sharp and queasy place as he lumbered through to the toilet.

Then back to bed again.

To hell with the day.

The padlock tumblers squeak beneath his blue fingertips. The hasp falls to the ground, followed by the lock as he pushes the door wide.

Its hinges creak like a coffin lid and he steps into the foetid darkness.

'Stephen?' The word comes out in a plume of breath, pale as a ghost. 'It's OK, you're safe now . . .'

No he isn't.

The torchlight swings its yellow septic eye across stacks of poles and saws and chains, logs and a cast-iron stove. Settles on a pile of filthy blankets.

Don't do it.

But his hand reaches out anyway. What choice does it have?

He grips the barbed-wire fabric and pulls.

'Stephen?'

The body lies on its side, curled up on a wooden pallet that's stained crimson and black. The gaps between the slats are dark and hollow, like the gaping mouth. Gums torn and ragged where the teeth had been ripped out. Fingers bent and twisted, as if someone had taken a hammer to them. Thick strips of silver duct tape wrapped over the eyes. Dried blood caked around the empty groin and filthy buttocks. More blood across the swollen chest. Chains around the wrists and ankles, heavy and rusted.

He's dead. He *has* to be dead.

A fist of gravel catches in Logan's throat. He swallows it. Forces it down into his chest, sharp and hard and cold. 'I'm sorry.'

And then that ruined blind head turns and *screams* . . .

The toilet bowl was cool against Logan's cheek. Breath slowing. The pounding in his temples settled to a galley-slave beat, battering the drums in time with his heart.

Sitting on the bathroom floor, Logan howched and spat out streamers of bile-yellow spittle. Groaned.

Pulled himself upright.

The man in the mirror looked like an extra from *The Walking Dead*.

He rinsed out his mouth. Washed his face. Dried it. Couldn't look at it any more.

His stomach gurgled and he froze, one hand pressing against the scars that criss-crossed his abdomen. Then it settled.

Never drinking cheap own-brand whisky ever again.

Ever.

Especially not half a bottle of it.

He slumped back to the bedroom. Stood, looking down at the crumpled, sweat-soaked sheets.

Yeah, sod going back to bed.

*   *   *

Sun streamed through the window, turning the air into golden syrup, flecked with glowing dust motes. The ward's quiet was punctuated by the hum and hiss of ventilators. The wub-wub-wub of a far-off floor polisher. The squeak of comfortable shoes on blue terrazzo flooring.

Logan knocked on the doorframe. 'Shop?'

Louise looked up from a clipboard. Smiled. 'Logan. Isn't it a lovely day?' Her pixie-cut was about twenty years too young for her, bleached blonde, the fringe gelled into a jagged curl above a pair of heavy dark eyebrows. White linen shirt, boot-cut jeans, black trainers. She picked up a large manila envelope from her desk, then pointed over his shoulder. 'Shall we grab a cuppa?'

Louise picked her way out onto the balcony, clipboard tucked under her arm, carrying a tray in both hands. One teapot, one cafetiere, two cups, and a plate of tiny triangular sandwiches. She lowered the tray onto the table. 'Sorry that took so long.'

Sunny Glen was living up to its name. The timber walls shone in the sunshine, the glass-and-chrome balustrade glinting. Logan had picked the table on the upper terrace, in the shade, with a view down the valley and out to sea. A neon-orange supply vessel ploughed its way towards the horizon, leaving a wake of shimmering white.

And, more importantly, the upper terrace overlooked the lower one.

Down there, a handful of wheelchairs were arrayed across the tiled floor. Some of the residents wearing hats, others baseball caps, a couple bare-headed.

Louise poured tea into Logan's cup. Nodded at the manila envelope. 'All signed and sealed?'

He pushed the thing across the small table towards her. 'Now what?'

'Now we give it to the lawyers, they give it to the Sheriff, he declares Samantha incapable, and you're appointed her financial and welfare guardian. Should only take a couple of weeks.'

Logan shifted in his seat. 'She's not incapable, she's ill, it's not the same thing.'

'I know, but it has to be done. She hasn't got anyone else. If her mum and dad were still alive . . .' A shrug. Then Louise smiled. Nodded towards the lower terrace. 'She's looking well, isn't she?'

Samantha's wheelchair sat over by the railing, her back turned to them. Her hair was almost solid brown now, just a tiny fringe of its former colour holding on at the tips. Red, faded to a dirty pinky-grey. Arms curled against her chest. Knees together. Head tilted on one side. As if some great fist had taken hold of her and squeezed till she was twisted out of shape. Far enough away that she couldn't hear them talking about her.

'So, about this chest infection . . .?'

A shrug. 'You know what it's like. She's less susceptible to them now she's sitting up more of the time. But it's always the same with brain injuries.

177

Chest infections, urinary infections. At least her temperature control's a lot better: she hasn't had a storm in months.'

The tea was hot but underbrewed. Thin and anaemic. A pale shadow of what it should have been.

Louise pressed the plunger on her cafetiere. 'Samantha's made remarkable progress since she got here. In fact, if she keeps this up, I think we should aim for a cranioplasty in August or September. Get them to patch the hole in her skull with a metal plate.'

'A metal plate.'

'Well, assuming the intracranial pressure remains within safe limits . . . But there's no reason to suppose it won't. And she'll look a lot more like her normal self without that big dip in her head.' Louise poured the coffee. Sipped. 'She smiled yesterday.'

He sat up straight. 'What?'

A grin. 'Isn't that great? First time she's reacted to anything. I tried calling you. Didn't you get my message?'

Don't get your hopes up. Small steps. Remember what the neurosurgeon said.

'What was it? What made her smile?'

Logan hunkered down on his haunches next to the wheelchair. Looked up into Samantha's face. Frowned. Took out his handkerchief and wiped a line of dribble from the side of her mouth. 'I hear you've been smiling at the guy who rubs your feet. You hussy.'

No reaction. But then there never was.

Two thick Velcro straps held her upright in the chair, wrapped around the metal frame, then across her chest. Stopped her slumping over, or falling out.

'Louise says you're now officially a *ten* on the Glasgow Coma Scale. How cool is that?'

Nothing.

'And we're having you declared incapable, that's nice, isn't it?' He puffed out his cheeks. 'Held them off for as long as I could, but apparently I haven't got a choice any more. I'm going to be your guardian. Like Bruce Wayne and Thingy the Boy Wonder. Only you don't have to wear a stupid yellow cape and big green pants over your tights.'

Still nothing.

He wiped away another line of dribble.

'Anyway, they're talking about putting a metal plate in your head. Maybe September, if you keep going the way you are. That'll be fun, won't it?' He brushed a strand of long brown hair from her face. Doing his best not to touch the big dent over her left ear where they removed a chunk of skull to relieve the pressure on her brain. 'You could wear hats again. Or maybe we could stick fridge magnets on it . . .'

He settled his back against the glass balustrade. 'We caught a dead wee girl, Monday night. Down by the swimming pool. Steel's up with the MIT.

179

Susan's tests came back and there's only a one in five hundred chance of the baby having Down's. That's good, isn't it?'

Samantha didn't move, staring straight through him as usual.

He cleared his throat. Turned his head. 'Yeah, that's what I thought.'

The supply boat was smaller now, churning away across the slab of navy blue.

'I screwed up. Graham Stirling's going to get away with what he did to Stephen Bisset. He's going to beat the charges and walk . . . because of me.'

A herring gull flapped to the ground on the other side of the glass railing. Strutted up and down, glaring at him with its yellow eyes.

'Should be spending the rest of his life in prison, and instead: they're going to let him go . . .'

The gull cocked its head and crawked at him. Pacing. Demanding. Shouting. Like a miniature DCI Steel.

'Hissing Sid's trying to make out that I fitted Stirling up. Can you imagine that? Me?' A small laugh that tasted as bitter as the spittle he'd left in the toilet bowl. 'Never fitted anyone up in my life.'

It raised its wings and screamed at him, high-pitched and grating. Digging into his brain with sharp little claws.

'Spent half my life trying to put bastards like him behind bars, and the courts let them go. If

I'd been fitting him up, I'd have made damn sure he couldn't wriggle out of it . . .' Logan scowled at the seagull. It glared back at him. 'Tell you what I *should* do: I should go round to Stirling's house, middle of the night, and batter his head in with a crowbar.'

A sigh.

'Well, we can always dream, can't we?' Logan stood. Brushed the dust off his jeans. 'You don't want to hear about this crap, do you? Course you don't. It's just me being a whinge.' He clapped his hands, fetched a chair from the nearest table and set it down next to Samantha. 'Now, how about we watch the ships and the seagulls for a bit?'

'Yeah, hold on . . .' Logan pinned the phone between his ear and his shoulder, shifted the heavy shopping bags to his other hand, then dug his keys out of his pocket. 'Sorry, what?'

On the other end, Biohazard sounded as if he was chewing bits of broken glass. *'Could've bloody swung for him. I swear to God, right there in the middle of the court. Homophobic? Me?'*

'So we're screwed then.'

'Said, and I quote, "How long have Police Scotland been operating a vendetta against Aberdeen's lesbian, gay, bisexual, and transgendered communities?" And you know why? Because Stirling was in that dress when we caught him, and I called him Danny the Drag Queen!'

'It's not . . .' Logan slid his key into the lock.

'Look, there was nothing we could do. We saved Stephen Bisset's life. At least that's something.'

'*Tell* that *to his kids.*'

Logan let himself into the Sergeant's Hoose. Closed the door behind him. Locked it. Held the phone against his chest. 'Cthulhu? Daddy's home.' No sign of her in the lounge. Or the kitchen. Back to Biohazard. 'Professional Standards say anything to you?'

'*What do you think? Spent the last two hours getting my ear chewed off about gender bias and equal opportunities for trannies and drag queens.*'

He dumped the big bag of value tatties in the cupboard under the sink. Stuck the kettle on. 'They say anything about me?'

'*No way the jury's going to convict the slimy little git now. No confession, no forensics, and no corroboration. All we've got is a couple of adverts placed in the lonely hearts column.*'

'Biohazard: focus. What did Napier say about me?'

'*No idea, got my spanking off Inspector Laird. Sourfaced nettle-licking old bag. Far as I know, they're coming after you next.*'

Wonderful.

'*Tell you: when this whole thing collapses, you, me, and the boy Rennie, are going to be up to our ears in a septic-tank hot tub.*'

'And on that cheery note.'

'*Exactly. Now, if you'll excuse me, I'm off to get blootered.*' Biohazard hung up.

Logan stood in the kitchen, staring out of the window at Banff police station.

Might be a good idea to get the resignation in early. Take what he could get before they kicked him out. Go work offshore or something where you didn't have to haul on a stabproof vest to start your working day. And you got decent regular shifts. And more money. And loads of time off . . .

Tempting.

But then, who'd look after Cthulhu while he was away on the rigs?

He dug her special saucer out, then went looking for a pouch of wet food. Whistled two notes, high-then-low. Stood at the kitchen door with the saucer in his hand. 'Cthulhu?'

No prooping noise. No sound of surprisingly heavy paws thumping down the stairs.

He climbed up to the first floor.

Stood in the hallway and listened to the rhythmic asymmetrical purr.

Let his head fall back, and *swore*.

Placed one hand on the bedroom door and pushed.

Steel was lying flat on her back, in his bed, one bare foot and one hand sticking out from beneath the duvet. Mouth hanging open, snoring.

A pile of clothes lay crumpled on the floor by the window. A copy of *Fifty Shades of Grey* on the bedside cabinet.

Cthulhu raised her head from the pillow, gave

a wide triangular yawn, stood. Turned around, and settled down to sleep again.

Typical.

Logan put the saucer of cat food on the chest of drawers and poked Steel in the shoulder. 'Hoy!'

'Mmmnnnghphhhhh . . .' Her mouth made glistening wet circles. Then the snoring started again.

'WAKEY, WAKEY!'

'Gnph . . .!' She scrambled up in bed, eyes wide and blinking. 'What? I never touched her . . .'

Oh. Dear. God.

Steel wasn't wearing anything . . .

Logan swallowed. Flinched back a step. A sour taste filled his mouth. 'Oh God, not *again*!'

'Noooo . . .' Then she grabbed the covers and hauled them up to her chin. Scowled at him. 'You rotten sod. I was dreaming about Claudia Schiffer!' More blinking. 'What time is it?'

'What are you doing in my bed? Naked. Why are you naked in my bed?' He backed up till he hit the wall. 'You swore this wouldn't happen again. You promised!'

Steel thumped back onto the pillow. 'She was all covered in Nutella and everything.'

'You know what? Tough.' Deep breath. Then Logan straightened. 'I'm not running a B-and-B here.' He crossed to the window and yanked the curtains open. 'Up.'

'Gah! Don't be a scumbag!' She pulled the duvet over her head, exposing naked shins and knees.

'Couldn't stay in the hotel, some moron was snoring.'

'That was probably you. Come on, out.'

The lump under the duvet didn't move. 'I *don't* snore.'

'Bloody well do. You sound like a drunk pig trapped in a wheelie bin.' He picked up the pile of clothes and dropped them on her. 'Downstairs. Five minutes.'

Steel scuffed into the kitchen wearing a hotel bathrobe and Logan's slippers. Thumped into the single wooden chair and cracked a huge yawn, showing off her fillings. 'Coffee.'

'In my sodding bed!'

'Oh, don't be such a girl. I changed the sheets and duvet cover first. Wasn't going to get into *your* filthy pit, God knows what I might catch.' Another yawn. 'Got any toast?'

'It wasn't my fault: Graham Stirling. I did what I had to and I'm not apologizing for it any more. They don't like it, tough.'

She stuck one hand down the front of her robe and had a scratch. 'Probably should've put on a bra . . .'

Oh God. Not again. Once was bad enough.

He turned his back. Stuck the kettle on to boil again. 'If you want to shout at me, you can get your stuff and bugger off. My shift starts at three: till then, I don't care.'

'Course you do.' She picked the bottle of supermarket whisky from the floor. Gave it a shoogle.

'Otherwise you wouldn't be drinking this pish.'

'And while I'm at it, how the hell did you get in here?'

Another yawn. 'You left me a key, remember?'

Outside the kitchen window, a knot of uniform in high-vis waistcoats clambered into the back of a big police van. Probably off to search the cliffs or the road again. As if that was going to make any difference.

He took two mugs from the cupboard and spooned instant coffee into them. 'You got an ID on your victim yet?'

'I wish.' A little deflating noise came from behind him. 'She's no' in the misper database, so Finnie went on the news last night with a picture and did an appeal for info. No prizes for guessing what happened next.'

'Nothing at all?'

'Six hundred phone calls, and no' a decent bit of intel between them.' More yawning. 'Don't know why we bother.'

The kettle's clicking grumble built to a rattling boil.

He stuck two slices of floppy white bread in the toaster. Put on his casual voice. 'We still on for that raid today? Four OSU and a dog team?'

'You've got a cheek. After your performance yesterday?'

He poured boiling water into the mugs. 'I can still throw your arse out on the street. In your stolen dressing gown.'

She shrugged. 'Try it.'

. . .

Fair enough.

He poured the water over the coffee granules. Stared out of the window as the police van pulled away. 'I need a success, OK? Biohazard says Professional Standards are coming after me.'

'Wondered when we'd get to that. Poor Logan, oh pity poor Logan, look at him all sad and unloved, he's only little, etc.' Steel went in for another scratch. 'Mind you, Biohazard's no' wrong. The rubber heelers are going to be all over you for yesterday. Right now you're about one screw-up away from getting booted off the force.'

— WEDNESDAY BACKSHIFT —

SOME PEOPLE JUST NEED A CLIP ROUND THE EAR . . .

CHAPTER 15

Logan pulled his epaulettes from his fleece pockets, huffed a breath over the chrome-plated sergeant's bars, and polished them on the leg of his trousers. Clipped them into place on the shoulders of his police T-shirt. Stared at his computer screen.

The STORM system was full of actions from yesterday's unsupervised backshift. A lot of which still needed updating. Tufty was the worst offender: from the look of things, he hadn't actually done a single bit of work yesterday. Well *today* he was going to be busy, even if it was only trying to extract a size-nine boot from his backside.

The desk phone burst into its annoying electronic trill.

So much for the peace and quiet.

Logan had a sip of tea, then answered the phone. 'Banff station.'

A woman's voice, hesitant and slightly hushed. Faint hint of an Ayrshire accent The sound of a grumbling diesel engine in the background. *'I need to speak to someone about the . . . the little girl's body they found.'*

He pulled out his notebook. 'Do you have some information?' Pen poised.

'*Can I . . . Can I see her?*'

Great. Another nutter.

'Police Scotland don't do general viewings for people who want to look at murder victims. It's considered insensitive. Thank you for calling.'

'*Wait! I . . .*' She cleared her throat. '*I think she might be my daughter.*'

'OK.' He peered at the phone's display and jotted down the mobile number she was calling from. 'Can I get your name please?'

'*It's Helen. Helen Edwards. My daughter's name is Natasha. Natasha Clara Edwards. She . . . She'd be six now. I haven't seen her for three years.*'

'Can you hang on a second?' He pinned the phone between his ear and shoulder, logged into the Missing Person system and hammered 'NATASHA EDWARDS' into the search box. Got back a raft of results for the surname Edwards, Edward, and Edwardson. Natasha Clara Edwards was halfway down the screen.

A click, and the summary appeared.

Abducted on the eve of her third birthday, three years ago, from the family home in Falkirk. Blah, blah, blah . . . Investigating officers were sure it was her father who snatched her – he disappeared at the same time, two weeks before financial irregularities surfaced at the firm of accountants he worked for. The assumption was that she'd been wheeched off to Spain where her dad had family.

Enquiries with the Spanish authorities fizzled out and the case was shelved.

He opened a web browser and had a bash on Google. Lots of red-top tabloid outrage about wee kids getting snatched by their estranged dads and what were the police going to do about it?

The photo beneath the headlines was pretty standard across the newspapers and editions: a little girl sitting in a paddling pool. Ash-blonde hair tumbling over her shoulders, eyebrows so pale they almost weren't there. Big grin. Spade in one hand. Ducks on her swimming costume.

Add three years and she could easily be the girl found in Tarlair Outdoor Swimming Pool.

'OK, sorry about that.' He underlined the name in his notebook. 'Mrs Edwards, can you remember any distinguishing features your daughter has? Birthmarks? Scars? Did she break any bones when she was small? Moles? Anything like that?' Dental records might help . . . assuming she'd had a lot of work done when she was tiny and those teeth hadn't fallen out yet. But it wasn't likely.

'Do you need DNA, or something? I've got a lock of her hair.'

There was a knock on the door. 'Logan?' Inspector McGregor stepped into the room. 'Are we all set for the raid on Klingon and Gerbil's place?'

He pointed at the phone in his other hand. Mouthed the words, 'Murdered girl.'

That got him a raised eyebrow.

'Before we go down the DNA route, we need to see if there's anything obvious to rule Natasha in or out.' He scribbled the words 'Tarlair Body – Might Be Her Mum On Phone' on a Post-it and held it out.

The Inspector took it, raised an eyebrow. Then perched on the edge of the desk.

'*Oh, I see . . .*'

'No point wasting your time coming all the way up here if it definitely isn't her.'

'*Too late. I got the train to Aberdeen this afternoon. I'm on the bus to Banff now.*'

'Right . . . Well . . . When are you going to arrive?'

'*Quarter past five?*'

Which gave them about two hours.

'OK, I'll get someone to meet you at the bus stop and we'll see what we can do.'

'*Thanks.*' She hung up.

Logan put the phone back on the hook. Frowned at it.

The Inspector craned her neck to peer at the search results on his monitor. 'Credible?'

'No idea. Maybe.' He pointed at the wee girl grinning out from the front page of the *Daily Mail* on his computer screen. 'Looks a bit like her. After three years . . .?' A shrug.

'Well, make sure you let the MIT know.' Inspector McGregor folded her arms. 'Anything I need to worry about today?'

'Should be fine, Guv. We've got Syd Fraser

coming over with his dogs and a four-person team from the Operational Support Unit. Plan is to go in soon as everyone's here.'

'I see. Well, make sure you keep an eye on Constable Quirrel – you know how excitable he gets.' She dumped an ID sheet on Logan's desk. Pointed at the lined face glowering out of the photograph. Skin tanned to an oaky brown, a mop of curly blond hair. 'Divisional Intelligence Unit says Stevie Moran's back in the country. Chances are he'll put in an appearance on our patch sooner or later, visiting his mum. Be nice if we could make his stay a bit more permanent this time. Say, six to eight years.'

Logan added the sheet to his in-tray. 'I'll tell the teams to keep an eye out.'

'Good. There's cakes and-slash-or pastries for whoever arrests him.' She slipped her glasses off, huffed a breath onto the lenses, and polished them. Kept her voice nonchalant. 'Now, do you want to tell me about what happened yesterday?'

Not really.

Deep breath. 'Hissing Sid made it look as if I was on a mission to stitch-up Graham Stirling. I'm too arrogant to follow procedure, but too incompetent to make my lies stick. So unless Stephen Bisset wakes up and dobs Stirling in, there's nothing we can do.'

A bit more chewing. Then, 'There are going to be repercussions, you know that, don't you? The vultures will be circling, looking for a scapegoat, and you're the most goat-like thing we've got right now.'

He slumped in his seat. Rubbed a hand over his face. 'What was I supposed to do, let Stephen Bisset die?'

Inspector McGregor stood. 'I'll have a word with a few people. See if there's any wiggle room.' She marched for the door, then stopped on the threshold. 'Meantime, it might be a good idea to get yourself a result at Klingon and Gerbil's. Bigger the better.'

Logan waited till the door clunked shut behind her before rolling his eyes. 'Yeah, thanks for that.' Then he punched the internal number for the MIT's incident room on the top floor.

It rang for a while, then a while longer, then finally: *'DS McKenzie.'*

'Took your time.'

'We're short-staffed today. What do you want?'

'I got a call from someone who thinks they might be your victim's mother.' Logan passed on Helen Edwards's details. 'She gets into Banff at quarter past five. Bus stop on Low Street.'

'I'll let the Boss know.'

Clunk – she hung up on him.

'You're very sodding welcome.' He popped the handset back in its cradle, grabbing his briefing notes, and headed out into the main office.

The usual newspapers were draped over the side of Maggie's cubicle: an *Evening Express* and an *Aberdeen Examiner*, joined by a *Scottish Sun*. 'CASE

AGAINST GRAHAM STIRLING SET TO COLLAPSE', 'POLICE "BUNGLED" INVESTIGATION', and 'LEFT-FEET FOUND IN CLYDESIDE SHOCK'.

Logan grabbed the *Evening Express* and the *Aberdeen Examiner* and dumped them in the nearest bin. In for a penny . . . The *Sun* joined them.

Maggie meerkatted her head over the parapet. 'You want me to make you a nice cup of tea?'

'I appreciate the thought, but I'm OK. Really.'

Her eyebrows peaked in the middle. 'Are you sure? You didn't collect your messages when you came in. And . . . well . . .' She held up a small stack of Post-its. 'Maybe I should dig out some biscuits?'

'Oh God. Is it that bad?'

She handed the notes over and he thumbed through them. Two from the Area Commander. Three from Steel. One from Detective Chief Superintendent Finnie. All pretty much the same thing: how had he managed to screw up the Graham Stirling trial? And, right at the bottom, one from Professional Standards. A mobile number was printed across the top in Maggie's perfect handwriting, followed by 'CALL CHIEF SUPT. NAPIER. HE SAYS "YOU KNOW WHY."'

Brilliant. Just bloody *brilliant*.

Well, couldn't say Biohazard hadn't warned him.

Septic-tank hot tub time.

Logan scrunched the notes up and stuffed them

in his pocket. 'If Napier calls again, I'm out running an operation. You don't know when I'll get back.' The phone rang on the desk facing Maggie's, but there was no one there to answer it. 'Where is everyone? Shouldn't the MIT be doing something?'

'Didn't you hear?' Maggie lowered her voice to a whisper. 'DS Dawson had to be *hospitalized*.'

Ah . . .

'Apparently his insides are all outside now. And—'

'Right, well, I'd better get on with it.' Logan backed towards the door. 'Got a . . . house to raid.' And escape.

Through in the Constables' Office, Deano poked at his keyboard with two fingers. Nicholson hunched over a stack of evidence bags, cross-referencing their labels with the official log. Tufty was slumped in his seat – arms dangling, head back. Swivelling left, then right again.

Logan thumped the door shut.

Tufty almost collapsed off his chair. 'Careful, Sarge, frightened the life out of me.'

'Tell me, Constable Quirrel, are you up to date with all your actions on STORM? Because last time I checked – which was, ooh . . .' Logan popped his arm out, flashing his watch, 'five minutes ago – there were ten you haven't touched for a week.'

'Ah . . .'

Logan loomed over him. 'Now I don't normally

approve of workplace bullying, but I'm going to start giving you a clip round the ear for every action you've done sod all about.'

'But—'

'No. No buts.' He jabbed a finger at Tufty's monitor. 'Get your backside in gear before I skelp the ears right off you!'

'Yes, Sarge. Sorry, Sarge.' Tufty spun the chair around and logged in. Fingers clattering across the keyboard.

'Better.' Logan pinned the ID sheet for Stevie Moran up on the corkboard by the radiator, adding his ugly face to the collection of druggies, dealers, burglars, and other dodgy sods currently at liberty in Banff and Macduff. 'Inspector McGregor says Stevie Moran's back in the area. Keep your eyes peeled: there's a fancy piece for whoever nabs him.'

Nicholson stared at the photograph for a bit. Then held up a biscuit tin. 'We doing presumptive testing, or just sending it off?'

A frown. Biscuit tin . . .? Ah, OK: the one hidden under a sofa seat cushion in Kirstin Rattray's fleapit flat. 'Do me a favour and mark it as "pending" till we're done with Klingon and Gerbil. Might want to put her on the books if the dunt goes well.'

Janet put the tin to one side. 'Sarge, about yesterday,' she glanced at Deano and Tufty, 'we want you to know that we're behind you. If there's anything you need us to do? You know, like—'

The door opened and she clicked her mouth shut.

But it wasn't Steel, or one of DS Dawson's team of tossers, it was PC Syd Fraser. Leather dog leads draped around his neck and fastened behind his back. Fleece all tatty and worn. Checked 'POLICE' baseball cap on his head. 'Afternoon, strange people. We knocking on someone's door today, then?'

'Waiting for the OSU.'

'They're outside, in the van, having a singsong.' Syd clapped his hands together. 'Time for a cup of tea?'

Nicholson jumped to her feet. 'I'll get it, Syd. Sarge? Deano? Tufty?'

OK . . . No way *that* was suspicious.

Logan shook his head. 'I'm good, thanks. And Constable Quirrel is far too *busy* to drink tea. Aren't you, Constable Quirrel?'

'Yes, Sarge.'

'Right.' She squeezed past Syd and out of the room.

Deano's Airwave bleeped. *'All units be on the lookout for a blue BMW – driving erratically on the A97 near Aberchirder. Possible drink driver . . .'* He turned it down. Pointed at his screen. 'Sarge, got another misper. Linda Andrews, eighty-two, dementia sufferer. Gardenstown. Husband says he got back from the shops half an hour ago and she was gone.'

Logan drummed his fingers on the worktop. Couldn't cancel the drugs bust *twice*. No way they'd let him have the extra bodies again. Not after yesterday. And he needed this.

So what was he supposed to do, ignore a vulnerable adult wandering lost somewhere on his patch? No thanks.

He stood, thumped a hand down on Tufty's shoulder, making the little sod flinch. 'Constable Quirrel. You are hereby granted a temporary reprieve. Get out there and find Mrs Andrews before something happens to her.'

Tufty scrambled out of his seat. 'But, Sarge, I want to go on the dunt, can't someone else . . .' He must have finally recognized the look on Logan's face, because he swallowed. Cleared his throat. 'I mean, "Yes, Sarge."'

'Damn right you do. And soon as you've found her, I want those actions completed.'

'Right, Sarge.' He grabbed his peaked cap and his equipment belt and legged it, nearly colliding with Nicholson on her way back in.

'Hoy, watch it!' She jerked to a halt, Syd's tea swinging in one hand, the milky contents tidalwaving from one side of the mug to the other as he scrambled past. 'Idiot.' She handed it to Syd as a barrage of 'excuse me's came from the corridor behind her.

The Operational Support Unit lumbered into the room. Four of them, all dressed in black, all looking as if they'd been carved from granite. One even had to stoop to get through the door.

He peered at Logan for a beat then stuck his paw out. 'You'll be McRae, then?'

It was like shaking a bench vice – the thick fingers

dwarfed Logan's hand, crushing it. 'Sergeant Mitchell?'

'Rob.' He nodded at his fellow mountains. 'Baz, Davy, and Carole.' They waved. 'Sorry we're late – "Bohemian Rhapsody" came on as we were pulling up. Can't pass up something like that, can you?'

Logan pulled the briefing sheets from the folder and handed them out. Front page: a photo of Gerbil and one of Klingon, along with a potted bio of each. Gerbil's red hair was cut in some weird 1920s throwback style – a number one at the sides, bowl haircut with extra fringe on top. Wide face. Little eyes. Klingon's dirty blond mop of curly hair hung in spaniel curls around thin, suspicious features. A wet, pouty mouth. Thick-rimmed glasses. 'We have a warrant to enter and search the residence of one Colin Spinney. He and his associate, Kevin McEwan, have a *lot* of form for dealing. You'll find the list of recent intel on page two.'

Everyone dutifully turned the page.

'Property is number thirty-six Fairholme Place. Page three has a photo of the house and a map. Any comments, questions, or concerns?'

Silence. Then Carole put her hand up. 'What kind of door we looking at?'

Logan went back into his folder and came out with the Method of Entry form. 'Brown UPVC with glazed panels.' He passed it over.

She skimmed the form, a crease between her

eyebrows. Then nodded. 'You want to snap the lock, Rob, or pop the whole thing in with the Big Red Door Key?'

'Hmm . . .' A frown creased Sergeant Mitchell's slab of a face. 'Any chance they've barricaded the door?'

Logan shook his head. 'Doubt it. It's Spinney's mum's house.'

'Oh.' Those huge shoulders dipped a bit. 'Shame. Been ages since we've used the chainsaw. OK, we go with popping.'

Carole's hand was up again. 'What about dogs? Kids? Firearms?'

'None that we know of.'

'Sweet.'

Logan produced the last bit of paperwork. 'Now, I need everyone to read the warrant and sign it on the back. Then we'll go do this dunt.'

'Right, stop here.' Logan hauled a baggy red hoodie on over his stabproof vest. The bulky padding made it look as if he'd put on two stone. Like the cuddly chunky-monkey Steel claimed to miss so much. A green baseball cap completed the look.

The OSU van pulled in to the side of the road. The thing was all big and white, with 'POLICE' down the side in reflective lettering. Riot grille raised. Not exactly subtle.

Sitting opposite, Deano buttoned up an over-sized checked shirt. Then pulled a pair of grey joggy bottoms on over his black trousers.

Nicholson sniffed. 'You both look ridiculous.'

'Thanks.' Logan hauled the van's side door open and hopped out onto the pavement. His fold-down seat snapped back up like a shot going off. 'OK, I need everyone to set their Airwaves channel to Shire Event Two. No chatter on open comms. Soon as we know someone's home, we'll give you the shout.'

Deano climbed out after him, then thumped the door shut and waved as the van pulled away. He followed Logan up the narrow alley joining Harvey Place and Victoria Place. 'Sarge?'

'You should have gone before we left the station.'

The sun pounded the tarmac and the houses all around. The smell of freshly cut grass sharp and green on the warm air.

'No, Sarge. We need to talk about Tufty.'

Out onto Victoria. Quick check left and right, then across the road. 'What's he done now?'

'The STORM actions. He's done the actual work, he's just a bit . . . lackadaisical when it comes to updating the system.'

'"Lackadaisical"? Hark at you with your big words.'

They headed right, keeping on up the hill. The wee traditional houses on the other side of the road petered out, exposing a straight run of grass down to the cliffs and the sea beyond. This side of the road, a shoulder-high wall kept a swathe of raised lawns in place. Big Eighties-style bungalows sitting well above street level.

'Maybe, you could cut him a little slack? I know you're pissed off about the Graham Stirling case, but that's not Tufty's fault.'

True. But still . . .

The 35A bus grumbled past, heading for the hedonistic delights of Elgin.

Logan tucked his hands into the pockets of his hoodie. 'A boss once told me, there are two kinds of people in this world – carrot people, and stick people.' To the left, a set of steps were cut into the wall between two of the properties. He took them. 'You and Janet are carrot people. Tufty couldn't be more of a stick if he tried.'

'Probably . . .' Up the stairs, along the path, up another set of stairs. Deano was beginning to look a bit puffed. Not surprising. It was baking hot, and the silly sod was wearing two pairs of trousers. 'But try slipping Tufty the carrot every now and then, eh? If all he ever gets is stick, he'll end up one big lump of gristle and bruises.'

'Thought you were his tutor, not his mum.'

'You want him thinking, "Sod this, I could go work offshore instead"?'

Fair point.

Another set of steps.

'OK – next time he does something right, I'll give it a go.' The stairs came to an end and they emerged onto Provost Gordon Terrace. 'Talking of carrots, Janet wants to know why she's not got a nickname. Thinks it's because she's a girl.'

This bit of the street was a line of semidetached

houses down one side, and the strange front/back gardens of the houses with the raised lawns they'd walked past on Victoria Place. Parking areas and garages and caravans and wheelie bins.

A nice area. Blighted by the presence of two drug-dealing tossers in the next street.

Down to the end of the road, then through a little alley and onto Fairholme Place.

Deano tipped his head at one of the semi-detacheds. 'That it?'

'Yup.' To be honest, they all looked alike: two storeys of grey harling with grey pantile roofs. Two windows upstairs. Two down – one belonging to a built-out porch. The only distinguishing feature being that Klingon's mum had painted her garage door a revolting day-glo purple.

Logan and Deano wandered down the street, hands in pockets. Not a care in the world. Two mates out for an afternoon stroll. Nothing to see here. All nice and innocent.

Deano sniffed. 'Janet say what kind of nickname she wanted?'

'I think it's meant to be up to us.'

'Clock the car parked outside Klingon's house. That not Gerbil's?'

A shabby Honda Civic hatchback with alloy wheels and a red go-faster stripe running across the white paintwork. The passenger door had obviously come from another car – it was a rusty orange colour. A buckled bumper on the rear driver's side.

'Yup. We've got movement inside too. Top floor, left.'

'What about . . . "Killer"? Or, we could go sarcastic with "Cuddles"?'

'Given the way she makes a cup of tea, we should call her Crippen.' Logan slipped the Airwave out of his hoodie pocket. Knelt as if he was about to tie his shoelace. Pressed the button. 'Operation Schofield is go. Silent approach.'

Sergeant Mitchell's voice crackled out of the handset. *'And there's me with "Ride of the Valkyries" all ready to pound out the PA speakers.'* Deep breath. *'Spartans, tonight we dine in Banff!'*

Logan put his Airwave away and looked up at the house. The only way into the back garden was through, or over, the six-foot-high gate. And going by the big yellow padlock on it, *through* wasn't really an option. 'You want front or back?'

'Rock, paper, scissors?'

Logan held out his fist next to Deano's. 'Three, two, one.'

'Aw . . . *pants.*' Deano pulled up his joggy bottoms and marched across the drive, past the garage and jumped for the top of the fence. Struggled and wriggled over it as the OSU's van roared around the corner.

It screeched to a halt right in front of Klingon's mum's house, the doors sprang open, and Sergeant Mitchell's team piled out. All done up in their riot gear – crash helmets, elbow and hand pads. Shin guards. Faces obscured behind visors and scarves.

They swarmed over the low garden wall. One of them had the hoolie bar – like a three-foot long metal ice-axe with two prongs on the other end. Another clutched the small red battering ram by its carrying handles. That had to be Mitchell: he was nearly six inches taller than everyone else.

Mitchell swung the Big Red Door Key back and up, then hammered it forwards, right into the middle of the UPVC door – right above the letterbox, between the glass panels. It went right through, collapsing the whole middle of the door, leaving nothing but the outer frame behind.

Then Mitchell flattened himself to the wall and the other three bundled inside.

'POLICE! NOBODY MOVE!'

He dropped the Big Red Door Key and charged in after them.

Nicholson stepped down from the van. 'Beautiful sight, isn't it, Sarge?'

'Few better.' Logan pulled the hoodie over his head and chucked it into the van. 'Listen, about the . . . The round of teas and coffees we did on Monday night . . .'

'Ah.' She bared her teeth for a second. 'Yes.'

'I think it'd probably be best if you and I never talked about it to anyone. Ever. Just in case.'

'Is it true Dawson's ended up in hospital?'

'We'll keep it as our little secret. OK?' He cleared his throat. 'So, what did you and the rest of the Wombles get up to last night? Anything I should know about?'

'The usual. Spun a few druggies, dealt with a drink driver, two housebreakings, two counts of piddling in doorways. Thrilling stuff.'

'*Shire Uniform Seven, safe to talk?*'

Logan pressed the button, talking into his shoulder. 'Spank away, Maggie.'

'*We've had a call. Someone spotted Ian Dickinson getting off the bus, with a woman, in Cullen. You've got a lookout request for—*'

'Ian Dickinson? Five years old, brown hair, blue eyes? The same Ian Dickinson we found last Thursday? Has he gone missing again, or have they forgotten to take down the posters?'

'*I don't know.*'

'Was he with a big woman with curly hair and a walking stick?'

'*Yes.*'

'That's his mum. Maggie, do me a favour – get onto someone and make sure they cancel the lookout *properly* this time. And tell them to take down those damn posters.'

A second Transit van rumbled down the road. Parked behind the OSU's sing-along wagon. Constable Syd Fraser waved at them from behind the wheel, then creaked open the van's door. 'Place secure yet?'

'Working on it.' He turned back to Nicholson. 'Anything else?'

Nicholson shrugged. 'Well, Deano and Tufty stopped a fight outside the Seafield Hotel. There was a break-in at the Spotty Bag Shop. Someone set fire to a bin on Castle Street. I investigated reports of a peeping tom on Melrose Crescent – no joy. And I picked up that old woman wandering up and down Market Street again. That's two nights in a row. Said she couldn't sleep in her bed because it was full of rats.'

Syd wandered over to a soundtrack of dogs barking in the back of his Transit. 'What's full of rats?'

'Auld wifie thinks her bed is. Every night they crawl out of the walls and under her duvet. Says it's driving her mad. I get her back inside and she gives me an earful of abuse about how nobody cares and we're all bastards. *Again.*'

A sigh. 'What idiot thought "Care in the Community" was a good thing?' Syd leaned back against the OSU van. 'What are we on for here: heroin? Bit of coke? Weed?'

Logan nodded. 'Probably.'

'Good. As long as it isn't Valium. Enzo's not been trained to find Valium.'

Nicholson smiled. 'Aye, aye, getting the excuses in early, are we?'

Logan's Airwave bleeped.

'Operation Schofield sont arrivé. Deux hommes dans des handcuffs.'

He smiled. Pressed the talk button. 'Couldn't remember the French for handcuffs then?'

'Everyone's a critic. Rejoice, sinner, for thy crime scene is secured.'

He fixed the Airwave to the clip on his stabproof

210

vest. Picked his peaked cap from the van and settled it on his head. 'Right, Syd, time for the hairy boys to shine.'

And please, dear God, let them *find* something.

CHAPTER 16

Gerbil and Klingon sat side by side on the grubby couch. The whole place was grubby – carpet, walls, curtains. Even the ceiling had its own collection of stains. Filth streaked the floor around the couch, as if whoever usually sat there couldn't be arsed getting up to use the bin, just tossed it where they sat.

Sergeant Mitchell stood behind Gerbil and Klingon, a hand on each of their shoulders. The pair of them doing their best not to make eye-contact with anyone else in the room.

A sagging coffee table sat in the middle of the carpet, a set of digital scales and a spoon parked on a red-top tabloid: 'NONCE ON THE RUN ~ DID MISSING SICKO WOOD CLAIM ANOTHER VICTIM?'

Logan pulled on a pair of blue nitrile gloves. 'Right, you want to save us the bother and tell us where the stuff is?'

Gerbil stared at his knees. Klingon blinked behind those thick NHS-style glasses. Not a single word.

'OK.' Logan removed the elastic band holding his body-worn video closed, and slid the front panel down, setting it recording. 'Sergeant Logan McRae, five minutes past four p.m., twenty-first of May, thirty-six Fairholme Place. Constable Fraser?'

Syd unclipped the lead from Enzo's collar, then slipped a fluorescent yellow vest thing over his head. Fastened the strap behind the Labrador's front legs. The dog was huge – big fluffy golden ruff, big fluffy tail, big block-shaped head. 'Come on, Enzo, off you go . . .'

The dog bounced his front legs from one side to the other, then scampered off, tail wagging, nose down.

Syd slung the lead over his head, clipped it behind his back in one fluid movement. 'The first ninety seconds, he's not really working. Having a bit of a sniff about. Too excited at being somewhere new.'

The dog reappeared from behind the couch and went straight for his master's legs. Bounced about a bit again.

'Come on, Enzo, calm down and get your nose in gear.'

Gerbil shifted in his seat. Squared his shoulders. Then came out with a Glaswegian accent you could cut soap with. 'I want a lawyer, and aw that. Ma rights, in't it?'

Deano stared. 'Seriously? You're from Peterhead, Kevin, what's with the mock Weegie?'

'I'm no' answering anything else till I see a lawyer, but.'

He sighed. Raised his eyebrows at Logan. 'Tell you, they do eighteen months in Polmont and they come out sounding like Begbie.'

The Labrador did another circuit of the lounge. Only this time there was a lot less bouncing about and lot more snuffling.

'There we go, he's got his working head on now.' Syd waved an arm up and out, as if he was introducing the wall. Enzo turned and followed the direction of the gesture, sniffing his way along the skirting board. Around the sofa. Then settled down in front of Klingon and stared at him.

Sergeant Mitchell took his hand off Gerbil's shoulder and hauled Klingon to his feet, getting an involuntary squeak from those wet rubbery lips. 'Think it's strip-search time, don't you?'

'Come on, Enzo, let's try the kitchen.' Syd clicked his fingers and did the same magician's apprentice gesture, this time aiming at the hallway.

Logan followed them, keeping the dog more-or-less in range of the BWV lens.

Through the hall, past the stairs, and into a small kitchen.

If the lounge was grubby, the kitchen was a pigsty. Dishes piled up in the sink. Food smears on the walls above the cooker. Everywhere covered in opened tins and takeaway containers. The bin overflowing with pizza boxes and kebab papers. A curdling reek of spoiled food and cigarette ash. The lazy burrr of bluebottles, dancing a slow-motion waltz through the foetid air. Pausing now and then to bang their heads against the window.

Logan curled his top lip. 'Can you *imagine* living like this?'

'Pff . . .' Syd puffed out his cheeks as Enzo did the rounds. 'You think this is bad? Had to search a place once, and they kept a bucket at the end of the couch. Not for rubbish, it was so they wouldn't have to leave the room to take a crap or have a pee. Never bothered to empty it either. Dear Jesus, the *smell*.'

Logan opened the cupboard nearest the door. It was stuffed with boxes of baby milk formula. 'Looks like they've stocked up stuff to cut it with.'

'Probably be more milk than heroin by the time it hits the streets. Honestly, if Trading Standards had to regulate drug dealers . . .' A smile. 'There we go.'

Enzo sat down in front of the cooker, giving it the same stare he'd treated Klingon to.

'Onwards and upwards.' He ushered the Labrador up the stairs.

Logan stuck his head into the living room. Nicholson and Carole were nowhere to be seen, but, sadly, the same couldn't be said of Klingon.

He was stripped to his pants in the middle of the room, hands cuffed behind his back, palms up. Muscles stood out on his arms and legs like elastic bands, his chest sunken, ribs on show, a proper full-on six pack. Standing there with his shoulders hunched and his back curved, showing off every bump and hollow of his spine. Blue-and-purple bruises rippled across his stomach and up one side. A wonky tattoo of the starship *Enterprise* and Captain Picard covered one arm from shoulder to elbow. Or at least, it was probably *meant* to be Captain Picard. It looked more like a constipated potato.

Wafts of bitter onion stink came off him like hungry tendrils. Burrowing their way into Logan's sinuses.

Mitchell was pulling a second pair of nitrile gloves on over the ones he was already wearing. Not taking any chances. 'Now, have you banked anything, Colin? Am I going to have to go spelunking here?'

Definitely not planning on hanging around for that. Logan pointed at the kitchen. 'When you're done here, try around the cooker. Got a hit from the dog.'

Then out again before the saggy grey pants came off.

Upstairs.

A greasy smear ran along the wallpaper at shoulder height.

Logan kept his hands away from the banister and picked his way down the middle of the landing, staying away from the manky wall. With most crime scenes, no one touched anything in case they contaminated the evidence. Here it was more about not wanting to catch anything.

The master-bedroom door lay open – Syd stood on the threshold and Enzo's tail was just visible

216

on the other side of the bed. No sheet on the mattress, no cover on the squashed pillow. Both were covered in yellow-brown stains, saggy, threadbare. Mounds of dirty clothes surrounded the bed. A framed picture of Jesus had pride of place on the wall above the headboard.

Syd looked over his shoulder. 'I'm saving the bathroom till last.'

Yes, because that was going to be *such* a treat.

They gave Enzo a couple of minutes, then held the wardrobe doors open for him.

Nothing.

The second, smaller bedroom was the same, only messier. A single mattress lay on the floor, a large brown stain covering one side, complete with its own collection of spiralling bluebottles. A windowsill laden with dead flies and wasps.

Other than a bong and a little drift of burnt tinfoil on the windowsill, Enzo didn't find anything there either.

A stepladder leaned up against the wall, in the corner of the room. Free of dirty socks, pants, T-shirts, or trousers.

Logan nodded at it. 'Does that look a bit suspicious to you?'

Back onto the landing. Staring up at the ceiling.

A hatch led up into the attic, right outside the single bedroom. The hatch's edges were filthy with layers and layers of dirty fingerprints.

He pointed. 'You think we can get Enzo up there?'

'Not without giving us both a hernia.'

Logan grabbed the stepladder and carried it through. Popped it open beneath the hatch. Climbed up the first couple of steps. Looked down over the side of the banister to the bottom of the stairs. Long way down. 'Do me a favour and hold the ladder for a minute?'

Better safe than sorry.

He climbed, pushed the hatch up and slid it to the side. Blackness. Logan's torch sent a beam of white LED light scorching across the roof beams. Another couple of steps and his head popped over the threshold into the loft space. Warm up here. Stuffy too. Partially floored.

He played the torch beam around him: boxes and boxes and shadows and boxes, and . . .

'Oh, ho. What have we here?'

It was a baseball bat, duct tape wrapped around the handle, the wooden end scraped and scarred. Smeared with what *looked* like dark-red jam but had the coppery smell of raw meat. It wasn't the only smell up here. There was something rank and sewage-like too.

Another couple of steps up, till his whole torso was in the attic.

Boxes and boxes. He popped one open. Grinned.

Syd's voice came up from below. 'Anything?'

'Either Klingon and Gerbil are stockpiling bags of cornflower up here, or we've hit the jackpot. It's . . .'

What was that?

A hand tugged at his trouser leg. 'You OK up there?'

'Shhh . . .'

He moved his foot to the top rung of the step-ladder. Wobbled for a moment. Then a bit of a struggle and he was in the attic, kneeling on the edge of the hatch. One hand on the nearest roof beam, the torch clutched in the other. Swinging the beam slowly left and right, causing the shadows to dance. Catching motes of dust in the stuffy space and making them glow.

There it was again. A sort of scratching snuffling sound.

Rats?

They'd have to be bloody huge if it was.

'Police. Is somebody there?'

He shuffled forwards. Let go of the roof beam. Reached out and pushed one of the boxes to the side. It fell over with a crash, spilling dusty crockery shrapnel over the chipboard flooring.

A man lay on his side, arms behind his back, ankles held together with a thick binding of duct tape. Gag over his mouth. Dried blood streaked the side of his face nearest the ground. One eye stuck closed with dried gore, the other slitted, only the white showing. Prominent cheekbones, pierced ears and nose. Jagged tribal tattoos on his neck.

In real life he was missing the Hitler moustache, glasses, and bolts out the side of his neck, but there was no mistaking everyone's favourite drug-dealing scumbag. Only reported missing because he owed his granny money.

Jack Simpson.

So *that's* where he'd been all this time . . .

CHAPTER 17

Logan hunched over the disposable tester, rubbing the tips of his gloved fingers together. 'Come on, you can do it . . .'

Silence filled the Sergeants' Office, only broken by the occasional creak and murmured cough from the gathered hordes. They packed the room – Syd, Sergeant Mitchell and two of his team. Nicholson, Tufty, and Deano were off doing things, but most of the dayshift were squeezed in around the edges, killing the last ten minutes before they could clock off.

Maggie appeared in the doorway. 'Well?'

Dirty pink spread along the thin display strip that took up one side of the flat, black, pen-sized bit of plastic. 'Red line, red line, red line . . .'

And there it was. Right where it was supposed to be, alongside the notch in the tester.

Logan straightened up. Held out the test, so everyone could see it. 'It's a boy!'

Mitchell let out a whistle. Stared down at the cardboard box they'd removed from Klingon's attic. 'Got to be, what: eighty, a hundred grand's worth there?'

Syd grinned. 'More if it's not been cut yet.'

Logan popped the tester into an evidence bag. 'Ladies and gentlemen, I hereby declare Operation Schofield a *massive* sodding success.'

Thank God.

Cue smiles. Laughter. Slapping of backs.

He stripped off his stabproof vest and propped it in the corner. 'Maggie, I need you to get everything bagged up, labelled, in the system, then into the productions store.'

'My pleasure.'

Logan headed out to the main office and up the stairs to the first floor, taking them two at a time. Whistling 'We're in the Money' all the way.

The sound of phones and voices filtered down from the top floor. That would be the MIT, going through whatever motions they thought would make it look as if they were actually doing something other than generating paperwork and excuses.

Unlike *Logan's* team.

The Duty Inspector's door was open, so he knocked on the frame and stepped inside.

Inspector McGregor was behind her desk, faint purple bags lurking beneath her eyes. She took her glasses off and waved them at the man sitting opposite. 'Ah, Sergeant McRae. I believe you know Detective Superintendent Young?'

Crap . . .

Young wouldn't have looked out of place on Sergeant Mitchell's Operational Support Unit. Broad shouldered with huge hands – the knuckles a map of scar tissue. Grey hair shorn close to the scalp. A crisp white shirt and dark-blue tie. Black suit jacket draped over the back of his chair. He nodded. 'Sergeant.'

'Sir.'

A smile. 'It's all right, I'm not with Professional Standards any more, you don't have to stand at attention.'

'Force of habit.' Warmth spread across Logan's cheeks. Back to the Inspector. 'Sorry to bother you, Guv, but thought you'd like to know: we've recovered at *least* eighty grand's worth of heroin from Klingon's house. Won't know for sure till the labs get through with it, but if it's uncut . . .'

'We'd be looking at two, maybe three hundred thousand.' She nodded. 'Excellent. Glad to hear you took my advice to heart about getting a big win.'

'*Plus* half a brick of cannabis resin hidden in the oven. And best of all, we've finally found Jack Simpson: battered, gagged, and tied up in Klingon's attic.'

'Still alive?'

'Just. Constable Scott's keeping an eye on him in case he regains consciousness and says some-thing coherent.'

'First time for everything.' She rubbed her hands together. 'Excellent result, don't you think, Superintendent? Shows what divisional policing can achieve with the right people.'

Young stretched his neck to one side, as if

working out a line of knots. 'And who's inter-viewing this . . . Klingon, is it?'

'Colin "Klingon" Spinney – local dealer.' Logan pointed at the map of Banff and Macduff on the Inspector's wall, where a cluster of red thumbtacks measled the streets. 'He and his mate Kevin "Gerbil" McEwan have been trying to move up to the premier league for a *long* time. I've sent them both straight off to Fraserburgh for processing. Soon as the Broch have booked them in, and the usual lawyer nonsense is out of the way, I'll head over and—'

'Actually, I'm afraid that's not really going to be possible.'

Logan straightened his shoulders. 'Thanks for your concern, sir, but I think my team are more than capable of—'

'I know, I know.' Young held up one of those huge, scarred hands. 'But if this pair had eighty grand's worth of gear stashed in the house, they've obviously got links to some serious players. Which means we're going to have to assign a Major Investigation Team. Get the Divisional Intelligence Office involved and see where this fits into the drug web. Liaise with whichever area of the country it all came from. Probably coordinate a cross-border operation . . .'

Inspector McGregor slipped her glasses back on. Scanned the intel section of the Operation Schofield briefing sheet. Her face soured. 'All we have at the moment is, the delivery was "from somewhere down south".'

'Guv, I think we—'

'Logan. Please.' Young pinched the bridge of his nose. 'It's not a case of someone else taking credit for your work. You and your team will still get the mention in dispatches and all the pats on the back you deserve, but *this* much heroin?' A half-shrug. 'It's too big to be handled at a divisional level. I'm sorry, but that's the way things work these days.'

'I see.'

Inspector McGregor sighed. Pulled a thick manila folder from her in-tray. 'And while we've got the Detective Superintendent in the house, I thought we should consult him on this.' She opened the folder and pulled out a wodge of A4 stapled in one corner. 'We got a call from Aberdeen City Division: the case against Graham Stirling collapsed half an hour ago. It's over.'

Logan closed his eyes and swore. Curled his hands into fists. 'But he *did* it. They can't let him walk!'

'The Judge ruled most of the evidence inadmissible. The Fiscal's office is spitting blood. And Professional Standards have requested copies of every complaint, reprimand, and comment made about you in the last five months.'

The paperwork thumped onto her desk.

'He tortured Stephen Bisset. He broke every one of his fingers, he ripped out his teeth, he castrated—'

'We know what he did.' The Inspector opened the folder. 'That's why we need to go over this.'

Logan stuck his chin out. 'You *always* get

complaints when you're in uniform. You're in contact with the public the whole time: people don't like being arrested or searched. And not a single one of those was upheld!'

'That's not—'

'The only way you don't get any complaints against you, is by sitting behind a desk all day.'

She stared at him. 'Meaning?'

Ah. Too far.

He cleared his throat. 'Meaning Professional Standards have no idea what it's like to break up a fight outside a Peterhead nightclub at two in the morning. People whinge. It's what they do.'

'Logan, we've received a formal complaint that you've been taking bribes from drug dealers.'

'First I've heard of it.'

She checked the top sheet of her pile of paper. 'Complaint was made this morning, by a Mr Brown.'

'Buster Brown? Are you kidding me?'

Young folded his arms. 'We take allegations of corruption *very* seriously.'

'I arrested him last week for possession with intent. This is his idea of revenge.'

'Sergeant,' Young leaned back in his seat, 'if you'll take a bit of advice: given the allegations made against you yesterday, my former colleagues are going to be all over you like flies on a turd. You need to minimize your exposure to anything that smells of shite.' He poked the paperwork. '*This*, smells.'

'I didn't have any choice! Graham Stirling—'

'It doesn't matter if you had a choice or not. It's how the thing looks in hindsight that matters to Professional Standards. Now, is there anything to this complaint about you taking money from dealers?'

'Of course there isn't. Two months ago, Buster Brown claimed I'd knocked him off his bicycle and broken both his legs. I did him for shoplifting and possession the week before, so he was getting his own back. Didn't seem to occur to Buster that being in a wheelchair for the last fifteen years *kind* of undermined his story.'

Inspector McGregor peered at the sheet again. 'That was him? Thought it was Ricky Welsh.'

'No, Ricky was the fake assault in custody.'

'Ah. So he was.' She spread her hands on the desk. 'Well, you'll have my full support when the rubber heelers get here. I consider you an asset to B Division, Logan – this morning's warrant proves that – but the Superintendent's right, you need to be squeakier than clean.'

As if Buster Brown's fictional complaints were anywhere near as serious as the Graham Stirling fiasco. As if they'd make any difference. As if Chief Superintendent Napier hadn't already made up his mind to rain down a monsoon of crap on Logan's head.

Still, when you're drowning . . .

Logan nodded. 'Yes, Guv.'

'In the meantime,' Young stood, 'as the press

seems to have decided Neil Wood was responsible for our dead wee girl, I think it's about time we posted an officer outside his bed-and-breakfast full time. His father gets out of hospital later today and I don't want him winding up on a mortuary slab for the sins of his son. Can you sort that, Wendy?'

Inspector McGregor's face didn't move for a moment. As if she'd pulled on a mask. 'I'll put in a request and see what the Big Boss says. Staffing levels are tight across the division as it is.' She stuffed the stack of complaints back into their folder. 'But we'll do what we can.'

'Thank you.' A nod. 'Good to see you again, Logan. Remember what I said. Keep your head down and your nose clean. Don't give Napier any more rope than he already has.' Young paused on the threshold. 'And phone him back. If there's one thing Napier hates, it's being ignored.'

The Inspector waited till the door swung shut behind Detective Superintendent Young before sagging in her seat. 'How, exactly, am I supposed to magic up an extra body to go stand in front of someone's house? Do we not have enough to deal with as it is?'

Logan curled forward and thumped his forehead against her desk. 'They're letting him go . . .'

A sigh. 'Had two people hand in their notice this month already. The Mire's a plague ship and we're dropping like flies.'

'How can they let Graham Stirling go? Did you *see* what he did to Stephen Bisset?'

'Logan, we—'

'And he's not going to stop at one, is he? Not now he knows he can get away with it!' Another thump. 'Gah . . .' Logan sat back, rubbed at the line above his eyebrows. 'How could they let him *go*?'

She grimaced. Swivelled her chair around and stared out of the window.

Blue sky, blue sea, herring gulls making lazy swirls in the sunlight.

Should've been raining.

Logan slouched further into the seat. Stared at the ceiling tiles. 'I'm completely screwed, aren't I?'

No answer.

Eventually, the Inspector cleared her throat. 'They got the post-mortem report in, late yesterday. Most of our little girl's recent injuries appear to have happened after she died. Probably caused by rocks as she got chucked about by the waves.'

'Completely and utterly screwed . . .'

'Logan!'

A sigh. 'Thought it wasn't our case any more.'

'Humour me.' McGregor didn't look around, kept her face to the window where he couldn't see it. 'A dead six-year-old girl washes up on our doorstep and no one reports her missing. Why?'

'OK . . . Cause of death?'

'Someone stove her head in with a length of metal pipe. Then dumped her in the water. Young says there's evidence of abuse too. Probably long term.'

Poor little soul.

Logan puffed out his cheeks. Let the breath escape slowly. 'Which brings us back to Neil Wood.'

'How do we prove it? The sea's not that forgiving with DNA and trace. We don't even know where she went into the water. Official line from the pathologist is a child of our victim's size and weight would have neutral buoyancy – she could have been dumped where she was found and the tide washed her out and back in again. Or she could have come down the coast on the current. Impossible to tell.'

'That's a big bag of no sodding help.'

The Inspector stuck one foot up on the window-sill, laced her fingers behind the back of her head. Stared out at the expanse of rolling blue. 'I know you're hacked off about what happened with Graham Stirling, but grumping about it isn't helping. You want me to give you some time off?'

'Yeah, because *that's* going to look good when Professional Standards get here. Suspended without pay, pending investigation.' He covered his face with his hands. Groaned. 'Brilliant. I should have let Stephen Bisset die in the woods. I should've been a good little boy, stuck to procedure, and left him to die.'

'No one's saying that.'

'No?' Logan sat up. 'That's *exactly* what they're saying. Do what you're told, be a parochial plod, don't think for yourself. We're nothing but robots in peaked caps and itchy bloody trousers. No wonder they won't trust us to run our own drugs investigation.'

She didn't turn around. 'Are you finished?'

'Sorry, Guv.'

'OK: it's frustrating that we don't get to pursue the drugs bust, but that's the world we live in now. Deal with it.'

'Not just the drugs, though, is it? There's no point talking about the dead little girl, because they took that off us too. Every time we turn up something big, someone comes in and takes it off us.' He knocked on the desk with his knuckles. 'And at least *I* got a result! More than Young's MIT can say.'

Outside the gulls drifted and screamed.

Waves made thin white lines against the shore.

A car drove by on the road below, music bellowing its distorted 'Bmmmmtshhh-bmmmmtshhh-bmmmmtshhh' as it passed. Fading into silence.

Inspector McGregor frowned at the ceiling. 'So why *hasn't* anyone reported her missing? Who doesn't miss a dead little girl?'

Back to that again.

Fine.

'Well . . .' Logan frowned, dredging stuff up from the black, inky depths. 'I had a case, years ago, back when I joined CID: unidentified dead wee girl. Turned out her mum was trafficked into prostitution from the Eastern Block. She was dead by the time the kid went missing, so no report.'

'Not a lot of help.'

'Our victim could be staying with friends or relatives while her parents are out of the country? Or . . . what if she *has* been reported missing, but it was a long time ago?'

'Hmm . . .' Inspector McGregor chewed on the inside of her cheek for a bit. 'If it was you, why would you dress her up as a schoolgirl, then kill her?'

'You mean, apart from the obvious? These people like little girls to look like little girls.'

'True.'

He stared at the thick file of complaints on the Inspector's desk. 'But why kill her? Why not keep her and . . . keep doing what you've been doing?'

'Accident maybe? Or maybe she tried to escape? And maybe she's not dressed up, maybe she *is* a schoolgirl.'

Logan took out his notebook. 'It's term time. Even if she *was* staying with relatives, the school would know she wasn't in class. Might be worth chasing up?'

Inspector McGregor nodded. 'Well, the MIT have probably thought of that, but let them know anyway. And when you've finished writing up this morning's raid, let's have a chat about how you're going to achieve your appraisal development actions. All that community liaison stuff.'

Wonderful.

'Don't suppose Young gave you a time of death?'

'On the girl? Probably sometime over the weekend.

232

Friday at a push. Water's still pretty cold, even in May.'

'What was the point of doing a post mortem if they couldn't come up with anything useful?'

'You're a little ray of sunshine, Logan. Did anyone ever tell you that?' The Inspector took her feet off the windowsill and swivelled back round to her desk. 'Anything else?'

'My Chiz – the one who gave us Klingon and Gerbil – when we picked her up she was in possession of Class A and B drugs, and a heap of stolen property too.'

'I see.' McGregor pulled a notepad out from beneath a pile of forms and opened it. 'And this Covert Human Intelligence Source of yours, is she on the books?'

'Not yet. She's got a wee girl of her own. Doesn't get to see her very often. If we do her for the drugs and stolen goods . . .'

'You've promised her something?' Inspector McGregor rummaged through the piles on her desk again. Then sat back and scowled at her notepad. 'I don't believe it. That's three pens Hector's had off me this week and it's only Wednesday.'

'I haven't promised my Chiz anything. Mind you, today her intel netted us at least *eight grand's* worth of heroin, so . . .?'

A sigh. 'I'll see what the Big Boss says. But if we're keeping her on, we do it properly. She goes on the books with Aberdeen and everything is firewalled. Info comes through the Dedicated Source Unit – no more informal tip-offs.'

He stood. 'Thanks, Guv.'

'And phone Napier back!'

CHAPTER 18

L ogan finished the background section and moved onto the main body of the report of the raid on Klingon and Gerbil's love-nest slash drug-den. Torturing the English language as only a trained police officer could.

He'd got to the bit where,

> Four trained MOE specialists from the OSU removed the property's front door by means of concussive force in order to gain entry. This was successful.

. . . when the Sergeants' Office door thumped open and in walked Steel.

She had her fake cigarette in one hand and a mug in the other. 'This where you been hiding, is it?'

He went back to his form. 'Have you sorted someone to pick Helen Edwards up from the bus?'

'I'm doing the questioning here, Disaster Boy.' She dropped into the chair behind the opposing desk. 'How could you screw up the Stirling case?'

'I'm not asking you to fly to the moon, I'm asking

you to go collect the person who might be able to identify *your* murder victim from the bus stop. How hard can it be?'

'You got any idea how much crap I'm getting from the Great Pointy Hats because of you?' She dumped her mug on the desk and dug a finger into her ear. As if she was searching for a brain. 'Been on that phone for the last hour.'

'Look, Helen Edwards might be your victim's mother. The *least* you can do is—'

'You're in no position to lecture anyone, Laz – no' after yesterday's wee fiasco. Lucky they've no' fired you yet, screwing up like that.'

'I saved Stephen Bisset's life!' He glared at her. 'You know what? Enough. I seized about a hundred grand's worth of drugs today. How about you? How much success have *you* had lately?'

'Don't be such a fairy princess.' Steel poked her e-cigarette at him. 'Get off your magic pony and go pick Helen Edwards up. You organized it, it's your—'

'Fine!' Logan shoved his chair back, thumping it into the wall. 'I'll go and do *your* job for you. As sodding usual!' He grabbed his hat and stormed out.

Her voice followed him into the main office. 'And get some decent biscuits while you're at it!'

Nicholson rested her forearms on the steering wheel. 'I think Tufty's parents got him a subscription to *New Scientist*.'

236

Logan settled back in his seat and scowled out through the windscreen. 'They all out of New Idiot?'

The sun beat down on Low Street, glittering back from the Perspex cover over the bus stop. A handful of Banffers strolled along the pavement, as if they were taking the air on the Riviera. Arm in arm, basking in the warmth.

Bloody Steel. All this time and he was *still* running around after her.

He sniffed. Wrinkled his nose. 'And what is that horrible smell?' Eggy, dirty, and rancid. The kind of stench Biohazard Bob would've been proud of.

Nicholson shrugged. 'Told you. We've had the windows rolled down all day as well. Going to have to get one of those air freshener things . . .' She sat forward in her seat. 'Oh-ho, here we go.'

A big rectangular single-decker bus grumbled around the corner.

It pulled up at the stop with a hiss of air brakes as Logan climbed out.

He pulled his peaked cap on and marched across the road, in time to catch the doors opening and the first passenger getting off. It was an auld mannie, all dressed in grey and beige. Presumably from Old-Farts-R-Us. Next a pregnant woman with a red face and a screaming toddler.

Then nothing.

Then another, older woman, and finally the last person stepped down onto the pavement. The bus door hissed shut. The engine growled and the thing lurched away.

Then everyone else did the same, leaving the last passenger standing there with a holdall at her feet.

Logan stopped by the public information point. 'Ms Edwards?'

She shuffled her feet. Picked up her bag. 'Sorry.' Dirty-blonde hair hung in a curly bob around a heart-shaped face, like broken springs. Bags under dark eyes. Dark lipstick beneath a long thin nose. Pretty, in a haunted kind of way. Grey woolly jumper and blue jeans. Some sort of puffa jacket, folded over one arm. 'Actually, it's Helen.' A faint Ayrshire accent, almost buried beneath generic queen's English.

'Helen.' He held out a hand for her bag. 'Sergeant McRae, we spoke when you were coming up on the bus? I'm going to take you back to the station, so you can meet with the Detective Chief Inspector running this part of the investigation. Want to give me your coat too?'

'Oh. OK. Thanks.' A small smile. 'Sorry. Didn't think it'd be this warm. Raining in Edinburgh this morning.'

He led her back to the Big Car. 'Have you got somewhere to stay?'

She wrinkled her top lip, made creases around her eyes. 'Just grabbed my bag and jumped on the first train north.'

'I'm sure they'll sort something out.' He opened

the back door on the driver's side. 'Probably as quick walking, but thought you'd like to be met.'

A small smile. 'Thanks.' She dug into her handbag and came out with a pink envelope – the kind that came with birthday cards for little girls. Held it out. 'I've got those hair samples.'

'Better save that for DCI Steel.'

'Oh. Yes. Sorry.' A breath, then she looked away. 'You've got other things to do.'

'Don't worry: we've got a dedicated Major Investigation Team working on the case. PC Nicholson and I do the day-to-day policing up here. We want to make sure you give those to the right person.'

'Right. Of course. Sorry.' She climbed into the back of the car and Logan clunked the door shut.

Nicholson pulled a three-point turn and headed back to Banff police station.

Helen sat in silence for the five-minute ride. Nose twitching from time to time, as if she was trying to figure out where the funny smell was coming from.

'*All units, be on the lookout for a stolen John Deere tractor in the Strichen area . . .*'

The Big Car pulled up outside the station entrance.

Clunk. Clunk. Helen Edwards frowned in the rear-view mirror. Then tried the door handle again. 'It's stuck.'

'Child locks.' Logan climbed out and opened

the door from the outside. 'Sometimes the people in the back try to make a run for it.'

'Oh. Right.' She climbed out. Looked up at the little portico with its carved curls and fake columns.

'It'll be OK. I'll take you into the reception area and someone will look after you.'

A crease appeared between Helen's eyebrows. 'Are you not . . .?'

'We've got to go patrol. But don't worry, everything will be fine. If you need anything.' He dug out a business card and printed his mobile number on the back. Handed it over. 'The Major Investigation Team are doing everything they can.'

'Thank you.' She tucked the card away in her handbag, accepted her coat and holdall, then walked up the steps and into the station.

The sour stench of BO rolled off the stick-thin man in waves as he held up his arms. Hands trembling. It was nearly impossible to tell what colour his tracksuit had started off as. Now it was the colour of rancid liquid leaking from a broken bin. Smelled about the same too.

Nicholson snapped on a pair of blue nitriles. 'Now, before we start, is there anything in your pockets I need to know about, Sammy? Needles, knives, anything sharp?'

'Nah.' The word slumped out on rotting corpse breath. Sammy Wilson's skin was nearly translucent, stretched tight across a large skull with prominent cheeks like knife blades, the bones sticking out in his wrists. Fingers like dirty twigs. Thin silver lines ran from his nose to his top lip. Pupils constricted to full-stop dots. 'But, you know, take your time in the front pockets, yeah?' A bloodshot wink. 'I like it nice and *slow*.'

Logan tried not to breathe the stench in. 'Who are you buying from now, Sammy? You still Klingon's client?'

A shrug. 'I'm, like, nondenominational. Secular. And I don't do . . . don't do drugs no more . . .' His eyes half-closed, then a slow smile spread across his face as Nicholson eased her gloved fingers into his front pocket. 'Oh yeah . . . Nice and slow . . .'

The Big Car's blues-and-twos cut a path through the evening traffic, the engine roaring as Nicholson floored it.

Logan hung onto the grab handle above the door, thumbed his Airwave's talk button again. 'Sorry, Control, missed that last bit, say again?'

'Roger: we're getting reports about people going in and out of a Francis "Frankie" Ferris's house, fifteen Rundle Avenue. Caller said it's probably drug dealing.'

'Any idea who?'

A squeal of tyres as Nicholson swung them around the corner and onto School Lane, drifting onto the other side of the road as the back end kicked out. Barely missing a big red removal van. Their brand-new Magic Tree air freshener swung like a pendulum from the rear-view mirror.

'*Caller can't ID any of them, but we're getting descriptions.*'

Worth a go. 'Tell Constable Scott to get over there and dragnet the surrounding streets. Anyone matching the descriptions gets a free stop-and-search. With any luck we'll get enough for a warrant on Frankie's hovel.'

'*Will do.*'

The car battered across the junction with Main Street, ignoring the stop sign. Little granite houses flashed by the Big Car's windows. An old lady stopped to gawk as they roared past in a blare of lights and sirens.

Logan let go of the talk button. 'Are you channelling Jeremy Clarkson today?'

Nicholson spared him a quick grin. 'Urgent danger to life, Sarge.'

Across North Street, the needle hitting sixty as they battered past the 'TWENTY'S PLENTY' limit.

Back on to Control. 'You got an ETA for the fire brigade?'

'*En route . . . Board shows them fifteen miles away.*'

Sodding hell.

A hard right, and there it was – Taylor Drive. But instead of flames searing through broken windows, crackling roof timbers, and palls of black smoke streaking the blue sky, there was a middle-aged man standing in the middle of the road wearing a 'KISS THE COOK' apron. Face blackened with soot.

He held his hands up, as if expecting to be shot, as Logan and Nicholson scrambled out of the car.

'Sorry, sorry, my fault.'

Logan hurried over. 'Is everyone out of the house?'

'No, it's a bit of a disaster. Sorry. I put a *tiny* bit too much lighter fluid on the barbecue and . . . well . . . the shed, sort of, caught fire. Just a little. We put it out with the garden hose.' A thin, uncomfortable smile. 'Sorry.'

'Nah, sod all so far.' Deano's sigh rasped out of the Airwave's speaker. *'Been round this block so many times, Tufty's getting dizzy.'*

Logan reclined his seat an inch. 'All we need's to get lucky once.'

Sun glittered on the windscreen, catching the flecks of dust and sticky fingerprints left behind by whoever did the Big Car's service. But Nicholson was still visible as she knocked on the red door. Stood there, hands tucked into her stabproof. Rocking back and forward on the balls of her feet.

Mind you, whoever serviced the car had left more behind than fingerprints, going by the smell. It was like something dead was being marinated in Biohazard Bob's eggiest of farts.

'If this was TV we could batter Frankie's door in, quick search montage, and back to the station in time for the ad break.'

A petite brunette opened the door, looked up

243

and down the street, then disappeared inside again. Nicholson followed her into the house. Closed the door behind her.

'That's because made-up cops never have to deal with Professional Standards.'

'*Or paperwork. Tell you, I was watching something last night and . . . Hold on, Sarge. Tufty: over there – bloke in the green hoodie and orange joggy bottoms.*'

Silence.

A kid went by on his BMX, standing on the back bar.

Still nothing from Deano.

Logan pulled out his phone and checked his text messages.

Puffed out his cheeks.

Played a game of solitaire on the little screen.

Lost.

Sat where he was, sniffing.

The smell wasn't coming from the back, or the passenger side. That left the driver's side.

Logan climbed out into the sun, opened the driver's door and sniffed at the seat.

Definitely something stinky going on there. Maybe someone had an accident?

He squatted down and peered under the seat. Yeah: there was something there.

Then Deano was back. '*Sorry about that, Sarge.*'

'Get anything?' He reached into the gap, fingers searching along the gritty carpet.

'*Not so much as a joint.*'

'Ah well, worth a go.' Almost there . . . Got it.

The smile died on Logan's face as his fingers sank into something squishy. Urgh.

'Looks like our info's a load of old wank. That's the new Police Scotland technical term, in case you're wondering.'

Bile caught at the back of his throat.

Oh God. Why didn't he put on a pair of gloves? Too late now.

He pulled the squishy thing out. A half-eaten egg sandwich, the bread and filling gone green and hairy. 'Dirty . . .' He dropped it in the gutter, then dragged his hand along the kerb, trying to wipe off the sticky bits.

'Sarge?'

'No wonder the Big Car's been stinking. Some filthy sod left half a sandwich going mouldy under the seat!' He got back into the passenger side. Popped open the glove compartment and pulled out the emergency packet of baby wipes. Scrubbed his fingers clean.

'Bet it was nightshift. You want me and Tufty to keep at it here?'

The red door opened again and Nicholson stepped out into the sunshine. Turned to face the house, obviously saying something. Then nodded and marched back towards the car.

'Give it another ten minutes, then go see if you can find something useful to do instead.'

'Thanks, Sarge.'

Nicholson opened the driver's door and slid in behind the wheel. Rearranged her equipment belt so the extendable baton wasn't jabbing into the handbrake. 'Safe-and-well check done.'

Logan twisted his Airwave handset back into the clip on his vest. 'And?'

'Usual lies.' Nicholson turned the engine over. Pulled away from the kerb. 'Alex has changed. Alex is sorry. Alex promises it'll never happen again. They *love* each other.' Around the corner, heading back towards the middle of town. 'Tell you, Sarge, some people are too thick to realize they've got their hand in a blender till the love of their life turns it on.'

CHAPTER 19

The driver wrapped his hands tight around the steering wheel. Cheeks flushed. Jaw muscles working like an industrial clamp. He stared straight ahead as Logan checked the proffered driving licence.

'Thank you, Mr Clifton.' Logan handed it back. Then followed it up with the fixed-penalty notice.

It was snatched out of his hand. Crushed in a fist. A strangled, 'Thank you,' forced out between gritted teeth.

Logan patted the roof of the car. 'Drive safely.'

A trembling hand reached up and pulled the safety belt down, and clipped it into place. Then the BMW pulled away from the kerb.

Nicholson zipped her ticket book away in a pocket. 'If he'd done that in the first place, would've saved himself a hundred quid.'

'. . . reported break-in at Aberdeen Heritage in Mintlaw, anyone free to attend?'

'You know what bugs me?' Nicholson took the patrol car up onto the bridge across the River Deveron. 'If he'd hit someone coming the other

247

way, he would've been through that windscreen like a bowling ball. Splat. Probably dead.'

The dull grey water glinted beneath them. Waves crashed in white arcs at the mouth of the bay. Over the bridge and right, towards Macduff.

'Aye, this is Sergeant Smith, pit me and King-Kong down as attending.'

'Hmm . . .' Logan sniffed his fingertips – talc and chemicals – then reached for the car radio and clicked it on, poking the buttons till Northsound burbled out of the speakers. Some boy-band nonsense, all bland and anaemic, droning away over the Airwave's chatter. 'Can you imagine what that must be like? You hear about a dead girl and you rush up the country with DNA samples.'

'And do you know what? Odds on, when he goes home tonight, it's not about us saving his life, it's about the police screwing innocent motorists for every penny we can. And why aren't we out there catching real crooks instead of harassing road users?'

'Do you think she hopes it's her daughter?' He frowned out at the water. '"Hope" is probably the wrong word. Maybe she's looking for closure?'

Over the bridge and right as the bland-boy-band was replaced by an identikit replica. The auditory equivalent of wallpaper paste.

Nicholson pulled a face. 'I remember this one bloke, hit a lamp post. Bang – sixty-to-zero in fourteen inches. Found him twenty feet down the road. Half his scalp came off when he hit the tarmac.'

Of course, it was daft listening to the radio and not just because of the horrible music. Sooner or later the news would come on with details of the Stirling case falling apart. It was like picking at a scab, or a hangnail. Knowing it would hurt and bleed.

Speaking of which, should really get Nicholson to pull over, so he could make that call to Napier. But she was still going on about her car crash.

'There were these . . . *hairy* strips of it every-where. Course I was the probationer, so I got the job of picking them all up. All cold and slimy.' A shudder.

Christ only knew what Stephen Bisset's family were going through. Probably something not too far removed from what Helen Edwards was. That was the thing about violent crime, in the end it always came down to pain and loss.

'Was almost finished when this cat ran out from someone's garden and grabbed the last chunk. Wheeched off with it into the gorse on the other side of the road.' She slowed down. Indicated. 'I mean, what was I supposed to do, charge in there after it? Sod that.'

Logan stretched out in his seat. 'Suppose it must've looked like a big mouse . . .'

'There!' Logan slapped one hand on his hat, the other grabbing his extendable baton as he hammered past the newsagent's. A hard, screeching right turn onto Cullen Street. 'Stevie Moran: come back here!'

The big man glanced over his shoulder, swore, and sped up. Down the hill. Past the post office. Red tracksuit jacket flapping behind him, paint-spattered jeans and dirty trainers. Long greying brown hair streaming out behind him. A face carved from driftwood.

Old-fashioned houses lined the street in various shades of grey. Raw stone and oatmeal harling. The thump of boots on tarmac.

Nicholson appeared at Logan's shoulder, elbows and knees pumping. Police bowler hat wedged down over her ears. Breath hissing in and out.

And then she was past.

Moran threw a left turn, both arms windmilling to keep himself upright.

Then Nicholson – almost colliding with the stop sign on the corner of Low Street.

Logan gritted his teeth and pushed harder, catching up with her as Moran hopped a waist-high stone wall, scrambled through a long narrow garden, trampling the flowers and bushes, then over the wall on the other side. Nearly went head-long, but managed to stay upright. Thumped into the wall below the Church Street sign.

The houses were even older here – three-storey merchant jobs on one side, ancient featureless slabs on the other.

Moran charged down an alleyway, Nicholson right behind him.

Logan didn't follow her. He cut down the side of the Shore Inn, skiffed the whitewashed stone-work with his shoulder, burst out into the sunshine again.

They'd run out of town.

Now the only thing between them and the North Sea was the harbour.

Stevie Moran sprinted for the harbour wall.

Nicholson lunged. Missed. Went crashing into a brown park bench as Moran hurdled the wall and disappeared.

Logan slithered to a halt on the warm tarmac. Peered over the edge.

On the other side of the wall was a ten foot drop onto shingle and rocks. Stevie Moran lay sprawled on his front. Groaning.

'All right, Stevie, that's enough.'

But he levered himself upright and limped towards the water, one arm clutched against his chest.

'What are you going to do, swim to Norway?'

A pause. Then a slip on the seaweed-covered stone and he was on his knees again at the edge of the lapping water.

'You'll sink before you get half a mile out. Give it up.'

His shoulders sagged. 'Arseholes . . .'

'And you'll never guess who we bumped into in Portsoy: Stephen "Stevie" Moran.' Logan hung back a bit, following Nicholson and Moran up North High Street, back towards the patrol car.

The pair of them limped and puffed and groaned. Moran with both hands cuffed behind his back, Nicholson with a death grip on the plastic bar between the metal arms. Making sure he didn't go for the five hundred metres record again.

On the other end of the Airwave, Deano sounded as if he was sitting in an echo chamber. *'How long's he been on the run: eight months? Ten?'*

'Silly sod should've stayed in Ireland.'

'Speaking of silly sods, your old guvnor wants a word.'

Steel's gruff smokey voice boomed out, *'Hoy, I heard that!'*

'Here.'

And she was on. *'Why haven't you called Napier yet?'* A small pause. Then, *'All right, Constable Smartarse, you can sod off now.'* Another pause. Then the muffled thump of a door closing. *'Well? You looking to get fired?'*

'Been busy arresting people.'

The road opened up, widening as it joined onto the square, with its regimented grid of white-line parking spaces in the middle.

'Putting it off's only making it worse. You know what Napier's like.'

'All right, all right, I'll call him.' And with any luck, Napier would have gone home for the night. Putting it off for another day.

A grey van rumbled past, the driver ducking his right hand down below the dashboard. As if that

252

would stop Logan from seeing the mobile phone clutched in it.

'*Good. And while we're on it, your merry band of local nonces – any of them got form for drugs? No' taking them: slipping them to kiddies. Got a positive off the blood tox screen for phenobarbital.*'

'Maybe . . . Probably. Pretty sure Dr Gilcomston did something like that. Barbiturates and house-calls? Check the files.'

'*Detective Chief Inspector, remember? What's the point of keeping flying monkeys if I have to check my own files?*'

Stevie Moran lunged to the right, but Nicholson hauled the cuffs up, and he went down on his knees in the middle of the car park, wheezing out a barrage of swearing.

'So get one of your flying monkeys to do it. I'm busy.'

'*You're hiding.*'

True. But that didn't mean he was going to admit it.

Nicholson pulled Moran to his feet. 'Try that again, please. I'd *love* another go.' And they both limped off towards the Big Car again.

'Bad enough I had to pick up your victim's mother – well, potential mother – without having to do all your legwork.'

'*Ah . . . I wondered how long it'd take you to bring her up. Pretty young woman with curly hair and pouty lips? All distressed and vulnerable? Right up your alley.*'

Logan paused, letting a shiny new Mini drive

past before stepping out onto the road. 'I barely met the woman.'

'Blah, blah, blah. You're fooling no one.' A sniff. *'You ask me, it's all a bit creepy.'*

'I didn't.'

'Dotting about from crime scene to crime scene, like an abduction tourist. Creepy-weird. No wonder you like her.'

Nicholson plipped the car's locks, then wrenched open the back door and bundled Stevie Moran into the passenger side. Buckled the seatbelt for him, pinning him in. Slammed the door closed. Leaned back against it. Raised her left foot off the ground and flexed it one way, then the other. Rubbed at her left elbow. 'Oww . . .'

'You know what she's doing right now? Hanging about outside the station like a stalker. Woman that screwed up? I'm amazed you've no' tried to shag her yet.'

'OK, I'm hanging up now.'

'Don't be daft. If I—'

Logan switched his Airwave off. Clipped it back onto his vest.

Nicholson's eyebrows pinched together, her mouth turned down, working on a pout. 'Think I ruptured something when I hit that bench.'

'We got him, though: eight counts of robbery, two of resetting, possession of a Class A, an assault, and breach of bail conditions. And we can add resisting arrest.' Logan opened the passenger door. 'Best of all, now Police Scotland has to buy us *both* a fancy piece for nabbing him. I'm having a Danish pastry.'

'Custard slice for me.' She poked and prodded at the elbow again. Baring her top teeth. 'Oww . . .'

Logan checked his watch. 'If we hurry, we can get him to Fraserburgh, process him, and pick up our reward in time for tenses.' Add on the time sodding about waiting for a lawyer, initial interview . . . Probably wouldn't make it back to Banff for dinner. 'Have to pop past the station on the way though. Haven't got my soup.'

Nicholson sank into the driver's seat. 'You're obsessed with soup.'

'Yeah, well. Glutton for punishment.'

'I'll only be a minute.' Logan clunked the passenger door shut and pulled on his peaked cap.

The sun was an orb of gold, dripping its way down to the border between the sky and the North Sea. It sparked rubies from the water, painted the Sergeant's Hoose with fire. Turned the shadows a deep midnight blue.

The Big Car idled at the kerb – Nicholson peering out from behind the wheel, Stevie Moran glowering out from the back seat as Logan let himself into the Sergeant's Hoose.

Quick rummage in the kitchen for a tin of lentil and two slices of cheap floppy white bread, stuff the lot in a carrier bag, and out again. All in under two minutes.

Logan locked the door, then turned. Stopped.

A figure leaned on the sea wall, staring out across the bay. Dirty-blonde hair, hanging in corkscrew curls around her head.

Logan popped his dinner on the Big Car's roof. Crossed the road. And stepped up onto the kerb beside her. 'Ms Edwards? Helen? You OK?'

She didn't look around. 'There's dolphins.'

'They come in from time to time.'

She pointed out into the bay as a sleek shape arced out of the water then disappeared again. 'Never seen one in real life before.'

'It's a beautiful place.' He leaned his elbows on the wall beside her. From here, the ground fell sharply away to the beach eight or twelve feet below. The sand turned dark orange by the setting sun. 'You sure you're OK?'

She picked at a fleck of lichen, growing on the concrete wall. 'They wouldn't take Natasha's hair for DNA testing. Said it wouldn't work because it was cut; they needed the roots attached. So they took a swab from my cheek instead.'

'That'll be enough to go on.'

Out in the bay, the dolphins danced.

'I don't know whether to hope for a positive match or not. If it matches, she's dead. If it doesn't . . .' Helen swept a wodge of curls out of her eyes. Her hand trembled, the fingernails bitten down to the quick.

'Why do you think it might be your daughter? Maybe she's in . . . is it Spain? With her father?'

'Because *he's* not in Spain. Hasn't been for years.

I hired a very expensive private investigator to track Brian down. Trail went cold in Middlesbrough two years ago.'

The sun sank lower, the colours richer.

'Well, it's—'

'Brian had a drink problem and a temper on him. Oh, butter wouldn't melt when we started going out, but then I got pregnant . . .' Another bit of lichen was peeled off by a ragged thumbnail. 'Most days it was like trying to defuse a bomb with boxing gloves on. He'd get drunk and bang – the smallest thing would cause an explosion.'

'Must've been hard.'

'I can't even change my name back. I have to be Mrs Edwards till I find Natasha. Soon as people think I'm not her mother, that's it: up go the barricades. Till then I can't even wash his stink off me.' She rubbed her hands up and down her arms, as if trying to scrub her ex-husband away. 'So this is my life. Every time they find a little girl my private investigator lets me know, and off I go, getting my hopes up. Maybe *this* one will be her? Maybe. But it never is. So I lurch from one crime scene or abduction or accident to the next. Three years.'

Logan pointed back towards the station. 'Do you want a cup of tea, or something? I'm off to Fraserburgh, but I can get someone to—'

'Do you have any idea what it's like to love someone who's completely lost? At least if they were dead you could start moving on. But they won't

257

give you that, they keep dangling that *sliver* of hope just out of reach.'

Warmth spread between his shoulder blades, curled its claws around his throat. Choked down the words. 'It's difficult.'

'Sorry.' She let go of her arms and stared up at the darkening sky. 'Didn't mean to bang on like a crazy person. Helen Edwards, the broken record of doom and gloom.'

Logan glanced at the Big Car.

Nicholson was staring out through the windscreen at them, eyebrows up.

He backed towards the car. 'We've got a prisoner. Sorry.'

'Yes. No. Don't worry about it. I'm fine.' Helen turned and stared out into the bay again as glittering beads of sunlight scattered and died in the water.

Logan let himself into the empty office and closed the door behind him. Outside, the floorboards creaked and groaned as someone walked past. Fraserburgh police station had to be at least a hundred years newer than Banff's, but it sounded like a galleon in full sail anytime anyone set foot in the corridor.

Through the office window, the granite buildings were washed in golden light as the sun sank. A few high wisps of cloud painted impossible shades of pink and orange.

Might as well get it over with.

He settled his backside into a creaky office chair, sooked the last sticky remnants of Danish pastry from his fingers, pulled out his mobile phone and the stack of Post-its Maggie had given him way back at the start of the shift. Called the number.

It rang.

Straight to voicemail. Straight to voicemail. Straight to voicemail.

Please.

And then a click came down the line. *'Napier.'*

The Voice of Darkness.

Logan closed his eyes. Let his head fall back. Tried not to sound like a man standing on the gallows trapdoor with a noose around his neck. 'Chief Superintendent. Hi. Sergeant McRae. You wanted to speak to me . . .'

'You OK, Sarge?' The Police Custody and Security Officer peered at him over the booking-in desk. A big bloke, with broad shoulders and thistles tattooed up both arms, disappearing into the short sleeves of his illicit 'GRAMPIAN POLICE' polo shirt. 'Look like you've seen a ghost.'

Logan leaned on the worktop. 'Professional Standards.'

The PCSO sucked air in through a grimace, eyes screwed shut. 'I remember it well. Like riding a horse through a minefield with haemorrhoids. Fancy a cuppa? I'm making anyway.'

'Thanks.'

He disappeared through the door behind the

259

desk, into the tiny galley kitchen bolted onto the side. 'Milk and sugar?'

'Just milk.' Logan turned and peered into the detention block. The wide grey-and-beige hall had doors off to one side for detainees, stores, and processing; one at the end for the Custody Sergeant's office; and two heavy barred gates through to the actual cells. No sign of life. 'You've not seen Constable Nicholson on her rounds, have you?'

'The delightful Janet?' He reappeared, placed a Police Scotland mug down in front of Logan. Put a polystyrene cup next to it. 'She's helping Suzanne strip-search a young lady caught breaking into the chemist's next to Farmfoods.' He pointed at the closed detention-room door. 'Pretty certain they'll have heard the screaming and swearing in Inverness. 'Scuse me . . .' He squeezed past, carrying the polystyrene cup in one hand, as if it was full of liquid explosives. Rattled his keys in the other. 'I'm afraid one of our charges is in need of tea and sympathy.'

Logan followed him through into the male cell-block. Clanged the heavy barred gate shut behind him. 'Any idea how long Nicholson's going to be?'

'Depends how much of a pain in the buttocks our novice burglar is when she's being searched.' A right, down a short beige corridor. Halfway down, the cells stretched off to one side – ten of them. Five on the left, five on the right. Most had their doors lying wide open – the stainless-steel backs making the place look like something out of a science fiction movie. But three were shut. The front painted the same dark blue as the skirting and architraves.

The PCSO led the way down to the far end, where sobbing oozed through the thick cell door. 'You know, I had a probationer like your Nicholson, back when I was a PC in Mintlaw. Same fire in her. Couldn't wait to climb the slippery ladder to CID. Never would take a telling.'

'What did you do?'

A shrug. 'Only thing I could do. Married her.' He grabbed the big metal slider on the safety hatch and pulled it down, lining the rectangular glass partition up with the rectangular hole in the door. Exposing the warning about the hatch now being unsafe, and the little patch of plastic where the occupant's details were scribbled up. Whether they were a biter, or a spitter. A self-harmer, or prone to outbursts of violence. This one had 'REALLY NEEDS A WASH!!!' printed on it in wobbly black marker.

The PSCO peered through the window, then unlocked the door. Stepped inside as the wails and sobs went on. 'Come on, it's not that bad, is it?'

Logan stayed where he was as a wave of mouldy body odour crashed out into the hall. Rancid, cloying bitter onions, and the ammonia nip of clothes left too long in the washing machine. 'Dear God . . .'

A cough. Blinking as the stench tried to sand-paper his irises off.

Kevin 'the Gerbil' McEwan sat on the thin concrete ledge that ran along one wall. He was hunched over with his forehead on his knees and his hands wrapped around his head. Ginger hair poked through the gaps in his fingers. Shoulders quivering in time with the sobs.

The PCSO put the polystyrene cup on the ledge, an inch or two out of reach. 'Look, if you tell the truth, it'll be OK.' He looked back at Logan. 'Won't it?'

'I'm not allowed to talk to him. Don't want to contravene his human rights.'

Gerbil raised his head. Cheeks pink and shiny, clean bits showing through the dirt where he'd been crying. Snot did a Magnum PI on his top lip. Eyes like bullet holes. Barely able to get the words out. 'They're . . . they're going to . . . going to . . . *kill* me!' All traces of the hard-man Weegie accent was gone. Now it was pure, terrified, Teuchter.

The PCSO tutted. 'No one's going to kill you, son.'

'They're . . . going to find . . . find out we lost . . . lost their stash.'

'Well, it's not the end of the world, is it?'

'I'll . . . I'll go to . . . prison and they'll kill me. They'll get someone to kill me!'

Logan didn't move.

Don't get involved. Follow procedure like a good little robot.

Wasn't even his case any more.

Remember what Napier said.

Logan cleared his throat. Turned his back. And walked away.

CHAPTER 20

'Don't understand why you didn't eat it for tenses.' Logan took the Big Car out through the Fraserburgh limits, heading back to base. The sky was a patchwork of indigo and black, covered in stars.

Nicholson took another big bite of her custard slice, getting pastry flakes all down the front of her stabproof vest. Little Tesco carrier bag tucked around her neck like a bib. 'Delayed gratification – you should try it sometime.'

Her Airwave crackled away to itself: *'Anyone in the vicinity of Dales Industrial Estate, Peterhead – reports of a break-in to the container yard round the back of the Marathon building . . .'*

'And don't get icing and stuff all over the passenger seat. Bad enough with manky sods planking mouldy egg sandwiches—'

'Not the half-eaten sarnie rant, *again.*' She grinned, talking with her mouth full. 'Think they should make it compulsory for Police Scotland to buy you cakes if you've got to do a full-on body-cavity search?'

'I'll vote for that.'

'It was like Aladdin's cave in there. She'd banked three tubs of Temazepam, one of Diclofenac, and one of Oxycodone. To be fair, that last lot *are* actually suppositories, but you're meant to take them out of the packaging first.'

He clicked on the radio. Yet more bland boy-band rubbish. 'Is this national horrible music day?'

The road twisted and turned, the hills and dips accompanied by the hiss of tyres and beige singing.

'Sarge?'

Here we go. 'Deano suggested "Killer" or "Snuggles". I quite like "Crippen".'

A frown. 'No . . . I wanted to know if there were any, you know, opportunities going on the Tarlair murder MIT. When we went to see all those sex offenders, I did a good job with the sneaking and searching, didn't I? I mean, I know I didn't *find* anything, but that's not my fault if there's nothing *to* find.'

'*Reports of a grey BMW people carrier being driven erratically on the Keith road, north of Huntly . . .*'

Shadowed fields rippled past the car windows, the lights of distant farms and cottages like glowing amber eyes in the darkness.

'You want to jump ship? OK, I've got a nickname for you: Rat. And we're not even sinking.'

'Oh, come on, Sarge, I want a bit of *excitement*. Like on the telly. Catching murderers, kicking in doors, high-speed car chases, the full Sweeney.'

'We had a high-speed last week. Harry Valentine: dog fighting and assault. We kicked a door in this morning and got eighty grand's worth of heroin. *And* we chased down Stevie Moran: remember that? How much more Sweeney do you want?'

'*Anyone in Banff? We've got reports of a domestic—*'

'You know what I mean. It's—'

'Shhhhh!' Logan tilted his head. 'Where was that domestic? Was that Alex Williams's address?'

She clicked the button on her Airwave. 'Shire Uniform Seven here – can you repeat the address for that domestic, Control?'

'*Flat thirty-nine B, Colleonard Heights. Are you attending?*'

Not Alex Williams after all.

Logan waved a hand at her. 'Tufty and Deano will get there long before we can.'

'Negative, Control, we've just left Fraserburgh. Constables Scott and Quirrel should be closer.' She settled back in her seat. Let go of her handset. 'Anyway, I don't see how it's disloyal to want to solve a murder.'

'That's what all the rats say.'

'Couldn't you put in a word with your old boss?'

A truck thundered past, going the other way, the 'FILLITIN' FINE FISH' logo glowing in the Big Car's headlights.

'OK, I'll see what I can do. *Assuming* we can get someone in to backfill for you.'

A huge smile. 'Thanks, Sarge.'

'You know they'll lumber you with all the rubbish jobs, don't you? Piddle Patrol's a highlight, everything else will be—'

'Shire Uniform Seven, safe to talk?'

She clicked the button again. 'Batter on.'

'We've had a call from Highlands and Islands – there's been a fatal RTC on the Kessock Bridge, Inverness side. Ford Fiesta went under an articulated. Wife's OK, but the husband and four-year-old boy are dead. Next of kin are in Gardenstown.'

Logan closed his eyes. No prizes for guessing where this was going. 'H-and-I want someone to deliver the death message, don't they?'

Of course they did.

Pale yellow streetlights lit the way down the steep hill to the North Sea. A string of fireflies, trapped in the darkness below the stretch of grey granite houses where Nicholson parked the Big Car.

Gardenstown perched on the side of the cliff, its streets winding their way to the small harbour at the bottom.

She killed the engine. Took a deep breath. 'We got the names?'

Logan read them out of his notebook. 'Joyce Gordon – serious condition in Raigmore Hospital. Ian and Colin Gordon both pronounced dead at the scene.' He puffed out his cheeks. 'Four-years old.'

Nicholson wiped her palms on her trousers. 'I hate this bit.'

'Me too.' He undid his seatbelt and stepped out into the night.

Stars blazed down from the inky sky, reaching from horizon to horizon, crystal clear.

They let themselves through the gate and walked up the path to a semidetached two-storey house. Roses and honeysuckle around the door, turning the cool air sickly sweet.

'Right.' Nicholson straightened her shoulders. 'No point putting it off.' She reached out and rang the bell. 'Ian, Joyce, Colin. Ian, Joyce, Colin. Ian, Joyce, Colin.'

No reply. So she leaned on the bell again, keeping her thumb on it till lights flickered on inside the house.

Logan blew out a breath. 'It's OK. I'll do it.'

She nodded. 'Thanks, Sarge.'

The front door creaked open and a white-haired man scowled out at them, pink dressing gown wrapped tight around his thin body. 'Have you got *any* idea what time it is?'

Logan stepped up. 'Mr Gordon, can we come in? I'm afraid I have some bad news . . .'

The living room was an oven, decked out in seascapes and photographs. A collection of little greenstone carvings on the mantelpiece above the blazing electric fire.

Mr Gordon sat on the couch, staring out into nothing, one hand holding onto his wife's as she sniffled and sobbed.

Nicholson squatted on the floor beside her, holding her other hand. 'Shh . . .'

The only other sound was the clock ticking away on the wall.

Then Logan's phone burst into the 'Imperial March' from Star Wars. Loud enough to make everyone flinch.

Didn't need to check the screen to know who it was: Steel.

'I'm really sorry about this.' He hurried out into the corridor and closed the door behind him, before dragging his phone out. 'What?'

DCI Steel's voice growled in his ear. *'You're no' answering your Airwave.'*

He marched down the hall and into the kitchen. 'I'm busy.' A small room, bright-red walls, black tile floor, wooden work surfaces. Lots of stainless-steel appliances. Expensive looking.

'Don't care.' A sooking noise. *'Listen—'*

'You get anything from the schools?'

'Of course we didn't. And in case you're wondering, we looked into that long *before you stuck your nose in.'*

Might as well do something useful while he was in here.

Logan put the kettle on to boil. 'Well . . . Did you check on kids who're meant to be off sick, or on holiday?'

'You about done telling me how to suck eggs? No one knows her, no one recognizes her, no one misses her.'

Poor little soul.

He found mugs in the cupboard above the kettle. Tea and sugar was there too.

'Probably not in school then. He dressed her up.'

The sarcasm positively dripped from the phone's speaker. *'Do you* think?' Then another sooking noise – probably Steel's e-cigarette. *'Got Becky to go digging. Uniform's all from Asda's "Back to School" collection. No way to know which store. Nothing specific about it, so we've no' clue which school he's pretending she's from.'*

A frown. 'She's wearing red shoes. That can't be normal.'

'Your head's no' normal.' More sooking. *'And speaking of no' normal: how come you've no' asked about your Mrs Edwards, up from Edinburgh, yet? The first flush of ardour fading, is it?'*

Logan pinned the phone between his ear and shoulder, then dumped teabags into mugs. 'Did she ID the body?'

'No distinguishing features or childhood broken bones. According to the pathologist, that matches what we've got. Yeah, there's signs of breakages, but no' till she's four or five. So we're going to try a DNA match with the mum. Aberdeen labs are still down, so it's off to sunny Dundee with the samples. Going to be a couple of days before we know for sure.'

Well, at least that was something.

'I've got to go: we're on a death message. RTC, one of the fatalities was only four—'

'Listen, about your complete and utter cocking disaster yesterday . . .'

Logan closed his eyes and dunted his forehead

off the wall unit. Here we go. 'I told you: I'm not apologizing for saving Stephen Bisset's life.'

'Aye. Very noble of you. Turns out it doesn't matter anyway.'

The kettle rattled to a boil. Clicked and fell silent.

Then Nicholson's muffled voice came from the hall outside. The clunk of a door closing.

And still nothing from Steel.

He poured hot water into each mug. 'Come on then, I'll bite. What cutting bit of sarcasm have you got for me?'

'It's no' a joke, Laz. Graham Stirling got set free at half four. And fifteen minutes ago, some nurse found Stephen Bisset. Dead. All alone in his hospital bed. Someone suffocated him.'

Oh that was just . . . perfect.

Brilliant end to a brilliant sodding day.

Logan thumped his head against the unit again. Stayed there. 'Please tell me someone's arrested Stirling.'

Nicholson slipped into the kitchen, face pink, scrubbing at her eyes with the heel of her hand. She saw Logan and froze. Blinked. Straightened her stabproof vest. 'Sarge.'

He pointed at the phone in his other hand. 'Have they arrested Stirling, or haven't they?'

'So all that grief and running about was for nothing, wasn't it? So much for bending the rules to save the poor bugger's life. Stephen Bisset still wound up dead, only he got to suffer for four months first.'

So, he'd been wrong. Today *could* get worse.

CHAPTER 21

Nicholson pulled into the only free parking space anywhere near Banff station. The MIT's collection of ragged pool cars and the search team's Transit vans clogged everything else. Wouldn't be long before the people living either side started complaining.

'All units, be on the lookout for an IC-One male wearing a dark hoodie and baseball cap. Mid-twenties with a moustache and soul patch. Chipped front tooth. Attempted sexual assault in Stuartfield . . .'

Logan climbed out. 'Right. Cup of tea, then get your actions up to date. We're going to be out of here bang on time for a change. Two o'clock on the dot.'

She nodded – eyes all puffy and red in the light spilling out from the station windows. 'Sarge.'

The main office had its familiar contingent of two uniforms battering away at a computer, while Steel's right-hand woman scowled away at the other. She looked up and let Logan enjoy that scowl for a bit, before going back to whatever was blighting her life on the screen.

Nice to see you too.

The Sergeants' Office was empty for once. Logan fought his way out of his protective gear and settled into his chair with a sigh. Spread his hands out on the desktop. No DS Dawson. How lovely . . .

And then a small barb of guilt hooked itself into his throat; and *why* was DS Dawson not there? Yes, well.

Still, it wasn't as if anyone ever died from an overdose of laxatives. Was it?

Hope not.

Logan logged into STORM and wrote up their visit to Gardenstown. Then started in on the team's actions.

The office door thumped open and Steel marched into the room. Scowled at him. Put her mug down on top of his notebook. 'Where the hell *you* been?'

'I told you: death message.' He moved the mug. Went back to his keyboard. 'If you want something, it'll have to wait. Got everyone's actions to review. Then I'm going home.'

'Pffff . . .' She thumped down into the chair opposite and heaved her feet up onto the desk. 'Don't be such a wheenge – night's barely getting started. Got a kid killer to catch.' Then stuck two fingers in her mouth and let out a piercing whistle. 'BECKY, BUMHOLE FRONT AND CENTRE!'

There was some muttered swearing from the main office, then Detective Sergeant McKenzie stomped to a halt on the threshold. Her bun was coming loose on one side, a handful of frizzy brown hair breaking free to puff around her ear. 'Don't have to bellow like that. You could pick up the phone.'

'Blah, blah, blah.' Steel dug into an inside pocket and came out with a small evidence bag. Then scribbled something down on one of Logan's Post-its. 'Get that sent off to this address. And *don't* stick it in the post. I want it hand-delivered by someone in a shiny uniform. Tell them, if it's no' in Dundee by lunchtime I'm going to take my fist and turn them into a glove puppet.'

DS McKenzie's cheeks flushed. 'Yes, Boss.' Then she snatched the evidence bag and Post-it off the desk and stormed out. Slamming the door behind her.

Logan waited for the echoes to fade. 'Did you have to?'

'Ah, she loves it really.' Steel delved into her cleavage for a scratch. 'Probably die of old age before those lazy sods get back with the DNA, but my new bestest friend – Professor Whatshisname, at that institute in Dundee – says if I get him some samples from our wee dead girl, he'll run stable isotope analysis on them. On the sly. No charge, just the warm fuzzy feeling of helping catch whichever dirty sod killed her. And a bottle of malt whisky.'

'Seriously, if you don't lighten up on DS McKenzie she'll either go off on the stress, or come after you with a meat cleaver.'

'Could only get my hands on some hair, but it's

better than nothing. With any luck, the Prof gets back to us with where our victim's from, and where she's been. Postcode would be nice, but probably asking a bit much.' A sniff. 'Aye, assuming Becky doesn't cock it up and send the sample to Glasgow, or Timbuctoo.'

'There's no point talking to you, is there?'

'Nope.' Steel clicked her fake cigarette on and stuck it in her gob. 'How about you and me head out to rattle a few more sex offenders?'

'Shift's over in fifteen minutes. And then I'm going home and having two rest days. So if you want someone to run around after you, you better get one of your minions to do it.'

'I don't like my minions. My minions are no fun.' She waved her fake cigarette about, like a conductor's baton. 'My old minions were much better.'

'Tough.'

She stared at him. 'Laz, in the old days, we'd dig through a dead tramp's used knickers if we thought it'd catch a killer. What happened to you?'

'What happened? *Seriously*? You can't be—'

Three knocks on the door and Nicholson stuck her head in. 'Sarge, do you . . . Oh, sorry, didn't know you had company.' Her puffy eyes were back to normal. Couldn't even tell she'd had a wee cry in the kitchen of an elderly couple who'd lost their son and grandchild in a stupid car accident. 'Can I get—'

'Do us a favour, Constable?' Steel held up her

mug. 'Coffee: two and a coo. Laz here'll have a milky tea.'

That got her a frown. 'Sarge?'

Steel waggled the mug. 'Give us a minute, eh? Got some motivating to do.'

Logan closed his eyes and swore.

Nicholson blinked a couple of times, then pulled on an uncomfortable-looking smile. Accepted the proffered mug. Backed away a couple of paces. 'Yes, fine. No problem.' Then turned and disappeared back through the door. Closed it behind her.

Steel had a dig at an armpit. 'Alone at last.'

Here we go . . . 'Look, if you're trying to bully me into staying late, you can—'

'We need to talk about Stephen Bisset.'

Oh.

Steel fiddled with the buttons on her suit jacket. Looked at her reflection in the dark office window. 'Media's going to have a field day: "Pervert victim killed in hospital!" Demanding to know why we didn't have a guard on his bed. Why we wasted all that money on a half-arsed excuse of a trial, only to let Graham Stirling walk away scot-free.'

She gave up on the buttons and had a fiddle with her bra strap instead. 'Jump in any time you like.'

'Have they arrested Stirling for the murder yet?'

A small sharp laugh barked out. 'Of course they haven't. He was with his scumbag lawyer when it happened. Probably trying to figure out how much he can screw us for wrongful prosecution.'

'God's sake . . .' Logan slumped in his seat. Scrubbed a hand across his forehead. 'OK, so it's someone else. Stirling's got an accomplice, or a relative, or someone with a vested interest in making sure Stephen Bisset never woke up and identified him.'

'That's—'

'We get the CCTV from the hospital and we comb through it, looking for anyone with a connection to Stirling.'

'Aye, believe it or no' we did *actually* think of that. Nada.' She shook her head. 'This time tomorrow there won't be a front page, news bulletin, or chat show that doesn't have Bisset's family all over it. Telling everyone how incompetent we are.'

Maybe they'd be right.

Logan let his head fall back against the shelves. 'Top brass are looking for a scapegoat, aren't they?' And no prizes for guessing who *that* would be.

Silence.

Steel cleared her throat. 'Listen, why don't you come back to work for me? Told you, my minions are pants. Rennie's useless and Becky's got a face only a baboon's backside could love. Don't know what's crawled up her today, but it's laid eggs.'

'I can't.'

'Course you can. I could *protect* you.'

'How?' Logan threw his arms out. 'How the hell are you going to protect me from Napier? He's a one-man jihad and I'm sodding America.'

'Don't know yet, but I'll figure something out. We get you seconded to my MIT and I make you invaluable. We set stuff up so it looks like you're Sherlock Holmes and Robocop all rolled into one. They won't *dare* sack you.'

Good luck with that.

'You can't magically—'

'All we need to do is find Neil Wood, batter a confession out of him, and tell everyone you saved the day.'

'That's your plan? You and me solve the case when a whole MIT can't? Just like that? And I suppose we're going to do it before Napier does his suicide-bomber thing?'

She scowled at him. 'Well, I'm no' hearing any brilliant plans coming from *your* side of the desk!'

'There *is* no plan. I'm screwed, OK? That's it. Me. Screwed.' He covered his face with his hands. 'I was acting DI for four years. *Four years*, and they wouldn't promote me. You think they're *ever* going to make me an inspector if I wimp out on Banff after three months? I'll be a sergeant for the rest of my career.' He let his arms fall to dangle at his sides. 'Gah . . .'

'So you're giving up? Wimping out.'

'No! That's exactly what I'm *not* doing. I'm staying here and I'm sticking it out.'

A knock on the door.

'Hallelujah. Come in, Janet.'

Nicholson pushed her way in, carrying two mugs.

A packet of Ginger Nuts tucked under one arm. 'Sorry, Sarge, didn't want it getting cold.'

Steel sniffed. 'Constable, your Sergeant here wants to call it a night.'

'Oh. OK . . .' She placed a mug on the desk. 'Well, if you're needing help with something, I could—'

'No.' Logan held up his hand. 'Shift ends in . . .' He checked his watch. 'Twenty minutes. Home on time for a change.'

'But, *Saaa-aaarge.*'

'He's no' bothered that there's crime afoot. That the good people of Banff can't sleep safe in their beds at night, for fear of blah, blah, blah.' Steel had a slurp of coffee. 'What happened to that can-do CID spirit, Sergeant McRae?'

'It disappeared soon as *you* got me transferred out to uniform.'

Nicholson scuffed forward. Held out the mug of tea. 'But it'd be great experience for me, wouldn't it? Working on an MIT?'

'You want to do it? You do it. With my blessing.' He pointed at Steel. 'You're covering the overtime though.'

Steel peered out at him from the passenger seat. 'I'm serious, Laz – we can beat this.'

'No we can't. And stick to your hotel room this time, I'm not running a B-and-B.'

She stuck her nose in the air. 'You're such a whiny princess.' Then Steel reached across and thumped Nicholson on the shoulder. 'Onward to justice!'

Logan stood on the pavement as the Big Car's tail lights dwindled to tiny red dots, then disappeared around the corner.

Pair of idiots.

Light blazed from the station windows. Normally, they'd only leave a single bulb on in the main office, so it looked as if someone was in. Well, it wouldn't do to have some scrote break into the place and make off with seized narcotics, electronics, and firearms, would it? But tonight, the whole top floor, half the middle, and the ground floor glowed like it was Christmas.

The MIT burning the quarter-to-two-in-the-morning oil.

As if he and Steel could catch a wee girl's killer when all this lot couldn't.

Even if half of them couldn't investigate their own pants for genitals.

A long slow breath hissed out of him.

It wasn't possible.

If he was going to look indispensable, it would have to be something closer to home. Something achievable.

He keyed in Deano's shoulder number. 'Shire Uniform Seven. Deano, you safe to talk?'

A pause, then: *'Fire on, Sarge.'*

'How'd you get on at that domestic?'

'Storm in a teapot. Big fight about going to EuroDisney or Lossiemouth with the grandkids this summer. Only thing that got battered was a tea set.'

'Tufty?'

'*Good as gold. Might even buy him a lolly.*'

Wonders would never cease.

'Glad to hear it. You still dealing with your drink driver, or are you Foxtrot Oscar?'

'*Up the hospital again. Silly sod's so blootered he can barely stand, but he thinks he's safe to drive. No one at home to take care of him, so he's the NHS's problem till he sobers up. Remember the good old days when we could chuck them in a cell for the night?*'

'OK, well, I'm finishing up soon. Make sure Tufty updates his actions *before* he goes back to his tree, or he's in for a swift kick in the acorns.'

'*Sarge.*'

Logan let himself back into the station.

Something closer to home . . .

He pressed the button again. 'Deano, do me a favour while you're up the hospital? Pop in and see if Jack Simpson's got over his time in Klingon and Gerbil's attic. If you can't get me on the Airwave, I'll be on my mobile.'

Worth a try anyway.

Back to the Sergeants' Office.

Logan finished updating the actions on STORM. Logged off. Shut down the computer. Stuck his dirty mug in the canteen sink. Unlocked the little blue door to his Airwave locker. More of a sealed pigeonhole than anything, set amongst twenty-eight identical little blue sealed pigeonholes. He pulled out the charging cable.

The Airwave bleeped at him and Deano's

shoulder number appeared on the screen. *'Sarge, you safe to talk?'*

'Thump away.'

'Jack Simpson. Docs say he's going to be under for at least a couple more days. Klingon and Gerbil really did a number on his head with that baseball bat. They're keeping him sedated till the swelling goes down a bit.'

Because that worked *so* well for Samantha.

'Thanks, Deano.'

Logan switched the handset off. Plugged in the charging cable. Stuck the lot back in its sealable pigeonhole and locked the door.

Just have to look somewhere else for salvation.

Logan slouched out of the station's side door. Made sure it was closed. Then stood there on the pavement and let a huge yawn shudder its way up from his knees. Sagged.

So much for finding a case he could crack quickly to get Napier off his back. Nothing was anywhere near big enough to make up for what happened at the Graham Stirling trial. A spate of shoplifting wasn't even going to put a dent in that.

He dumped his peaked cap on his head and cut across the car park . . . Then stopped.

A figure was huddled against the wall that separated the road from the beach. Bum on the pavement, knees up against its chest, arms wrapped around itself. Face hidden in the depths of a parka's periscope hood.

Logan walked over. 'Are you OK? Hello?'

The figure jerked, then looked up at him. Peeled back the hood to reveal an explosion-in-a-spring-factory haircut. Helen Edwards – the woman with the missing daughter. She blinked a couple of times, then pulled her shoulders in. 'Cold.'

'Have you been out here all this time?' He helped her to her feet.

It took a while, her knees didn't seem to be working properly. 'Sorry . . .'

'Honestly, you can go back to your hotel, we'll call you as soon as we know anything.'

She stumbled a little. Grabbed the wall. Stretched out her left leg. 'Foot's gone to sleep.'

'I can give you a lift, if you like?'

'Don't have a hotel. I didn't want to . . .' A shrug. 'What if something happened and I wasn't here?'

'So you were going to sit out here, in the dark, all night? And all tomorrow as well? You do know it's going to take a few days for the DNA results to come in?'

'What else can I do?'

Logan dug out his keys. 'Have you eaten anything today?'

'I know, I'm an idiot.' Her head dipped. 'Argh . . . pins and needles.'

Helen Edwards limped around the kitchen as the microwave burrrrrrred away to itself, and the kettle grumbled to a boil. She stopped in front of the row of framed photos next to the calendar. May's picture

283

was a cat and a pony playing in a field, executed in crayon and glitter. 'You've got kids?'

Logan dumped teabags in two mugs. 'Not really. Sort of. It's complicated.' The kettle clicked to a stop. 'You take sugar?'

'One, please.'

He filled the mugs with hot water. 'My boss and her wife wanted a kid, so I donated. Jasmine's six now. Made me the calendar for Christmas. You want to get the milk and spready butter from the fridge?'

'She's very talented.'

'Doesn't get it from my side of the family.' He dug the loaf of cheapo white from the breadbin and placed it on the kitchen table.

'Your girlfriend?' Helen Edwards pointed at one of the photos that hung squint on the wall. Logan and Samantha eating ice cream outside the Inversnecky Café down at Aberdeen beach. Samantha's hair was post-box scarlet, a dribble of vanilla snaked down her hand, chocolate flake posed at a jaunty angle. Big smile. Logan grinning. As if the world wasn't a cruel, dark, hollow, pit of a place.

Helen straightened the frame. 'She's pretty.'

Ah . . . 'That's complicated too.' He fished out the teabags and put the mugs next to the loaf.

'It always is.' She got the milk and the butter. 'I remember when it was like that for Brian and me. The smiles and the chips and the lazy Sunday mornings . . . Before the shouting and the swearing and the constant criticism eating away at you like acid.'

The microwave gave its triumphant bleeps of completion. The bowl was almost too hot to touch, but Logan got it onto the kitchen table with only second-degree burns to the fingers. 'Sorry, it's only lentil.'

'I like lentil.'

'Gets a bit samey after a couple of weeks.' He handed her a plate and a spoon. Then slopped some milk in his mug and took it over to the sink. Rinsed out the soup tin.

'It's lovely, thank you.' The slurp and crunch of soup and toast sounded behind him as she tucked in. 'Very good.'

'It's complicated, because Samantha was in a coma for four years.'

Silence.

He stuck the tin on the draining board. 'She's what they call "minimally conscious" now.'

'I'm sorry.'

A long slow breath made his shoulders sink. 'She can't speak. Can't move on her own. And there's a big hole in her skull so her brain doesn't swell up and kill her.'

'Must be hard.'

'Don't even know if she's in there any more. I mean, I talk to her, but . . .' Yes, well. No point going down that road. A small laugh forced its way out, leaving a bitter taste behind. 'Sorry. Must be my turn to play Captain Gloom and Doom.'

He gave himself a small shake. 'Anyway, would you like some hot sauce? Perks a bowl of lentil up no end.'

'Are you sure it's OK?'

Logan handed her the pillow. 'It's fine, seriously. You look reasonably honest, and I've got sod all worth stealing anyway.'

She lay back on the couch and pulled the duvet up under her chin. 'Thank you.'

Click, and the room was plunged into darkness. He stepped out into the hall. 'I'm not on duty tomorrow, so it won't be an early start.'

Her voice came from the dark. 'Logan?'

'What?'

'You remember what I said? About knowing what it's like to love someone who's completely lost? And if they were dead you could start moving on?'

'Yeah.'

'I'm sorry.'

'I am too.'

He closed the door, and headed upstairs to bed.

— THURSDAY: REST DAY —

CHAPTER 22

A yawn. A stretch. A scratch. Then Logan slumped back into his pillow.

Sunlight glared around the border of the curtains, revealing the peeling wallpaper around the window in all its hideous glory. Have to get that stripped off today. Well, it was that or paint the living room. Or the stairs. Or do one of the other hundred jobs that—

What was that?

He sat up, ears straining to catch the noise again.

A clunk came from somewhere downstairs.

There was someone in the house.

Need a weapon. Extendable baton. Not as good as a shotgun, but it'd do.

His hand fumbled down the side of the mattress, fingertips searching for the equipment belt and . . .

Idiot.

Of course there was someone in the house: Helen Edwards. She was going to the toilet, wasn't she. There wasn't one on the ground floor, so she'd climbed the stairs.

Who was it going to be, Freddy Krueger?

He lay back. Slow calm breaths, until the thudding beat in his chest faded a bit.

Idiot.

Five more minutes: then up.

Logan hauled the T-shirt over his head and scuffed his way downstairs. A handful of fliers for the local takeaways lay scattered beneath the letterbox, along with a collection of canvassing leaflets for the upcoming by-election. Vote for me, I'm not a scumbag!

Yeah, right.

He scooped the lot up and carried them through to the kitchen.

Helen Edwards stood at the sink, elbow-deep in suds. Pots and pans were piled up on the draining board, while what looked like every plate in the place was stacked on the other side.

Logan stopped at the doorway. 'Is everything really that filthy?'

She turned. Pink spread across her cheeks. 'It . . . No. I just . . .' She pushed a dirty-blonde curl out of her eyes with a soapy finger. 'I was sitting about and I thought, I know, I'll do something useful – I'll clean the kitchen.'

He clicked the kettle on. 'You want tea?'

'Please.'

For a minute, the only sound was the clicking rattle of the water boiling.

Logan cleared his throat.

Cthulhu padded into the room and hopped up

onto the windowsill in one fluid motion. Arched her back, then sat down, tail in the air, front paws at ten to two, like a small fuzzy ballet dancer. Logan reached out and scratched her behind the ears, getting a deep rumbling purr for his troubles.

Behind her, sunlight washed the face of Banff police station. Gave its sandstone cheeks a rosy glow.

An old man went by on a bicycle.

Helen cleared *her* throat.

Yeah, this wasn't awkward at all.

Click.

Logan made the tea. 'I'm heading off to see Samantha later.'

'Do you . . . Do you think they'll hear about the DNA today?'

'Probably not. They're upgrading the equipment in Aberdeen so everything's going to Dundee instead. And they've *always* got a backlog these days – rapes, murders, severed feet. It's Thursday now. Lucky if it's done before the weekend, to be honest.'

'Oh.' Helen's head drooped.

'DCI Steel will be kicking up a fuss, try to get it prioritized, but there's only so much she can do.'

The last pot got added to the clean pile. 'Can I see it?'

'See what?'

She took the first plate from the stack and slipped it into the foamy deep. Kept her face turned away from him. 'The swimming pool. Where they found her.'

Logan pulled up at the brow of the hill. From here the North Sea was a polished slab of blue slate, edged with white where it hushed against the pebble beach below.

The coastline stretched away ahead – the reaching cliffs paling and turning blue as they faded into the distance. Stone fingers reaching for the horizon.

Tarlair Outdoor Swimming Pool's nest of white cubist buildings nestled in the depths of the rocky bowl, walls shimmering in the morning sun.

His rusty Clio's engine sounded like a screwdriver scraping along a breezeblock.

'You sure you want to do this?'

Helen nodded.

'OK.' He put the car into gear and slid them down the hill, around the dog-leg bend, and onto the patchwork stretch of potholes and rutted tarmac.

A Police Pod sat in the car park, in front of the burned-out remains of the bin, but the door was shut. No sign of life.

He parked next to it. 'If you feel uncomfortable, or sick, or anything like that, let me know and we'll get you out of here. It's not a problem.'

'Right. Yes.' She unclipped her seatbelt. Blew out a breath. Brushed the curls from her face. 'You can do this . . .' Then opened the door and stepped out into the sun.

Logan joined her. Locked the car – as if anyone

would be desperate enough to steal a rattly heap like that.

A line of blue-and-white 'POLICE' tape stretched across the gap in the rock that acted as a gateway to the site. He pulled it up and ushered her through.

She glanced back at the pod. 'This is all right, isn't it? We're not going to get into trouble?'

'I called DCI Steel – they've finished the search. The barrier tape's there to stop weirdoes and grief-tourists snooping.'

She picked her way along the path, past the pebble beach with its stone archway and kelp bones. Stopped in front of the Aberdeenshire Council sign:

TARLAIR POOL IS CLOSED

THIS AREA CAN BE

<u>DANGEROUS!</u>

<u>SWIMMING IS NOT PERMITTED</u>

The water is not treated or monitored.
There is no supervision.
The structure is <u>unsafe</u>.
<u>Beware of slippery surface</u>.
Do <u>NOT</u> walk on the sea wall,
it is <u>unsafe</u> to do so.
There is a two metre drop on the seaward side.
Young children must be supervised at all times.

She stared at it for a while. Then took a deep breath and walked past, making for the boxy art deco buildings.

'You're sure you're OK?'

A nod. 'It's fine. I'm fine.' She wrapped her arms around herself. Holding it in. Stopped at the top of the apron.

Three wide tiers of dark concrete, edged in white, led down to the inner pool. Little more than a rock-strewn swathe of cracked grey.

Helen puffed out her cheeks. There was no inflection in her voice at all. 'Where did you find her?'

He pointed at the corner of the outer pool. The water level had gone down since Monday evening – evaporated in the sun, or drained out through cracks in the sea wall.

She followed him, past the main building with its grime-streaked walls, around the edge of the amphitheatre space, and out onto the side apron.

'Watch your footing.'

The walkway got worse the closer they got to the outer pool, crumbling away to expose massive holes strewn with rock and pebbles. Bits of broken glass and sun-bleached crisp packets nestled amongst the weeds.

Logan came to a halt at the corner of the outer pool. 'This is it.'

The whole place obviously got battered with huge storm surges, going by the size and the number of rocks that made a drift against this side of the pool. The force needed to shift them must've been massive.

Helen sank down on the edge of the pool, feet dangling over the stones. Stared down into the water. Closed her eyes. Bit her bottom lip. Her shoulders quivered. A sniff. Then the tears came.

Logan swallowed. Looked away.

Stood there in silence and listened to her grief.

'Look, all I'm saying is light a fire under them, OK?' Logan leaned on the roof of the car. 'She needs to know if it's her daughter or not.'

On the other end of the phone, Steel sounded as if she was crumpling tinfoil. *'Oh aye, and how come you're so interested all of a sudden? Yesterday it wasn't your case. You had beddy-byes to go to.'*

'How would you feel if it was Jasmine?'

'Don't you sodding dare.'

'Well, give the lab a kick then. It's a dead wee girl we're talking about.'

'Anyone touches Jasmine, I'll make the Spanish inquisition look like a WRI meeting. Doesn't matter how fast or far they run, I'll find them and skin them alive.'

'And how could you not find Helen anywhere to stay?'

'Make them wear their arse for a face.'

'She slept on my couch last night. It was that or stick her in the cells.'

Helen stood on the pebble beach, at the water's edge, staring out to sea.

'Oh, I see. You've taken her in and now finding the wee kid's killer's a top priority, is it? What, did she polish your truncheon for you last night?'

'She thinks her daughter's dead. And you find it *funny?*'

A sigh. '*No.*' Steel took a deep breath. '*Look, I told McKenzie to sort it out – accommodation, contact details, next of kin, the lot. I'll get it done. And I'll tell the lab to get a shift on. OK?*'

'Thanks.'

'*Going to be a right pain in the backside though. His Royal Finnieness has decreed there's no point having all these bodies on the ground up here. Operational priorities.*'

'Doesn't want to pay the overtime?'

'*Half the team's back to Aberdeen tomorrow. They won't even let me keep Rennie, you believe that? Rennie! He's about as much use as a cardboard dildo, but he's better than DS Sulkypants McKenzie.*'

'Don't be such a moan. And make sure you give the lab a kicking, OK? I've got to go.' He hung up. Put the phone back in his pocket.

The pebbles scrunched beneath his feet.

Helen's eyes were bloodshot and swollen, the tip of her nose flushed and pink.

Logan shuffled to a halt beside her. 'You all right?'

She nodded, then wiped her eyes with the heel of one hand. 'Sorry. Being stupid.'

'They're going to chase up the DNA match. See if they can't get the lab to bump it up the list.' Way out to sea, a scarlet fishing boat carved a line of white across the blue. 'They're sorry about the mix-up with the hotel. DCI Steel says she's going to make sure they get somewhere organized for you, so you don't have to crash on my couch.'

'Oh.' Helen picked at the corner of a fingernail. 'That's very kind.' Her shoulders curled in.

'You sure you're OK?'

She looked away. 'I don't want to be a burden. It's just . . . I don't want to be on my own. I'm always on my own, in B-and-B's and hotels and buses and trains and it's really nice to have someone to talk to. Someone who understands what it's like.'

Logan stared at her.

Pink bloomed on the back of her neck. Spread to her cheeks. 'And I could help out – my father was a painter and decorator with Glasgow City Council . . .?' She cleared her throat. Looked down at her feet. 'Sorry. Being stupid again.'

He put a hand on her shoulder. 'I've got to go see Samantha. You any good at stripping wall-paper?'

A massive supply vessel dragged a wake of white behind it, making for the horizon. The sky made a perfect blue dome, wrapping around the jagged coastline, punctuated with the wheeling slashes of herring gulls. Faint screeches and craws drifting down to the balcony.

All the wheelchairs faced out to sea, their occupants slumped and slouching against their chest restraints. Propped up in the sunshine.

Logan swapped his phone to his other hand, then dabbed a tissue at the corner of Samantha's mouth. 'Yeah, sorry.'

On the other end, Deano sighed. *'And you're sure?'*

'Can't. Something's come up and I'm stuck.'

'You do remember I've got ribeye steaks the size of your head?'

'I know. I'd love to, Deano, but I can't.'

Samantha's forehead was getting a bit red. Have to get her a big hat or something.

'We've got a heap of beer too.'

A groan escaped Logan's lips. 'You're not making this any easier.'

Well, it wasn't as if he could abandon Helen to do the DIY while he went out and got stuffed and hammered, could he? And there was no way in hell he could take her with him. Turn up to a barbecue with what might be the dead little girl's mother in tow? It wouldn't be fair on her. *Or* the team.

How were they supposed to relax and enjoy themselves if they had to be on their best behaviour the whole time?

He'd never hear the end of it.

'Well, if you're sure you're sure.'

'Trust me: if I could, I would.'

After all, there would be other barbecues. Other steaks.

Logan's stomach growled.

And it wasn't as if he didn't have plenty tins of lentil soup at home.

Logan pinned his phone between his ear and shoulder while he tied up the third bin-bag. 'You're kidding. Not till *Monday*?'

On the other end, Steel sniffed. *'Two high-profile rapes, and another three severed feet in the Clyde today.'*

Logan glanced towards the bedroom door. No sign of Helen, but he dropped his voice anyway. 'Surely a murdered little girl trumps three severed feet?'

'In a sensible world, yes. Here? No. Even tried getting Big Tony Campbell to weigh in, but no doing. We're in the queue.'

'Someone needs a stiff kick in the balls.' Logan unfurled another bin-bag and stuffed a wodge of stripped wallpaper into it.

The room looked a lot better without the peeling mess of sickly purple paper. Now the walls were stripped back to the pink plaster – speckled with fresh white filler. A going over with sugar soap and a coat of white emulsion had faded the stains on the ceiling a bit, but nowhere near enough. The air tasted sticky and plasticky from the paint fumes.

'Which reminds me: I gave Becky a chewing out for no' getting a hotel arranged for our victim's mother. So off she goes, looking like she's about to burst one, and gets everything sorted.'

'Ah . . .'

'Only, you know what Ms Helen It-Might-Be-My-Dead-Daughter Edwards says when Becky tells her there's a room booked for her? "No thanks, I'm staying with a friend."'

'Well, maybe—'

'Ungrateful cow.' Something crunched down the line, and Steel's voice went all muffled, as if her mouth was full. 'In other news: you want to play the voice of sanity for a change?'

The last of the stripped-off wallpaper went in the bin-bag. 'What did you do?'

'Only reason those feet are higher up the list is because the media's got their teeth into them. What if someone leaked it? "Police labs ignore murdered six-year-old's DNA in half-arsed PR grab?"' More crunching. 'Or something snappier: "Scumbag Labs DNA Cock-up." You know the kind of thing.'

'No.'

'Well, you come up with a better headline then.'

'No, I mean: no. Don't do it. You leak it after rattling everyone's cages, it'll get back to you. You really that keen to spend more time with Napier?' Logan tied the last bag and added it to the pile. 'You can't leak it. They'll nail you to the ceiling.'

'So I get Rennie to do it.'

'Yeah, because there's no way that could *possibly* be tied back to you.' He gathered the bin-bags together and struggled them out onto the landing.

Tuneless whistling came from the bathroom.

Logan hefted the debris downstairs. 'How'd you get on with Nicholson last night?'

'*Well, what about Becky then? I could get her to do it.*'

'No.'

'*Pfff . . .*' More crunching. '*Your girl Nicholson's a bit keen, isn't she?*'

He dumped the bin-bags at the front door. 'Let me guess, you didn't get anything.'

'*Two hours of sod all. Well, no' counting nasty cups of tea and dirty looks. Dr Kidfiddler says he's putting in a complaint about harassment.*' The grin shone through Steel's voice, '*Turns out he doesn't like being roused at three in the morning and grilled about access to barbiturates. Poor baby. Should've thought about that before he started molesting wee kids.*'

Upstairs, the toilet flushed. She'd be down in a minute.

'Look, I've got to go.'

'*Oh aye, got a hot date, have we? Rosy palm bringing round her five sisters for a gangbang?*'

'I'm hanging up.'

'*Hope you've got protection. A Marigold glove would probably do if—*'

He poked the button, then slid the phone back in his pocket as Helen appeared at the top of the stairs.

She tucked a curl behind one ear. Smiled. 'What's for dinner?'

'Lentil soup.'

The smile froze. 'Again?'

— FRIDAY: REST DAY —

CHAPTER 23

'. . . *going to be with us for the next hour, but first here's Carol with all your lunchtime news, travel, and weather. Carol.'*

'*Thanks, Justin. Greater Glasgow Police are refusing to confirm or deny rumours that three severed feet found in the Clyde yesterday are part of a sectarian feud . . .'*

Logan pulled his rattly Clio into the kerb, opposite the Sergeant's Hoose. Dug out his phone and checked his messages.

Voicemail from his mother. That got deleted.

A text from Rennie about a dead tramp he'd had to peel out of a wheelie bin back in Aberdeen. Delete.

'. . . *confirmed that sex-attack-victim Stephen Bisset's death in Aberdeen Royal Infirmary on Wednesday night is being treated as suspicious. After the collapse of the trial against—'*

Logan killed the engine.

Sat in the silence.

Went back to his phone.

A text from Steel was next – moaning about him not going to Jasmine's dance competition tomorrow.

Delete. And another from her about chasing up on Neil Wood's connections in the sex-offender underground.

And one from Biohazard Bob.

> Napier was round here 2day asking loads of questions about U.

> Kept asking if U gone mental on this case. Obsessed & that.

> Watch Ur back: knives R out!

'Great.' He thumbed out a response and sent it off. Sat there, staring at the glittering expanse of the North Sea.

Could do a Reginald Perrin. Strip off at the water's edge and walk out into the waves. Sod off somewhere else . . .

Then what would Samantha do? Who'd pay her bills?

Yeah. Exactly.

Logan put his phone away and climbed out into the sunshine.

A knot of scruffy blokes and well-dressed women were gathered outside the front of Banff station. Some doing pieces to camera, others smoking and drinking from Styrofoam cups.

What the hell was wrong with Steel? She'd blabbed to the press, even though he'd *told* her not to.

Idiot.

Out with the phone again.

She picked up on the fourth ring. *'I'm no' telling you again: I'm no' giving you any more money!'*

'What?'

'What?' She cleared her throat. *'Oh . . . Thought you were someone else. Why are—'*

'What did I tell you last night?' He stomped across the road to the Sergeant's Hoose. 'You leak it, they're going to trace it right back to you! How could you be so stupid?'

'Who are you *calling stupid? I should—'*

'Telling the media – you really think that's not going to blow up in your—'

'Hold your sodding horses right there, Tonto. I didn't tip anyone off about anything.'

He stuck his head around the corner. The pack of journalists were still there. 'Then why am I looking at a bunch of idiots from the national press and TV hanging about outside Banff station?'

Silence.

Yeah, she didn't have an answer to that, did she.

He let himself into the house. 'What were you thinking?'

Still nothing.

Inside, the sound of tuneless whistling came from the open kitchen door, floating on an air of rich meaty scents.

'Hello? You still there?'

Helen's mess of explosive curls poked out of the kitchen. 'Logan. Hi. Thought I heard something.

You're right on time.' Her face glowed, the skin pink and shiny.

He closed the front door. 'Hi. Sorry.' He pointed at the phone in his other hand.

'Ah, right. Sorry.' She backed into the kitchen.

Back to the phone. 'OK, I'm hanging up. You have—'

'I didn't leak sod all to anyone. For your information, Chuckles, the press mosh-pit outside the front door isn't there for the Tarlair case. It's no' there because of me, it's there because of you.'

Sand and gravel filled Logan's mouth. 'Me?'

'Aye, you. Who's the idiot now?'

He cleared his throat. Peered through the open kitchen door and out through the window. There had to be at least a dozen of them out there, with their cameras and their microphones and their notepads. 'Why are they after me?'

'Why do you think? You screwed up the Graham Stirling case and now Stephen Bisset's dead.'

Oh God . . .

Logan stepped away from the door. 'I'm off duty. Tell them to go away.'

'Free country. They can hang about if they like, long as they don't cause a disturbance.'

He rested his head back against the wall. Closed his eyes. 'It's not my fault.'

'Aye, well remember that next time you try calling me an idiot.*'*

The line went dead.

Perfect. As if Napier's witch-hunt wasn't bad

enough, without the press banging the drum for a full-on crusade.

'Logan? You OK?'

Excellent. Couldn't be better.

He opened his eyes and Helen was standing in the doorway again.

Little wrinkles appeared between her eyebrows. 'Did something happen at the care home? Is Samantha OK?'

'Everything's fine. Just . . . work.' He put his phone away. 'You know what it's like. Always something.'

'Anyway, I couldn't find anything in the kitchen for lunch except tins of lentil soup.' She turned and headed back into the kitchen. 'And I know it must be a favourite, otherwise you wouldn't buy so much of it, but there's only so much lentil I can take.'

He followed her through. Forced a smile. 'Smells good, whatever it is.'

'Mince and tatties. I'm a carrots and peas kind of girl. You didn't have any Bisto.'

'Sorry.'

'Or carrots. Or peas. Or mince. Or onions. You did have potatoes though.' She produced a pair of plates. 'Mash, or boiled?'

'Mash.'

'Good choice.' She poured the tatties, then put them back on the stove with milk and a wodge of butter. Stood mashing away with her back to him. 'It's Natasha's favourite.' Helen fidgeted with her fingers. Looked away. 'Well, it was when she was wee. "Mint an' tatties." I always make too much.' She pointed at the table, set for two – complete with napkins and glasses of water. 'Ready to serve up if you are.'

'Thanks.'

'Mint an' tatties. Markanory cheese an' chibs. She used to love anything you could gloop about with a fork . . .' Helen dug the potato masher out of the drawer. 'Of course *Brian* always wanted her to eat paella and chorizo and all the rest of it. She told him pale ella tastes of worms. And it'd all kick off again. How I was disrespecting his Spanish heritage. And I'd point out he wasn't *actually* Spanish, he was born in Dalkeith. Didn't even visit Spain till he was three.' Helen's head dipped. 'Same age Natasha was when he abducted her.'

She battered the potatoes into submission. 'So I'd shut up and make his stupid paella and maybe he wouldn't scream at me. Or maybe he would. And this, children, is how we play happy families.'

More potato battering.

'Why didn't you leave him?'

'Right, I think we're about ready.' She glopped tatties and mince onto two plates. Then sank into the chair opposite.

Logan dug a fork into the mash, scooped up a glob of mince – dark brown, flecked with glistening slivers of onion and emerald green peas.

She rubbed her fingertips across her stomach.

Mouth pinched into a circular scar, eyebrows pinched. 'Is it OK?'

He swallowed. Dug out another forkful. 'Thanks. It's lovely.'

'Are you *sure* it's OK? I know lentil soup's your favourite, but . . .?'

'Honestly, it's great. I've got loads of lentil soup because it's cheap. And you can sling it in a carrier bag and not worry about it going off if you've left it in the car, in the sun, for four hours. Every station's got a microwave and a toaster.'

She watched him shovel down another forkful. 'So you live on cheap soup and pound-shop bread?'

'A whole pound? Are you kidding? It's nowhere near as expensive as that.'

Helen swirled her fork through her mashed potatoes, leaving it raked like a Zen garden. 'Logan, the thing with work: it wasn't about Natasha, was it?'

'No. It's another case. The labs are still trying to push through the DNA sample you gave us, but . . .' A shrug. 'Not supposed to talk about it, but those severed feet turning up in the Clyde are probably a serial killer. So it's all hands to the pumps on that before he kills someone else. Or the media find out it's not some Protestant sectarian gang thing.'

'I see.'

'They swear blind our samples will be ready Monday.'

She kept her eyes on her plate. 'Right.'

They ate in silence for a bit.

Logan tried for a laugh. Didn't quite make it. 'Suppose that means you're stuck with me for the weekend.'

The clock on the wall ticked.

Helen had a sip of water. 'I was thinking, if we finish painting the bedroom today, I could get cracking on the lounge tomorrow while you're at work. If that's all right?'

He reached across the table and took her hand. 'If I could get them to go any faster, I would. I promise.'

'I know.'

— SATURDAY EARLYSHIFT —

HINDSIGHT IS A TREACHEROUS MIRROR.

CHAPTER 24

'. . . every single time: rats in her bed. And she *hates* the police.' Nicholson clicked the mouse, sending the morning briefing PowerPoint onto the next slide. A grainy CCTV image of what looked like a mosh pit outside a pub. 'OK, so there was a mass altercation outside the Fish and Futrit, in Peterhead, last night – wedding reception got a bit out of hand.'

She looked at Logan.

He took a sip of tea. 'As a result, the Peterhead cells are full and the overspill's in Fraserburgh. Which means . . .?' He thumped a hand down on Tufty's shoulder, making him flinch.

'Er . . . They've got to have two people manning the cell blocks, because it's the law?'

'And when do the courts open again?'

'Monday?'

'So?'

'So . . .' Frown. Think. Think. Think. 'They're going to be short-staffed all weekend?'

'Correct. You win a Crackerjack pencil.' That got him a confused look. 'We're close to minimum staffing levels everywhere, so losing two officers in

315

Peterhead *and* Fraserburgh means we're going to have to pick up the slack.'

Groans.

'Yes, I know. Take it up with the bride and groom's families.'

Tufty stuck his hand up. 'Can't we get some bodies from the Tarlair MIT?'

'They've scaled back the team. Going to run the bulk of it out of Aberdeen instead, to – and I quote – "maximize operational efficiencies". AKA: so they don't have to pay overnights or accommodation.'

Deano twiddled his CS gas canister in its holder. 'Meaning: they've achieved sod all, and now they're running away home.'

'Couldn't possibly comment.' Logan nodded at Nicholson. 'Janet?'

'Luckily it's pretty q . . .' She cleared her throat. 'We're not anticipating much happening on a Saturday morning.'

Deano hissed a breath in through his teeth. 'Ooh, so close to jinxing the whole shift.'

'Shut up.' Back to the slides. 'Anyway. Other things last night: house fire in Rosehearty – one of the cottages on North Street went up. Not being treated as suspicious at this point. Four break-ins at Pennan during the wee small hours – variety of electrical goods, books, knick-knacks, and some jewellery reported missing.'

Logan put his mug down. 'Deano, you and Tufty go past and do the CSI thing. Photos and fingerprints. Fly the flag.'

'Sarge.'

'Four break-ins is a *lot* for somewhere that wee. Door-to-door the whole village. I want to get a result on this one.'

Nicholson moved on. 'Two drink drivers taken – one outside Strichen, the other on the A947 north of Keilhill. Silly sod left the road and ended up on his roof in a field. And last, but not least, our boy the peeper's prowling Melrose Crescent again. We now have a description.' Click, and the screen changed to a hazy identikit picture of a man. 'Vague and blurry and sod all use.'

She sat back in her seat. 'Sarge?'

'Good. Right, first off: I understand congratulations are in order for Deano's barbecue on Thursday night . . .'

Nicholson and Tufty clapped while Deano did a slow three-sixty spin on his office chair, both hands in the air as if he'd just run a marathon, or been asked to hand over his wallet at gunpoint. 'Thank you, thank you.'

A grin from Tufty. 'Should've been there, Sarge. We had a bouncy castle!'

'Seriously?'

Nicholson nodded. 'My uncle's got one. Says we can have it for the station open day in June, if we want.'

'Done.' Logan pulled out his notebook and scribbled it down. 'Secondly: Klingon and Gerbil have been remanded without bail. Pair of them are going to be banged up in Craiginches till it's time to try them. Word from Queen Street is that our involvement will be restricted to giving evidence in court, they've set up an MIT to handle everything else.'

Deano puffed out his cheeks. 'Big of them.'

'And thirdly: I don't care if the Tarlair MIT is slinking off back to Aberdeen with its tail between its legs, it doesn't mean *we're* giving up. Keep your eyes *open* when you're out there, OK? Neil Wood didn't vanish off the face of the earth, he went to ground. He has to come out sometime.' Logan thumped his notebook closed. 'And when he does, we're going to be there to nab him.'

There was a knock on the Sergeants' Office door, and Tufty stuck his head in. 'Sarge? Did you know there's a tramp sleeping in the canteen?'

Logan looked up from his keyboard. Frowned. 'Tramp?'

'Half sprawled across the table. Snoring and farting.'

He sat back in his seat. Narrowed his eyes. 'Male or female?'

'Woman. Hair all Albert Einstein meets semtex.'

Of course it was.

'Better put the kettle on, Tufty. One coffee: milk and two. I'll have a tea.'

'Sarge.'

'And give your tramp a poke. Send her through.'

Logan went back to his screen, checking the other Banff station teams were up to date with their actions. Adding comments. Flagging a couple to follow up.

Next up: Crimefile.

'Gnnnph . . .' Steel slumped against the doorframe, looking as if she'd hired a drunken gorilla as a personal stylist. Her mouth cracked wide in a long shuddering yawn that ended with a little burp. Then some blinking.

He checked his watch. 'It's not even eight yet. To what do we owe this honour?'

'I *hate* dayshift.' Another yawn.

Tufty reappeared with a mug in either hand. Put one down on Logan's desk, then looked from him to the scruffy monster slouched on the threshold and back again. 'Sarge?'

Steel stuck out both hands. 'Coffee. Coffee, now. Coffee make feel better.'

Logan logged into Crimefile. 'Constable Stewart Quirrel, meet Detective Chief Inspector Roberta Steel. Tarlair Major Investigation Team.'

'Ah. OK. Here you go, Boss.' He passed her the other mug.

She buried her face in it, making slurping noises.

Tufty pulled his eyebrows up and his mouth down at the edges, doing a fair impression of a startled frog. Then jerked his head at Steel a couple of times. Creased his nose, as if he'd caught a whiff of something stinky. Steel still hadn't looked up from her coffee.

'All right, Tufty, that's enough. Go find something useful to do.'

'You want me and Deano to hit Pennan?'

'Have you finished updating your actions?'

Pink bloomed across Tufty's cheeks. 'Sarge.'

Soon as he was gone, Steel scuffed her way over to the desk that backed onto Logan's and collapsed into the chair. Cracked another huge juddering yawn. 'Pfff . . . Your bed's a lot comfier than that manky hotel.'

'You look like you climbed out of a skip.'

'I hate you . . .' More slurping at the mug. 'Why haven't I got any biscuits?'

'Ask your boyfriend, DS Dawson.' Logan checked his Crimefile in-tray. Three requests to put a tweet out about a serious assault in Mintlaw. The face of modern policing.

'Do you a swap: your hovel for my nice luxurious hotel room. Wee bottles of shampoo and all the fresh towels you can eat.'

'Nope. What's happening with your Tarlair case?'

'You get breakfast too. Sausage, egg, and tattie scones. You'd like that. Put a bit of meat on your bones.'

'Did you come in here to moan, or are you planning on doing some actual work today?'

She hunched forward in her seat, both hands wrapped around her mug as if it was the only thing keeping her from freezing to death. 'They're winding us back again. Four days and we've no' got a single sodding clue about who the wee girl is, or who killed her.'

'I heard.' He popped onto Twitter and hammered

320

in the requested appeal for witnesses. Fighting crime 140 characters at a time. 'So you're heading back to Aberdeen then.'

At least that meant they'd get their station back. Could throw open a few windows and get rid of the stink of desperation, failure, and the aftermath of too many laxatives.

'You should be so lucky.' She stretched out her arms, twisted her head to one side and arched her back. Grunted. Yawned. Shuddered. 'Skeleton staff are staying behind to direct B Division in its enquiries.'

Of course they were.

'So, basically, the MIT couldn't find its own backside in a sleeping bag, and now it's *our* problem.' He closed his eyes, folded forward and dunked his forehead off the desk. 'Oh, *lucky* us.'

'You're in no position to be sarcastic. Stephen Bisset's dead, remember?'

As if he could forget, with it being all over the papers for the last two days. At least they'd given up hanging about outside the station.

Steel poked him in the shoulder. 'And do you know what they found when they went through the CCTV from the hospital? Sod all. Ran all the faces through the system and not one of them's got anything to do with Stirling. So your "accomplice" theory's about as much use as DS Rennie.' She cricked her head from side to side. Rubbed at the base of her neck. 'Still can't believe no one saw anything.'

'Are you sure you don't want to head back to Aberdeen with the rest of them? Maybe leave someone less annoying behind instead?'

'You'd think they'd notice a bloke going in, having a wank over Stephen Bisset, and suffocating him, wouldn't you? Got to be a *wee* bit conspicuous, standing there with your sausage d'amour in one hand and a pillow in the other.'

Logan stared at her. 'They found semen on the body? Do a DNA match!'

'Aye, thank you, Hercule Poirot, we had actually thought of that. No hit from the database. Tell you, the press will go ape when it comes out.' She blew out a sigh, slurped down some more coffee. 'Was bad enough when they only had Graham Stirling to batter us with, but this? This piles on extra baboons. Wee sod might be keeping his head down right now, but you can bet your itchy police trousers he'll be back with a massive law suit, and it'll all flange up again. See if I was you? I'd be sucking up to anyone in a position to deflect a bit of the crap away from me.'

'I told you: I'm not joining your MIT. I *can't*.'

She held up her hands. 'Just saying.'

'Well, just don't. It's bad enough—'

Three quick knocks on the door, and Steel's right-hand woman stuck her head into the Sergeants' Office. 'Boss?'

Steel didn't even look at her. 'For the last time, Becky, you're no' escaping back to Aberdeen till Dawson gets out of hospital. You're no' much, but you're all I've got to keep these bunnets in line.'

DS McKenzie's neck darkened and the creases around the bottom of her mouth deepened. 'It's about the CCTV footage from the hospital. There's no one on it that isn't meant to be, right? I mean we've got doctors, nurses, volunteers, that consultant urologist . . .' She left a dramatic pause. 'And Bisset's kids.'

Steel rested her elbows on the desk, head dangling over the coffee cup. 'You seriously suggesting it was his kids?'

McKenzie stepped into the room and closed the door behind her. 'I know it's a long shot, but think about it. They—'

'Laz, I'm too knackered. You do it.'

Logan pointed at the spare seat. 'You want to sit?'

She didn't. Instead she leaned on Steel's side of the desk. 'Come on, Boss, no one's ever going to suspect them, are they?'

He bit down on his lips. Be nice. 'Well . . .' Frown. No point making her look stupid, but it wouldn't be easy. 'I can see where you're coming from, DS McKenzie, but it doesn't really tally with the semen they found on Stephen Bisset's body.'

Silence. Then McKenzie's face creased in around her nose. 'Sod.'

Steel must have decided that she could be bothered after all, because she sat up. Pointed. 'They're brother and sister, Becky. They're no' likely to murder their dear old dad then crack one off over his still-warm corpse, are they? It's Aberdeen, no' *Game of Sodding Thrones.*'

The flush on DS McKenzie's neck deepened. She forced a smile that looked painful as a whole-pineapple suppository. 'I see . . .' Deep breath. Her chin came up. 'Anything else?'

Steel waved a hand in the vague direction of the door. 'Away and see if anyone's spotted Neil Wood yet. Nonces don't vanish into thin air.'

A curt nod. 'Boss.' Then daggers at Logan, as if somehow it was his fault. '*Sergeant.*' And she was off, slamming the door on the way.

The blast of air ruffled the Post-its stuck to Logan's desk.

He blew out a breath. 'That went well.'

'Told you – one poke away from an aneurism.'

'So stop poking her.' He skiffed his fingertips back and forth on the desktop a couple of times. Looked out of the window as the guilt twisted a little knife into his chest. 'DS Dawson's still in hospital then?'

'Serves him right. Never trust a kebab, that's my motto.' She slurped at her coffee again, then frowned. 'Sure you've no' got any biscuits?'

The familiar, depressing sounds of a hospital ticking over, hummed and buzzed and clanked and murmured down the corridor. Logan stuck his back to the wall and his finger in his other ear. 'Say again, Deano?'

'Aye, that's us going round and round Rundle Avenue again. Got a call your mate Frankie Ferris was getting a lot of visitors.'

Logan checked his watch. 'At twenty past eight on a Saturday morning? Only way he's awake this early is if he didn't go to bed last night.'

'My thoughts exactly. But we got the call, so we diverted from Pennan to drive round and round in circles looking for early-riser druggies who don't exist.'

The door at the end of the corridor opened and a young woman in pale blue scrubs stepped out. Stack of folders pinned under one arm. Short brown hair, twin scars reaching from beneath her nose and through her top lip.

'OK: give it another couple of laps then call it. With Klingon and Gerbil out of the way, someone's got to be picking up the slack. Might as well be Frankie Ferris.' Logan stuck his Airwave back on his shoulder and walked over. 'Doctor?'

She flashed him a smile that looked as if it needed another eight hours' sleep. 'Can I help you?'

Logan pointed at the door she'd come out of. 'Jack Simpson.'

'Ah, right.' One of the folders came out and she rummaged inside it. Produced a sheet of paper and squinted at it. 'Concussion, ruptured spleen, fractured skull, broken ribs, left femur, right tibula and fibula, left humerus and—'

'That's the one. He awake yet?'

She pursed her lips for a moment. Sniffed. Probably not used to being cut off mid-flow. 'Mr Simpson regained consciousness this morning. The swelling's gone down, so we're confident he'll make a complete recovery. Though, obviously, he's going to need a *lot* of physiotherapy.'

'Can I talk to him?'

'I've got to warn you, he's a bit . . . fractious.'

No surprise there – Jack Simpson probably hadn't had a day off the heroin in years. Still, at least he'd have been sedated through the worst of the withdrawal symptoms.

Logan slipped into the room.

The blinds were half open, throwing bars of light across the floor and bed. A TV set was mounted to the wall, the picture flickering in time with some far-off machinery. A reporter in a suit was doing a piece to camera, microphone held like a knuckleduster in one hand. '. . . *Prime Minister announced today that Detective Constable Mary Ann Nasrallah of Merseyside Police would be posthumously awarded the Queen's Police Medal for Gallantry. We're over live to Westminster . . .*'

Jack Simpson lay spread out on top of the sheets: both arms and both legs in plaster, a neck brace squeezing his chin up, bandages around his head. Face a dark swathe of purple and yellow. Lips swollen and lined with scabs.

'. . . *dedicated undercover officer whose tragic shooting last Sunday only goes to demonstrate—*'

Logan killed the TV with the remote. Gave Jack

326

Simpson a smile. 'Klingon and Gerbil really did a number on you, didn't they, Jack?'

Two bloodshot eyes blinked back at him. 'Gntt sttfffd.'

'Now, now, is that any way to talk to the guy who saved your life?' He carried the plastic chair from the corner to the bedside. Settled into it. 'Sorry, didn't bring you any grapes.'

'Mm nntt saynn nthnn.'

'OK, how about you listen for a bit instead? When I found you in Klingon's attic, you were half dead. Between the internal bleeding, toxic shock, and dehydration, the doctors say you'd have lasted maybe another day. Maybe two. Max.'

Simpson lay there, scowling at the ceiling.

'They tried to kill you, Jack. They nearly battered you to death, then they stuck you in the attic. If I hadn't looked up there, that would've been it. No more Jack Simpson.'

Not that anyone would really have mourned *that* loss. There wasn't a single 'GET WELL SOON' card in the room; no teddy bears, Mylar balloons, or bunches of flowers. The only things decorating the unit by the bed were a sippy cup and a box of tissues.

But then who was going to wish a drug dealer a speedy recovery? By now his customers would have found someone else to sell their favourite poison. Not even his mum and dad cared about poor old Jack Simpson.

Logan leaned forward and knocked on the cast encasing Simpson's right arm. 'Do you want Klingon and Gerbil to get away with it? Let bygones be bygones?'

A breath hissed out between the cracked lips. 'Klll thmmm.'

'How you going to do that, Jack?' He pointed at the bag hanging on a stand beneath the level of the bed, connected to a tube that disappeared under Simpson's hospital gown. 'You can't even pee on your own.'

Logan sat forward. Lowered his voice. 'Right now, they'll be cutting a deal. Ratting out whoever sold them the drugs in exchange for a reduced sentence. Who knows, if the intel's good enough, they might even walk. That what you want?'

A cough. Then another one. Spittle flying from his lips. Eyes squeezed shut, chipped teeth bared with every convulsion. Till it was over and he slumped back into his pillow. Dragging in rattly breaths. Face nearly scarlet between the bruises. 'Watrr . . .'

Logan took the sippy cup from the beside unit and held it to Simpson's lips. 'Slow and steady. That's it. Don't choke yourself.'

The breathing slowed, his face returning to its normal unhealthy pallor.

'Better?'

'Am I under arrest?' The words came out with a slight lisp.

'Nope. You're the victim here, Jack. All we want

is to make sure the guys who did this to you don't get away with it.'

He frowned at the ceiling for a bit.

A trolley clattered by in the corridor outside.

Voices faded in the distance.

Then Simpson nodded – not much, just a small bob of the chin, restrained by the neck brace. 'A scummer from down south supplied the stuff.'

'Hold on.' Logan slipped the elastic band off his body-worn video and set it recording. 'Sergeant Logan McRae, eight thirty-two a.m., twenty-fourth of May, Chalmers Hospital. Interview with Jack Simpson.' Pulled out his notebook. 'OK, back to the beginning. Who supplied the heroin in Colin Spinney's mum's house?'

That got him a look. 'His mum's house? You mental? She's been gone for, like, years.'

'Years? I know she's in Australia, but—'

'Guy who supplied the drugs was a Geordie, or a Scouser. Somewhere like that with the accent, you know?'

Logan scribbled it down. 'What's his name?' Probably a waste of time: Klingon and Gerbil would have spilled their guts to whoever was running the investigation in five minutes flat. By now, their supplier would be under arrest, or on the run. Either way, he wouldn't be hanging around Banff. But still . . .

'Nah.' Simpson looked as if he was trying to frown, but his battered face wasn't cooperating. 'Called him some stupid nickname, like . . .

Candleman? Or Candlestick Man? Something like that. Only met him once: short, and broad, you know? Like a wee rugby player, or a boxer. Hard man.'

'Age? Hair colour? Distinguishing features?'

'Vicious bastard stood there, egging Gerbil and Klingon on while they took turns with the baseball bat . . .' Tears glistened Simpson's eyes. Spilled over onto his bruised cheeks. 'Told them they had to . . . had to keep . . .' He pulled his head back an inch, fighting against the neck brace, pushing himself into the pillows. Blinking it back. 'I'm lying there on the garage floor, screaming and trying to cover my head, and they're hammering away at me, and everything's . . . God it hurt so bad.' The tears were flowing freely now, a line of silver bubbling out of one nostril as he shook. 'And they *laughed*! They laughed as they battered the crap out of me.' A shudder ran up his body, setting the casts twitching. Deep breaths, wheezing on the way in, hissing on the way out.

Logan put his pen down. 'You want a break?'

'Want a sodding hit. The morphine here's pish . . .'

It took a couple of minutes, but the shudders passed, and Simpson's breathing returned to normal.

Logan pulled two tissues from the unit by the bed. Stood and dabbed at Simpson's face with them. Cleared up the tears and the worst of the snot. 'What did you do, Jack? Why did the . . .'

He sat down again and checked his notes. 'Why did this Candlestick Man want Kevin McEwan and Colin Spinney to kill you?'

'Kill us? Naw, that was just day one.' What was probably meant to be a laugh crowbarred its way out of Jack Simpson's ruined mouth. 'Scummers hauled me out the attic next day and did it again. And the day after. I *begged* them to kill me.'

'But they wouldn't.'

'Candleboy told them this was how they built a rep. A week of . . . of breaking every bone in my body, then turf me out on the street. And when word got round no one would ever screw with them again.' He bared the jagged stumps of his teeth. 'Wasn't personal, it was business.'

'So why'd they pick you?'

A tiny little smile curled one side of Simpson's mouth. 'Turns out they don't like it when you help yourself to free samples . . .'

CHAPTER 25

Logan stood on the pavement outside the hospital, flicking back through his notebook to last Monday. Found Kirstin Rattray's number and keyed it into his mobile. Listened to it ring. And ring. And ring. And—

'*Pmmmmph . . .*' A thick, muggy yawn came from the other end. The words sticky and malformed. '*Whtmisit?*'

'Kirstin? It's Sergeant McRae.'

A small whimper. Then a man's voice in the background. '*Who the hell's that?*'

'*It's . . . my mum. Something's up with Amy. Dunno . . . school stuff.*' Back to the phone. '*Mum, hold on, I'll go make a cuppa and we can chat.*'

'*And close the bloody door.*'

Clunk. Then she was back, voice a low whisper. '*Are you mental? You can't call me at home!*'

'Better put the kettle on. Don't want whoever it is to wonder why they can't hear it boiling.'

'*If Klingon and Gerbil find out I talked to the cops they'll kill me!*'

'After what we found in their house? No chance.

332

The pair of them are going away for at least sixteen years.'

'*And what about the guy supplied them? You think he'll be happy all his gear's been thieved by the plod?*'

'Well, we'll just have to do something about him, won't we? My boss wants you registered as a Covert Human Intelligence Source, so we can—'

'*You told your* boss? *God's sake . . .*' Some rattling and thumping, then the click-rumble-rattle of a kettle. '*You want me dead, that what you want? You want my wee Amy to end up an orphan?*'

'That's why it's better to go on the books.'

'*Don't understand why you can't leave us alone. Never did nothing to you.*'

'It all gets handled through Aberdeen, you never even have to speak to me again.'

'*You got any idea what they do to grasses? Like all my fingers where they are, thank you very much!*'

'It's not grassing, it's helping keep your community safe. You want little Amy to grow up somewhere safe, don't you?' He shifted the phone to his other ear as a manky old Land Rover rattled past, haunted by the cloud of blue-grey smoke billowing out of its exhaust pipe. 'Have you ever heard of someone called the Candleman? Maybe Candlestick Man?'

'*Are you off your head?*'

'He'd be from Newcastle or Liverpool. Wee guy, but fancies himself a bit dangerous?'

'*No.*'

A little old lady stepped off the kerb, shoulders hunched, pulling an ancient Westie behind her. It walked on stiff limbs, its once-white coat stained like a smoker's teeth.

The Land Rover's driver leaned on his horn, forcing out an asthmatic honk.

The old lady scurried back to the kerb and glowered as it passed. Stepped out onto the road again and stuck two fingers up at the departing smokescreen. The manky Westie managed a bark.

Auld wifies, got to love them.

'. . . *are you even listening to me?*'

Ah, right. Back to the phone. 'Sure you don't know him?'

'*Can I go back to bed now?*'

Ah well, it'd been worth a try. 'Give whoever it is my best when you get there.'

The old woman doddered across the road towards him, grumbling and swearing away to herself. Westie lumbering behind her like a broken wind-up toy.

Hmm . . .

'. . . *can go bugger yourself with a—*'

'Listen, while I've got you: Klingon's mum.'

Pause. '*What about her?*'

'You said she'd gone to Australia. When?'

'*Dunno. Couple of months? Does it matter?*'

'What was she like: scruffy? Drunk? Bit of a druggie?'

'*You're kidding, aren't you? Like she was born starched, holding a can of Mr Sheen in one hand and*'

334

a vacuum in the other. Had to take your shoes off at the door.'

She was in for a shock when she came home and saw the state of the place, then.

'Don't suppose you've got a contact number for her, do you?'

'Yeah, cause my middle name's "Yellow Sodding Pages". God's sake . . .' And Kirstin was gone. Back to bed with whoever was financing her habit today.

A couple of months in Australia. Long enough for Kevin and Gerbil to turn the house into the sub-slum pit they'd raided?

Maybe. Maybe not.

The old lady was getting closer, brows down, mouth chewing through a buffet of profanity.

Logan keyed Maggie's number into his Airwave handset. 'Aye, Maggie: does your Bill still work for the Council?'

'Depends on your definition of "working."'

'Do me a favour – see if he's got any friends in Housing. I need them to find out who's paying rent on Klingon and Gerbil's place.'

'On a Saturday?'

'They don't call you the miracle worker for nothing.'

The old lady came to a halt in a waft of Ralgex and peppermint. She jabbed a twisted finger in the direction of the dissipating exhaust fumes. Flashed her dentures like she was about to bite him. 'Did you see that?' Up close, she barely came up to his breast pocket.

'*Well, I'll see what I can do. But no promises.*'

'Thanks, Maggie. And put the kettle on, I'll be back at the ranch in five.' He put his Airwave handset back on its mount 'Now, how can I help?'

'People like that should be taken out and shot! Beeping his horn, like it's *my* fault. Little sod. I'm eighty-two!'

'Well, at least you're OK, that's the important—'

'They've got no manners at all. None. It's like living in the *Lord of the Flies*.' She sniffed. Chewed for a bit. 'Got a good mind to get myself a shotgun and teach them all a lesson.'

'Yeah. Probably not such a good idea.'

'I blame the parents. This is what happens when you tell people they can't smack their children. I'm eighty-two and my father would leather the living hell out of me and my brothers for leaving the *toilet lid* up! Never mind cheeking my elders.'

Behind her, the Westie sank its backside onto the pavement and sat there puffing and panting with its mouth hanging open, tongue lolling over a row of stumpy brown teeth.

She gave a little yank on the lead, hauling the dog back to its feet again. 'And have you *seen* what they've done to the billboard by the bridge? A great big purple willy, painted right across the nice man from the SNP. It's a disgrace.'

Wonderful – Geoffrey Lovejoy, their resident political analyst, strikes again.

Logan nodded. Backed away a step. 'Right. Yes. A disgrace.'

'I wouldn't put it past the Tories to do something like this. It's their level. It's not a by-election, it's a war zone.' Getting closer with every word, forcing him back against the wall.

Logan put his cap on his head. Slipped sideways out of the gap between her and the hospital's granite blocks. 'Right, well . . .' He pointed over his shoulder back towards the bay and the bridge and the big purple willy. 'I'd better go see what we can do about that billboard.'

Her parting call growled out behind him. 'I'm eighty-sodding-two!'

'Roger that, we are two minutes away . . .' Logan clutched at the grab handle above the passenger door as Nicholson roared past a joiner's van. The Big Car's blue lights strobed through the morning air, accompanying the siren's throbbing wail.

They flashed through the town limits. 'WELCOME TO PORTSOY PLEASE DRIVE CAREFULLY'. So much for that – the needle on the speedo ticked up past seventy.

Be advised, perpetrators are still at the scene.

Bungalows on one side of the road, fields of lustrous green on the other.

Logan clicked the button again, talking into the Airwave pinned to his stabproof. 'Copy that.'

Nicholson turned and flashed him a grin. 'We're going to catch them red-handed!'

'Just watch the road.'

The bungalows gave way to old-style Scottish

granite, then trees – whipping past the Big Car's windows. Then into Portsoy proper, with its ancient, flat-fronted granite. A hard right onto Seafield Street, the engine howling as Nicholson battered down the gears and hit the brakes, then on with the power again. Accelerating past shops and little old ladies. A minibus with 'C'MON THE SOY !!!!' lettered down the side, little kids dressed in black-and-white-striped football tops staring as the car wheeched by.

Logan jabbed a finger. 'There.'

Nicholson hammered on the brakes, slithering them to a halt outside the bus stop.

Little cubes of glass, tins, packets, and jars spread across the road in front of the Co-op. The signage above the windows was buckled out on the side closest to them, the support beneath the word 'Co-operative' missing – the glass it held in place reduced to a sagging web around the edges. A hole ripped through the knee-high blockwork beneath it.

No sign of whoever did it.

Logan jumped out, grabbed his peaked cap. 'You!' pointing at a young woman with a push-chair. 'Which way did they go? What are they driving?'

There was a pause, then her arm came up. 'One of them big four-by-fours. Erm . . . blue? I think?'

He got back in. Thumped the dashboard. 'Go!'

Nicholson put her foot down again and the Big Car roared forward.

'Shire Uniform Seven to Control, perpetrators have fled the scene. Witness says they took the Cullen road. We're in pursuit.'

'Do you have visual?'

The car powered past leafy gardens and someone walking their dog.

'Negative.'

Three cars, a bus, a removal van, and a tanker – all coming the other way – pulled into the side of the road, giving them a clear run at it. More than could be said for the idiot with the caravan blocking this side of the road.

Nicholson thumped the steering wheel. 'Out of the way you mouldy old sod!' Soon as they'd cleared the tanker she wrenched the Big Car onto the other side of the road and accelerated past the caravan. 'Can't have missed them by much . . .'

Logan clicked his Airwave again. 'Where's everyone else?'

'Units are on their way. Closest is fifteen minutes away.'

'Tell them to hit the A98 soon as they can. We're looking for a blue four-by-four. No make or model known, but the back end will be all dented in.'

A petrol station whizzed by on the left, then a plumber's, then the fringe of a housing estate. The speedo hit ninety as they flashed through the limits and out into the countryside again.

'Roger that.'

Ten seconds later the lookout request crackled from the Big Car's radio. *'All units be on the lookout for a blue four-wheel-drive vehicle heading west on the A98 . . .'*

With any luck, this time, they were actually going to catch them.

CHAPTER 26

'Anything?'

Nicholson looked up from her Airwave and shook her head. 'No sign of them anywhere.'

Logan tied the end of the 'POLICE' tape to the downpipe between the two parts of the Co-op. On one side it took up the bottom floor of a three-storey granite building, but the main entrance – the side that had been raided – was a single-storey extension, painted white with green buckled frontage. A red post box positioned by the entrance. The other end of the blue-and-white cordon was wrapped around it, like the ribbon on a very boring present, then stretched out to an orange cone in the middle of the road in front of it, and on to another in front of the downpipe. A nice big rectangle, protecting the scene.

The Big Car blocked the other side of the road, its lights spinning in the sunshine.

A bleep from his Airwave. Then, *'Sarge, it's Deano. Safe to talk?'*

'Fire away.'

'Me and Tufty have been round the burglaries in

Pennan. No witnesses. Got some pretty odd stuff gone missing though. There's the usual iPads and DVDs and phones, bit of cash and jewellery, but one lot's missing a bible from 1875, a First World War bayonet, and a Georgian vase. House next door's missing paintings from the 1920s. One next to that's lost a crystal decanter set from the Cutty Sark.'

Logan hauled open the Big Car's boot. 'M.O.E.?'

'Popped a pane of glass in the back doors. Thing is, Sarge, how'd you know to take a decanter set and ignore a CD player?'

'Stealing to order maybe? That or he's got an interest. Run a check on the PNC, maybe we can get a quick result on this one.' Logan pulled the dustpan and long-handled broom from the boot. 'Keep me up to date, OK?'

'Will do.'

He handed the broom and dustpan to Nicholson. 'And before you start moaning, it's not because you're a woman, it's because you're a constable.'

Her face drooped. 'Sarge.'

'Clear this side of the road. Soon as it's done, shift the car and get traffic moving again. Don't sweep up anything inside the cordon.' He picked his way through the scattered debris into the store. Inside, it looked as if a bomb had gone off. Ground Zero was the gap where the two windows had been, spreading impulse-buy items, tins, and lottery tickets out in a fan of destruction. A display stand of newspapers was smashed in half, canted over – spilling out its collection of red-top tabloids, gossip magazines, and issues of *Farmers Weekly*.

A handful of breezeblocks from the caved-in sill.

The manager sat behind the counter, cup of tea and packet of Rennies in front of her, mobile phone to her ear. Green shirt and black fleece. 'STACEY', according to her name badge. Round-shouldered, going grey, and smelling of pepper-mint. She crunched down another antacid. 'I don't know, Mike. It's up to the police. But the whole place . . .' She stared out at it. Sagged a little further. 'I'll let you know soon as I do.'

Logan stood at the counter, amongst the drifts of newsprint and lotto tickets.

It could be you.

But today it was Stacey.

She blinked up at him. 'Got to go.' Hung up. Put her phone down. 'Sorry. Head office. Wanted to know if everyone was OK.'

Logan nodded at the hole where the two windows used to be. The rest of them were blocked off with shelves and display units. 'Where was the cash machine?'

She pointed over the counter at a clean rectan-gular patch on the floor, with four sheared bolts and a snapped length of electrical flex. 'It was like . . . I don't know. The window exploded and there was glass and things everywhere and it was over so quickly.' Stacey wrapped her hands around her tea. 'Thought everything was supposed to slow down, but: *whoosh*.' A shudder.

343

'How about CCTV?'

A nod. Then a deep breath. 'Yes. CCTV. We can do that.'

She led him through the wreckage to much cleaner aisles. Past the crisps and cat food to a double door. Pushed into a backroom store full of cages of breakfast cereal and tatties. A little office sat on one side. Stacey opened the door and ushered him inside. 'Three cameras cover the front of the shop: two inside, one out.'

A worktop desk ran along two walls, complete with computer, two phones, and a pair of office chairs. A monitor was mounted in the corner, above a bank of digital recording stuff. Eight views of the shop filled the screen, each with a little timer ticking over in the corner. Only one view was nothing but static.

Stacey picked a remote from the top of the recording boxes and sank into one of the chairs. She poked at the buttons, sending the timers clattering backwards.

Ten minutes. Twenty. Thirty. Forty – and the static disappeared, replaced by a view of the shop from a point above the display stand where people were meant to fill out their lottery tickets.

'Here we go.'

The screens froze.

Camera four showed an old man juggling a basket and a two-litre bottle of Irn-Bru. Six had a young girl dangling a teddy bear by its leg, while an older woman weighed up the difference between two loaves of bread. Camera one was an exterior shot from above the front door. And camera two had Stacey, sitting behind the counter hunched over some sort of paperwork.

Play.

The old man dropped the basket. The little girl skipped along the aisle.

A big blue four-by-four reversed into shot on camera one, swung round and its rear-end smashed into the window beside the door.

Camera two filled with exploding glass and dust, flying tins and packets. All in perfect silence.

Debris blocked the view of cameras two-to-three, but the others showed shelves shaking. The older woman clasping the bread to her chest like a parachute.

Camera three went to static.

It took a couple of seconds for camera two to clear, and when it did the back half of the huge four-by-four jutted into the shop. Not a Range Rover or a sporty job, a proper huge one with a loadbay and canopy. Toyota Hilux, or a Mitsubishi Warrior? Difficult to tell from this angle. Maybe it was an Isuzu? Something like that. The sort of thing you could chuck bales of hay or a couple of sheep into.

Ceiling tiles and tins lay on top of the canopy.

Camera one: the car's back doors popped open and two figures swarmed out and into the shop, climbing through the shattered hole where the windows used to be. Black ski masks, gloves, tracksuits. One had a length of heavy-duty chain in his hands. He wrapped it around the base of the cash machine, while his mate clipped the other end onto the four-by-four's towbar.

Mr Towbar jumped back and thumped on the side of the vehicle. Mr Chain hurried behind the cash machine as whoever was at the wheel put their foot down, snapping the chain taut and ripping the whole machine from its moorings.

Then Mr Chain and Mr Towbar opened the canopy lid, thumped down the tailgate, and humped the cash machine into the loadbay. Shut everything up and clambered out through the broken window again.

Camera one caught them clambering back into the four-by-four and it roared off. Inside the shop, a chunk of ceiling tiles collapsed.

Pause. Two. Three. Four. And then Stacey peeked out from behind the counter.

The whole thing had taken a little over a minute.

Brilliant. So much for *'Be advised, perpetrators are still at the scene.'*

Logan put a mug of tea on Nicholson's desk.

'Thanks, Sarge.' She cleared her throat, leaned over in her seat to peer out through the open Constables' Office door. Then back again, voice lowered to a whisper. 'Maggie told me that DS Dawson's *still* in hospital.'

'Yup.' He took a sip of his own tea. Hot and milky. 'We're never mentioning it again, remember?'

'Yeah, but, Sarge, maybe, you know, if they knew

what caused it, they might have more luck fixing him? I don't know, we could do it anonymously, or something? They wouldn't have to know it was us . . .'

'They'd know. And *you'll* never make it in CID if you can't keep a secret.'

She pulled a face. 'Yes, Sarge.'

He headed back through to the Sergeants' Office.

Inspector McGregor sat in the other chair, digging through the contents of a large cardboard box. 'Do we have any triple-A batteries? All I can find are double-A's. Hundreds and hundreds of double-A's . . .'

'Sorry, Guv – the Alcometers are all double.' Logan settled in behind his desk. 'I can get Tufty to pick some up on his way back?'

She pushed the box away. 'A little bird tells me there was a crowd of journalists outside most of yesterday.'

Ah. He took a sip of tea. Arranged his notepad, Post-its, and keyboard into a straight line. Tried for a nonchalant shrug. 'Didn't notice. I was busy painting the house.'

'They were very interested in talking to you. Apparently, now Stephen Bisset's dead, the story's become a lot more shiny. Anything you want to tell me?'

His head dropped. 'It wasn't my fault.'

'I don't like journalists staking out my stations, Logan, it makes the public nervous. Makes it look like we've done something wrong.'

'It wasn't my fault! I did what . . .' He sighed. 'We've been over this.'

'Of course, things might have gone a bit better if you'd actually caught the Cashline Ram-Raiders this morning, instead of letting them get away.'

'I didn't *lose* them, they were long gone by the time we got there. I saw the security-camera footage: whole thing was over in eighty-two seconds.' He sat forward and poked the desk with a finger. 'The only way we could've got to Portsoy *before* they sodded off is if Police Scotland issued us with a TARDIS.'

'Thought they were still at the scene?'

'I checked with the control room – turns out the guy who said the Ram-Raiders were still there was blootered. Not bad going for half nine on a Saturday morning.'

The Inspector picked up a manila folder. Tapped the edge against the desk. 'Did you hear? Traffic stopped a blue Isuzu D-max a mile north of Keith.'

A smile bloomed on Logan's face. 'That's great. Did—'

'Wasn't them. Still, it's not our problem any more, it's DI McCulloch and his MIT's.'

The smile faded. 'Does it really not bug you? Every time something big comes up, we've got to hand it over?'

She dumped the folder on his desk. 'Appraisal results, hot off the press from Division Headquarters. The Big Boss says Maggie can have two and a half percent and not a penny more.'

'Better than nothing.' He opened the folder, pulled out the printouts. 'Oh, I spoke to Jack Simpson this morning.'

'And how is everyone's favourite drug-dealing minker?'

'Lucky to be alive, and feeling vindictive. Got a sworn statement off him, fingering Klingon and Gerbil for assault. They weren't trying to kill him, they were trying to put the fear of God into everyone else. *And* whoever supplied the drugs is down as an accessory. So, soon as the MIT are done with their drugs charges, we can ask the PF to prosecute.'

'Excellent.' She hopped down from the desk. Straightened her police-issue T-shirt. 'Don't suppose he ID'd the supplier?'

'Best he could do is: wee hardman from Newcastle or Liverpool, calling himself the Candleman, or Candlestick Man. Doesn't know his real name. I'm going to call round, see if anyone recognizes the alias.'

'Well, keep me informed.' She paused in the doorway. 'It *does* bother me when the MITs swoop in and grab everything. But it is what it is. We just have to try and get one in under the radar every now and then.'

CHAPTER 27

Logan folded his arms and leaned against the alley wall. 'Really?'

Sammy Wilson blinked a couple of times with his good eye – the other swollen and darkened, the skin turned purple-blue and green. Looked down at the paper bag in his grubby skeletal hand. Licked his thin lips with a pale tongue. Then sniffed. 'Yeah . . . I wasn't . . . This . . .' He looked over his shoulder where Nicholson blocked his escape route.

A cough.

Another sniff.

Then Sammy's working eye raked the ground around his manky trainers. 'Found it.'

'Did you now?'

He rubbed his other hand along the grass-stain streaks on his tracksuit top. 'Bag was kinda lying there.'

'I'll bet it was.'

Nicholson stepped up close. Opened her mouth to say something. Wrinkled her nose. Then stepped back and tried again from a safer distance. 'Why'd you run then, Sammy?'

'Had to catch a bus. Yeah, a bus, can't be late for the bus or they drive off, don't they? Like, you know, the Ninky Nonk . . .' He peeled open the paper bag. 'Wow, look at that, got rowies in it, rowies, yeah, not that big a deal is it? Bagarowies? Found them.'

She pointed. 'Where'd you get the black eye, Sammy?'

'Found it.' Sammy swayed from side to side. 'You don't need me, right? I'm not, like, on your radar or nothing and I was just nipping past the baker's . . . to get something for Jack Simpson. Yeah, a present, cause of him being in hospital with the beatings and that.' Sammy's smile was a graveyard of yellow and brown. 'Cause of Klingon and Gerbil. Bad stuff, eh? Bad stuff. You don't need me, right?'

'Thought you said you'd found it?'

Logan took a deep breath. Regretted it. The air tasted of rotting meat and onions. 'Normal people bring flowers and grapes, Sammy. Not rowies.'

'Yeah. Right. Forgot. Flowers not rowies.' Another brown gap-toothed smile. 'Get them confused. You should see my mum's grave, like.'

'Sammy, you ever heard of a drug dealer from down south, calls himself the Candleman? Maybe Candlestick Man, something like that? Wee tough nut from Newcastle or Liverpool?'

'Yeah, nah, I don't know no drug dealers. Don't do drugs. Nah, used to, but I'm clean as a . . . you know, these days? Clean, clean, clean.'

Logan kept his mouth shut and stared.

One set of filthy fingers beat a tattoo on his pigeon chest.

Dirty trainers shuffled on the pavement.

'Nope. No drug dealers. Never.' Sammy cleared his throat. Looked down at his scabby arms. 'Couldn't lend us a tenner, could you? You know, for a cuppa tea and that? To go with me rowies . . .'

Silence.

'Twenty gets me the name of the guy Klingon and Gerbil got their stuff from. His *real* name. And where I can find him.'

Sammy swallowed. Upped the tattoo on his chest. Bit his bottom lip. Then his hand trembled out, palm open, fingers spread.

Logan took out his wallet. Produced the last two fivers from the thing. Leaving nothing but lint till the end of the month. Held the notes up. 'I'm warning you, Sammy – you get me that name, or I come after you. We clear?'

That single bloodshot eye sparkled like a rat's. Hand *reaching*. 'Yeah, yeah, his name and where you can find him.'

'Half now, half later.'

'Promise on my mother's grave and that . . .' Fingers twitching.

Logan dropped the cash and he snatched the falling notes from the air like a cat taking a pair of birds.

'Now, get out of here and find me that name.'

'Yeah, right, right, got to go and see Jack Simpson. And find the name. Name, name, name.' He jammed the money in a tracksuit pocket and lurched off, legs stiff, like a wind-up automaton with heroin as the cranking key.

Nicholson joined Logan by the wall. Frowning as Sammy disappeared around the corner onto Kingswell Lane. 'You sure that's a good idea?'

'Nope.' Logan put his empty wallet away. 'I'm skint now.'

'Well, that's one tenner you're never going to see again.' She waved a hand back and forth. 'Think he's ever seen a bar of soap in his life?'

'You never know, maybe he'll come up with something.' Logan headed back towards Big Car – parked half on the pavement where they'd abandoned it to give chase.

Nicholson shook her head. 'Why are you bothering anyway? Klingon and Gerbil have the backbone of an earthworm. They'll have sold out their supplier quicker than you can say "wriggle".'

Because the Inspector was right – sometimes you had to slip something in under the radar.

'Shire Uniform Seven, safe to talk?'

Logan pressed the button. 'Batter on, Maggie.'

'Got another misper sighting for you. Liam Barden – spotted in the Dundee Waterstones this morning.'

Nicholson took the Big Car along the waterfront. Macduff harbour shone sapphire blue, a couple of small fishing boats tied up against the walls. The wheeling shriek of herring gulls. Windows down, letting in the crisp tang of seaweed and ozone.

Logan reached out and poked her in the shoulder. 'See? Told you he's not visiting the Co-op on the High Street.' Back to the Airwave. 'Maggie, can you get onto Tayside and ask them to check the bookshop CCTV? Might not be him, but it'd be nice if we can let his family know he's OK.'

'Will do. And I spoke to Bill, he's asking round his fishing buddies for you about who's paying Klingon and Gerbil's rent.'

'Thanks, Maggie.'

Out the window, the streets of Macduff gave way to the A98, skirting the bay.

Logan twisted his Airwave back onto its holder. 'So . . . Liam Barden's in Dundee.'

Nicholson stuck her chin up. 'Can't help it if I'm thorough.'

He grinned. 'Deluded, more like.'

'I'm not the one who gave Stinky Sammy Wilson my last ten quid.'

Ah . . . True.

Up and over the bridge into Banff.

A billboard sat at the side of the road, not far from the football ground. The horrible little old lady was right – someone *had* drawn a huge willy over the local SNP candidate's campaign poster. A big purple willy. Geoffrey Lovejoy strikes again.

Still, at least it looked as if their one-man Marxist

revolution was being even-handed in his coverage of the issue. And the candidates.

'All units, be on the lookout for an IC-One female, five two, slim build, ginger hair, in the Peterhead area. Wanted in connection with an assault on a Salvation Army volunteer.'

'Sorry.' Logan turned the volume down, until the Airwave's babble was barely audible.

Steam fogged the kitchen window, the air full of the rich meaty scent of mince and earthy mashed tatties. He dug his fork into his plateful again. 'Very good.'

Sitting opposite, Helen smiled. 'Natasha wouldn't have mince and tatties without peas and carrots in it. Wouldn't touch either on their own, but soon as you cooked them with mince: best thing ever.'

'Much better than lentil soup for lunch.'

She cracked some black pepper over hers. 'Are you heading up to see Samantha later?'

'When the shift's finished. Shouldn't be too late.'

'Good. You can give me a hand finishing the living room. Going to look nice when it's done. Then, I was thinking, maybe steak for tea?'

'Steak?' More mince. More mashed potato. Logan swallowed. Had a sip of water. 'Don't know when I last—'

His Airwave gave its four point-to-point beeps.

God's sake. 'Can I not get *five* minutes?' He picked it up, turned up the volume. 'Sorry.' Pressed the button. 'Shire Uniform Seven.'

Inspector McGregor's voice crackled into the room. *'Logan? Are you safe to talk?'*

'Give me a minute, Guv.' He scraped his chair back. 'I have to take this. Only be a minute.'

Then out of the kitchen and through into the lounge.

The sofa lurked in the middle of the room, along with the bookcase and the TV, their shapes making tell-tale humps in the dustsheet draped over them. Above, the ceiling was a perfect field of white. Must've taken Helen at least three coats to get it looking that clean.

Logan eased the door shut and pressed the button. 'Bang away.'

'Where are you?'

'Lunch. Nicholson's got some shopping to do, so we're getting together at quarter-to and heading over to Macduff again. Canvas Melrose Crescent and see if we can dig anything up on our peeping tom.'

'You'll have to leave that till later: you've got a visitor.'

No doubt another fine upstanding Banff citizen in to complain about wheelie bins going out on the wrong day, or their neighbour's dog, or Martians stealing their tins of Tartan Special and getting the cat pregnant. God bless Care in the Community. 'Can Deano deal with it?'

'Logan, you—'

'Oh, and while you're on: can you do me a favour, Guv? Can you ask whoever's running the

Klingon and Gerbil investigation if they've got a name for their supplier yet? I'm hearing rumours.'

'*It's not our case any more. You* know *that.*'

'Yes, but if more drugs are on their way up here, it'd help if we knew what we were dealing with *before* it hits the streets. And who's dealing it.'

'*Well, I suppose that's valid. Now, before I return to my rapidly chilling baked potato, your visitor—*'

'Genuinely: Deano would be best. I'm up to my ears with nutters as it is today.'

'*Have you fallen on your* head, *Logan?*' Her voice dropped to a dramatic stage whisper. '*You do not let anyone hear you calling him a "nutter". What if he found out? God knows, he's scary enough as it is.*'

Logan cleared his throat. 'Guv?'

'*Chief Superintendent Napier's come all the way up from Aberdeen, just for you. And I don't think I've ever seen him looking so happy in my life.*'

Napier was happy?

Why did that sound like a very, *very* bad thing?

CHAPTER 28

Chief Superintendent Napier steepled his fingers, rested his elbows on the desk, and stared. He'd commandeered the Major Incident Room on the top floor, sitting at the head of the long conference table with his back to the windows, so the light would be in Logan's eyes.

The sun caught his thinning nimbus of ginger hair and made it glow like a halo of fire. A smile spread across his face, causing the end of his long nose to twitch.

He didn't look very comfortable in the police-issue black T-shirt. Probably didn't have enough shiny buttons for him. Or a place to hang his good conduct medal. Nothing to intimidate anyone with but the silver crown and single pip on each epaulette.

Logan sat perfectly still in his seat.

The Inspector who'd arrived with Napier fiddled with a digital video camera mounted on a tripod. Muttering to herself as she played with the settings. Then a red light appeared on the thing and she nodded. Middle-aged and gaunt, with a brown fringe swept forward in an attempt to cover the toast-rack wrinkles that crossed her forehead.

She settled into a chair diagonally opposite Logan. Put a digital dictaphone on the table between them. Then delved into a leather satchel and came out with a memo pad and a thick folder. Lined them up. Took the top off her pen. Cleared her throat. 'Saturday twenty-fourth of May, two forty-seven p.m.' Her voice was surprisingly light and girly. 'Present are Chief Superintendent Napier, Inspector Gibb, and Sergeant Logan McRae.' She turned and nodded to her boss.

His smile widened. 'Sergeant McRae, how *kind* of you to take time out of your busy schedule to talk to us today.'

Rule number one of being recorded during interview: keep your gob shut unless you're asked a direct question.

Napier rested his chin on the tips of his steepled fingers. 'Perhaps you'd like to get something off your chest before we begin? Something that's weighing on your conscience.'

Still no actual question. Logan kept his gob shut.

'Well, perhaps later.' He checked the file lying open on the desk in front of him. 'For example: I see that you've been spending an inordinate amount of time on one Francis "Frankie" Ferris. Hundreds of man-hours spent for no result at all. Do you really think that's a worthwhile expenditure of police resources?'

'Yes.' Rule number two: only answer the question

you've been asked, nothing more. Never volunteer anything. Never go off on a tangent.

'Really?' A frown creased Napier's forehead. 'Can you explain?'

'Raids disrupt the flow of drugs and keep the dealers unsettled. It makes the environment more dangerous for them to deal in.' Not quite word-for-word from the B Division drug-prevention strategy document, but near enough. 'It's proactive policing.'

There was no way Napier came all the way up from Aberdeen to ask about Frankie Ferris. This was just starters for whatever horrible meal he had planned. A prawn cocktail before the main course arrived.

He couldn't be leading up to something about Stephen Bisset dying in hospital, could he? Already had a big moan about that over the phone on Wednesday night. Why do it again, in person?

Inspector Gibb sat with pen poised. She hadn't taken a single note so far.

Logan narrowed his eyes. Opened his mouth . . . then shut it again. Rule three: never ask a question you don't already know the answer to.

Napier let the silence stretch. Then tilted his head to one side. 'You have a girlfriend, called Samantha Mackie, do you not?'

'Yes.'

'She's currently residing at a private care home not far up the coast from here, I believe. Sunny Glen?'

'That's right.'

'Hmm . . .' The head came up, then tilted to the other side. 'From what I understand, it's a rather expensive facility. Full-time care for someone in a vegetative state – that must be difficult to afford on a Sergeant's salary.'

Never volunteer anything.

'So tell me, Sergeant, how exactly *do* you pay for Miss Mackie's care?'

Inspector Gibb's pen scrawled across her memo pad.

OK, that *was* a question. 'I sold my flat in town. I was going to rent it out, but it wouldn't bring in enough to cover Samantha's care.'

'So you sold your flat to take care of your sick girlfriend. How very noble of you.'

Please don't ask who he'd sold it to. Stay far, *far* away from that particular wasps' nest.

Logan spread his hands on the desktop, felt the muscles in his shoulders bunch. 'She was hurt as a *direct* result of an ongoing investigation, she should've been covered under occupational health!'

Napier settled back in his seat. 'Your investigations have a habit of creating collateral damage, don't they, Sergeant McRae? Other people's misery follows you around like an unwelcome stench.'

'That wasn't . . .' He closed his mouth. Stupid. That's what he got for breaking rule number two. Don't go off on a tangent.

'And speaking of collateral damage, we have Stephen Bisset. Murdered in his hospital bed,

361

much to the delight of the press.' Napier flicked a finger in Inspector Gibb's direction and she dug into her thick folder.

Gibb pulled out a small stack of newsprint – the front pages of six or seven papers – then spread them out in front of Logan. 'A small selection from the *Daily Mail, Daily Record, Scottish Sun, Aberdeen Examiner, Evening Express, Scotsman,* and last, but not least, the *Press and Journal.*'

The headlines ran from, 'Tragic Dad Murdered In His Bed' to 'Pervert's Victim Killed With Hospital Pillow'. The *Aberdeen Examiner* had gone with, '"Dad Wasn't A Sex Freak!" Say Grieving Family'.

Each came with a photo of Stephen Bisset, all smiles and happy families. Not lying beneath a filthy blanket, covered in his own blood and filth, in a shack, hidden away in the depths of a snow-covered forest.

One had a little inset picture of Logan in his full dress uniform, getting a commendation for catching the Mastrick Monster. 'Police "Hero" Accused Of "Fitting-Up" Graham Stirling.' Another had '"Officer Fabricated Evidence" Jury Told.'

So that was it.

This wasn't about someone killing Stephen Bisset, or Samantha's care-home expenses, it was about Logan not following procedure back in January. Because obeying the rules mattered more than someone's life.

He kept his mouth shut.

Napier pursed his lips. 'Tell me, Sergeant . . .' dramatic pause, 'where were you last night between the hours of eleven p.m. and three a.m.?'

What?

OK, wasn't expecting that.

Logan stared at him. 'Why?'

'It's a simple question. Where were you?'

'I was at home, painting the bedroom.'

Napier did the head-tilting thing again. 'Until three in the morning?'

'No, about one. Then I went to bed.' Rule Number Two.

That pointy smug smile of his never wavered, it sat there on his stupid face like it'd been welded on. 'And can anyone vouch for that?'

Yeah, because Logan was going to tell him *all* about Helen Edwards staying at his house.

The red light on the digital camcorder glowed like an ember, the lens a dead, black, eye.

Logan shuffled his chair back from the table an inch. To hell with the rules. 'Do I need to have a Federation rep in here with me?'

'Do you think you need one?'

'I want it made clear – for the record – that I haven't been cautioned, nor am I under oath, nor have I been informed what the hell is going on.' Back another inch.

Napier spread his hands, palms up, fingers out. Like a Bond villain about to disclose his master plan. 'It's interesting that you think you've done something which merits being interviewed under caution.'

Logan stood. 'We're done here.'

'Do you remember discussing Graham Stirling with Miss Mackie on the morning of Wednesday the twenty-first?'

'Discussing? Is that meant to be a *joke*?' His hands made fists, the knuckles hard, skin stretched tight. 'Samantha hasn't spoken a word in four years.'

'Did you discuss—'

'*No.*' Go on, swing for him. One last glorious act as a police officer – batter Napier's head clean off his bloody shoulders.

'Inspector Gibb?'

She reached into her folder again and came out with two sheets of paper, stapled together. 'We have a statement from a Mr Kevin Cooper, an orderly at Sunny Glen. On the twenty-first of May he heard you talking to Miss Mackie about the collapse of Graham Stirling's trial. He quotes you as saying, "I'll go to Graham Stirling's house in the middle of the night, and bash his head in with a crowbar."'

Napier sat back and crossed his legs. He wasn't wearing a nice solid pair of black boots – like everyone else in uniform – instead his tiny leather brogues were polished to an onyx shine. Couldn't be more than a size six. Probably didn't need anything bigger to cover his cloven hooves. One hand made a lazy circle in the air. 'Do you remember saying that, Sergeant McRae?'

'No. Maybe. I don't know. If I did, it was—'

'The reason I ask, is that Graham Stirling's missing. His sister went to his house at nine o'clock this morning and, in her words . . .?' Napier gave Inspector Gibb a smile.

She picked up a sheet from her folder. '"I let myself in using my key. I shouted for Graham, but there was no answer. I went into the kitchen and it was like a bomb had gone off. There were broken cups and plates, and a chair with its legs all snapped. And there was blood on the floor and on the fridge."'

Ah . . .

Logan sat down again. 'I had nothing to do with that. *Nothing.*'

'But you *can* see why we'd be interested in talking to you? Here you are,' one hand described a brief circle, taking in the room, and presumably the whole of Banff station and the area beyond, 'reduced in circumstance, downgraded from a high-flying career in CID to Duty Sergeant in the back of beyond—'

'I have *not* been downgraded. This was Chief Superintendent Campbell's—'

'Don't interrupt. I understand you've been complaining that certain investigations have been removed from your remit and assigned to Major Investigation Teams better suited to completing them. So: reduced, downgraded, and frustrated.' The fingers steepled again. Chin resting on the tips. That Cheshire Cat smile welded in place. 'And then the case against Graham Stirling collapses,

because you seem to think that following procedure is beneath you. Why not mete out a little
justice of your own? Judge, jury, and executioner.'

'I did *not* kill Graham Stirling!' Logan shoved
his chair back. Stood with his fists curled on the
conference table. 'And if you had any evidence
we wouldn't be having this *little chat* up here, we'd
be in an interview room with a lawyer and a
Federation rep. So you can take your accusations
and shove them!'

Napier didn't flinch. His smile didn't waver. He
sat there, watching.

Logan stood back. 'Now, if you'll excuse me,
I've got *real* police work to do.' He turned and
marched for the door.

He was reaching for the handle when Napier's
voice cut through the room.

'What would you say if I told you we know who
killed Stephen Bisset.'

Logan wrenched the door open. 'If you're
implying it was me, you can—'

'Hoy!' Steel barged into the room, hoicking up
her trousers with one hand, holding a mobile
phone in the other. She glowered at Logan, then
at Napier. Then at the little digital camcorder.
'Someone going to clue me in?'

Napier held up a finger, 'Sergeant McRae has
been assisting us in understanding the slick of
destruction he seems to leave behind him like a
leaky oil tanker. Dead bodies. People in comas.
Things like that.'

'Well . . . keep it down. Some of us are trying to work up here. And *you*,' she poked Logan in the chest, 'you're meant to be helping me catch a wee girl's killer, so say goodbye to your little friends and get your arse in my office. Now.'

Napier stood, the smile never wavering. 'You didn't answer my question, Sergeant. Can anyone vouch for your whereabouts last night?'

Steel had another haul at her trousers. 'Sergeant McRae was with me last night. We were painting his manky house. Magnolia, I think it was.'

Inspector Gibb scribbled down another note.

Her boss licked his lips. Lowered himself back into his seat. 'I see. Well, in that case, by all means get on with some "real" police work, Sergeant. Our business is concluded for the moment.'

'Should think so too.' Steel shoved Logan out of the room, into the corridor. 'And keep it down in here.' She thumped the door shut. Then crept along the grey carpet to the next office. Ushered Logan inside.

She closed the door behind her and slumped back against it. Dropped her voice to a whisper. 'Christ on an emu, that was close.'

Steel's office was furnished with two ancient lockers, a filing cabinet, an office chair, and a desk covered in stacks of paperwork. A laptop, with a screensaver that seemed to consist of kittens peeking out of boots and teapots, sat between the piles and every available inch of wall space was covered in maps and pinboards. The latter plastered with index cards, connected by lines of red twine.

She pulled out her phone and poked at the screen as she made her way behind the desk. 'You know I'm missing Jasmine's dance competition for this, don't you?'

'How is it *my* fault?'

'If you hadn't found that dead wee girl, I'd be sitting in a school gym right now, surrounded by other parents, watching their stinky kids lollop around the floor like drunken elephants . . .' A sniff. 'So it's not all bad.' She sank into her chair. 'Sit.'

The only other seat in the room was a blue swivel job, but the backrest was missing, leaving the support poking up like a broken spine. She pointed at it. 'Bum. There.'

He did, sticking to the front edge. 'Thanks for backing me up with Napier. How did—'

'Shhh!' Finger to lips. 'Nosferatu next door's got ears like an NSA listening station.' She narrowed her eyes at him. 'What did I just alibi you for? What are we saying you've no' done?'

'Kill Graham Stirling.'

Her mouth collapsed, till it was a round, wet, cave. Then snapped shut again. Her eyes widened. 'You didn't, *did* you?'

'Of course I didn't!'

'Pfff . . . At least that's something.'

Muffled voices came through the wall. Then what sounded like laughter.

Logan turned and stared.

Should march right back in there and introduce Napier's teeth to Napier's rectum.

There was the *thunk* of a door closing, then Napier and Gibb's voices faded down the stairs. The pair of them off to blight someone else's life.

Logan sank back in his chair. Froze. Yanked himself upright before he went over the broken spine. 'Gah . . .'

Steel grinned. 'Good, isn't it? Stops the lower ranks from drifting off when you're bollocking them.'

'How did you know?'

'Been doing it to Rennie for months. Sometimes I try and be extra boring, to see if I can get him to cowp over backwards. All you've got to do is wheech out a couple of screws and the back comes right off.'

'No, I meant how did you know I was painting?'

'Did I no' say you need someone to protect you?' She pulled a blank index card from the box on her desk, frowned, then went rummaging through the drawers. 'Sodding hell, no' *again*. Place is like the Bermuda Triangle for pens . . .'

'Told you: it's Hector.'

The index cards on the board each had the name of a sex offender written on them, along with details of offence and length of time served. Everyone they'd visited on Monday night was there, along with a few others. All caught on the scarlet threads of a spider's web. With a photo of the dead girl in the centre.

He pointed at it. 'You getting anywhere?'

'Do I look like I'm getting anywhere? Does this look like the buzzing hub of a successful investigation?' She printed something on the card. 'All I do is tramp round sex offenders' houses and rescue silly-sod sergeants who should know better.'

He dropped his gaze to the carpet. 'Thanks for alibiing me in there. You took a big risk, guessing like that.'

'Pfff . . . You've got wee speckles of paint on your ears and in that kiwi-fruit-skin shambles you call a haircut. How else would they get there?' A smile. 'Plus, I lugged at Napier's door for a bit before barging to the rescue.'

'He says they know who killed Stephen Bisset.'

'Found out an hour ago.' She shifted a pile of paper and turned her laptop around, so the screen was facing Logan, then poked a couple of keys. 'Look.' The kittens disappeared, replaced by a window that took up most of the desktop. CCTV footage. What was probably a wall-mounted camera in a hospital – people marching about in scrubs with clipboards, or in pyjamas being wheeled about in porter's chairs. Everyone looking miserable and defeated. The time-stamp in the corner of the image put it at Wednesday night. Seven minutes after eight. 'This is outside the ward where Bisset was.'

Steel poked another button and the footage

spooled forward at double speed, then eight times, then twelve. Doctors, nurses, and patients whizzed in and out of shot. What looked like Bisset's kids whooshed past, going in with a big bunch of flowers, then out again. Poor wee sods.

Then Steel leaned forward and poked the keyboard again, setting the speed back to normal. 'There.'

The time-stamp clicked over to ten p.m.

'Where?'

A sigh. 'Seriously? Rennie spotted it right off.'

CHAPTER 29

Logan peered at the screen. What the hell was he supposed to . . . 'The guy in the long coat? Must be sweltering: Aberdeen Royal Infirmary keeps the heating cranked up to stifling.'

'Nurses didn't think anything was unusual, because this bloke's been volunteering at the hospital for years. Talks to coma patients, plays their favourite music, reads them their favourite books. That kind of thing. Been visiting Stephen Bisset almost every day for the last month and a half.'

Exactly what Logan had spent nearly four years doing with Sam. 'How do you know it's him?'

A fire-hazard smile burned across her face. 'Elementary, my dear Logan: he's a pervert. Marlon Brodie. Got one of those websites where he writes about bizarre fetishes and freaky kinks. What do they call it, sexblogging?' The smile crackled brighter. 'Rennie spotted him, and *you* didn't. Beaten by Rennie, how rubbish can you be?'

He scowled at her. 'How about the fact I haven't seen the footage till now, and I don't visit sexbloggers' websites.' He poked at the keyboard, zooming in on the figure in the long overcoat. An unremarkable man: average height, average build, features slightly blurred and pixelated. 'And the DNA . . .?'

'Course it does. Finnie got Ding-Dong to drag him in, test him, and one rush-job later: bingo. It's Marlon Brodie's semen on Stephen Bisset's dead body.' She sank back into her chair, swivelled it left and right a couple of times. 'Course, Finnie's trying to claim credit for it, but I'll figure something out.'

Logan closed the laptop. 'You got a one-hour test? What about Helen Edwards? She's been waiting since *Wednesday*.'

'Yeah, well, if you hadn't been such a damp blouse and let me leak it to the papers we could've had it by now. But no, Mr Morals knows best.' She spun the laptop back around to face her. 'Happy?'

'Oh, don't start. You know I'm right, or you'd have gone ahead and done it anyway.' He turned to look up at the board with its index cards and paedophiles. 'Does the family know? About Marlon Brodie?'

'So much for Detective Sergeant Barmy Becky's theory. The *kids* did it. Moron.'

'You should go easy on her. Keep treating her like the village idiot and she'll turn into one. More carrot, less stick.'

'Blah, blah, blah.' Steel waved a hand, as if wafting away a foul smell. 'Marlon Brodie denies suffocating Stephen Bisset, but what do you expect? And what kind of sadist calls their kid "Marlon" anyway? Asking for trouble. No wonder he turned into a killer. And a pervert. You seen his website? Got stuff on there that'd make *me* blush.'

'Well . . . at least it's—'

'Shire Uniform Seven, safe to talk?'

'God's sake.' Logan slumped, 'Aaargh . . .' caught himself before he tipped over the back of the broken chair, and sat upright again. Scowled at Steel. 'You trying to get me killed?' Clicked the button on his Airwave. 'Go ahead.'

'Sergeant McRae? It's Maggie. I've got a tip-off from your friend about dealing on Rundle Avenue again. Says there's been three of them in and out in the last fifteen minutes.'

'Thanks, Maggie. Is Nicholson back yet?'

'Just walked in.'

'Good. Tell her to get the Big Car fired up, we're going trawling for druggies.' Though knowing the way his luck was going these days . . .

Steel stood. Grabbed her suit jacket. 'What we waiting for?'

He backed towards the door. 'It's some local thing. Not important. You've got a dead wee girl's killer to catch, remember?'

'Oh no you don't. Every time I let you out of my sight, you get in trouble. And I call shotgun.'

Of course she did.

★　　★　　★

'Pfffff . . .' Steel wriggled further down into her seat, shoulders barely clearing the car windowsill. 'Is this *it*? Is this all you do?'

Nicholson took them round the corner, onto Rundle Avenue again. Grey harled semidetacheds on one side, a Morse code of short wood-panelled terraces on the other. Like oversized garden sheds, painted Cuprinol Brown. Knee-high garden walls holding back an onslaught of gravel, lawns, and associated shrubbery, depending on the property.

The speedo barely nudged fifteen miles an hour.

Sitting in the back, Logan peered up and down the road. No sign of anyone. 'You didn't have to come.'

Steel puffed out another sigh. 'I'm bored.'

'We can't kick the door in, because we don't have a warrant. So we cruise round and pick up anyone we see coming out of the place, and search them.'

'As if anyone's going to be daft enough to go buy drugs when they see you circling in a dirty big patrol car.'

The shed-style terraces gave way to white harled ones.

Nicholson took a left, across Tannery Street and onto Alberta Place. 'Oh, you'd be surprised.'

Off in the distance, a small wedge of North Sea peeked out between two houses in another street. Crystal blue beneath a shining sky.

Logan tapped a finger against the back of Nicholson's seat. 'When they were interviewing

Klingon, do we know if he said anything about his mother? Where she was, when she'd be back, anything like that?'

'No idea. Last time I spoke to the Custody Sergeant up there he said it was like something off a spy thriller. Everyone stomping about in sunglasses and suits. No talking to the prisoners. Top hush secret.' She stuck the car in reverse and did a three-point turn, going back the way they'd come.

Logan leaned forward and tried Steel instead. 'You must have heard something. You and all your MIT buddies.'

A sniff. 'You're kidding, right? Only way you get info out of another team is if you use a lead pipe and pliers.'

'Do me a favour then – ask about. See if it came up.'

Her eyes narrowed. 'Why? What are you up to?'

Shrug. 'Just a hunch.'

Left, onto Tannery Street, then a quick right. No houses here: a line of about thirty garages, with identical blue up-and-over doors, lined either side of a short dead-end road. No sign of anyone.

Steel puffed out a breath. 'I'm still bored. *And* hungry. Time for lunch.'

Another three-point turn.

Logan twisted his Airwave from its clip. 'We're working.'

'Lunch, lunch, lunch, lunch, lunch!'

'Shire Uniform Seven, you there, Maggie?'

'*Safe to talk.*'

'We got any more descriptions?'

'*Last one was an IC-one female, wearing grey joggies and an orange hoodie. Ugg boots.*'

Now there was a fashion statement.

The street slipped past the window. Quiet suburbia. Manicured gardens and pedicured cars – their owners out giving them their Saturday once-over with sponge and shammy.

'Lunch, lunch, lunch, lunch, lunch!'

Logan closed his eyes, pinched the bridge of his nose. 'If we stop at the baker's, will you *promise* to shut up?'

The smell of chicken curry pies filled the Big Car with earthy notes of cardamom and cumin, playing off against Scotland's real national dish: chips. Steel stuffed a couple into her mouth, chewing through the words, 'Told you.'

Sitting in the driver's seat, Nicholson ripped a bite out of her pie. Then made ooking monkey noises, mouth open in a little circle. 'Hot . . .'

Logan sat in the back, stomach grumbling. 'Ten minutes, then we're back looking for druggies to spin.'

'*Shire Uniform Seven, safe to talk?*'

'Thump away, Maggie.'

'*Tayside have been through the CCTV from the Dundee Waterstones. It wasn't Liam Barden. Sorry.*'

'Ah well, it was worth a go.'

'*And Traffic say they've got a burned-out Toyota*'

Hilux in a field outside New Pitsligo. The vehicle matches one stolen from a farm north of Strichen three days ago, but apparently *now the back end's all bashed in.'*

Probably where it reversed, at speed, through the front window of the Portsoy Co-op.

'Cashline Ram-Raiders.'

'Inspector McGregor's out there now.'

'OK, let me know if we need to do anything.' He ended the call as a roll of thunder growled out from the depths of his innards, loud enough to make Steel and Nicholson turn and stare at him.

'Sure you don't want some chips?' Steel wiggled the polystyrene carton.

Pause. Then he helped himself to a small handful.

She snatched the carton away. 'Hoy! I said, "some", not "all".'

He climbed out into the sunshine with his pilfered chips. Popped one in his mouth and twisted his Airwave free from its clip. Picked Deano's shoulder number into the keypad with a greasy fingertip. 'Deano, safe to talk?'

'Give us a minute, Sarge.'

Tiny Scottish cottages lined one side of the curving road, but the other was a line of grass and gorse that died at the edge of the cliff. Beyond that, it was all sea and sky. Tiny fishing boats bobbed in the water, their brightly coloured hulls glowing like neon against the rich blue.

Logan munched the last couple of chips. Not as nice as the plate of mince and tatties he'd left congealing on the kitchen table back home, but better than a kick in the knee.

Then Deano was back. *'Batter on.'*

'You run a PNC check on those burglaries in Pennan? Find us any suspects?' Logan sooked the last smear of salt and grease from his finger-tips.

'All the historical stuff? Yeah. Came back with a couple of hits. One guy's doing a sixer in Barlinnie – so it's not him. The other's called Tony Wishart. Bit of a history freak, according to his social worker. Outstanding apprehension warrant for doing over that wee Aberdeenshire Heritage place in Mintlaw. So we're already looking for him.'

At least that was something.

'We're going to be another twenty or so. If you've got a chance, swing past Alex Williams's for a safe-and-well check. And make sure Tufty stays in the car. Don't want a repeat of last time.'

The Big Car looped around onto Tannery Street again. Going the long way around. Steel lolled in the passenger seat, head on the window. Her breathing deepened, then little snuffling noises burrowed their way out of her open mouth.

Nicholson sniffed from the back seat. 'What do we do if she starts to snore?'

Logan poked the car radio, bringing it to life. Not an anodyne boy-band this time, but an insipid all-girl outfit, close-harmonying their way through another beige tune. 'Think we're probably onto a loser here. Might as well go back to the station and try again tomorrow.'

The song limped to its bland conclusion, replaced by whatever idiot was manning the microphone. *'I swear that gets better every time I hear it. Don't forget: we'll be going live to Liverpool Cathedral for the memorial service of Detective Constable Mary Ann Nasrallah, tragically shot on Sunday. So stay tuned for that. Now though, it's time to catch a bit of Bieber Fever!'*

Nicholson poked Logan in the shoulder. 'Noooo!'

'Gah!' He jabbed the button just in time, and classical music filled the speakers. Logan let out the breath he'd been holding. Thank God for that . . . 'One last drift past Frankie's place and we're done.'

She stuck her head forward, between the two front seats. 'You know what hacks me off about this undercover officer getting shot? How come you only ever get politicians lining up to say what a great job we do when one of us dies? What about the rest of the time?'

'I know.'

'Oh yeah, we do a spectacular job when we're *dead*, but other than that, nothing.'

'Preaching to the choir, Janet.' He took them back onto Rundle Avenue with its dot-dot-dash of terraced shed-like houses. Grass. Grass. Gravel. More Grass.

Another poke in the shoulder. 'Sarge? Back there – shiny new blue Ford Fiesta. Does that not belong to the ugly bloke we stopped Monday for being on his mobile phone?' A small pause, then the delicate crackle of flipping paper. 'Here we go: Martyn Baker. AKA Paul Butcher, AKA Dave Brooks. Possession. Possession with intent . . .'

OK, so Martyn-with-a-'Y''s car wasn't parked right outside Frankie Ferris's house, but it wasn't exactly a million miles to walk. 'Think he's buying or supplying?'

'Yes.'

'Me too.' Logan pulled in to the kerb. Killed the engine and the music.

Steel sat up. 'What? I was listening to that.' A yawn. 'Where are we?'

Nicholson pointed at the blue Fiesta. 'Belongs to a dealer from down south.'

'Good for him.' She dug a hand in under her left breast and had a scratch. 'Why's there no coffee? Thought you bunnets were all about the coffee and doughnuts.'

Logan climbed out into the sunshine. Pulled his peaked cap on. Then turned and opened Nicholson's door for her.

She joined him on the pavement, wedging her bowler down so far it bent the top of her ears. 'We got a plan?'

Rundle Avenue didn't exactly have a lot of places to lay low. No alleys to lurk in and keep an eye on Frankie's place. No convenient trees or hulking rhododendron bushes. 'Right, you go that way,' he pointed back towards the Fiesta, 'back onto

Tannery, left, down to the end, round onto Golden Knowes, and come from the other direction. Find something to hide behind. I'll watch from this end. We catch him coming out and we search him.'

And please, dear God, let him be carrying enough Class A drugs to put him away for a long, long time.

Logan crossed the road as Nicholson headed off. Staying on the same side of the street as Frankie Ferris's house. He ducked behind a Transit with 'Big Jeemie's Bug Control ~ Who You Gonna Call?' stencilled down the side, complete with rip-off Ghostbusters logo.

'*Shire Uniform Seven, safe to talk?*'

'Bang away, Maggie.'

'*Bill says the rent on thirty-six Fairholme Place got paid every four weeks by direct debit from a Mrs Lesley Spinney's TSB account until ten months ago. Then there was a couple of months paying cash.*'

Overhead the herring gulls soared. An ice-cream van chimed in the distance.

Logan pressed the talk button. 'Are you trying to build up dramatic tension here, Maggie? Only I'm dying of old age.'

'*Sorry, someone's at the front desk. The rent now gets direct-debited from a Mr Colin Spinney's account – Bank of Scotland.*'

So Klingon's mum stopped paying rent nearly a year ago and trusted her wee boy to look after it instead. Really? Why would *anyone* put a drug-dealing wee scruff like Klingon in charge of the rent? Pretty much guaranteed to wake up one morning to an eviction notice.

What if she didn't stop? What if her direct debit stopped because her account was emptied?

'*Sergeant McRae, are you still there, only the front desk—*'

'Yes, thanks, Maggie. Tell Bill he's a star from me.'

What if she never went to Australia after all?

Logan settled his bum down on the kerb and peered around the van.

It'd probably take Nicholson five minutes to get around to the other end of the street. Then all they had to do was wait till Martyn-with-a-'Y' finished his business with Frankie, find out what happened to Klingon's mum, catch whoever killed the little girl out at Tarlair Outdoor Swimming Pool, arrest the Cashline Ram-Raiders, solve all the burglaries in Pennan, find Neil Wood before he molested any more children, and all would be right with the world.

How hard could it be?

A wheeze sounded at Logan's shoulder. 'I'm bored.'

He closed his eyes, rested his forehead against the bug van's painted side. 'So go back to the station and do *your* job instead of moaning about mine.' He turned and pointed back along the road. 'Go. That way. Down to the bottom of the hill, cross the road, and follow the signs for the harbour. It'll take you ten, fifteen minutes, tops.'

Steel pursed her lips around the e-cigarette that poked from her lips. 'Give us a lift.'

'We're trying to catch a drug dealer. That OK with you?'

'You lowly Sergeant, me Detective Chief Inspector. Me want lift, you give lift.'

'No.' He turned back to the house. 'You're meant to be catching whoever killed that little girl. Go do it.'

'Tell you what: why don't I *wave* my magic wand and summon up the killer? Of course! Why'd I no' think of that before? Hang on . . .' Steel swooped her fake cigarette through the air. Then frowned. 'Nope. That's strange, it was working this morning.'

Still no sign of movement inside.

'Well, what about your stable isotope analysis?'

Steel popped her magic wand back in her gob and gave it a sook. 'Good job I outsourced it. Nothing like a bottle of eighteen-year-old Macallan to well-oil the wheels. My Dundee guru ran hair samples from the body last night – according to him, our wee girl spent the last four months dotting round the northeast, year before that in Glasgow, and the rest of the time's split between the south coast of Wales and north London.'

Logan scribbled it down in his notebook. 'What about further back?'

'Can't say without a bone sample, or one of her teeth. Got a request in with the Procurator Fiscal.'

'So why are you sodding about here instead of chasing him up? You know what the Fiscal's like!'

384

Logan turned and stared at her. 'This is what happens when there's no one running around after you, isn't it? Everything goes to crap.'

A scowl. Then a smile greased its way across her face and her voice went all sing-song. 'Give us a lift, or I won't tell you what DI Porter said.'

Not so much as a hint of remorse or guilt. Typical.

Deep breath. Sigh. Back to watching the house.

Maybe Frankie and Martyn-with-a-'Y' had settled down in front of the football? Couple of beers and some crisps. Jammy sod.

Steel poked Logan. 'Aren't you going to ask?'

'Fine: who the hell is DI Porter?'

'No lift, no intel.'

His shoulders dipped. 'Look, this is what we do, OK? This is us working.'

Steel tugged at his sleeve. 'But I'm *bored*.'

'You know what I haven't missed? This. Babysitting you, like a small whiny child.' He pulled his arm out of her grasp. 'If you want to go: go. I'm staying here, till Martyn Baker comes out.'

'Be like that, then.'

The sound of her boots scuffed away into the distance.

Finally.

He peered around the other side of the van. Nicholson was crouched down behind a Fiat Punto about a hundred yards down the road. She was using her bowler hat as a fan, wafting air over her shiny face. Not surprising. Day like today, with the sun hammering down? Not exactly the best time to be dressed all in black with a stab-proof corset on.

A trickle of sweat made its way down Logan's spine and into his underwear.

'Come on, Martyn, where the hell are you?'

Hang around like this much longer and someone was going to get suspicious. Assuming Logan and Nicholson didn't keel over with heat-exhaustion first.

A sharp *crump* of shattering plastic broke the stillness. Then did it again.

Nicholson stepped out onto the pavement, staring past where Logan was lurking.

The booming clang of dented metal was swiftly followed by the discordant, outraged wail of a car alarm.

He turned and there was Steel, standing on the pavement, hands behind her back. She grinned at Logan, e-cigarette dangling from the corner of her mouth. 'What?'

Martyn Baker's shiny new Ford Fiesta had two broken headlights and a big dent in the passenger door. Its indicators flashed, horn blaring.

Steel shrugged. Raised her voice over the skirl of the alarm. 'What, this?' Nodding at the car. 'Was like that when I found it.'

Great – and Logan was the one Professional Standards wanted to shaft.

'Are you *insane*?'

A door banged open and there was Martyn-with-a-'Y', face flushed, teeth bared. 'MY CAR!' His Birmingham accent stretched the last word out, like a small scream. Only it wasn't Frankie's drug-dealing hovel he'd come out of, it was the house opposite his blinking wailing Fiesta. The one with the rose bushes, water feature, and plastic Wendy house.

He lurched down the path and onto the pavement, mouth moving as if trying to chew out the words, eyes bugging. Presumably taking in the fresh dents and shattered plastic. Then he turned on Steel. 'DID YOU—'

'A big boy did it and ran away.' She flashed her warrant card. 'One of my colleagues is in hot pursuit. Mr . . .?'

He laid his palms flat on the roof of the Fiesta, as if he could summon the Power of the Lord to heal the afflicted. 'My car!'

'This your vehicle, Mr Mycar? Any chance you could turn off the alarm, only it's doing my head in.'

His lips made a creased snarl. Then he stepped back, pulled out his keys and pressed the fob.

Silence.

'Much better.' Steel dug a finger into her ear and wiggled it. 'You staying in the area, Mr Mycar?'

Martyn-with-a-'Y' narrowed his eyes, jaw muscles knotting the line of spots along his chin. 'See if I get my hands on the little—'

'Aye probably best no'.' She took the fake fag from her mouth and waved it up the street towards

Frankie Ferris's house. 'You been visiting across the road there? Number fifteen? Manky house with the lime-green door and funky smell?'

Logan stepped up behind him, blocking any escape. 'Is there a problem, Mr Baker?'

'Look at what those little bas—'

'Baker? Hang on,' Steel popped the e-cigarette back in, 'he told me his name was Mycar. Don't you know it's an offence to give a false name to the police, Mr Baker?' She flashed a smile at Logan. 'I think that's just cause for a stop-and-search, don't you, Sergeant?'

Logan snapped on a pair of blue nitriles. 'If you can put your arms out for me, Mr Baker.'

Steel took a long slow drag as Logan patted Baker down. 'Didn't answer my question, by the way. Have you been visiting your friendly neighbourhood drug dealer? Maybe picking something up, or dropping it off?'

If that jaw clenched any tighter, one of those spotty Vesuviuses was going to blow. 'You arresting me?'

'Depends what my Sergeant finds, doesn't it?'

Logan finished running his hands down Martyn-with-a-'Y''s legs. 'Have you got anything in your pockets I should know about? Anything sharp – knives, needles, blades?'

He bared his teeth. 'This is harassment.'

'Paul?' A woman appeared from the same doorway, with a Brummie accent thick as a breezeblock. Cut-off jeans and a 'BARNEY MUST DIE'

T-shirt. Her bare toes made little feet fists as she stepped out onto the path. 'Everything OK?' A toddler wobbled up behind her and stood clinging to her leg, thumb firmly planted in mouth.

The scowl faded, and Baker turned his head to her, face stretched in a smile. 'It's OK, Elsie. You and Mandy go back inside and stick the kettle on, yeah?'

'Paul?'

The fake smile slipped a bit. 'I *said* it's OK. Someone vandalized the car and these . . . officers are being a bit jobsworth. Go back inside.'

A little nod, then she disappeared back into the house. The toddler froze on the top step, looking back at them. Then Martyn-with-a-'Y' gave her a little wave and she followed her mum. The door swung shut.

Martyn Baker assumed the position again. 'Let's get this over with.'

CHAPTER 30

'So who's Paul when he's at home?' Steel turned to peer through the back window as the Big Car headed off down the road. 'Well, no' "at home" so much as "slumming it in Teuchter Town with some leggy blonde tart".'

'Alias.' Nicholson took them straight through the roundabout onto Whinhill Terrace, hands slip-sliding around the wheel in proper I'm-trying-to-pass-my-driving-test manner. 'Martyn Baker also goes by Paul Butcher and Dave Brooks.'

'So the poor cow he's shagging doesn't even know his real name? That no' a wee bit sad?'

Sitting in the back, Logan stuffed his blue nitrile gloves into an old Tesco carrier bag and stuffed that into one of the pockets on his stabproof. 'Can't believe he didn't have anything on him.'

Nicholson shrugged. 'Maybe next time?'

'Would it no' be really weird for him as well, though? There he is, humping away, and she's screaming, "Oh, Paul, you magnificent stallion. Harder, Paul, harder!" and he's thinking, "Who the hell is *Paul*? . . . Oh, right, it's me." You'd think that would put him off his stroke.'

Logan's Airwave bleeped. *'Shire Uniform Seven, safe to talk?'*

'Thump away, Maggie.'

'Are we still looking for a Charles "Craggie" Anderson? 'Cos we've got a sighting this morning of him getting off a bus in Inverness.'

Steel took a sook on her e-cigarette, setting the tip glowing. 'Do you think the wee kid's his? Imagine growing up no' knowing your dad's real name.'

'We sure it's Charles Anderson?'

'Not really. You know what it's like. Someone sees someone that vaguely looks like someone on a missing person poster they can barely remember, so they call us.'

'Anything else?'

'Deano and Tufty got themselves an overdose in Keilhill, ambulance is on the scene.'

'Thanks, Maggie.'

Nicholson took them right, onto Castle Street. It was busy with couples and families. Baby buggies and carrier bags.

Nicholson slammed on the brakes. Pointed. 'There! It's *definitely* him this time!'

A chunky middle-aged man, balding at the back, lurched along the pavement, carrying a pair of wooden kitchen chairs with the labels still attached.

She undid her seatbelt. Hopped out of the car. 'Liam Barden?' No response. 'HOY, LIAM!' Still nothing. She grabbed her bowler hat, wedged it on, and hurried after him on foot.

Steel half turned in her seat. 'Why are you lot obsessed with this Liam bloke?'

'It's not him.' Logan shifted forward in his seat. 'So, come on then, you're getting a lift back to the station. What did your DI Porter say?'

A blank look wafted across her face, then it must've clicked. 'Aye, Porter. She's in charge of the day-to-day on that big drugs bust – what is it, Kevin and Gherkin?'

'Klingon and Gerbil.'

'Takes all sorts.' Steel had a long drag on her fake cigarette. 'You wanted to know about Kevin's mum.'

'*Klingon's* mum. She's supposed to be in Australia for a couple of months, but word is she's not been at her home address for a long, long time.'

'So?'

'So I want to know if Klingon or Gerbil said anything about Klingon's mum.'

Another puff. 'Why?'

'You didn't see the state of the place. No way they caused that much mess in a couple of weeks. That house has been a slum for *months*. She's a neat freak. And according to the Council, even though the place is still in her name, Klingon's been paying the rent for nearly a year. So what happened to her?'

'That's what you've got? The place is dirty?' Steel pointed a chipped red fingernail at her cheek. 'Does this look like a face that gives a toss about two junkies' housekeeping skills? By the time the pair of them get out of prison, she'll have tidied it all up anyway.'

A family of five shambled past the patrol car, the father and mother looking as if they'd never seen a happy day in their lives.

Logan lowered his voice. 'What if she never went to Australia in the first place?'

'Still not caring.'

'What if she's dead?'

Steel clicked her cigarette off and slipped it back into her pocket. 'You think this Kevin's the kind of bloke to kill off his dear old mum?'

'For God's sake, it's *Klingon*. Kevin is Gerbil's real name.' Logan sat back in his seat. 'Maybe they killed her, or maybe she had an accident, but something's not right.' He drummed his fingers on the driver's headrest. 'Wonder if she's still drawing money from her bank account? Think we can find out?'

Steel produced her phone and poked away at the screen for a bit.

Logan poked her. 'Well?'

'Well what?'

God's sake. 'What did DI Porter say? About Klingon's mum?'

'Nothing. Never came up.' She held out her phone. A photo of Susan and Jasmine glowed on the screen. The two of them were in a school hall, Susan in a floral dress that could've walked straight off the set of a Doris Day film, Jasmine in a black leotard with a green tutu – grinning away, clutching a tiny golden trophy. That would be at the dance competition. 'She came third. Think I should ask them to come up to Banff for a couple of days?'

'They didn't mention his mum at all?'

'Course they couldn't stay at Craphole House with you, but it'd be nice, wouldn't it? Trip up here, in the sun.'

'How could she not ask?'

'They could jump in the car today, spend the night, and go back on the Sunday. Be nice to have them for longer, but these idiot teachers throw a wobbly if you take kids out of school in term time.' Steel stared at the picture. 'We could have a barbecue. Go for a walk along the beach. Swim in the sea.'

'Are you even listening to me?'

'Nope.'

Fine. If she wasn't going to help . . .

He took out his own phone and scrolled through the contacts list. Selected one, then listened to it ring. And ring. And ring.

And then a man's voice came on the line, very well spoken with a faint Essex twang. *'Department of Administrative Support.'*

'Derek? It's Logan McRae. We met at the big security briefing weekend for the Commonwealth Games? You and your boss were getting chucked out of that strip—'

'Ah yes, Logan. Of course. Yes. How are you?' He cleared his throat. *'I thought we weren't going to talk about that again.'*

'You still with the Secret Squirrel Squad?'

Steel changed the photo on her phone to Susan and Jasmine in bathing suits on a white sandy beach, with palm trees and tins of Irn-Bru.

Derek was silent for a moment. *'I have no idea what you're talking about.'*

'I'll take that as a yes then. Listen, I need to find out if someone's left the country. She's supposed to be on holiday in Australia. Any chance you can find out when, and *if*, she went?'

Steel turned and held the phone out to him. 'Tiree. Got sunburnt every morning, eaten alive by midges every evening, and loved every minute.'

'Logan, the Department of Administrative Support doesn't do counter-terrorism, it does requisitions for staplers and Bic pens. Photocopier maintenance contracts. All very mundane.'

'Sure it does. And you still owe me one, remember? The strip—'

'It wasn't . . .' Deep breath. *'Yes, well, perhaps I can make some discreet enquiries on your behalf. Name?'*

Logan dug it out of his notebook. 'Lesley Spinney, born in Fraserburgh, eighth of April, 1971.'

'I'll see what I can do.' He hung up.

Steel held out her mobile again. The three of them sitting around a camp fire with fish on sticks. 'That's us in Lossiemouth. Went out fishing in a wee boat.' A grin. 'Susan caught this mackerel; got it off the hook and it starts wriggling like a mad

395

thing. Slaps her in the face with its tail, and sods off back into the water. Fish: one, Susan: nil.' A sigh. 'I'm going to call them.'

The driver's door clunked open and Nicholson slumped in behind the wheel. Sighed.

Logan put his phone away. 'Let me guess: it wasn't him.'

'*Looked* like him.'

'It's the same bloke as last time, isn't it? The one you chased into the Co-op. No moustache. Supports the wrong football team.'

'Well . . . what sort of idiot goes about looking like a missing person? That's asking for trouble.' Nicholson stayed where she was for a moment, then turned the key in the ignition. 'Could've sworn it was him.'

'*Shire Uniform Seven – urgent.*'

Logan unhooked his Airwave. 'Safe to talk.'

'*Reports of raised voices and screaming at number sixteen, Chapel Hillock Crescent. You've got a grade one flag on that—*'

'Alex Williams.' He thumped a hand down on Nicholson's shoulder. 'Go!'

She shifted gears then jabbed the 999 button setting the lights and siren blazing. Put her foot down.

The Big Car's back end wriggled for a moment, rear wheels spinning, then they caught and the whole thing rocketed forwards, pushing Logan into his seat.

Traffic parted before them, Saturday shoppers

stopping on the pavement to gawp as the patrol car flashed and wailed past.

Logan clicked the talk button. 'Roger that, we are en route. Who reported it?' He snatched at the grab handle above the door as Nicholson Silverstoned around the sweeping curve at the bottom of Castle Street. Bushes, trees, and lampposts flashed by the windows. Out onto the wrong side of the road to overtake a lorry full of cattle.

'Next-door neighbours. Say they can hear plates and things smashing.'

Nicholson hunched forward, closer to the wheel. 'Told you, Sarge: all fun and games till someone turns on the blender.'

Steel shoogled in her seat. 'This is more like it. Bit of excitement for a change.'

He thumbed Deano's shoulder number into the handset. 'Deano, where are you?'

'We're up the hospital. Again. *Our overdose took offence at getting a shot of Narcan. Nearly ripped the head off the paramedic who injected her. What's up?'*

'Alex Williams.'

'Crap. Right, give us a minute. We'll be there, soon as.'

The football ground came and went, then the bridge into Macduff. Tearing through the streets of the town, walls of granite flashing past the windows.

The Big Car screeched around the corner onto Chapel Hillock Crescent. Cookie-cutter houses in the familiar pattern of semidetached houses and mini-terraces. Grey harling. White harling. Red pantile roofs.

Nicholson stamped on the brakes, bringing them to an abrupt halt outside number sixteen. She jumped out, reached back and opened Logan's door.

He'd got one foot on the pavement when his Airwave gave its point-to-point bleeps.

'DCI McInnes to Shire Uniform Seven.'

Who the hell was DCI McInnes?

Logan lunged out of the car and hit the button, talking into his shoulder. 'Have to call you back, sir, we're—'

'No you won't! You will talk to me now or I will personally get someone over there to kick a hole in your backside big enough to drive a bus through!'

Nicholson scrambled up the path to the red front door. Hammered on it. 'POLICE! OPEN UP!'

'I'm attending a domestic. You do what you want.'

More hammering. 'POLICE!'

He let go of the Airwave. 'Kick it in.'

Nicholson stepped back and hammered her foot into the UPVC, an inch below the handle. The thing gave a wobbling *BOOM*, but it didn't seem to do anything. She gave it another go. *BOOM*.

'Sergeant, I am warning you!'

Steel got out and made a loudhailer out of her hands. 'TRY THE HANDLE, YOU IDIOT!'

Nicholson did. And the front door swung open. The sound of raised voices battered out into the afternoon. Then something smashing.

She charged inside, Logan right behind her. Steel puffing along at the rear.

It was a short hallway with a set of stairs on one side, heading up to a small landing. Downstairs, two doors lay wide open. One to a kitchen, the other—

A scream – off to the right.

Nicholson threw herself into the lounge, clacked out her extendable baton. 'POLICE! NOBODY MOVE!'

An older man stood with his fist raised, ready to snap forward. Little shards of white clung to his grey hair and the shoulders of his torn shirt. Scarlet dripped from the lobe of one ear.

A young woman scrambled back on the couch, trying to push herself into the cushions. One eye was screwed shut, the skin already starting to redden around it. Blood made a greasy smear at the side of her mouth. Long brown hair, a tangled mess around her face.

Logan snapped out his extendable baton. 'ENOUGH!'

The man's arm trembled. Then he dropped the fist and stood there with his shoulders slumping. Chest heaving. 'I'm . . . I'm sorry . . .'

Steel appeared at Logan's shoulder. 'Aye, you sodding well will be.'

She stepped into the room. Flashed her warrant card. 'Detective Chief Inspector Steel.' She pointed at Logan and Nicholson, then at the shaking man. 'Get him out of here.'

★   ★   ★

Sunlight bathed the back garden, making the grass and shrubs glisten impossibly green. Logan sat on the top step of a section of decking, Airwave pressed to his ear. Other hand massaging his forehead. Doing nothing to shift the rusty tin cans rattling about behind his eyes.

'*Do I make myself clear?*'

'Perfectly.'

'*I will not have you trying to circumvent my Major Investigation Team. And if I hear you've been bothering DI Porter again—*'

'I didn't . . .' What was the point? 'Yes, sir.'

'*You will stay away from Operation Troposphere, or by God I'll make you wish you had.*'

'Operation Troposphere?'

A couple of gardens over, a dog barked, setting off a chain reaction further down the road. A staccato rhythm with lawnmower solo and the shrieking chorus of happy children.

'*Yes, Operation Troposphere. You really think you know best, because you stumbled across the drugs in the first place? Well, you don't. And what the* hell *were you thinking, calling it Operation Schofield? Anyone with half a brain could connect that to someone called "Kevin the Gerbil". Were you* trying *to get him killed?*'

'No, sir. It—'

'*This is why we use random name generators,* Sergeant, *to prevent stupid cock-ups like that. It's not your investigation any more. All aspects of Operation Troposphere are off limits.*'

Deep breath. One last go. 'Sir, with all due

respect, we'll have to deal with the fall-out on the ground. If there's a major influx of drugs on the way to Banff, we need to know what we—'

'*No you don't. I decide what you need to know, Sergeant. And right now you need to mind your own business. Keep your nose out of my investigation!*'

Silence from the handset.

Logan checked the display – Detective Chief Inspector McInnes had gone.

A long, slow breath hissed out between gritted teeth. 'Up yours, *sir*.' He twisted the Airwave handset back onto its mount. Turned to face the kitchen.

Nicholson had her back to him in the kitchen window. Behind her, the top of a grey-haired head was just visible above the sill. Probably sitting at the kitchen table trying to justify the whole thing. Alex was sorry. Alex didn't mean it. Alex wouldn't ever do it again. They loved each other.

Right up till the time one of them ended up in the hospital or the cemetery.

No wonder so many police officers drank.

Logan let himself in the back door. Leaned on the working surface. 'Well?'

The floor was littered with broken crockery and spilled cutlery. Rorschach inkblots spattered the walls, marking the death-throes of half a dozen bottles and jars. Their shattered glass corpses lay slumped on the floor below.

Nicholson pulled her face into a grimace. 'Usual. Started off with an argument over who was going to get voted off *The Voice* tonight, ended up with threats to kill.'

The door through to the hall crashed open and Steel stomped in. Scowled. Pointed a finger at the figure slumped at the table. 'Think yourself lucky, sunshine. See if I have to come back here?' She slammed her palm down on the tabletop.

He flinched, covered his head with his hands. 'I'm so sorry . . .'

'You're on your final warning.' Steel snapped her fingers. 'Tweedle Dum, Tweedle Dee – we're out of here.' No one moved. '*Now!*'

Logan and Nicholson followed her down the hallway.

The door to the living room was still open. A broken coffee table. A picture ripped from the wall. A small figure curled on the edge of the couch, watching as they passed, her eye well on its way from red to black.

Logan stepped out through the front door and closed it behind him.

Nicholson sniffed. 'Bloody disaster. Next time it's going to be all ambulances and trauma teams.'

'Tell me about it.'

Steel was halfway to the car, puffing away on her e-cigarette when she stopped, turned and jabbed a fist at the house. 'Makes me want to *scream.*'

'So why didn't we arrest—'

'How could she no' want to press charges? What the goat-buggering hell is wrong with her?'

Logan pulled his chin in. 'What?'

'But it's OK, because they *love* each other. Well, that's all right then, isn't it?' Steel kicked the head off a scarlet rose growing in the front border. An explosion of blood drops drifted to the ground. 'You don't put up with that crap, OK? You don't!'

Logan took a step towards her. Frowning. 'What are you talking about?'

'The bastard hit her!' The e-cigarette's end glowed fierce and cold. 'But don't you worry, I had a good *long* chat with her. Told her: no one gets to treat her like that. See if it was me, I'd hack the bastard's balls off with a rusty spoon.'

The frown slipped. 'You did *what*?'

Nicholson swallowed. 'Oh God . . .'

Steel kicked the head off another rose. 'How can a grown man do that to a wee girl?'

'WHAT?' Logan stared back at the house. 'You told her to hack . . .? No, no, no, no, no!'

Nicholson was already sprinting up the path. She barged past him and grabbed the door handle, yanked it up and down. 'It's locked!'

Steel stared at them both from the pavement. 'What the hell are you pair playing at? I sorted it.'

Logan snapped out his extendable baton. 'Alex Williams isn't the old man, it's *her*, you idiot. She's been in and out of prison for domestic assault ever since she was sixteen, and you told her to hack her partner's balls off!'

Muffled screams came from somewhere inside.

Steel's mouth fell open. The e-cigarette tumbled from between her lips and clattered against the paving slabs. 'Don't just stand there, kick the bloody door in!'

CHAPTER 31

The siren drowned out the voice on the other end of the phone, then the ambulance engine roared and it was off, blue lights flashing.

Logan turned his back on the noise. 'Sorry, I didn't get that, Derek. Can you repeat?'

A sigh. *'I said, there's no sign of her. Border Agency have got no record of her passport being scanned on the way out of the country. Theoretically, she could have travelled to another EU country using her driving licence as photo ID and flown out from there, but there's no record of an Electronic Travel Authority being issued to let her into Australia.'*

Alex Williams stared out at him from the back of the Big Car, wearing a black eye and a pout. I'm sorry, I didn't mean it, it'll never happen again. We love each other.

'So Kevin Spinney's mother never went to Australia.'

'Not unless she's got forged papers, no. Now, I think I've fulfilled my obligation, don't you?'

'Thanks, Derek.'

'*Don't mention it. Please. Don't mention it to anyone.*' He hung up.

Steel grumbled her way out of the house, on the phone to someone. 'No, it . . . She shouldn't have been let out in the first place. The team here did everything they could.' Steel looked up and scanned the road. Neighbours stood behind a cordon of 'POLICE' tape, all having a good gawp at the house and its uniformed comings and goings. Then Steel must've spotted Logan, because she waved and marched over. 'Yes, sir. . . . I'm sure it will . . . Thank you, sir.' She slid the phone into an inside pocket. Grimaced. Stood right next to him and lowered her voice to barely a murmur. 'We are royally screwed soon as anyone finds out.'

Logan stared down at her. 'What do you mean, "we"? "*We*" didn't tell her to cut her partner's balls off, that was all you.'

The murmur became a growl. 'You remembering who alibied you to the Ginger Ninja?'

He nodded at the Big Car and Alex Williams in the back seat. 'Not me you've got to worry about, it's her. Probably well on the way to convincing herself that you made her do it.'

'Well . . . At least . . .' Steel frowned. 'Looking on the bright side . . .' She scuffed a toe along the pavement. Pulled out her e-cigarette. 'No, I've got nothing.'

Singing echoed out through one of the closed cell doors, reverberating down the corridor. It was an

406

old Elvis number about Mr Presley setting his soul on fire, only sung in a thick Northeast accent with the chorus changed to, 'Viva, Pee-Ter-Heed'.

The Police Custody and Security Officer undid Alex Williams's cuffs, then stepped back out of the cell as Alex rubbed at her wrists.

He closed the door with a solid, final *thump*. Then slid down the observation hatch. The female cellblock was old-fashioned compared to the new male wing. No science-fiction row of stainless steel with fancy fittings here, it was all dark blue and industrial.

The PCSO took out a whiteboard marker and printed the words, 'VIOLENT ~ DO NOT TRUST!' on the hatch. Knocked on the door. 'If you need anything before your lawyer gets here, use the intercom button by the door.'

Alex stepped up close to the hatch and looked past the PCSO's shoulder at Logan. 'I do love him, you know?' A little smile. 'He just . . . annoys me sometimes.'

Logan reached forward and clicked the hatch shut. Turned and marched back out through the barred gate and into the custody suite. 'Total utter nutjob.'

'Tell me about it.' The PCSO swung the gate shut with a clang and locked it. 'Place is full of them after last night. Knocking lumps out of each other during the wedding, now they're all taking turns to start a singsong. It's going to be a *long* weekend.'

Away in the male cell wing, someone launched into, '*Welcome to the Hotel Fraserburgh, such a lovely place . . .*' Soon joined by half a dozen other voices.

The PCSO shrugged. 'Still, at least they're in tune. And it's better than the usual swearing.'

Logan followed him back to the booking desk with its posters and notices and leaflets. Stopped, one hand on the countertop. 'When Kevin McEwan and Colin Spinney were in here, did they say anything about Spinney's mum?'

'Gerbil and Klingon?' The PCSO scratched at one of his tattooed arms with the bunch of keys. 'Hmm . . .' One eye squeezed closed and the scratching intensified. Then stopped. 'She's gone to Australia? Sydney or Perth, something like that.'

No she sodding hadn't.

'Thanks.'

'I can ask, if you like? Got a mate works as a Prison Officer in Craiginches.'

'Keep it low key. Someone finds out I'm taking an interest, I'll get my testicles handed to me.' Speaking of which. 'Sorry, got to make a call.'

He slipped out the side door and into the car park at the back of the building. A couple of patrol cars were parked next to the tradesman's entrance. One Transit van sagging to the right with a flat front tyre. And a couple of everyday family saloons. No one about.

Logan pulled out his phone and called Nicholson's mobile. Listened to it ring for a bit.

Then she was on the line. *'Sarge? Why didn't you use the Airwave?'*

Because this way they wouldn't be monitored or recorded.

'How is he?'

'Lost a lot of blood. Going to be in surgery for at least another two hours.'

Deep breath. 'Listen, if anyone asks about what happened today—'

'I didn't hear anything. Not until someone screamed inside.'

'Janet, DCI Steel—'

'Think there must've been something coming over my handset at the time, because I didn't hear her say anything.'

'Janet. You tell the truth: no mitigation, no spin. A cock-up's OK – a cover-up isn't. We don't synchronize our stories, that's when the rot sets in.'

Nothing from the other end.

'Janet, you with me?'

'Yes, Sarge.'

'Good.' He hung up. Pushed back into the detention suite.

His Airwave bleeped.

'Shire Uniform Seven, safe to talk?'

Can't even get two minutes . . . Logan pressed the button and talked into his shoulder. 'Hammer on, Maggie.'

'Sergeant McRae, I'm afraid we've got a problem with this evening's lateshift. Sergeant Muir's broken his leg.'

The Fraserburgh Cellblock Choir must've reached a difficult bit in their song, because the words were replaced by lots of 'la, la, la,' until they hit the chorus again.

Logan closed his eyes. 'What happened?'

'Unfortunate encounter with a springer spaniel. He fell off his mountain bike.'

'Let me guess: Inspector McGregor wants someone to fill in for Muir. No one else free?'

'Sorry.'

Of course there wasn't.

So much for helping Helen paint the living room tonight. Still, at least it meant overtime. 'Yeah, OK. Put me down for a green shift.'

Logan swivelled his chair left and right, and back again. Every movement coming with a free squeak, like the whole mechanism was resting on top of an angry mouse. 'No, I'm going to be stuck at work. Just wanted to check in and see if the new antibiotics were working.'

On the other end of the phone, Louise from Sunny Glen Care Home made a little humming noise. *'It'll take a couple of days, but I think we've finally got Sam's chest infection under control. And I've spoken to the consultant at Aberdeen Royal Infirmary – the next free surgical slot is in three months' time. You could go private, but it'd cost a fortune, and it'll be the same people doing it, so . . .?'*

'Does it make any difference to whether she gets better or not, if we do it now or later?'

Squeak. Squeak. Squeak.

The Fraserburgh Sergeants' Office was a lot more modern than the one back at Banff station. No architraves, panelled doors, or high corniced ceilings here. Instead it was all ceiling tiles, yellow walls, minimalist furniture, creaky computers, and creakier floors. A lot bigger too – at least three times the size, with desks all the way around the outside and a clothes rail hung with high-vis jackets and stabproof vests.

'Hello? You still there?'

'Logan, I know it's difficult, but we've talked about this. The chances of Sam making a full recovery are . . .' A sigh. *'Why don't we take it one day at a time?'*

His stabproof hung from the rail like all the others, but some days its crushing grip on his chest never went away.

'You think we should go with the later surgical slot.'

'I really do. Anyway, look, I'd better run.' She paused. *'Take care of yourself, Logan.'*

'OK.'

He slid his phone back into his pocket. Stared out of the window at the hulking Victorian pile on the other side of the street.

We've talked about this.

Yeah. Didn't make it any easier, though.

A sigh pulled the air out of him, leaving him slumped.

Better give Helen a call. Let her know she was on her own tonight.

Her mobile rang twice, then she was on, breath-less, voice a quarter octave higher than normal. *'Hello, yes?'*

'Helen, it's Logan, I've—'

'Have they run the DNA? Is it Natasha?'

'They're still working on it. Look, I'm going to be stuck at work tonight – the Duty Sergeant who usually does backshift broke his leg.'

'Oh . . . But I got steak for tea.'

'I know. I'm sorry.' He picked at a scar in the desktop, working his nail under the laminate. 'How did you get on with the living room?'

'We were going to have chips and mushrooms and onion rings.'

'You're talking to a man who's lived on lentil soup for the last four weeks. Believe me: I'm really, *really* sorry.'

The Sergeants' Office door opened and a scowling Steel slumped in and pulled a face like a dying fish. Then shuffled over and collapsed into the chair on the other side of the desk in an avalanche of grunts and groans. 'Knackered.'

Helen's voice took on a brittle cheerfulness. *'Well, not to worry: we'll have steak tomorrow. I'll make something else.'*

Steel had a dig at an armpit. 'Haven't got any crisps, have you?'

Logan swivelled his chair around till his back was to her. 'OK, well, I'll talk to you later. Bye.'

'Suppose I'll go back to the painting then . . .'

He hung up and slipped the phone back in his pocket.

A sniff. 'Come on then, who was that?'

'Just a . . . witness to a case. Fly-tipping. Nothing serious.' He swivelled round again. 'How did it go?'

The dying fish finally gave up the ghost. 'Lucky for me, Napier's already up here, isn't it? Saved me having to go all the way down to Aberdeen for my bollocking.' She drooped even further, head back, staring up at the fluorescent lights. 'If I'd known *she* was Alex instead of *him* . . .'

Hindsight. Got to love it.

'You might want to get a lift back to Banff with Deano. I'm going to be here for a bit.' Logan logged on to the computer.

'And because *that's* not enough: Susan can't get here till tomorrow. She's got her lump of a mum visiting. I swear, soon as I leave the house that woman swoops in like a frumpy vulture. Digging her beak in.' Steel grimaced at the ceiling tiles. Silence. 'You know what we should do, Laz? We should hit the town. Get some pints, then a curry, then more pints. And to hell with Napier, and Alex Williams, and Susan's horrible mum, and everyone else.'

'Can't: got a division to run.'

She waved a hand at him. 'You used to be more fun . . .' Then blew a wet raspberry. 'On second thoughts, you've always been a miserable git.'

'Feel free to sod off any time you like.' He pulled up the shift roster for Saturday's lateshift and wrote everyone's name and shoulder number down in the A4 hardback notepad he'd lifted from the stationery cupboard, listing each of them by operational area. It was nearly half four now, so they'd start drifting into their various stations in fifteen minutes, ready to start another *fun* Saturday evening arresting drunks, breaking up fights, and stopping people from peeing in doorways.

Yeah, divisional policing was where all the cool kids were.

Steel pulled out her fake cigarette and poked it in her mouth. 'You hear about DS "Squirty" Dawson?'

Logan cleared his throat, kept his eyes on the notepad. 'Still in hospital.'

They had four PCs in Banff and another two in Mintlaw. Should be six in Peterhead, and four in Fraserburgh, but that included the two officers needed to watch each cellblock, so really only four and two. For a Saturday night.

If anyone had any idea how few police officers they had to look after huge tracts of Scotland, there'd be panic in the streets.

Steel dug a hand into her armpit and had a rummage. 'Picture him up there, getting sponge-baths from all those lovely nurses. Lucky sod.'

'Believe it or not, a stay in hospital isn't all it's cracked up to be.'

So, two officers from Banff to Fraserburgh? Or one to Fraserburgh and one to Peterhead?

'The doctors did that palpitating thing to his

stomach when he wouldn't stop exploding. Found a lump.'

Maybe one from Mintlaw to Peterhead, and one from Banff to Fraserburgh instead? Bit more fair. Everyone would be one body down, and it wasn't as if Mintlaw was a hotbed of . . . Wait a minute. 'They found a *lump*?'

'Cancer. Caught it just in time to do something about it.' She nodded, took a long draw on her e-cigarette. 'Tell you, Laz, never mock a dodgy kebab, it could save your life.'

Silence.

Steel squinted at him. 'You feeling OK? Only you look like someone's stuffed a Kinder Surprise up your bum.'

He closed his mouth with a click. Blinked. Smiled. 'Yes. Good. Well, that's great news, isn't it? Dose of the squits saved his life. Excellent.'

At least now Nicholson could stop feeling guilty.

Steel laced her hands behind her head. 'OK, so if you knew you could get away with it, how would you kill Napier the Ginger Whinger?'

Logan went back to his notepad. 'Thought you had a little girl's murder to solve?'

'I think I'd go for a claw-hammer. I know, I know: it's a trope of the genre, but would you no' get a load more satisfaction battering his brains out than stabbing him?'

'You've got no idea what you're doing on that case, do you?'

415

'Stabbing's for wee boys and tossers. Claw-hammer, that's a *real* woman's weapon.' She raised her arm above her head and mimed raining hammer blows down on an imaginary Napier. 'Bang, thunk, thud, crack, splinter, squish, squelch—'

'You know Helen . . . *Mrs Edwards* is probably sitting somewhere, eating her nails down to the elbow, while you're here playing silly buggers?'

Steel sighed, then placed her invisible hammer on the desk. 'What are we supposed to do?' She counted each thing off on her fingers. 'There's no trace, there's no DNA, there's no witnesses, and we don't know who she is. If we can find the murder weapon they can probably match flakes of metal to the wound in her scalp, but that's sod all use if we've no idea where it is.'

'But—'

'The only suspect we've got is Neil Wood, and he's vanished. You're right, other than tramping round the stots and nonces again and rattling their teeth till someone talks, I've no' a sodding clue.' She folded her arms and hoicked up her bosom. 'Come on then, Angela Lansbury, tell us what you'd do.'

Silence.

Logan bit his bottom lip. Stared down at the point of his pen. 'Well . . .'

'Aye, no' so easy, is it?'

'National appeal for—'

'Done it. Got the nutters out in force, that one.' She jerked her chin up. 'Anything else?'

'How about tidal patterns? You could predict where the body—'

'Already got a team of marine biologists from Aberdeen University doing it. Next?'

Logan tapped his pen against his pad. Looked out of the window. Then down at the carpet. 'Someone has to know where Neil Wood is.'

'And we're back to rattling sex offenders again.' Steel huffed out a breath. 'Face it, we're going round in circles till we get a break. God knows where it's going to come from, though.'

All units, be on the lookout for a stolen poodle taken from outside the Lidl in Peterhead. Answers to the name of "Knitted Doug".'

She checked her watch. 'All this achieving sod all is making me hungry. When's dinner?'

'There has to be *something* we can do.'

'Soon as you think what it is, let me know and I'll take the credit.'

— SATURDAY LATESHIFT —

YOUNG LOVE.

CHAPTER 32

Someone walked past outside, setting the floorboards singing. Logan put ticks against each member of the Banff lateshift in his new notepad. Pressed the talk button again. 'OK, thanks, Joe. I'm going to be out and about for most of the night, but give me a shout if you need anything.'

'*Will do, Sarge.*' And that was it – they were good to go till three in the morning.

Nothing like running a team that didn't actually need supervision.

Logan stuck his body-worn video unit into the charger next to the steam-powered computer and set everything the BWV had recorded downloading onto the system. Then picked up the phone and called Peterhead.

'Stubby, it's Logan. What are you and your hired thugs up to the night, then?'

Sergeant Jane Stubbs blew a raspberry down the line. '*That's what. You really Duty Sergeant tonight? You not learn after last time?*'

'Glutton for punishment. Listen, I'm slinging someone up from Mintlaw to help you. Don't break them.'

'*No promises. We've got the usual checks on licensed premises to do, probably be a barney at some point – usually is on a Saturday – then there's couple of housebreakings to follow up on, some bail violations, and there's a wee sod selling pills in the clubs. Says they're Viagra, but they're really GHB.*'

Logan jotted it all in the notepad. 'Someone's in for a shock come bedtime.'

'*I want to catch the wee sod before he kills someone.*'

'Good. Do me a favour and keep an eye out for Neil Wood, would you? Oh, and speaking of housebreakings, if anyone spots Tony Wishart knocking about, bang him up and give me a call.'

'*Will do. Have a Q-one.*' Then Stubby was gone.

Next up: call the Mintlaw station to break the good news about them having to lend Peterhead a body tonight. Then head downstairs to prioritize jobs with the Fraserburgh Sergeant – currently playing babysitter to the Cellblock Singers, as per regulations. At least that meant Logan wouldn't have to sod about with the official Twitter account for the rest of the shift – if Sergeant McCulloch was going to be sitting on his bum all night, *he* could deal with it.

And after that . . .

Logan performed a little drum solo on his pad with the end of his biro.

There had to be something out there that was solvable without a team of three thousand and access to a HOLMES suite. Something he could bring in on his own and get a bit of credit for. Something to get Napier off his back.

Something that wouldn't blow up in his face.

Logan took a big bite out of his burger, chewing through lettuce and meat, onions and cheese, bun and thousand island dressing. Proper food. Food you didn't eat with a spoon.

Sitting in the Big Car's passenger seat, Steel had a napkin tucked into the collar of her shirt and pink smeared either side of her mouth. 'Didn't know Wimpy still existed.'

From their little patch of gravel, just off the Fraserburgh to Sandhaven road, the sea was a wall of blue, fringed with white where it nudged against the shore. A towering cliff of cumulonimbus reared up from the horizon, caught in the spotlight of the evening sun.

With the car's windows down, the iodine scent of seaweed and the skirling craw of herring gulls filled the warm air.

A couple of chips, then a scoof of Fanta. 'I've been thinking about what Jack Simpson said about the guy who supplied Klingon and Gerbil's drugs.'

Steel licked a dribble of sauce off her wrist. 'Who?'

'Jack Simpson: the guy we found half-dead in Klingon's attic.'

'Don't care.' She sooked a fingertip clean. 'I mean, what kind of place still has a *Wimpy*? What is this, the 1980s? Welcome to Fraserburgh, look at our cool digital watches, mullets, and shoulder pads.' Another bite, chewing with her mouth open. 'No' that I'm complaining, mind. Haven't had one of these in years.'

'Jack said he was called the Candleman, or Candlestick Man. What if he got it wrong? I mean, they're battering the living hell out of him, and he's probably off his face on heroin at the time.'

'You're obsessed with this Candlebloke.'

'What if it's the Candlestick *Maker*. "Maker", not "Man".' He raised his eyebrows at her. 'Well?'

His Airwave bleeped. '*All units from Control. Be on the lookout for a green Audi estate, failure to stop following an RTC on the A95 north of Cornhill . . .*'

'Can you no' turn that down?'

'Duty Sergeant, remember?'

Munch, munch, munch. Chew, chew, chew. 'Fine. But if I finish my chips before you do, I get to steal yours. It's the rules.'

'Since when?'

'Since I had to buy your dinner.'

Fair enough. He popped a couple of them before that happened. 'Come on: who do we know who'd use "Candlestick Maker" as an alias?'

She ripped another bit out of her burger. 'Mmmnnghmmmph.'

'Martyn Baker, *that's* who. AKA: Paul Butcher. The Butcher, the Baker, and the Candlestick Maker—'

'Went to sea in a beautiful pea-green boat.'

'That's the Owl and the Pussycat.' He pulled another chip from the pile and waved it at the view outside the windscreen. 'We got thrown off the scent because Jack Simpson said Klingon's supplier had a Newcastle or Liverpool accent. But the Candlestick Maker's not a Geordie or a Scouser, he's a Brummie – Simpson was too doped up and concussed to tell the difference. Martyn Baker's our guy.'

Steel polished off the last of her chips. 'Aye, well done, Miss Marple. Shame there's sod all you can do with it. Porter and her crew will have got there on day one. He'll be under surveillance till he gets his next shipment, then *boom*, they come down on him like the Fist of God.' A sniff. 'You really want to get in the way of that? 'Cos they'll squish you into mush if you do.'

True.

'Anyone in the vicinity of King Edward? We've got reports of a break-in . . .'

Logan took another bite, but the burger didn't taste as good as it had a minute ago. Could've been at home eating steak instead . . . Still, it was miles better than the tin of lentil soup waiting for him back at the station. 'The fact that they're watching Martyn Baker doesn't stop him being an accessory to Jack Simpson's beatings.'

'Aye, good luck with that.' She reached over and helped herself to a couple of Logan's chips. 'Laz, you and me are on a sinking ship, adrift on the Sea of Jobbies. If we're getting a lifeboat big enough for two, it'll have to be a different case. What else you got on?'

'Not counting your murdered wee girl at Tarlair Outdoor Swimming Pool? Only other big thing's the Cashline Ram-Raiders.'

'Hmm . . .' Steel narrowed her eyes at the horizon and chewed the rest of the way through her burger in silence, with the odd pause to swig down a mouthful of Diet Coke.

'What if we got Jack Simpson to ID the three of them from a VIPER line-up? I know we've got video of Klingon and Gerbil. And there has to be one on file for Martyn Baker.'

'Don't be daft. Told you: they won't let you anywhere near Baker.' She dipped into Logan's chips again, so he handed the whole container over. She wolfed down a couple. 'Tell me about these Ram-Raiders.'

'Going by past experience, it's probably a gang up from down south.' He stuck the last wedge of burger in his mouth. 'They get themselves a van, or a minibus, and they go on a wee tour of wee towns, boosting cash machines from wee shops. Take the lot back down south and break them up away from . . .' He wiped his face with the napkin. Frowned out at the rolling surf. 'Hold on, if they've got Martyn Baker under surveillance, why did they let you vandalize his car this morning?'

'Told you: it was like that when I found it.'

'But we *searched* him. What if he was carrying product? We would've arrested—'

426

'And you'd have got your bum handed to you on a stick, soon as you got back to the station.'

The traffic was beginning to pick up. Not that rush hour was much to write home about in Sandhaven. Two cars going one way, a tractor going the other.

'All units, cancel that lookout request on the green Audi estate. Been found wrapped around a signpost on the B9025.'

Steel polished off the last of the chips, then dabbed up the remaining dribbles of special sauce with a fingertip. 'What kind of wee shops are they hitting?'

'All Co-ops. Well, except for that place in Fraserburgh: Broch Braw Buys.'

'Interesting.' She licked the fingertip clean, then wiped her hands on her trousers and dug out her phone. Made greasy prints on the screen. 'Hold on. . . . Aye, Andy? It's Roberta. . . . Yeah, still stuck with the Mire's Bunnit Brigade. . . . Really?' She laughed, setting a crevasse of wrinkly cleavage jiggling. 'Listen, Andy, you're in charge of the Cashline thing, right? Anyone looked at it being an inside job? Maybe it's someone from the Co-op, or whoever it is supplies the cash machines?'

A removal van grumbled past on the road, 'BLOO TOON SHIFTERS ~ TOUGH ENOUGH TO SHIFT YOUR STUFF!' stencilled down the side with a cartoon of a haddock carrying a packing case.

Steel nodded. 'Uh-huh. . . . Yeah, thought so. Never mind, worth a try. Give Dawn a big wet

427

kiss and a grope from me, OK? . . . Yeah, you too, Andy.' She hung up. Pursed her lips at the phone for a second. Then thumped Logan on the arm. 'Told you it was a stupid idea.'

'Yeah, what *was* I thinking?' He finished off his Fanta. 'Think they'll keep hitting Co-op stores?'

'Suppose we could stick a bunnit in every Co-op in the northeast. That'd do it.'

'Do you have any idea how thin we're stretched as it is? Where are we supposed to find the bodies?'

'There is that.'

A minibus drove past with its windows down. Everyone in the back was wearing a black-and-white striped football shirt, as if they were all referees off on a jolly. The words, 'One-Nil! One-Nil!' Dopplered by, battered out on the wings of far too much lager and not enough tune.

Logan's Airwave bleeped. He wiped his hands on a napkin. 'Safe to talk.'

'*Sarge? Deano.*'

'What you still doing on, Deano? Shift ended an hour ago.'

'*Had to break into an auld wifie's house. Daughter was convinced the old girl was dead at the bottom of the stairs.*'

'No?'

'*Nah, drunk as a badger. Found her in the down-stairs bog, all covered in sick.*' The clunk of a door closing, muffled out of the handset's speaker. '*Listen, turns out the auld wifie's husband did six years for abusing wee girls. Ran his own photography*' *business. You know the sort of thing: come get glamour shots of your kids. "Oh, don't worry, you can leave wee Jeanie with me, and I'll be done by the time you've finished your shopping." Kind of thing.'*

Logan crushed the empty Fanta can and dropped it into the bag his burger had come in. 'At it again, is he?'

'Not unless it's from beyond the grave. Died last year. His shop caught fire with him in it.'

At least that was something.

'And . . .?'

Sitting in the passenger seat, Steel indulged herself with a post-Wimpy e-cigarette, blowing malformed vapour rings at the windscreen.

'And no one's going to hire a paedo photographer, so when he got out of prison he started taking pics for competitions. Got some of them up in the house.'

'Deano, I'm losing the will to live here.'

'Fifth place in the Aberdeen Examiner *portrait competition from four years ago. It's Neil Wood, cooking eggs in his B-and-B. Two years ago, it's third place for a photo of Charles "Craggie" Anderson standing alongside his ship in dry dock. Our missing person's got his portrait up on a paedo's wall, Sarge.'*

And Neil Wood wasn't the only one who disappeared just before that wee girl's body turned up.

CHAPTER 33

Logan propped his pilfered notepad open against the steering wheel, and frowned at the short list of names doing lateshift in Banff that evening. Big Paul, Penny, Kate, and Joe. Of the four of them, Joe had the lowest shoulder number so the most time served. Logan called him on the Airwave. 'Shire Uniform Seven. You there, Joe?'

'Aye, Sarge. Safe to talk.'

Outside, Steel scuffed up the steps to her hotel with her phone clamped to her ear and her fake cigarette waving about like a conductor's baton.

The wind was getting up, making her shirttails flap as she disappeared inside.

Logan pressed the button again. 'Where are you?'

'Castle Street. Me and Penny's doing the rounds.'

'Good. What about the others?'

'Kate's off to Fraserburgh for the night, and Big Paul's away following up on a couple of tractor thefts around Portsoy.'

Nice and low-maintenance. Got to love it.

'Do me a favour – nip back to the ranch when you've got a minute and run a full PNC on a misper for me: Charles "Craggie" Anderson. All his details are on the briefing slide. Go digging. I want to know if there's any soft intelligence out there about him.'

A pause. *'Am I looking for anything in particular?'*

'Yes, but I'm not prejudicing your enquiries.'

'Then I'll go digging.'

'Thanks, Joe.'

He hooked his Airwave back in place. Stuck the notepad on the passenger seat. According to the dashboard clock, it was gone ten past six. Time to patrol.

'All units, please be on the lookout for one Mark Lee, outstanding apprehension warrant for assault.'

Logan climbed into the Big Car and tossed his cap into the back.

The old woman stood at the front door of her tiny cottage, watching as he pulled away. One arm wrapped around herself, the other giving a small half-hearted wave. Holes in her cardigan, holes in the ancient slippers on her feet.

He called it in. 'That shed break-in in King Edward: looks like they got away with a lawnmower, strimmer, and a chainsaw. Victim's got no idea when it happened – any time over the last three weeks.'

'Got that. Shed was locked?'

Nope. But then that meant the insurance company could weasel out of paying for what had been nicked. 'Yeah, they popped one of the windows in. It's boarded up now.'

431

'OK. Thanks.'

He took the back roads, past fields and lonely farmhouses, turned amber and gold in the sunlight. A herd of sheep glowed like bronze statues against a field of emeralds.

Trees and hedges blurred by the windows.

'Anyone in the vicinity of Cruden Bay, we've got reports of a fight outside the Golf Club . . .'

With any luck, they'd have stopped by the time a patrol car got there from Peterhead. The last thing they needed tonight was more people in the cells, taking up space till the courts opened for business on Monday morning.

Stubby's voice growled out of the speakers. *'Roger that, Control. Show Sierra Two One responding.'*

Past the big graveyard on the outskirts of Macduff, the rows of the dead cold beneath the sun-warmed grass. Plenty of space for more to join them.

God, that was cheery.

Logan twisted his Airwave out of its clasp and thumbed Joe's shoulder number into the keypad. 'Joe, safe to talk?'

Silence.

Then, *'Sorry, Sarge, we're doing a stop-and-search.'*

'OK. I'm on my way back to the station. Wanted to know if you'd found anything out. Give me a shout when you're free.'

'Will do.'

The River Deveron was a sheet of beaten copper at the side of the road, glittering its way to the North Sea.

Why was Broch Braw Buys the only non-Co-op hit by the Cashline Ram-Raiders? It wasn't as if it was anything special – just another wee shop. Maybe there was some sort of personal connection? A grudge against the owner? It wasn't the first in the series, so it wasn't as if they were getting their eye in. Or maybe it was simply an easy shop to hit?

Might be worth popping past tomorrow when it was open and having a word with the owner. See if he'd made any enemies in the last few months.

Probably a waste of time, but you never knew . . .

Around, over the bridge, past the Spotty Bag Shop, and along Carmelite Street.

A gaggle of women in short skirts and high heels clacked and cackled their way along the pavement. They all wore pink Stetsons, except for the one in the middle who had a white veil and learner plates on. They cheered and waved as Logan drove past.

Give it a couple of hours and at least one of them would be face-down in a pub toilet, or being sick in a bus shelter.

'Shire Uniform Seven from Control, safe to talk?'

He hit the button. 'Go ahead.'

'Got a Sergeant Creegan for you from Kirkwall station.'

There was a *click*, then a man's voice came from the Airwave's speaker, sounding a lot more Inverness than Orkney. *'Hullo? Yes, are you the one*

433

who put a lookout request on the Copper-Tun
Wanderer? *Cause we've found it.'*

'Great. Thanks. Is the skipper there: Charles
Anderson?' Logan eased past the much smaller,
much older graveyard opposite Banff's little Tesco
supermarket. Ancient lichen-flecked headstones,
squeezed in cheek to jowl. No more room for the
dead.

'Ah . . . Yes, and no.'

'So he's not there?'

A troupe of lads in tight jeans, tattoos, and
numbered T-shirts lurched across the road, two of
them holding up a bloke in a kiss-me-quick porkpie
hat. All of them singing 'Flower of Scotland' with
the complete lack of skill and self-awareness that
comes free with lots and lots of booze. Looked as
if the stag do had headed out a lot earlier than
the hen night. Eight o'clock and they were already
lurching.

*'We found the boat on the rocks, off the coast of
South Ronaldsay. There was a fire on board, looks like
Friday night. It's pretty much a hulk now, everything
burnable's burned. There's not much left of the wheelhouse, or Mr Anderson.'*

'He's dead.'

'Very. Looks like part of the roof came down on him.'

At least with Steel's monkeys back off to
Aberdeen, there were plenty of parking spaces in
front of the station again. Logan reversed into the
one by the front door.

'OK. Well, thanks for letting me know.' Not

exactly a great result, but at least they could stop looking for him now. Mind you, with Anderson dead, they might never find out what happened to the wee girl they'd hauled out of the water at Tarlair.

The stag party must've been on their way to the Ship Inn, because they lurched along the road on the other side of the public car park. Skirted a woman, standing on her own by the wall that separated the road from the bay. Their rendition of 'Flower of Scotland' segued into a chorus of wolf whistles and blown kisses as they passed her.

She turned to watch them go, then went back to staring out across the water.

'Suppose he'd just had enough. Happens sometimes with fishermen. They want to go out like Vikings.'

Logan grabbed his peaked cap and climbed out into the warm evening. 'You're saying it wasn't an accident?'

'Best guess: two bottles of whisky, two litres of petrol, and a match. Nothing left but bones and ash. Hell of a way to die.'

And maybe Hell was where Charles Anderson deserved to be.

Logan ran through his warrant request one last time. Changed a couple of words, then emailed it off to Inspector McGregor. OK, so DCI McInnes had been *very* clear about Logan keeping his nose out of Operation Troposphere, but that didn't mean Klingon, Gerbil, and their new mate Martyn

Baker should get away with battering Jack Simpson half to death.

Next up – more paperwork . . .

The tradesmen's entrance banged, then the sound of heavy feet thumped along the corridor.

PC Penny Griffiths stuck her head into the Sergeants' Office. A small woman, red hair pulled back from her round face. Big smile. 'Evening, Sarge, you want a tea? Joe's making.'

'Thanks. How's it out there?'

She pursed her lips for a moment, eyebrows up. 'Well, we had to caution a bloke in a stupid porkpie hat for peeing off the harbour wall, but other than that it's pretty you-know-what.'

Good. And with any luck it would stay you-know-what till the shift ended.

Penny pointed back into the main office, where the newspapers were hung over Maggie's cubicle wall. 'You see the late editions? They got someone for killing Stephen Bisset. Mad, isn't it? Can you imagine what those poor kids must be going through?'

'Yeah, I know.'

She turned to go. 'We've got doughnuts as well, if you want one?'

'You're a star, Penny – and anyone who says different is a moron.'

Soon as she was gone, he wandered out into the main office and helped himself to the *Aberdeen Examiner*. Its headline – 'PERVERT VOLUNTEER ARRESTED FOR BISSET KILLING' – sat above a photo of a smiling man with a bald head, soup-strainer moustache, and soul-patch. He was in a bar with a couple of other people, their features pixelated out by the newspaper. It was captioned, 'MARLON BRODIE WROTE AN ONLINE JOURNAL ABOUT EXTREME SEXUAL PRACTICES'.

They didn't give the web address, but it didn't take long to Google it up.

According to the home page, Brodie was taking his inspiration from a book called *The Encyclopaedia of Unusual Sexual Practices* by someone called, appropriately, Brenda Love. It looked as if Brodie was flitting his way through the A-to-Z of kinks in no particular order, then arranging his adventures into categories, along with musings and plans for the future.

Logan skimmed through a couple of pages. Pausing to wince at the one about Brodie getting an ex-girlfriend to staple his scrotum to the kitchen table. Then laugh at the photo where he had a bash at anaclitism – anyone who found wearing a nappy sexy had no business posting pictures of themselves doing it on the internet. Another laugh at the failed attempt to negotiate a threesome to check troilism off the list. Another wince for the bee-sting fetish – complete with before and after photos that had Logan crossing his legs. And finally, a rather sad story about Brodie paying a woman he'd met at a party to let him have sex with her armpit. Axillism? Apparently also known as 'having a bagpipe'.

Took all sorts.

Logan found the button to arrange Marlon Brodie's posts by date order, rather than topic, and there it was, top of the list: pseudonecrophilia.

Joe appeared in the doorway, mug in one hand, brown paper bag in the other. 'One white tea, one jammy doughnut.' He'd dumped his protective gear, leaving a black Police T-shirt stretched tight across a huge barrel chest. The same DIY-style haircut as Logan's sat above a big square face with a scar through one thick eyebrow.

'Ta.' Logan reached for the mug. 'Did you manage to dig anything up on Charles Anderson?'

'Other than the fact he's dead?'

The tea was hot and milky. 'Well, that's a good start.'

'Family man. Coached the under-twelves five-a-side team in Macduff for a couple of years.'

'Any hints he was doing more than coaching them?'

'Nope.'

'But?' Logan dipped into the brown paper bag, and came out with a sugary disc of squidgy delight.

Joe sat back against the desk, arms folded. 'Wife divorced him three years ago. Irreconcilable differences.'

'They say what those differences were?' The first bite of doughnut was yieldingly soft and sweet, with a wee squirt of raspberry jam in the middle. Mince and tatties, a burger, *and* a jammy doughnut, all in the same day. It was like having Christmas in May.

'They had a son: Andrew. Went missing five years

ago. Thinking was he'd been playing on the edge of the cliff by the family home and gone over the edge. Officers found a couple of toys up there, but no sign of the body – must've washed out to sea. Andrew was four.'

Poor wee sod.

A slurp of hot milky tea to wash the stodgy mouthful down. 'No suggestion the father was involved?'

Joe shook his head. 'Opposite. He was *convinced* someone had snatched his kid. Banged on about it to anyone who'd listen. Got bits in the paper, put up posters, but . . .' A shrug. 'Wee Andrew wasn't that photogenic, so eventually everyone forgot about it.'

'Except Charles "Craggie" Anderson.'

'And there's your irreconcilable differences. Ex-wife lives in Devon now. She wanted to up sticks and start over somewhere else. He wouldn't budge.'

Another bite of squidgy doughnut. 'If it was your kid, would you?'

A smile spread across Joe's big square face. All teeth and menace. 'If someone touched one of my kids, I'd rip their leg off and jam it up their backside like a lollypop stick.' The smile faded. 'You want to know the spooky coincidence? Andrew died five years ago, yesterday.'

The same day Charles Anderson set fire to the *Copper-Tun Wanderer* and gave himself a Viking's funeral.

Did that make it more, or less likely that he'd

been responsible for killing the little girl at Tarlair Swimming Pool? He might have been overcome with the grief of losing his son, or it might have been guilt . . .

Difficult to tell.

'Sarge?'

Blink. Logan sooked the sugar off his fingertips. 'Sorry, thinking. Thanks, Joe.'

'No probs.'

Soon as he was alone, Logan read the last entry posted on Marlon Brodie's exploration of kinky sex. Drummed his fingertips against the desktop. Frowned at the screen some more. Swore. Then logged into STORM.

A couple of clicks brought up the personnel working on the Major Investigation Team looking into Stephen Bisset's death. Logan picked the DCI in charge from the list, poked her number into the phone and let it ring.

No answer. But then, it *was* nearly nine o'clock on a Saturday night. Have to find someone further down the pecking order who might actually still be working.

Logan dialled the next in line.

Luckily, the DI had a better work ethic than his boss.

He picked up on the fifth ring. *'For God's sake, what now?'*

'Detective Inspector Jackson? Sergeant McRae, B Division. I need to talk to you about the guy you've got in custody for killing Stephen Bisset.'

The rustling of paper came down the line. *'McRae, McRae, McRae . . . Ah, right. It's you. Wondered when you'd come sniffing about.'* Pause. *'If you're looking to put your oar in: don't. You've done quite enough.'*

'It's important. Did—'

'Case should have been airtight and you blew it. Now if there's nothing else, I've got work to do.'

Logan stuck two fingers up at the phone. 'No, you're fine. Good luck with your miscarriage of justice.' He thumped the handset down.

One, one-thousand.

Two, one-thousand.

Three, one-thousand.

Right on cue, the desk phone rang. He picked it up. 'Banff station.'

'What do you mean, "miscarriage of justice"?'

CHAPTER 34

On the other end of the phone, Jackson groaned. Swore. Puffed out a sigh. *'But we've got his DNA . . .'*

'Yeah, and I'll bet you anything you like, if you get the IB to take surface swabs from the other coma patients, you'll find traces of Marlon Brodie's semen.'

More swearing.

'It's all there on his sexblog. He's been trying his hand at pseudonecrophilia. Only he doesn't have to pay someone to pretend to be dead, he's got loads of them lying about in the hospital for free.'

'Well . . .' The faint sound of drumming filled the silence, as if DI Jackson was beating out a tattoo with his fingers. *'Maybe he decided to take it all the way? No more "pseudo". Holds a pillow over Stephen Bisset's face so he's got a real live dead body to have sex with?'*

'There's no mention of murder on his blog. He writes about what he's done and what he'd like to do. I think he saw an opportunity and he took it.'

'But we've got his DNA, and . . . Bloody hell. It's all circumstantial, isn't it?'

'He saying anything about why he did it?'

'His solicitor's told him to "no comment" everything.' More drumming. *'Could still be him. Gah . . . If it isn't him, who is it?'*

'You think you've got it bad: my girlfriend was in a coma there for four years. Don't know how many times he was in her room, unsupervised.' Logan's jaw tightened.

OK, so they couldn't do Marlon Brodie for murder any more, but they could do him for sexually exploiting vulnerable people.

And with any luck, someone in prison would rip the damn thing off and make him eat it.

'No, just wanted to see how you're getting on.' Logan drifted the Big Car along Rundle Avenue again. Still no sign of anyone coming or going from Frankie Ferris's drug den.

On the other end of the phone, Helen coughed. *'Sorry, paint fumes are getting to me a bit.'*

'Then stop. Put your feet up. Read a book.' He slowed down and took a left into a small cul-de-sac. Did a three-point turn.

'Is there any news?'

'They're still working on it.' Logan turned off the engine and sat there, parked beneath a street-light, with a perfect view of Frankie Ferris's front door. 'Helen, when you've been to crime scenes before, have they tried tracking down your ex-husband? Done tax searches, Land Registry, benefits office, pensions, things like that?'

'*And every mortuary, hospital, and graveyard. Brian's disappeared.*'

'Got to be somewhere.'

An old man scuffed past on the pavement opposite, being taken for a walk by a tiny Staffordshire Bull Terrier puppy.

'How was your tea?'

A sigh. '*The MIT don't have any leads, do they?*'

Not a single one.

'Early days yet.'

Silence.

The dog snuffled around a lamppost for a bit while its companion poked away at a mobile phone.

'Helen?'

'*The living room's nearly done. One more coat on the skirting boards to go.*'

'We'll get there. I promise. We'll find—'

'*Don't.*' There was a catch in her voice, as if something had got stuck. '*Don't promise something you can't.* Please. *I've been here too often.*'

The line went quiet again. Only when Logan checked his mobile's screen it showed the call was over. She'd hung up.

And she was right. He had no business promising anything, because there was sod all he could do.

'. . . *break-in at New Pitsligo. Anyone free to attend?*'

He turned the key in the lock. It was a new shiny brass Yale job, set into a bog-standard blank UPVC door that opened on the stinking hovel Colin 'Klingon' Spinney called home.

444

Logan stepped over the threshold into the enveloping reek of rotting garbage, stale body odour, and greasy filth. Closed the door behind him. Clicked on the lights.

The lounge was as they'd left it on Wednesday after the raid, but in the kitchen, someone had pulled the cooker away from the wall. Probably DCI McInnes's Major Investigation Team, giving the place another going over. They'd done the same with the fridge-freezer, getting the white goods out of the way so they could search behind them.

A door off the hall led into the garage. A gloomy, dusty space full of cobwebs and discarded beer tins. Cigarette butts. Roaches. Shelves all higgledy-piggledy with cardboard boxes, paint tins, and filthy gardening equipment.

Dark-brown stains covered the middle of the concrete floor, beneath the fluorescent strip light. That would be where Jack Simpson got used for batting practice, before they stuffed him in the attic ready for tomorrow's beating.

Back into the house proper. Up the sticky stairs.

Logan's Airwave gave its point-to-point beeps as he reached the landing. He unhooked it and wandered into the smaller of the two bedrooms. 'Safe to talk.'

'*McRae? It's DI Jackson.*'

Here we go. 'How did you get on with Marlon Brodie?'

Piles of clothes and dirt and bin-bags. The view

through the window would have been great in daylight – out across the rooftops to the sea – but the moon had been smothered by clouds, leaving everything shrouded in darkness beyond the street-light's glow.

Jackson sighed. *'He says Stephen Bisset was dead when he got there.'*

'What happened to "no comment"?' Back onto the landing.

'Brodie had a change of mind when we told him we'd read his blog.'

'Uh-huh?' Should've done that in the first place.

The bigger bedroom had all its filth piled up in one corner and the mattress leaning against the wardrobe. The painting of Jesus was squint on its nail. Logan walked over to the window and pulled the curtain back.

'He's admitting to masturbating over multiple patients in the coma ward, male and *female. Says them lying there all cool and still and almost dead was one of the sexiest things he's ever seen. Claims he wasn't really hurting anyone. And definitely denying murder.'*

The garden was caught in the glow from the kitchen window, the garage, and the houses on either side. Weeds mostly. Docken and rosebay willowherb jabbed their spears at the dark sky. A patch of brambles in the corner. No shed, but there was a whirly washing line – canted over to the left, its stainless-steel branches buckled and twisted like a tree caught in a storm. The grass had grown in long tufts and clumps, its blades turned rusty and brittle in the recent spate of hot weather.

'You believe him?'

'*Probably. We went through it a dozen times and he didn't change his story once. He got into the room, he saw Stephen Bisset was dead, and he grabbed the chance to crack one out over a* genuine *corpse for a change.*'

'You going to throw the book at him for it?'

'*Going to try.*'

'Good.'

One patch was denser than the others. Over by the back fence, the grass and weeds were shorter and a more luscious shade of green. As if someone had cut a chunk out of some other garden and dropped it into the scrubby wasteland Klingon and Gerbil had ruled over.

'*Listen, McRae, I'm sorry about your girlfriend. We can't tell if he . . . you know. But I'll make sure he's going away for as long as we can get.*'

Why just that patch? Why wasn't it half-dead and choked like the rest of the garden?

'*Trouble is, if he's telling the truth and he didn't kill Stephen Bisset, who did?*'

It was as if there was something under the surface, feeding the plants.

Couldn't really see Klingon and Gerbil out there with the Baby Bio. They weren't exactly *Gardeners' Question Time* kind of guys.

'*McRae? You still there?*'

Logan let the curtain fall shut and pressed the talk button. 'Sorry. Yeah. Listen, has anyone spoken to Bisset's kids?'

'*Not specifically. I spoke to the mother soon as we picked Brodie up. She knows we arrested someone for her husband's death, but not who. Well, assuming she was sober enough to take any of it in.*'

Out onto the landing and down the stairs. 'No, I mean there's no one on the CCTV footage going into Stephen Bisset's room between his kids leaving and the time Marlon Brodie turns up. Don't know about you, but I think they *might* have noticed if their dad was dead. So if he was alive when they went in, and dead by the time Marlon Brodie visited . . .?'

'*Why the hell would they murder their own—*'

'It wouldn't be murder for them, it'd be a mercy killing. Or it's because they're ashamed of the sex thing. Or maybe they couldn't face the thought of their father lying there like a corpse for the rest of his life. Doesn't really matter, does it?'

Steel's right-hand woman, Becky, had been right after all. Even if she was a sour-faced moaning pain in the backside.

Logan marched along the hall and through the kitchen.

The key was still in the door. He unlocked it and stepped out into the back garden.

'*Unbelievable . . .*' A sigh crackled out of the Airwave's speaker. '*OK, I'll get them picked up.*'

Cool air caressed his face, bringing with it the

aniseed-and-petrol smell of wood preservative and the gritty scent of dusty vegetation. He twisted his LED torch free from its catch. Clicked it on.

The grass was soft beneath his boots, like walking on a dying mattress.

'McRae? Thanks. I owe you one.'

There it was. The only patch of healthy-looking weeds in the whole jungle. Definitely shorter than the rest, as if it'd been trimmed down, or only recently grown. Lush and green and healthy in the LED's hard white spotlight.

'Do me a favour? Go easy on them. They're pretty screwed up as it is.'

'I'll see what I can do.' Then DI Jackson ended the call.

Logan tapped the Airwave handset against his leg.

The patch was about five foot by three. Perfect size, if you wanted to get rid of a body.

He thumbed Syd Fraser's shoulder number into the Airwave. No response. So he dug out his phone and tried Syd's mobile instead.

'Hello?'

'Syd, it's Logan. Logan McRae, from Banff? You busy?'

'Sitting here with a cup of tea, watching The Wrong Trousers, *that count?'*

'Am I remembering right: does one of your dogs do cadavers?'

'Hold on.' A scrunching squelch came from the handset's speaker, then a muffled, *'It's work. Only*

449

be a minute.' Some clunking. Another scrunch, and Syd was back. *Lusso did a bit of training as a cadaver dog before I got him. Dog handler who had him ended up falling off a railway bridge after a bottle of vodka, twelve packs of paracetamol, and a note.*

'The other guy named him Lusso? Dog Section full of Ferrari freaks is it?'

Nah, the idiot named him "Goldie". Don't know how much of the training stuck, though; I've been using Lusso as a cash and explosives dog for years. Hidden firearms, things like that. He's good at it.

Better than nothing.

Logan stared at the patch of verdant green. Could just dig it up and see what was down there, but the powers-that-be were already hacked off about him not following procedure. No point giving them another stick to beat him with.

'Any chance you're free tomorrow? I'm at what *might* be a deposition site.'

You there right now? Some more clunking. Then that scrunching squelch again, and a muffled, *Think I'm going to take the wee hairy lads out to stretch their legs before bedtime. Don't wait up if I'm late.* Another clunk and he was back, full volume. *OK, where am I going?*

Yeah, attempted suicide. Not much of an attempt, mind: made a right hash of slashing his wrists. Wasn't hard to stop the bleeding.

Logan rested his elbows on the windowsill. 'OK, thanks Penny. Soon as the ambulance gets there, can you and Joe do another licensed premises check? Want to keep a tight lid on things tonight.'

'*No room at the inn?*'

'Think we've got about four cells free in Fraserburgh. After that we'll have to open up the Banff ones, or start shipping people to Elgin. And you know how that's going to go.'

'*Do my best, Sarge.*'

A pair of headlights worked their way up the street. Then Syd's police Transit van parked outside Klingon's mum's house.

Logan twisted his handset back into place before heading downstairs and opening the front door.

A minute later, Syd came lumbering up the path, being towed by a large golden retriever. He'd changed into his dog handler outfit – webbing waistcoat over a black fleece, black cargo pants, and DM boots. That tatty, ragged old police cap on his head. 'Evening all.'

'Thought you were off duty?'

'Special dispensation from the wife and the Duty Inspector. In that order. Long as I don't put in for overtime, we're fine.'

'Right.' Logan backed into the hall. 'There's a—'

'Nope.' Syd held up a hand. 'Don't tell me. Don't want to prejudice Lusso. If you tell me where you think the cadaver is she'll pick it up from my body language.'

'OK. Then you can get cracking.'

Syd stepped inside and froze, nose wrinkling. '*Stinks* in here.'

'You get used to it.' He removed the elastic band holding his body-worn video shut and set it recording. 'Ten forty p.m., Saturday the twenty-fourth of May. Present: Sergeant Logan McRae and Police Dog Handler Syd Fraser.' A nod. 'Off you go, Syd.'

He let the dog off its lead. 'Come on then, Lusso. Find the body.'

The golden retriever bounded up and down the hall a couple of times, then settled into a sniffing routine. Trotting around the outside edges of the room, nose down, tail up.

'So . . .' Logan laced his hands behind his back. '*The Wrong Trousers*?'

'What's wrong with *The Wrong Trousers*?'

Through into the living room. Lusso did the same tour of the skirting boards.

'Never said a word.'

'It's a film about a man and his faithful canine companion, solving a crime and catching the bad guy. What's not to like?'

'Speaks to your inner dog handler, does it?'

'Damn right.' The golden retriever sniffed back and forth across the floor. Circled the tatty sofa a couple of times. 'Anyone who doesn't like Wallace and Gromit needs a boot up the backside. There's nothing in here, by the way.' Syd stepped back out into the hall. 'Come on, Lusso, kitchen.'

Logan's Airwave bleeped at him. He hung back while Syd directed his own personal Gromit around the filthy room. 'Safe to talk.'

'Sergeant McRae? It's DI Jackson. We sent a car to Stephen Bisset's house. There's no sign of David or Catherine. Their mother says she's not seen them since Wednesday evening.'

That would be just before they put their dear old dad out of his misery.

'They didn't take anything with them. No tooth-brushes, clothes, makeup, or toiletries. The only thing missing is Catherine's favourite teddy bear. So it doesn't look as if it was premeditated.'

'They went missing Wednesday evening, and the mother didn't bother telling us?'

'Don't think she's seen the outside of a gin bottle for about a week. I'm getting an apprehension warrant and a lookout request circulated.'

Well, with any luck, someone would find them before the guilt and grief caught up and made them do something stupid – like Lusso's former owner. 'Thanks for keeping me in the loop, I appreciate it. If you find them . . .?'

'Will do.' And DI Jackson was gone.

Syd emerged from the kitchen. 'Got a positive off the bin, but there's God knows what mould-ering away in there, so it's not surprising he picked up a bit of cadaverine. Going to try the garage next.'

Logan twisted his Airwave back into its holder. 'Dried blood on the concrete floor.'

'OK.'

He followed Syd and Lusso into the dusty space. Leaned back against the wall as the golden retriever sniffed and snuffled around the outside, then lay down in the middle of the floor on top of the blood spatter. Which was to be expected.

'Good boy.' Syd swept an arm towards the door. 'Upstairs next.'

'All units, be on the lookout for a David and Catherine Bisset. IC-One male: seventeen years old. And IC-One female: fourteen. Both with shoulder-length black hair. Apprehension warrant is pending.'

Not exactly a happy ending, but at least the whole sorry mess would be over soon.

He followed Syd up to the landing, filming as Lusso went from room to room.

They'd probably cop a plea. No Procurator Fiscal was going to want to do two grieving kids for the murder of their coma-stricken dad. The media would whip the country into a frenzy.

Then again . . .

A frown.

Graham Stirling: missing, kitchen full of broken chairs and dishes, blood on the floor and the fridge.

You don't batter your crippled dad to death, do you? No, you smother him gently with a pillow. The guy who mutilated him, on the other hand – the guy who abducted him and smeared filth across his memory; you take your time caving his head in with a claw-hammer.

No way they'd let Graham Stirling live. Not after what he'd done to their father.

And if they'd made it quick, his body would still be there, mashed and bloody in the kitchen.

Whatever they had planned, it was going to take a while and hurt a *lot*.

Good.

But that didn't mean they should get away with it.

Logan unhooked his Airwave and dialled DI Jackson again. 'I think I know what David and Catherine Bisset were doing on Friday night.'

'If you're about to say, "Abducting Graham Stirling," you're five minutes too late. I've told the labs to try matching their DNA with trace found at the scene.'

Oh. OK.

'Don't mean to be rude, Sergeant, but I've got a manhunt to organize. Anything else?'

'No, sorry. Thought you'd want to know.'

He put his Airwave back on its holder. So much for that.

Syd puffed out his cheeks as Lusso emerged from the cholera-cesspit toilet. 'Looks like we're a corpse free zone.'

'Yeah. Well, while you're here, we might as well try the front and back gardens too.' Keeping it nice and light. No hints or tips. All nonchalant.

They thumped downstairs, and out through the kitchen door.

The wind's cold fingers pinched at Logan's ears as the golden retriever sniffed his way around the garden fence. Straight over the top of the patch of healthy weeds. Not so much as a twitch.

Sodding hell.

Logan leaned against the doorframe. 'When

he *was* a cadaver dog, any idea if he was any good?'

'Not a clue.'

Lusso snuffled his way across the lawn and back again.

Still nothing.

Syd took off his cap and had a scratch at the shiny scalp beneath. 'No overtime, middle of the night, wandering about in a druggie's back garden.' A smile. 'We must be off our rockers doing this for a living.'

'True.' Logan stuck his hands in his pockets. Nodded at the dog. 'This isn't working, is it?'

'Nope.'

'Sorry I dragged you out.'

'Meh, worth a go.' He unclipped the lead from behind his back. 'Come on, Lusso, time for home.'

But the dog didn't come. He was back at the fence, circling that patch of healthy weeds. Then he lay down right in the middle of it.

Bingo.

CHAPTER 35

'*G*od, *Klingon and Gerbil are the gift that keeps on giving, aren't they?*' The words came out flat and nasal, as if the backshift Duty Inspector needed a good clean out with a drain rod. He paused for a sneeze. Then a sniff. '*And you're sure it's her?*'

'Well . . . not a hundred percent, but there's definitely something there, Guv.' Logan stepped back as a line of anonymous figures in white SOC suits rustled past and out the back door. 'The IB's ready to start digging.'

Outside the window, a blue marquee snapped and rippled in the wind. Hiding the deposition site from prying eyes.

'*They killed his mum, and buried her in the back garden? Are they mental?*'

'Well, Klingon and Gerbil were never the sharpest spoons in the drawer.'

'*Why didn't they chuck her in the sea? Or take her out to the middle of nowhere? Not like we don't have excellent body-burying opportunities round here.*'

'Some people are just lazy.'

'*Place should be a Mecca for people looking to get*

457

rid of their no-longer-loved-ones. We could sell spades and souvenir T-shirts.'

There was a knock on the door and Constable Griffiths poked her head into the kitchen. Her eyebrows were up, the edges of her mouth down. 'Sarge, there's a boss outside and he's foaming. Big Paul won't let him in, 'cos it's a crime scene.'

Oh. Logan sucked a breath in through his top teeth. 'Any idea who it is?'

'A Detective Chief Inspector McInnes?'

The guy in charge of Operation Troposphere. This wasn't going to be fun.

'OK, thanks Penny.' Back to the handset. 'Sorry, Guv, got to go. Someone wants to give me a bollocking for doing my job.'

'I'll be over soon as I can.'

Logan clipped his Airwave back into place, slipped the elastic band off his body-worn video, pulled his chin up, and marched out of the kitchen, down the hall, and into the porch.

Big Paul stood on the top step, blocking the front door, towering over a figure wearing a suit, a tie, and a homicidal expression. That would be McInnes, then.

Big Paul tapped the clipboard in his other huge hand. His voice was a collection of rumbling bass notes that vibrated everything for twenty yards. 'I know that, sir, but this is a crime scene and I'm not going to let you in until the Scenes Examination Branch tell me it's OK. Those are the rules.'

McInnes paced up and down on the short path. Streetlight glinted off the bald patch at the back of his head every time he turned around, like a lighthouse in a sea of short curly grey hair. A thin face with permanent lines etched past the sides of his mouth, a gathering storm of them between his eyebrows. He was at least a foot shorter than Big Paul, but didn't seem to let it bother him. Too used to getting his own way. 'Don't make me call your Divisional Commander!'

'Feel free.' Big Paul leaned forward, voice dropping to an even more menacing rumble. 'Now get behind that barrier tape, before I—'

'All right.' Logan tapped him on the arm. Solid muscle, bunched tight beneath the black T-shirt. 'Thanks, Paul, I'll take it from here.'

He turned. Smiled. 'Sarge.' Then stepped to one side, letting Logan squeeze past onto the path. Before returning to blocking the front door. Both huge arms crossed over his huge chest.

McInnes jabbed a finger at Logan. 'What the hell do you think you're playing at?' The auld-mannie scent of Old Spice wafted off him like cheap vodka.

'We're—'

'Did I, or did I not expressly forbid you from interfering in Operation Troposphere? Because I'm pretty sure I told you to keep your damn nose out of it!'

'Sir, I need you to—'

'THIS!' Another finger, but this one made

contact, stabbing Logan's stabproof vest. 'THIS IS WHAT I WAS TALKING ABOUT!'

'Sir, I need you to calm down. Shouting the odds isn't helping.'

'DON'T YOU BLOODY TELL ME TO CALM DOWN!'

'The curtains are already twitching all along the street. Do you really want to see yourself having a rant posted on YouTube by some nosy neighbour?'

McInnes hissed a couple of breaths in and out through gritted teeth. Then, 'Fine.' His voice dropped to a growling whisper. 'You listen to me, *Sergeant*, and you listen well. This isn't some halfwit divisional bumfest, it's an extremely high-profile inter-agency cross-border operation, and what you're doing is screwing it about!'

Logan pulled his shoulders back. 'With all due respect—'

'Shut up! I've given you chance after chance, but somehow, because you lucked into the initial bust, you think that gives you the right to decide how a thousand-man-hour operation is run?'

'I didn't—'

'You think I don't know you've been asking people to question Kevin McEwan and Colin Spinney in Craiginches? And now here you are, digging up MY BLOODY CRIME SCENE!'

The dogs in Syd's Transit must have finally had enough, because shotgun barks boomed out through the open windows.

McInnes marched down the path to the line of blue-and-white 'POLICE' tape and back again. 'You will stay the hell away from Kevin "Gerbil" McEwan and Colin "Klingon" Spinney. You will stay away from their house. You will stay away from their friends. And if I hear so much as a whisper about you coming anywhere near Operation Troposphere there's going to be a lifetime of misery coming your way.' He dipped into his pocket and produced a smartphone. 'And so we're clear: right now, I'm going to call *my* guvnor and get him to rain crap on *your* area commander's head from a great height. You enjoy the fall-out, Sergeant. You've had your last warning.'

'No, Guv, with all due respect, that's—'

'Don't you dare "all due respect" me, Sergeant.' The backshift Duty Inspector's cold didn't sound as if it had improved any. *'This isn't an "all due respect" situation, it's "shut up and do what you're told".'*

'Guv, I—'

'McInnes called his boss. His boss called the Chief Constable, who opened the sewage floodgates. It's cascading all the way down through B Division from way on high and I don't appreciate being in the bloody flood zone! You will stay the hell away from Klingon, Gerbil, and Operation Troposphere, do I make myself clear?'

'But we found—'

'I don't care if you found Shergar, the Ark of the

Covenant, and the entrance to sodding Narnia: no more! It's done. Now get out there and do your job.'

The muscles in Logan's jaw ached. He prised his teeth apart, barely far enough to squeeze the words out, 'Yes, Guv.'

And the Duty Inspector was gone.

The handset creaked in Logan's fist.

Slow calm breaths.

Don't smash the thing against the pavement. Then gather up the broken shards and ram them up McInnes's backside.

Fifteen minutes. That's how long it had taken for McInnes's crap to roll all the way downhill. Fifteen minutes.

A hand thumped down on Logan's shoulder. Syd. 'You look like you're going to kill someone.'

'Don't tempt me.'

'Only saying.' He hauled back the sliding door on his Transit van, getting a few low yowls of welcome from the dogs. A couple of fold-down seats and some plastic crates filled the space between the Transit's cab and a partition wall with four hatches set into it – each one marked with a little sticky label. 'ENZO' and 'LUSSO' on the bottom two, 'DINO' and 'DO NOT USE!' on the top ones.

The smell of dog was thick as bargain-basement lentil soup. Gritty and sweaty and meaty, all at the same time. Syd hauled a large plastic container from one of the crates and sloshed water in a metal bowl. 'Look on the bright side, at least we found something. Powers that be spent all that time cutting the Dog Section by half, and you know what? We *still* deliver the goods.'

Yeah. Just in time for McInnes to show up, throw a hissy fit, then take the credit.

'All units, be on the lookout for a red Isuzu Trooper. Suspected involvement in the ram-raid on the Gardenstown Co-op. Last seen heading off on the Dubford road.'

Fifteen minutes.

Thank you, Detective Chief Inspector McInnes.

Logan drummed his fingers against the Big Car's steering wheel.

'We've got reports of an assault on Broad Street, Fraserburgh, two hundred yards down from the Crown Bar . . .'

Rundle Avenue was quiet. Here and there, lights glowed through living-room and bedroom curtains, but other than that, the houses were dark. A ginger tabby slunk across the road two cars down from where Logan was parked. It hopped up onto the low garden wall and paused for a second, before jumping down and disappearing around the side of the house that Martyn Baker shared with his girlfriend and kid.

Stay away from Operation Troposphere.

Do what you're told.

Be a good little parochial plod.

Logan wrapped his hands around the steering wheel and squeezed till his forearms trembled.

'Anyone in the vicinity of Crimond, we're getting reports of multiple break-ins . . .'

Could just *manufacture* something to bring Baker down. Not exactly ethical, but then what did ethics get you? Ethics meant people like Graham Stirling got away with torturing Stephen Bisset. Ethics meant letting the bad guys walk, even when you *knew* they were guilty.

And Martyn Baker was guilty.

'Shire Uniform Seven, you safe to talk?'

Logan peeled his fingers off the steering wheel. The knuckles were all white and stiff. 'Go ahead.'

'Sarge, it's Penny. We've got a problem in Macduff, any chance of an assist?'

Of course they did. He sagged back in his seat, stared at the car's ceiling.

'Sarge? You there?'

'Yeah. OK.' A big, long sigh hollowed him out. 'Give me the address.'

Market Street was another collection of small Scottish houses – most of them tiny with dormer windows above a single floor, gable ends, chimney stacks, and grey slate roofs. A line of parked cars were squeezed down one side of the road, single yellows on the other. All bathed in the sickly septic glow of a sodium streetlight.

Logan parked the Big Car with two wheels on the pavement. Not quite blocking the road, but narrowing it a hell of a lot.

Deep breath. Then he picked his peaked cap

off the passenger seat and climbed out into the night.

Wind snatched at his trousers. It dragged the scent of seaweed and iodine all the way from the sea at the end of the road. Sent an empty crisp packet twirling along the kerb.

A faint tang of salt in the air.

Penny stepped out of a doorway two houses down and waved at him. 'Thanks, Sarge.'

He stamped his way over, jamming his hat on his head. 'Still don't see why you couldn't sort this yourselves.'

'She won't listen to us. Says there's rats in her bed.'

Logan stopped. Stared at the cracked, moss-lined, concrete pavement. The muscles in his jaw tightened, so he had to force the words out between gritted teeth. 'That's not a police issue, that's a Care in the Community one!'

When he looked back up again, Penny had folded her arms across her chest, mouth set in a down-ward curl. 'I know that, Sarge.'

Another sigh. He pinched the bridge of his nose. 'Sorry. It's been a long day.' A long, long, crappy day.

'We tried Social Services, they say they can't send anyone out till Monday. Mrs Ellis has been wandering up and down the road, every night for two weeks. In her *jammies*. She's eighty-two.'

The wind snatched and tugged at Logan's hat. Eighty-two, and she was walking about in this, in the dark. Wouldn't be long till she caught her death of cold, or ended up under a car.

Logan's shoulders dipped. 'Come on then, let's get this over with.' Chin up. Force a smile. It wasn't Penny's fault, or the auld wifie. It was whatever scumbag thought turfing vulnerable people out on the streets to fend for themselves was a good idea in the first place.

'Sarge.' Penny led the way into a narrow hallway lined with shelves festooned with little porcelain figurines. Dogs and cats, mostly, but the odd saccharine child in pantaloons or nightshirts too. Dark wood on the walls, a low-wattage bulb in a table lamp. Penny nodded towards a closed door. 'She's in there.'

Logan opened it and stepped into a small living room. More dark wood. More shelves. More creepy porcelain effigies, lit by a single standard lamp. Painted eyes glittered at him from the heavy shadows.

A carriage clock sat amongst the figures on the mantelpiece, click-clacking its thin brass arms around.

Big Paul sat on a two-seater sofa, knees nearly up to his chest. When he stood, he had to stoop to avoid banging his bullet-shaped head on the ceiling. A nod. 'Sarge. This is Mrs Ellis.'

The room's other occupant was a little old lady, thin as a rolling pin. Her thinning silver hair hung around a lined face that looked as if it had seen a lot more pain than anyone should ever have to.

As if every one of those eighty-two years had been carved into her face with a blade. She was dressed in an old pair of winceyette pyjamas, the fabric worn see-through on the knees and elbows. One hand made a brittle claw on the arm of her chair. The other clutched a long breadknife.

OK. Logan took off his hat. 'Are we making sandwiches, Mrs Ellis?'

She blinked her sunken eyes. 'It's meant to be a carving knife, but I don't have one. And they're not mice, they're rats.'

'Rats.'

She bared a set of yellow-grey teeth, each one perfectly regular, set into dark-brown plastic gums. 'Rats in the walls. Rats under the floorboards.' She pulled her knees together and rocked back and forward in her chair. 'They come out at night and they . . . climb into my bed. Scurrying about under the blankets with their sharp little claws and shiny dead eyes.'

The clock on the mantelpiece clacked and clicked, while the porcelain figurines stared from the gloom.

Logan tucked his hat beneath his arm, then held his other hand out. 'How about you put the breadknife down, Mrs Ellis?'

She held it tight against her chest. 'They scratch and they bite and they won't let me sleep. Why won't they let me sleep?'

'OK.' Mad as a fish. He turned to Penny. 'Bedroom?'

She pointed above their heads.

'Thanks. Come on, Mrs Ellis, let's go see these rats.'

The stairs were off the narrow hallway. They creaked and groaned all the way up to a landing barely tall enough to stand up in. A single door led off it. Logan pushed through into a claustrophobic room with a coombed ceiling, a small wardrobe, and a double bed that teetered on the cusp between antique and firewood. The mattress wasn't much better. It sagged in the middle, dragging the layers of itchy blankets and comforters with it.

Floorboards complained as he walked around to the other side of the saggy bed.

Mrs Ellis stayed on the landing, cowering behind the doorframe, breadknife clutched in both hands. 'See? What did I tell you?'

He nodded at the blankets. 'Are the rats there now?'

She blinked at him. 'Of course they are! Can't you see them?'

'No, what I mean is: are they *all* there? In the bed. Not in the walls or the floors, all in the bed?'

A nod.

'Right.' Logan unclipped his extendable baton, slid it out of its holster, clacked it out to full length . . . then battered the hell out of the blankets, comforter, and pillows. Slamming the metal rod down again, and again, and again.

Bloody McInnes and his bloody – *thump* – bloody

– *thump* – Operation – *thump* – bloody – *thump* – Troposphere – *thump, thump, slam, thump.* Bloody Martyn Bloody Baker. Bloody Klingon. Bloody Gerbil. Bloody Napier. *Slam, thump, thump, thump.* The blankets jumped and danced beneath their hammering. Bloody every bloody body. *Thump, slam, thump.*

CHAPTER 36

Logan lowered the baton and stepped back. Chest heaving. Air searing in his throat and lungs. Arm aching. Tingling numbness stretching from his fingertips to his elbow. Face burning. Sweat trickling down between his shoulder blades.

He looked up, puffing and panting. 'Wh . . . What?'

Mrs Ellis stood on the threshold, one hand covering her mouth, eyes wide.

Penny was on the landing behind her, looking much the same. 'Sarge?'

Took a bit of time for the air to stop wheezing in and out. He pointed at the bed. 'There . . . there you . . . go. No . . . no more . . . rats.'

The old lady doddered forwards, reached out a hand, and pulled the covers back.

Dents covered the sagging mattress.

She looked up at him and a smile spread across her face. 'They're gone!' Then she climbed into bed, pulled the blankets up around her chin, closed her eyes, and within five or six seconds was breathing slow and deep.

OK . . .

Logan backed out of the room and switched off the light.

They let themselves out.

'. . . reports of a white Volvo estate driving erratically on the A950 between Longside and Mintlaw . . .'

Logan watched in the rear-view mirror as Penny and Big Paul's patrol car pulled away from the kerb and disappeared into the streets of Macduff. Off to do licensed premises checks on the small handful of places still open at half-one on a Sunday morning.

Mrs Ellis's house lay all locked up and dark. Just the old woman and her collection of creepy porcelain, now that all the rats were dead.

'Anyone free to attend an attempted mugging on King Street, Peterhead?'

He stuck the Big Car into gear and headed down Market Street. Past the rows of little houses. Past the Plough Inn – all quiet. More little houses. The wind was picking up, gusts shoving at the bodywork. Past the wee fish shop and that was it: he'd run out of town.

Macduff aquarium was the only thing between him and the rolling black mass of the North Sea. Half of the car park's lights were out, leaving most of the bays in darkness.

The caravan parked outside the line of temporary fencing rocked in a gust of wind. Its plasticky white walls sparkled with amber beads.

And a manky skeletal figure in a mankier track-suit sat on the top step. Sammy Wilson.

'Not again.'

Logan pulled into the car park and drove over. Buzzed down the window. 'Sammy?'

He was sitting with his head thrown back, face to the dark sky. One arm limp in his lap, the other dangling by his side. Legs bent and splayed.

'Sammy? You OK?'

Nothing.

So much for staying in the car where it was dry and warm.

Logan stuck his hat on his head and climbed out into the wind.

Wet drizzled against his face. Not rain, but spray from the pounding sea. The waves growled and boomed against the rocks, hissed back through the shingle.

The smell of rotting meat and onions surrounded Sammy Wilson like a protective blanket.

Still no movement.

Silly sod had probably overdosed. Again. Time for yet another wheech up to hospital and a dose of Narcan to spoil his high. Well, unless it was already too late?

'Sammy?' Logan reached out and poked him.

'Gaaaaaaah!' Sammy's arms flailed up and out, feet and legs thrashing like a dying frog against the car park's tarmac. Eyes wide, mouth hanging open.

The smell went up by fifty percent.

BOOM – another wave hit the rocky shore.

Logan backed away a couple of steps. 'What the hell are you doing out here? You *trying* to catch your death?'

A puff. A pant. A sickly hissing sound. Then he wiped a bony hand across his grubby face. 'Thought you were . . .' He cleared his throat. 'Yeah. Right. No.'

'Looked like you'd overdosed.'

Sammy blew out a breath. Closed his eyes and let his head fall back against the caravan again. 'Nah. You know, enjoying the night air in sunny Macduff. S'lovely.'

Aye right. Found somewhere quiet to shoot up was more like it. Still, there had to be somewhere drier and warmer to do it than the aquarium car park.

Logan nudged his leg with a boot. 'Thought I told you not to hang about here.'

'Hanging about? Not me, no, no, no. Sammy's not hanging about, he's James Bond waiting for his contact, yeah? Finding out about the Candleman-Maker-Man for twenty quid. Cash for questions.'

BOOM.

Another batter of spray rattled the caravan, nipping at Logan's ear like a thousand midge bites. 'You couldn't find somewhere drier to do it?'

'You got my other ten quid? Ten quid down, ten for questions. Twenty quid.' A filthy hand came out, fingers trembling. 'No win no fee.'

'Come on then: who is he? Who's Klingon and Gerbil's supplier?'

The hand wavered for a moment, then slowly went back to its filthy owner with a sigh. 'Still asking.'

'Then you're getting sod all. And stop hanging around the aquarium. Go find somewhere warm to sleep instead.' Logan turned back to the car. 'Don't make me tell you again.'

Wind rattled the lampposts, making the pools of yellow light dance and writhe as the Big Car drifted through the quiet streets.

Macduff slept. No cars, no taxis; nothing but tarmac and stone and wind and darkness.

Up to the monument. Around past the golf course. Through the middle of town. Then one more check on the aquarium – no sign of Sammy Wilson – and on to the harbour. Then Macduff disappeared in the rear-view mirror. Over the bridge and into Banff, quartering the town, checking on all the little streets where the drug dealers played. Only none of them were daft enough to be out this late in this weather.

Three circuits of Rundle Avenue turned up nothing.

Ah well. There was always tomorrow.

He headed back towards the station, cutting down the Strait Path, between the Royal Bank and the M&Co. Past boarded-up windows and shops for let. Driving down the middle of the steep lane.

'Bravo India from Control, reports of a car fire in a field off the A981 north of Strichen.'

The Duty Inspector's voice crackled out of the handset after it, all bunged up and nasal. *'And I care because?'*

'It's a red Isuzu Trooper. Could be the one that ram-raided the Copey in Strichen.'

'Gah . . . They couldn't have waited another twenty minutes? Shift's nearly over.' A sigh. *'Fine. OK, I'll be there soon as I can.'*

Down to the bottom, and left. Not a living soul to be seen.

A speck of rain snapped against his cheek. Then another one.

Perfect.

Round the corner and left onto High Shore, with its ancient buildings. Past the other end of the old cemetery . . . Logan stopped. Put the Big Car in reverse and backed up a couple of feet. A pink Stetson was poked up between the old headstones, rising and falling.

He buzzed down the window, letting in the moaning wind and a duet of grunts and groans, keeping time with the Stetson's motion.

God's sake, was that what passed for romance these days? A quick shag in a graveyard in the middle of the night?

Logan reached for the button marked 'RIGHT ALLEY'.

Then again, just because he was having a rotten

night, it didn't mean he had to spread the misery. Even if they *were* breaking the law.

The grunts and groans were getting quicker and louder.

Leave the poor sods in peace to enjoy their knee-trembler. Wasn't as if anyone was going to see them at quarter to three on a Sunday morning, was it?

Besides, arresting them would mean more forms, more cautions, another trip to Fraserburgh and not getting home till after four.

He buzzed the window back up again.

Go back to the station, finish up the shift's paperwork, then home.

A huge yawn cracked at his jaws and left him sagged in his seat as he powered down the computer.

All done. He pushed back his chair and hauled himself to his feet.

The station was like a mortuary. Devoid of life, but redolent with the weird smells that always came with the guys on nightshift. God alone knew what they'd had for their lunch, but the stench was all through the building.

Logan locked his notebook away, grabbed his stabproof vest and peaked cap. 'Night, Hector.' Then slouched out into the night.

The wind howled across the bay, pounding surf against the beach. At least the rain hadn't come to much more than an intermittent drizzle.

He hurried across the car park, fumbled his keys

out and let himself into the Sergeant's Hoose. Stood there in the darkness.

The house was quiet, not so much as a creak or a thump. Which probably meant Cthulhu was in the lounge, sleeping with Helen again. Disloyal fuzzy little sod.

Logan scritched the Velcro fasteners off his stabproof then hung the whole thing over the back of a kitchen chair. Checked the fridge. A pair of thick rib-eye steaks sat on a plate, glistening, raw, and dark. One of Steel's confiscated beers sat behind what looked like leftover macaroni cheese.

Wasn't as if he didn't deserve it, after a crappy day like today.

A creak.

Logan's eyes flickered open. Sunlight licked at the chinks in the curtain, but the clock-radio glowed 04:40 in the gloom.

Another creak, right outside the room.

Then the door opened.

A whisper in the dark. 'Logan? Are you awake?'

He sat up. 'You need something?'

'Can't stay down there any more: paint fumes are killing me.' The door closed again. Feet scuffed on the bare floorboards. Then she slid into bed. 'Don't say anything, OK?' She wrapped her arm across his chest and rested her head against his shoulder. 'This isn't a big thing. I just . . . I just want to sleep.'

He cleared his throat. 'OK. But I'm not actually wearing anything.'

Silence.

'Helen?'

Her breathing was deep and regular. She was already gone.

CHAPTER 37

The alarm-clock radio sprung into a spirited accordion-and-fiddles rendition of the Barenaked Ladies' 'One Week'.

Logan puffed out a breath. Groaned. Reached out and hit snooze.

Five more minutes.

He turned over and flinched. The world was full of dirty-blonde corkscrews. A breath pulled in a mouthful of hair.

'Gnnn . . .' Helen Edwards rolled over. Blinked at him. 'Wht time ist?'

He flinched again. The words had oozed across the pillow in a wave of what could only be described as broken-drain stink. He angled his mouth away, in case his own morning breath was as bad. 'Nine.'

'Too early.' She draped an arm across his chest again, hooked her leg around his. Closed her eyes. 'Sleep.' Then opened them again and stared at him. 'What's that?'

Warmth bloomed in his cheeks and ears. He scooted away until he was barely hanging on to the edge of the bed. 'It's a morning thing, OK? It . . . Look, I told you I was naked in here!'

479

'Logan—'

'Nothing's going to happen. It's just . . .' He fumbled about on the floor for yesterday's pants. 'You're not exactly a bag of spanners, and certain male bits have a mind of their own, and can you *please* stop staring at me like I'm a sex offender.' He pointed at the far wall. 'Look over there.' Then hauled his pants on under the duvet. Half climbed, half fell out of bed. Turned his back so she wouldn't see the awkward bulge. Struggled his way into his jeans.

Helen peered out at him, through a mask of curls. 'What happened to your stomach?'

Logan ran a hand across the knotted scars, then pulled on a T-shirt. 'I got stabbed. I died for a bit. I got better. No big deal.' He grabbed a towel from the dresser. 'Look, I've got to take a shower. Go back to sleep if you like. It's OK.'

'You're blushing.'

He backed out of the room. Collided with the doorframe and came within an inch of falling on his backside.

Smooth, Logan. Really smooth . . .

— SUNDAY EARLYSHIFT —

DRUGS FOR A FAIRY PRINCESS.

CHAPTER 38

'What time do you call this?' DCI Steel slouched against the doorframe of the Sergeants' Office, fake cigarette dangling from the corner of her mouth. 'Dayshift starts at seven.'

Logan went back to STORM, scrolling through the teams' actions. 'I was on till three. Technically I'm allowed eleven hours between ending one shift and starting the next, so sod off.'

A sniff. 'At home to Mr Grumpy this morning, are we? Know what causes that? Not enough sex. Makes you irritable.' She dug a hand down the front of her shirt and had a rummage. 'That's why I'm a picture of sweetness and light all the time.'

It looked as if Tufty had updated *all* of his actions for once. Wonders would never cease.

'Thought you were missing Susan.'

'Seriously, all that gunk in your junk will be backing up. Don't get rid of it at some point and you're going to burst like a big spermy pluke.'

'OK, you can go away now.' A couple of burglaries needed looking into. Some witness statements taken for a hit-and-run in Cornhill. An unlawful removal in New Pitsligo. The peeping tom was back in Macduff, and someone had set fire to a shed in Gardenstown. Hopefully it wouldn't be an idiot with his own barbecue this time.

'Don't want that, do we? You, getting every woman in three hundred feet pregnant.'

He scribbled them all down in his new notepad. 'Are you still here?'

'Susan's getting everything packed in the car now. Says she's made a picnic lunch: chicken, beetroot, sausages, egg sarnies, and that weirdo potato salad with gherkins you like because you're a freak.'

'You're the freak.' He picked his Airwave off the desk. Punched in Janet's number. 'Safe to talk?'

'Sarge: you're awake! Feeling OK?'

'No.' Logan glowered at Steel for a moment. 'Janet, I need you and—' The desk phone rang. It was the Duty Inspector's number on the screen. 'Hold on.' He grabbed the handset. 'Guv?'

Inspector McGregor's voice could have made it snow in July. *'Sergeant McRae. My office. Now!'*

'I didn't say you could sit.'

Caught, halfway down into the chair, Logan stood again. Feet shoulder-width apart, hands clasped behind his back. 'Ma'am.'

The Inspector took off her glasses and sighed. 'Do you know what I got when I arrived at work this morning, Sergeant? I got a bollocking from the Area Commander, because apparently I'm incapable of controlling my own staff.'

'Guv, it wasn't—'

'Did I say you could talk?'

Logan closed his mouth.

McGregor swept a spare strand of greying hair from her face. Then let her shoulders droop, all the ice gone from her voice. 'I *was* going to haul you over the coals, but to be honest, I'm more disappointed than angry.' She shook her head. 'What did I do wrong, Logan? What did I do that made you decide I wasn't fit to be your commanding officer?'

Logan swallowed down a groan. Stuffed it down into his ribcage where it could marinate in the spreading guilt.

Through the window behind her, the sky was a uniform lid of granite, flecked with wheeling herring gulls. Grey sky, grey sea, grey Sunday.

The only sound was the hum of her computer's fan.

She pointed at herself. 'Do you have problems taking orders from a woman, is that it? I thought we'd developed a rapport, Logan. That you had at least a *sliver* of respect for me.'

The guilt seeped out through his ribs, oozing down into his stomach, climbing up into his throat. Making his cheeks burn.

He let out a breath. 'No, Guv. I mean, yes. I mean . . .' This was going well. Why couldn't she have yelled at him and had done with it? A straight-up rant would've been a lot easier to deal with. And she bloody well knew it. 'I don't have a problem taking orders from a woman, and I *do* respect you.'

More silence.

He cleared his throat. 'I wanted to . . . When we talked about getting stuff under the radar, I thought this could be one of those things.' God knew what colour his cheeks were by now, but his ears were probably going to burst into flame any minute.

Inspector McGregor sagged back in her seat. 'Logan, I know you mean well on this one, I really do, but you have to stop. We're officially on our final warning. DCI McInnes has taken over the scene at Fairholme Place. All digging stopped till further notice.'

Count to ten. Don't say anything.

Sod it. 'Ma'am, with all due respect to the Detective Chief Inspector, he's an idiot. Klingon's mum never made it to Australia. There's no sign of her leaving the country. She's buried in the back garden, and Klingon and Gerbil killed her.'

'That's as may be, but until McInnes says other-wise, no one's digging her up. And yes, I think that's wrong. And I think it's wrong we're not getting to prosecute for the serious assaults on Jack Simpson. But it doesn't matter what I think, because we have *no* say in this. It's over.'

A weight settled on Logan's shoulders, dragging them down. 'Yes, ma'am.' The carpet was blue and tufted, he stared at it for a bit. Shuffled his feet. 'Might be a *bit* of a problem there.'

Another sigh. 'What did you do?'

'I gave Sammy Wilson a tenner to sniff out information on the Candlestick Maker, AKA: Martyn Baker.'

A laugh burst its way free of the Inspector. She rocked back in her chair, all her teeth on display. Hooting.

What happened to the disappointed expression and *we're-all-doomed* voice?

Then, when the fit passed, McGregor wiped her eyes with the back of her hand. 'Classic. You trusted Stinky Sammy Wilson with ten pounds? I wouldn't trust Stinky Sammy Wilson with a snotty hankie. A knitted condom would be more reliable than him.' She waved a hand at the door. 'Go on, you can take ten quid from the petty cash and I'll sign for it. Worth it for the laugh.'

Logan dumped a teabag in his mug and put the kettle on to boil. From the Tupperware containers on the canteen table, it looked as if someone had brought in cakes that morning, but all that was left were crumbs and smears of icing.

Typical. Nothing left for Logan.

Steel's whipping girl, DS McKenzie, lumbered in on her mobile. 'Yeah . . . No, I don't think so, but we'll follow it up . . . OK. Thanks.' She hung up and dug a mug out of the cupboard. Then nodded at Logan, setting the frizzy ponytail-bun thing wobbling. 'Sergeant.' All the warmth of yesterday's vomit and just as bitter.

Logan nodded back. 'Did you get some cake?'

The creases between her eyebrows deepened. 'There was cake?'

'Yeah, I didn't get any either.'

'How come no one said there was cake?' She thumped her mug down next to Logan's.

He dug the huge carton of semi-skimmed out of the fridge. 'You want a bit of unsolicited advice?'

'No.'

'Tough. Detective Chief Inspector Roberta Steel can be a massive pain in the arse. I know, because for ten years it was *my* arse she was a pain in. Do this, do that, go here, go there—'

'Fetch this, carry that.' A small smile cracked itself on McKenzie's face. 'Do all my paperwork for me.'

'Exactly. But she's also—'

'And all the swearing, and the blasphemy, and the innuendo, and the sexual comments, and the sarcasm, and the *scratching*!' DS McKenzie threw her arms wide, hands curled into claws.

'Yes, but—'

'Forever digging at her bits and her boobs. And look at her! Like someone ran over Columbo with a lawnmower, how's that supposed to command respect?'

'You finished?'

A shrug. McKenzie dropped her arms by her sides. 'You know what she's like.'

'Yes, and I also know she's incredibly loyal. If

you screw up, she'll rip you a new one in private, but she'll slap down anyone who has a go in public. She's got your back and she trusts you to do a decent job, not like some bosses.'

Silence.

Then McKenzie stuck her chin out. Stared down her nose at him. 'Yeah, maybe she trusts *you*. The sainted Logan McRae.' Her voice took on a gravelly edge, not the best impression of Steel, but not bad either: '"Logan wouldn't do that", "When Logan was my DS everything was much better", "Logan's wonderful, Logan's perfect, everything you can't do, he'd be great at."'

The kettle rattled to a halt.

'Really?'

'You're the stick she beats me with every day.'

'Then don't rise to it. If she finds a crack she'll dig and poke till the whole thing breaks, or it gets fixed. Fix it.'

Nicholson appeared in the canteen doorway. 'There you are, Sarge. Been calling you.'

'Airwave's back in the office. What can I do for you, Janet.'

She pulled her mouth into a sad-frog frown. 'Got another anonymous tip: our mate Frankie Ferris is at it again.'

So much for a nice cup of tea.

Nicholson took a right onto Rundle Avenue. Again. 'You know, I'm beginning to think someone's having a laugh.'

489

Logan slumped in the passenger seat, staring out of the window. 'You ever wonder why we bother, Janet?'

'We get, what, six calls a day about Frankie dealing from his house? So round we dutifully trot. And round and round we go. But do we ever catch anyone?'

The white harled houses gave way to the timber semi-shed ones.

'I mean, this: right here, it's the perfect metaphor for the job, isn't it? We go round and round in circles, but what do we really achieve?'

She narrowed her eyes. 'You know what I think? I think someone's figured out that this is a *really* easy way to get us out of the way for an hour.'

'End of the day, people still keep doing horrible things to each other, and we're trying to keep everything together with string and old chewing gum.'

'Yeah, I heard Inspector McGregor had a go at you this morning.' Nicholson shifted her grip on the wheel. 'What did you get: the full shouty savaging, or the guilt trip?'

'Guilt trip.'

'Urgh, I *hate* it when she does that. "I'm not angry with you, Janet, just *disappointed*."' Nicholson grimaced. 'She's even better at it than my mother, and that's saying something. Last time, I had to go eat a whole tub of ice cream afterwards, and I still felt like an utter failure.' Nicholson pulled the Big Car to the kerb, opposite Frankie's place. Frowned through the windscreen. 'What if he doesn't deal from his own house any more? What if this is all make-work to keep us away from where the real action's going down?'

Logan frowned at her. 'Have you been watching old repeats of *The Sweeney* again?'

'When did we last arrest someone coming out of Frankie Ferris's Den of Dodgy Drugs?'

True.

'Not as if we can ignore the tip-off though, is it? Soon as we do, something horrible will happen: Sod's Law. Give it one more pass, then back to the station.' He dug out his mobile and called Steel. 'Anything back from the labs yet?'

'*What? No, I won't come into the office. I told you, my wife's more important to me than any job.*'

Brilliant. Logan closed his eyes and massaged his forehead. 'Susan's there, listening, isn't she?'

'*Get DS McKenzie to do it. I'm spending time with my family for a change.*'

'Yes or no: have the labs done the DNA match with Helen Edwards yet?'

'*Damn it, sir, I'm no' a miracle worker. These things take time.*'

'For God's sake, you were supposed to chase them up! Do I have to do everything?'

'*Thank you, sir. I'll see you when I get back to the station.*'

Unbelievable. Logan hung up, unhooked his Airwave and got Control to put him through to the Dundee Lab as Nicholson took them on another tour of the back streets.

'Come on, answer the sodding— Hello? I need to speak to whoever's processing the Tarlair MIT samples. Can you . . .' He held the handset out. 'I'm on hold.'

Nicholson tapped her two index fingers on the steering wheel, like searching antenna. 'Or maybe it's someone who likes screwing with the police? Calls us up, gets his giggles watching us driving about like idiots . . .' A frown. 'What if it's *Frankie* doing the tipping-off?'

'About his own dealing? Nah.'

A one-eyed smile spread across her face. 'Yeah, think about it: he calls us with these bogus tip-offs when he knows there's no one there buying his product. Waste our time often enough, and we stop taking tip-offs seriously.'

A thick Glaswegian accent curled out of the Airwave's speaker. '*Yellow?*'

Logan pressed the talk button. 'Sergeant McRae: B Division. Where are you with the DNA comparison on the wee girl and Helen Edwards?'

'*Ah . . .*' A sooking noise – getting ready to break the bad news. '*Between you and me: going to have to be Tuesday or Wednesday. Can't get to it any sooner than that.*'

'You've had it for nearly a week!'

'*Aye, well, there's a load on in the labs right now. Everyone's upgrading their kit but us, so we're getting nine divisions' worth of stuff. And Renfrewshire-and-Inverclyde are going* mental *with all these feet washing up in—*'

'No.' Logan jabbed a finger against the dash-board. 'Trust me on this, there is *nothing* you've got on that's more important than identifying our victim. Other people might tell you there is, but they're not going to turn up on your doorstep at four in the morning and knee your testicles out through your ears. Are we clear?'

'But the severed feet—'

'Would you rather have severed testicles?'

A cough. A pause. *'Look, this isn't my choice, OK? I have to do what I'm—'*

'And can you imagine how many people will be lining up to lend a knee when it gets out you've been dragging your heels? When *that* gets splashed across the front pages?' Logan shook his head. 'Dear, oh dear. Here's us trying to catch a little girl's killer, and you're messing about with feet? Think your bosses are going to stand behind you on that one? Or are they going to tie sausages round your neck and throw you to the sharks?'

Nothing.

'Take your time.'

The voice dropped to a whisper. *'OK. OK. I'll bump it up the list. But . . . I'm only doing my job, here.'*

'Then do it faster. I want that result on my desk by close of play.' Logan ended the call and twisted his Airwave back on its holder. Looked up to find Nicholson grinning at him. 'What?'

'Oh, Sergeant McRae: you're so *masterful!*'

CHAPTER 39

Nicholson drifted the Big Car through the little side streets, keeping the speed under twenty. 'What do you fancy doing for Sunday lunch?'

'Nice big carvery. Rare roast beef; fluffy Yorkshire puddings; crispy roast potatoes done in goose fat; carrots and peas and gravy. All you can eat.'

'Sounds cool. What are you *actually* having?'

'Lentil soup.'

A billboard for home insurance slid by at the end of the road. A happy nuclear family, grinning away at a Plasticine dog. Someone had spray-painted a big purple willy right across the lot of them.

Nicholson pointed at it. 'You know, I'm beginning to get the feeling our graffiting wee Marxist friend isn't all that interested in the political process. I think he just likes painting willies on things.'

'Think you're right. Suppose that means we'll have to pay Comrade Geoffrey a visit. There's—'

'Shire Uniform Seven, safe to talk?'

'Here we go.' He pressed the button. 'Hammer away.'

'We've got reports of cows on the road: A947, between Keilhill and the farm shop.'

Nicholson slowed them to a stop, then curled forward and boinged her head off the steering wheel. 'Not again.'

'Roger that, show us responding.' He reached out and poked her in the arm. 'Come on, Calamity Janet, time to go play cowboys. Yehaw, ornery critters, circle the wagons, etcetera.'

'Yeah, right here's fine.' The Big Car drifted to a halt outside the Sergeant's Hoose, and Logan popped the door. 'You going home, or you using the shower in the station?'

Nicholson scowled across from the driver's side. 'It's sodding *everywhere*.' Drying mud made pale beige streaks across her cheeks, clumped in her hair, stained the sleeves of her black Police T-shirt and the pale arms sticking out of it. More on her trousers and stabproof vest.

'If you're worried about Hector spying on you in the shower, go home. I think we can spot you an extra half-hour for lunch today, after your sterling efforts thwarting the Great Bovine Rebellion.'

'Oh, you're funny now, are you?'

Logan climbed out into the dreich afternoon. 'I'll be here all week. Try the fish.' He clunked the door shut and waved as Nicholson bared her teeth for a bit, then pulled away from the kerb. Heading back to the station and a hot shower.

He crossed the road, dug out his keys and let himself into the house. No point carting soup about the whole time when home was a two-minute walk away.

The living-room door was open, showing off four nice cream walls and shiny white skirting boards. Next up – carpet.

Logan unVelcroed his stabproof and hung it over the bannister. 'Helen?' No reply. 'Hello?'

Through to the kitchen. Not there.

Oh.

Cthulhu yawned from the windowsill – perched between the herbs – stretched, turned around to show Logan her bum, then settled down to sleep again.

So much for the big welcome.

He checked the fridge. Both steaks were still in residence. As was the leftover macaroni cheese. Lunch.

Logan pulled it out, popped a couple of holes in the clingfilm, and stuck it in the microwave. Put the kettle on.

A clunk from the front of the house. *'Logan?'*

He stuck his head out into the hall. 'How does macaroni-cheese on toast sound?'

Helen dumped her bulging contingent of carrier bags on the bare floorboards and wiped a sheen of water from her face, hair hanging in frizzy brown-tinged coils. 'Urgh . . . So much for summer.' A shudder. Then she pointed at the bags. 'Want to give me a hand?'

They unpacked them in the kitchen as the microwave droned. Salad. Pickles. Salmon fillets. Sausages. Potatoes. Onions. Chocolate. Wine.

Warmth bloomed in Logan's cheeks. 'You don't have to, you know.'

She put a squeezy bottle of salad cream away in the cupboard. 'Don't have to what?'

'This: buy loads of things. Cook for me.'

Her eyebrows drifted up an inch, the edges of her mouth going in the opposite direction.

Logan held out his hands. 'No – it's great, seriously, I've not eaten this well in months, but I don't want you to think you *have* to. It's not . . .' He cleared his throat. 'I don't want to be taking advantage.'

She put a jar of mustard down on the counter. Looked at it. 'You want me to go.'

'No! No, I don't, I'm only . . .' He shrugged at the pile of food. 'You're doing all this for me, and I'm doing nothing in return.'

'Yes you are.' Helen stepped in so close that the scent of apricots coiled around him from her damp hair. Joined by the warmth of her body. 'You're finding my daughter.'

She placed her hand on the small of his back.

Ding. The microwave came to a halt.

Logan swallowed. Took hold of her shoulders.

Helen looked up, lips parted.

OK.

Deep breath. And—

'LAZ?' The word barged in from the front of

the house, wearing smoky hobnail boots. 'YOU IN THERE?'

'Gah . . .' He flinched. Stared at the kitchen door. Not *now*.

Helen shrank back a step. Bit her top lip. Blushed.

Logan dropped his voice to a whisper. 'Maybe if we're really quiet, she'll give up and go away?'

The kitchen door battered open, and a whirl-wind in pink top and blue jeans charged into the room, ash-blonde hair streaming out behind her. 'Daddy!' She grabbed Logan's waist for a quick hug then ran over to the windowsill. 'Cthulhu!'

Stroking and petting and rubbing of ears and purring.

Upstaged by the cat. As usual.

Helen crossed her arms. Pulled back against the working surface. 'Yes. Right. Sorry.'

'Gah, what a day.' Susan lurched into the room and dumped a cool-bag on the table. She'd pulled her blonde hair back into a ponytail, and when she smiled, dimples appeared in her round cheeks. Little wrinkles deepened around her eyes. 'Logan. How are you? We haven't seen you in ages. Jasmine was so disappointed you couldn't make the dance competition.' Susan marched over and gave him a kiss. Then turned and clapped her hands. 'Come on, Little Monkey, wash up, time for lunch.'

'But, Mu-um—'

'No buts. Upstairs. Wash. Don't make your dad

498

arrest you.' Susan peeled off her jacket as Jasmine skipped out of the room. Her belly was a little swollen, but not that much more than usual. 'Honestly, I love her to bits, but I swear to God: sometimes . . .' She turned to Helen and rolled her eyes. 'Sorry, I'm all over the place today. Two hours in a car with the loudest six-year-old on the planet.' Stuck her hand out. 'Susan.'

A pause. 'Helen.'

'Helen. I love your hair, all mine ever does is hang there like mince. With Jasmine, soon as I hit the third trimester it was like I was channelling Tina Turner, so there's that to look forward to.' She unzipped the cool-bag. 'Do you like roast chicken and watermelon salad? I've made about enough for twenty.'

'It . . . I should probably . . .'

Susan turned and took a deep breath. 'ROBERTA! DON'T FORGET THE DRINKS!'

Steel's voice boomed through from the hall. 'I'M ON THE PHONE!'

'Of course you are.' Susan pulled a stack of Tupperware from her cool-bag. 'You're always on the phone.'

The sound of the toilet flushing came from upstairs. Then Steel lurched into the room, carrying a big plastic box. Fake cigarette sticking out of the corner of her mouth. Phone pinned between her shoulder and her ear. 'I'm no' telling you again, Becky – get those lazy sods out there door-to-dooring with Neil Wood's picture. . . .'

I don't care if it's raining, snowing, or . . .' She stopped. Stared at Helen. Stood there for a bit, bottom lip hanging open. Then, 'Just sort it. Gotta go.'

Helen wrung her fingers into a knot. 'Has something happened? Have they got the test results back?'

Steel dumped the plastic box on the kitchen floor. Stuffed her phone in a pocket. 'Mrs Edwards?' Then she had a raised-eyebrow ogle at Logan. 'OK . . .' Then back to Helen. 'I'm sorry, Mrs Edwards, it's going to take a bit of time. Everyone watches these stupid detective TV things and thinks you can get it done in fifteen minutes, but it's no' that easy in real life.'

'Oh.' She stared at her feet for a moment. 'Of course. I'm being stupid.'

'No problem. Didn't know you were here.'

Susan put a hand against her stomach, fingers splayed over the bump. 'Oh, I'm so sorry, I thought you were a friend of Logan's. And here's me rabbiting on.' She creased her eyes up. 'If you'd like to join us for lunch, that'd be—'

'Why don't you lay the table, Sooz?' Steel pointed over Helen's shoulder. 'I need to borrow Sergeant McRae for a wee minute.'

Logan grabbed a glance at Helen, then followed Steel down the hall and out into the gloomy afternoon. The slate-grey sea mirrored the granite sky. 'You could have called!'

'What the hell are you playing at?' Steel

punched him on the upper arm. 'I can't believe you're shagging our dead kid's mum! Are you *insane*?'

'Ow!' He rubbed at the spot. 'Nothing happened, OK? Not that it's any of your business.' He pulled the front door shut.

'Aye, and my bum's the Queen of Sheba. You were at it, weren't you?'

'She wouldn't have to crash at mine if you'd got your finger out and organized somewhere for her in the first place.'

'Oh my God, it's you, isn't it? The "friend" she's staying with. I *knew* it.'

'She thinks it's her daughter lying in the mortuary, OK? She just wants someone to talk to.'

'Shouldn't even be anywhere near her.' She hit him again. 'What's wrong with you? You—'

'Ow! Cut it out, or—'

'—when you're investigating the damn case! It's unethical.'

Logan marched off a couple of paces. Then back again, hands jabbing the air for emphasis. 'Nothing happened! And I'm not *on* the case, I'm barely case-adjacent. You can hardly *see* the case from where I am.'

Steel crossed her arms, hoicking up her bosom. 'Nothing happened? *Really*?'

'Nothing happened!'

She hissed out a breath. 'Well, no wonder you had a face like an unemptied scrotum this morning. See – told you. Sexual frustration.'

He rubbed a hand across his face. 'We were eating lunch. That's all.'

'Fine.' Steel poked him in the chest. 'And make sure you keep your hands where I can see them.'

Tufty indicated left, then sniffed. 'Why can I smell chicken?'

The Big Car drifted back onto Rundle Avenue, making its third pass in fifteen minutes.

Still no sign of anyone that looked even vaguely like the descriptions Maggie had shouted through.

Logan shifted in his seat. The equipment belt was digging into his stomach's full load of chicken and sausage rolls and potato salad. Every burp burned. Should really loosen it. But if he did, the damn thing would fall off if they had to chase anyone. 'So, come on then: what did you do?'

The tips of Tufty's ears turned pink. 'Maybe I wanted to learn from the master for a bit?'

'What did you do?'

A breath of drizzle fogged the windscreen. The windscreen wipers squealed it away, but it was back a couple of beats later. The tips of Tufty's ears darkened.

'Well?'

He shrugged one shoulder. 'Deano just gets a bit grumpy sometimes.'

'Tufty!'

'All I said was, Einstein states that as an object's velocity approaches the speed of light, its inertial mass tends towards infinity, right? Well, what about photons? They travel at the speed of light, because they *are* light.'

'There,' Logan pointed, 'woman in the tracksuit.'

She was trudging along through the drizzle, head down, woolly hat pulled low over her ears.

Tufty shook his head. 'Should be wearing a green hoodie. Anyway: light's both a wave and a particle, right? And it's travelling *at* the speed of light, so the particle bit of it should have near-infinite mass, even if the wave bit doesn't. So maybe *that's* what dark matter is? All that excess inertial mass?'

'You think dark matter is light?'

'Well, it's not gerbils, is it? Stands to reason . . .'

'Janet's right – we should've had you tested.' Logan dug out his phone, found Helen's number, and thumbed in a text.

Sorry about lunch – didn't know they were coming.

They can be a bit much at times.

He frowned at the screen. Say something about the almost-kiss, or not? What if she didn't mean it? What if it was a misunderstanding? He'd end up looking like a right idiot. Or a pervert. Or a massive dickhead.

Gah, it was like being a spotty teenager again.

Play it cool.

If I can get free we could try grabbing
dinner?

His finger hovered over 'SEND'.

Nah. That last bit looked desperate.

He deleted the line, then sent the text off into
the digital void.

All nice and bland and unembarrassing.

The phone went back into his trouser pocket.

Outside the car windows, the damp streets
glistened.

Tufty sucked on his teeth for a bit. Then, 'You
ever wonder about the origins of the universe,
Sarge?'

Logan hit the button on his Airwave and talked
into his shoulder. 'Maggie, any more sightings?'

*'Aye, we've got an IC-One female wearing Ugg
boots, blue jogging bottoms, and an orange sweatshirt.'*

Tufty stuck on the brakes. Then reversed downhill. 'Got her.' He swung the Big Car right, onto
Ardanes Brae.

And there she was, hurrying along the pavement,
bent into the wind, a carrier bag dangling from
one hand.

'OK, wait till she's level with the white Passat
. . . Go.'

Tufty slid alongside, then pulled into the kerb.
Grabbed his peaked cap and jumped out into the
drizzle.

Logan went the other way, around the back of
the Passat, cutting off the retreat.

She looked up, just in time to avoid walking straight into Tufty. Stopped. Took a step back. Turned. Saw Logan. Swore.

Kirstin Rattray screwed her bony face into a fist, then slumped. Licked her thin, pale lips. 'Was . . . out for a walk.'

'Afternoon, Kirstin.'

No one moved.

She wrapped one bony arm around herself, the skeletal hand gripping her other arm. 'Going to see Amy.' She jiggled the carrier bag. 'Got her some toys and a pretty dress. 'Cos . . . 'Cos it's her birthday.'

Logan pointed over her shoulder. 'Kirstin Rattray, I have reason to believe that you're in possession of a controlled substance, so I'm detaining you in terms of Section Twenty-Three of the Misuse of Drugs Act 1971 for the purpose of a search.'

She curled in on herself, folding at the knees and wrapping her arms around her head. 'Noo . . .'

'We are unable to search you here, as I don't have a female officer to do it. So we're going to take you to the station until one becomes available. You're not obliged to say anything, but anything you do say—'

'Please . . .' Her voice came out muffled and strangled. 'Please, if they put me away I'll never get to see my wee Amy again. Please . . .'

Tufty shifted from foot to foot. 'Sarge?'

'She's only *three*!'

The same age Helen's daughter was when she disappeared.

'Sarge, maybe we could . . . I don't know. Something?'

Kirstin stayed where she was, rocking back and forward slightly. Crying.

Logan stared up at the lid of grey that loomed over the town. The drizzle caressed his face with its cold clammy hands. Three years old.

Ah, sod it. It wasn't always about banging people up. 'Kirstin.'

'Please . . .'

'Kirstin, come on: stand up, I'm not going to arrest you.'

She peered up at him with bloodshot eyes. 'My Amy's only—'

'I know. I'm not arresting you. Up.'

She stood, sniffling and gulping. Wiped the snot off her top lip with a skeletal hand. 'I can go?'

'Not yet.' He snapped on a single blue nitrile glove. 'What did Frankie Ferris give you?'

The skeletal hand scrubbed at her eyes. 'I didn't—'

'You were seen, Kirstin. What did he give you? You can give it to me, or you can come down the station and wait to be searched. And when we find it, we arrest you and confiscate it anyway. Your choice.'

She nodded. Sniffed. Then dug into the front pocket of her joggy bottoms. Came out with a small plastic baggie with brown powder in it.

Rubbed the thing between her fingertips, like the world's tiniest violin. Licked her lips again. Cleared her throat.

He held out his gloved hand. 'Kirstin?'

A hatchback went past, the sound of music turned up too loud grinding out through the rolled-up windows.

'Come on, Kirstin. What's more important: getting high, or your daughter?'

The drizzle fell.

Tufty shifted his feet again.

And finally Kirstin dropped the little packet on Logan's palm. Her fingertips hovered over it for a moment, then she snatched her hand away and pressed them against her throat. 'It . . . Sometimes it's . . .' She looked away. 'I found it.'

'Of course you did. Does Frankie have a big stash? Is it worth my while paying him a visit?'

She hauled one shoulder up to her ear. 'Didn't see anything. He was, you know, working the hall, never got to see anywhere else.'

'OK.' Logan pointed. 'Can I see inside the carrier bag?'

She held it out and open.

Inside was a little pink princess dress, a set of pink fairy wings, and a pink magic wand.

He stepped back. 'Thanks. You tell Amy the nice policemen said hello, OK?'

A nod. Then she scuffed her Ugg boots on the pavement. 'She's all I've got.'

'Off you go then.'

She scurried away, carrier bag clutched to her chest. Getting smaller and smaller, until the hill and the drizzle swallowed her up.

Tufty grinned. 'Catch-and-release. Like it.'

'Right. Back to work.'

While Tufty got in behind the wheel, Logan closed his fist around the little package of heroin, then pulled the glove inside out, trapping it inside. Slipped it into one of his stabproof vest's zippy pockets. Couldn't sign it into evidence without implicating Kirstin. Just have to lose it down a drain somewhere.

The drizzle thickened, the drops turning heavier and wetter.

He climbed into the passenger seat. Clunked the door shut. 'Right, a couple more goes, then we're off to Gardenstown to see about that shed fire.' He pulled his Airwave free as Tufty crossed Tannery Street and started yet another long slow loop of Rundle Avenue.

'Sarge?'

'Is this about Einstein again?' He thumbed the Duty Inspector's shoulder number into his Airwave. 'Bravo India from Shire Uniform Seven, safe to talk?'

'You know the Big Bang?'

'*Go ahead, Logan.*'

'Any chance I can get a warrant to dunt in Frankie Ferris's door? We're getting a lot of tip-offs about him dealing today. Sounds as if he's got a new batch of heroin in.'

'You doing stop-and-searches?'

'On it now.'

'Good. I want you copping a feel of everyone who comes out of that place. You get me one solid bit intel and I'll get you a warrant.' There was a bit of rustling at her end. Then, 'I've no spare bodies for a dunt today. Have to be tomorrow or Tuesday.'

Might all be gone by tomorrow or Tuesday. But it was better than nothing. 'Thanks, Guv.'

Tufty took them out the end of the street and onto Golden Knowes Road. It was the Westernmost edge of town, no houses on the left side of the road, from here on it was fields and cattle all the way to Whitehills. 'If we hadn't let Kirstin Rattray off with a caution, you'd have got your warrant.'

'And make sure she never saw her kid again? Thought you were all in favour of catch-and-release.'

'Yeah, but . . .' A small frown and a little chewing on the inside of his cheek. Then whatever ethical dilemma was raging inside that misshapen little head of his must have passed. 'Anyway, so we know that the universe goes from nothing to everything: boom, in teeny wee fraction of a second.' He took his hands off the steering wheel and mimed an explosion.

'Anyone in the vicinity of St Fergus, got reports of a campervan with German plates acting suspiciously. MOD staff want them picked up . . .'

A right, onto Windy Brae, making another long loop.

'So there's nothing, then there's inflation, then there's expansion, then there's everything, right?'

'I'm beginning to know how Deano felt.'

Little houses, terraced bungalows, all darkening in the rain.

'All units be on the lookout for an IC-Two female, suspected of robbing a Big Issue vendor in Peterhead, Back Street . . .'

'So, in that first trillionth of a trillionth of a trillionth of a second, all this primordial quantum foam is accelerating faster than the speed of light—'

'How about him?' Logan pointed through the windscreen at a man in a scuffed bomber jacket with a hoodie underneath, marching on through the rain.

'Should be green cargo pants, not stonewashed jeans. But it's the same thing, isn't it? Closer you get to the speed of light, the greater your inertial mass, so if it wasn't for that tiny fraction of a second wheeching everything up to uber-fast speeds, there wouldn't be any mass in the universe. We're made of speed, not stuff.'

Logan stared at him.

'What?'

'I swear to God, Tufty, I was this close to being nice to you today.' He held one hand up, thumb and forefinger less than an inch apart.

Right, onto Meavie Place, then another quick right onto Ardanes Brae again.

'Only trying to get a bit of intelligent debate going.'

510

There was blissful silence all the way back to Rundle Avenue. Well, except for the rhythmic squeak-and-groan of the windscreen wipers.

Tufty heaved a big sigh. 'Must be weird, living in one of the wood-clad houses. Think it's a bit like moving into a two-storey shed?'

'Don't know what's worse, your cosmology, or your social commentary . . .' Logan sat forward in his seat. Peered out through the rain-smeared windscreen. 'Up there. Is that not our good friend, Martyn Baker?' And he was going into Frankie Ferris's delightful little drug den too. Logan grinned. Rubbed his hands together. 'Right, park the car around the corner. Soon as he comes out, we've got ourselves a winner.'

And best of all, he had plausible deniability. The Duty Inspector gave the order to stop-and-search everyone who comes out of Frankie's place. *Everyone*. And that included Martyn Baker.

Yes, DCI McInnes would blow a vein, but sod him.

About time these MIT scumbags learned what a real police officer looked like.

CHAPTER 40

'**M**r Baker, what a nice surprise.' Logan stepped out from behind the mouldy Transit van. Rain pattered on the brim of his peaked cap, bounced off the shoulders of his fluorescent yellow jacket. Not exactly subtle, but Martyn-with-a-'Y' still hadn't seen him.

A narrowing of the eyes. Probably weighing up the odds of doing a runner, but then Tufty stepped onto the pavement behind him.

'Sarge?'

Baker took his hands out of his pockets, curled them into fists. The tendons on his neck tightened, stretching the skin. Rain soaked into his bomber jacket, slicking the red fabric. 'What?' Those thick eyebrows glowered like storm clouds.

'I see you've been visiting with Frankie Ferris.'

'Nothing illegal, is it? Visiting someone?' His Brummie accent thickened with every word. 'Youse jocks are harassing us.'

Logan smiled at him. Smiled at the gel-spiked hair drooping in the rain. Smiled at the nuclear-furnace plooks ready to blow along his jaw. Then slipped the elastic band off the body-worn video

512

unit and set it recording. 'Martyn Baker, I have reason to believe that you're in possession of a controlled substance—'

'Don't.' He bared his teeth. 'Don't you *bloody* don't.'

'—under Section Twenty-Three of the Misuse of Drugs—'

'You've already got my phone, that not enough for you!'

'—detained for the purposes of search—'

All the air vanished from Logan's lungs, as a fist smashed into his stomach hard enough to skid him back a couple of inches on the pavement. Yeah, a stabproof vest might be a pain to lug about all day, but if it didn't let a kitchen knife through, a fist wasn't going to have much luck.

He snapped his hand up and out, palm forward, fingers splayed, channelling his weight through his hip. The heel of his hand slammed into the underside of Baker's chin. 'Back!'

Baker's head jerked up, and his feet went out from underneath him. Windmilling arms and a gurgling moan, all the way down to the pavement. He hit like a sack of tatties, and lay there, blinking up at the rain.

Tufty lunged, whipping out the cuffs and snapping them on one wrist, before hauling him over onto his front and flicking the other one into place. He looked up at Logan. 'You OK, Sarge?'

'Never better, Officer Quirrel. Never better.'

★   ★   ★

513

They stood him in the middle of the custody suite and searched him.

The Fraserburgh Cellblock Choir did a round-robin of 'Soft Kitty' as Tufty worked his way along Martyn Baker's limbs, then through his turn-ups and pockets.

The PCSO puffed out his cheeks and stirred his tea. 'You're lucky you weren't here this morning: we got the Spice Girls' greatest hits. Can you imagine spending your honeymoon in the cells, waiting for the courts to open Monday morning? Singing about wanting a zigazig-ah?'

Logan leaned back against the custody desk and lowered his voice to a whisper. 'I want Baker processed ASAFP, but keep it low key, OK?'

The Police Custody and Security Officer folded his thick, thistle-tattooed arms. 'You hiding him from anyone in particular?'

'Not hiding him, I'm ensuring his safety. In case someone decides to throw a fit.'

'So . . .?'

'I want to be done before anyone from Operation Troposphere, or some MIT numptie comes sniffing about. Baker calls his lawyer, then we get him in an interview room. And make sure you give me a shout, soon as he's ready. We burst him, we throw a party, then everyone gets medals.'

Tufty came to the end of his search, then held out his gloved hand to Logan. A ziplock plastic bag of dried green herbs sat in the middle of the palm. Not a huge bag, not even big enough for a charge of possession with intent.

Logan walked over and picked it out of Tufty's hand. 'This it?'

A shrug. 'Sorry, Sarge.'

He walked around to face Martyn Baker. 'Well, Mr Baker? Anything else on, or in, your person I should know about?'

Martyn Baker's jaw clenched and ground, the muscles writhing beneath the skin. Making the spots ripple. His feet made restless patterns on the grey floor, following the steps of some obscure, guilty dance. His eyes flicked from side to side, never meeting Logan's. 'I want my lawyer.'

'I'll bet you do.'

Logan rinsed the empty mug under the hot tap, then added it to the pile on the draining board. A couple of support staff sat around the TV in the canteen, having a deep and meaningful conversation about the new series of *Danger Mouse*.

A buzzing sensation worked its way into Logan's thigh, followed by the tell-tale sound of a new text message arriving. He dug his phone out of his pocket.

> Srry for being all wierd at Inch I just didnt expect all the ppl Im not usd to all th family anymore Still gt steak fr tea if U want it? I cn make chips

How could any gentleman refuse an offer of chips?

He hit reply, then stopped. Put his mobile away and headed back along the groaning corridor to the Sergeants' Office. Picked up the internal phone.

'Cellblock.'

'Hi, it's Sergeant McRae. Any word on our friend Martyn Baker yet?'

'Still on the phone to his solicitor. Takes a while to remember to say "no comment" to everything. Takes practice.'

'OK, well I'm heading out for a bit. Give me a shout soon as he's ready.'

Out the door, down the stairs, and onto the rear car park.

Slivers of blue jabbed their way through the grey cloud. The leaching drizzle and unforgiving rain had gone, leaving the windscreens and bodywork of the parked patrol cars and van dulled to a pewter sheen.

He pulled out his mobile, found Helen's number, and—

'Sarge?' Tufty.

Logan froze. 'Martyn Baker said something?'

'Well . . . No. PCSO said you were heading out. So, you need backup? Shall I get the Big Car?'

Yes, because that was going to make it *so* much easier to phone Helen.

Think fast.

A patrol car rocked over the speedbump and

516

into the car park. There had to be a job out there that needed seeing to.

Logan turned to watch the officer behind the wheel make a pig's ear of parking. 'Actually, I'm going to wander down to Broch Braw Buys. See if the owner's got any idea why the Cashline Ram-Raiders picked him instead of another Co-op.'

A nod. 'Right, I'll get my hat.'

'No, you're all right. You stay here and . . .' Come on – what could he get Tufty to do instead of playing gooseberry? 'Do me a favour – Helen Edwards. If she is our Tarlair little girl's mother, I want to know about the father. See what you can dig up.'

'Sarge.'

'. . . *possible drugs death in Peterhead. Ambulance is on its way.*'

Next door to Fraserburgh police station, the houses were grand and granite. Bungalows on one side, two-storey jobs with bay windows on the other.

Logan wandered down Finlayson Street, mobile phone to his ear as the Airwave cackled away to itself. 'I don't really know. They've still not got a replacement for Sergeant Muir, so unless they can find someone else I've got to pull another green shift. Officially two, maybe half-two tomorrow morning?'

Helen's voice sank a bit. *'That's a shame.'*

'Sorry.' He crossed the road. 'I don't know if I'll get home for dinner, but I'll do my best. It all depends what happens this evening. If something kicks off or not.'

'Well, I can always put the steaks back in the fridge and eat all the chips myself.'

He groaned. 'Don't tempt me with chips, that's police kryptonite.'

On the left, the houses gave way to the car park outside Riteway. The homeware store's boxy frontage was stained dark grey. A handful of kids rattled skateboards up and down in front of it, doing low-level tricks and falling off.

'Helen: you're sure you've not heard anything from your ex-husband? Nothing at all?'

'One postcard. It was the Cathedral Church of Saint Martin, in Ourense. It was three months after he took her.'

'And nothing since?'

'"Don't bother trying to find us. You had your shot poisoning her against me. You'll never see her again, you jealous frigid bitch. You'll die alone, because no one could ever love a useless ugly cow like you."' A shuddering breath. Then a pause. *'It was post-marked Ourense. My private investigator spent two weeks there, looking for them.'*

Logan stopped at the crossroads, where Finlayson Street met Gallowhill Road. 'Brian sounds like a proper charmer.' And in need of a good sodding kicking.

'I paid for adverts in the local papers, from A Coruña

518

to Zamora, but no one recognized Brian's photo, or Natasha's. Like they'd vanished . . .'

On the other side of the road, Broch Braw Buys was sandwiched between the betting shop and the chipper. The boards over the shattered window had gone, replaced instead by a nice sheet of shiny new glass, already disappearing under a plastering of offers and notices.

'I'm sorry.'

'I know it makes me a bad person, but if I got my hands on Brian, I'd kill him. I wouldn't care about going to prison. I'd kill him.'

A Fiat Panda growled past, followed by a motorbike, a rusty Land Rover, and a Council Transit with rusty wings.

Yeah . . . Probably best to change the subject.

'Helen, about today, before Steel and Susan and Jasmine—'

'It's OK. Really. I shouldn't have . . .' Deep breath. *'Look at me, wittering away. I should let you get back to work.'*

'Yes. Right. Well, I'll see you for dinner. If I can.' He forced a smile. 'You know, if there's chips?'

Nothing.

'Helen?'

She was already gone.

He sighed. Put his phone away. Waited for a break in the traffic, then crossed over.

A couple of old men stood outside the Kenyan Bar and Lounge, smoking rollups and moaning

519

about getting booted out at three, yet again, same as they were every Sunday.

'All units, be on the lookout for a Raymond Goldmann, IC-One male, grey beard and bald head. Apprehension warrant issued for indecent exposure.'

Speaking of apprehension warrants. He unhooked his Airwave. 'Shire Uniform Seven. Has there been any update on David or Catherine Bisset?'

The two old men eyed him for a moment, then shuffled off.

'Roger that, we've had a dozen sightings from Dundee to Oban, via Edinburgh and Kilmarnoch. Local officers are looking into them. You want me to put you on the update list?'

Why not? 'Thanks.'

Wouldn't have thought it was that easy to kill two people and then disappear, but apparently it was. He hooked his Airwave in place and turned back to the shop.

Broch Braw Buys was deeper than it was wide, with racks of breakfast cereals barely visible through the blizzard of notes and signs. The one offering a thousand quid to anyone who helped ID the Ram-Raiders – so the shop owner could break their legs – had pride of place in the middle, over the Coco Pops.

The door bleeped as Logan stepped inside.

Rows of shelves, aisles of shelves, everywhere: shelves, all heaped with food and tat. The smell was a strange mixture of fust and dust, overlaid with fresh paint and glazier's putty. Big circular mirrors were dotted about above head height, presumably arranged so that whoever was behind the counter could see every nook and cranny in the shop from there. A CCTV camera sat not far below the ceiling in every corner, red lights glowing.

'I help you?' A wee man with a tweed waistcoat and post-box eyes appeared at Logan's elbow. Stubble covered his nub of a chin, the hair on his head trimmed into a bowl around a smooth shiny crown.

Logan pointed at the floor, where four drill holes marked out a relatively clean rectangle on the ancient linoleum. 'They haven't fitted a new cash machine?'

'What's it look like to you? Course they haven't. Insurance company are playing silly buggers. Oh, you're not covered for that, you're not covered for this, have you not read the small print?' His face soured. 'Thieving bunch of scum. Come the revolution, they're first against the wall.'

The wee man scuffed the toe of his trainers over the clean rectangle. 'Only agreed to cough up for the window yesterday. Had thirty-five thousand quid's worth of my stock nicked, and do they care? Do they hell.'

'It was only twenty-seven thousand last week.'

He jammed his hands in his pockets. 'Inflation. Now, what do you want? I don't do discounts for plod till you catch the thieving sods who robbed me.'

Logan looked up at the security camera, mounted above the door. 'I need to see the footage from the raid.'

The front door bleeped again, and a wee girl in denim shorts and a Chainsaw Teddy T-shirt skipped in, all smiles, dimples, and pigtails, a Hello Kitty skateboard tucked under one arm.

'You! Get out, you're banned. Go on!' He grabbed Logan's arm. 'Look, I've got the police here. You get out of here now, or he'll arrest you!'

She stuck her middle finger up at the pair of them, spat on the floor, then turned and skipped back out of the shop again. Couldn't have been much more than five years old.

The shopkeeper let go of Logan's arm, and spread his hand across his own chest, fingertips trembling. 'They're like jackals.'

'What about the CCTV?'

'They come in here in packs and they steal and they make threats and they break things and they spit.'

'Do you have security footage, or don't you?'

He sniffed. 'Don't. What we had, the police took after the robbery.'

Which meant it would be locked away in the evidence store at Queen Street, Aberdeen. No way they'd let Logan anywhere near it. But it'd been worth a try.

Logan stopped on his way back to the door. 'Why you?'

'Of course, you try to talk to the parents, but

do they do anything? Of course not. Between you and me, they're scared of their own children.'

'Why did the Ram-Raiders pick this place? All the other shops they've hit are Co-ops. Why you?'

He straightened a stack of toilet rolls. 'I'm a hardworking businessman who pays his taxes and does the right thing and these people are the scum of the earth. Come the revolution—'

'Yeah, I heard. Up against the wall.' Logan pointed at the patch where the cash machine had been. 'Why you? Someone come round threatening you, or wanting protection money? Something like that?'

'The children. All the time. Money, threats, spitting. I should get a gun to protect myself.'

'Don't be an idiot.' Logan opened the door. 'And take down that stupid reward sign. You're not breaking anyone's legs.'

'Children? They're not children, they're *monsters*.'

The door bleeped shut as Logan stepped out onto the pavement again.

OK, so Broch Braw Buys was a non-starter for CCTV. No sign of cameras on the chip shop next door, but the Kenyan Bar and Lounge had one of the black dome security cameras above the door on Gallowhill Road. There was another next to the painted sign, and a third above the door on Finlayson Street.

Perfect.

Logan knocked on the barred gate. No reply.

A couple of posters sat in the recess behind the

gate, either side of the door. One was for the open-mike night on Tuesdays, and the other was for the new and improved Pubwatch scheme. 'ALL SECURITY CAMERAS IN THIS ESTABLISHMENT ARE CONNECTED TO FRASERBURGH POLICE STATION. AGGRESSION TOWARDS STAFF OR OTHER CLIENTS WILL NOT BE TOLERATED.'

Even better.

Fraserburgh's Cellblock Gospel Singers roared their way through 'The Ballad of Eskimo Nell' somewhere below Logan's feet, giving every verse the full-throated Whitney Houston warble. The viewing equipment was temporarily stacked on a scarred desk, jammed into the corner of a disused office while the viewing suite waited for a fresh lick of paint that never came.

'Anything else?' He shifted the phone to his other hand and had a sip of tea.

It sounded as if Big Paul was checking his paperwork. *'We're still after witnesses to that hit-and-run. Couple of house-breakings to look into. Someone's been smashing windows in Inverboyndie. And I want to make a nuisance of myself on Newton Drive – our old friend Lumpy Patrick's dealing again. Going to disrupt his business.'*

'Good.' Logan checked his notepad. 'I need you to send Kate over to backfill at Fraserburgh again. And I want you to take a swing past Frankie Ferris's place on Rundle Avenue every couple of hours. Let's make it a bad day to be dealing drugs all round. Other than that, you, Penny, and Joe have a good shift. I'll see you when I see you.'

'*Right, Sarge.*'

Logan slid the next cartridge out of the rack and into the machine. Had a slurp of tea while it whirred and groaned. Then Gallowhill Road filled the screen.

The camera had obviously been set up to monitor events outside the front of the Kenyan Bar, that bit of the picture was sharp and clear, the rest of the street was caught in the distorting glare of the wide-angle lens. Getting more stretched and distorted the further away things got from its target area.

Logan spooled the controller forward. The time-stamp in the bottom-right corner wheeched along at thirty times normal speed.

Right on cue, a dark green Mitsubishi Warrior drove past the pub, slammed on its brakes, then reversed at speed through the window of Broch Braw Buys. All in perfect silence. The back end kicked up as it smashed through the glass, sending packets and tins flying. Two masked men leapt out – one from the passenger side, the other from the back – and battered in through the broken window. Forty-five seconds later, the Warrior leapt forward, yanking the cash machine from its moorings and out into the street. The thing got heaved into the four-by-four's loadbed, and they were off.

One minute and fifty seconds from start to finish.

Longer than it took them to ram-raid the Co-op

in Portsoy, but then they'd had a lot more practice by then.

Logan sat back in his seat and tapped fingertips against the desk. One minute, fifty seconds. That wasn't brave, it was idiotic – the shop was, what, a three-minute walk from the police station? Less than a minute in a car. You'd have to be pretty sure of yourself before risking that.

Mind you, it'd probably take a minute and a half to call 999 and tell them what was going on. Call it a minute to get over the shock in the first place. Then another five minutes for a team to scramble from the station. One more to actually get there . . .

Nearly nine minutes.

By the time the police turned up at Broch Braw Buys, the Ram-Raiders could be in Rosehearty without even breaking the speed limit.

Still, it was a big risk.

Either they were very, *very* lucky, or really knew what they were doing.

And given how many other cash machines they'd wheeched out of convenience stores, it couldn't be luck.

Logan sent the recording spinning backwards again. No way they picked Broch Braw Buys at random. They would've cased the joint, made sure they knew where the machine was inside the shop.

He drummed his fingertips against the desktop.

If you were smashing a stolen four-by-four backwards through a shop window, would you grit your

526

teeth and go with it, to hell with the consequences? Or would you cruise by first, making sure no one was standing behind all the notices and special offers, ready to be flattened? Maybe drop off a spotter to give you a call when it was safe to go.

And you wouldn't want to swap vehicles, would you? Not before the raid. *After*: yes. But the less messing about beforehand the better. Which meant that, sooner or later, the stolen four-by-four would drift past the Pubwatch camera, only the people in it wouldn't be wearing masks. They'd pull over, and someone would get out, walk into the shop, and find out what they were looking at. All caught on camera.

He reversed all the way back to the beginning of the recording, but there was no sign of the Mitsubishi Warrior.

Logan checked the paperwork again. The four-by-four wasn't reported stolen until after the police turned up at the owner's door to arrest him. The silly sod hadn't even noticed the thing was missing until it was found two days after the raid, burned out in a field north of Woodhead.

Maybe they dropped their spotter off around the corner and let him walk?

Logan ran the footage again, but no one loitered about on the street looking shifty with a mobile phone.

OK, try the previous day.

He ejected the hard cartridge and slotted in Sunday's instead.

Let it run while he punched Tufty's shoulder number into the Airwave. 'Shire Uniform Seven, safe to talk?'

'They're onto verse forty-six, Sarge. This Eskimo Nell sounds—'

'What's happening with Martyn Baker?'

'SLAB have set him up with some lawyer down in Dundee.'

'Dundee? That's a lot of sodding use. Is he coming up?'

'Verse forty-seven. You'd think she'd get tired of all the—'

'Tufty!'

'Sorry. Don't know, Sarge. He's still on the phone.'

'OK, let me know soon as he's done.' Logan put the handset down. Frowned at the screen.

On it, a rainy Sunday morning in Fraserburgh drizzled along in silence. A handful of people hurried past in ones and twos, shoulders hunched, backs bent against the wind. None of them optimistic enough to sport an umbrella.

No point looking for the Mitsubishi Warrior. He checked the paperwork again. According to the owner, the last time he'd driven it was Friday night. They wouldn't have stolen it then – not that long before the raid. As soon as it was reported stolen there'd be a lookout request, all the Automatic Number Plate Recognition cameras would flag it up. All they'd have to do is drive past a traffic car and they'd be nabbed.

So they must've used another vehicle to stake the place out.

He frowned his way through the day's footage on six-times speed. No suspicious cars. And the only people loitering about looking shifty were the same pair of auld mannies outside the Kenyan Bar.

Mind you, just because the Ram-Raiders weren't lurking on *this* camera, it didn't mean they weren't on one of the pub's other two.

He reached for the eject button . . . Stopped. Pressed pause instead. Squinted at the screen. There – stepping out of Broch Braw Buys – a young man in a blue outdoor-hill-climby jacket, earphones on, carrier bag in one hand.

Play.

He walked towards the camera, features getting less distorted with every step, until he was clear in perfect focus.

Logan hit pause again. Fiddled with the controls to zoom in. Short dark hair, long-ish nose, a designer-stubble goatee. 'Well, well, well.'

Print.

The machine whirred and clunked, then produced a full-colour printout of the man on the screen. Tony Wishart. History buff and burglar.

Play.

Wishart walked beneath the camera then off the screen.

Eject.

Logan slotted in the cartridge for the next camera and spooled it forward to the right time.

Tony Wishart walked into shot, under the camera. Stopped at the crossroads. Looked left, then right, then left again. Waited for a Fiat Panda to judder past, then crossed over Finlayson Street. Turned left . . . And disappeared behind a big black removal van with 'MAGNUS HOGG & SON ~ MOVING FAMILIES HOME EST 1965' down the side.

A red Fiat drove past. Then a blue Audi.

Still no sign of Tony Wishart.

A slouch of children zombie'd past, followed by their mums – leaning heavily on pushchairs.

Where the hell was he?

Four minutes and counting.

Either he'd got into the removal van, or he'd gone into one of the houses hidden behind it.

Logan tried camera number three, but it was the same.

So . . . was Wishart robbing the house, or laying low there?

Print.

Only one way to find out.

CHAPTER 41

The Big Car slid along Gallowhill Road, making for the crossroads with Finlayson Street. Logan nodded at Tufty. 'Go on then.'

A nod. 'Right.'

Sitting in the back seat, Constables King Kong McMahon, and Dundee Bill eased forward. Dundee was big enough, but King Kong's head scraped the car's ceiling. His large square head was topped with a fine felt of hair, big sideburns, thick features and a beaming smile. Dundee, on the other hand, looked like someone had squeezed a coatrack into a police uniform. Large ears, long thin nose, enough creases on his face to put a linen suit to shame.

Tufty glanced at them in the rear-view mirror. 'Tony Wishart. IC-One male, eighteen years old, wanted on eighteen counts of burglary. Likes to help himself to historic memorabilia along with the usual laptops, mobile phones, and jewellery. Not known to be violent, but there's always a first time.'

A thick finger poked into Tufty's shoulder. King

Kong's voice was a lot posher than it should have been. 'So, are we looking at a dog here? Or a firearm?'

'Sarge?'

Logan shook his head. 'No dogs, no guns.'

'Good. I hate getting bits of Rottweiler all over my uniform. Takes ages to wash out.'

Dundee Bill grinned. No two of his teeth seemed to be pointing in the same direction. 'Remember yon time we were up that block of flats with Spooney Birch?' Dundee stuck a hand on Tufty's other shoulder. 'I do the dunt, and Spooney's the first in. Charges right in there, screaming, "POLICE, EVERYONE ON THE FLOOR NOW!"'

King Kong sighed. 'Come on, it wasn't Spooney's fault.'

'And then there's this high-pitched yippy barking, and Spooney screams. And I mean a *proper* scream, a real dig-down-to-your-socks-and-bellow kind of noise. So we all swarm in, and there's Spooney doing the highland fling in the middle of the living room.'

'He had thirty-two stitches, I don't think that's very funny.'

'Only instead of a sporran, it's a Jack Russell terrier latched onto his bits. Growling and shaking away while he's trying to batter the thing off with his extendable baton. Billy Smith recorded the whole thing on his phone.' The grin got wider. 'Haven't laughed so much since Jimmy Deacon fell in the harbour.'

'You're not a very good friend, are you, Dundee?'

'Nope.'

The little line of shops came up on the left-hand side.

Logan held up the printout from the Pubwatch camera as they neared the crossroads. A cluster of new-build houses sat all clean and shiny, opposite the Kenyan Bar. Only the closest one would've been blocked by the removal van. He pointed at it. 'Here we go.'

'Lights and music, Sarge?'

'Knock yourself out.'

Tufty poked the 999 button on the central console, and put his foot down. The Big Car surged forward, screeched around the corner and slithered to a halt in front of the nearest new-build.

They piled out into the dull afternoon, Tufty and Dundee hopping the fence into the back garden while Logan and King Kong marched up the short path to the front door.

King Kong cricked his head to one side, then the other. 'You want me to batter it in?'

'Let's try the old-fashioned way first, eh?' Logan reached out and pressed the doorbell.

It buzzed slightly.

No reply.

King Kong's knees popped as he squatted down and peered in through the letterbox. The sound of frenetic drums and guitars stuttered out through the gap. 'Think there's definitely someone in there.'

'Is it locked?'

A quick turn of the handle, and the door swung open. They stepped inside.

A nice hall, bit bland and magnolia, but other than that it was OK. An old leather bible sat on the hall table, next to the phone, its edges scuffed, the gilt lettering flaking and cracked.

The music was coming from somewhere further down the hall, all the words hammering out in barrages, interspersed with a weird blend of electronic rock and heavy metal guitars.

Lounge: empty.

Dining room: empty.

King Kong eased a door open on a tiny toilet. Also empty.

That left the kitchen.

Logan stopped at the door. It was open a couple of inches. Nice new kitchen, certainly a lot more expensive-looking than the one he'd put in at the Sergeant's Hoose. Lots of black work surface, slate tiles, and oak units. A portable speaker sat in the middle of the breakfast bar with an MP3 player plugged into the top.

A flash of purple T-shirt and black jeans in the gap between the door and frame then gone again. It sounded as if whoever was in there was having a bit of a singalong. And not doing a very good job of it. The words were all there, but the tune had stormed off in a huff.

Logan put a hand on the door and pushed.

It swung all the way.

A young man stood by the conservatory doors,

with his back to the room, pouring what looked like Irn-Bru from a crystal decanter into a tall glass. Battering out the words in time with whoever was battering out of the speakers. The liquorice smell of star anise combined with the aroma of coriander and pepper, presumably coming from the trio of takeaway containers sitting on the breakfast bar. Noodles, something prawny, and what was probably spare ribs. A bag of prawn crackers lay next to them.

Logan's stomach growled like an angry badger.

Who said crime didn't pay?

The guy still hadn't turned around, so Logan crept into the kitchen and pressed the power button on the speaker-dock.

What almost passed for singing continued for a couple of beats, 'Old School Hollywood . . .' then faded away. The singer cleared his throat. 'There's someone there, isn't there?' He turned around. And his eyes went wide. 'Crap.'

Logan smiled. 'Tony Wishart, I believe. How nice. Tell me, Tony: the bible out in the hall, that the one you stole from Pennan?'

He put the decanter down on the work surface. Licked his lips. 'I don't know what you're talking about.'

'Is this your house, Tony?'

Wishart shuffled left a bit. 'I'm . . . looking after it for a lovely old lady. Poor dear's got Alzheimer's. She fell and broke her hip, so while she's in hospital, I'm, you know, doing my bit.'

'Doesn't look like an old lady's house.' Logan pointed. 'Let me guess, that's the ship's decanter from the *Cutty Sark*?'

Wishart pulled his lips in, squeezing his jaws together. Look left, look right. He was going to run for it. Getting up on the balls of his feet. Tensing up. Ready to go.

Constable King Kong McMahon stepped into the kitchen doorway, filling it. 'Oh no you don't.'

'Oh yes I do!' And Wishart was off in the opposite direction, yanking open the conservatory doors, sprinting past the wicker furniture and out the far side, into the garden.

King Kong lumbered after him with Logan not far behind.

Dundee Bill appeared from nowhere, arms open like a goalkeeper, and Wishart ducked, scrambled past him, once round the garden with Dundee and Tufty in hot pursuit. Then bang – he jumped for the high wooden fence, using a plastic compost bin for a boost, up and over the top.

Tufty didn't stop in time and hammered into the fence. Bounced. Landed flat on his back with a, 'Whoooof!'

King Kong charged up onto the compost bin and over the fence.

Logan slid to a halt on the wet grass and grabbed the wood, peering out like Kilroy.

Wishart was legging it down Mid Street as fast as his skinny legs would carry him, the mounded bulk of King Kong pounding along behind him. Gathering momentum.

Dundee Bill thumped to a halt next to Logan, grinning. Made a loudhailer from his hands. 'RUN, FORREST, RUN!'

Nope, Wishart was faster. Little sod was going to get away . . .

Then a bicycle appeared from between two parked cars and *CRASH*. Arms and legs and wheels and swearing.

Dundee winced. 'That's gotta hurt.'

Tony Wishart lay sprawled across the tarmac, with one foot still tangled in the bicycle's skeleton. He struggled to his knees, just in time to get rugby-tackled by King Kong.

'Ooh . . .' Dundee sucked a breath in through his crooked teeth. 'But not as much as that.'

'All units be on the lookout for a dark-red Vauxhall Astra, stolen from outside the chip shop in Gardenstown . . .'

Tony Wishart sat at the breakfast bar, a bag of frozen sweetcorn pressed to the left side of his face. 'Think I chipped a tooth.' The stubble on his chin was all matted with drying blood, where he'd smashed into the road surface.

Logan sat down opposite and helped himself to a prawn cracker. Cold, but still good. 'So, when I search this place, what am I going to find, Tony? First World War bayonet? Maybe some paintings from the Twenties?' Another cracker, crunching through the words. 'How about all the stuff that got nicked from the Aberdeen Heritage Centre in Mintlaw?'

He peeled the bag of sweetcorn from his cheek. There was the beginnings of a nice shiner there. 'Don't suppose it'd help if I told you I'd found it?'

'Not really.'

'Pfff . . .' Wishart dumped the sweetcorn on the worktop. Cracked his way through all eight fingers, then did the thumbs as well. 'How did you know to find me? Someone ratted me out, didn't they? Was it Baz? I bet it was Baz, he's always been a tosser.'

Logan pulled out the two printouts from the Pubwatch recordings, holding them up one at a time. 'This is you coming out of Broch Braw Buys. And this is you disappearing behind a removal van. You didn't come out, so you must've gone into the house behind it.' He laid them out on the counter. Frowned. There was something . . .

'I only went in for teabags.' Wishart's shoulders slumped. 'Can I at least eat my carryout?'

'Sorry.' Logan clicked the plastic tops back on the containers. 'But I'll do you a deal. You show me everything you've squirrelled away here, tell us what you did with the rest of it, and I'll make sure the Sheriff knows you cooperated.'

Tufty lowered the last cardboard box into the Big Car. A brass sextant poked out of the top, nestled amongst old gramophone records and rolled-up

538

maps. He stepped back and closed the boot. 'That's the lot.'

'Good.'

Tony Wishart was squeezed into the back seat with his bag of frozen sweetcorn, and a stack of boxes full of historical memorabilia. Paintings, bowls, vases, a medical bag from the Crimean War, pens, pipes, photographs, books . . . A full-sized porcelain bust of some long-dead man in a naval uniform sat on the passenger seat, held in place by a set of fluorescent-yellow limb restraints.

'Sure you're OK to walk, Sarge?'

'It's two minutes up the road. Go.'

Tufty climbed in behind the wheel.

Logan stood on the pavement as the Big Car pulled away. OK, so Tony Wishart wasn't exactly Hannibal Lecter meets Professor Moriarty, but at least the good people of Pennan, and other points north, would get their antique knick-knacks back.

King Kong clunked the front door shut and locked it. Pocketed the key. 'That'll put a dent in the unsolved burglaries.'

'How's the leg?'

He glanced down at the hole in his trousers, where a scabby knee showed through. 'My own silly fault for rugby-tackling him.' King Kong stepped to the kerb. 'You filling in for Davey Muir again?'

'For my sins.' Logan picked up the carrier bag from behind the garden gate, then they set off up the street, hands behind their backs, feet swinging out with metronome regularity. Not walking: proceeding.

They'd barely made it halfway up the street before Logan stopped. Popped the carrier bag on a garden wall, and dug out the printouts again.

'Sarge?'

He handed them to King Kong. 'What am I not seeing?'

Frown. Scowl. Peer. 'No idea. Missing person, maybe? Stolen car? You recognize any of the registrations?'

'No.' He stuffed them back in his pocket and picked up the bag again. 'But there's something.'

Logan paced away from the kitchen area, then back again, phone pressed hard against his ear. 'What do you mean, "he's not there"?'

'Went home for the night.'

The Fraserburgh station canteen was deserted except for Logan, the TV – on mute – and the howl of the microwave.

Useless, half-arsed, lazy, lying little tosser.

'He was supposed to get me DNA results for close of play!'

'What can I say? He went home for the night. His shift starts at nine tomorrow morning, so feel free to call up and shout at him then. Me? I've got work to do.'

Logan jabbed his finger at the disconnect button. Stood and glowered at the TV.

Why could no one do their bloody job?

Just as well he hadn't told Helen about chasing up the lab results. Wouldn't exactly have showered himself in glory there.

The microwave's drone climaxed with a ping and Logan dug the plastic containers out with scorched fingertips. 'Ooh, hot, hot, hot . . .' He clunked them all onto one plate, grabbed a fork and hurried back to the canteen table.

'Shire Uniform Seven, safe to talk?'

Couldn't even get five minutes to himself.

He sank into his seat. 'Bang away.'

'You've got a lookout request on the go for a Charles "Craggie" Anderson. He's been spotted buying pile cream from a chemist's in Peterhead.'

'That's a good trick – they found his body on Saturday morning, up in Orkney. So unless it's a ghost, it's *probably* someone else.' Logan creaked the tops off the containers, letting out a waft of oriental steam. 'Can you cancel the lookout request?'

'Will do.'

He stuck the Airwave handset back on the table. Licked his lips.

The spare ribs were almost too hot to touch – silky and spicy and meaty and . . . God's sake.

'Sarge.' Tufty settled into the seat opposite. 'Ooh, prawn crackers!' He helped himself.

Logan sooked the sauce from his fingers and dropped the naked bone onto the plate. 'Should you not be off home? Shift ended twenty minutes ago.'

Crunch, crunch, crunch. 'Wanted to make sure you got the intel. Martyn Baker's talked to his solicitor, and now he's sitting in Interview Two, waiting to no-comment everything.' Little flecks of prawn-cracker dandruff drifted their way down Tufty's black T-shirt. 'You want me to sit in on the interview? There's never anything on the telly, Sunday nights.' Crunch, crunch, crunch.

Another bone got denuded and dumped. 'OK, but only because I'm not sending you home with the Big Car.' He sooked his fingers clean again, and produced the printouts. Tossed them across the table to Tufty. 'You recognize anyone or anything there?'

He helped himself to another prawn cracker. Crunched his way through a frown. 'Is it this?' He pointed at a blue Kia, driving up Mid Street towards the Kenyan Bar. 'Number plate's a bit fuzzy, but it could be the one got nicked from Peterhead? Was on the Monday briefing slides.'

'You remember a number plate from Monday?'

Crunch, crunch, crunch. 'It's easy: you make them into words. This one looks a bit like, "Moontihum". Want me to run it through the system?'

'Thanks.'

Tufty scribbled the Kia's registration, make, and colour down in his notebook. Then paused. Looked up, his eyebrows knitted together as if something dramatic had suddenly occurred to him. 'Sarge?'

'What?'

'Can I have a rib?'

A little burp worked its way up Logan's throat, bringing with it the taste of kung po king prawns with special fried noodles and honey chilli ribs.

Martyn Baker fidgeted on the other side of the interview table. 'No comment.'

'I only asked you how you'd describe your voice, Martyn. I'm not trying to trip you up.'

'No comment.'

Logan gave Tufty the nod.

He placed the small baggie of weed on the table with a flourish. 'I am now showing Mr Baker the container of cannabis weed I discovered on his person when I searched him this afternoon.'

Logan gave it a poke. 'Not a huge amount, is it, Martyn? Thought a big-time dealer from down south would have more on him.'

'No comment.' It looked as if he'd been at his spots in the cell. Two were now all swollen and red, one an empty crater plugged by a dark-red scab.

'Are you planning on expanding into all of Aberdeenshire, or is it just the bit around Banff?'

'No comment.' He scowled out from beneath his heavy eyebrows. 'And I'm not expanding nothing nowhere. I'm up on holiday with me bab and me kid. Three of us been here for weeks.'

'How do you know Colin "Klingon" Spinney and Kevin "Gerbil" McEwan?'

'No comment.'

'How do you know Francis "Frankie" Ferris?'

'No comment.'

'So was this wee bag a sample or something? Are you drumming up business?'

'No comment.' His fingers wouldn't sit still, they skittered back and forth along the edge of the scarred tabletop.

'All right.' Logan dug into the folder and came out with a little cardboard box. The form printed on it was filled out in blue biro – where the phone had been seized, by whom, where, and when. Maggie had managed to spell his last name wrong again. He opened the box, took out the big Samsung. 'This is your phone. Remember it? We confiscated it because you were using it while driving.'

Baker licked his lips. Kept his eyes on his twitchy fingers. 'No comment.'

'When we send it down to get analysed, what do you think we're going to find? Lots of little secrets and deals, I'm betting. Lots of . . .'

Baker's head drooped, then his shoulders quivered. Once. Twice. Three times. Then a sob burst free. Followed by a moan. Little drops of water exploded between his trembling fingers.

Bit extreme.

Then again, maybe he'd finally realized that he was going down for attempted murder.

Logan tapped on the table. 'Something you want to tell us, Martyn? We know it all anyway, might as well put your side of the story.'

Martyn Baker seemed to get three sizes smaller, his back hunched, shoulders up around his scarlet ears, hands curled against his chest. 'Wasn't meant to happen. Was only meant to be a warning . . .'

'Kind of heavy-handed for a warning, wasn't it?' Battering someone with a baseball bat didn't exactly reek of subtlety.

'Meant to be a *warning*. Stay the hell off our turf. I didn't want it to . . . It was an accident.'

An accident. With a baseball bat?

'Are you kidding? How do you accidentally—'

'Bullet must've, I don't know, bounced off something. I wasn't aiming for her, I swear.' He looked up with bloodshot eyes. 'On my little girl's *life*, it was an accident.'

Bullet? OK, not exactly what was expected.

Tufty opened his mouth to say something, so Logan kicked him under the table.

'Ow!'

A warning finger.

Tufty shut his mouth again.

Baker's head fell. 'I didn't mean to shoot her. Had to go lie low for a bit, far, far away from civilization and that.' His shoulders rose and fell. 'Told Elsie to chuck some stuff in a bag while I fetched Mandy from her nan's. We piled in the car and just drove. Got the hell out of it.' A sniff. 'Then the telly said she was an undercover cop.'

Logan let out a long, slow breath. 'You shot the undercover officer in Liverpool, and you ran away to Banff to hide.'

'I didn't mean to. I didn't. It was an *accident.*'

Holy mother of fish. 'Where's the gun?'

'Was meant to be a couple of shots in the air, you know, to scare them.'

'Martyn, what did you do with the gun? We—'

A knock on the interview-room door.

Oh for . . .

Logan's head dipped. Whoever was out there, they couldn't have timed it worse if they'd tried. He curled his hand into a fist and pressed it against his leg. Kept his voice calm. 'Constable Quirrel: go see who it is.'

Tufty scraped his chair back and scurried off to the door. A clunk. Some murmuring. Then he was back, lips an inch from Logan's ear, voice low. 'Sarge, it's a DCI McInnes and he looks like someone's taped his bits to an angry Rottweiler.'

Logan kept his eyes on Martyn Baker. 'Tell him I'm busy.'

'Yeah . . . He's kinda insistent. And really, *really* angry.'

'Fine. Interview is suspended at eighteen-hundred. Sergeant McRae leaving the room.' He stood. Pushed a blank notepad across the table. 'Maybe you'd like to write it down, Martyn. Get it all on paper. Might make you feel better.' Logan stepped out into the corridor, closed the interview-room door behind him.

McInnes took up as much space as possible, arms raised, hands curled into claws. The creases either side of his mouth looked as if they'd been carved with a chainsaw, his features dark and flushed, teeth bared in a vicious smile. But his voice was remarkably calm. 'What, exactly, do you think you're doing, Sergeant?'

'I'm interviewing my suspect, so—'

'Did I, or did I not, tell you to stay away from Operation Troposphere? Because I'm pretty certain I did.'

Logan pulled his shoulders back. 'I carried out a routine stop-and-search and found Class B drugs. I was doing my job.'

'No, you were trying to screw with me and my operation.' He stepped closer. 'You arrested that man, dragged him over here from Banff, and told everyone to keep it a secret from me. Did you *really* think I wouldn't find out?' The smile got even less pleasant. 'You've got no idea what you're doing, have you?'

'What, because I got the Candleman before you? Sounds like I know *exactly* what I'm doing.'

One eyebrow went up. 'Candleman? What the hell is a "Candleman"?'

'The guy who supplied Kevin McEwan and Colin Spinney?'

McInnes laughed. A proper full-on belly laugh that left him panting and wiping his eyes. 'Not Candleman, you idiot, *Candy* Man. The supplier's called the Candy Man. And that isn't him.'

Oh . . . Logan stared at the ceiling. 'The Candy Man.' So he'd spent the last day and a half chasing a ghost that didn't even exist. Thank you, Jack Simpson.

Idiot.

'You thought you were screwing with Operation Troposphere. I told you to stay the hell away from every*one* and every*thing* to do with it, and you went ahead and arrested Martyn Baker anyway.'

Logan shook his head. 'You just said he didn't have anything to do with Klingon or Gerbil, so—'

'Yeah, but you thought he *did*.' McInnes took another step. Now he was close enough that his breath was warm against Logan's cheek. It stank of cigarettes and extra-strong mints. 'You thought he did and you picked him up anyway, even though you knew I'd told you not to. You did your best to screw me and my operation over.' The creases either side of McInnes's mouth deepened. 'You really think I'm going to let that go, Sergeant?'

Of course he sodding wasn't.

'It had *nothing* to do with your case.'

'You screwed up.' The Detective Chief Inspector poked him in the chest. 'And you know what? I wouldn't have found out if you hadn't tried to cover it up.' McInnes turned on his heel, and sauntered away down the corridor. 'I told you, you were on your last warning, McRae. What happens now: you've only got yourself to blame.'

Great.

— SUNDAY BACKSHIFT —

BURN.

CHAPTER 42

Logan sank back in his chair and put a hand over his eyes. For some reason, the temporary viewing suite had developed a distinctly cheesy smell. Like a big block of Stilton, abandoned in a small car on a hot day. 'Well, how was I supposed to know Jack Simpson got it wrong?'

On the other end of the phone, the backshift Duty Inspector puffed out a sigh. Still sounding as if he had a bag of marbles stuffed up each nostril. *'He was off his face on heroin and getting battered to death at the time. How accurate would you be?'*

Yeah, that wasn't helping.

'But, on the bright side, we've solved the murder of an undercover police officer. Be some brownie points for you there, Logan. Not sure if it'll be enough to stop McInnes from shafting you, though.'

Still not helping. 'We've got a signed confession and he's rolling on two of his gang mates, so—'

A knock on the door.

'Sarge?' When Logan uncovered his eyes, there was Tufty, with two steaming mugs and a copy of the *Sunday Post*. He popped a tea down in front

551

of Logan and mouthed the words, 'I'm hunting biscuits.'

He was retreating when Logan waved him over and muffled the mouthpiece with a hand. 'Watch: and see if you can spot anything weird.' Logan scooted his chair back out of the way and pointed at the screen. The view from camera number three flickered on pause – looking out across the street at the removal van and the zombie children. Logan uncovered the mouthpiece. 'Sorry about that, Inspector, someone came in.'

'I'll get onto Merseyside Police. They'll probably want to send a car up to get him, but I'm pretty certain the Chief Constable's not letting Martyn Baker go anywhere till we've done a joint press conference. We're not having a bunch of Scousers taking all the credit.' The grin was audible in his voice. *'That's my job.'*

Tufty squatted down in front of the viewer and fiddled with the controls, sending the picture streaking into fast-forward.

'Trouble is, we've still got no idea who supplied Klingon and Gerbil with their gear.'

'Yeah, well, I'm sure DCI McInnes will tell us when he deems fit. And not before. Meantime, what are you and the rest of my sticky minions up to in B Division the night?'

Logan ran through the duty roster and the open caseload while Tufty wheeched back and forth through time. Logan clunked his notepad shut. 'Guv, don't suppose there's any news about my warrant to dunt Frankie Ferris's door in, is there?'

'*I'll check. When you going in?*'

'Tomorrow, if I can get the bodies. Might try the OSU.'

'*OK – do that. But make sure the cellblock know Martyn Baker's going nowhere and talking to no one until I say so.*'

'Yes, Guv.'

'*And Logan? Good work.*'

Good grief: praise. For once.

'*But please, for the love of God, stay the hell away from DCI McInnes!*'

He hung up the office phone.

Tufty was still fiddling with the dial.

'Are you having fun?'

'Wonder who's flitting.'

Logan stared at him. 'What?'

'Who's moving house? The removal van sits there the whole time. Nobody loads anything into it, nobody takes anything out of it. Maybe they're parked up for the day?'

Logan blinked at the screen. 'Try one of the other cassettes.'

Tufty hit eject, then slotted in the one that came after the one they were watching. Twisted the dial and set everything whooshing forwards. Nothing. Nothing. Nothing. Then four men in overalls wandered up Mid Street, carrying brown paper bags that looked as if they might have come from the Wimpy on Hanover Street. They climbed into the removal van, and sat there eating. Then finally buckled their seatbelts and drove away.

'Just a bunch of gadgies, parked up for lunch.'

Tufty ejected the cassette, and replaced it with the one before the one they'd been looking at before this one. 'A four-hour lunch break? Tell you, we're in the wrong job.' He sent the footage spinning backwards, then hunched forward, nose inches from the screen. 'If you were the Cashline Ram-Raiders, you'd want to stake the place out, right? Find out when it got stocked up by the bank, or whatever. Maybe we need to find when the security car turns up and look round about then?'

People lurched in reverse across the screen. Cars and bicycles all going backwards too. Everything except that removal van.

Nothing went into it, nothing came out of it.

Then the four men backed across the road and climbed into the van, started it up, and reversed out of shot.

'. . . Sarge? Yoohoo, Sarge?' Tufty was waving at him. 'You OK?'

'Get the footage for camera one. Same time-stamp.'

A shrug. But he did what he was told, slotting the new cartridge into place, then spinning the dial until one of the four men walked backwards into Broch Braw Buys: big, with long brown hair and green overalls.

All that time, and the only things they did were buy burgers and visit the shop that got ram-raided the very next day.

Removal van. Removal van.

No . . .

It was. *That* was what looked familiar, not the people or the cars.

A slow smile spread across Logan's face. 'Tufty, never thought I'd say this, but you're a genius.'

'I am? Cool.' He puffed out his chest. Then frowned. 'What did I do? And do I get a badge, or something?'

Logan pulled out his notebook and flipped back through to yesterday morning. Found the number for the Portsoy Co-op's manager, and dialled it.

The phone rang, and rang, and rang, until finally: *click.* *'Hello, you've reached the voicemail of—'* Another click. *'Hello? Can I help you?'*

'Hi, Stacey? It's Sergeant McRae, we met yesterday morning. After the ram-raid?'

'Sorry, I was stocktaking the walk-in freezer. You have no idea how many bags of oven chips we go through.'

'Can you do me a favour? Take a look on your CCTV footage for a removal van. Might have to go back a couple of days.'

'If you think it'll help.'

With any luck . . .

His Airwave handset crackled away to itself. *'Anyone in the vicinity of Aberchirder? We've got a report of cows loose on the A97 south of Castlebrae . . .'*

'How does half seven, quarter to eight sound?' Logan pinned the phone between his ear and shoulder and rummaged through the next shelf down. Why did no one put things back where they came from? The Big Car's CCTV cartridges were supposed to be ordered chronologically, oldest to newest, on the sodding shelf below the monitor. There was even a sodding label on the sodding shelf *saying* that.

'*Aye, aye, Control, show Big Paul and the Dreaded Penny attending. On our way.*'

Seven o'clock and he had the whole of Banff station to himself. Made a nice change.

Or it would do if he could sodding find anything.

Squeaking rattling noises came from the other end of the phone. God knew what Helen was doing, but it sounded like she was washing a bag of robot mice. '*Steak, mushroom, onion rings and chips?*'

On top of confiscated Chinese?

Never look a gift meal in the mouth.

'Sounds great.'

Finally – there they were, two shelves down, stuffed in willy-nilly behind a stack of evidence bags. Idiots. Supposed to be one for every day of the fortnight, with one spare. If they were all jumbled up, how was anyone meant to find what they were looking for?

'*I got the hall done. Ceiling above the stairs was a bit of a sod, but it's looking a lot better now.*'

He stacked all fourteen cartridges into a big wobbly pile and carried them back to his desk. 'You got all that done in one day? You should go into business.'

556

Now where was the lead to connect them with the computer?

'Alleged dog attack on Williams Crescent, Fraserburgh. Anyone free to attend?'

It was buried under a slew of triple-A batteries, elastic bands, and paperclips in the bottom drawer.

Whole place was like living with the bloody Borrowers. And it couldn't *all* be Hector's fault.

'Right, I'll finish cleaning the roller and brushes, then it'll be time to get dinner on the go.'

'Looking forward to it.' Logan hung up, put all the cartridges into order, then plugged the lead into yesterday's one. The computer groaned, and creaked, a little green light came on in the cartridge. Whirring. A couple of bleeps. Then the loading bar appeared on the screen.

Might as well go make a cup of tea, this would take a while.

An *Aberdeen Sunday Examiner* was folded over the edge of Maggie's cubicle. 'TRAGIC END FOR MISSING FISHERMAN' sat above a photo of Charles Anderson with an inset of his boat. Logan grabbed the paper and took it through to the canteen. Spread it out on the table and stuck the kettle on.

Had a bit of a sing as the water grumbled and pinged: 'Steak for tea, steak for tea, la-la-la-la steak for tea . . .'

According to the *Examiner*, Charles 'Craggie' Anderson's life had been blighted by the loss of his son five years ago. There wasn't much more info than Big Paul had dug up from the official files, but the reporter had sexed it up as much as possible. Anderson's campaign to find the paedophile he was sure had abducted his wee boy. The collapse of his marriage. The drinking. And his fiery Viking death.

They'd even managed to track down Anderson's wife, now living in Devon under her maiden name. A tearful quote about lost chances, tragedy, and grief.

The kettle growled to a boil.

No suggestion that Anderson was anything other than a broken man on his way to the inevitable grave. No hint that he was responsible for his son's death, or that he was the kind of guy who would abduct a little girl, abuse her, then cave her head in with a metal pipe.

Logan made a cuppa, checked to make sure no one was looking, and nicked a Jammie Dodger from Inspector McGregor's stash at the back of the cupboard. She wouldn't be in again till tomorrow morning, so nightshift could take the blame.

Maybe it was just a coincidence that Anderson had gone missing at the same time as Neil Wood? And a coincidence that a wee girl's body washed up at Tarlair Outdoor Swimming Pool not long after.

Or, maybe, Wood and Anderson were in it together. Wouldn't be the first time a pair of scumbags had teamed up to abuse kids.

'*Shire Uniform Seven, safe to talk?*'

Logan checked the screen. It was the Duty Inspector's shoulder number. 'Batter on, Guv.'

'Got a delay on your warrant for Frankie Ferris's house. Something about operational pressures. They said to try again tomorrow. Meantime, let me know if you need a hand leaning on the Operational Support Unit for extra bodies.'

'Thanks, Guv.'

Logan took his tea and pilfered biscuit back through to the Sergeants' Office, in time to see the progress bar hit 100 percent. Half of the screen filled with a static view of the car park outside Banff police station. The other half was a list of time-stamps – each one representing a block of data when the camera was activated.

He scrolled through it, and clicked on the one for half-nine yesterday morning.

The screen jumped to an image of a winding road, trees and bushes reduced to a green blur by the speeding car as its siren wailed out of the computer's nasty little speakers. A readout in the corner of the picture put Nicholson's speed at eighty-five. The 'WELCOME TO PORTSOY' sign flashed past. Houses. Cars. Then onto the main street.

Bottles and cartons and tins covered the road in a slick outside the Co-op with its ruptured window. The car screeched to a halt. Some clunking. Then Logan appeared on the screen, pulling on his peaked cap.

'You! Which way did they go? What are they driving?'

The young woman with the pushchair pointed,

mouth moving, but she was too far away for the microphone to pick up any words.

Logan jumped back in. There was a *thump*. Then, *'Go!'*

And they were off again, tearing along the street, past houses and cars and stunned pedestrians.

'Shire Uniform Seven to Control, perpetrators have fled the scene. Witness says they took the Cullen road. We're in pursuit.'

Whatever Control said in reply, it got reduced to a tinny burr.

His own voice again: *'Negative.'*

A caravan blocked the left side of the road, ignoring the flashing lights and screaming siren. Cars coming the other way . . . There.

Logan hit pause. Three cars. A bus. A removal van. And a milk tanker. All pulling into the side of the road to let them past. The van was big and black, with 'MAGNUS HOGG & SON ~ MOVING FAMILIES HOME EST 1965' down the side in curly red lettering.

Same one that was sitting outside the Kenyan Bar in Fraserburgh the day before Broch Braw Buys got ram-raided. Only this time the number plate was clearly visible. He copied it down into his notebook and called up the PNC interface.

'Shire Uniform Seven, safe to talk?'

Logan grabbed his Airwave and checked the screen. No idea whose shoulder number that was, but it was a low one, so maybe a boss. He pressed the button. 'Go ahead.'

'*Ah, Sergeant McRae, it's DCI McInnes.*'

Oh joy. Here it came – McInnes's revenge.

Logan typed the registration in one-handed. 'What can I do for you?'

'*You can join me at thirty-six Fairholme Place, that's what you can do. Right now, would be good.*'

Brilliant. 'Sir.'

The screen filled with ownership details for the removal van – a firm down in Bristol. The next page had the insurance details, and who was insured to drive the thing. None of the names seemed familiar.

Mind you, there was no guarantee there was actually anything dodgy about the thing. So it had turned up near two ram-raids, so what? Coincidences happened all the time.

Still . . .

But it'd have to wait. No point winding McInnes up any more than he already was.

Logan grabbed his hat and his keys.

Logan pulled the Big Car into the kerb, behind the Scene Examination Branch's manky white Transit van. Someone had finger-painted 'IF YOUR MUM WAS THIS DIRTY I WOULDN'T NEED PORN!' in the grime covering the back doors.

OK. Might as well get this over with.

He climbed out into the drizzle. The tips of his ears burned in the cold. So much for May, felt more like December.

His phone launched into its generic tune. He

pulled it out as he walked along the pavement towards Klingon's mum's house. 'Hello?'

'*Sergeant McRae? It's Stacey from Portsoy. I've looked through the CCTV like you asked.*'

He ducked under the cordon of blue-and-white 'Police' tape. 'And?'

'*Why did you want me to look for a removal van?*'

'We . . .' Good question. 'We think they might have witnessed a crime, we're trying to track them down so we can get a statement.' OK, so it was a lie, but she didn't know that.

There wasn't an officer on the front door, so Logan let himself in.

'*OK. Well, I found one. Had to go back to Wednesday to do it, but there's a removal van parked opposite the shop for a couple of hours in the morning.*'

The smell of burst bin-bags and rotting filth was like a wall across the porch.

'Let me guess: blue, with Duncan Smith Movers down the side?'

'*Oh . . . No. It's black. Magnus Hogg & Son.*'

Bingo.

There was a thump from somewhere inside, followed by a shrill woman's voice, 'NO I WILL NOT CALM DOWN! LOOK AT IT!'

Logan paused. 'Forgot to ask earlier: when do they refill your cash machine?'

'*Friday evening. Usually. Sometimes Saturday if there's a problem at the bank, or they're busy.*'

'LOOK AT IT!'

'OK, thanks. I'll let you know if anything comes

up.' He hung up. Took a deep breath. Regretted it. The air tasted of mank. He coughed a couple of times. Then stepped into the hall.

The shouting was coming through the open kitchen door.

He walked over and knocked on the frame.

McInnes leaned back against the work surface, arms folded, while a PC tried to placate a battle-ship of a woman in stonewashed jeans and a Burberry coat.

HMS Angry jabbed a finger at the kitchen window. 'AND WHAT THE HELL DO YOU THINK YOU'RE DOING TO MY GARDEN?'

McInnes turned his head in Logan's direction and pulled on a cold smile. 'Ah, Sergeant, good. *So* glad you could join us. Have you two met?' He pointed at the quivering mound of irate woman. 'This is Lesley Spinney. Colin Spinney's mother.'

Ah . . . So maybe she wasn't dead and buried after all.

CHAPTER 43

Detective Chief Inspector McInnes held out his arms. 'Doesn't she look good for a corpse?'

Klingon's mum turned her considerable scowl on him. 'Are you being funny?'

'Not at all, Lesley. Would you mind telling Sergeant McRae where you've been for the last four months?'

'And what happened to my house? It was just decorated before I left!'

'Please.' He patted her on the shoulder. 'Tell the Sergeant where you were.'

'I was in Perth, looking after my brother Sydney. Pancreatic cancer. We buried him, Wednesday.'

McInnes's smile grew. 'Not Perth, Australia, mind you, but Perth, Scotland. One hundred and thirty miles away, not nine *thousand*.'

No wonder Derek Stratman couldn't find her visa application.

Logan shifted his feet. 'I see.'

Not in Australia. And not dead.

How could she not be dead? The council records Maggie's partner dug up yesterday showed Klingon's mum hadn't paid the rent for nearly a year. How could *any* sane human being put Colin Klingon Spinney in charge of keeping a roof over their heads?

'But . . .' He cleared his throat. 'Why did you cancel your direct debit ten months ago? For the rent? Why did you let Colin take over?'

'None of your damned business, that's why.' She thumped over and glowered at him. 'Now what happened to my bloody house?'

Logan pulled his shoulders back. 'I'm afraid it's a crime scene.'

'No it isn't.'

'Your son and Kevin McEwan were dealing drugs and—'

'How dare you! No they were not!'

'—attempted murder of Jack Simpson—'

'My Colin's a good boy! How *dare* you talk about him like that.'

Logan stared at her. 'We recovered over a hundred thousand pounds' worth of heroin from the attic, and Jack Simpson's battered body.'

She shook her head. 'No you didn't. This is all *lies*.'

'I was there. I saw it. I *found* it!'

'No, you planted it. You're a liar and I'm making a formal complaint.' Klingon's mum pulled herself up to her full height. 'You won't get away with this!'

And today had been going so well . . .

★   ★   ★

'Well . . . I thought she *was*, OK?' Logan leaned back against the garden fence.

'Doesn't look dead to me. Does she look dead to you?' McInnes produced a packet of cigarettes, dug one out of the plain packaging and lit it. 'Thought they might have covered the difference between a living person and a dead one when you were at police college. Did you skip that day?'

Drizzle crawled down from the gunmetal sky, cold and damp.

'Everyone said she'd gone to Australia . . .'

There was a *crash*, and the Scenes Examination Branch tent lurched to one side. A white-suited figure emerged from the blue plastic edifice, carrying a metal pole. She dumped it on the ground with a clang. Her colleague cracked his knuckles, then went in to get his own pole. SOC-tent Jenga had begun.

McInnes took a long draw on his cigarette, then blew the resulting smoke in Logan's face. 'See, everyone's going to be patting you on the back. "Well done, Sergeant McRae, you caught the drug-dealing scumbag who shot Constable Mary Ann Nasrallah." Oh, the press are going to be shining your backside with their tongues for a bit, but you and I know different.' Another puff. At least this one went off to the side. 'You only lucked into that because you tried to screw me over.'

Logan shrugged a shoulder. 'It was a legitimate—'

'Don't even try.' McInnes stepped in close

enough that the glowing end of his cigarette cast a warm glow against Logan's cheek. 'You think you're the dog's balls, don't you, McRae? But you're nothing but a jumped-up little squirt in an itchy uniform and a bad haircut. And you're *right* at the top of my list.'

Silence.

Another clang, then the first SOC tech went in for the next pole.

McInnes took a step back. 'Oh, I can't touch you right now. But see when the dust settles, and everyone's over Constable Nasrallah getting shot? I'm coming for you.'

Logan parked the Big Car outside the Sergeant's Hoose. Slumped in his seat. Thumped his forehead off the steering wheel a couple of times.

Typical. It'd been going *really* well today, but they couldn't let him have that, could they? No. Of course they couldn't. One step forward, three steps sodding backward.

How could she not be dead? Syd's dog found her body, for God's sake.

He hissed out a long, slow breath. It was a dead family pet, or an old chicken carcass, wasn't it? Or maybe Syd's golden retriever was every bit as thick as every other retriever in the world.

'Gah . . .'

Come on. Finger out.

Logan flipped through his notebook, then pressed the talk button on his Airwave. 'Shire

Uniform Seven, I need a lookout request on a black removals van . . .' He rattled off the description and the number plate. 'Suspected involvement in the Cashline Ram-Raiders. Stop and search.'

'*Roger that.*'

And with any luck, he wouldn't end up looking like an idiot on that one as well.

He climbed out into the damp evening. Slammed the car door. Then hurried across the road and let himself into the house. The dark earthy smell of frying mushrooms met him at the door. 'Hello?'

'In here.'

He followed the scent into the kitchen. 'Sorry – got caught up at work.'

'Don't worry. Timed it perfectly.' Helen stood at the stove, wooden spatula in hand, poking away at the contents of the frying pan. Then nodded at the twin steaks sitting on their plate, raw and purple. 'Rare, or medium rare? I don't do well done.'

He settled at the kitchen table. 'Rare. Thanks.'

She brushed a handful of tarnished-golden curls from her face. The bags under her eyes were smaller than yesterday, and the day before. 'Chips will be ready in a minute.' She hunched her shoulders, poured the mushrooms into a bowl. Turned up the heat under the frying pan. 'Look, about last night—'

'It's OK. Really. Not a problem.' He cleared his throat. 'Sorry about the . . . you know. It . . .' A small cough. Warmth tingled the tips of his ears.

'Been a while since . . .' Yeah, probably best not to bring up an awkward erection at the dinner table. Sniff. 'Anyway. Steak and chips, eh? Been looking forward to this since yesterday.'

'Only I didn't want you to think that I'm some sort of tease and . . . I'm really . . .'

'No, don't worry about it.'

'And it's just so *lonely*, you know? The never knowing drives me insane.'

'Yeah.'

The steaks hissed and crackled in the hot pan.

She cricked her neck to one side. 'I know it's difficult. With Samantha.'

Difficult.

'It's been four years since she went into a coma. Four years and seven days. That's longer than we were together in the first place. I've known her longer like this than I did . . . It's . . .' A long slow breath took all the air from him. Made his back bend and his shoulders sag. 'Yeah. Difficult's a good word for it.'

Helen didn't turn around. 'And in all that time, did you never . . .?'

He stared at the back of her head. 'Yes. A couple of times. An old girlfriend. She's separated now.'

'I see.'

Logan put a bit of steel in his voice. 'I'm not *proud* of it.'

She lifted the steaks out of the pan. 'I haven't. And I'm not proud of that either.'

A timer bleeped, and she bent down and opened

the oven door, letting out the enticing aroma of fake chips.

He rearranged the cutlery.

She put the oven tray on the stovetop.

He lined up the salt, pepper, mustard, and vinegar. Looked down at his hands. 'I'm going to be late again tonight: probably half-two. Something like that.'

'Oh. OK. I'll probably read a book.'

'Good. Right.'

The chips rattled onto both plates like finger bones.

'Any unit in the vicinity of Bunthlaw, we've got a report of indecent assault at the caravan park . . .'

He turned down the volume on his handset. 'Sorry.'

The steaks were thick and bloody. Glistening and rich. And they ate them in total silence.

Half-past eight and the rain had faded away to nothing, leaving the streets slick and dark. The sun had found the chink between the sea and the lowering clouds, spreading its golden rays across the fields and houses as it sank towards America.

Logan took the Big Car around onto Rundle Avenue again.

Never knew your luck.

'Shire Uniform Seven, safe to talk?'

'Batter on.'

'You're on the update list for David and Catherine

Bisset? We've got a sighting of them getting on the Megabus from Dundee to London.'

'Someone stopping it?'

'On their way.'

'Thanks.'

No sign of anyone on Rundle Avenue. Frankie Ferris's customers would all be indoors, eating their microwave dinners in front of the telly. Moaning about how there was never anything decent on.

Wasting his time here.

Well, except for the whole deterring trade thing. With any luck Frankie's customers would shy off for a bit. Meaning all those lovely drugs would still be there when Logan battered his door down and raided the place.

Speaking of which: he keyed Sergeant Mitchell's shoulder number into the Airwave handset. 'Shire Uniform Seven, safe to talk?'

A crackle. A pause. Then Mitchell's booming rumble sounded. *'Sergeant McRae. Hear you're to thank for catching the scummer who shot that under-cover cop. Well done. The Operational Support Unit salutes you.'*

'Bit short notice, but are you and your Singalong Troupe free tomorrow for another dunt? Well, assuming I can get the Sheriff to stop being a pain in the hoop long enough to cough up my warrant.'

'Love to, but we're booked tomorrow. Could do the day after though, we'll be up your neck of the woods anyway. First thing Tuesday morning?'

'Deal.'

'Don't suppose there's any chance we'll get to use the chainsaw . . .?'

'I think we can swing that.'

'Then it's a date!'

And maybe this time they'd actually get Frankie Ferris for something more impressive than possession of a Class A.

Logan turned the car around and headed back towards the town centre.

'All units be on the lookout for a grey Volvo estate, driving erratically on the A98 east of Blakeshouse . . .'

He drifted through the rain-slicked streets – all nice and quiet – then over the bridge to Macduff.

The harbour was dead, and so was High Shore. No one hanging about outside the pubs, hotels, or chip shop.

Maybe it was the rain that had chased everyone inside? Sent them off to batten down the hatches and weather the storm. A little slice of December in May.

He stopped at the top of the hill, looking down the curling sweep of the road to where Tarlair Outdoor Swimming Pool nestled at the base of the cliffs. The cordons of police tape were gone, the place abandoned to the ghosts of bathers past, and a murdered little girl.

Yeah . . . this was getting a bit morbid.

So what if McInnes wanted to come after him, what was the baldy wee sod going to do? All mouth and shiny trousers, that's what *he* was. He wasn't the one who'd solved a murder from the other end of the country, was he? No. That was Logan, thank you very much.

Even if it had been a complete accident.

Long blue shadows reached across the weed-slicked water of the two swimming pools, then swallowed them entirely.

One dead little girl, head caved in with a metal pipe. Two missing men.

'All units: reports of a domestic disturbance on Fair Isle Crescent, Peterhead. Urgent response required.'

'Sierra Two Four, roger that. We are en route.'

No sign of Neil Wood – probably not even in the area any more. He'd have jumped the first bus out of there, set up shop in Edinburgh or Dundee. Somewhere big enough to blend in. Get himself a bit of anonymity. Difficult not to stick out in wee communities like the ones around here.

And then there was Charles 'Craggie' Anderson, burned to death on the bridge of his own boat . . .

Logan narrowed his eyes, blurring the swimming pool. Drummed his fingers on the steering wheel.

What if they *were* in it together? What if Neil Wood *didn't* hop a bus? What if he hopped on Anderson's boat instead? The pair of them make a run for it. There's a fight when they get to Orkney, and Neil Wood wins. Kills Anderson. Burns the boat to hide any evidence. Then disappears.

Mind you, if it was difficult to blend into the scenery in Aberdeenshire, it'd be almost impossible on Orkney . . .

Logan pulled a three-point turn and headed back to the main road.

If Wood and Anderson were working together, there'd be a trail, wouldn't there? Something more tangible to connect the pair of them than a photograph on a dead paedophile's wall.

Steel and her team would've been all over Neil Wood's bed-and-breakfast, but no one had given Charles Anderson's house more than a quick once-over – making sure he really *was* missing and not lying dead in the bath.

Time to change that.

Anderson's house was all on one level, with a grey slate roof. Chimney stacks at both gable ends, the pots cracked. Twig fingers reaching out of the tops, where the rooks had set up home. Warm light washed the cottage walls, made the white paint glow beneath the heavy black and blue clouds. Like the sky was one big bruise.

Dockens and thistles rampaged through the garden. Dandelion seeds stuck to nearly every surface – a plague of gossamer spiders in the long grass and overgrown borders.

Logan locked the Big Car and crunched across the gravel driveway to the front door.

The house sat all on its own, halfway between Macduff and Gardenstown. Isolated from its nearest neighbours by fields of neon rapeseed, down the end of a rutted track, about fifty feet from the edge of the cliff.

574

No prying eyes to see Anderson getting up to anything.

Front door was locked, so Logan tried around the side, wading through the knee-high grass, getting his itchy black trousers clarted with willow-herb tufts.

Back door was locked too.

Logan's mobile launched into 'The Imperial March'. He paused. Swore. Dug the thing out of his pocket. 'What?'

'Laz, that's no way to talk to a superior officer. Bit of respect, eh?'

'I'm busy. Leave me alone.'

There was probably a key, in a file, in a police station somewhere, but that wasn't much use right now. He tried above the back door.

Nothing.

'Ungrateful wee sod. There was me phoning up to congratulate you on catching the guy who shot Constable Nasrallah, and what do I get?'

'Yeah, that was all you were calling about.' Nothing under the pot plants either side of the door either.

'But now you come to mention it – you might be getting a call from Susan about a big family dinner to celebrate the test results. I need you to tell her she can't invite her mother. Or yours.'

'She's *your* wife, you tell her.' There was a garage, built onto the far side of the house. A bit ramshackle. Made of nailed-together boards. The paint peeling, exposing the wood beneath. Wasps had been at that, leaving the surface fuzzy and grey. No windows, but it probably wouldn't be too hard to lever a couple of boards free and squeeze inside.

Be easier to break one of the panes of glass in the back door though.

He snapped on a pair of blue nitrile gloves.

'Don't want to upset Susan, do I? Tell her . . . I don't know, your mum's giving you a hard time and if she finds out Susan's mum was there and she wasn't, she'll jump off a bridge or something.'

'I should be so lucky.' Logan grabbed a book-sized rock from the weeds by the door. 'Anyway, it's not my job to keep you safe from your mother-in-law.'

The back door had nine small glass panes set into the top half. The rock smashed through the bottom right one, sending shards of glass crashing to the kitchen floor.

'Why can I hear breaking glass?'

'Grow a pair and tell Susan how you feel. Stop weaselling, and do something about it.' He unsheathed his extendable baton and jabbed it into the hole. Raked it round the edges to clear off any jagged remnants.

'Laz, you're no' doing something you shouldn't, are you?'

'I'm busy.'

He stuck his gloved hand through the hole and felt about . . . Door knob. Down a bit. There – the key was still in the lock.

Logan turned it, then did the same with the knob. Pushed the door open and stepped inside. 'Got to go.'

'Oh no you don't. If you think I'm alibiing you again, you're off your head. Whatever you're doing: stop.'

The kitchen felt cold and damp, as if no one had lived there for years. A crust of moss clung to the inside corners of the window frames. Everything smelled of mould and dust. Not dirty, just neglected.

'Laz, I'm warning you – they've got GPS in the Airwave handsets. It works even when they're turned off. If you're up to something, they'll know where you are.'

Through the kitchen and into the long, narrow hall. Three other doors off the sides, one at either end.

'No one's going to complain, OK? The home-owner's dead. No one else lives here.'

Door number one opened on a living room that must have died years ago. Ancient wallpaper, a sagging couch, a frayed rug on scuffed floorboards.

Steel's voice dropped to a hard whisper. *'Why are you breaking into a dead man's house?'*

'I'm not breaking in. Who said anything about breaking in?'

Door number two opened on a bathroom – white tiles on the walls, white enamel bath, white sink. All the warmth of a fridge.

'Laz, don't be a dick! This isn't—'

'I got here and I noticed there was a broken

pane of glass in the back door. I went inside to make sure no one had stolen anything. All perfectly above board.'

Door number three opened on a bedroom. Double bed, sagging mattress, no pictures or paintings on the walls. The closed net curtains gave it a funeral parlour air.

'God's sake . . . Where are you?'

He tried the bedside cabinet nearest the door. 'Why?'

Socks. Pants. Hankies. Assorted junk.

'Because I'm coming over there and kicking your backside for you!'

The other cabinet was much the same, only with a small bundle of well-thumbed porn mags in the bottom drawer.

'Some of us have work to do, OK?'

Logan flicked through them with his gloved fingers. Nothing too extreme, nothing too kinky, and definitely no kids.

'We're supposed to be a team! You, me: the two musketeers, remember?'

The clothes in the wardrobe were grey and dated, sagging on their hangers as if they didn't want to face another day.

Back into the hall.

'I'm at Charles Anderson's house.'

Door number four opened on a child's bedroom. Blue football wallpaper; posters of bands and film stars; a row of picture books, fading on the windowsill. Bart Simpson duvet cover.

A little shrine to a boy who died five years ago.

His photo sat in a big silver frame on the bedside cabinet. Bright-red hair. Dimpled cheeks. Big grin and a threadbare teddy bear.

'Who the hell's Charles Anderson when he's deid?'

Door number five, at the far end of the corridor, opened on the wooden garage. With no windows, the only light was what filtered through from the hallway behind Logan.

Furniture and boxes lurked in the gloom. Things on the walls.

A light switch was mounted on the wall by the door. He clicked it on and a strip light buzzed, clicked, and pinged its way slowly awake.

'Laz? Hello? You still there?'

A soft whistle escaped from his lips.

The things on the walls were corkboards, like the one in Steel's commandeered office at Banff station. And like Steel's they were covered in photographs and densely scribbled index cards, all linked together with grey string and red ribbons.

A single card sat at the centre of the web, with 'LIVESTOCK MART?' printed on it in marker pen and underlined three times.

He blinked a couple of times. The Livestock Mart. Oh, you wee beauty . . .

'Logan! What the hell's going on?'

He stepped in close. Ran his fingers across one of the photos. It was Neil Wood, caught somewhere on a long-lens, paparazzi style. That one over there was Mark Brussels, with the patchwork scars he got in Peterhead Prison. And Dr William Gilcomston, with his grey hair and high forehead, caught in the supermarket. Mrs Bartholomew, the owner of the big Victorian pile on Church Street, putting her wheelie bin out.

There were others too – about two dozen of them, all snapped from a distance. Some familiar faces, some not. All connected to each other with bits of string. All connected to the Livestock Mart.

'*LOGAN!*'

He blinked. 'They're all paedophiles. Paedophiles and sex offenders.'

The red ribbons led to pictures cut from newspapers and magazines, or printed off the internet. Pictures of children. Each one was connected to at least one grown-up. One little girl to three of them. But one kid was out on his own: a wee red-haired boy, standing on a local beach in shorts and a Bart Simpson T-shirt, playing with a bucket and spade. His grin made puncture-mark dimples in both cheeks. The picture surrounded by a band of black ribbon.

It was the boy from the shrine in the other room.

'*Who're all . . .? Have you been drinking?*'

Only one other child looked familiar. A young girl, no more than six years old. She'd looked . . . different when she was alive. Without the big dent in her forehead where someone had smashed her brains in with a metal pipe. Without the sea-bleached tone to her skin.

Her picture wasn't a cut-out, it was a telephoto

snap like the grown-ups. Caught outside some-where – leaves in the foreground, something black, out of focus behind her. Big, rectangular. A door? Maybe a van? And her red ribbon didn't go to Neil Wood, it went to Dr William Gilcomston.

'Charles Anderson was mapping out a paedo-phile ring.'

Because he was blackmailing it? Because he was part of it?

'All right, that's it, I'm getting in the car. Don't touch anything!'

The corkboard on the opposite wall had chil-dren's drawings and little bits of jewellery pinned to it. Ear rings, a bracelet, a couple of watches, and some necklaces. One was a gold chain with a thistle on it. It glittered in Logan's palm.

Gold chain with a thistle . . .

He went back to the photo board. Scanned the faces.

A heavyset balding bloke with a smile full of teeth and a third-world moustache looked out of one picture with shining eyes. It must've been taken in a pub somewhere, the pumps on the bar pin-sharp in the background. He was halfway out of his seat, arms coming up, celebrating a goal. Wearing the same blue-and-red Caley Thistle replica shirt and gold chain he had on in his missing person's pic.

It was Liam Barden, the father of two Nicholson seemed obsessed with spotting on Castle Street.

But Barden wasn't on the Sex Offenders' Register

– it would've come up when they put together the misper file on him. So why was he on Charles Anderson's pinboard?

Logan turned the necklace over in his hands. The metal was cool through the nitrile gloves. Tiny flecks of dark red clung to the inside of the links either side of the thistle.

Dried blood.

There was more, clinging to the indentations of the inscription on the back. 'To LIAM ~ LOVE KATHY ~ FOR EVER!!!'

He cleared his throat. 'You still there?'

Huffing and puffing came from the earpiece. 'No.'

'Yeah, neither am I. Think we'd better get a warrant and come back and discover this officially.' He slipped Liam Barden's necklace back onto its pin. Backed out of the room and switched off the light.

As long as Logan was one of the first in when they got the warrant, no one would wonder why his DNA was all over the room. All above board. No breaking and entering and contaminating the crime scene here, thank you very much.

Yes, there'd be the broken pane of glass in the back door, but that'd be easy enough to blame on someone else. Nothing for Napier to complain about . . .

And all Logan had to do was—

CHAPTER 44

'Unngh . . .' There was a jackhammer in his skull, battering away, trying to separate it from his spine. Forehead pounding. Face prickly. A million bells ringing in his ears. Warm though.

Not warm, *hot*. All down one side.

Logan peeled one eye open, squinting out at the crackling yellow light.

Gravel dug into his cheek.

Why was he lying down?

What?

It took a couple of blinks to get the world into focus.

He was on his side, next to the Big Car, bathed in the light of Charles 'Craggie' Anderson's burning house. Flames roared from the open windows, crackling and bellowing in the light of the dying sun. Sparks flew like fireflies, swirling away into the bruised sky.

God . . .

Logan struggled to his knees and stayed there – eyes closed, thumping forehead resting against the car door.

Don't be sick.

His trembling hand came away wet from the back of his head. Sticky.

A booming crash sounded behind him.

Get *up*.

Deep breath.

He pulled himself up the side of the car. Wobbled there for a moment. Then turned and slumped back against the bodywork. Opened his eyes.

Half the roof had caved in, exposing rafters like the ribs of a skeletal ship. The garage was a solid block of snapping flame.

So much for getting a warrant.

He ran his fingertips along the back of his head again. Winced. Yeah, that was blood.

Headlights bounced along the rutted track, getting closer. Then an MX-5 emerged from the gloom, grinding and scraping through the potholes. Steel clambered out from behind the wheel and stood there with her mouth hanging open. 'What the hell did you do?'

The fire engine's diesel growl cut through the night, its swirling lights casting strobe patterns that interfered with the ones from the ambulance and the patrol car.

'Ow!' Sitting on the ambulance's back step, Logan winced. 'Easy!'

'Don't be such a baby.' The paramedic went in for another go with the antiseptic, tongue poking out the side of her mouth as she tortured him. 'When was your last tetanus shot?'

Acid-dipped needles tattooed across his scalp. 'Ow!'

'Bleeding's stopped – won't even need stitches.' She liberated a wad of gauze from its sterile packaging and pressed it against the back of his head. 'Now: tetanus?'

'Couple of years.'

'Should be fine then.' A smile. 'Do you want a bandage and a lollypop, or are you putting your big-boy pants on?'

Logan sniffed. 'You don't like people very much, do you?'

'God, no.' She tried to jab a finger all the way into his skull.

'Ow!'

'You'll live.' The paramedic snapped off her surgical gloves and turned to Steel. 'Right, he's all yours. Need to keep an eye out for a concussion – says he didn't black-out, but if you believe that . . .' A shrug. Then back to Logan. 'Medical advice time: a concussion can mean subdural haematoma or a subarachnoid haemorrhage, dizziness, nausea, confusion, and – worst-case scenario – death.' She hooked a thumb in Steel's direction. 'So you should probably stay at your mum's the night. Make sure you don't die in your sleep.' Then she shooed Logan off the back step, closed the back doors, climbed in behind the wheel and drove off, while Steel stood there and spluttered.

Thank you, Florence Nightingale.

'Your *mum*?'

Don't smile, it'll only make it worse. 'I know, nerve of the woman.'

Steel threw her arms up, as if she was going to tear the clouds from the sky. 'One: I am nothing like that frumpy scheming battleaxe. Two: I'm nowhere near old enough. And three: if I was your mother you wouldn't be so sodding ugly!'

'Finished?'

'She thinks I'm your mum! How can I be your mum? I mean, look at me: in my prime here.'

He peeled the gauze off and squinted at it in the patrol car's swirling lights. A thin line of scarlet, marred with dark-orange blobs.

'Are you listening to me?'

'Not really.'

Gouts of white steam tumbled upwards into the air, eating away at the black smoke.

'*Shire Uniform Seven, safe to talk?*'

Steel grabbed his Airwave. 'No he's not. And if he opens his mouth again, I'm going to finish the job!'

'*OK . . . Well, tell him that Tayside have stopped that Megabus and it's not David and Catherine Bisset. Sighting was wrong.*'

'What a shock.' She chucked it back at him. 'How come you're on the update list for the Killer Bissets?'

'Because.' He probed the lump on the back of his head. Winced. 'Lucky I'm not dead.'

Steel sooked on her fake cigarette. Dribbled the steam out of her nose. Then nodded at the burning house. 'So?'

He dabbed the gauze pad against the sore bit again. 'Probably got a cracked skull.'

'Did you see anyone? Did someone hit you, or did you just trip and bang your head like an auld wifie?'

'What, and then dragged myself outside and set the house on fire?' Another dab. 'Ow.'

The fire flickered, dimmed, then went out, plunging the surrounding area into darkness again. Well, except for the swirling lights of the assembled emergency services.

Four firefighters in their bulky brown-and-high-vis outfits wrestled with a pair of hoses, deluging what was left of Charles Anderson's house.

Steel pulled the e-cigarette from her mouth and bared her bottom teeth. 'And you've no idea who did it? Thought you said you didn't black out.'

'Blah, blah, blah. You heard Nurse Crippen: I'm fine.' Still stung though.

'Maybe it was someone in this paedophile ring? Found out you knew about them and decided to make it go away?'

'How would they even know I was there?' He crumpled up the gauze and stuffed it into his pocket. 'Anderson had it all mapped out on his board. About a dozen names and faces, all linked to the Livestock Mart.'

Steel stared at him. Then the burning garage. Then back again. 'You *what*?' Then she hit him.

'Ow! Cut it out.'

'We've been after a lead on the Livestock Mart for *years*, and you let it go up in flames? What's wrong with you?' Another thump.

'Get off!' He backed away. 'I got bashed over the head. What was I supposed to do, wake up and wade back into the fire?'

Steel stormed off a half-dozen paces, then back again. 'What was on the board. Who? How did it all link up?'

'I can't remember. It—'

'Why didn't you take a picture? You've got a camera on your sodding phone, *use it!*'

He jabbed a finger at the smouldering house. 'I'm not psychic. How was I supposed to know they were going to set fire to the place? I could've died!'

Steel turned her face to the dark, oily clouds. 'Give me strength . . .' A sigh. She screwed her eyes shut. 'Can you remember *any* of it at all?'

'The wee dead girl from Tarlair – she was on there, connected to Dr Gilcomston.'

'Wee Willy Gilcomston? Dr Kidfiddler?' A raised eyebrow. 'Why?'

Logan headed across to the Big Car. 'No idea. Let's find out.'

'No, I don't. I told you this before, and I resent having to repeat myself.' William Gilcomston's eyebrows dipped over those eerie blue eyes. Tonight's cardigan was bottle green, with a small heart-shaped pin in the collar. The kind they gave to blood donors. 'Now, if there's nothing else?'

The house sat in silent isolation, surrounded by gardens on all four sides. His standing in the community might have taken a tumble after the court case, but the family home stood firm. Three storeys of grime-streaked granite with mature trees out front, a sweeping gravel driveway, a separate garage, and a low wall separating it from the street.

An old-fashioned Jaguar was parked out front, hubcaps gleaming in the house's security lights.

Steel kept her foot wedged in the doorway – keeping it open. 'Can we come in, Billyboy?'

He stiffened his back, pulling himself up to his full height, and glared down at Steel. 'Do you have a warrant?'

'I can get one.'

'Then the answer is no. Now remove your foot from my property, I'm under no obligation to entertain your nonsense any further.'

The sound of a television, turned up a little bit too loud, came from somewhere inside. A serious man's voice doing the news: '. . . *confirm that an arrest has been made in the Scottish town of Banff, connected to the fatal shooting of undercover police officer, Mary Ann Nasrallah . . .*'

Logan stepped up. 'Dr Gilcomston, do you know

a man called Charles Anderson? Also goes by the nickname, "Craggie"?'

'. . . *go live to Aberdeenshire. Kim, have Police Scotland released any details about the individual involved?*'

Gilcomston pursed his lips. 'I believe he's some sort of dead fisherman. There was an article in the paper about him setting fire to his boat.'

'Yes, but did you know him before that? Before he went missing?'

'No. Now please go.'

'. . . *as Martyn Baker, a twenty-one-year-old man from Birmingham.*'

Steel pulled her foot back. 'OK, play hard-to-get if you like, Billyboy, but we'll no' be far away.' She winked at him. 'Stay out of trouble, eh?' Then turned and marched down the path toward her little sports car.

'. . . *plead guilty or not guilty, when Mr Baker comes up before the Sheriff Court at nine a.m. tomorrow morning.*'

The tendons in Gilcomston's neck tightened for a beat, then he turned his blue eyes on Logan. 'I'll be making a complaint about your superior. This is harassment.'

Logan stared back in silence.

'*Thank you, Kim. And we'll have more on that later, when the Police Scotland press conference starts.*'

A herring gull cawed and shrieked somewhere in the darkness.

'*This, of course, ends a week-long manhunt for the person or people who shot and killed Mary Ann Nasrallah . . .*'

A car rumbled past.

'*. . . to Liverpool now, where Constable Nasrallah's family have been holding a prayer vigil . . .*'

Gilcomston cleared his throat. Looked away. 'I have nothing further to say to you.'

'Charles Anderson thought you were involved in the death of the little girl we found at Tarlair. What would give him that idea?'

'I'm sorry, I have to go.' Gilcomston closed the door. Then the sound of bolts and locks shooting home clicked and clacked out through the wood.

Logan gave it a count of ten, then turned and joined Steel on the pavement.

She was leaning back against her MX-5, arms folded, e-cigarette sticking out the corner of her mouth. 'He's a slimy git.'

'Anderson must've seen her. The picture on the board: it wasn't from a newspaper or off the internet, it was a photograph. He took it. So he must have seen her when she was alive.'

'And he probably saw her with Dr Kidfiddler.' Steel blew a stream of steam at the heavy clouds. 'Laz, could you no' have saved the evidence, instead of swooning like a Victorian heroine?'

'Thanks. Yes, it was all my fault someone tried to bash my brains in, how *very* careless of me.'

591

He dug his hands deep into his pockets. 'Could've died. Bit of sympathy might not go amiss.'

'Wah, wah, wah. Don't be so melodramatic. If they wanted you dead, they would've left you in the house when they set fire to it.'

CHAPTER 45

Logan drove the Big Car up the kerb, over the pavement, and onto the half-moon of blockwork opposite the Threadneedle Street Car Park. Well, it was easier than messing about with the automatic gate that secured the loading area at the back of Peterhead police station.

Nearly half-past eleven, and the place was dead. The occasional car drifted past – with horrible music *bmmmtshhh, bmmmtshhh, bmmmtshhh*ing out through the windows – but other than that, the Blue Toon was as quiet as it ever got.

Logan locked up and stepped out.

The surrounding wall of terraced houses cut the wind down to a dull roar, leaving the drizzle to sway down from the burnt-orange sky in clammy waves. He tucked his notepad under his arm, rammed his hat on his head—

'Ow . . .' Knives and needles jabbed through the skin and into his skull, radiating out from the brand-new lump. 'Sodding hell.'

He tucked his hat under his arm instead and hurried up the street. From the front, Peterhead station looked like a bank – all granite and tall windows, an imposing frontage with pillars and a portico – but the other three sides were knobbly red sandstone, stitched together with thick lines of grey mortar.

'All units, be on the lookout for a brown Ford Ranger, number plate unknown, but the back end's all dented. Just ram-raided the Co-op in Strichen. Last seen battering away down the New Deer road.'

He dug out his key and let himself into the blue side door.

It opened on a manky magnolia hall, with temporary lockers and building works on one side. Singing came through the bars separating the cellblock from the rest of the building. It sounded as if all the talented members of the wedding party had ended up in Fraserburgh's cells, leaving only the tone deaf behind.

Logan nipped up the wee flight of stairs, past the three banks of Airwave lockers, and into the stairwell. Stood at the bottom and stared up into the darkness. 'SHOP!'

The only answer was the echo. *Shop . . . Shop . . . Shop . . .*

OK. Up three flights to the first floor.

'Anyone in the vicinity of New Aberdour? Mrs Tobias has gone walkabout again.'

Where the hell was everyone?

The canteen had the same collection of chipped Formica, cheap kitchen units, and unwashed mugs as every other station in the northeast. It was separated into two bits with a wee archway in the middle. One half held the vending machine and a handful of tables and chairs. Posters on the walls about integrity, fairness, and respect. One about dialling 101 if it wasn't an emergency, and another about being on the lookout for suicidal colleagues. The other half had the kitchen: worktops; fridge – covered with notices and dire warnings about not stealing other people's food; toaster; cooker; and not one but *two* microwaves. Fancy.

He helped himself to a mug and a teabag, then filled it from the special boiling-water tap mounted on the wall. Must've been someone's birthday, because the last two slices of a chocolate cake sat on the kitchen table. He helped himself to one of those too.

Then picked up the wall phone and pressed the button for the cellblock. Listened to it ring.

'*Aye, aye?*'

'Stubby? It's Logan. Whose birthday was it?'

'*Well, as I live and breathe – our very own B Division Duty Sergeant! To what do we lowly peasants owe the honour?*'

'Don't be like that, I was here last night, wasn't I?'

'*No.*'

Fair enough. 'Anything going on I should know about?'

'*Aye, Glen's forty the day. Doesn't look out of nappies yet, does he?*'

'I got hit on the head, so I'm stealing a slice of his cake.'

'Other than that, we've still got a full set after Friday night's wedding. Can't wait for the courts to open tomorrow, it's smelling a bit ripe down here.'

He took a bite of cake, chewing around the words. 'Anything new?'

'Domestic earlier: bloke's off to Fraserburgh for the night. She's off to the hospital. Picked up a guy for getting hot and heavy with, and I kid you not, a Shetland pony. Silly sod filmed it on his own phone. And there's a couple of unlawful removals we're looking into. Found one up at the Flaggie earlier. Other than that, it's been pretty Q-word.'

'Wish I could say the same.' He washed the cake down with a mouthful of tea. 'Stubby, did you ever deal with Neil Wood?'

'Our missing paedo? Yeah, couple of times when I was in the Offender Management Unit. He wasn't mine, but I had to fill in now and then. Sniffly, runny, sticky kind of bloke. You know the type people always think of when someone says "child molester"? That.'

'You been to his B-and-B since he went missing?' The last of the cake disappeared.

'Got enough on my plate as it is. Why?'

'Looking for a link with one Charles "Craggie" Anderson. Tell Glen happy birthday from me, OK?'

'You sticking around for a bit?'

'Depends what comes up.' Logan put the phone down, grabbed the remaining slice of cake, and headed for the Sergeants' Office.

It wasn't that much different to the one back

at Banff – high ceilings, cornices and moulded architraves being slowly buried under layers of white gloss. Two desks, back to back, and computers almost powerful enough to pull the skin off a cold cup of coffee.

He settled into the seat, slurped, munched, and logged on to the system.

Didn't take long to catch up with the day's actions. Everyone was up to date, even Tufty.

A dull ache seeped around Logan's skull, starting at the back of his head and ending up right behind his eyes. The paramedic's paracetamol was wearing off.

Paracetamol for a cracked skull – how was *that* supposed to help? Whatever happened to coco-damol, voltarol, naproxen, or oxycodone? Ah, the good old days.

He went rummaging through the desk till he turned up a battered packet of aspirin. Better than nothing, but not much. Two got washed down with a swig of cold tea.

Of course, Steel was right – if they'd wanted him dead, they'd have left him to burn with the house. Still . . .

He checked the clock on the computer. Gone half eleven. Far too late to be calling civilians. But . . . He pulled out his phone and dialled.

Ringing. Ringing. Then an Aberdonian accent trying very hard to sound posh came on the line. 'Aberdeen Examiner, *news desk, how can I help you?*'

'Is Colin Miller there? Tell him it's an old friend.'

'One moment, I'll put you through . . .' *Click.*

Ravel's 'Bolero' droned out of the handset, sounding as if it was being played in an elevator by drunken monkeys.

Logan finished off his tea.

More 'Bolero'.

He pulled over a sheet of paper and drew a rectangular box in the middle. Wrote 'LIVESTOCK MART' in it. Next came the names: Gilcomston, Brussels, Wood, Barden, and what was the woman called? The one living in the big Victorian house with twinset, pearls, and death threats. Ah, right: Mrs Bartholomew. What else? Who else was on the board?

He tapped his pen against the desk. Steel was right: should've taken a photograph. Be easier than trying to piece it together from memory, after a thump to the head.

Who else was—

Click. And on came an unabashed Glaswegian accent. '*Logie? That you? Long time no hear, man. How's life in the sticks? You hear anything about this Martyn Baker joker?*'

'You're still in the office, Colin? Don't you have a wife and three kids to get home to?'

'*Alfie's teething, so I've come down with a nasty dose of "stuff what needs written for Monday's edition". Longer I stay out of the house, the better. What you after?*'

'Did you write that piece on Charles Anderson in the *Examiner* today?'

'*You kidding? The day I use that many adverbs in one story, you've got my permission to shoot us. It was that neep, Finnegan.*'

'I need to speak to Anderson's ex-wife. Any chance you can dig out her details for me?'

A small hungry pause. '*Something juicy on the go?*'

'Nah, standard follow-up stuff.'

'*Cause if something juicy comes up, you're no' gonnae forget your old pal Colin, are you?*'

'When have I ever?'

'*Aye, right.*'

Somewhere in the distance church bells gave twelve sonorous cries of doom, while the canteen microwave droned.

The sound of scuffing feet. Then someone cleared their throat. 'Sarge.'

Bleeep.

Logan glanced over his shoulder. 'Hi.'

The wee loon couldn't have been much over twenty. Spots clung to the sides of his forehead, disappearing into the felt-style haircut. A full-moon face with chubby child cheeks. Quick peek at the shoulder numbers on his epaulettes showed he was one of this year's gaggle of newbies. He produced something between a smile and a wince. 'PC Matthews. Ted.'

'Right. Ted.' Logan made a half-arsed set of oven gloves out of a tea towel and liberated his bowl of lentil soup from the microwave. 'How's it hanging, Ted?'

The smile got more wincey. 'Yeah. Great. Thanks.'

'Good.' He carried his soup through to the sit-down part of the canteen, then went back for his toast.

'Anyone free to attend? Got complaints about a man urinating in the Iceland shop doorway, Fraserburgh.'

'Sarge?'

'What can I do for you, Ted?'

Constable Matthews sank into the chair opposite. 'How do you . . . If . . . I mean . . .' Pink bloomed on his cheeks and the tips of his ears.

Surely he wasn't asking for a talk on the birds and the bees.

He cleared his throat. 'I found a body today. Old man, hadn't been seen for a week and his neighbours were worried.'

Logan put down his spoon. 'It happens a lot more often than people think.'

'He'd hung himself, on the stairs. Wrapped a belt round the bannister and his neck.' Matthews puffed out his cheeks. 'Place was a tip. I mean, really, *really* horrible. Everything sticky and filthy and the smell was unbelievable.'

A bite of toast. 'I know it sounds daft, but you get used to it. Never gets any better, but you do get used to it.'

'He had the heating up full pelt, and he'd been hanging there for seven days . . . Face all black and crawling with flies . . .' A shudder.

'Update on the piddler: turns out there's a woman

with him and she's having a wee there too. Can someone attend, please?'

Should really have had a squint through the cupboard first – found out if anyone had any hot sauce. Couldn't do it with Matthews here. Not with all those signs about not nicking other people's food glaring down from the fridge door.

'You know what I spent the morning doing, Sarge? Getting spat at. Sworn at. Shouted at. Someone threw up on my shoes.' He slumped inside his stabproof vest, making it look as if he'd shrunk. 'Don't know if I can do this any more.'

Have to buy something different next time. No more lentil soup. Maybe cream of tomato? Pff . . . Who was he kidding. The decent stuff cost more than the budget would allow. Tattie and leek?

'And it's the same people, day after day, shift after shift. All the time, the same manky minks, with their filthy houses and smelly clothes and drug habits. Or drink. Or both. Never mind the nutters . . .'

Of course, the ideal thing would be to go buy a bunch of vegetables and *make* soup. But then he'd have to trust it to the canteen fridge, and everyone knew what a bunch of thieving sods police officers were when it came to food. Oh, you could leave cash and jewellery and electronics lying about for weeks and no one would touch it. But see if you put a custard cream down and turned your back for five seconds? Gone.

601

'Joined the police to help people, and all I'm doing is babysitting scumbags who hate me.'

That was the thing about tins, you could hide them. Didn't need refrigerating.

'And the pension's a joke now, isn't it? Get to work till I'm sixty, for a pittance. Can you see us as a bunch of sixty-year-olds, dunting in some druggie's door and fighting off his Rottweiler?' He shrank a little more. 'Got a friend who works on the rigs.'

'I know.' Logan dipped a chunk of toast in his soup. 'The pay here's rubbish, the shifts are rubbish, and the pension's rubbish. Job's well and truly screwed.' He popped the soggy morsel in his mouth and chewed. 'But we get to *change* people's lives. We get to keep them safe. And when something horrible happens, and they end up dead or damaged, we get them justice. Try doing that on an oilrig.'

Matthews raised his eyebrows. 'Yeah . . .' Then lowered them again. Curled his top lip 'Suppose.'

'It's nothing but milky tea and porn out there anyway.'

CHAPTER 46

Logan scuffed in through the door to Banff station. 'Pff . . .'

Joe emerged from the canteen. 'Sarge, how's the head?'

'Like a bowling ball full of angry mice.'

A nod. 'You want a coffee? I'm doing the rounds.'

'You're a star.'

Big Paul and Penny were in the Constables' Office. The pair of them sitting with their backs to the open door, thumping away at their keyboards. Getting everything tidied away for the two o'clock end of business.

No sign of the nightshift.

Logan slouched through the main office and into the Sergeants' room. Peeled off his stabproof vest and dumped it behind his desk, then followed it with the equipment belt. A whole stone lighter, just like that. He collapsed into his chair. Stared at the high ceiling for a bit. Then sighed and pulled the keyboard over and logged in.

Joe knocked, then let himself in. Mug in one hand, packet of Ginger Snaps in the other. 'You get your fax?'

A frown. Logan took the mug of coffee. 'What fax?'

'Should be in your pigeonhole – came in about five-ish.'

'Oh. No.'

'We're planning on writing everything up, then work up some targets for next week before home-time. Thought we'd have a bash at antisocial behaviour and car thefts.'

Logan had a dig into his desk drawer and came out with a packet of aspirin. 'Do me a favour and stick drugs on your list? I'm declaring war.'

'Will do.'

Joe wandered off and Logan threw back four tablets. Washed them down with a slurp of hot coffee.

Someone had given the angry mice chainsaws, and the little sods were on a mission to cut their way out of his skull.

'Fax.' He pulled himself out of his seat and through into the main office. The pigeonholes weren't really pigeonholes, they were a collection of red plastic in-and-out-trays, stacked four-high in a recess by the door through to the front of the building. Logan's was stuffed with sponsorship forms, takeaway menus, a couple of leaflets for local businesses, and a newspaper clipping about a dirty wee scumbag climbing up onto someone's roof to have a crap down their chimney pot. There was even a photo.

But right at the bottom was an internal mail envelope.

He opened it and took out the three sheets of A4 from inside.

DNA RESULT ON TARLAIR REMAINS.

According to the fax's time-stamp, it arrived at 16:58 – the guy from the labs had managed to get it done by close of play after all.

Logan skimmed over the intro paragraphs and procedural bits, the graphs and diagrams on page two, and went straight to the results at the back.

Puffed out his cheeks.

Leaned against the wall and stared at the sheet. No match with Helen's DNA.

It wasn't her daughter.

'Night, Sarge. Night, Hector.' Penny gave him a wave. Then followed Joe and Big Paul out into the night. Bang on two in the morning.

The door clunked shut, leaving Logan alone with his ghosts.

A dozen names now featured on the sheet of paper he'd started in Peterhead – trying to recreate Charles Anderson's paedophile wall chart. Some had question marks next to them, others were underlined. Like Dr William Gilcomston, AKA: Dr Kidfiddler, connected by a thick red line to 'TARLAIR WEE GIRL'.

Didn't get them any closer to catching her killer though, did it? Not when Gilcomston could simply deny everything. They needed some evidence. Some information. Something to justify getting a warrant from the Sheriff and ransacking the place.

But that was a job for tomorrow.

Logan logged off. Pushed the keyboard away. Yawned. Then sagged in his seat.

No point hanging about, putting it off any longer. Time to go home.

More mice had joined the throng, and these ones were armed with sledgehammers. Battering away at his brain in time to the thump of his pulse. Need more pills. And something stronger than aspirin.

He scrubbed his hands across his face.

Come on. Home. Bed.

Yeah . . . But what if Helen was there again – in his bed?

Wear pants. No more embarrassing early-morning protuberances.

Not much of a plan, but it was better than nothing.

He slouched out of the station, leaving it to Hector and the darkness. Crossed the car park.

The moon was a heavy crescent, glowing down through a gap between the clouds, reflecting back from the churned steel surface of the bay. Waves roared and hissed against the beach.

A smatter of rain needled out of the darkness, hurrying him inside.

He eased the door closed again. Locked it.

The living-room door was closed too. No light seeping out from the cracks around it, or the big gap left by the absent carpet below.

Logan crept up the stairs, keeping to the outside of the steps to minimize the creaking.

She'd made a great job of painting the hall – a hell of a lot better than he'd made of the kitchen.

Place looked ready for getting some flooring down. Maybe he could nick the police van for a couple of hours and pick a load up from the B&Q in Elgin?

Yeah, Napier would *love* that if he found out.

Have to wait till Wednesday instead, when this block of double-shifts finished. See how much laminate they could fit in his manky old Clio.

Up to the landing.

Rain rattled the skylight.

Teeth. Quick wash. Two Nurofen. Then through into the bedroom.

Pale orange oozed in through the window from the streetlight outside. It caught the mound in the middle of the bed. Glinted off the corkscrew curls. She shifted in her sleep, murmured, smacked her lips together a couple of times, then settled down again.

OK.

You can do this.

Wake her up and tell her what the DNA results said. Tell her it's not her daughter.

Helen's face was soft and smooth, the creases around her eyes and between her eyebrows almost gone. At least now, wherever she was in her dreams, she'd found a moment of peace with herself.

Why ruin it? Why wake her up and get her worrying all over again?

It still wouldn't be her daughter in the morning.

Let her dream.

Logan stripped off and slipped in beside her.

But he kept his pants on.

CHAPTER 47

'. . . *after the news. But right now it's over to Tim. Tim?*'

'*Thanks, Bill. Police in Banff, Aberdeenshire, announced last night that they'd arrested a Birmingham man for the murder of undercover police officer, Constable Mary Ann Nasrallah. The man, Martyn Baker*—'

Logan thumped the snooze button. Looked across the pillow.

Helen turned onto her side. 'Fv mr mnnt . . .'

He slipped out of bed and headed for the shower.

Froze at the top of the stairs.

Noises, coming from the living room. Was that the TV?

Back into the bedroom. A quick struggle into a pair of jeans and some slippers. He unclipped the extendable baton from the equipment belt in the corner.

Then gave Helen's shoulder a shoogle.

Her eyes creaked open, then her mouth.

'Shh . . .' He put a hand over it. Her lips were warm and moist against his palm. Logan dropped his voice to a whisper. 'I need you to stay up here. No sound. OK?'

Blink. Blink. Blink. Then a nod.

'OK.'

Out onto the landing again. Then down the stairs, keeping to the outsides of the treads.

It was definitely the TV. '. . . *and that's a lovely shot, straight down the fairway and onto the green . . .*'

'*She's having a great game.*'

'*She is indeed.*'

A floorboard groaned behind the living-room door. Then another one. Whoever it was, they were moving around.

Logan shifted his grip on the baton.

Three.

Two.

One.

He barged through the door, clacked the baton out to its full length. 'ON THE FLOOR NOW!'

Cthulhu scrambled off the coffee table and bolted for the gap behind the couch.

Steel didn't even flinch. Just sat there, shovelling a spoonful of cornflakes into her mouth. Muffling the words, 'Aye, very impressive. Remind me to swoon.'

'*Ooh, and Michelle's not going to be happy with that. Straight into the bunker.*'

He lowered his baton. 'What the hell are you doing here?'

'Watching the golf.' She pointed with her spoon. 'Your cornflakes taste awful, by the way.'

On screen, a very curvy red-haired woman in a *tiny* bikini stepped down into a bunker.

'Is this porn?'

The woman lined up her shot and spanked the ball up onto the green. Everything wobbled.

'Like eating waxed cardboard. Whatever happened to Crunchy Nut?'

'*Ooh, that's a super recovery.*'

'Can't afford it. Why are you watching porn on my couch?'

'*And this is for one under par . . .*'

A blonde in an even tinier blue bikini lined up a putt. The camera went in for a close-up, until two round, tanned buttocks filled the screen – wiggling left to right.

'It's not porn, it's Bikini Golf.' More waxy cornflakes disappeared. 'Got to love Channel Five.'

God's sake. 'I'm going for a shower.'

'Don't forget to wash behind your ears.'

He clumped back up to the top of the stairs.

Helen stood on the landing, peering down below. Her T-shirt had a hippo on it, and her shorts showed off a pair of legs that glowed a bit with blonde stubble. She barely moved her mouth. 'Is it burglars?'

'No, it's a pervert.'

Logan marched down the stairs, all done up in his black Police Scotland ninja finery. He stopped, outside the living-room door. Paused with one hand on the knob.

Helen's voice came through the wood. '*I don't get it.* Why *are they wearing bikinis?*'

Then it was Steel's turn. *'You got something against sexy women in bikinis?'*

Yeah. Maybe going in there wasn't the best of ideas.

He clipped the epaulettes onto the straps on his T-shirt's shoulders.

'But isn't it a bit, well, sexist?'

'Nah, the Bikini Golf Masters is open to everyone – male, female, and transgender – doesn't matter, as long as they're in a bikini.'

'Men in bikinis?'

'Aye. Can you imagine Colin Montgomery, squatting down to check the lie of the green, in a polkadot bikini? One of his wee hairy gentlemen dangling out the side?'

A snort of laughter.

Oh joy, they were bonding.

He got himself a cup of tea and a slice of toast. Consumed both standing at the work surface. Then couldn't put it off any longer. He pushed through into the living room.

The pair of them were on the couch with Cthulhu curled up on Helen's lap, purring.

'. . . number four on the leader board. And it's Svenga to tee-off first.' Svenga was a statuesque brunette with an unfeasibly large pair of breasts barely contained by two scraps of floral-patterned fabric and some string.

He cleared his throat. 'Helen, can I have a quick word?'

Helen looked up at him. 'Is it about lunch?'

'In private.'

Steel pursed her lips. Narrowed her eyes. 'You know what? I think Helen's quite happy where she is. Aren't you, Helen?'

Logan squatted down in front of her. Put a hand on her knee. 'We got the DNA results back. The little girl at Tarlair Swimming Pool – she's not Natasha.'

'*Ooh, and that's a cracking drive, right down the fairway.*'

Cthulhu stretched out a paw.

'*It's difficult to see how the others are going to recover from this.*'

One shoulder came up and Helen stared down at the cat in her lap. 'Oh . . .'

'Are you OK?'

The creases deepened between her eyebrows. 'I don't know. Every time: I tell myself that it'd be better to *know*. That if I knew she was dead I could mourn and move on. But . . .' The other shoulder joined it. 'She might still be alive.'

Steel patted her on the shoulder. 'I'm sure she is.' Then stood. 'Right, I better escort Sergeant McRae to the station. He's going to help me with my enquiries.'

She waited for him to stick a tin of lentil soup and two slices of cheap white into a carrier bag, then ushered him outside.

Wind whipped spray off the churning waves, hurling it over the sea wall like cold salty nails. The sun hidden behind heavy, grey, threatening clouds.

Steel closed the door behind them. Then slapped him on the arm. *Hard.*

'Ow!'

'She was a potential witness, and you're shagging her!' Another slap.

'Stop hitting me!' He backed away. 'Nothing happened.'

'Really? You're sharing a *bed* and nothing happened?'

'We're not sharing—'

'You sodding well are. I'm a detective chief inspector, no' an idiot!'

'Nothing happened. OK?' Logan marched towards the station, Steel close behind him. 'And nothing's *going* to happen. The dead wee girl isn't her daughter. She's hardly going to hang around, is she?'

'Have you got any idea what Napier's going to do when he finds out? How could you be so bloody *stupid*? I told you to keep it in your trousers, but you'll no' take a telling, will—'

'STOP IT!' He turned, threw his hands out. 'Enough! I'm not you and Susan's personal sperm bank. I can see who I like and it's none of your business.'

'Don't you—'

'No! We're not talking about this any more.' Logan thumped into the station and slammed the door in her face.

Who the hell did she think she was? Telling him what he could and couldn't do.

And he wasn't even *doing* anything.

Chance would be a fine thing.

'Sarge? You OK?' Nicholson froze in the corridor, outside the canteen, two mugs in her hands. 'Only, looks like you're about to murder someone.'

'And I'm making a list.'

'Right. Well . . .' She backed away. 'I'd better . . .' And she was gone.

He stormed through to the main office.

Bloody Steel. Good mind to go back out there and jam his—

'Sergeant McRae?' Maggie looked up from her keyboard. 'Inspector McGregor said she wants to see you soon as you're in.'

His shoulders slumped. 'Did she—'

'She's waiting for you now.'

Of course she was.

— MONDAY EARLYSHIFT —

THE OTHER SHOE.

CHAPTER 48

The Inspector swivelled her chair from side to side. Behind her, the North Sea raged beneath a sky of clay. A spattering of raindrops killed themselves against the window. 'I'm not sure if I should congratulate you, or give you the bollocking of your life.'

Logan didn't try sinking into one of the visitors' chairs. 'Guv?'

'They did an overnight on Martyn Baker's phone. Even if he changes his mind about the confession, there's enough text messages on there to tie him to the shooting. Telling him to go to the scene and put the fear of the righteous man into the other gang. Others telling him to sod off to the back-end of nowhere and lie low afterwards. A couple panicking when they found out she was an undercover cop.'

'Good. Does that mean they can tie whoever sent the messages to this as well?'

The chair swivelled left and right. Left and right.

'The Chief Constable's been on the phone, congratulating B Division for catching Mary Ann Nasrallah's killer. Here's us, a wee police station on the northernmost edge of the northeast of Scotland, and we're solving the biggest crime on the national news. Police Scotland saves the day.'

OK . . . As far as bollockings went, this one was surprisingly painless.

'There's going to be a letter of commendation going into your file, maybe even an award. How does that sound?'

He smiled. 'That's sounds—'

She slammed a hand down on the desk, rattling the keyboard. 'Now, what the *hell* were you thinking?'

Not so painless after all. 'Well, it—'

'I gave you a *direct* order to stay away from Operation Troposphere, and you went ahead and arrested Martyn Baker. And don't tell me he wasn't connected with it, you *thought* he was and you arrested him anyway!'

Logan shut his mouth and kept it that way.

'For God's sake, Sergeant, did I not make myself *perfectly* clear?' She jabbed a finger at him. 'Someone goes into a nightclub and tells people he's selling them Ecstasy when it's really Smarties, we still do him for selling Ecstasy. The intention is what counts. And you thought he was the Candleman!'

She glowered at him for a bit. 'Well?'

'Sorry.'

'If you can't be arsed obeying orders, how are the rest of the team supposed to? You're the Duty Sergeant, and you're acting like a bloody probationer. No, you know what? That's not being fair on probationers. Tufty has more professionalism in his hairy wee backside than you just showed!'

Rain hammered against the glass behind her.

The Inspector drummed her fingers against the desk. 'Are you finding the role too demanding, Sergeant McRae? Would you be more comfortable if I had you transferred somewhere else?'

'No, Guv. It wasn't meant to . . .' Deep breath. 'I apologize.'

'Damn right you do.' More staring. Then she sat back. Folded her arms. Swivelled her chair around to face the window. 'There's going to be celebratory drinks after work tonight. The Chief Constable's *personally* put cash in for the kitty. It would be a good idea for you to stay out of my sight till then.'

Logan let himself out.

His footsteps rung like funeral bells, all the way down the stairs, echoing back at him.

You'd think catching a cop-killer would be all parades and champagne. Not threats of demotion and reassignment.

What a *great* sodding day this was turning out to be.

He stopped at the bottom of the stairs. Pulled his shoulders back and his chin up.

Hissed out a breath.

Onward ever downwards.

Logan opened the door and marched through

into the main office. Right: quick squint at the papers, cup of coffee, check the computer for actions, then get the hell out of here before something else went wrong.

An *Aberdeen Examiner* hung over the partition of Maggie's cubicle. 'HUNT CONTINUES FOR BISSET CHILDREN' and a photo of the pair of them taken outside the High Court. Thin faces, identical shoulder-length black hair. Matching expressions of grief and loss and shock.

The article beneath the picture was a rehash of the stories published over the last couple of days, no real detail, enquiries are continuing, sightings coming in from all over the country. And a completely pointless account from one of the passengers on the Megabus that *didn't* have David and Catherine on it.

The *Scottish Sun*, on the other hand, had gone for 'MORE SEVERED FEET FOUND IN CLYDE ~ "NOT A SERIAL KILLER" SAYS TOP COP.' Yeah, good luck with that.

Maggie struggled in from the corridor, carrying a large cardboard box. 'Sergeant McRae?'

'I'm hanging by a thread here, Maggie. Is it good news?'

'There's a woman at the front desk for you.'

So probably not then.

Chin up, shoulders back. He slipped behind the partition with all its notices and posters, and up to the desk.

An old woman sat on one of the plastic seats in

the hallway on the other side of the opening. Her big heavy coat glistened with water, a pair of rubbery ankle boots poking out from her tweed skirt on chicken-bone legs. What looked like a Tupperware box nestled in her lap.

Great. There was going to be something dead in there. Something dead and very smelly.

Lovely.

Logan's shoulders dipped a bit. 'Can I help you?'

She looked up and smiled with all her dentures. 'I wanted to say thank you.' It took a bit of effort, but she levered herself upright and squeaked her rubber over-boots across the damp tiled floor. 'You killed them all. It's wonderful.'

He shrank back from the hatch. 'I did?'

'All the rats. You beat them to death with your truncheon and they've never come back.'

OK . . .

But at least now he knew who she was. 'Mrs Ellis. It was my pleasure.'

'I've slept like a baby these last two nights and I wanted to say thank you.' She held out the box in her trembling claws. 'For you.'

There was a dead rat inside, wasn't there? A big, stinky, dead rat.

Logan forced a smile. 'Thank you. You shouldn't have.' *Really*.

'Nonsense! I've won prizes with these – my mother's secret recipe.' A wink rearranged the lines on her face.

Crispy rat. Great.

Try to look pleased. 'Thank you.'

'You deserve them.'

The Big Car drifted around back onto Rundle Avenue, windscreen wipers screech-and-groaning their way across the glass. Nicholson sniffed. 'Nothing doing the day.'

'Probably too early.' Logan shook his head. 'But thing is: it wasn't full of dead rats, it was a big box of cheese scones. Can you believe that?'

'Well . . .' A frown worked its way across Nicholson's face. 'I once caught the guy who assaulted a mother of three, and she baked me a cake.'

'Sometimes, people are lovely.'

'All units, be on the lookout for a Julian Martin, IC-One female, thirty-two. Apprehension warrant for making indecent images of a child.'

Not all of them, obviously.

They made a left onto Tannery Street again.

'You sure you're all right, Sarge? Back of your head looks like a hairy aubergine.'

Logan's fingers reached up and stroked the bruised lump. A line of scabs marked the path of whatever it was he'd been brained with. Still stung like a hundred tiny wasps. 'I'm fine.'

'Come on: if it was me or Tufty who got thumped, you wouldn't let us back to work for a week.'

A shrug. 'Yeah, well, maybe *your* commanding officer is nicer than mine.'

Nicholson hunched over the steering wheel, peering left and right. 'Rain's not helping, is it? Not even druggies want to be trudging about in this.'

'Probably not. Call it quits: we'll try again later.'

She turned the car around. Back onto Rundle Avenue. Up to the end of the road.

The lights were off in the house Martyn Baker had been staying in. The curtains drawn. Would his girlfriend hang around for a bit, or take the kid and head back down the road to Birmingham? Assuming the opposing gang didn't go after her as retribution for what Baker had done.

That was the trouble with drug wars, no one fighting them ever gave a toss about the collateral damage.

Right onto Golden Knowes Road.

Nicholson slammed on the brakes. 'Not *again*!'

A billboard stood in the field, on the other side of the fence: 'BANFF HEIGHTS ~ EXCLUSIVE DEVELOPMENT OF EXECUTIVE VILLAS ~ COMING SOON.' A happy family stood in front of an architect's drawing of a boxy house. Only someone had spray-painted a big purple willy over the whole thing.

Logan reached forward and pressed the '999' button, setting the siren and flashing lights going. 'Foot down, Janet, we've got a master criminal to confront.'

They left the Big Car's blues on, spinning their accusatory light outside the Lovejoy household. That'd get the neighbours' curtains twitching.

Rain peppered the living-room window, the drops gathering together and running like tears. Inside, the fake-gas fire was hot enough to make toast. The place was laden with doilies and lace thingies, porcelain clowns and glass vases full of silk flowers. Plates decorated with painted teddy bears on the walls.

Classy.

'Well?' Logan folded his arms and did his best loom. 'Is that what you want, Geoffrey? Because that's what's going to happen.'

The wee sod sat in the middle of the couch, knees together, fingers coiled into the strings of his hoodie. Head down. Shoulders hunched. Sniffing. Biting his bottom lip. Tears running down his freckled cheeks. One trainered foot jerked and twitched on the Turkish rug. Not so much as a peep out of him about class struggle or the workers controlling the means of anything.

Apparently it was only OK to be a Marxist when his mum wasn't watching.

A bit more looming. 'Is – that – what – you – want?'

Geoffrey shook his head, setting the mop of red curls bobbing. He made a choked mumbly noise, but if there were words in there they were inaudible.

His mum thwacked him on the back of the head. 'Don't sit there snivelling; answer the nice policeman!'

'I'm . . . I'm . . . I'm sor— sorry.' So now it was hiccups as well.

One last loom. 'No more painting willies on things, or we're going to come back here and you're off to prison.'

'Plea— please don— please, I'm— sorry . . .'

'Right.' He hooked a finger at Nicholson. 'We're off, but we'll be watching you.'

Geoffrey's mum hit him again. 'Say thank you to the nice policeman for not sending you to the jail.'

'Than— thank — you . . .'

Nicholson stopped and looked back at the house. 'You know, if my parents called me "Geoffrey Lovejoy" I'd probably spray-paint willies all over the place too.'

'Will you get your finger out and unlock the doors? It's bucketing.'

They ducked into the Big Car and thumped the doors shut.

Rain drummed on the roof, bounced off the bonnet.

She started the engine. 'Sarge, these—'

'Shire Uniform Seven, safe to talk?'

Logan pressed the button. 'Stab away.'

'It's Tango Bravo One Two, guess what we found?'

Nicholson pointed at the handset, raised an eyebrow. 'Who're they?'

'Traffic car, out of Mintlaw.' He pressed the button again. 'What have you got?'

'One large black removal van, with "Magnus Hogg and Son, Moving Families Home Est 1965" down the side. Parked on the High Street in New Aberdour.'

The rain picked up pace. Thumped on the roof. Spattered against the windscreen. Danced back from the pavement.

An old man trudged past, wrestling with an unruly umbrella.

Logan gave it a count of ten, then: 'Are you actually going to tell me, or am I supposed to be psychic now?'

'*Psychic?*'

God's sake . . .

'What happened when you searched it?'

'*We didn't. It's still parked there. We're waiting for the driver to appear. So if you hurry . . .?*'

A grin cracked across Logan's face. 'Thanks.' He biffed Nicholson on the shoulder. 'Blues-and-twos – and put your foot down, we're going to New Aberdour.'

CHAPTER 49

Trees and hedges made a green blur outside the Big Car's windows as Nicholson hammered along the coastal road. The windscreen wipers thumped back and forth across the glass.

'*All units, be on the lookout for a blue Transit van towing a caravan in the Peterhead area, believed to contain a stolen Labrador . . .*'

Logan snatched at the grab-handle above his door, as the Big Car cleared a hump in the road and took to the air for a heartbeat. Then battered down onto the tarmac again. 'This isn't the Dukes of Hazard!'

Nicholson didn't look round. 'You want to get there in time, or don't you?'

'Calamity Janet rides again.'

A small ding sounded somewhere inside Logan's stabproof vest, followed by a buzzing sensation in his ribs. That would be a text message coming in. He pulled out his phone and checked the screen.

> Got an address for you
> Alison hay – was alison anderson – 19
> rooks crescent, tiverton, devon
> Mobile number to follow
> You owe me, right?

Say what you liked about Colin Miller; he might be a chubby Weegie shortarse, but he knew how to dig up info.

Logan punched the number for the Mintlaw traffic car into his Airwave. 'Tango Bravo One Two, from Shire Uniform Seven.'

Whatever the response was, it was inaudible over the siren. Logan poked the button to switch it off, leaving the lights going.

'Say again?'

'I said, "Safe to talk".'

'Is the van still empty?' They went airborne again, slinging his stomach up into his ribs and then down again.

'No sign of them yet, but three men went into the baker's opposite a minute ago, and there's a fourth outside with a big black umbrella – on his phone, having a fag.'

Sounded as if the whole gang was there.

'Is your car marked or unmarked?'

'We're buck-naked the day. Blending right in.'

'Perfect. With any luck they'll hang around till we get there. Who else you got in the area?'

Nicholson jabbed the brakes, changing down to rally their way into a gorge and round a hairpin bend, accelerating up the other side.

'*Sierra One One's approaching from Sandhaven. Tango Bravo One Four's on its way from Strichen.*' Which didn't leave a lot of ways to escape the place.

'OK, shout if anything happens. We'll be there in . . . call it ten.'

A ping and a burr announced the arrival of Colin's second text message. It contained the promised mobile phone number. Logan selected it and made the call.

A small voice barked in his ear. '*Hello? Yes? Hello? Yes?*'

'Hello, can I speak to your mummy?'

'*I has a fire engine.*'

'That's great, I has a police car.'

Nicholson threw it around another corner, pressing Logan up against his door.

'*I has a fire engine, and a tiger, and the Tooth Fairy gave me a whole pound for—*'

'*All right, sweetie, that's enough.*' There was some crackling, probably the phone being confiscated. '*Can I help you?*'

'Is this Alison Hay, formerly Alison Anderson?'

A sigh. '*Look, I'm not giving any more interviews, so please, leave me and my family—*'

'My name's Sergeant Logan McRae, Police Scotland. We were investigating your ex-husband's disappearance.'

The Big Car nipped onto the wrong side of the road for just long enough to pass a people carrier, and end up right in the crash zone of a massive tractor coming the other way.

Logan's hand tightened around the grab handle, eyes wide, something solid jamming his throat. Nicholson wrenched the wheel and they jerked back into the left lane before the tractor turned them into police pâté.

Oh God . . .

It rumbled past, hauling up a thick mist of road spray behind it. The world went opaque for a second, then the wipers caught it.

'Craggie isn't missing any more, he's dead. To be honest, he died years ago. We want to move on.'

Might be best to close his eyes.

'I can understand that, and I'm sorry to bother you, but I need to ask about what happened five years ago. It's important.'

A pause. Then another sigh. A scrunching noise muffled her voice. *'Sweetie, go play in the living room for a bit. Mummy needs to talk to the man.'* Then she was back. *'Andrew . . .'* She cleared her throat. *'Sorry, it's been a long time since I've said his name.'*

'It's OK.'

'He'd run around the garden like a mad thing. We got him a plastic sword and a shield and he'd be Spartacus, or Bilbo, or whoever it was this week. Fighting dragons and skeletons. We always told him to stay away from the far field, because of the cliffs, but . . .' Silence. *'I only turned my back for five minutes. I was making tattie and leek soup for tea, and . . .'* A small hissing noise escaped from the handset. *'We found his sword and shield. We'd been looking for Andrew for hours,*

and there they were, lying against the drystane dyke at the edge of the far field.'

'I'm sorry.'

'They called the Coast Guard, and they searched the cliffs and the rocks, but there was nothing. Andrew . . . They told us he'd been swept out to sea.'

Logan's stomach lurched against his lungs again as Nicholson took them over another bump at speed. 'Did Charles say anything?'

'Say anything?' She gave him a small bitter laugh. *'That's all he'd talk about. How it wasn't right. Andrew wasn't dead, he was missing. There wasn't a body, how could he be dead? Someone must've snatched him.'*

'But there wasn't any proof?'

'He was obsessed. Put posters up everywhere, adverts in the newspapers, handed out fliers at football matches and the supermarkets, till they told him to move on. Two years I made allowances, I lived with it, because he was grieving. But do you know what? I was grieving too.'

Logan sneaked a peek. Fields and trees hammered past, Nicholson put her foot down to overtake a plumber's van. He closed his eyes again. 'Did he ever find anything? Ever connect anyone to Andrew's disappearance?'

No reply.

'Ms Hay?'

'I remarried. We've got a little girl. Andrew's dead and I don't want to speak about it ever again.' Click. She'd hung up on him.

Nicholson's voice rose above the roar of the engine. 'You can open your eyes now, Sarge. We're here.'

The thirty limit flashed past and she stood on the brakes, taking them down to a more respectable thirty. Then poked the button switching the swirling blue lights off.

A graveyard with plenty of room went by on the left.

Rain battered the Big Car, sounding like a million tiny hammers.

She pulled up outside the church. 'What's the plan?'

Logan hit the button again. 'Shire Uniform Seven to Tango Bravo One Two. Safe to talk?'

'You made it?'

'By the skin of our teeth. Any news on the suspects?'

'Still in the baker's. Been ten minutes.'

'What about the one on the phone?'

'On his third fag, stomping up and down the pavement, jabbing his elbows about as he talks. Looks like he's giving someone a bollocking . . . Oh ho. Hold on. He's hung up and got a set of keys out. . . . Making for the van. . . . Come on, Chuckles, do it for Uncle Ed . . .'

Nicholson bounced up and down a couple of times in the driver's seat.

'He's in. Repeat, Chuckles has got in behind the wheel.'

Logan stuck a hand out and shoved Nicholson back into her seat. 'What about the other three?'

'Still in the . . . Nope, that's them coming out now. Lots of paper bags and Styrofoam cups.'

Nicholson slipped the Big Car into gear. 'Here we go . . .'

'Which way's the van facing: south, or north?'

'They pull out now, they'll be on the road to Strichen.'

'OK, they're not going to do a three-point turn in a removal van. You're unmarked, right? When they go, I want you ahead of them. We let them get half a mile then you block in front and we block behind.'

'Chuckles has started the van. OK, we're heading out first . . . Nice and slow . . . He's following.'

'Tell me when you've cleared the end of town.'

'There's four of them, what if they've got guns?'

'You want me to go first?'

'You saying Traffic's full of Jessies? . . . OK, that's us cleared the limits on the Strichen road. Chuckles is right behind.'

Logan gave Nicholson the nod. 'Nice and easy.'

She pulled the Big Car onto the High Street.

Little grey houses, all in a straight line, slipped past the windows. Sulking beneath the hammering rain. At the bottom of the road, they took a left, following the sign for Strichen. Past another couple of houses, then around the corner and out into the countryside.

The road stretched out ahead, the boxy black bulk of the removal van sticking out like a lump of coal between fields of waving gold.

Logan pressed the button. 'Tango Bravo One

Two, that's us cleared the limits. We have visual. Closing on you now.'

'*Roger that. Slowing to a halt. . . . And we're blocking the road. Chuckles has stopped.*'

Nicholson accelerated, taking them right up behind the van, then slamming on the brakes.

Logan poked the siren button, letting it wail as he unleashed his body-worn video from its elastic band. 'Let's do it.'

Out into the downpour. He wedged the peaked cap firmly over his ears – froze for a second and winced as it caught the lump on his head – grabbed a yellow high-vis from the rear seat and hauled it on as the rain trickled down the back of his neck.

Nicholson scrambled out the other side, pulling on her coat as they sploshed through the puddles either side of the removal van. Up to the cab.

The guy behind the wheel, Chuckles, didn't move. Kept his hands at ten to two. The three men sitting next to him did their best to look relaxed. Nothing to see here. Move along.

The two-person crew of Tango Bravo One Two appeared in their high-vis. Four against four.

Logan reached up and knocked on the driver's window.

A pause.

Rain thumped out a tattoo on Logan's peaked cap. Pattered against his fluorescent-yellow shoulders.

Then the window buzzed down.

A smile pulled Chuckles's cheeks into rosy apples.

'Something up, Officer?' Not a local accent, but still Scottish. Dundee maybe? Not sing-song enough for Fife. Big lad, his head almost scraping the top of the cab. Long brown hair. Green overalls.

'This your vehicle, sir?'

'Nah, I'm just the driver. Know what it's like with these removal firms, eh? All we do is drive about and hump the heavy stuff from A to B.'

'And your name?'

'And it's always at the top of the stairs, isn't it lads? The heavier the bit of furniture, the more flights you've got to lug it up.'

His mates nodded. Made agreeing noises that weren't actually words. All of them in green overalls, all of them big enough to give Constable King Kong McMahon a thump for his money. Larry, Curly, and Moe.

'Your *name*, sir.'

'Yeah, of course. It's Russell. Russell McNee. Was I speeding or something?'

'I need you to give me the keys and step out of the vehicle, sir.'

'Come on, I wasn't speeding, I know I wasn't. This is—'

'Keys. Please.' Logan stuck his hand out.

No one moved.

Rain.

'All units, be on the lookout for Terrence and Jon McAuley. Both have apprehension warrants for an aggravated assault on Saturday night.'

635

More rain.

This was it. Either they came quietly, or—

Moe – the one on the far side – broke. He yanked off his seatbelt and threw the passenger door open. It slammed into Nicholson, sending her crashing back into a barbed-wire knot of brambles. And he was off, jumping the fence and charging into the field of wheat.

It took less than two seconds for Nicholson to swear herself back upright and hammer after him, bowler hat tumbling off as she ran.

Closer . . . Closer . . . Closer . . . Then *thump*, she slammed into him and they went down in a tangle of arms and legs that disappeared beneath the surface of the wheat.

McNee looked down at Logan. Sighed. Then pulled the keys from the ignition and handed them over. 'He always was an idiot.'

One of the officers from Tango Bravo One Two scrambled over the fence and waded into the field. He'd barely gone six feet before Nicholson emerged from the wheat, hauling her new captive up with her – both hands cuffed behind his back.

Don't mess with Calamity Janet.

Logan jerked his head towards the removal van's big black box. 'You want to show me what's inside?'

'Not really.' But McNee climbed down from the cab anyway, stomped around to the back roller doors, unlocked the heavy padlock. Then hauled on the lever. The door clattered up, revealing the back end of a brown Ford Ranger. Thick scrapes buckled and scarred the paintwork, the bumper all dented and barely hanging on. A set of metal ramps were secured against the van wall. Four ratchet straps fixed the battered four-by-four to tie-down points on the floor.

Logan raised an eyebrow. 'Well, well, well.' No wonder they could never find the cars that did the actual ram-raiding.

McNee licked his lips. Dropped his voice to a whisper. 'Look: I drive the van. I do what I'm told. It's the other guys who're in charge.'

'Aye, right. And where's the cash machine you boosted from the Strichen Co-op last night? That in the back too?'

He ran a hand across his face, pulling it out of shape. 'Knew it was going to be a bad day when I woke up this morning.'

CHAPTER 50

A uniformed officer hurried across the car park behind Fraserburgh station, an Asda carrier bag dangling from one hand, the other pinning his peaked cap to his head. Rain bounced off the shoulders of his high-vis jacket, dripping off the hem like a personal waterfall. He gave the Big Car a quick nod as he passed, then disappeared through the back door into the place.

Sitting in the driver's seat, Nicholson raised an eyebrow, mouth contorted into a half-smile, half-frown. Little red lines scratched around the side of her cheeks, each bearing tiny dots of dried blood like jewels on a necklace. 'The Cashline Ram-Raiders, *and* the scumbag who shot Constable Mary Ann Nasrallah. Not bad for an old man.'

A grin cracked across Logan's face. 'Shut up and drive.' He poked the Duty Inspector's number into his Airwave handset. 'Bravo India from Shire Uniform Seven, safe to talk?'

'*Go ahead, Sergeant.*'

So he was still 'Sergeant', was he? Time to change that.

'We've caught the Cashline Ram-Raiders.'

Nothing.

Nicholson pulled away from Fraserburgh station, joining the steady stream of lunchtime traffic.

'You still there, Guv?'

'You caught them?'

'And done the preliminary interviews. Three of the gang are no-commenting, but the guy who drives the removal van has dobbed the lot of them in. Get the feeling they'll reciprocate soon as they find out he's shafted them.'

'When did this happen?'

'Three hours ago, about a mile south of New Aberdour. Got backup from Mintlaw Traffic.'

The houses thinned, then disappeared in the rear-view mirror.

'And it's definitely them?'

'They do the raid with a stolen car, race off to where they've got a big removal van waiting, down some quiet wee country road, and they load the four-by-four into the back using a pair of metal ramps. Strap the car down, close the door, and drive the van back the way they came. Any police pursuit wheechs right past them like a bunch of numpties with all lights blazing.'

Blue patches peeked through between the heavy clouds. A rainbow marked the death of the fallen rain.

'Logan, that's excellent. Really, excellent.'

And he was 'Logan' again. 'Couldn't have done it without Constables Nicholson, Scott, and Quirrel. Proper team effort.'

Sitting behind the wheel, Nicholson beamed.

'*Then we're on for drinks tonight. I may even spring for chips.*'

'Thanks, Guv.'

'*Where are you?*'

'Heading back to Banff now. Late lunch, then off patrolling again.'

A shaft of sunlight made it through the lid of grey, making the fields glow.

Nicholson glanced at him. 'Did they get a replacement for Sergeant Muir then?'

'No idea.'

'Well, how are you going to make chips and drinks if you're pulling a green shift?'

Good point. He pressed the button again. 'Guv, you still there? Anyone standing in for Davey Muir tonight?'

'*Damn.*' There was a pause. '*No, not yet. Let me have a rake around. Must be someone who needs the overtime.*'

'Thanks, Guv.' Beer and chips . . . The smile died on his face. What about Helen? Assuming, of course, she was still there when he got back. It wasn't her daughter, why would she hang around a wee town on the north coast of Aberdeenshire? No, she'd be off to the next abduction scene. Chasing the hope. Goodbye, Banff. Goodbye, Logan.

Couldn't really blame her.

But it had been nice to have someone there for a change. Even if it was only for a—

Nicholson poked him in the arm. 'Sarge, you OK?' She pointed at the Airwave in his hand.

'Hello? Logan? You still there?'

'Sorry, Guv, thought I saw something.'

'Logan, when you've eaten, I need you back in the station. You've got an appointment.'

'I do? OK.' That was news. 'Anyone in particular?'

'Chief Superintendent Napier.'

Again?

Typical: couldn't even enjoy half an hour of success without the ginger whinger swooping down and spoiling everything.

'He say what it's about?'

'Operation Troposphere.'

Great. Just great.

Nicholson pulled up outside the Sergeant's Hoose. Cleared her throat, and kept her eyes dead ahead. 'Sarge, is it true you're . . . Well, that you and the dead wee kid's mum are . . . You know?'

'No. Now go get yourself some lunch and I'll see you back in the station at quarter to.'

A small sigh. 'Sarge.'

He climbed out into the sun. Leaned back into the car. 'And get some Savlon on those scratches.' Then thunked the door closed and watched the Big Car drive away.

Logan pulled out his phone and selected Steel ~ Mob from his contacts. Above his head, clouds chased each other across the dark-grey sky, wind whipping the weeds growing in the Sergeant's Hoose gutters. Have to do something about that.

A plastic bag went tumbling by.

Then, *'Aye, this is Steel. No' answering the phone right now, but you can blah, blah, blah . . .' Beeeeep.*

'It's Logan. Listen, Napier's turned up at Banff station wanting to give me another bollocking about Operation Troposphere. Call me back, OK?'

He put his phone away, then let himself in through the front door. 'Helen? You there?'

Silence.

Of course she wasn't. She was on her way back to Edinburgh, looking for the next lead on her missing daughter.

His shoulders dipped a little.

Then thump, thump, thump, as Cthulhu pooked her way down the stairs. She wound herself around his ankles, purring and meeping.

'Still got each other, haven't we?' He bent and scooped her up, turning her upside down and rubbing her tummy as she stretched out her arms and legs, rumbling like ball bearings in a tumble drier. 'Who's Daddy's best kitten?' He carried her down the hall towards the kitchen. 'You are. Yes you are. You're my pretty little girl.'

He pushed the door open and stopped.

Helen sat at the little table, with a mug of what probably used to be tea and a bottle of supermarket brandy. When she looked up her eyes were red, her nose too. She sniffed, wiped the back of a hand across her eyes. 'Sorry.'

'What happened?'

'She's not dead.'

Logan turned Cthulhu the right way up and lowered her onto the table. 'I thought that was a good thing this morning?'

The cat stood where she was for a moment, then butted her head against Helen's shoulder and thumped down to the floor. Wandered off with her tail in the air and her bumhole on display.

'It is. It isn't.' She poured a slug of brandy into her mug, then took a sip. 'Like being beaten up, every time.'

He sank into the chair opposite. 'I'm sorry it's not her. And I'm glad she's not dead.'

'I didn't even make anything for lunch.'

'Don't worry about it. There's still some leftover mince and tatties, I could microwave that? Or we could tart it up with baked beans and make Mexican mince? Be like the Seventies all over again.'

She stared at the bitten fingernails resting against the brandy bottle. 'Logan . . .'

'I know.' He stood. Fought his way out of his protective gear. 'You have to go.' He took the bowl of mince out of the fridge and topped it up with a tin of own-brand beans. Chucked in some chilli powder and stirred the lot into a gloopy mush. Kept his eyes on the lumpy surface, not looking at her. 'But you don't have to go right now, do you? You're welcome to stay as long as you like.' It went in the microwave, at full power. 'Why not stay till your next lead comes up? It's . . . nice having you here.'

Lunch buzzed around in its slow pirouette.

Behind him: the sound of a chair scraping backwards. Then her arms wrapped around his chest, squeezing. He put a hand on hers.

She kissed the back of his neck. 'Your poor head's all bruised.'

'Helen, I—'

'Shh . . . No talking.'

By the time the microwave went *ping*, they were already upstairs.

Nicholson frowned at him. 'What happened?'

'Nothing happened.' Logan chucked his teabag in the bin. 'I smile like this all the time.'

'No you don't. Your cheeks are all rosy too.'

'Had a good lunch.' Milk. Stir. Let the spoon clang and clatter in the stainless-steel sink. 'You seen Tufty? I popped past the Spotty Bag Shop and made him a badge.'

'Out patrolling with Deano.'

Logan dug into his pocket and produced the paper bag the badge came in. Held it out.

Nicholson peered inside. 'Oh. Erm . . .' Wrinkles appeared between her eyebrows. She chewed on her bottom lip for a moment. 'Not to be funny, Sarge, but that's not how you spell "genius".'

'I know. How long do you think it'll take him to notice?'

'Fiver says Wednesday.'

'I bet he's still wearing it when we start back on nights, Friday.' Logan took a sip of tea. Glanced up at the ceiling. Two floors up, Napier was waiting. Ah well. 'Right, I've got a meeting. Take the Big Car and drift about on Rundle for a bit, then head over to Macduff and see if you can find something out about that peeping tom. Look for patterns – are there specific days he likes to peep? What about times?'

'Sarge.'

Logan took his tea through to the Sergeants' Office. Someone had dumped a big box of stolen garden gnomes on his desk, so he shifted them to the other side. Then stood, staring out of the window.

Steel was out there, marching up and down in the courtyard behind the building, phone pressed to her ear.

'Sergeant McRae?'

He turned.

Maggie stood in the doorway holding a short stack of Post-it notes. 'Got some messages.'

'Let me guess: I've won the lottery?'

'Sorry.' She peered at Post-it number one. 'A Lesley Spinney's been in three times, demanding to know when she can get back in her house. Klingon's mother?'

'No idea. She'll have to ask DCI McInnes – I'm not allowed to interfere.' A point that Napier was no doubt about to ram home with a tiny size-six boot.

Post-it number two. 'We've had a complaint about an . . . ahem, "aroused" male dancing naked down Harbour Road in Gardenstown?'

'Tell Deano and Tufty to take a swing by, see if anyone recognizes this fine upstanding member of the community.'

Post-it number three. 'Sean MacLauchlan called – he's running the investigation into the fire last night. Says it was definitely deliberate. Apparently something about the burn patterns means the place was doused with petrol first, then torched.'

Not exactly a huge surprise, but at least they were doing something.

'Thanks, Maggie.'

He took his tea through to the main office. Deano appeared in the doorway, head down, shoulders back, face like a Rottweiler eating nettles, storming by on his way to the Constables' Office. Thirty seconds later, Tufty lumbered by, straining under the weight of a large plastic crate.

Logan pointed. 'What did you do to Deano?'

'Wasn't me, Sarge.' Tufty shuffled into the room and lowered his crate down onto an empty desk. 'God, these weigh a ton.'

'Come on: he looked like he was about to murder someone.'

Tufty reached into the crate and produced a garden gnome. 'Found them planked in the grave-yard, posed like they were having a wee orgy.' He pulled another one out and made them kiss. 'Oh yeah, you're so sexy Mr Fishy Gnome. I love you too Mr Diggy Gnome.' He puckered his lips and made kissy-kissy noises. Looked up. 'What?'

'Never mind, I know what you did.'

The gnomes went back in the crate. 'I went digging, like you asked, Sarge.' Tufty produced his notepad. 'Helen Edwards's ex-husband, Brian Menendez Edwards: thirty-eight, IC-Two male, born in Kilmarnock. Went to Stirling University studying—'

'Skip to the relevant bit, while we're all still young enough to enjoy it.'

'Oh. Right.' He flipped forward a couple of pages. 'Here we go: Brian Edwards did a runner from the accountants he worked at not long before a massive fraud turned up. Firm says he got away with quarter of a million. Went out to lunch, picked up his daughter from school – middle of a PE lesson – and got the next flight to Spain from Edinburgh airport.'

'He pack bags and things?'

'Yup. Bought his tickets in advance as well. Looks like he'd been planning it for weeks. Far as local plod could tell, he got met at the airport by a cousin from Vilar.' Tufty waved his other hand from side to side. 'Sort of in the west of the country, not that touristy. His mum's family have a farm in the hills around there.'

'Extradition?'

'No joy. Sounds like a pretty half-arsed investigation to be honest. I checked births, marriages, and death records online, but nothing for Brian Edwards. So I tried the family name, Guerra, in case he changed his, you know, to blend in? A Brian Menendez Guerra got married in the Iglesia Catedral de San Martín, Ourense.' Tufty put on a Spanish accent for the place names. 'That was three months after Brian Menendez Edwards got off the plane with his kidnapped wee girl. So technically he'd still be married to Helen Edwards at the time.'

Three months after he snatched his daughter – exactly the time he sent that postcard from Ourense, telling Helen she was a useless ugly cow and no one would ever love her. Did he post it before, or after the wedding ceremony?

Yeah, Brian Edwards just got lovelier and lovelier.

A nod. 'Thanks Tufty.'

That got a beaming smile. 'I did good?'

'You did good. Now have a dig around for Brian Menendez Guerra – did he ever come to the UK? Where is he now, are there photos of him on Facebook, that kind of thing.'

'Will do, Sarge.' Tufty put his snogging gnomes in their box again and humped the lot off to the Constables' Office.

Logan checked his watch. Napier would be waiting. Sharpening his knives.

Need to do something first, though.

Steel was still wandering back and forth in the courtyard behind the station, so Logan went through the door by the reception hatch, into the hall, past the stairwell, left at the interview rooms, and finally out of the old cellblock door.

The building acted as a windbreak on three sides, with its plain stone walls and barred windows. Cracks broke the concrete courtyard into a chessboard patchwork, and the only thing winning was the moss. All of it bathed in a spotlight of sunshine.

Steel got to the far end, then turned and marched back towards him. '. . . I've no idea, Susan, I really don't. . . . I know. I've tried, but he says he really can't stand your mother. Says if she comes to the dinner, he won't. . . . I know, he's a complete . . .' Her head came up. She blinked at Logan a couple of times. 'I'll call you back.' The phone went in an inside pocket. 'Well, well, if it's no' Mr Grumpy.'

'Did you get my message?'

She crossed the last couple of feet between them and plucked the mug of tea from his fingers. 'Ta.' Took a slurp. 'What happened to the sugar?'

'It's not your sodding tea.'

'Is now.' The fake cigarette came out, and got plugged into the side of her mouth. 'Got any biscuits?'

'Napier's upstairs waiting for me.'

'Again? He must fancy you something rotten.'

'Wants to shout at me for interfering with Operation Troposphere.'

'Serves you right.' She had a couple of puffs, then dribbled steam out of her nose. 'You know where I spent most of the morning? Peterhead, rummaging through Neil Wood's bed and breakfast. There's three hours I'm never getting back. And his taste in soft furnishings is abysmal. Worse than your mum's.'

'Hard to believe.' Logan stared at the cracked concrete around his feet. 'Look, if you wanted to interrupt my interview and drag me away again, I'd be OK with that. I don't know, we could traipse round all the sex offenders again, if you like?'

Another slurp of tea, then she turned and pointed at an old granite stone, mounted above the Constables' Office window. All the stone bricks were the colour of slate, but this one was an ancient grey, sitting next to a coat of arms above the lintel. The words carved into it were still chisel sharp:

> **SAY · NA · MAIR ·**
> **ON · ME · THAN ·**
> **YOV · VALD · I ·**
> **SAID · ON · YE · A · S**

'That no' a strange thing to put on a police station?'

'Wasn't always a police station. Used to be a bank at one point. And they cannibalized something else to make that. Probably a merchant's house. It basically says, "Don't bear false witness".'

'No it doesn't, it says, "Nobody likes a clype".'

'Speaking of which: Napier.'

'Can't. I've got a conference call with Finnie in two. You'll have to take your medicine like a big boy . . .' She narrowed her eyes. Tilted her head to one side. 'You've been up to something, haven't you? You're all rosy and glowing.'

'Not you as well.' Logan folded his arms. 'I haven't been up to anything. Now, if you'll—'

'You *have*. What is it? What did you do?'

Don't flinch. Don't let her know about Helen. 'I caught the Cashline Ram-Raiders. They had a whole MIT on that for a fortnight, and who solved it? Me.'

'Aye, well done, Inspector Morse.' She took the e-cigarette from her mouth. 'Don't suppose your little grey cells have come up with anything about our wee dead girl, have they?'

'Grey cells are Poirot, not Morse.' He dug into his pocket and produced the sheet of paper with its boxes and lines and paedophiles' names. Unfolded it and handed it over. 'That's all I can remember from Charles Anderson's garage. The ones with question marks, I'm not sure of.'

A sniff. 'Better than nothing, I suppose.'

He turned and marched back inside. Stopped at the door. 'You sure you can't interrupt Napier?'

'You want a bit of advice about dealing with the Ginger Ninja?'

'If it'll help.'

Steel grinned. 'Grope his bum when he's not looking. Gives him the willies.'

★   ★   ★

651

Rain clattered against the Major Incident Room's window. At the head of the table, Napier steepled his fingers. Again. 'And you're certain of that?'

'Yes.'

The camera's dead eye stared at Logan, little red light glowing like an ember. Sitting next to it, Inspector Gibb made a note in her pad.

'So, to be clear, you're categorically certain, *on the record*, that you haven't seen Graham Stirling since the trial collapsed.'

'No. I haven't seen him since Tuesday morning. *Before* the trial was called off.'

Napier's smile widened. 'We're still looking for him, by the way. It may take a while, but we'll find him.'

The camcorder whirred in the silence.

Logan narrowed his eyes. 'I thought this was supposed to be about Operation Troposphere: Klingon, Gerbil, Klingon's mum.'

'Oh, don't worry, we'll get to that. In the meantime: when we *do* find Graham Stirling, what would you like to bet he'll be face-down in a ditch? Or do you favour a shallow grave, Sergeant McRae?'

'I think the more important question would be, "Where are David and Catherine Bisset?"'

'Enquiries are proceeding.' He sat forward, resting his elbows on the desk and his chin on his fingertips. 'Do *you* know where they are, Sergeant?'

'No.'

'Are you sure? Because a more cynical man than I might come to the conclusion that if you're unable to exert justice-slash-vengeance on your own, who better to recruit to your cause than the children of the man you couldn't save?'

'I don't know where they are.'

'Graham Stirling walked free, because you couldn't be bothered following procedure. We know you don't feel bound by the same rules as the rest of us mere mortals. What's a little conspiracy to commit murder between friends?'

Logan stared at him.

Napier smiled back. 'You see, the DNA results came in this morning: we know that David and Catherine Bisset were in Stirling's kitchen. Did you send them there? Did you tell them they could kill Graham Stirling and get away with it?'

Inspector Gibb raised her head, eyes glittering. Pen poised, ready to take notes.

So he'd been right – they'd put their father out of his misery, then broken into Stirling's house and killed him. It was just a case of waiting now till the body turned up and David and Catherine Bisset went down for twelve years to life.

Logan kept his mouth shut. Let the silence stretch.

'Well, Sergeant? Would you care to—'

Then Logan's Airwave gave its four point-to-point bleeps. *'Shire Uniform Seven, safe to talk?'*

He glanced at the screen. No idea whose shoulder number it was, but it was low, so might be a boss.

Napier held up a finger. 'I don't think so.' He put his hand out. 'If you don't mind.'

'And if I do?'

His shoulder rose, then dipped. 'Well, for a start, I'm a chief superintendent, and you're a sergeant, so that makes me, let's see: four steps further up the ladder? If you can't have the common courtesy to switch off your Airwave when you're in a meeting, I shall do it for you. Now: the handset, please.'

No point fighting – it wasn't as if he was ever going to win.

Logan unclipped his handset and passed it across.

'Thank you.' Napier glanced down at the screen as he reached for the off switch. Then stopped, fingers hovering over the control. 'Ah . . .' He pursed his lips. 'I think you probably better take this one.' Then stood, walked around behind Logan, on those silent little feet, and placed the Airwave on the table in front of him. 'It's the Chief Constable.'

The breath wheezed out of Logan, dragging heart and lungs down into his bowels. Great – a tag-team bollocking.

He pressed the button. 'Shire Uniform Seven, safe to talk.'

Napier settled back into his seat, that Night-of-the-Living-Dead smile twitching at the corner of his lips.

Inspector Gibb's pen hovered over her notepad.

And then the Chief Constable's voice thumped out into the room. *'Sergeant McRae – Logan – it's John.'*

'Sir.'

Here we go . . .

'I wanted to call you anyway; say congratulations on catching the man who shot Constable Mary Ann Nasrallah. Excellent result, especially given the case was a national priority. First-rate job there. Really showed the power of good old-fashioned divisional policing.'

Logan blinked at the handset a couple of times. OK . . . 'Thank you, sir.'

Time for the other shoe, not so much to drop as get rammed home into his groin.

'And now I hear you've been instrumental in arresting the Cashline Ram-Raiders.'

Warmth bloomed in his cheeks. 'Thank you, sir, but it was a team effort.'

'That's what I like to hear, Logan: shoulder the blame when things go wrong, share the credit when they don't. That's the kind of leadership I want in Police Scotland.'

Logan raised an eyebrow at Napier. 'Glad to hear it, sir.'

'The media lot are putting out a statement, and believe me when I say you're going to get a glowing write-up. Well done again. We could do with a lot more Logan McRaes out there, Sergeant.'

'Thank you, sir.' But the Chief Constable was already gone. Logan placed his Airwave handset back on the tabletop. Gave Napier his widest smile. 'Now, I think you were busy implying that I colluded with David and Catherine Bisset to kill Graham Stirling?'

Napier pulled his chin in. Bit his top lip. Closed his eyes. Let out a small sigh. 'Inspector Gibb, switch off the camera: this meeting is concluded. I'm sure Sergeant McRae has lots more vital work to be getting on with.'

And, escape.

CHAPTER 51

'Interview suspended at sixteen hundred hours.' Logan gathered his papers together and stood.

The guy on the other side of the table squinted back at him. The green overalls were gone, replaced by a white paper oversuit with bootee feet. The skin across his left cheek had darkened to a thundercloud of blue and purple, marbled with yellow. That's what he got for doing a runner on Nicholson's watch. He sniffed, rubbed at his nose with cuffed-together hands. 'You'll make sure McNee goes down for it, aye? Rest of us was only doing what we was told.'

The solicitor from the Scottish Legal Aid Board polished a pair of little round specs. 'Albert, there's no need for you to continue talking. The interview's over.'

He pulled one shoulder up till it almost touched his ear. 'Just want to make sure, like.'

Logan looked down at the dirty fingernails, the thick hands, the cuffs. 'Why Broch Braw Buys?'

'Eh?'

A sigh from Mr Solicitor. 'Sergeant McRae, this interview has been terminated.'

'I'm curious.'

'Was McNee's idea.' Albert picked at the wart on the back of one thumb. 'We was hungry, so we parked up to get a burger. McNee went into the shop for a paper. Said there was this wee blonde girl comes skipping in and the gadgie running the place is shouting and swearing and kicks her out. Tiny wee girl, all dressed in pink with a skateboard. Wouldn't hurt a fly.'

Another sigh. 'Albert, I really have to advise *against* this.'

'So McNee comes back and he says, "We're doing that miserable old git next." Said it was payback for being cruel to kids and that.'

At least that was one mystery solved.

Logan shifted his Airwave to the other hand and had a slurp of tea. 'I thought Billy was doing it.'

'Can't, he's been summoned to Tulliallan to explain that firearms thing from two weeks ago.' Inspector McGregor sounded as if she was in a wind tunnel. *'Sorry.'*

Creaks and groans came from outside the Sergeants' Office door as someone stalked Fraserburgh station's wonky corridors.

'Gah . . .' Logan folded forward and rested his forehead against the keyboard. 'We're supposed to be going out tonight to celebrate.' And then home to celebrate some more with Helen. Hopefully twice.

'It's just for tonight. Billy will be back tomorrow evening, we'll do it then.'

'Chips and beer.'

'I wouldn't ask, but we need a duty sergeant.'

Logan groaned. Swore. Then hit the button. 'OK, put me down for a green shift.'

'And we need someone to fill in for Big Paul as well. He's stood down tonight because he's got court first thing tomorrow – that attempted murder in Peterhead three months ago.'

'I'll have a word with the team.'

'Good. Now, where are we at?'

'Finished the last interview half an hour ago. Soon as the other three heard the van driver had rolled over on them, they all changed their plea. According to them, he's the mastermind behind the Cashline Ram-Raiders. It's like a competition to see who can shaft him the hardest. I'm writing it up now.'

'So they're all pleading guilty?'

'That's the plan.'

'Excellent. What else?'

There was a knock on the door and Nicholson stuck her head into the room. 'You want a tea before we head off, Sarge? Nearly home time.'

'Got one, thanks.' He flipped over a couple of pages in his notepad. Keyed the talk button again. 'Right, we've got two drink drivers and one driving while disqualified, a break-in at Peterhead Cinema, an aggravated assault in Gardenstown, and a mum of three's gone missing from Aberchirder. Friends say she's never done it before, but rumour has it she's got a fancy man in Cullen. I've asked the Moray lot to keep an eye out for her.'

'*All pretty calm for a Monday.*'

'Don't knock it.'

'*And we'll do chips and beer tomorrow. Promise.*'

Assuming nothing went wrong between now and then. And knowing his luck . . .

Logan finished off writing up the interview notes, then headed through to the canteen.

Nicholson sat in one of the purple couches in front of the TV, Syd Fraser in the other one. The pair of them froze, hands dipped into a box of Maltesers.

Then Nicholson grinned. 'Sarge, frightened the life out of us.' She nabbed a Malteser and popped it in her mouth and went straight back for another one. Munching. 'Thought you were the owner.'

Syd scooped up a clicking palmful of little chocolate balls. 'They were planked in the back of the cupboard. Dig in before whoever bought them finds out.'

Logan helped himself. All malty and chocolaty and melty and crunchy. 'Did you hear Klingon's mum's not dead?'

A shrug. More Maltesers. 'To be fair, I did say Lusso's not been a cadaver dog for years. They lose the nose for it if they don't practise.'

'Yeah.' Crunch. Munch. Sook. 'Would've been nice though.'

Syd rubbed a hand across his shiny bald head. Frowned. 'OK, so it's not Klingon's mum buried in the back garden. So what? That doesn't mean someone else isn't. You got any missing druggies on the books?'

Nicholson grabbed another couple. 'Always. And no one ever tells us if they turn up again.'

Syd took one more palmful, leaving the box virtually empty.

'Pair of you are like vultures.' Logan grabbed the last Malteser before anyone else could. 'Still, it's sod all to do with us now. DCI McInnes won't let us anywhere near Klingon's place.'

Syd squished the empty box flat. Folded it in half. Then dumped it in the bin and covered it with yesterday's colour supplement. Burying the evidence. 'Shame. Otherwise we could nip round there with a couple of shovels and do a bit of grave-robbing. Don't think they'll be letting Klingon's mum move back in any time soon.'

True.

Logan hooked a finger at Nicholson. 'Come on, Calamity, time to get you back to the station.'

Syd raised a chocolaty hand in salute. 'Give us a call if you fancy playing Burke and Hare.'

Nicholson followed Logan out into the hallway. 'Calamity?'

'Calamity Janet rides again. You're the one who wanted a nickname.'

They clumped down the stairs.

'Yeah, but—'

'No buts. You said people weren't allowed to pick for themselves. So as of now, you're Calamity.'

All units, we've got a fatal RTC on the A90 between

Boddam and the Cruden Bay turn-off. Anyone free to attend?'

Out into the car park at the back of the station. Drizzle greyed the breezeblock and tarmac, misted the windscreens.

A couple of CID types leaned against a pool car, smoking cigarettes and drinking coffee. They looked up as Nicholson plipped the locks on the Big Car.

One seemed to think a Kevin Keegan perm was a good idea, the other looked as if the Ugly Fairy had paid him a visit and never left. Keegan jerked his chin up. 'You McRae?'

'Yes. You?'

'Brogan, MIT. You got the Ram-Raiders?'

'One removal van, one four-by-four, one boosted cash machine, and four guys in boiler suits.'

Ugly pinged the butt of his cigarette away into the drizzle. 'Yeah, we're going to take it from here.'

'Be my guest.' Logan swept an arm towards the cellblock door. 'Mind you, there's not far to take it. The other thing we got was four confessions. Job's done.' He climbed into the passenger seat. 'You have fun though.'

Nicholson started the engine, drowning out whatever Brogan's reply was.

She chewed on the inside of her cheek as she steered the Big Car out onto the street. 'Curlytop didn't look too happy.'

'Poor wee soul probably thought he could swoop down at the last minute and take all the credit.

662

Only to find the bunnets had got there first. Boo hoo. Nobody loves him. Etcetera.'

'My heart bleeds.' She took them out past the fish-processing plants, slowing down to peer into the car parks. 'Shout if you see an old red BMW Z4. Driver's disqualified.'

Grey hatchbacks and saloons: all sitting in ordered little rows, waiting for their fishy owners to do the five o'clock dash.

No BMW.

Logan adjusted his equipment belt, so the extendable baton wasn't poking into his leg. 'Fancy a green shift? Big Paul's got court in the morning.'

'Thought we were hitting the town for beer and chips.'

'Can't. Got to fill in for Davey Muir again.'

'Yeah, well my mates are heading off to Ellon to see that new Johnny Depp where everyone's zombies except him and Bill Bailey. If there's no beer and chips, I'm joining them.'

Just have to ask Deano then.

Logan pointed through the windscreen at the glowering sky beyond. 'Home, Calamity, and don't spare the horses.'

— MONDAY BACKSHIFT —

BROKEN BONES.

CHAPTER 52

'... *absolutely dinging it down.*'

Logan pressed the talk button. 'Well, don't hang about too long then, Joe. Don't want you and Penny catching pneumonia.'

Heat wafted through the Sergeants' Office, making spider-webs of steam on the mullioned window. A clatter of rain against the glass made it shiver.

'*Definitely. We'll finish up the last interview and be back in time for eightses. Penny's got chocolate éclairs.*'

Logan put his Airwave back on the desk and bashed in comments against two or three actions that needed following up. Shockingly, none of them belonged to Tufty. And speaking of Constable Quirrel . . .

His thin face appeared at the door. Cheeks shiny and red, with nose and ears to match. 'Ooh, it's perishing out there. Fancy a cuppa?'

Logan held out his mug. 'Any news?'

'Hospital say it wasn't as bad as it looked. A broken leg and a couple of ribs. Not bad for getting knocked down by a bus.' He pulled off his hat and a dribble of rainwater pattered against the carpet tiles.

Logan dug into his pocket and came out with a small paper bag. Tossed it on the desk. 'Before I forget, that's for you.'

'Is it cola bottles?' Tufty picked up the bag and peered inside. 'It's a badge.'

'For your help yesterday with the CCTV.' A smile. 'Put it on then.'

Tufty unzipped his high-vis jacket and pinned the badge to his stabproof. Round and red, with 'GENIOUS' on it in little white letters. He beamed. 'Thanks, Sarge!'

'No problem. You earned it.'

'You've got a visitor, by the way. Outside.'

'In this?' Logan grabbed his waterproof high-vis gear. 'Not supposed to leave members of the public out in the rain, Constable. Sends a bad message.'

'Yeah . . . Didn't want to let him into the building. Not after what he did to the Big Car. It's Stinky Sammy Wilson and, going by the smell, I think he's here to report his own death.'

'I've changed my mind: you're an idiot.' Logan hauled on the vest, the jacket, and fastened his equipment belt over the top on his way to the tradesmen's exit. Instantly a stone heavier. 'Go make the tea – Penny and Joe are on their way back for eightses.'

'Sarge.'

He let himself out the door, pulling his peaked cap on, high-vis collar up.

Joe and Tufty were right, it was a foul evening. Not far off eight o'clock and it didn't look as if the sun would ever shine again. The sky was a slab of grey marble, mottled with black, and from it icy needles hurled themselves down to bounce off the houses, tarmac, and cars. Making dark lakes on the pavement that spread out across the roads from swollen gutters.

A fist of wind rocked Logan back on his heels.

Yeah, tonight was going to be one for staying indoors and doing paperwork. No villain with half a brain would be out and about in this.

He narrowed his eyes against the rain, and there was Sammy Wilson, huddled in the lee of the portico over the station's front door. Not that it gave much protection from the horizontal weather. Sammy's trademark filthy tracksuit hung baggy and shiny, soaked through. But in a fit of inspiration he'd fashioned a balaclava from a Tesco carrier bag – the handles tied beneath his chin.

Tufty had been right about the stench as well. Even from here the reek of rotting onions and spoiled meat was enough to catch the back of the throat.

Logan blinked, working the sting out of his eyes. 'Sammy?'

He looked up, eyes dark pits in the bony hole of his face. The blue-and-white 'POLICE' sign above his head gave his skin a sickly pallor, making him look as dead as he smelled. 'Sergeant, Sergeant, yeah, right, hi.' Those grimy twig fingers knotted themselves in front of his chest. 'Yeah, been looking into it, you know? Doing some James Bond on the down and out. Like you asked.'

'It doesn't matter – you can stop looking.'

A cough, then a sniff. 'You got my ten quid, right? Ten quid for Samuel Ewan Wilson, half now, half earlier, cause I asked questions. Questions, questions. Who *is* the Candleman?'

'Sammy: it's over. It's not my case any more.' Besides, DCI McInnes was hacked off enough already. He'd go thermonuclear if he found out Sammy Wilson was sniffing around Operation Troposphere on Logan's behalf. Didn't matter if the Chief Constable *had* called Logan personally to say what a good little boy he was – the explosion would be horrendous and the fall-out? It'd last for years.

'I asked them high, and I asked them low, and they never suspected I was James Bond and they were all stupid and I was slicker than a monkey, I was. Yeah. Questions. You got my ten quid?' His fingers disengaged and one hand reached for Logan, palm up, eyes glittering. 'Ten quid for a cuppa tea and that?'

'Here.' Logan dug in his pocket and came out with five pound coins and some smush. 'It's all I've got.' He tipped it into Sammy's open palm and it got snatched back against the sodden, dirty tracksuit.

'Tenner, we said, ten quid for questions, right? Ten quid, not . . .' His lips moved as he counted. 'Six pound twenty-three.'

'I've nothing else. That's it. I'm skint till the end of the month. Now give it up. No more asking questions. It's *over*.'

The eyebrows went up. 'No more James Bond? I've been asking and asking for ten quid, only we're three pound seventy-seven short. Can't give any of the questions back, sale is final: no receipt, no returns.'

'Let it go, Sammy. Thanks for the help, and I'll get you the other three quid when I've got it.'

'Three seventy-seven.' Another cough – this one longer and deeper – had his back heaving. His knees bent until he was almost in two. Hacking and wheezing to a stop. Then a deep gasp hauled him upright again. 'Sammy's dying . . .'

A car ploughed its way along the road in front of the sea wall, sending up plumes of water.

Wind rattled the station windows.

Logan cleared his throat. 'Have you got somewhere to stay tonight? A bed at the shelter, a friend's couch?'

Samuel Ewan Wilson stepped in close enough for the heat radiating off him to seep into Logan's skin. 'If I find out his name, I get my three pounds seventy-seven, right?'

'No!' Rain dripped from the brim of Logan's hat. 'It's over, understand, Sammy? It's *over*. Stay away from the whole thing. Take the cash and go get some chips or something. A kebab. I don't want you asking any more questions.'

The skeletal face tilted to the left, eyebrows

pinched together. Breath like a ruptured bin-bag. 'You don't want to know who he is? Why don't you want to know? Police always want to know, right? Why don't you want to know?'

'Drop it. And find somewhere warm and dry to sleep. Don't spend the night out in this. You'll catch your death.'

'I still get my three pound seventy-seven though, right? Ten quid for asking questions. We had a deal, that was the deal, ten quid.'

'Sarge?' The word came from the rain behind Logan. He turned and there were Penny and Joe. 'You OK there, Sarge?'

'I'm fine. See you inside.'

A pause. Then, 'OK.' And they let themselves in the tradesmen's entrance.

And when Logan turned back, Sammy Wilson was lumbering off into the gloom, rain sparking off his plastic-bag hat.

'All units be aware: we've got a lorry fire on the B9093, between New Pitsligo and Strichen . . .'

Tufty tapped his fingers along the top of the steering wheel. 'You know what I don't understand?'

Logan scrolled through the text messages on his phone. 'Here we go.'

Outside, the day had given up. Wind rocked the lampposts, the rain making shimmering golden orbs around their sodium bulbs. The windscreen wipers thunked back and forth across the glass, engine barely ticking over. They'd parked facing the road to Macduff, lurking beside a council bin, overflowing with newspapers and plastic bags. Someone's broken umbrella poked out of the side, its black-ribbed skin making it look like something with bat wings was trying to escape from within.

'No. Look, everyone who's like of northern European decent has got a chunk of Neanderthal DNA in them, right? Because somewhere back in the dawn of time our ancestors fancied a bit of caveman. So they *can't* have been a different species, can they? Whole point of speciation is you can't breed with the rest of them any more.'

'Are you finished?'

'Well, makes you think, doesn't it?'

'No.' Logan settled back into his seat.

A shrug. Then he launched into whistling the theme tune to *Bonanza*.

'Tufty!'

'Sorry.' Back to tapping his fingers along the steering wheel. 'Can't believe I wasted all that time digging up info on Brian Menendez Guerra.'

'Who?'

'Brian Menendez Guerra – Helen Edwards's ex-husband. Snatched their daughter? Spent ages on that.'

Logan checked his phone for text messages. Nothing. 'Why wasted?'

'Well, no one cares now, do they? The wee girl we found at Tarlair wasn't Natasha Edwards, so no one cares her dad's dead.'

'Brian Edwards is dead?'

'Hit-and-run in Middlesbrough two years ago.'

Couldn't have happened to a nicer scumbag.

Mind you, it showed how rubbish Helen's private investigator was. Tufty had dug up the fact that Edwards was dead in a couple of hours, while all Sam Spade ever managed was 'he disappeared'. Yeah, he was *definitely* worth whatever Helen had been paying him all these years.

Idiot.

'What about the daughter?'

'No record. Probably still at home with Ex-Wife Number Two in Spain. She got shot of him for battering her and the kids.'

Why the hell would Helen *marry* someone like that?

'Do me a favour, Tufty, text me the address in Spain. Might be worth following up.'

'*Shire Uniform Seven, safe to talk?*'

Logan talked into his shoulder. 'Bang away.'

'*We've had another three sightings of David and Catherine Bisset: Inverness, Carlisle, and Ellon. Local forces are investigating.*'

'Thanks.' He let go of the button.

Tufty was looking at him.

'What?'

'If it was your dad, if you were David Bisset, what would you do? Would you kill Graham Stirling?'

'It wasn't, and I'm not, so I wouldn't.'

A nod. 'Don't know if I could kill someone, not

674

even if they'd done horrible things to my dad. Well, maybe. I mean, if they'd done something to my *mum*, then yeah. I'd crack them open like a pistachio nut.'

'You're supposed to be a police officer, Constable Quirrel. We don't "crack people open", we arrest them and we prosecute them.'

'Yeah, but if it was your mum . . .'

A rust-flecked Transit growled past on the way to Macduff, towing a plume of oily black smoke from its exhaust. The driver had his elbow on the windowsill, mobile phone clamped to his ear. He wasn't wearing a seatbelt either.

Logan pointed. 'We're on.'

Tufty clicked on the headlights and pulled out onto the road.

'Shire Uniform Seven, safe to talk?'

'We're in hot pursuit at the moment.' The speedo had barely nudged thirty and they were already catching up with the Transit's greasy cloud. 'Well, lukewarm pursuit.'

'Got an assault victim up at Elgin A-and-E with your business card in her pocket.'

'Elgin? You got a name?' Logan reached out a finger and hit the button marked 'BLUES'. The lights on top of the Big Car flickered to life.

'Yeah, one Kirstin Rattray. IC-One female, thin, twenty-four but looks forty-five. Well, she looks like she's been run over by a tractor, but you know what I mean.'

Kirstin Rattray?

The Transit's driver clearly wasn't looking in his mirrors. So Logan gave the 'SIREN' button a go too. Its wail cut through the downpour. But the Transit kept on trundling up onto the bridge across the Deveron.

Right: Kirstin Rattray. Shoplifter extraordinaire and drug addict. The woman who'd tipped them off about Klingon and Gerbil in the first place.

'Someone attacked her?'

'Doctor thinks they used a crowbar. Broke her jaw, her cheekbone, and her nose. Fractured skull, one leg, and both arms. Seven cracked ribs, three cracked vertebrae, and a shattered right kneecap. She's waiting for a scan to see if they've ruptured her spleen too.'

Logan sucked air in through his teeth. 'Oooh . . .' That didn't sound like an assault, that sounded like attempted murder. He poked Tufty in the shoulder. 'Are you planning on pulling this guy over any time soon, or are we going to follow him all the way to Fraserburgh?'

'Sorry, Sarge.' Tufty drifted out into the other lane and overtook the Transit. Slowed in front of it, all lights blazing.

Back to the Airwave. 'She conscious?'

'Nope. According to the doctors, she's lucky whoever it was didn't kill her.'

Finally, the Transit's driver seemed to get it through his thick skull. He pulled in to the side of the road with his load of burnt-oil smog.

Logan stared at it in the wing mirror. The Transit's driver still hadn't put down his mobile phone. Or pulled his seatbelt on. Had to admire stupidity that thick. 'Why Elgin? Why did she turn up there?'

'What's wrong with Elgin?'

'She lives in Banff, why did she end up thirty-five miles away? Not as if she could've walked it with a broken leg and shattered kneecap.' He held the Airwave against his chest, then poked Tufty again. 'You sitting there for a reason, Constable?'

Tufty curled his top lip. 'But it's bucketing down.'

Another poke. 'You're not going to sodding melt. Now get out there and see how many things you can do him for. And if you come back with less than three, I'm sending you out to try again.'

His face drooped with his shoulders. 'Yes, Sarge.' Then he stuffed the peaked cap on his head, grabbed his high-vis jacket, and scrambled out into the rain.

'You still there?'

'Had to motivate my constable.' Logan pulled out his notebook and scribbled down Kirstin's name, the date and the time. 'How did she get to the hospital?'

'Ambulance. Pair of caravanners found her in a lay-by, east of Fochabers. Thought she'd been in a hit-and-run; called it in.'

Logan tapped his pen against the notebook for a bit. 'OK, thanks for letting me know. If something happens – if she wakes up, or anything like that – give me a shout, OK?'

'*Will do.*'

He hooked his Airwave back into place, frowned at the windscreen as the wipers thumped and groaned their curves against the glass.

OK, so Kirstin was a drug addict, and sometimes drug addicts made poor choices and plenty of enemies. But still . . .

She was the one who dobbed Klingon and Gerbil in. Cost their supplier a hundred grand's worth of heroin.

What if the Candy Man found out?

Maybe Jack Simpson wasn't the only one who'd be serving as an object lesson.

Which meant it was Logan's fault.

Wonderful.

Wasn't as if he'd had any choice, was it? Couldn't turn a blind eye to drug dealing, just in case someone got hurt.

A long slow breath hissed out between his teeth, leaving his shoulders slumped.

Poor Kirstin.

Should probably hand it over to Operation Troposphere. Assuming they didn't already know about it.

Mind you, what if it wasn't the Candy Man? What if someone *else* decided she needed her skeleton rearranged with a crowbar?

Wouldn't hurt to ask about a bit first. See if anyone knew anything.

The driver's door clunked open and Tufty avalanched in behind the wheel, dripping on the upholstery. 'Dear Lord, it's wet . . .' He cranked the blowers up to full, then dumped his damp hat in the back. Held out his notebook. 'Driving without a seatbelt. Driving while using a mobile phone. Using a vehicle which has faulty lights. Using a vehicle which is in a dangerous condition. And two bald tyres in contravention of Section Twenty-Seven of the Road Vehicles, Construction and Use, Regulations 1986. Oh, and his road tax is three weeks out of date too.'

'And?'

'Says he was on his way to the garage to get it all fixed and didn't know about the tax. So I gave him an on-the-spot fine and fourteen days to attend a police station with evidence it's all been fixed, or we're confiscating the vehicle and doing him.'

'Good.' Logan pointed through the rain-shimmered glass. 'Now get a move on, we've got some druggies to spin.'

'And you've got nothing on your person I should know about?' Tufty snapped on a pair of blue nitrile gloves. 'No knives, needles or blades?'

A sniff caught the drop on the end of Lumpy Patrick's nose and hauled it back in. 'Nah, I'm, you know, clean and that . . .' His arms were like sticks, knotted around with rope. Thin hands with thick black crusts under the fingernails. Sunken cheeks and bloodshot eyes.

He stood in the battered glow of a lamppost on

Low Street, shielded from the wind and rain by the triangular frontage of a sheltered housing block.

Lumpy assumed the position and Tufty ran his hands along the outside of his manky sweatshirt. 'I hear you're dealing again.'

'Nah, not me, no, not dealing. Don't deal no more. Nah, someone's lying.'

Logan dug his hands deeper into his pockets, out of the cold. 'You hear about Kirstin Rattray, Lumpy?'

His head wobbled round to blink with two bloodshot eyes. He'd lost a couple of teeth since last time. 'She pregnant again?'

'No. Someone battered the living hell out of her. Left her for dead in a lay-by.'

One eyebrow crawled its way up Lumpy's forehead. 'Oh. Right. No.' He sent a pale tongue slithering across greying gums. 'No. Didn't know that. No.'

'You sure?'

'Nah.' Pause. 'Yes.'

Tufty finished the pat down. 'Right: pockets.' Then dipped into them.

Lumpy sniffed back another droplet. 'I hear stuff from time to time, though. Yeah, everyone thinks I don't, but I do.'

'Like what?'

A grin. 'Like Stinky Sammy Wilson saying you gave him fifty quid to dig out someone called the Candleman. You can't trust Sammy Wilson, but you can trust *me*. Totally. For fifty quid I could be, like, your eyes and ears and that. Much better than Sammy Wilson; man's a moron and a liar.'

No honour amongst addicts.

And what the hell was Sammy doing *telling* everyone he was asking after the Candleman? Silly sod was leaving a trail a mile wide that led right back to Logan. And it wouldn't take much for McInnes to stumble across it. Then BOOM, followed by nuclear winter.

'Forget the Candleman. There *is* no Candleman. But if you find out who battered Kirstin Rattray, we'll talk about it.' He stuck a business card in Lumpy's fingers.

'Arms out, Bill, you know the drill.'

A sigh, then the arms came up, increasing the choking stench of old cheese and socks. Bill's red hoodie was smeared down the front, hanging like a scarlet shroud over his skeletal torso.

Wind moaned in the branches of the trees, rustling the leaves outside St Andrew's Episcopal Church. Rain pattered against the lanced windows and gothic frontage, darkening the granite. Making it glisten in the streetlight.

Tufty worked his way along Bill's arms.

Logan shifted himself into the church doorway, but it wasn't any drier there. 'So, Bill, what do you hear about Kirstin Rattray?'

A shrug. 'There something in it for me? Sammy

Wilson says he's getting eighty quid for info about who's supplying Klingon and Gerbil.'

Eighty quid? At this rate he'd be on more than Logan.

'Said it was top secret. Think he told everyone.'

Because Sammy Wilson was an idiot.

'Do you know anything, or don't you?'

'Do you a deal, I'll undercut Sammy: let's call it sixty quid?'

Rain lashed the Big Car as Tufty took it across the bridge and into Macduff. 'Get the feeling we're piddling in the wind on this one, Sarge.'

'Probably.'

'Seven druggies, and all we know for sure is that Stinky Sammy Wilson is a useless lying wee sod. Which we kinda knew to begin with.'

That and the fact someone had a damn good go at battering Kirstin Rattray to death.

Outside, the North Sea hacked at the bay with curled white claws.

OK, so she'd clyped on Klingon and Gerbil, but that didn't mean whoever attacked her had something to do with Operation Troposphere. Half the shopkeepers in Banff and Macduff would probably queue up to have a go. But maybe not with a crowbar.

Still, it wasn't as if they were making much headway here, was it? And given the way things had been going lately, it might not be such a bad idea to cover his own arse for a change.

Logan twisted his Airwave free of its holder. Rubbed his thumb across the face of the buttons. He poked a shoulder number into the keypad. Pressed the talk button. 'Shire Uniform Seven for DI Porter, safe to talk?'

Tufty pulled a face. 'Who's Porter?'

'Runs the investigation into Klingon and Gerbil for that nasty wee—'

'*Hello?*' Her voice crackled out of the handset. '*Who is this?*'

Here we go. 'It's Sergeant McRae in Banff.'

'*This better be important, Sergeant, I'm right in the middle of something here.*'

A couple of drunks weaved their way along the pavement, arms wrapped around each other's sodden shoulders, ignoring the howling wind and battering rain.

'I know I'm supposed to stay away from Operation Troposphere, but before you set your boss on me, there's something you need to know.'

'*Sergeant McRae, I think Detective Chief Inspector McInnes was* very *clear about this.*'

'I'm not interfering, I'm passing on information. Kirstin Rattray – she gave us the nod about Colin Spinney and Kevin McEwan in the first place. She's turned up at Elgin A-and-E. Someone's had a go at beating her to death.'

'*And you think our Candy Man found out this Rattray woman was clyping on him and decided to shut her up.*'

'Might be. Or it might be unrelated. Either way, I thought you should know.'

'*Thank you, Sergeant. I'll be in touch if I need anything else.*'

Logan peered at the Airwave's screen. She'd disconnected. 'My sodding pleasure.'

Tufty sucked at his teeth. 'So . . . This means we're done spinning druggies?'

'What do you think?'

CHAPTER 53

'Come on, I didn't do nothing.' The words clambered their way out of a mouth that looked as if it hadn't seen a toothbrush since puberty. 'This is harassment.' She'd dragged her hair back from her face with a couple of elastic bands, hard enough to pull her eyes out of shape. A hand reached down and scratched the underside of one buttock, poking out below the hem of an unbelievably short black skirt. No tights, just ice-cream skin, flecked with little red spots. A blue streak of varicose veins. Low-cut top showing off a stretch of ribby cleavage.

At least it was relatively sheltered here, in a little alleyway down the side of the post office, opposite the public car park where they'd found her.

Logan leaned against the rough stone wall. 'It's OK, Abby, want to ask you a couple of questions, that's all.'

She eyed Tufty like a dying snake. 'You're no' searching us?'

'Would you like us to?'

She shrugged one shoulder. 'What questions?'

'What have you heard about Kirstin Rattray?'

685

'That slag? Wouldn't pee on her if she was on fire.'

'Yeah, but would you try to beat the flames out with a crowbar?'

Abby's mouth clicked shut. She looked away. 'Didn't mean nothing. Was only . . .' She picked at her fingernails. 'Not saying she wouldn't deserve it, like. Doing what she did.'

Logan gave her a quick loom. 'And what was that?'

'Oh, come on, everyone knows she's shagging Judy Webster's husband.' Abby folded her arms across her bony chest. 'You don't shag someone else's man. You just don't. It's against the sisterhood, you know?'

Logan stared at her.

Colour bloomed across her pale cheeks. 'It's not the *same*. This is business.'

'Go home. No one's going to be kerb-crawling in this anyway.'

Abby stuck her nose in the air and clacked away on her too-high heels, staggering and lurching as she walked out of the alley and into the wind.

Tufty blew out a breath. 'Points for self-awareness?'

Logan shook his head. 'Might as well call it for tonight. Either no one's got a clue who attacked Kirstin, or they're all too scared to talk. Probably have to sit on our thumbs till she wakes up to find out.' Assuming she ever did.

They marched back to the Big Car, where the

wind tried to haul the door out of Logan's hand. He climbed inside and slammed it shut again.

It wasn't his fault. It *really* wasn't. Kirstin Rattray had been involved with dodgy people for years, sooner or later one of them was going to do something horrible. That's the way drug culture worked. Nothing to do with Logan.

So why did it feel as if something sharp and cold was grinding away deep inside him, filling his stomach with gravel and broken glass?

Maybe DI Porter would have more luck coming up with something. Hope so, anyway.

Tufty got in behind the wheel. Checked his watch. 'Quarter past ten. Back to the station for an early elevenses?'

'First we do a drift-by of Rundle Avenue. Keep Frankie Ferris's customers too scared to buy his wares. *Then* elevenses.'

Wind shook the Big Car as Tufty took them down the hill, past a couple of boarded-up houses, and out onto the harbour front. A couple of fishing boats bobbed in their berths, lights glimmering. More lights off in the distance – probably offshore supply boats, riding out the storm.

'*Shire Uniform Seven, safe to talk?*'

'Bash away.'

'*Got a report of someone breaking into one of the warehouses down at Macduff harbour. You're not far, right?*'

So much for elevenses. 'OK, we're on our way.'

★　　★　　★

'Anything?'

Tufty slowed the Big Car down to a crawl as they made another circuit of the harbour.

It wasn't exactly home to a huge fleet. Ten large fishing boats were tied up to the docks, most streaked with rust along the side where the nets were hauled in. Some nearly new, others that looked as if they could've fought in the Cod War. All bathed in the waxy glow of the harbour's lights.

Logan poked the 'LEFT ALLEY' button, and the side spotlight lanced out into the gap between two warehouses, illuminating a stack of yellow fish boxes.

'We're wasting our time, aren't we, Sarge?'

'Looks like it. Five more minutes, and back to the station.'

Another warehouse – breezeblocks on the bottom floor, with corrugated metal above painted a dusty orange. The spotlight shone back from the lower windows, glittered in the upper ones.

Tufty took a right, into the yard next door with its offshore containers, stacks of pallets, piles of thick metal pipes, and big chunks of machinery in wire cages. He poked 'RIGHT ALLEY' and the other spotlight came on, firing through the pallets and making skeletal shadows up the side of the warehouse. 'You know, if we put the blues, rear reds, and headlight flashers on, it'll be like driving about in a Christmas tree. Or we could have a disco.'

'Do you want me to take that badge back?'

The Big Car slowed to a halt in front of a short office-block attached to the side of the orange warehouse. The door was open. 'Oh-ho. Maybe not such a waste after all.' Tufty hauled on the handbrake. 'What do you think?'

They climbed out into the night.

Wind was picking up again, rattling the corrugated metal on the warehouse roof. Moaning through the chain-link fence.

Could've been eating chips, drinking beer, and celebrating instead of this . . .

Logan twisted his LED torch out of its holder and clicked it on. Swept it across the front of the office block. 'Might still be in there.'

'Right.' Tufty unclipped his extendable baton and clacked it out to its full length. Held it up and back, so it rested on his shoulder, torch in his other hand. 'You want me to go first?'

'No point keeping a dog and barking yourself.' Logan pulled out his own baton. Flicked his wrist and the end shot out, snapping into place. 'Remember – no hitting anyone unless I tell you it's OK.'

'It was only that one time, and I didn't do it hard.' He eased the door open and slipped inside.

The beam of Tufty's torch bobbed on the other side of the window.

Logan followed him in.

A cluttered open-plan office, with whiteboards and noticeboards covered in scrawled notes. Half a dozen desks with antique beige computers. A bank of filing cabinets. A coffee machine. And a bookshelf full of ring binders.

Tufty picked his way around the room, peering under desks. Then straightened up and shook his head. Pointed at the door in the opposite wall, by the filing cabinets.

'Go for it.'

A wince. Then a whisper. 'Are we not supposed to be sneaking about in secret?'

'We turned up in a dirty big patrol car with "Police" down the side and spotlights blazing. Not exactly subtle, is it?'

'Oh. OK.' He turned and opened the door through to the warehouse. Stepped through, with Logan right behind him.

Their footsteps echoed back from the high ceiling and metal walls. Racks of things and piles of stuff loomed in the darkness. Tufty played his torch across the nearest rack. Metal things, and plastic things, and things that were a combination of both. The place was huge. Bigger than it looked from the outside – with rack shelving laid out in long rows, like a cash-and-carry.

Ship's chandlers? Something like that. The bits and bobs looked kind of nautical.

Tufty crept out into the aisles, keeping his torch beam down.

Yeah, sod that. A bank of switches sat beside the door through to the office block. Logan swept a hand down them, clicking them all on.

Clunk. Then pinging and flickering as the fluo-rescent tubes warmed up.

Tufty froze, mid-creep. Then straightened up. Cleared his throat. 'OK. Or we could do that.'

Something clanged and thunked against the floor, somewhere deep inside the warehouse, the sound quickly smeared and distorted by its own echoes.

Logan clicked off his torch. 'Police! We know you're in here.'

in here . . . in here . . . in here . . .

The echo faded into nothing.

'Don't play silly sods, it's over.'

over . . . over . . . over . . .

Still nothing.

OK, if that was the way they wanted to play it.

He pointed Tufty towards the far corner of the warehouse.

A nod, then Constable Quirrel loped away into the racks.

'You're only making it worse for yourself.' Logan stepped into the gap between two sets of tall metal shelving. Look left: no one. Look right: no one. 'I'm sure we can work it out.' Through into the next aisle. No one. Same with the next aisle. 'Come on, don't be daft. Only one way this ends.'

Which was a lie: there were plenty of gaps between the racks, so as long as whoever it was timed it right, they could sneak away unseen while Logan and Tufty were still searching the place.

Another clunk.

Logan froze.

Then a crash battered out from the left.

'Sarge! There!'

'Where?' He spun in place.

Someone sprinted across the aisle, down by the far wall.

'Come back here!' Tufty appeared, then disappeared into the next row of shelving.

Move. Logan ran back the way he'd come, one hand holding the baton, the other pinning the peaked cap to his head. Past rows of meters and gauges, unidentifiable boxes, sections of plastic piping.

A bang rang out from the front of the building – a door.

Hard right turn, feet clattering on the concrete floor. Knees and elbows pumping. Equipment belt jouncing up and down on his hips. Come on, come on, come on . . .

There – a door lay wide open, showing off the harbour outside. Logan battered through it and skittered to a halt on the tarmac outside. Spun around in place. No sign of anyone. 'Tufty?'

Silence.

'Constable Quirrel!'

Still nothing.

Logan punched Tufty's shoulder number into the Airwave handset. 'Where the hell are you?'

His own voice crackled out of the darkness, somewhere to the right. *'Where the hell are you?'*

'Tufty?' Logan shifted his grip on his baton, clicked his torch on again.

A rusty van sat at the kerb, the company name faded to a shadow on the dented bodywork.

He picked his way forwards, baton resting back against his shoulder, ready to swing. Pressed the talk button again. 'Are you OK?'

'Are you OK?'

Definitely coming from behind the van.

Logan lunged around the corner. 'POLICE! NOBODY . . .'

Tufty was face down on the pavement, one arm twisted at his side, the other dangling over the kerb.

CHAPTER 54

'Shire Uniform Seven, I need backup to Banff harbour *now*. Officer down.' He knelt beside the crumpled body.

The back of Tufty's head glistened with dark red, matting his hair.

Logan grabbed his shoulder and shook. 'Tufty? You OK?'

Don't be dead. Don't be—

'Unngh . . .' Tufty raised his forehead off the pavement. 'Ow . . .'

Joe's voice boomed from the Airwave, crackling and panting, as if he was running. *'Roger that, Shire Uniform Seven, Penny and me are on our way. Is he OK?'*

'What happened?'

'My head . . .'

'It's still there. Luckily, you're all skull and no brain. Can you stand?'

'Shire Uniform Seven, from Control. Do you need an ambulance?'

'ASAP. We've got an officer with a head wound.'

'Ow . . .'

Logan helped him to his knees.

Then Tufty wobbled a bit and slumped back against the rusty van, sitting on the pavement, one hand probing the sticky mess of matted hair. When he pulled the fingers away, they were slick with blood. 'Ow . . .'

'Which way did he go?'

'Can you hear that? Sounds like sirens?'

Corrugated metal groaned and rattled in the wind. Rain clicked and pattered against the van. No sirens. But they'd be here soon enough.

'You had a thump on the head, but you're going to be OK. Now, *which way did he go?*'

Tufty prodded at the back of his skull again. Winced. 'Came out . . .' His eyebrows furrowed. 'That way?' A blood-sticky finger came up and wobbled in the direction of the Macduff Shipyards warehouse, where the dry docks marked the inner-most end of the harbour, furthest away from the exit out into the sea. And right now the security lights were blazing on the closest side of the ware-house.

Got you.

'Stay here.' Logan sprinted across the road and through the car park. His peaked cap flipped up and over in the wind, abandoning his head. Sod it. He could find it later.

The smell of diesel and iron grew with every thumping step, bringing with it the acidic reek of long-dead fish. Past the shipyard warehouse . . .

Where now?

'Shire Uniform Seven, ambulance is on its way.'

695

A pair of large fishing boats were propped up in the dry docks, their curved hulls scraped back to the metal beneath. They towered up on either side of the slipway down into the inky water.

Where the hell was he?

There – on the other side of the slipway, not running back towards town, but out along the harbour wall.

'COME BACK HERE!' As if that ever worked.

Logan ran to the dry dock's edge, scrambled down the ladder built into the concrete wall. Water lapped halfway up the slipway. He sploshed through it, picking his way over the weed-slicked surface. Cold and damp leached through his boots. Up the ladder on the other side.

The harbour curved around the edge of the town, a narrow strip of water less than two hundred feet wide in most places, fishing boats packed in nose-to-keel along both sides.

Somewhere behind him, the pained wail of a siren battered its way through the wind.

Keep going.

He lurched into a run again, socks squelching in his sodden boots. The North Sea battered against the sea wall, sending up jagged plumes of spray that smelled of salt and seaweed.

They crashed down onto the harbour's outer arm, making the concrete glisten in the light of swaying lampposts. Jabbed and stabbed at Logan's face and high-vis jacket. Soaked through his trousers.

Might as well jump in the sodding water, probably be drier than this.

Up ahead, the lights flickered on in one of the fishing boats rocking at the quayside.

Little sod was *not* getting away.

A figure clambered back onto the harbour side, by the boat, caught in the glow of its lights. Bent over, removing the lines tying it to its moorings. Then he jumped back onto the deck.

Closer. Come on. Only two boat-lengths to go . . .

A gurgling roar and the fishing boat pulled away.

Oh no you don't.

Logan picked up the pace, feet slapping against the spray-soaked concrete.

Jump it. Couldn't be more than six feet. Then eight. Then ten.

Even with the waves hammering the harbour wall on the seaward side, the water on this side was still and black. The fishing boat surged forwards, engine making a burbling roar, leaving a wake of churned white behind it.

Twelve feet.

Yeah, sod that.

He scrabbled to a halt on the lip of the harbour side, arms windmilling. 'YOU! TURN THAT BOAT AROUND NOW!'

The figure in the wheelhouse turned and stared at him. A leathery face, stretched in a grimace above waterproofs, greying hair hanging damp across his forehead.

Dear God: it was Charles 'Craggie' Anderson.
'YOU'RE SUPPOSED TO BE DEAD!'

The engine changed tone, dropping in pitch and ferocity. Coming to a halt, instead of forging away. 'PEERIE WULLIE'S RANT' was painted along the bow in red letters, over a thick white stripe that circled the hull. Charles Anderson opened the wheelroom window, picked up a radio handset – stretching the loops out of the coil of wire – and thumbed a button. His voice crackled out from the boat's PA system. *'I am* dead.*'*

Logan made a loud hailer out of his hands. 'WHO WAS IT IN THE BOAT, UP IN ORKNEY? IT WASN'T YOU BURNED TO DEATH.'

'Someone who deserved to die. He liked to play with little boys.'

'AND YOU KILLED HIM.'

'You let him go. You could've kept him in prison for ever, but you let him go. You let him run free, abusing children!'

'I DIDN'T, IT'S . . .' The boat wasn't holding position any more, it was edging forward, towards the next section of the harbour. Towards the exit. 'COME BACK AND WE CAN TALK ABOUT IT.'

No reply.

A stack of ancient lobster creels were piled at the foot of a flight of steps up onto the sea wall. Logan pulled out a Police Scotland business card and scrawled his mobile number on the back.

Stuck it in one of the creels. Then took a run and flung the thing out over the harbour side.

It twirled through the air, crossing twenty foot of inky water, then crashed down on the deck of the fishing boat. Slid back against the wheelhouse and jammed beneath a railing. 'MY NUMBER'S IN THERE. CALL ME AND WE CAN SORT SOMETHING OUT!'

But Charles Anderson stayed at the controls. '*Neil Wood was hanging about the Community Centre. He was following schoolboys into the changing rooms and giving them money to let him touch them. Not years ago,* two weeks *ago.*'

Logan kept pace with the boat. 'WHY DIDN'T YOU TELL ANYONE? WE COULD'VE DONE SOMETHING!'

'*I didn't know, till just before he died. Sometimes it takes a while for people like him to tell the truth.*'

The boat slipped through the bottleneck by the old fish market building. From here the harbour opened out, twisting around to the right, before narrowing one final time, then it was a straight run out to the sea. But Anderson kept *Peerie Wullie's Rant* twenty feet from the harbour wall where Logan was. Close enough to shout, but too far to jump.

'DON'T DO THIS. COME BACK AND WE CAN TALK ABOUT IT. WE DON'T—'

'*He told me about the Livestock Mart. He told me about what they were doing. Him and his nasty little ring. Told me about the little girl they'd bought to share.*'

Little girl. The one they'd found floating face-down in Tarlair Outdoor Swimming Pool. The one on the board in Charles Anderson's garage, connected by a red ribbon to Dr Gilcomston.

'It was Neil Wood's "turn".' The word came out as if it tasted of sick. *'He didn't even like little girls. I tried to save her. I couldn't. I tried, but I was too late.'*

On the other side of the harbour, an ambulance raced along Shore Street, lights flashing, siren wailing. It disappeared behind the fishing boat for a heartbeat, then screamed past. Siren dopplering away.

'IF YOU'VE GOT EVIDENCE, I CAN—'

'William Gilcomston, Neil Wood, Mark Brussels, and Liam Barden bought a little girl to share from the Livestock Mart. I know, because Liam Barden screamed their names before he died. Think they'd let you have a warrant based on that?'

Logan's Airwave gave its four point-to-point beeps. *'Shire Uniform Seven, ambulance is on scene now.'*

'WE CAN ARREST THEM. WE CAN SEARCH THEIR HOMES AND FIND SOMETHING CONNECTING THEM TO THE LITTLE GIRL: DNA, FIBRES—'

'They're not that stupid. The law isn't justice, it's the law. You lock them up and then you let them out and they never change.'

The boat accelerated, making for the narrowest part of the harbour. Definitely be able to jump on board there. Wouldn't be more than six or seven feet between the deck and the wall.

But the boat would be through, long before he got there.

Damn it.

Anderson stepped out of the wheelhouse and picked up the lobster creel. Turned it over in his hands as the fishing boat puttered towards the exit.

'CALL THE NUMBER!'

He stepped back inside the wheelhouse. Closed the door.

Another wave pounded against the sea wall, showering Logan with a spray of frigid brine.

'YOU CAN'T GO OUT THERE, THE SEA'S TOO ROUGH.'

'You never arrested Liam Barden. He was at it for years. Boys, girls: didn't matter to him.' The boat slipped through the narrow point. *'You know what else he told me before he died? He told me about Andrew. He told me about how he and Neil Wood shared my son.'*

Logan jogged to a halt. This was it, there was nothing between Charles Anderson and the raging sea. The fishing boat's bow reared in the swell as it lined up to exit the harbour. Last chance to jump on board and arrest him.

OK. Can do this. Bit of a run-up . . .

'Don't be an idiot. You'll miss: you'll get crushed between the hull and the harbour wall. Or you'll drown.'

Dragged down by a stone of stabproof vest and equipment belt.

701

'GIVE IT UP. I'LL CALL THE COASTGUARD AND THEY'LL CATCH YOU AND BRING YOU BACK ANYWAY.'

'No they won't. You said it: the sea's too rough.'

'THEN DON'T BE A BLOODY FOOL!'

'I've got work to do.'

God's sake.

Wind slammed a massive fist into him, and Logan lurched a pace to the left.

'PLEASE: CALL THE NUMBER!'

But the engine changed tone again, deepened to a dark diesel growl, and *Peerie Wullie's Rant* surged out into the crushing embrace of the North Sea. The bow bucked and reared through a twisted corkscrew path, propellers hammering the boat forward into the waves.

More sirens.

Logan turned.

A patrol car sped along Shore Street, its blue-and-whites making the hotels and shops flicker as it sped past.

At least Tufty would be—

Logan's phone rang in his pocket. He dragged it out. 'Hello?'

Charles Anderson. *'You're the only one knows I'm alive.'*

'Turn the boat around and come back.'

'If they come looking for me, I can't do what I need to do.'

'What you need to do is come back here before you kill yourself.'

702

'*So you can stick me in prison for the rest of my life? Don't think so.*'

Logan clambered up a set of steps, to the parapet running around the top of the sea wall. *Peerie Wullie's Rant* was getting smaller, surging up the face of the waves, then crashing down the other side in a plume of spray. 'You killed Neil Wood and Liam Barden.'

'*This why you joined the police? To let child molesters walk free?*'

'Of course I didn't. It—'

'*Child killers?*'

'Charles . . . Craggie, we're not allowed to play God, OK? We've got laws and rules and—'

'*Some people don't deserve the law. I find one of them, and I make sure he tells me everything I need to know. Then I move on to the next one.*'

'That's not justice, it's a witch hunt. You need to come back.'

A wave boomed against the sea wall, sending up a stinging explosion of salt water.

Logan hunched his shoulders, turned his face away as it crashed down around him.

'*Is your friend OK? I'm sorry I had to hit him, I really am.*'

He wiped the sea from his eyes. 'You have to stop this.'

'*Sorry I had to hit you too. Didn't really leave me any choice though, did you? Can't do what I need to from a prison cell.*'

'You didn't have to burn the house down.'

'I'm dead, I don't need a house. I died a long time ago.'

Peerie Wullie's Rant grew dimmer, the growl of its engines torn away by the wind. Its shape swallowed by the night.

'*They snatched Andrew, because he was there. Wasn't planned. Liam Barden saw him playing in the field by the cliff and told Neil Wood to stop the car. They got out. And abducted my son.*'

Cold spray whipped across the wall, rocking Logan back on his feet. 'I'm sorry.'

The only sign of the boat now was its running lights, fading away into the storm.

'*They used him for two days, then they strangled him so he wouldn't tell anyone. He was four. Nicest wee boy you could ever meet, and they killed him so no one would find out what they'd done.*'

'You can't just go around murdering paedophiles. An eye-for-an-eye is *not* how this works.'

'*And if I don't do it, who will? You can't even question them without their lawyer sitting there, telling them to lie. The whole system's rigged so the guilty get every chance their victims didn't.*'

Couldn't really argue with that. Not after what happened with Graham Stirling.

Logan puffed out a breath. 'What was her name? The little girl they bought?'

'*Wood didn't know. Neither did Barden. They said Gilcomston called her "Cherry", don't know if it was shorrrrrrrtttt . . . ing . . . Maybe it . . . be . . . better place if . . . innnnnnn . . . never.*'

'Hello?'

'. . . *if you tellllllll . . . won't . . . too imporrrrrrtant . . . ffffff . . . shhhhhhhh . . .*'

Then static.

Then silence.

The boat was out of range of the masts.

Couldn't even see its lights now. There was nothing but darkness and waves.

Logan turned his back and picked his way down the stairs. Wiped his mobile on the leg of his trousers and slipped it in his pocket.

Penny's voice clattered out of the Airwave. '*Shire Uniform Seven. Sarge? We've got Constable Quirrel. Where are you?*'

'How's Tufty?'

'*Think he might have a touch of concussion, but he's fine otherwise. They're playing it safe and taking him in for an X-ray, though.*'

'Good. I'm out by the harbour exit and I'm soaked. Do me a favour: come get me?'

CHAPTER 55

Logan dripped on the Inspector's carpet. The drops made little patting noises when they hit. 'The hospital rushed through an X-ray of his head, and apparently there *is* a brain in there.'

'Hmm . . .' Inspector Fettes swivelled in the chair for a bit, setting his mop of ginger hair shoogling like a badly fitted wig. He'd cleared some space on the desk for a framed photo of a spaniel. Other than that, it was just the way Inspector McGregor left it when she headed off at the end of the dayshift. Well, except for the nippy smell of menthol coming from Fettes every time he opened his mouth. The words sounded as if they were squeezing themselves individually down his red nose. 'And do we have any idea who did it?'

Right . . .

Logan stared at the wet patch, seeping into the carpet. What was he supposed to do, let Charles Anderson get away with two murders, assaulting two police officers, and the possible theft of a boat? Let him run free to punish child molesters? To get justice when the courts let them walk?

All those years, Liam Barden was doing the most horrific things to children, and the police never got anywhere near him. And if it wasn't for Charles Anderson, he'd still be doing it.

'Logan?'

Blink.

'Sorry, Guv. It was dark. Whoever it was hit Tufty from behind then ran off. I went after them, but . . .' It wasn't too late to pull this back. Stop this right here. Cover for Anderson, and it'd be perverting the course of justice, and culpability in any other murders he committed.

Was that really such a great idea?

Of course it wasn't. He shrugged and dripped some more. 'It was Charles Anderson.'

The Inspector frowned. 'But he's *dead*.'

'Not so much. I think the body they found in the boat is what's left of Neil Wood.'

'Wonderful.' A sigh. 'At least that would mean we could stop looking for Wood. Doubt there's enough left to run DNA on, but we can give it a try. And get the IB up – let's see if they can get some fingerprints off the chandler's warehouse.'

'I'll set up a lookout request on the boat he was using.'

'Might get lucky. Still—'

Logan's Airwave gave its point-to-point bleeps. *'Shire Uniform Seven, safe to talk?'*

He pointed at it. 'Is it OK if I . . .?'

The Inspector waved a hand. 'No skin off mine.'

Logan pressed the button and talked into his shoulder. 'Bash away.'

'Aye, you wanted to know when Kirstin Rattray woke up? That's her now.'

'She say anything about who attacked her?'

'Nah. I've seen headstones more talkative. You want to have a shot?'

He let go of the button. 'Guv?'

'Might as well. Not as if there's anything else we can do tonight anyway.'

Logan abandoned the Big Car in someone's reserved parking space and jogged back through the drizzle towards Accident and Emergency. Forty-five minutes: not bad from Banff to Elgin. Only had to use the blues-and-twos twice as well.

The town's lights reflected back from the heavy lid of cloud, casting a sickly burnt-orange glow across the hospital's bland grey façade. A handful of smokers choked the entrance to A & E, keeping out of the rain. Shuffling feet and fidgeting fingers, the streams of their cigarettes glowing in the harsh lighting.

He squeezed past into the depressing antiseptic blandness of the waiting area.

A nurse shuffled by in a pair of pink Crocs, clipboard clutched tightly to his chest as if it was the only thing keeping him upright.

Logan stepped in front of him. 'I'm looking for Kirstin Rattray.'

The nurse blinked at him. Grey-purple skin filled

708

the hollows beneath his eyes. A yawn shuddered its way through him, leaving him slumped around his clipboard. 'Sorry. Been a long shift. Who?'

'Kirstin Rattray, assaulted earlier today. Cracked skull, broken ribs, arms, leg . . .?'

'Yes. Right. Let's check the computer.'

The nurse stopped in the corridor and gave his clipboard another squeeze. 'I can only give you a couple of minutes. She's been through a lot.'

'I'll be quick.' Logan pushed through the door into the ward.

The room was caught in the dim glow of a reading light in the far corner. Eight beds, four to a side, but only three were occupied. One by an obese teenager, flat on her back and snoring. One by the old lady in the corner reading what looked like a trashy crime novel. And one by Kirstin Rattray.

Her face was a mess of plasters and patches of gauze. One arm propped up on a stick and plastered from fingers to armpit, the other in a sling across her chest. A boxy contraption made a square hump in the blankets where her right knee should have been. Tubes going in from drips, others going out to bags dangling under the bedframe.

Logan drew in a breath. It tasted of disinfectant and pain and despair. 'Is she . . .?'

The nurse dropped his voice to a whisper. 'You wouldn't *believe* how much morphine they gave her, and it barely touched the sides. No one wants to OD a patient by accident.'

Logan pulled up a chair, then slipped the elastic band off his BWV and set it recording. 'Kirstin? Can you hear me?'

The fingers poking out from the full-length cast twitched. Then her head turned. One eye taped shut, the other a mess of burst blood vessels. Kirstin's skin was an inkblot mess of darkening bruises. 'Hrrrts.' Her mouth barely moved.

'I know. I'm sorry.'

'Oiiiwwnt mmey Ammgheee . . .'

Oiiiwwnt mmey Ammgheee . . .? Then it dawned. 'You want Amy? Your daughter? I think they'd like you to get a bit better before they bring her to see you.' Logan forced a smile. 'Don't want to scare her.'

A little shake of the head. Then a wince. 'Dnnnnt lt thmmm tk hrrrrr awwwweyyyy.'

'Do you know who did it?'

'Hrrrts.'

No wonder.

Logan's hand went into one of the zippy pockets on his stabproof vest. The one where the tiny plastic baggie he'd confiscated from her was. A single wrap of heroin, concealed in an inside-out blue nitrile glove. That'd make a dent in Kirstin's pain.

Of course it could react really badly with whatever else they'd given her. And then she wouldn't hurt any more, she'd be dead.

710

Stupid idea.

Logan let go of the glove, left it where it was.

'I'll let your mum and dad know you're in here. They can arrange for Amy to come visit.'

The bloodshot eye squeezed shut, forcing out a couple of tears. She pulled her lips back, but there weren't any teeth to bare, just swollen gums spidered with stitches.

'I'm sorry.' Logan put a hand on Kirstin's shoulder. 'Who did this to you?'

The nurse's Crocs squeaked on the ward floor. 'Look, I think she's probably had enough. She's tired. She needs to—'

'Frrnnnkeee Frrrrs.'

Logan frowned. 'Who?'

'Look, I'm really going to have to insist.'

Her whole face clenched with the effort. 'Frrnnkeee *Frrrrrrrrrrs!*'

Logan took out his notebook and . . . Sodding Hector. He turned to the nurse. 'Can I borrow a pen?'

'This isn't—'

'She wants to ID the person who tried to kill her with a crowbar, OK? Now give me your pen.'

A pause, then a chewed blue biro was produced.

Logan held it out to Kirstin and she reached for it with the fingers of her other hand – the one poking out of the sling. Clutched it against the strip of fibreglass cast across her palm. Then picked out the name in painful wobbling capitals:

'FRANKIE FERRIS' and underlined it twice, before slumping back into the pillows, panting.

Logan held the notepad up so the BWV could capture what she'd written. 'You're saying Frankie Ferris attacked you?'

A nod. A gulping breath.

'And you're *sure* it was him?'

A pause. Then another nod.

Which meant Frankie Ferris was about to get his door battered in.

And if he resisted arrest and fell down the stairs a couple of times, that would be a bonus.

Dark fields flickered past the Big Car's windows, caught for a brief moment in the flashing lights, then disappearing into the night again.

Logan changed up and kept his foot down.

The headlights made glittering streaks on the wet road as the windscreen wipers *thunk-wonk*ed back and forth across the glass.

Logan pressed the talk button on the steering wheel. 'I'm about fifteen minutes away. No one moves till I get there, understood?'

Penny's voice crackled out of the speaker. '*Yup – we block both ends of the street and we wait for you. What about a warrant?*'

'Next on my list.'

The Big Car swept around a long bend, engine roaring.

He hit the button again. 'Shire Uniform Seven to Bravo India, safe to talk?'

'Go ahead.' Inspector Fettes paused for a sneeze. 'Urgh . . . Sorry about that. How's Kirstin Rattray?'

'Lucky to be alive. She's ID'd Frankie Ferris as the assailant. I'm on my way back to Banff now. I applied for a warrant to search his place yesterday, any chance you can light a fire under Sheriff Harding? He's dragging his heels and I need to—'

'Ah. Actually . . .' A cough. 'Logan, there's a reason Harding's not issued your warrant. He already gave a search-and-arrest one to DI Porter.'

'Porter?'

'Operation Troposphere dunted Frankie Ferris's door in half an hour ago.'

'Are you kidding me!'

'They've netted about eighty grand's worth of heroin, and another sixty of cocaine. Three bricks of resin, a big box of temazepam, and about thirty thousand in cash.'

'He was my suspect! I've been after him for months.'

'Well, yes, but look on the bright side: that's a substantial amount of drugs that are never going to hit our streets. You've got to be pleased about that.'

'Sodding months!'

Brilliant. Thank you DI Porter, DCI McInnes, and Operation Bloody Troposphere. Bunch of scumbag MIT tossers. Frankie Ferris was his. His pet project. His drug dealer. And McInnes waltzes in and wheechs him away, right from under Logan's nose. Not so much as a thank you.

It was his case in the first place, too.

Logan jabbed his thumb against the 'Blues' button on the central console and the strobing lights flickered out. No point hurrying now.

Rundle Avenue was blocked off. Three patrol cars, two unmarked CID Vauxhalls, Syd Fraser's dog van, and an OMU Transit with its riot grille up and its side door open. Logan parked in front of the cordon of blue-and-white 'Police' tape.

His dunt. His arrest. His bloody suspect.

Half the houses in the street had their lights on. Probably standing there with their mobile phones out, filming everything for posterity and YouTube.

He grabbed his peaked cap and climbed out into the rain.

Sergeant Mitchell waved from the open door of the Operational Support Unit van. Then held up a thermos. 'Dear God, do they issue every bunnet up here with tea-detecting radar? Haven't even opened it yet.'

Logan stood outside, water drumming on his high-vis shoulders, bouncing off his black-and-white cap. 'This is the thing you were doing, isn't it? Why you couldn't come on my dunt.'

'Bit of a result. Found heaps of gear under the floorboards in the bedroom. Like an Aladdin's cave for druggies.' He screwed the top off the thermos and poured a measure into a mug with 'World's Best Door-Kicker-In' on it. 'Shame you missed the dunt, though.' A grin. 'They let us use the chainsaw.'

'Glad someone's having a good night.' Logan turned his back and marched up the path to Frankie Ferris's house.

A uniformed PC slouched on the threshold, sheltering from the rain. He stood up straight. 'Sergeant.' Wasn't a local lad – definitely not from B Division. Probably a big-city boy up from Aberdeen. Big ears, small forehead, thick furry hair.

The outer edges of the door framed him like a particularly unattractive picture, its UPVC ragged where the chainsaw had ripped through it.

Logan gave him a nod. 'Your guvnor about?'

'DI Porter? Yeah.' He didn't move. Then it must have dawned on him. 'Oh, right. I'll shout her.' He turned, still blocking the entrance, and bellowed back into the house. 'Boss? There's a sergeant here to see you. Want me to let him in?'

Rain soaked through the collar of Logan's high-vis jacket.

PC Ugly pulled a face. 'Maybe she's in the bog?'

Then feet thumped down the stairs and a short woman in a grey suit appeared. Carefully manicured haircut. Shiny boots.

PC Ugly scrambled out of the way, without being asked, and Porter took his place. Looked Logan up and down. 'Well, you've saved me a phone call at least. Come to confess, have we?'

Logan tightened his hands into fists. 'You arrested Frankie Ferris.'

'Did you come all this way to stand in the rain and tell me things I already know? Or, let me

715

guess, are you here to stick your nose into my investigation instead?'

'He assaulted Kirstin Rattray earlier today, tried to batter her to death with a crowbar and left her for dead in a lay-by.'

'I know. You phoned me, remember?' Porter raised an eyebrow. 'Has your Kirstin Rattray ID'd him?'

Logan tapped his BWV unit. 'Did it on camera.'

'Well, we'll follow it up.' The rain continued to fall. 'Now, are you deaf, Sergeant, or just stupid? You were told time and time again to stay the hell away from Operation Troposphere, but you couldn't do it, could you?'

'I stayed away. I've *been* staying away.'

'Really? Then tell me, Sergeant McRae, when I dunted in Frankie Ferris's door, why did I find this?' She turned and nodded at PC Ugly. 'Bring the smelly one out.'

Smelly one?

PC Ugly reappeared with a dishevelled stick-figure in a manky tracksuit. Both hands were cuffed together in front. Stinky Sammy Wilson. Oh God . . .

Sammy sniffed, wiped his nose on a grimy sleeve. 'See? I told you, yeah? Told you. I'm like, on police business. Totally official.'

Porter's smile didn't look all that genuine. 'Well, Sergeant? Care to enlighten us how getting drug addicts to poke about in my investigation is "staying away"?'

'I told him not to! I told him it was over. Sammy, tell her – I told you to drop it.'

Sammy shook his head, setting his greasy hair swishing. 'I'm here undercover, yeah? Doing my bit. Asking questions for ten quid, questions for ten quid, questions, questions, questions.' Another sniff. Then he stared at Logan. 'You got my three seventy-seven, yeah? I found out for you – I found out who the Candleman is.'

'THERE ISN'T ANY CANDLEMAN!' Two steps away, then back again. Staring at DI Porter, but jabbing a finger at Sammy Wilson. 'I told him to quit it! He was outside the station and I told him to stay the *hell* away from this thing.'

'And yet, here we are.' She folded her arms. 'Anything else?'

He bit the inside of his cheek. Calm it down. Unclenched his fists. 'Do you know if your team's finished at Klingon's house yet?'

'Let me guess: his mum's been moaning about not being allowed home yet?'

'Something like that.'

A shrug. 'She can have it back any time she wants. Not a crime scene any more – we're focusing our efforts here on Rundle Avenue now.'

'Good.' He turned to go.

'Sergeant?'

Logan stopped. What now, more gloating?

DI Porter's voice softened. 'We're charging Colin Spinney and Kevin McEwan with the attempted murder of Jack Simpson. They're not

717

getting away with anything. Thought you'd like to know.'

Probably wouldn't make much difference to Klingon and Gerbil's sentences, but at least it was something.

And the day had started so well . . .

CHAPTER 56

'**Y**ou woke me up to tell me that?' A cough rattled down the phone. '*Urgh . . .*'

Logan stepped out into the rain and clunked the station door shut behind him. 'Thought you'd still be up watching porn.'

The streetlights made sickly yellow spheres in the downpour as he hurried across the street.

'*What you want me to do, pat you on the head and say, "There, there, poor Logan. Aunty Roberta kiss it all better"?*'

Down the steps to the car park – taking the quickest route to the Sergeant's Hoose. 'It was my case.'

'*You're no' six, Laz. For God's sake, grow a pair. If you flounce off in a huff every time some Major Investigation Team swoops in and takes over your case, you think anyone's going to care? This is how it works now.*'

He dragged in a deep breath, then huffed it out again. Hurrying between the puddles. 'I've been working on nailing Frankie Ferris for months.'

'*I'm going back to sleep now.*'

'Thanks for the sympathy.'

'*Laz, if you don't like MITs nicking your cases,*'

come back and work for me. *Be the nicker, not the nickee. Either way, stop whingeing.'*

'I'm not "whingeing", I'm getting screwed over. How is that "whingeing"?'

Nothing.

'Hello?'

She'd hung up on him. Lovely.

Across the road, around the corner. Water over-flowed the weed-blocked gutters, cascading down the side of the house. Yet another thing to stick on the to-do list.

He let himself in.

Darkness. No sound of television. No creak of floorboards.

Not really surprising at quarter to two on a Tuesday morning – Helen would be asleep – but it would've been nice.

A pair of eyes glittered at the top of the stairs, then *thump-poc, thump-poc, thump-poc,* and Cthulhu worked her way down. Wound herself around his ankles, purring. He bent down and picked her up. Soft and warm and fuzzy.

'Daddy's had a crappy day.'

He carried her back upstairs. Popped her down on the landing. Eased open the bedroom door. 'Helen?'

Grimy orange light spilled in through the window and onto the bed. Curtains weren't closed. And the bed was empty, still made from that morning.

Maybe she wanted to sleep on her own tonight?

Had he done something?

Back downstairs.

His knuckles made a dull thunk on the living-room door. 'Helen?'

Idiot. What was the point of whispering?

Knock again. Louder. 'Helen, you awake?'

Silence.

Maybe she'd been drinking again and passed out on the couch?

He opened the door. But there was no one there.

Kitchen.

Empty.

An envelope sat in the middle of the table, birthday-card sized, with 'LOGAN' written on the front. He tore the flap open.

Wasn't a birthday card after all, it was a thank-you one. A photo of a kitten wearing a jumper and John Lennon glasses looked out at him. The message inside was written in neat blue biro:

Dear Logan,

They've arrested a traveller family in Gwent and taken a little girl into care. They're all dark haired, but she's blonde. She's six. It might be Natasha.

Thank you so much for letting me stay with you. It's been a long time since I've let anyone get that close. And I'm sorry about the washing up.

Love,

Helen x

Brilliant. That was really sodding brilliant.

He pulled out his phone. Glared at the card.

Not even a goodbye.

Logan scrolled through his contacts. Found her number . . .

No.

He swiped down to Syd Fraser's details instead. Hit dial.

— TUESDAY EARLYSHIFT —

BREATHE.

CHAPTER 57

Syd Fraser wiped the sheen of sweat from his face. Leaned on his shovel. 'You know, when I said we should go grave-robbing, I didn't mean it literally.'

'Shouldn't have said it then.' Logan dug the blade of his spade into the turf and heaved. The grass roots crackled as they tore, letting out the rich dark smell of the soil beneath.

'It was more an expression of moral support.'

'I'd feel more supported if you were actually digging right now.'

Early morning sun dappled the back gardens of Fairholme Place, drying up yesterday's rain.

'All units, be advised that the lookout request on Ronnie Bronowski is cancelled. Found safe and well by his dad.'

Syd hacked out another patch of turf. 'Be easier if we didn't have to wear black the whole time.'

They'd staked out the corners of the lush patch of weeds and grass in Klingon's back garden.

'Told you, you could put on an SOC suit if you liked. They're white.'

'Yeah, and like wearing your very own sauna. No thank you.'

Another chunk of sod joined the pile. 'Moan, moan, moan.'

At least they were getting somewhere now.

'Shire Uniform Seven, safe to talk?'

Logan heaved the last chunk of green out of the plot. Pressed the button. 'Bang on, Calamity.'

'Me and Deano have been round Portsoy. Break-ins all look like they're done by one person. Even left us some fingerprints.'

'Good. Get them off to the lab, then see if you can't get hold of whoever's monitoring Mark Brussels and William Gilcomston. Both sex offenders.'

'Anything in particular you want to know?'

'Everything.'

'Sarge.'

Syd heaved out a lump of thick black soil. 'Course, you know this might be a complete waste of time?'

'Don't you start. Was hard enough convincing the Duty Inspector to let us have a bash.'

Dig. Dig. Dig.

'Look on the bright side, Sarge. Worst comes to worst, Klingon's mum gets a lovely tatty patch dug for her.'

They worked in silence for a bit, except for the occasional grunt and hiss.

Nearly a foot down now.

Syd stepped into the hole. 'If it *is* a dead body, who do you think it is?'

'Don't know. Toby Neish, maybe? He went missing about five months ago.'

Dig. Dig. Dig.

'How's Tufty's head today?'

'Every bit as empty as it was yesterday. Got two complaints from the hospital about him offering to show the nurses his "extendable baton".' Another shovel full of dirt.

Little chips of stone were appearing in the soil now. Like someone had dumped a bag of gravel.

Dig. Dig. Dig.

'Should've brought some tins of coke or something . . . Parched.'

Dig. Dig. *Thunk*.

Syd raised an eyebrow. 'Aye, aye. We have touchdown.' He poked his shovel into the earth again. *Thunk*. Then over a bit. *Thunk*. A big smile. 'Told you: best dogs in the country.'

They scraped the soil back. It was a wooden box, not quite as big as a coffin. But that didn't really matter if you weren't interested in the dear departed's comfort or dignity.

'What do you think, Sarge? Do we open it and risk contaminating anything, or leave it and call for backup?'

'Doesn't smell like a dead body.'

'Wouldn't if it was old enough. Everything would rot away.'

'Then how did Lusso smell it?' He dunked his spade off the lid a couple of times. 'We open it.' Logan climbed out of the hole and rummaged through the holdall from the Big Car's boot. Came out with the hoolie bar. 'This'll do it.'

He wedged the curved blade of metal from the pick-end into the wood where the lid joined the box. Leaned all his weight on the prongs. Nothing. OK, shoogle it about a bit. Then more pressure . . .

First a small pop, then a splintering crackle, and *thunk*: the lid sprung open at one corner. No sudden waft of rotting meat. Didn't take long to work the hoolie-bar's adze along the gap, levering out the groaning nails.

'Right, let's see what we've got.'

They pulled the lid free and propped it up against the fence.

Syd pursed his lips. Sooked in a breath. Then whistled.

Logan nodded. 'Looks like Lusso's not the best cadaver dog in the world after all.' But he *was* damn good at finding firearms and explosives. The box contained about a dozen rifles, four sawn-off shotguns, cardboard boxes of bullets and shells, and three semi-automatic pistols. 'Think they were planning to start a war?'

'Yes, well . . .' DI Porter clicked her head to the side. It pulled the hair out of her eyes, but left the bags under them. One hand came up to scratch at the mole on her cheek. 'Perhaps, in hindsight, we were a little hasty in declaring this no longer a crime scene.'

Logan raised an eyebrow. 'You don't say.'

She leaned back against the stained wallpaper

in Klingon's kitchen, watching as anonymous white-oversuited figures catalogued the contents of the gun coffin. 'Far as we can tell, they wanted to set up an American-style drug cartel here in Banff. Bring the stuff in on boats and shoot anyone who got in their way. Witnesses, rival drug dealers, police officers.'

'Pair of idiots.'

'Quite.' DI Porter tore her eyes away from the kitchen window long enough for a brief glance in Logan's direction. 'DCI McInnes thanks you for your input.'

'I'll bet he does.'

Pink flushed the tips of her ears. 'Don't push it, Sergeant. I'm still trying to talk him out of going after you with the career chainsaw. That thing with Sammy Wilson was . . .' A deep breath. 'What were you *thinking*?'

'Honestly: I told him to stop it. I really did.'

'This whole thing's been a cocking mess from the start.' She blew out a breath. 'Right, we'll take it from here.'

Logan turned and made for the kitchen door.

'And Sergeant?'

He stopped on the threshold. 'Ma'am?'

'Try to keep out of McInnes's way for a bit. Three or four years should do it.'

Syd was leaning back against his Dog Unit Transit van. Basking in a wedge of golden light. The sky was swaddled in thick purple clouds, overlaid by wisps of battleship grey, but right now

729

the sun was shining on Klingon's house. Syd lowered his face, held a hand above his eyes in a makeshift visor. 'We good?'

'Difficult to tell.' Logan clunked open the passenger door and climbed into a solid block of Labrador stink. 'Back to the station, young man, where we shall be fêted with tea and biscuits. If I can find any planked in the canteen.' He belted himself in and pulled out his Airwave. 'Shire Uniform Seven, safe to talk?'

Nicholson's voice came through the speaker. *'Go ahead, Sarge.'*

'That's us finished up at Klingon's. How are you getting on with those names?'

Syd pulled away from the kerb, did a quick three-point turn, and headed back towards the centre of town.

'Mark Brussels. Serial sex offender, assaulted at least twenty-three boys and girls over a decade, not one of them older than eight. Spent sixteen years in various prisons up and down the country. Kept getting targeted, so they kept moving him on. Someone in Shotts pinned him down and carved the names of every one of Brussels's victims into his skin with a sharpened spoon. Brussels's skin, not his own. Apparently it took three hours. Nearly died from shock and blood loss.'

'Supervision?'

'On the register for life, but he's been scoring consistently low on the ACUTE-2007 guide for a couple of years, so they've cut back his supervision.'

'No hint of anything?'

730

'His case officer says they wouldn't have cut it back if there was.'

Fair enough. 'What about Gilcomston?'

'Dr William Harris Gilcomston, no longer allowed to practise medicine, or come within three hundred yards of a school. Did eight years in Peterhead for assaulting wee girls in his surgery. Lots of very detailed, very unnecessary examinations. Youngest was four, oldest was nine. That one jumped off the Union Terrace Bridge on the eve of her tenth birthday. He'd been molesting her for five years by then.'

Houses drifted by the van's windows.

A rainbow reached from the bridge over the Deveron, up past Macduff and disappeared into the bruise-coloured clouds.

'Hello? Calamity, you still there?'

'Sorry, Sarge. It's just . . . people like Gilcomston and Brussels, you know?'

'What about his supervision?'

'Every week. He's still denying he did anything wrong, won't take responsibility for his actions, he's hostile to his case workers, claims he's being victimized.'

'You'd think he'd have learned to play the game by now.'

'Some people think they're untouchable.'

And then along comes Charles Anderson.

'OK, thanks.' He twisted his handset back into place.

Of course, in the good old days, they'd haul Gilcomston and Brussels in. Stick them in a couple of cells and grill them for a bit. See who cracked first. But that wasn't exactly legal any more. Hard to burst someone with a lawyer sitting there advising them to no-comment everything.

Didn't even have any grounds to arrest them.

Yes, Milord, we'd like a warrant. Why? Well, a man we thought was dead told me the accused had chipped in with two other paedophiles to buy a little girl they could share. Only those other paedophiles are now dead. What's that: you're calling security? I'm suspended? Oh dear . . .

'. . . there all day?'

'Hmm?' Logan frowned.

Syd was looking at him, as if he was expecting an answer.

'Er . . . In what way?'

'What way do you think? We're here. Now are you getting out or not?'

Ah, right. 'We're celebrating catching the Cashline Ram-Raiders and the guy who shot Constable Nasrallah tonight, you should tag along. We'll add "uncovering Klingon and Gerbil's weapons stash" to the list of B Division successes.' He climbed out. 'Inspector McGregor's buying everyone chips.'

'Wouldn't want to miss that. Right, better get back to it, got some woods to search for a missing eighty-four-year-old. Two guesses how *that's* going to turn out.'

Logan closed the door, and the van took a right, down past the car park, right again, and away towards Macduff.

Even with the threat of rain, a couple were walking their dog on the sands of the bay, throwing sticks and eliciting excited barks. A young man slouched past, cigarette dangling out of the corner of his mouth, tattoos up and down both arms, wheeling a pushchair full of screaming toddler. A thin young woman stood leaning against the sea wall, where Helen used to stand. Only she had shoulder-length black hair, instead of Helen's knot of dirty blonde curls.

Don't suppose he'd ever see those again.

He pulled out his phone. Fingers hovering over the contact list. Then put it away again and went inside. No way he was calling her first.

Banff station was quiet for once. Only the hum-and-click of the photocopier broke the silence.

Maggie looked up, caught in the act of feeding another sheet into the machine. 'Sergeant McRae, I've got those Biros you wanted. And you've got a visitor in your office.'

Logan stayed where he was. Lowered his voice to a whisper. 'Who is it?'

DCI Steel's smoke-roughened rasp filled the room. 'Who the hell do you think it is? It's your fairy bloody godmother with the "I'll give you three wishes" routine.'

'Maggie, we need a signal. Put a sock in the window if someone horrible's in my office so I know to steer clear.'

'I heard that!'

'You were meant to.' Logan thumped through

733

to the Sergeants' Office and peeled off his stab-proof vest. 'What do you want?'

'I'm getting a visit from Finnie this afternoon. Apparently I'm no' making enough progress on the Tarlair case.'

'Oh.' He sat in his chair. Frowned. 'What about Mark Brussels and Dr Gilcomston? Have you hauled them in?'

She collapsed into the seat opposite. 'Why, because you *think* you saw something in a burning house? Don't be—'

'Because of what Charles Anderson said last night. It was in the report.'

'There was a report?'

'I *sent* it to you. For goodness' sake, can you never—'

'Since when do I read reports? You want me to know something, sodding well tell me.'

Logan stared at the ceiling for a moment. 'Every time . . .' Back to Steel. 'Charles Anderson says Gilcomston and Brussels were part of a paedophile ring who bought the little girl. They killed her.'

'Is that it? That *all* you've got? A rumour from a dead man?'

'More than you've got.' He picked at a scar on the desk, right through the veneer to the chipboard below. 'We should take another look at them. Them, Liam Barden, and Neil Wood too.'

Steel covered her face with her hands. 'Neil Sharny Wood is the bane of my existence, second only to you.'

'So go have a bit of a dig. Speak to friends and neighbours. At least it'll look as if you're doing something when Finnie gets here.'

Logan killed the engine and climbed out onto Firth Place. The rain had passed, leaving the road glistening. Small puddles clung to the gutter. Overhead, the sky was grey as a shroud.

Steel slammed the car door. 'Still say this is a waste of time.'

Logan locked the Big Car and stepped across the road to Mark Brussels's front door. He leaned on the bell. 'Better than sitting about, moping.'

Mark Brussels's house loomed in silence. Curtains drawn.

He tried the bell again, letting it ring and ring and ring.

'Told you. He's no even *in*.'

'Do you have to complain about everything?' Logan knocked – three, loud and hard.

Still no reply.

He levered the letterbox up. 'MR BRUSSELS? HELLO?'

'Still don't see what playing postman's knock with Manky Marky Brussels is supposed to achieve. No' without a warrant.'

'You want to go back to the station and twiddle your thumbs till Finnie gets there, or do you want to actually do something?' One more go: 'MR BRUSSELS?' He straightened up. 'Better try round the back.'

Through a gate at the side of the house, and down the path into the rear garden: a small patch of seedy grass surrounded by thistles and bushes laden with redcurrants. A battered wooden door hung open a couple of inches, revealing a small utility room on the other side.

'Mr Brussels?' Logan snapped on a pair of blue nitrile gloves and pushed it all the way. 'Hello?'

The smell of bleach and washing powder drifted out into the garden. A puddle of water reached across the linoleum from the back door. 'Mr Brussels? It's the police.'

'Oh stop fannying about. Haven't got all day.' Steel barged past him, into the room, then through into the kitchen beyond. 'SHOP! Come out, come out, wherever you are!'

He followed her into an ancient-looking kitchen, with painted cabinets and an electric cooker.

'Game's a bogey, the cat's in the lobby.'

Logan stepped out into the hall. The smell of bleach was stronger here, and a patch of carpet at the foot of the stairs was a different colour to the rest of it: pale and yellowed.

He pushed open the living-room door.

It was exactly the same as they'd left it a week ago. Clock on the mantelpiece. TV on with the sound muted. Small terrier slumped in a tartan beanbag in the corner. Only difference was that this time it wasn't snoring and twitching, it was lying perfectly still. Not so much as a wheeze. Its chest wasn't rising and falling either.

Steel slumped into the room, hands in her pockets. 'Well, looks like Manky Marky B's no' in.'

'His dog's dead.'

'No . . .' Her face drooped. 'Poor wee thing. Spends his whole life being loyal to Brussels, never knowing his master's a child-molesting wee turd. And then he dies. No' much of an existence, is it?' A sniff. 'Maybe he's nipped out to buy the dog a wee coffin?'

'Yeah, maybe.' Or maybe Charles Anderson had paid a visit and covered his tracks with bleach afterwards. 'Can you give me a minute? I want to nip out and phone Tufty. Make sure he's OK after his bash on the head.'

'Knock yourself out.' She sank into Brussels's armchair, in front of the TV, and picked up the remote. Then poked at the buttons until a woman in a bikini appeared, lining up a shot off the tee.

Logan slipped out into the back garden. Took out his phone and checked the caller history. The entry he was looking for was right there – twenty-five to twelve, last night. He pressed the button and listened to it ring.

Checked over his shoulder to make sure Steel wasn't standing at the kitchen window, watching him.

Come on, come on . . .

'Hello?'

'Where are you?' Keeping his voice down.

'Who is this?'

'We spoke last night, remember? You were on the boat and I was on the harbour wall, getting drenched.'

'If you're trying to trace the call, you're—'

'I'm not.'

'Soon as I hang up, I'm ripping the SIM card out of this phone and destroying it.'

'I'm trying to trace Mark Brussels.'

'Ah . . . Mark can't come to the phone right now. You want to leave a message?'

Logan marched out onto the lawn. 'Whatever you're doing, stop. OK? Just stop. No more.'

'That's what I've been telling him. And do you know what he's been telling me?'

Silence.

'What?'

'He's been telling me about the Livestock Mart. He's been telling me about turning up in a barn in the middle of the night and picking a little girl to buy. He's been telling me lots *of interesting things he'd never tell you.'*

Logan checked the kitchen window again. Still no Steel. 'Then tell me. Tell me where it is, and who runs it, and I'll make sure they go away for a long, long time.'

A laugh. *'You* really *think I should trust you?'*

'Of course you bloody should!'

Silence.

A car drove by on the street outside.

A faint mist of drizzle caressed Logan's face with its clammy hand.

'Hello?'

'I don't know where it is. It floats around – they take over people's barns. Sometimes it's people like them, sometimes it's hired anonymously. If you're in the loop, you get a text telling you where to go on the night. Cash only.'

'When's the next one?'

'Brussels doesn't know, but probably not for a couple of months. Doesn't know who's running it either – changes every time.'

Well, that was sod all use.

Logan paced his way to the garden wall. 'Who killed her?'

Nothing.

'Come on, Charles, one of them has to know.'

A sigh came down the line. *'They all point the finger at each other. Well, while they've still got some. But it doesn't matter. They're all guilty. They all have to be punished.'*

Logan stopped. Stared down at the damp grass at his feet. 'It doesn't have to be like this, Charles.'

'Yes it does.' The line went dead. Charles Anderson was gone.

Logan leaned against the doorframe. 'You ready?'

'Hold on, Britney's going up for a putt.' Steel scooted forward in the armchair, elbows on knees, hands clasped together. 'Come on, Britney, check the lay of the green for Aunty Roberta . . . Oh yeah . . .'

He picked at his fingernails. 'If it was up to you, would we let paedophiles out of prison? Or keep them locked up for ever?'

'If it was up to me? I'd castrate the bastards. Make them wear their severed dicks round their necks in little tubes so everyone would know what they did. Show me a police officer who says different and I'll show you someone who's no' got kids of their own, or they're bucking for promotion.' A shrug. 'Or they're a moron. Maybe all three.'

'Time to go.' Logan picked up the remote and killed the TV. 'Let's go see if Dr Gilcomston's in.'

Steel jerked her head at the tartan beanbag. 'What about man's deadest friend?'

A bluebottle landed on the little brown-and-white body.

'He's not going anywhere.'

After all, it wasn't as if Mark Brussels was ever coming home.

CHAPTER 58

'Well, this *is* fun.' Steel clunked the passenger seat back a foot, then stuck both of hers on the dashboard. 'We should do this more often.'

On the other side of the road, Gilcomston's big granite house lurked behind its partial screen of trees and bushes.

'You didn't have to come.'

Her voice jumped up an octave. 'Ooh, look at me, my name's Logan, we should *totally* go sit about like a pair of morons outside Dr Kidfiddler's house for half an hour.'

'Was that supposed to be me? And it's only been ten minutes.'

She blew a wet raspberry. 'I'm bored.'

'Really? Because you're doing a *great* job of hiding it.'

Wind rattled the sycamore trees, sending a cascade of second-hand rain tumbling from their leaves. Up above, the sky loomed grey and black.

'*Shire Uniform Seven, safe to talk?*'

'Batter on, Maggie.'

'*They've had another sighting of Catherine and*

David Bisset: Waverley Centre. Edinburgh are attending.'

Probably a complete waste of time, but it had to be followed up anyway. 'Anything else?'

'Yes. Constable Quirrel has reported for duty. Am I letting him, or sending him home again.'

'He look OK to you?'

She lowered her voice. *'He's wearing a badge with "genius" on it, but it's spelled G.E.N.I.O.U.S.'*

'If Inspector McGregor's got no objections, send him out. But make sure Tufty sticks with Deano all day. No wandering off on his own.'

'Will do.'

He clipped his Airwave back into place.

Steel was staring at him. She narrowed her eyes. 'What?'

'Thought you said you were phoning him when we were at Mark Brussels's place.'

'I trust Maggie more than I trust Tufty. If she says he's OK, he's OK.'

Steel folded her arms and let her head fall back. 'Couldn't be more bored if I tried.'

'This is for *your* benefit! Your case, remember?'

'So let's kick the door in and ransack the place!'

A jackdaw hopped sideways across the driveway.

'We haven't got a warrant.'

'Then there's no point sitting here. He's hardly going to wander out and invite us in for quiche and a look at his stash of kiddy-porn, is he?' She hauled her feet off the dashboard. 'You know what? I'm no' doing this any more. Back to the ranch.'

Logan opened the door and climbed out onto the street.

'Hoy! I said back to the ranch.'

He clunked the door shut and walked across the road. Stood at the foot of Gilcomston's driveway. Wandered along the pavement, looking up at the house. No sign of life. So he tried the other side of the driveway.

Paused on the edge of the kerb.

From there, just outside the front left corner of the property, he had a clear view between the leaves of a rhododendron bush to a garage set back from the house. Black double doors. Difficult to tell for sure without the actual photograph for reference, but it looked a lot like the spot where Charles Anderson must have stood to take a photo of the little dead girl before she appeared face-down in Tarlair Outdoor Swimming Pool.

He unhooked his Airwave.

Steel was right, they needed a warrant.

Of course that didn't matter to Charles Anderson. No evidentiary procedures to follow. No slippery defence lawyers waiting to pick holes in everything. No letting people like Graham Stirling back on the streets. No worrying about—

A loud *Breeeeeeeeeeeeeeeeeeeep!* Sounded from the Big Car.

God's sake, it was like babysitting a drunken toddler.

Logan started back, then stopped. Stared down the street.

An ancient green Jaguar growled its way up the hill towards him, with Dr Gilcomston behind the wheel. The car didn't slow down as it swung into the driveway, crunching its way up the gravel drive.

Logan marched after it.

The driver's door creaked open, and Gilcomston stepped out. Shoulders back, chin up, scowling down his nose. 'This is harassment. I've already made a formal complaint about you and that *woman's* behaviour. Now please get off my property, I have nothing further to say to you.' Today's cardigan was purple. He walked around to the Jag's boot and popped it open. Took out a clutch of Asda carrier bags. Slammed the boot shut again.

'We know.'

He picked up his bags and scrunched along the gravel towards the house. A gust of wind snatched at his grey hair.

'We know about you, and Mark Brussels, and Neil Wood, and Liam Barden. We know about the little girl you bought.'

Gilcomston paused, one foot on the front doorstep. 'I have no idea what you're talking about.'

'She was six years old. You called her "Cherry". Did you pick her yourself, or did you put it to a vote?'

'Whoever you've been talking to is *lying*. This is nothing to do with me.'

'And we're not the only ones who know about

it. There's someone targeting people like you. And you're the only one of the ring left.'

His eyes darted to the garage, with its black doors. 'Please get off my property.'

'Neil Wood's dead. Liam Barden's dead. Mark Brussels is missing, so he's probably going to be joining them soon. That leaves you.'

He lowered one set of bags and dug out his keys.

'How long do you think it'll be before he comes after you too?'

Gilcomston unlocked the front door. 'Am I under arrest?'

'You come in voluntarily, you make a complete confession, and we get you somewhere safe.'

'If I'm not under arrest, you can leave now.'

He marched inside. Slammed the door closed.

Some people think they're untouchable.

Some people really needed to learn.

Logan clicked the talk button on his Airwave. 'Shire Uniform Seven to Bravo India, Safe to talk?'

Inspector McGregor's voice crackled out of the little speaker. *'What's up?'*

'We need to get a surveillance operation set up: Dr William Harris Gilcomston, eighteen Firth Place, Macduff. I need a twenty-four-hour observation on him for about a week. Week and a half. Starting now.'

'You are joking, aren't you? You're talking about at least two and a half thousand *man-hours. Have you any idea how much that would cost?'*

'Might be our best bet to catch Charles Anderson.'

A sigh. *'If it was up to me: I'd say go for it, but I haven't got the bodies, Logan. I'll try the Area Commander, but it'll take a while to get an operation of that scale approved. At least two or three days.'*

By which time Gilcomston would probably be dead.

Maybe it was for the best? Charles Anderson turns up and carts Gilcomston off somewhere painful for a chat. Then dumps whatever's left of him at sea. Couldn't exactly say he'd be a great loss to humanity.

Still . . .

Logan puffed out his cheeks. Let the breath slowly hiss out. There *was* one way to save the arrogant scumbag's life. Not exactly ethical, but it might work. 'OK, thanks, Guv. Let me know how it goes.' He twisted the handset back onto its holder.

'Are you no' done sodding about yet?'

Logan turned, and there was Steel, puffing away on her fake cigarette.

He nodded at the house. 'Detective Chief Inspector, was it my imagination, or did Dr Gilcomston seem unsteady on his feet when he emerged from his vehicle?'

'Eh?' She pulled her chin in. 'Why are you talking like that? Sound like you've swallowed your notebook.'

'I'm concerned that he may have been driving under the influence of either drink or drugs.' Logan thumbed the doorbell. Then gave the police-issue three loud knocks. Stepped back. Released the elastic band from his body-worn video and set it recording.

'You're off your head, Laz.'

The door yanked open, and there was Gilcomston glowering down at them. 'I think I made myself perfectly clear, *Sergeant*. I want you off my property.'

Logan wandered over to the Jaguar, hands tucked into the zippy pockets on his stabproof vest. 'Is this your vehicle, sir?'

'Of course it is. And it's taxed and insured.'

'I see.' Logan turned a smile on him. 'Have you been drinking, sir? Because you seem a little unsteady.'

'I have *not* been drinking. How dare you come here and accuse me!' Gilcomston stamped down onto the driveway and jabbed a finger in Logan's direction. 'I'll have your badge. Or warrant card. Or whatever it is you petty fascists have.'

'Sir, I have reason to suspect that you've been driving under the influence of drink or drugs in contravention of Section Two of the Road Traffic Act 1988. Are you sure you've not been drinking?'

'I'VE JUST TOLD YOU THAT!' Blood flushed his face, hands curled into fists at his sides, arms shaking.

Steel raised an eyebrow. 'Aye, aye, someone's no' been taking their happy pills.'

'If you've not been drinking, sir, I can only conclude that you may have taken, and be in possession of, a controlled substance.'

'I don't have to stand here and listen to this nonsense!'

'Sir, I'm detaining you in terms of Section Twenty-Three of the Misuse of Drugs Act, 1971 for the purpose of a search. Do you have anything in your pockets I should know about? Any knives, needles, anything sharp?'

'You are *not* searching me! I demand to speak to your superior.'

Steel gave him a grin. 'That would be me. You search away, young Logan. Methinks Dr Kidfiddler doth protest too much.' A wink. 'That's your actual Shakespeare.'

'Arms out, please, sir.' Logan snapped on a pair of blue nitrile gloves.

'I'll make damn sure the pair of you never work again. Do you hear me?'

'Yes, sir. Now: arms out, please.'

Logan ran his hands along the sleeves of Gilcomston's cardigan, then the legs of his corduroy trousers. Checked the turn-ups. Then the cardigan's pockets. The left one contained a pipe, and a packet of tobacco. The right one contained a box of matches. 'Well, well, well. Would you care to explain this, sir?' He held up a small plastic baggie with brown powder in it. Remarkably similar to the one he'd confiscated from Kirstin Rattray when she was on the way to her daughter's fairy princess party. Identical, in fact.

'It . . . I never . . .' Gilcomston's face darkened

748

again. 'YOU PLANTED THAT!' He lunged, fist swinging.

Logan grabbed the arm, locked the wrist, and thumped him chest-first into the Jaguar's passenger door.

'GET OFF ME! I'LL KILL YOU!'

'Possession of a Class A drug, resisting arrest, threats to kill.' Logan snapped on the cuffs. 'William Gilcomston, I'm detaining you under Section Fourteen of the Criminal Procedure – Scotland – Act 1995, because I suspect you of having committed an offence punishable by imprisonment . . .'

Wind whipped a fistful of rain against the Sergeants' Office window. Outside, Fraserburgh scowled beneath a swathe of grey clouds.

Logan pinned the phone between his ear and shoulder, and ran a thumbnail along the foil, between the KitKat's fingers. 'We did presumptive testing, and it's definitely heroin.'

The officer on the other end of the phone sighed. *'Never pegged him for a druggie, but I suppose there's a first time for everything.'* Her voice was big, round, and warm. The kind of voice that went with hot chocolate and marshmallows.

Click, and the two bits of biscuit snapped apart. 'I was wondering: is this a violation of his super-vision order?'

'Not explicitly. But given how prickly he is at the best of times, it's not a good sign. Did he admit to it?'

'Does he ever?' Logan crunched into one of them, sooking the chocolate off the wafer.

'Not that I've ever heard. You could catch him peeing in your shoe and he'd tell you someone else did it.'

The chair swivelled left, then right, then left again. 'Can you do me a favour? Get a search warrant for his house? If he's up to this, maybe he's up to something else?'

A pause.

Logan crunched down the rest of the finger, and started on the other one.

'Do you know something I don't?'

'Well . . . let's just say it might be worth taking a look around before he gets out and disposes of whatever it is he's hiding.'

'I'll see what I can do.'

The door opened and Steel bundled into the room, fastening her belt. 'You getting a search warrant?'

He put a chocolaty hand over the mouthpiece. 'Offender Management Unit are handling it. We could probably tag along, if you like?'

Little creases appeared between her eyebrows. 'How come you're no' doing it?'

'He's a registered sex offender. Thought it made more sense if they were in charge.' And it didn't hurt to put a little distance between himself and the warrant.

'Oh no you don't, it's *my* shout.'

Back to the phone. 'Can you give DCI Steel a bell when you're ready to go in? She's keeping an eye on him for something else. Wants to tag along.'

'Will do.'

Logan put the phone back in its cradle. Scrunched up the tinfoil wrapper and lobbed it in the bin. 'You ready to head back to the ranch? Gilcomston's solicitor's not going to be up till three-ish.'

Steel settled on the edge of the desk. 'Do you no' think it was a bit of a coincidence? You think he's acting a bit funny, you search him, and halle-lujah, praise the Lord, you find a wrap of heroin.'

Logan didn't look at her, gathered up his things instead. 'Sometimes you get lucky.' OK, so it wasn't ethical. And if anyone found out he'd done it, he'd be fired, then prosecuted. But he'd prob-ably just saved William Gilcomston's life.

She was still staring at him.

'What?'

Steel took out her fake cigarette, clicked it on. Took a puff. 'Nothing.'

Logan pushed through the tradesmen's entrance and into Banff station. 'No. The photo was taken outside Gilcomston's house. That means the wee girl was there. There's going to be DNA. Maybe photographs.'

Steel followed him into the canteen. 'Going to be hard to get him for killing her. Even if we get anything at the house, he's going to blame one of the others. Pass the corpse.'

Logan grabbed a couple of mugs from the

cupboard. 'We can still do him for the abuse. Maybe conspiracy to commit?'

'Well, that's sod all use, isn't it? I want to bang someone up for killing that wee girl, no' slap them on the wrist for being a nonce.'

'What am I supposed to do, magic up a witness?' Teabags.

'How about a wrapper of heroin, because—'

Logan's phone blared out its anonymous ringtone. Saved by the bells. 'McRae?'

What sounded like singing in the background, then, *'Logan? It's Helen. Helen Edwards?'*

'Hold on a minute.' He put his hand over the mouthpiece. 'I need to take this.'

Steel folded her arms. 'I'm no' stopping you.'

'In *private*.'

'Tough.'

'Fine. You make the teas.' He turned and marched back outside. 'Sorry. Had someone with me.'

'No, I'm sorry for running off. I didn't want to leave without talking to you, but I was running out of time and I had to get the bus, or I would've missed my train. I stayed for as long as I could.'

'You could've called me!'

'I know. I tried, but . . . I'm really, really sorry.'

A big stone weight dragged at his shoulders, pulling them down. 'Yeah, I'm sorry too.'

A handful of herring gulls swooped and crawed across the bay, glowing like diamonds when they hit a blade of sunlight, then fading to grey on the other side.

He cleared his throat. 'So: Gwent. Wales.'

'Took all night and all morning to get here. I'm at the police station.'

'Well . . . . make sure you get a B-and-B this time. No more sleeping rough waiting for nice police officers to take you in.'

'I really am sorry, Logan.'

A couple of cars drove past. An ugly man with an uglier child walked along the road.

The awkward silence stretched.

'It's OK. We knew it was going to happen sooner or later. But I kind of hoped we'd have a bit longer before it did.'

'And it's not as if you've got room to spare any more, right? Now you've got guests, you don't need me cluttering up the place.'

'Cluttering? You didn't . . .' Frown. 'Sorry? I've got *guests*?'

'Of course you do.'

'It's not Steel, is it? Because if it is, she can kiss my—'

'No: Samantha's cousins. They came round yesterday when I was waiting for you.' Helen made a hissing sound, as if she was sucking air in through her teeth. *'It was kind of awkward, really. They're asking questions about how she's getting on and if the care home's any good, and all I can think of is "I slept with her boyfriend."'*

Cousins?

'Samantha doesn't have any cousins. Her mum was an only child, her dad too. Are you sure they said—'

753

'Of course I am. Boy and a girl. He's, what, sixteen-ish? She's about fourteen? Both of them really needed feeding up, so I made fish fingers, beans, and chips. I would've washed up, but I didn't have time, and—'

'Helen, this is important. What did they look like?'

'Well, they were thin. Dark hair – they both had the same haircut, shoulder-length and straight – both really soft-spoken. Aberdeen accents?'

No. No. No. No.

The young woman, standing in Helen's spot by the sea wall earlier. Thin. Shoulder-length black hair. Samantha didn't have cousins.

He looked up and the girl was still there, leaning back against the concrete. A denim jacket, black jeans, big white trainers. Face dead and motionless.

Catherine Bisset. Stephen Bisset's daughter. The young woman who'd helped kill her own father. Who'd probably cheered her brother on while he battered Graham Stirling to death. Or did she join in?

Logan's throat tightened.

She'd been in his house, asking questions about Samantha.

He stepped out into the road.

CHAPTER 59

Sunlight caught the houses on the other side of the bay, making them shine against the hill. Then the clouds closed up, and they sank into darkness again.

Logan stepped into the spotlight surrounding Catherine.

'That's far enough.' She held up a mobile phone. 'David's on the other end.' Pink speckled her cheekbones and nose. She was thinner than she'd been the last time, back when the trial had collapsed. Two dead bodies ago.

He reached for the handcuffs on his equipment belt. 'What did you do?'

'How does it work? You've got a girlfriend in a coma, and another one living with you. Have you never even *heard* of loyalty?'

'Catherine, what – did – you – do?'

'We had a long talk with Helen yesterday. Found out all sorts of interesting things.'

'Catherine Bisset, I'm detaining you under Section Fourteen of the Criminal Procedure – Scotland—'

'No you're not.' She gave the phone a wiggle.

'David, remember? Don't you want to know where he is?'

Sand filled Logan's mouth. 'Where is he?'

'You lied about our father, didn't you? You lied about dad, and you did it in *court*.'

'I tried to save him. He—'

'YOU TOLD EVERYONE HE WAS A PERVERT!' Spit flew from her narrow lips. Then a couple of deep breaths pulled her back. 'David's right: you *lied*.'

Herring gulls wheeled overhead, screaming in the last slice of sunshine as it was swallowed by clouds.

Down on the sands of the bay, the couple with the excitable dog turned back and headed for home.

'He's at the care home, isn't he?' Logan pulled out his phone and flicked through the contacts. Tapped the one marked 'SUNNY GLEN' then listened to it ring. 'This isn't TV, you can't—'

'*Sunny Glen Care Home, how can I help you?*'

Catherine pinched her eyebrows together, poked out her bottom lip as if she was about to cry.

'Louise, it's Logan McRae. Has Samantha had any visitors today?'

That bottom lip trembled. Good.

'*She has indeed. Her cousin David came up from Edinburgh. Managed to get some time off from his uni course.*'

'Is he still there?'

Catherine's hand came up to cover her mouth.

'*Think so. You want to speak to him?*'

756

'Please. And Louise? Make sure you've got someone from security with you.'

'*Erm . . . OK . . .*' Clunks and thumps came from her end – doors and footsteps. '*I've got some good news, by the way: there's been a drop-out at Aberdeen Royal Infirmary. Samantha can get a place on the surgical rota in three weeks, if you don't mind it being a training opportunity with students watching? It's all done by camera though, they don't even get in the room.*'

A sniff. Catherine's eyes glistened. Shoulders trembling.

Yeah, go ahead and cry, see what good it does you.

Three knocks. '*Samantha? It's Louise.*' The sound of a door opening.

'Is he there?'

'*Oh . . . No. Hold on.*' A clunk. Then the beep-boop sound of a touchtone-phone dialling in the background. Louise's voice grew an echo from the care home's tannoy system. '*Good morning, everyone, can Samantha Mackie's cousin David please pick up the nearest courtesy phone? Thank you.*' Then a muffled, '*Hugh, go check the terrace. See if Miss Mackie's out there.*'

'Louise?'

'*They've probably gone for a cup of coffee.*'

And Catherine Bisset couldn't hold it in any more. She spluttered out a laugh. 'We're not *stupid*.'

'Louise, where the hell is Samantha?'

'*There's no reason to worry, I'm sure everything's all right.*'

The laughter faded and Catherine's face died again. 'I liked Helen. She told us all about her daughter, and how you thought she was the dead girl in the swimming pool.'

He took a step closer. 'What do you want?'

'Little limp body, floating face down in seawater, head all bashed in like that. Must've been horrible.' She frowned up at him. 'But it's more horrible for Samantha, isn't it? David and me know what it's like to have someone you love stuck in a hospital bed. Unable to move, or talk, or do anything. Needing someone to feed them and wipe their backside. Not really alive, are they?'

He lowered his voice. 'Catherine, I swear to God . . .'

'Logan? I'm sorry, there seems to be some sort of mix-up. We're having a bit of difficulty locating Samantha right now, but she's probably in one of the TV rooms. I'll give you a call back, OK? It—'

He hung up. Put his phone away. Unclipped his CS gas. 'What have you done to Samantha?'

'*You* did that to my father. You. You could've found him in time, but you didn't.'

'Where – is – she?'

'You let someone cut him and beat him and take him away from us. Nothing left but skin and bone and blood and *shame*.'

He flicked the safety off the canister.

'No. Because if you do . . .' She held out the phone. 'What do you think happens to her?'

The gulls screeched.

758

A patter of rain darkened the concrete wall.

Catherine shook her head. 'Really, *really* think about it.'

He slid the CS gas back in its clip. 'What do you want?'

'I want my father back.'

'Then you shouldn't have killed him.'

She pulled one shoulder up. 'He was dead long before that. We *saved* him. We had to, because you didn't.' Catherine pointed at a little Nissan Micra, the green paint scraped through to the metal down the passenger side. 'Do you want to come see Samantha? I'll give you a lift.'

'You're fourteen. And I can drive myself.'

She wiggled the phone at him again. 'No, you can't.'

Beneath the tartan blanket, everything smelled of dust and dog. It itched his cheeks and cut the light down to a multi-coloured gloom. Seatbelt clips dug into the small of his back as the car swung around to the right. 'Where are we going?'

Catherine's voice was muffled by the blanket. *'I'm not allowed to tell you. David says it'd spoil the surprise.'*

Lying on his side, on the backseat, Logan screwed his hands into fists. Should've hit the transmit button before handing over his Airwave. Stupid. Shouldn't have given her his phone. Stupider.

But what was he supposed to do? Climb up on his pedestal and let them kill Samantha?

759

Stay in the backseat. Stay under the blanket.

Hope to God they don't have a gun.

Or a knife.

Why did he take his stabproof vest off? *Idiot.*

A hard left this time, and the clips dug in again. 'David's not thinking clearly right now. He's grieving. You both are.'

'You didn't see him lying there in that hospital bed. All eaten away . . . We did the right thing.'

'I know. You did it because your dad was suffering. But this is *wrong*.'

'We cried, and cried, and he didn't even struggle, and . . .' A sniff. Then a long shuddering breath. *'No more talking.'*

Click and the radio came on. *'. . . and that's your news and weather. We'll have more at half nine, but first: here's Water's Edge, with "Love Fill Me Up" . . .'* A kitsch dollop of boy-band pop globbed out of the car radio.

A count of four, and Catherine joined in. *'I was empty as a picture of a bucket on the wall . . .'*

Still wasn't too late.

'Empty since she left me, I'm the loneliest of all . . .'

Sit up, wrap an arm around her throat and squeeze hard. Her phone was on the passenger seat, no way she could get to it – she'd be too busy pawing at his sleeve. Enough pressure and she wouldn't even get a squeak out.

'Hollowed out and broken, and battered, and so cold . . .'

And even if she did, so what? David Bisset would

have Samantha as a hostage, and Logan would have Catherine. Mexican standoff.

'*Then in my mind, I think I find, the price for all the lies she told . . .*'

Only they *all* knew that Logan wouldn't kill anyone.

And David had already proven he would. Twice.

'*Doooo doo, dooo-deee-doo la-dooo, as something taking hold . . .*'

Acceleration pushed Logan back against the seatbelt clips again. Either she was speeding, or they'd passed the town limits.

'*Love fill me up, to the top of my heart . . .*'

Climbing a slight incline. Not steep enough to be the road out to Fraserburgh. Not enough right turns to be the one heading south either.

'*Overflow, let it go, right off the chart . . .*'

Definitely came over the bridge into Macduff. So that only left one option.

'*Cause loving you's easy, and loving you's smart . . .*'

They were going to the outdoor swimming pool.

'*Love fill me up, to the top of my heart . . .*'

The car took a hard right, then descended a steep hill as Catherine ran out of words and went back to doo-dee-doo again.

It levelled out, then the Micra rocked and scraped its way through the potholes. Eased to a halt.

'*There we go.*'

She killed the engine and the music died with it.

'*It's OK, you can come out now. There's no one can see you.*'

Logan pulled the blanket off his head and sat up.

She tried for a smile, but it didn't really work. 'Told you it wouldn't take long.' Catherine climbed out of the car.

Rain clicked across the windscreen like the feet of tiny crabs.

OK. This was all doable. They were just a pair of kids.

He stepped into the grey morning. Turned to look back up the hill.

'There's a big sign up there, saying "Road Closed". No one's coming.' Catherine picked Logan's equipment belt off the passenger seat and clipped it on. Far too big – she had to hold it up with one hand. 'They're waiting for us.'

The North Sea surged, dark and heavy against the pebble beach.

She marched off, through the gap in the rock at the far end of the car park.

Just a pair of kids.

CHAPTER 60

He followed her along the old tarmac road: past the rocks and another pebble beach lined with the bones of old seaweed; past the warning sign about Tarlair pool being closed and dangerous. Past the crumbling concrete wall. Then onto the apron of rain-slicked grey that led out to the two derelict pools.

Tarlair's boxy art deco buildings stood like gravestones around the edge.

Catherine kept going. Down, onto the terraced steps leading to the water.

Both pools were nearly full – the one closest to the defunct changing rooms, and the one nearest the sea. Probably topped up by yesterday's storm. Three figures were on the walkway between the two – one standing, one kneeling, and one in a wheelchair.

Catherine glanced back over her shoulder at him. 'Do you like it here? I like it. It's all decayed and broken . . . A dead place, where the dead come. Like all of us.'

'This doesn't have to go this way, Catherine. It can be made right again.'

'Can it?' Her trainers squelched through vast puddles of standing water, the surface pebbled with rain.

'It can if you want it to be.'

They'd almost reached the concrete walkway separating the inner pool from the outer one. The water in both was nearly black, reflecting back the clouds and surrounding hills.

A boom, and a wall of spray leapt over the sea wall. It hissed down against the dark water.

They'd wheeled Samantha out to the middle of the walkway and parked her facing out to sea. Both arms were curled against her chest, knees lopsided and together. Head hanging on one side, as if she was trying to get something into focus.

Next to her was a man, on his knees, hands tied behind his back, a pillowcase over his head.

Catherine rubbed her palm down the side of her jacket, as if she was trying to remove a stain. 'David says everyone dies in the end. The unlucky ones keep on breathing afterwards.' She paused on the edge of the pool. 'Dad was unlucky. Watching him lie there, all cut up and broken, and dead, and still breathing . . .' She shook her head. 'It's not fair to make people suffer like that. If he'd been a dog, we wouldn't have let him suffer, we'd have put him down to spare the pain.'

'Catherine!' Logan grabbed her arm. 'I thought you were meant to be the sensible one. The one who kept David from doing something stupid. It's not too late.'

'Did you never think that about your girlfriend? That it'd be kinder to put her to sleep?'

He stared at her. 'Please. This doesn't have to—'

'We don't have any choice.' She marched out onto the walkway.

Logan stepped onto the strip of concrete. Had to be about five-foot wide, but they'd positioned Samantha's wheelchair with the small front wheels resting on the very edge.

David Bisset stood right behind her, leaning on the back of the chair.

Catherine walked up to him. Stopped. 'See? I brought him.'

'You did great.'

'And I got this too.' She unfastened the equipment belt and held it out to her brother. Then produced a four-inch kitchen knife from her denim jacket. Held it clenched in her fist. 'He thinks we're being stupid.'

Logan held his hands out, palms up. 'You are, but you don't have to. We can sort this out.'

Stubble made patchy blue-grey shadows on David's chin. His eyes had sunken into his head, underlined by the same bony cheeks as his sister. He stared back for a moment, then fastened the equipment belt around his waist. Pointed at the kneeling figure. 'Does this look stupid to you?'

David snatched a handful of pillowcase and pulled.

Graham Stirling blinked in the light. His face was a paisley-pattern of yellow and purple bruises, one nostril crusted with black. A thick wad of fabric poked out of his mouth, held in place by the gag tied behind his head. 'Mmmnnnnngh! Mnnngghhnnnghnnnphhhh!'

'He says he never touched our dad. Says you made it all up to frame him. That right?'

'No. He's sick and he's dangerous and he should be locked away for the rest of his life.'

'But he's not, is he? They let him go, and they let you call our father a pervert.'

David untied the gag and Stirling spat out the lump of fabric. Coughed. Spluttered. Retched. Then his shoulders drooped.

Stirling's voice creaked like an unoiled hinge. 'I didn't . . . I didn't touch . . . your father. I swear . . . I didn't touch him.'

'See? He says you're a liar, Sergeant McRae.'

'I'm not! I saw what he did – he led me there! He did it. But he needs to go to prison, not whatever this is.'

'I didn't . . . it's . . . it's all . . . lies.'

David's left hand drifted down to the extendable baton, thumb toying with the catch keeping it in its holder. *Pop* – it was off. *Click* – it was back on again. *Pop. Click.*

'He set . . . He set me up.'

'This doesn't help you, David.' Logan inched closer, hands still out. 'We know you killed your dad, but it was a mercy killing. He was suffering. It was an act of love. No jury's going to hold that against you.'

Pop. Click. Pop. Click.

'Stop this now, before it goes too far.'

Pop. Click. Pop. Click.

'Please . . . don't kill . . . don't kill me. I didn't . . .'

'He says he didn't do it, McRae.'

Pop. Click. Pop. Click.

'He's lying, because he's scared. Come on, let's all—'

'OK.' *Pop.* David yanked the baton free of its holder, hard enough to send the extendable end clacking out to full lock. Raised it high above his head, arm drawn back, teeth bared.

Stirling flinched, shoulders up, as if that was going to save him. 'Please! I didn't! I didn't do it!'

Oh Christ, David was going to kill him.

'NO!' Logan lunged, then stopped as Catherine rested the tip of her knife against the dip in Samantha's head, where the bone was missing.

Catherine stared at him. 'You stay where you are.'

'Please, don't do this. He's sick, OK? He's broken. He deserves to be locked away for ever, but he doesn't deserve to die.'

David lowered the baton. 'Doesn't deserve to die? After what he did to my dad, he DOESN'T DESERVE TO DIE?'

'David, please, I know you're upset, but—'

'HE DESERVES TO DIE!' The pale skin darkened, whites showing around the iris of his eyes. 'HE *DESERVES* TO BE TORN TO PIECES! I SHOULD SKIN HIM ALIVE!'

'David, you don't get to decide who lives and who—'

'I SHOULD CASTRATE HIM! CARVE HOLES IN HIS CHEST! RIP HIS BOWELS OUT HIS BACKSIDE!' David's arms and legs trembled, the extendable baton slapping against his own thigh. The tendons in his neck twitched. Teeth glittering with spittle in the gloom.

Catherine reached out her other hand and tugged on his sleeve. 'It's OK. Just do it like we practised.'

A couple of deep breaths. Then he nodded. 'But I can't do those things, because I'm not a pervert like him. So I'm going to bash his brains out. He's guilty. And he *does* deserve it.' The baton swooped up again.

'Stop! OK, you're right!' Logan held his hands out again. Flicked his eyes towards Graham Stirling – kneeling there with his eyes screwed shut and his teeth bared, waiting for the blow to come. Waiting to die. Logan cleared his throat. 'I was lying. He didn't do that to your dad. I picked him, because I didn't know who did it. Put the baton down.'

No one moved.

David stared at him. Then lowered his arm. The colour faded from his face, leaving him ghost-pale again. 'You were right.'

Stirling looked up. Smiled. 'What did I tell you? Sergeant McRae *lied*.' He worked his way to his feet. 'All that time, *lying* about me.' He pulled his hands apart. The rope had been wrapped around his wrists, not tied. It was all for show. 'A dirty, filthy, liar.'

Logan stepped back. 'You planned it?'

'I helped David and Catherine see through your lies, McRae. They came to me, and they were angry and upset, and I helped them.'

'I only said that because they were going to *kill* you!'

'See? I told you. He lies, and he schemes, and he could've saved your dad, but he was too busy fitting me up to care.'

David looked up at the lowering clouds.

Boom – another wave hit the sea wall, sending spray bursting over it like fireworks.

Then down again.

He turned to his sister. 'Like we practised.'

She grabbed hold of the wheelchair and wrenched the handles upwards, pitching it and Samantha forward into the pool.

CHAPTER 61

'NO!'

Samantha hit the water, and the weight of the wheelchair pulled her straight under.

Logan ran for the edge, then David crashed into him. A one-shouldered tackle that sent them both crunching onto the walkway.

A grunt, then pain flashed across Logan's ribs as the extendable baton cracked into them.

He raised an arm, covering his head. Kicked out, missed.

But David didn't. The baton smashed into Logan's upper arm. Numbness followed a wave of broken glass, from his shoulder to his fingertips. Flat on his back, one leg in the cold water.

David scrambled on top, hauled the baton up again.

Logan jerked up a knee and made contact. But it didn't make any difference.

The baton cracked down again, tearing into his scalp. Echoing through his skull on waves of burning coal.

His fist jabbed up and round. Caught David on

the side of the nose, snapping it. Warm blood pattered down.

'AAAAAAAAAAAAGH!' David reared back, one hand covering his ruined nose, bright red oozing between his fingers.

Logan forced himself up on his numb arm and battered his right elbow into David's face, mashing those bloody fingers into teeth and bone. Then grabbed a handful of long dark hair and yanked him forwards. Turning. Putting his weight behind it.

David's head bounced off the concrete with a dull *thunk*. Twice. Three times.

Catherine screamed.

Logan pushed the limp body off of him and tumbled into the swimming pool. Cold, squeezed his body, forcing the air out of his lungs.

The wheelchair was only a couple of feet underwater, on its front, pinning Samantha to the rocky floor of the pool. She wasn't moving. Wasn't trying to save herself. She sat there, face down, strapped in, still like the dead.

He wrapped his arms around the chair's back and heaved, dragging the whole thing up.

She flopped in her seat, head lolling, skin pale as ivory, lips granite grey. Water cascaded from her open mouth.

Thunder growled through the sky, reverberating back from the hills. A squall of rain pebbled the surface of the pool, bounced off the concrete walkway.

He snatched at the Velcro straps holding her in the chair. Tore them free, then dragged her out of it. Half wading, half swimming to the ramp at the side of the water leading up onto the tiered apron.

'Come on . . .' He pulled her up onto the walkway by her collar, knelt beside her and felt for a pulse. Nothing. 'No, no, no, no, no.'

Logan tipped her head to the side and shook it, till water stopped running from her mouth and nostrils. Chest compressions. One one-thousand. Two one-thousand. Three one-thousand.

Hands snatched at his back.

Catherine – eyes wide and bloodshot, face streaming with rainwater, black hair plastered to her head. 'I'LL KILL YOU!'

One one-thousand. Two one-thousand. Three one-thousand.

Then a fist thumped into his back.

'KILL YOU!'

One one-thousand. Two one-thousand. Three one-thousand.

A palm slapped the side of his head.

One one-thousand. Two one-thousand. Three one-thousand.

Nails dug into his neck.

He snapped an elbow back. Caught her in the mouth.

One one-thousand. Two one-thousand. Three one-thousand.

She stumbled back, moaning and spluttering.

Scarlet smeared her lips and chin, dripped onto her denim jacket, spreading into the damp fabric like poppy blooms. Then one white trainer caught in a crumbling pothole and she fell, arms out. The dull crack when her head hit the concrete was like a distant gun going off.

Logan laced his hands together and pushed against Samantha's chest again. 'Come on!'

One one-thousand. Two one-thousand. Three one-thousand.

He tilted Samantha's head back, pinched her nose and breathed for her. Did it again.

More chest compressions: one one-thousand. Two one-thousand. Three one-thousand.

Something solid cracked off his head, hard enough to send him sprawling as broken bells and sirens screamed through his skull. Gagh . . . Black and yellow dots sparkled in the dark clouds above his face, riding the wave of heat trying to push his eyeballs free.

Then everything faded to grey, hiding the pool and the hills and the buildings. Like being wrapped in a shroud that muffled the sound of rain and pounding blood in his ears.

. . .

Get up.

Nothing but grey.

. . .

Then the world snapped back into Technicolor.

Graham Stirling stood over him, extendable baton clutched in both hands like a baseball bat.

773

'Well, well, well. Looks like it's just you and me again.'

'Gnnn . . .'

'I'd really love to take my time, but this has all turned into a bit of a mess, hasn't it?'

The baton cracked into Logan's leg. Glass and barbed wire ripped through the muscle.

Up. Get up.

'You've spoiled it.'

It battered against his chest. Knives and needles, cracking through his ribs.

GET UP!

'I had them all nice and trained. But you couldn't . . .' He stopped. Stared off at the entrance to the outdoor pool.

The ringing in Logan's ears changed tone, wailing up and down, regular and electronic. And it wasn't in his head any more.

Stirling put his hands up and the baton clattered to the concrete apron as two patrol cars screeched to a halt by the pool buildings. 'Your word against mine again. David and Catherine tried to kill you. I tried to stop them, but I was so weak after they attacked me.'

The Big Car's doors sprang open and Nicholson and Steel charged out into the rain. Sprinting across the crumbling poolside. Tufty and Deano jumped out of the other car.

Oh, thank God.

'No jury's going to believe anything else.'

Logan rolled onto his front, forced himself to his knees, and shuffled over to Samantha.

One one-thousand. Two one-thousand. Three one-thousand.

Breathe . . .

One one-thousand. Two one-thousand. Three one-thousand.

Breathe.

'You lied about me last time, why would they think this was any different?'

One one-thousand. Two one-thousand. Three one-thousand.

SODDING BREATHE!

Samantha's chest convulsed and foul-smelling water spewed out of her mouth. Coughing and spluttering. Heaving in great ragged breaths, eyes wide, staring up into the thick black sky. Hands pressing against her chest.

He scooped her up and held her: cold, clammy, but warming up.

Steel's voice cut through the downpour. 'You! Where the hell do you think you're going?'

Graham Stirling faked a couple of sobs. 'They tried to kill me! They attacked me in my house and beat me and I was so scared.'

'Get your arse over here.'

'Samantha.' Logan brushed the hair from her face and she blinked up at him.

Frowned. 'L . . .' She licked her lips. Swallowed. 'Logan?'

Holy shit.

He almost dropped her. Squeezed her tighter instead as something warm burst inside his chest. 'Hey you.'

'Where am . . . Why am I all wet?' Samantha reached for his hand, but hers wouldn't work, the fingers stayed curled into a claw. 'What—'

'You haven't moved in four years. But it's going to be OK. I promise.' He leaned in and kissed her.

CHAPTER 62

Samantha's claw scraped down his cheek. Grey . . .

. . .

Cold . . .

Logan cracked open his eyes.

He was lying on his side, being dragged along the concrete walkway by one leg.

'Gnnnph . . .' His head throbbed, as if something living in there was trying to dig its way out.

'Oh, you're awake?' Graham Stirling gave his leg another tug. 'Good. Wouldn't want you to miss this. A man shouldn't be late for his own funeral.'

But . . . Where were the patrol cars? Where were Steel, Deano, Nicholson, and Tufty?

Samantha. Where the hell was Samantha?

Move. Get up.

But Logan's arms and legs were like strips of rubber. 'Nnngh . . .'

'Thought I'd hit you too hard there.'

They'd reached the middle of the walkway between the two pools, where David Bisset lay still as the grave. Rain bounced off his body, turning the pool of blood seeping out of his nose and mouth a delicate shade of pink.

Stirling let go and Logan's leg thumped against the walkway.

'Have to say, I'd expected more of them. But they're only kids, so what can you do?' He knelt and rummaged through the equipment belt fastened around David's waist. 'Limb restraints and hand-cuffs. You learn a lot about this kind of stuff when you're remanded for trial.'

He unrolled both of the bright yellow restraints. Then squeezed Logan's knees together and wrapped them tight. Then did the same with his ankles.

'Four months in that stinking cell with a *junkie*. You think that was nice for me?' Stirling unclipped the cuffs from their holder. 'He'd go to sleep every night, talking about all the things he was going to do to me if I didn't get him some money, or cigarettes, or drugs.'

MOVE.

Logan forced himself onto his side.

Samantha lay on the concrete apron, spread-eagled. Catherine wasn't far away, flat on her back with her arms outstretched. What happened to Nicholson and Steel? Where was the cavalry?

'Nnnng . . .'

'Where do you think you're going?'

'Kill . . . you.' The words hurt, echoing around his battered skull.

'Wrong way round.' Stirling put a foot against

Logan's shoulder and pushed him over onto his back. 'They broke into my house in the middle of the night. Little David and Catherine Bisset, all bitter and fired up and ready for revenge.'

Rain pattered down against his face.

Deep breath. And MOVE.

Stirling grabbed Logan's left wrist and snapped the handcuff on, squeezing the metal arm until it was far too tight.

COME ON AND BLOODY MOVE!

Logan's right hand trembled. He hauled it off the ground and fumbled at Stirling's face. Gouge his eyes out, rip them from his nasty bruised little face.

But Stirling pulled his head back, grabbed at the hand. Missed. Fought for it. 'It's time . . . for you . . . to go . . . *away*.'

Don't let him. Don't.

Click, the handcuff closed around the other wrist.

Stirling frowned. 'They were waiting for me, in the kitchen. Attacked me in my own house, can you believe that? Thought David was going to kill me.' A shudder. 'But I stuck to my guns: told them what they wanted to hear. It was all lies of course. You set me up. Their dad wasn't a pervert. And eventually, they stopped kicking me and hitting me and stamping on me and curled up against the fridge and cried instead.'

He stepped back. Took hold of the limb restraint around Logan's ankles and hauled – pulling them to the edge of the walkway.

'Was quite sweet really. They're so suggestible when they're that age, aren't they? Didn't take much to convince them to come after you and the coma girl.' Stirling wiped his hands down the front of his shirt. 'I've never worked in a team before. I like it. Definitely going to try this again.'

The words had to be forced out, like mouthfuls of stone. 'They'll . . . They'll find you. . . . They'll *stop* . . . you.'

'Don't be stupid.' He squatted down, patted Logan on the cheek. 'Now you go in the water, and you sink, and you die. And everyone thinks David and Catherine did it. Yet another horrible Jacobean revenge tragedy, played out in the northeast of Scotland.' A grin. 'You should see your—'

Logan snapped both wrists forward, slamming the cuff's centre bar into Stirling's face.

He went over backwards, into the water.

MOVE!

Logan groaned onto his side again and coiled up into the foetal position, fingers searching for the Velcro end of the limb restraints around his ankles. He scrabbled at the edge and yanked. The restraint ripped free. Knees next. Grab the end and—

Graham Stirling burst from the water, a thick slash of purple across his top lip, pouring blood down his face. 'AAAAGH!' He grabbed Logan and dragged him backward off the walkway and into the pool.

Cold water enveloped him in its jagged arms.

Dug its claws into the back of his head as Stirling climbed on top, keeping him under.

Logan opened his mouth. Salt water burned in his nose. One last tug and the restraint around his knees tore free. He kicked, shoved, and finally got his head above the surface. Gasped in a huge breath.

Sirens. *Real* ones this time, getting closer.

Graham Stirling backed off. 'It's your word against mine. They abducted me, and you tried to kill— Ulk . . .'

Logan grabbed two handfuls of Stirling's collar and pulled him off his feet, turned and forced his head beneath the water. Face up. Blood seeping from the gash in his top lip. Arms and legs thrashing. 'YOU DO *NOT* COME AFTER SAMANTHA!'

Fingers scrabbling at Logan's wrists. Grabbing at the handcuff's centre bar.

Eyes wide.

'YOU HEAR ME?' Logan shook him, forced him further under, arms locked, pushing until the water brushed his own chin. Held him there. 'NEVER AGAIN!'

Stirling's hands reached up, like they were trying to find the light.

The sirens were getting louder.

This was taking too long.

Any minute now they'd clear the hill and it would be all over. Graham Stirling would lie and weasel his way out of another attempted murder charge. And Samantha would never be safe.

No.

Charles Anderson was right. Some people didn't deserve the law.

He gave Stirling's collar a shake. 'DROWN DAMN YOU!'

'Logan.'

'DROWN AND DIE YOU FILTHY—'

'Logan.' A hand on his arm. 'Stop.'

He blinked. Looked around.

Samantha stood beside him, the water lapping around her chest. She shook her head. 'This isn't you, Logan. This is him.'

'But . . .' He turned. Samantha lay on the concrete apron, spread-eagled, motionless, where he'd left her. 'Are you . . .?' A lump formed in his throat, almost too big to swallow. 'Are you dead?'

'Let him go. Please.' Her hand was cool against his cheek. 'For me.'

A wave boomed against the sea wall, sending up an explosion of spray.

She lay on the concrete. She stood by his side. 'You know this isn't right. Let him go.'

Stirling's fingers clutched at the air, as if he could grab a handful and take it down beneath the water to breathe.

Logan let go. 'I miss you.'

'I know you do.' Her smile was a knife in his chest. 'Thank you.'

Graham Stirling thrashed to the surface, coughing and spluttering, face an unhealthy shade of purple. 'Aaaaaaaagh!'

'What for?'

'For everything.' She leaned in and kissed him on the cheek. 'For still being you.'

Stirling waded to the concrete walkway, clutched onto the edge, retching and trembling as a patrol car appeared at the entrance to the pool.

Its swirling blue-and-whites made sapphires and diamonds in the pounding rain. The doors sprang open and Deano, Tufty, and Nicholson jumped out. An ambulance screeched to a halt beside the patrol car, siren adding to the din.

Logan turned his back on them. 'Samantha, I . . .'

But she was gone.

CHAPTER 63

'Here.' Steel held out a plastic cup from the machine down the corridor. The smell of burned coffee and chemical creamer oozed into the air like a seeping wound.

'Thanks.' He reached up to take it. A line of dark-red bruising encircled his wrist, marking where the cuffs had dug in.

A nurse scuffed by, trainers making tortured squeaks on the green terrazzo floor.

Steel sank into the plastic seat next to his. 'I would've been here sooner, but we were searching Dr Kidfiddler's place. Found a digital camera in the garage with photos of the dead wee girl on them. Before she was dead, anyway. No' to mention a stash of phenobarbital – same stuff they found in her bloodstream.'

'Good.' The coffee tasted every bit as bad as it smelled.

'Denies it all, mind. Like that's a shock.' Steel had a good long frown at Logan's clothes. 'You should go home and change.'

'Nearly dry now.'

'Nothing's going to happen if you leave her for

half an hour. Go home, get something to eat.' She put a hand on his shoulder, warm and firm. 'I'll stay and make sure everything's under control.'

An old lady hobbled past, wheeling a drip on a stand, muttering to herself.

'Don't you have to go interview Gilcomston?'

Steel let loose a nasty little laugh. 'His esteemed highness, Darth Finnie, has decided to do it himself. Thinks a more senior officer would have a better shot at bursting him. Sod took it away from me.'

Logan toasted her with his horrible coffee. 'Welcome to my world.'

They sat in silence for a bit, as doctors and patients shambled by like something out of a zombie movie.

'Logan . . .' Steel looked off down the corridor. 'That wrapper of heroin. You planted it, didn't you?'

'Me?' He pulled the corners of his mouth down. 'Nah, doesn't sound like me.'

She lowered her voice. 'If you hadn't found it, we couldn't have arrested him. He'd still be at home and we'd no' be able to prove he had anything to do with that wee girl.'

A volunteer trundled by, pushing a trolley laden with clinking teacups and a big metal urn.

Steel waited until he'd disappeared down the corridor. 'More importantly, Gilcomston's no' getting released on bail: he's getting locked up till his trial. And if Charles Anderson really is on some sort of mission from God to bump off paedophiles – and he's killed the other three in the ring – you just saved Dr Kidfiddler's life.'

Logan stared down into the Brownian depths of his plastic cup. 'Proud day for us all.'

'Yeah.' She stretched out in her seat.

The clock on the wall ticked off another minute of their lives.

Steel had a dig at the underwire on her bra. 'While we're at it: you want to tell me what happened with Graham Stirling?'

A shrug. More horrible coffee. 'I got hit on the head a couple of times. It's a bit fuzzy.' Logan reached up and brushed his fingertips over the twin pads of gauze taped over the wounds. 'He tried to drown me. I fought back.'

'So all this stuff he's saying about you holding him under the water . . .?'

A shrug. 'Like I said: I fought back.'

'Don't sweat it. Everyone knows he's a lying wee sod anyway.' She closed one eye and really had a go at her cleavage, like a Labrador with fleas. 'Pffff . . . Well, Catherine Bisset's under observation for concussion. Brother David's been wheeched off to Aberdeen with intracranial swelling. They've put him in a medical coma. Won't get to charge him until . . . *if* he comes out of it.'

'*Shire Uniform Seven, safe to talk.*'

Logan groaned. Took the Airwave from his fleece pocket. 'Thump away, Maggie.'

'*Thought you'd like to know: the care home have*

got David Bisset on CCTV abducting Samantha. And there's a fax in for DCI Steel. Results of a Stable Isotope Analysis she ordered on a section of thighbone?'

Logan handed her the Airwave. 'For you.'

Steel stuck it to her ear. Stood. Marched off down the corridor. 'What's it say? . . . Uh-huh . . . Yeah . . . How long? . . . OK . . .'

A thickset nurse squeaked along the terrazzo floor and stopped right in front of him. He checked his clipboard. 'You're Sergeant McRae?'

As if Logan was going to be anyone else, sitting there in a damp Police Scotland uniform with sergeant's stripes on his shoulders. 'Is she all right?'

The clipboard got hugged against the nurse's chest. 'Right: so we've got Miss Mackie stable, but obviously there was a *lot* of water in her lungs. She's developed pneumonia on the left side. And it was pretty manky water too. Because she already had a chest infection, we're worried that this is going to exacerbate it. We're pumping her full of intravenous antibiotics, but you need to know it's very serious for someone in her condition.'

'Can I see her?'

The nurse bared his teeth in a grimacing smile. 'I'm sorry, but that's really not a good idea right now. Probably better give it three or four hours.'

Logan sagged in his seat, let his head thunk back against the wall. Flinched as the gauze pads hit it. Blinked. Swore. Winced.

'Are you all right?'

'Not really. Is she . . .?'

'We're doing everything we can, believe me. She couldn't get better care than she's getting.'

Steel thumped back up the corridor and collapsed into the seat next to Logan's. 'What did I miss?'

The nurse squatted down in front of him. 'You should go home and get some rest. You've got someone to look after you, haven't you? You've had a couple of nasty blows to the head; need to make sure you're not left alone in case you've got a concussion.' A smile, broad and friendly. He patted Steel on the knee. 'Maybe your mum will let you stay with her for a bit?'

Logan dumped his keys and phone on the coffee table, then slumped onto the couch. Yawned. Sighed.

Rain hammered the living-room window, the droplets turned amber by the streetlight outside, glowing against the raven sky.

So much for going out and celebrating.

A stilted trip to the pub, full of awkward silences, forced jovialness, and well-meaning assurances that Samantha was going to be OK. As if drowning someone in a minimally conscious state was going to be good for them.

Everyone dies in the end. The unlucky ones keep on breathing afterwards.

And Samantha couldn't even do *that* on her own any more.

A small burp gurgled free, followed a breath later by a wave of fire, radiating up inside his chest and throat. Hadn't even been nice fish and chips.

The rain fell.

Should really get up and close the curtains.

In a minute.

Cthulhu padded into the room as if she was wearing little fuzzy stilts. Hopped up onto his lap and dunked her forehead against his chest.

'At least I've still got you.' He rubbed her ear – she leaned into it, eyes closed, one long pointy tooth poking out the side of her mouth. 'And the rest of the world can go screw itself.'

Graham Stirling was off to Fraserburgh station, to spend a night in the cells before the courts opened tomorrow morning. Where he would lie and wheedle and wriggle.

Should have drowned the little sod when he had the chance. Held him under the water till he stopped struggling and his face turned blue. Leave him lying dead on the bottom of the pool with the stones and the silt, staring up into whatever hell he ended up in.

Charles Anderson was right, some people didn't deserve the law.

Logan picked up his phone, worked backwards through the call history till he got to Anderson's number. Pressed call.

It went straight to voicemail – didn't even ring. Probably no point leaving a message: not if Anderson had destroyed the SIM card as promised. *'Aye, you've got Craggie, I'm no here, but leave your name and number and I'll give you a call back when I can.'*

Logan hung up.

Stared at the screen.

Cthulhu jumped down again and made for the bowls in the corner, crunching away with her tail in the air.

Helen's number was right there.

His thumb hovered over the call button. What the hell?

It rang three times, and then her voice crept into his ear. *'Logan?'*

He cleared his throat. 'Just wanted to make sure you got somewhere to stay.'

'Are you OK? You sound . . . I don't know.' She sniffed. The words were strained, as if she was having to haul them up from somewhere dark and deep. *'Sorry. Been a long day.'*

'I know the feeling.'

'The girl in Gwent isn't Natasha.' Something broke, and the tears started. *'They did a blood test and it's the wrong type. I'm so stupid. I got my hopes up, I thought it was her, and now it's all gone again.'*

All that way for nothing. Helen could've stayed with him in Banff after all.

But that wasn't the way the world worked.

Logan's shoulders dropped another inch. 'We found out who the little girl in the swimming pool was. They measured the stable isotopes in her bones and traced her back to Carlisle. She went missing four years ago. Her mum and dad are coming up to identify her tomorrow.'

'That's . . . good.' A breath huffed down the

phone, followed by another sniff. *'I'm happy for them. They get to say goodbye.'*

'They were so grateful . . .' A deep breath. 'They're wrong though. Someone tried to kill Samantha today. They drowned her, but the paramedics managed to start her heart again.'

'I'm sorry.'

'I thought she was dead. For fifteen minutes I thought she was dead. Hope hurts. It's like a knife in the guts sometimes. But it's better than that.'

Cthulhu finished crunching and hopped onto the coffee table. Settled down on Logan's keys and washed her paws.

He huffed out a breath. Rubbed a hand across his eyes. 'Anyway. Yes. I got Tufty to do some digging. You don't need to worry about getting your hands on your ex-husband. Brian Edwards died two years ago in Middlesbrough. Hit-and-run.'

'I see . . .' The silence stretched.

'Helen?'

What sounded like laughter got muffled. *'I know it makes me a horrible person, but I'm* glad. *I'm glad he's dead. I hope he suffered.'*

'He'd changed his name, got married again, had a couple of kids with a Spanish woman. He beat her up, so she kicked him out. Got sole custody of the children.'

A breath, then it must've clicked. *'What about Natasha? Is she there? Is she OK?'*

'I don't know, but I've got an address in Spain I can text you.'

'Oh God, that's brilliant news! Thank you!' And the hope was back again, glowing in her voice like sunshine. *'I'll call the private investigator right away. Oh, Logan, what if she's OK? What if my little girl's not dead after all? Isn't it wonderful?'*

At least somebody could have a happy ending. God knew it would be about sodding time. Still . . .

He sagged back on the couch. 'Helen, maybe you'd be better off finding someone else. Your PI didn't even know Brian was dead. Doubt he could find his own bum in a kilt, never mind Natasha.'

'Oh.'

Silence.

'Look, I'm sorry. Forget I said anything.' He let his head fall back and stared up at the pristine ceiling. 'I'm having a bad day, that's all. Sure it'll be fine.'

The silence stretched.

'Helen? You still there?'

'Logan? Would you . . .' She swallowed. *'Would you like to come to Spain with me?'*